LOST SOULS

Also Published by the University of Minnesota Press

Lost Illusions

HONORÉ DE BALZAC

LOST SOULS

TRANSLATED
AND WITH AN INTRODUCTION BY
RAYMOND N. MacKENZIE

University of Minnesota Press
Minneapolis
London

This book was originally published as *Splendeurs et misères des courtisanes,* appearing in four parts from 1835 to 1847.

Translation copyright 2020 by Raymond N. MacKenzie

Published by the University of Minnesota Press
111 Third Avenue South, Suite 290
Minneapolis, MN 55401-2520
http://www.upress.umn.edu

ISBN 978-1-5179-0544-6

A Cataloging-in-Publication record for this book is available from the Library of Congress.

Printed in the United States of America on acid-free paper

The University of Minnesota is an equal-opportunity educator and employer.

27   26   25   24   23   22   21   10   9   8   7   6   5   4   3   2   1

CONTENTS

TRANSLATOR'S INTRODUCTION
Raymond N. MacKenzie

Lost Souls is the title given to this new translation of Balzac's *Splendeurs et misères des courtisanes.* That French title loses its subtleties and its tonalities when carried directly into English. Ellen Marriage's translation was titled *A Harlot's Progress,* a good title, though it evokes Hogarth more than anything in the novel does.[1] More recently, Rayner Heppenstall gave his translation the title *A Harlot High and Low,* which is clever but a little too amusing to suit the contents of Balzac's book.[2] My own title is, intentionally, more somber. The title choice also underlines how this novel is in some ways a continuation of *Lost Illusions,* bringing the stories of Lucien Chardon de Rubempré and Jacques Collin/Vautrin to a conclusion. All Balzac's fiction, at least all of his mature, post-1829 fiction, is richly interconnected: characters, families, events, even locations appear and reappear across the roughly one hundred tales that make up the *Comédie humaine.* But every one of those tales can also be appreciated in its own right. *Lost Souls* is a fine example of both points: it is intimately connected with other works but remains a uniquely satisfying, hugely ambitious novel read entirely in isolation from those others.

As his fame and his audience grew, Balzac crafted an image of himself, one that remains fixed in the public mind even in our time. We imagine him up all night, wearing his white Carthusian monk's robe (depicted in the famous portrait by Louis Boulanger), consuming dozens of cups of coffee, practicing a kind of manic chastity to maximize his written productivity, generating tale after tale, spinning out fiction the way a silkworm spins out silk, as Marx said of Milton and poetry. In his lifetime, stories circulated and at least one novel was written about him, stressing some of his hallmark eccentricities.[3] Later biographies only solidified the image, and the "eureka moment," when Balzac realized what his true life's work should be, has become part of the myth. A good example is in the biography the Austrian Stefan Zweig was working on when he died in 1942; it was an admiring, enthusiastic biography of a novelist by a novelist, and Zweig clearly understood the great engine that made the *Comédie humaine* run:

> Balzac had discovered the great secret. Everything was raw material. Reality was an inexhaustible mine. One only had to observe from the right angle and everybody became an actor in the human comedy. There was no distinction between high and low. One could choose everything, one had to choose everything. That was the decisive point for Balzac. An author who wished to portray the world could not afford to ignore any of its aspects. Every grade of the social hierarchy had to be represented, the artist as well as the lawyer and the physician, the wine-grower, the porter's wife, the general and the private, the duchess and the woman of the street, the water-carrier and the banker. All these spheres were interwoven.[4]

The artist of "all," the titan, the indefatigable: all this has passed into the popular conception of Balzac (helped along by imagery—not only that monk's robe but also Rodin's startling sculpture of him as a kind of colossus).

That popular image is largely correct, as the man was indeed startlingly prolific, with work habits that would put almost anyone else to shame. But among the many surprises Balzac offers the reader, one of the most striking is the fact that yes, his productivity was enormous, with some one hundred tales and novels making up the vast *Comédie humaine,* but he was at the same time an almost obsessive reviser of his own work. His younger friend and colleague Théophile Gautier tells us that he would cover even the tenth iteration of a page proof with corrections, that "he tortured himself horribly in his quest for style, and in his anxieties over correctness, would consult people who were a hundred times his inferiors. . . ."[5] He continued his revisions even after a book had been published, tinkering with stylistic details in succeeding editions, and often making substantive changes as well.

Composing the Novel

Lost Souls went through an even longer, even more complicated process— longer and more complicated than that of any of his other works. The novel is divided into four parts, each of which had its own (sometimes labyrinthine) publication history, and each of which had at least some life as a separate book.[6] The character of Vautrin, given his real name of Jacques Collin only in this novel, originated in 1834, during the composition of *Père Goriot,* and the policeman Corentin appears as far back as the 1829 *Le Dernier Chouan.* But with regard to the actual plot of *Lost Souls,* we can date the beginning around 1835, when Balzac was referring to a work, yet to be written, to be titled *La Torpille,* the "professional" name of a courtesan so beautiful that the observer felt stunned, as if by an electric ray or *torpille.*[7] When writing the story of the Jewish moneylender Gobseck in that year, he added a few lines about a great-niece of the old man, the first hints of the character Esther. Balzac sold the idea of the story about "La Torpille"—the idea only, that is, because when he made the sale he had not yet begun writing it—to the *Chronique de Paris,* but the editor began worrying about the possible reaction to so racy a subject, and when he ended up rejecting it, Balzac went on with other work, including the story of the wealthy Alsatian banker Nucingen.

In 1838, in Milan, Balzac thought in more specific terms about his Torpille story: the courtesan would be named Esther and would be a suicide (originally she was to have drowned herself in the Seine), and he now began work in earnest, with the full work, titled *La Torpille,* seeing publication that December. But he was already dissatisfied with the work as it stood, realizing it needed to be a much fuller, longer study; he tried out various titles for this new, larger work: *The Loves of an Aging Millionaire* was one possibility, though this soon changed to *Esther, or The Loves of a Lynx,*[8] and segments of the story began to appear serially under those and similar titles in 1843. In August 1844 he collected all he had so far written of the story of Esther and Lucien under the title *Splendeurs et misères des courtisanes.* But this was only the equivalent of the first three parts of the novel as we now have it. The final part, to be titled "Vautrin's Last Incarnation" (or, in one version, "Transformation of Vautrin"), was begun that same August, but other tasks intervened, and it was only in the summer of 1847 that he published the sections we know today as "Where Evil Pathways Lead" and "Vautrin's Last Incarnation" (Parts III and IV of the finished novel) as separate works. We know from his notes that Balzac intended these to be part of the larger novel of Esther and Lucien, but he died before being able to publish all the parts together as one book. Surprisingly, there are only one or two places where the seams show, so to speak, the chief one being the repetition of Lucien's letter in Parts III and IV.

All this makes the gestation period of the novel *Lost Souls* the longest of all Balzac's work, from 1835 to 1847. It's natural to assume, then, that it also reflects most of the preoccupations, themes, and insights that he developed over that exceptionally productive twelve-year period.

Courtesans and Esther

To begin with the courtesans of the French title: prostitution is a ready metaphor in all Balzac's work for the way the modern world turns everything into a commodity. The term *courtesan* has an interesting history, coming into use in Italian first and originally meaning simply a female courtier. But that soon changed. The 1606 dictionary *Thresor de la langue francoyse tant ancienne que moderne* tells us that properly speaking the word means a female courtier, but it had lately acquired an "odious signification," connoting a prostitute. Less than a century later, the *Dictionnaire de l'Académie Française* simply defined the term as *fille publique,* or prostitute. But by Balzac's day the term had taken on a new shading: in the 1836 edition of the same dictionary, a courtesan is defined as a "woman with a disordered way of life, but one distinguished by a certain elegance of manners who charges for her favors. The term is used especially for such women in antiquity, and in the great cities of Italy. . . . Today the term is used of a woman with a low way of life who is nonetheless of higher status than a common prostitute."[9]

A low way of life but a higher status: this describes the women Balzac calls courtesans. We know little about the realities of the lower-status woman who engaged in prostitution, the women who populated the legally regulated brothels, as few of them got the chance to tell their stories. What we do know comes from the sociological, almost anthropological, research done by Aléxandre Parent-Duchâtelet.[10] Novelists (Eugène Sue and Balzac among the first) made heavy use of the information Parent-Duchâtelet compiled; his work was so widely read and accepted that, as Jill Harsin notes, "the nineteenth-century view of the prostitute was essentially that of Parent-Duchâtelet."[11] He provided not only statistical information but a great deal of interpretation as well, including so-called facts such as the prostitute's habit of lying at all times, as well as her tendency to a superstitious brand of religiosity—traits we see reflected in the way Balzac's Esther can lie to Nucingen so expertly, and in her intense religious sensibility. The prostitutes Parent-Duchâtelet studied were considered a threat to public health and morality, and regulations concerning the brothels—significantly termed *maisons closes,* "closed houses"—abounded as the 1820s progressed. Balzac tells us that Esther had been registered as a prostitute, a "numbered, registered girl" (*fille à numéro*), as the category was named, and worked in such a house until she met Lucien. But, surprisingly, Balzac tells us almost nothing about the brothel and the brothel life; the novel, as Antoine Adam notes, never presents us with "the sordid, ignoble reality that Parent-Duchâtelet describes in abundant detail."[12] Given Balzac's penchant for elaborate, detailed descriptions, especially of interiors, this silence is a little surprising. Evidently, he is less interested in the reality of the brothel, wanting instead to use it simply as a point on the arc of Esther's story, a nadir from which she has risen and to which she could any day return (as the false priest Carlos Herrera threatens more than once). Balzac turns away from it as subject matter—perhaps because the "sordid, ignoble" reality would overwhelm the rest of the story. Other interpretations include that of Charles Bernheimer, who argues that Balzac wants to focus on the "desire she generates," in order to associate that desire with "biological degeneration and the collapse of social differences."[13] Bernheimer's analysis is intriguing, but what strikes me is the difference in prostitution as both topic and trope, subject and symbol, between the two novels *Lost Illusions* and *Lost Souls*.

In *Lost Souls* Balzac seems less interested in seeing the courtesan as a metaphor, the way he did in *Lost Illusions*. There the corrupt journalist Lousteau draws an explicit parallel between the world of the writer and the world of the prostitute:

> "This reputation that we [writers] desire so badly is almost always a kind of prostitution that goes about wearing a crown. Yes, the lowest types of literature are like the poor girl shivering on the street corner; and as for the second-rate literature, that's the kept mistress who has made her way out of the brothels of journalism, and she's the one I'm trying to master. Successful literature—she's the glittering, insolent courtesan with furnished apartments, who pays her taxes, who receives grand lords, treating them well or badly as she likes, who has liveried servants and a fine carriage and the power to keep her creditors at bay. But oh, for the men who see her—as I did not long ago, and for you, who still see her that way—as an angel with diaphanous wings, dressed in white, . . . finally growing wealthy but only through her virtue, rising back up to the heavens with her immaculate character intact—as long as she does not go to her pauper's grave soiled, despoiled, raped, and forgotten: men like that need to build a fence of bronze around their minds, and find a way to keep their hearts warm despite the ice storms of experience, and men like that are very rare in the place you see spread

out before you." As he said this he gestured out toward the great
city, its smoke rising up in the dusk. (*Lost Illusions*, 20)

Esther herself is scarcely identified with the kind of grasping material-
ism Lousteau describes; instead, she transcends this image of venality
and corruption, only being forced into making cunning financial negotiations for sex because of Herrera's plot. In a highly Romantic touch,
Balzac allows her to purify herself through her selfless and absolute
love for Lucien—and in a rich irony, her return, for one single night, to
her life of prostitution is both her downfall and her redemption. Born
in 1805 or 1807 and dead in 1830, she is the heart of the novel, in more
senses than one.[14] A number of other novels from the period sympathet-
ically depicted prostitutes who tried to reform, as Jann Matlock notes,
and these may have had some influence on how Balzac came to envision
his character Esther.[15]

   That biblical name of hers is suggestive. Traditional Christian biblical interpretation had a tendency to read the two Testaments in a "typological" manner, in which a character or event in the Hebrew or Old
Testament foreshadowed its greater manifestation in the Christian or
New. Thus, for example, the fatal tree with forbidden fruit in Genesis
foreshadows the tree of the cross with its salvific fruit. It may be useful
to read the intertextuality of *Lost Illusions* and *Lost Souls* in a similar
way, with the teenage actress Coralie in the earlier novel foreshadowing the even more spectacularly self-sacrificing Esther, or David's arrest
and incarceration in the earlier book foreshadowing Lucien's, and so on.
Esther dies so that Lucien may live and succeed in his grand plan for
rising up into the aristocracy. But this typological reading carries with
it an implicit tragic irony, for while biblical typology for the Christian
emphasizes redemption and salvation, the Balzacian version only underlines and amplifies the losses, the wasted possibilities, the failures of
nerve and integrity, and, as Othello might say, the pity of it that dominate the second volume.

Melodrama and Realism

Esther is one of a handful of characters in Balzac's world—Ursule Mirouët, from the novel that bears her name, is another major example—
whose love seems to come from some other world far from that of the
Comédie humaine, and from some time other than the nineteenth century; Balzac's conception of Esther seems a vision of almost celestial
purity. This is one of a number of features that make *Lost Souls* feel as if

its world is not quite the same as that of *Lost Illusions,* despite the presence of many of the same characters and some of the same ideas and motifs. The presence of the angelic Esther and the satanic Jacques Collin suggests we are in the realm of melodrama, but *Lost Souls* is too original, too unusual a narrative to fit that category exactly. Northrop Frye's definition is valuable:

> In melodrama two themes are important: the triumph of moral virtue over villainy, and the consequent idealizing of the moral views assumed to be held by the audience. In the melodrama of the brutal thriller we come as close as it is normally possible for art to come to the pure self-righteousness of the lynching mob.[16]

Flattering his audience's sense of morality is not Balzac's aim, in this or any other of his novels. And if the audience expects evil to be punished and good rewarded, Balzac will rarely come through. Indeed, as Christopher Prendergast puts it, Balzac's plots, and especially the one in this novel, tend to reject any traditional moral hierarchy, stressing instead "the moral similarities of protagonists and antagonists."[17] The difference between the police and the criminal is simply one of legal sanction; the difference between a common thief and the financier Nucingen is simply a matter of scale. Seeing such similarity is hardly a new insight. Shakespeare had it too, and he put it into the mouth of his suffering King Lear:

> A man may see how this world goes with no eyes. Look with thine ears. See how yond justice rails upon yond simple thief. Hark in thine ear. Change places, and handy-dandy, which is the justice, which is the thief?[18]

The changing of places is literalized in *Lost Souls,* with Vautrin's "last incarnation," the arch-criminal easily changing into the master police operative. All this is concrete, detailed social criticism, not melodrama. Indeed, Balzac's social criticism deserves greater emphasis than it is given today. Critics with a Marxian orientation have long stressed, and highly valued, exactly this aspect of his work. Georg Lukács, for example, saw Balzac's work as a kind of "mourning over the slavery that capitalism has brought on mankind."[19] For Walter Benjamin, Balzac's social criticism was more predictive or prophetic than descriptive, as the world described in his novels became the real world as the century progressed.[20] To reduce *Lost Souls* to melodrama, one needs to overlook a great deal of what happens on virtually every page of the novel.

But having said that, it is also true that *Lost Souls* does include some departures from social realism, that it does flirt, at least, with some hall-marks of melodrama, such as scarcely credible coincidences and the presence of both extreme villainy and extreme virtue—extreme in the sense of being difficult for a reader to credit. And in these respects there is no doubt that Balzac was directly influenced by the supreme purveyor of the novel as melodrama in his day, Eugène Sue.

Sue's *Les Mystères de Paris* was serialized in the *Journal des débats* (the paper for which Balzac's fictional character Blondet writes), running from June 1842 to October 1843, and, as Peter Brooks says, it would be hard to overstate its success:

> It was certainly the runaway bestseller of nineteenth-century France, possibly the greatest bestseller of all time. It's hard to estimate its readership, since each episode was read aloud, in village cafes and in workshops and offices throughout France. Diplomats were late to meetings, countesses were late to balls, because they had to catch up on the latest episode.[21]

This was the kind of success Balzac could only dream of—and living as he did in constant debt, trying to stay one step ahead of his creditors, he must have dreamed of it a great deal. Balzac had known Sue personally for over a decade before Sue's great triumph with the *Mystères*, speaking of him with some affection in 1833 as "a true child of nature," but by 1838 he had changed his view, describing him then as having a "narrow and bourgeois mind."[22] But when Sue's *Mystères* became so enormously popular, Balzac seems to have become obsessed with him, seeing him representing a complex of qualities, many of them dubious. As Christopher Prendergast puts it, for Balzac

> Sue is the living image of the prosperity and popularity achieved by a particular style of writing. Hence, in Balzac's mind Sue often appears as a kind of symbolic figure, an embodiment of every-thing that materially Balzac would like to possess and therefore, in terms of literary and creative values, of the temptations that in all conscience he must resist.[23]

Sue is both attractant and repellant, and no doubt some aspects of *Lost Souls* owe their being to Balzac's conflicted view of him and the kind of writing that seems to appeal to the widest possible public. That is the kind of writing that, as Frye said, flatters and idealizes the morality of the audience. Balzac couldn't quite force himself to do that, but at the same time he couldn't quite turn away from the desire for the material success and readership such toadying could bring, either.

Perhaps this accounts for some of the elements in *Lost Souls* that so strain credibility, and that seem to belong to what we today call genre fiction—the preposterously impenetrable disguises, the fiendishly complicated scheming, the languages only the initiates know, the sentimentalizing touches that crop up from time to time. But there are other ways of reading, even appreciating, those aspects of the book that have led some critics to dismiss it as an inferior production. The emphasis on crime and criminals is especially indebted to Sue, and both authors helped establish the ongoing taste for novels about the criminal and crime.[24] The criminal is in need of disguise, and disguises, especially the disguises of Jacques Collin, certainly strain the reader's willing suspension of disbelief—though perhaps Balzac's disguises are no more difficult to believe in than the same plot device in, say, *Twelfth Night* or *The Merchant of Venice*. But when we reflect that disguise is a controlling metaphor throughout the novel, we may forgive the lapse in verisimilitude and instead welcome the suggestiveness of the trope. Disguise—the pretense at being something other than what one is—is precisely the mainspring governing Lucien's entire project, and arguably his entire life. To become the Marquis de Rubempré is to wear the mask that will cover up for all time the reality, the indignity, of being Lucien Chardon, son of a pharmacist and a midwife, brother of a laundress, a nobody from Angoulême.

Calling Lucien a nobody seems more apt with *Lost Souls* than it does with the previous novel. In *Lost Souls* he is scarcely an agent anymore, appearing to have become almost entirely the puppet of his mentor, the abbé Carlos Herrera. We see him lounging about at home with a hookah, awaiting orders, and we see him rushing home from parties at homes like those of the Grandlieus to tell all the details of every evening to Herrera. And if in *Lost Illusions* he was guilty of many moral failures, at least he was making decisions and acting on them, often out of ignorance. But here he goes so far as to lose the reader's sympathy altogether in agreeing to sell (literally) the woman who loves him, all for his own advancement.

Balzac brings Lucien to a point of complete erasure of his integrity, in a powerful scene at the end of Part I. Herrera takes Lucien and Esther together to a forest outside Paris, where the three of them sit down "on the trunk of a felled poplar, looking off at that view, one of the finest in the world, one that takes in the Seine, Montmartre, Paris, even Saint-Denis." Herrera explains the plan, involving Esther giving Lucien up and prostituting herself to Nucingen, all in order to further Lucien's ascent into the world of the aristocracy. Herrera sends Lucien off for a moment, in order to be alone with Esther; he dismisses Lucien, almost contemptuously, telling him to go pick some flowers, a sarcastic reference to his volume of poems, titled *Marguerites*. When he returns, the poet, ostensibly in love with Esther, now abases himself even further, more than vaguely aware of what is at stake, and casting "a pleading look at Esther, one of those looks common with weak and greedy men, a look filled with the tenderness of the heart and the cowardice of the soul." The moment, comprising Lucien's moral nadir, Esther's realization of her tragic fate, and Herrera's complete dominion over the two of them, is played out like a tableau against the great scenic backdrop of Paris. Balzac created a similar, and similarly powerful, effect against such a backdrop at the end of *Père Goriot*, with Rastignac looking down on Paris from the height of the Père Lachaise cemetery and resolving to win in his struggle with all that the city represents. And that very scene will be echoed yet again toward the end of *Lost Souls*. Such scenes that constellate the individual, the cityscape, and the moral moment function like a kind of refrain resounding over the entire *Comédie humaine*.

Lucien's end is ignoble, pathetic, the result, as so often in his life, of faulty information, faulty inference, and, perhaps, a too-belated sense of responsibility and, with it, shame. But there is a kind of tragic grandeur in the arc of his life story, the slow, at first, but sure, and soon accelerating fall from innocence and artistic idealism to a cell in the Conciergerie. Perhaps against our better judgment, he seduces us readers yet again into sympathy and pity and regret. One of the mourners was Oscar Wilde:

> A steady course of Balzac reduces our living friends to shadows, and our acquaintances to the shadows of shades. His characters have a kind of fervent fiery-coloured existence. They dominate us, and defy scepticism. One of the greatest tragedies of my life is the death of Lucien de Rubempré. It is a grief from which I have never been able completely to rid myself. It haunts me in my moments of pleasure. I remember it when I laugh.[25]

Wilde is given to paradox, but the description of Balzac's characters and their effects on the reader is right. And because of the sheer size of his canvas, Balzac is able to imply that the fall of Lucien is part of a much larger fall, a more universal tragedy.

What Lucien meant to Balzac is ambiguous. At some points, especially in *Lost Illusions*, he functions as an innocent, whose naïve point of view allows the novelist to remind us how shocking some things are, even ones we have come to take for granted in the modern world—such as the omnipotence of money. But though Lucien is or was a writer, and though he encountered many of the same issues that Balzac had involving the power of the newspaper press, for example, Balzac never treats him as an alter ego. He is beautiful, "this half-woman man" with feminine hands, feminine hips; women fall in love with him instantly—Coralie and Esther, but also Peyrade's daughter Lydie, not to mention a suite of married aristocrats—and so do men, or at least the one supremely important man, Collin/Carlos Herrera/Vautrin. As Peter Brooks points out, Lucien's body plays the role the female courtesan's body is expected to: arousing desire.

> Lucien's body is a consistent clue to his inconsistent career. It has an absolute appeal, to women and to the homosexual Collin; loving and desiring Lucien never needs justification or textual motivation, but is simply the natural and unquestioned response to his beauty.[26]

He has the kind of power over others that Circe had—though it is Esther who Balzac compares to Circe. Both are supreme seducers, both effortlessly so. Early in the novel, Lousteau says of Esther exactly what might be said of Lucien:

> "At eighteen years of age, that girl has already experienced the highest levels of opulence, the lowest depths of poverty, and men at every stage along the way. She has a magic wand, so to speak, and she can use it to unleash the animal instincts in men who otherwise keep them violently repressed, men in politics, in science, in literature, in art. There's no other woman in Paris who can be so effective in saying to the Animal, 'Come out of your cage!' And the Animal comes out, and he rolls and wallows in excess; she leads you to the table, up to your chin, and she helps you to a drink, a cigar."

All this lends a kind of timelessness, a certain allegorical haze to the tale, as if *Lost Souls* were in part a modern *Odyssey*, or a modern morality play. It is, of course. But the morality, being modern, is knotty and difficult rather than straightforward and clear.

Vautrin/Herrera/Collin

Both courtesans, Esther and Lucien, become the property of the bizarre figure of the false Spanish priest, who conceals within him the ex-convict, as well as the future policeman. He has so many identities that Balzac seems frequently unsure about what he ought to call him. Vautrin, Deathcheater, Carlos Herrera, Jacques Collin—all those names are used nearly interchangeably. Amusingly, there's a moment in Part IV when our narrator announces that Jacques Collin "from now on, shall be referred to only under that name," but in the next paragraph he slips and calls him Vautrin again. Even his gender is represented as unfixed, indeterminate: while he acts as, and almost seems to believe that he is, Lucien's father, he used quite different terms at the end of *Lost Illusions,* when he was tempting Lucien to give himself up completely: "Obey me as a wife obeys her husband, as a child obeys its mother," he says.[27] The self of the man never quite settles and takes final shape; perhaps the best way to understand him is to recall the peeled onion image in Ibsen's *Peer Gynt,* suggesting the self is only layer upon layer with no stable core or center. The one definite, ineffaceable marker, the sign that is meant to define him permanently, is the brand he wears on his back from his time in the penal colonies, a state-inflicted indicator, reminiscent of the ancient Roman custom of branding a slave on his face. But even this permanent sign, this *marque infamante,* has been so disguised that the prosecutor and witnesses cannot be sure whether it's there on his shoulder or not. His identity is always in question.

And yet for someone so evanescent, he plays a powerfully solid role, the backbone of the whole long narrative, as Balzac says: Jacques Collin is "the vertebral column whose evil influence stitches together *Père Goriot* with *Lost Illusions,* and *Lost Illusions* with the present work." The reader first encountered him as Vautrin, the ex-convict, in the 1835 *Père Goriot,* attempting to seduce Eugène de Rastignac into crime, even murder, to help further his ascent in the Parisian social world; Vautrin fails, but he is defeated only by circumstance, for Rastignac was in fact weakening. Vautrin returns on the scene in the guise of the Spanish priest Carlos Herrera in the final pages of *Lost Illusions,* now attempting the seduction of the stunningly beautiful Lucien, who appears out of a meadow clutching a bouquet of flowers he's just picked. In a masterful moment of narrative orchestration, the two get up into Herrera's carriage, and they pass a lane that leads to ... the family home of Rastignac. Herrera gets out, gazes down the lane at the house for a moment from the highway, with what feelings the reader can only infer, and then climbs back into the carriage to continue his temptation of Lucien. He serves as a vertebral column of "evil influence," then, for three different novels. Vautrin/Herrera/Collin had been on Balzac's mind for just about as long as the composition of *Lost Souls,* some twelve years.

In 1840 *Vautrin,* a stage play Balzac wrote, exploiting the notoriety of the character, was produced. The plot largely follows that of the novel, with the Lucien character being renamed Raoul de Frescas. The play might have been a hit, but the lead actor (Frédérick Lemaître, who had had a great success playing another popular criminal character, Robert Macaire) decided to have Vautrin wear a wig that would make him look like the king, Louis-Philippe, and the authorities swept in and closed the play down after one night. It was one thing to suggest a likeness between the criminal and the ruling class in a novel, but quite another to do it on the stage.

There was a living, breathing inspiration for the idea of a character who turned from master criminal to master policeman: Eugène-François Vidocq (1775–1857). Imprisoned several times for a range of crimes from forgery and theft to assault, he escaped again and again, disguising himself variously, sometimes as a sailor, once even as a nun. In 1809, arrested yet again, he agreed to become an informant, and after a number of coups in that role, he was allowed to organize a special "security" force, the Brigade de la Sûreté, a plainclothes police unit that was considered a great success. Many of his men were ex-prisoners themselves, recruited by Vidocq. Balzac had met him socially many times. In 1824 the memoirs of the famous police chief who had served under both the revolutionary Directory and Napoleon's empire, Joseph Fouché, were published to considerable interest and success, and this no doubt inspired Vidocq to write his own. It was easy to interest a publisher; Vidocq was no writer, and the publisher assigned a ghostwriter, Émile Morice, to work with him. Morice and Vidocq quarreled, however, and Vidocq ended up with a second publisher, who assigned a second ghostwriter, Louis-François L'Heritier, a friend of and sometime collaborator with Balzac, and the result was a wildly popular book, even if its veracity is highly questionable.[28] Vidocq became famous, so much so that no contemporary could possibly read about Balzac's Vautrin and fail to think of Vidocq. Thus, Balzac grounds his most evanescent character about as firmly in reality as could possibly be done.

One more important aspect of Herrera/Collin/Vautrin deserves some attention: he explicitly compares himself to an author. In *Lost Illusions* he says he wants to make Lucien his creation:

"I want to love my creation, to fashion it, to sculpt it to my own uses—to love it the way a father loves his child. I'll ride in your chic carriage, my boy, taking joy in your successes with women. I'll say, 'That beautiful young man, that's me! That Marquis de Rubempré, I created him, I set him down in the aristocratic world; his greatness is all my work, and when he speaks, it's my voice. . . .'" (Part III, 532)

And in *Lost Souls* the metaphor is explicit: "I am the author, and you are the play; if you aren't a success, I'm the one they'll hiss," he tells Lucien. He is like an author in another sense, too, for as he pours himself into various characters, he experiences, and creates, a multiple self. Bernheimer draws our attention to the image of the author in Baudelaire's prose poem "Les Foules" ("Crowds").[29] Baudelaire writes:

Multitude, solitude: terms that are equivalent and interchangeable for the active and fertile poet. . . . The poet enjoys this incomparable privilege, that he can be, just as he likes, either himself or somebody else. Like those wandering souls in search of a body, he enters, whenever he likes, into the characters of everyone.[30]

This is the condition that Vautrin inhabits, far more than the "real" poet, Lucien. Perhaps the suggestion is that Vautrin is the more completely modern man. D. A. Miller suggests something along these lines when he writes that Balzac depicts a social order that neither "values or even requires a fixed self" but instead aspires "to the condition of money: to its lack of particularity, to the mobility of its exchange, to its infinitely removed finality."[31]

Money and Nucingen

Money, as most readers know, is Balzac's primary field of investigation, all across the *Comédie humaine*. From the inheritance concerns in *Eugénie Grandet* and *Ursule Mirouët* to the lawsuits in *L'Interdiction* and *Le Curé de Tours,* money is explicitly foregrounded in the lives of nearly all of his characters. As Harry Levin once put it, "it is Balzac's zeal for tracing financial relationships that links cause to effect, plot to character, and volume to volume in the *Comédie humaine*."[32] Money is nowhere more crucial than it is in *Lost Souls,* where much of the plot centers on the scheme to sell Esther to the wealthy banker Nucingen. The background story of his wealth is given (though in less detail than one might wish) in the novella-length *La Maison Nucingen* (1838), which tells about one particular shady scheme that helped build up Nucingen's vast wealth. In *Lost Souls* we get a glimpse of his heartless, rapacious business dealings as he swoops in to profit from the downfall of his one-time employee Jacques Falleix and snatch for himself the house Falleix had purchased. And we repeatedly hear (though from Herrera and his aunt, not always the soundest sources) allusions to his being a thief on the grand scale. After he sees Esther in the midnight forest, like a fairy vision, he is smitten with love for the first time in his life, and Herrera smells opportunity in the situation: he gets Esther's debts bought up, threatening her with prison, and this leads to Nucingen eagerly stepping forward to help her, at which point, to use Balzac's metaphor, the cashbox is open.[33]

Nucingen, then, is detestable because of his rapacious, immoral business dealings, and he is comic in his absurd infatuation with Esther. He is sixty, and in Balzac's era this passed for old age, so his passion thus places him as the stock too-old lover in the long tradition of May–December tales, such as those in the medieval fabliaux. He is also made absurd by Balzac's insistence on his fractured French. The modern reader will be less inclined to see him as simply comic, however, because Nucingen is Jewish (as is Esther, though she doesn't know it). Maurice Samuels argues that "the radical otherness of Nucingen—rendered through an opaque, phonetically transcribed Germanic accent . . . inhibits our identification with him."[34] Samuels also notes that although Balzac deploys racial stereotypes, he is not bound to them, making the successful novelist Nathan, for example, a Jew and concluding that while the "cultivated, liberal French audience" might view Jewish artists as exotic, they "did not relegate them to the margins" (23). It is difficult to deny the presence of at least the odor of anti-Semitism, for Balzac's Jews are often stereotypically obsessed with money.[35] But the author also questions the validity of racial and ethnic stereotypes in a remarkable passage in *Lost Illusions:*

> Yes, the Spaniard is generous, as the Italian loves poisons and is jealous, as the Frenchman is superficial, as the German is frank and open, as the Jew is despicable, as the Englishman is noble. But reverse these old saws and you'll be nearer the truth. Jews have stockpiled gold, and they have written *Robert le Diable,* performed the role of Phèdre, sung *William Tell,* erected palaces, written *Reisebilder* and admirable poetry; they're more powerful than ever, their religion is accepted, and they even lend money to the Pope! In Germany, people insist on contracts for even the smallest matters, so given to double dealings are they. In France, people have been applauding for fifty years now at the Theater of National Absurdity; they continue to wear idiotic hats, and

> they accept a change in government only on the condition that it
> is the same as the previous government! ... The English openly
> display their perfidy to the world, and it is only exceeded by their
> greed. The Spaniards had their hands on the gold of both Indies,
> and now they're penniless. There's no country in the world where
> you'll find less poisoning going on than in Italy, where manners
> are easy and courteous. (530)

We find Balzac making use of racialized generalizations, but his cynicism tells him to beware of them, helping him keep an ironic distance from them. How to read Nucingen as Jew—or rather, how to read Balzac's reading of him—must be left to the modern reader.[36]

This intersection with the evolution of European anti-Semitism is but one of many connections *Lost Souls* makes to the culture of its day. Its treatment of homosexuality, in the relationship between Deathcheater and Théodore Calvi, for example, and of course between Herrera and Lucien, likewise makes a claim on the modern reader's attention. For Theodor Adorno, Balzac "discovered homosexuality for literature":

> In view of the irresistible ascendancy of the exchange principle,
> he may have dreamed of something like love in its undistorted
> form occurring in a despised and inherently hopeless love: it is
> the false cleric, the bandit chief who cancels the exchange of
> equivalents, whom he believes capable of it.[37]

This may be overstatement, but there is truth in it, for Balzac never marginalizes, condemns, or mocks Collin's homosexuality. The warden of the Conciergerie expresses disgust when he gestures toward the cells where the "aunts" are housed, but the narrator does not, and the passage feels like a prefiguration of the prison narratives of Jean Genet.[38] How homosexuality intersects with power and money, and whether, as Adorno suggests, it subverts those twin idols of modernity, is yet another question *Lost Souls* invites us to consider.[39]

Lost Souls in its day was one of Balzac's most popular, best-selling works,[40] but today it is less widely read than it deserves to be. Arguably it is Exhibit A in the category Henry James called the loose, baggy monster novel, growing as it did more by accumulation than any grand, architectonic vision. And the bag is quite large: we meet some 273 named characters in the novel,[41] and a great many of those not only recur but are actually main characters in other works in the *Comédie*, creating a rich dimensionality. The grand tapestry of *Lost Souls* excludes nothing: serious social criticism sits next to bedroom farce (as in the scene duping Nucingen), fast-paced crime-novel material next to the deeply tragic, casually referenced horrors like the phenomenon of the Opéra "rats," or the abduction of Peyrade's daughter, next to the almost super-human, perfect love of an Esther. The story runs from the gutters to the palaces of Paris, from the provinces to the capital, from the cell of the condemned criminal to the cabinet of the king, touching on nearly every theme in the whole *Comédie*. In the course of its twelve-year gestation, the scope continued to expand, and the result is one of the most ener-getic, compulsively readable works in all Balzac's canon.

On the Translation

In undertaking a new translation of *Splendeurs et misères des courti-sanes,* the first question is which text to use. As I have detailed here, the text went through many partial publications and many different versions. Most modern editions use the so-called Furne edition: the collected edi-tion of the *Comédie humaine* that began to be published in 1842. Charles Furne was one of several publishers who collaborated on a revised and corrected publication of the *Comédie humaine,* a major and dauntingly complex editing enterprise, one made even more complex by an author who never stopped revising and reshuffling his works. Seventeen vol-umes appeared between 1842 and 1848; a suspension followed, and Bal-zac died in 1850, but then the project was taken up again by a different group of publishers between 1853 and 1855. The Furne edition of *Splen-deurs et misères des courtisanes* dates from 1847.[42]

I have relied on three modern editions: Antoine Adam, editor, *Splen-deurs et misères des courtisanes* (Paris: Classiques Garnier, 1958); Pierre-Georges Castex and Pierre Citron et al., editors, *La Comédie humaine VI* (Paris: Gallimard [Bibliothèque de la Pléiade], 1977); and Pierre Barbéris, editor, *Splendeurs et misères des courtisanes* (Paris: Gallimard [Folio Classique], 1973).

I occasionally quoted from those editors' notes in my own endnotes, and when that is the case I indicated them by last name: Adam, Citron, or Barbéris. Adam and Barbéris retain the chapter titles that Balzac had used in earlier editions, and I have kept them, too. I followed the same procedure in my translation of *Lost Illusions,* believing that omitting the chapter titles is a real loss: they help the reader find her or his way through the long and winding road that is this novel, and they are often clever or interesting in themselves.

As with my translation of *Lost Illusions,* I have striven for accuracy and, just as important, for reproducing the *feel* of Balzac's style and stance as much as possible. This means that I maintained his sometimes enormous paragraphs and many (though not all) of his sometimes overloaded sentences.

I have allowed myself to be freer with dialogue. Balzac's dialogue, especially in this novel, is always natural, never stilted, and to get that natural effect one must sometimes seek analogs rather than simply producing a literal translation. There are two special challenges in the dialogue of *Lost Souls*: first is Nucingen's fractured French, and second is the heavy use of criminal slang or argot. I used a somewhat cartoonish Katzenjammer German–like accent for Nucingen (and it is just as cartoonish in French). This can, frankly, try the reader's patience, I know; but the French version is just as trying, and there are moments where Nucingen's speech is stunningly opaque. May the reader pardon me for attempting to create the same effect in English.

More complicated, and more interesting, is the matter of the slang. It is clear from the text of the novel that Balzac was deliberate and serious in his documentation of actual criminal slang of the period, so much so that he italicizes terms to be sure the reader notices them. He loves the vitality and energy of slang, devoting one entire chapter to a "Philosophic, Linguistic, and Literary Essay on Slang, Whores, and Thieves," where he expresses his enthusiasm:

> Slang is always on the move, everywhere. It follows right behind civilization, right on its heels, enriching it with new expressions constantly. The potato, introduced into France by Louis XVI and Parmentier, is quickly turned by argot into *pigs' oranges.* Bank notes are invented, and the prison world soon calls them *garatted flimsies,* after Garat, the cashier whose name is printed on them. *Flimsies!* Doesn't it make you hear the very rustle of that thin paper? A thousand-franc note is *a male flimsy,* the five-hundred a *female flimsy.*

He usually italicizes the slang term, and often follows it with a parenthetical definition. I have generally followed him in this format, though sometimes I've sought to simplify things without, I hope, losing any of the flavor or the zest of Balzac's use of criminal slang.[43]

Many of his slang terms come directly from Vidocq's *Mémoires,* which gives them the stamp of authenticity. Victor Hugo's *Le Dernier Jour d'un condamné (The Last Day of a Condemned Man,* 1829) and later Sue's *Mystères de Paris* used underworld slang extensively, establishing something of an expectation for the novelist dealing with criminals and the world of crime.[44] The translator must walk a tightrope, avoiding, on the one hand, sounding quaint and dated (avoiding, that is, having Balzac's characters sound like they belong in a Damon Runyon story), and on the other making the characters sound too modern or too American. I have resorted to varying approaches, depending on the term. With a few terms, such as *largue* for a criminal's girlfriend, or *fanandel* for a member of the criminal organization, the etymology is unclear, making it difficult to find an analog, and in those cases I've simply retained the French word. Some English words are timeless enough to work well: thus, in the Part IV chapter "His Majesty the Boss," *dab* becomes "boss," and the repeated italics signal that the term was criminal argot in the original. If the slang sometimes seems forced or simply odd, I must plead that it does in the original too, but it also carries with it an energy, those italics functioning like the enthusiastic presence of the author, eagerly pointing out the extraordinary details of the life he is documenting.

Lost Souls is in fact partly motivated by Balzac's ongoing desire to document, to get down on the page the realities of his Paris. But the novel is no museum piece: in its unique mix of horror, satire, romance, and tragedy, it remains as vital, as alive as if it were written yesterday. And while we might be struck, even put off somewhat, by the melodramatic elements, we would do well to remember how Balzac was seen by his contemporary readers, not the least of whom were Jules and Edmond de Goncourt, who wrote this remarkable summation in their journal for September 1857, just seven years after the novelist had died:

> No one has called Balzac a statesman, but he might be the greatest statesman of our time, a great social statesman, the only one who has plumbed the depths of our malaise, the only one who has a broad perspective on the disintegration of France since 1789, of the manners beneath the laws, the fact beneath the word, the anarchy of unbridled interests beneath the apparent order, the abuses replaced by influences, privileges by more privileges, equality before the law annihilated by inequality before the judge, in short the whole great lie of '89 that managed to accomplish nothing but replacing names with 100-sou pieces, and replacing the marquis with the banker. . . . And to think it took a novelist to see all this![45]

LOST SOULS

I ❧

HOW WOMEN LOVE

A View of the Opéra Ball

In 1824, at the last Opéra Ball of the season,[1] a number of masked women were dazzled by the beauty of a young man they saw prowling around the hallways and the foyer; he had the air of a man seeking everywhere for a woman who had been kept at home by some unexpected turn of events. But the secret meaning of his restless pacing—sometimes slow and lazy, sometimes quickening—was clear only to those with the skills to understand it, that is, women of a certain age, and a few flâneurs. In a huge gathering such as this, the crowd doesn't really study the crowd, for each one is absorbed in his own particular passion; even idleness itself is preoccupied. The young dandy himself was so absorbed in his restless search that he didn't see his own success: he never heard the ironic exclamations emanating from behind those masks, nor the more serious expressions, nor the biting taunts, nor the softer phrases: he heard none of it, saw none of it. While his beauty put him in the class of exceptional people who came to the Opéra Ball expecting to find an adventure there, one which awaited him just as surely as a lucky spin of the roulette wheel awaited him in the era of Frascati's,[2] the young man seemed so sure of the evening ahead as to be complacent; he must, certainly, have been the hero of one of those three-actor mysteries that define the masked Opéra Ball but which are known only to those who have a role to play in them. To anyone else—the young women who attend only in order to be able to say "I was there"; the provincials; the young men of little experience; the foreigners—to all of them, the Opéra Ball must be the very palace of fatigue and boredom. To such as them, that black-clad crowd busily creeping along, turning this way and that like a great serpent, going up stairs and back down, looks like nothing so much as an army of ants on a woodpile, and to them the sight is about as comprehensible as the national debt is to a Brittany peasant. With rare exceptions, the men in Paris do not wear masks; a man in a domino would look ridiculous. And here we observe the national genius: men who want to keep their good fortune secret may head off for the ball but fail to arrive, while the masked women are forced to go in and then leave as soon as they can. A highly amusing spectacle is to be seen at the doorways just when the ball is getting started, for here is a pent-up flood of those making their escape and others pushing their way in. Any man in a mask must be a jealous husband who comes to spy on his wife—or a husband who has stumbled into a little good luck and who wishes not to be spied upon by his wife—and both situations are equally comical. Now our young man was being followed, though he did not know it, by what appeared to be a masked assassin, short and heavy, rolling along behind him like a barrel. To an experienced ball-goer, the masked man could only be some broker or agent, some banker or notary, some species of bourgeois who suspected his wife of infidelity. In the higher realms of society, of course, no one goes running after evidence that would only be humiliating. Already a number of masks had been laughing at the monstrous-looking person, while some others had called out to him, and a few younger ones had openly made fun of him, but he maintained his same posture and bearing, evidently immune to their barbs. He continued to go wherever the young man went, his gait resembling that of a hunted boar who carries on running, evidently uninterested in the bullets whizzing about him and the dogs barking behind him. At first the observer would think that pleasure and anxiety were wearing the same costume, that illustrious Venetian black robe, and that here at the Opéra Ball everything was muddled up together, but the various circles of which Parisian society is composed do in fact recognize each other, encounter each other, and observe each other here. Certain notions are so precisely understood by the initiated that they can read this occult book as readily as they can a novel, and with just as much amusement. The habitués would observe this particular scene and conclude that the man in the mask was not in a good situation, for otherwise he would infallibly have worn some little mark they could have deciphered, some hint of red or white or green indicating that some happy encounter was planned. Was it a matter of revenge? Watching the masked man so closely tailing the fortunate young man, some of the idle observers turned to gaze again upon the handsome face that pleasure had surrounded with its divine halo. That young man was interesting: the more he walked around the place, the more curiosity he aroused. Everything about him suggested an elegantly lived life. But in accordance with a fatal law of our era, there is little difference, whether physical or moral, between the most distinguished, the best brought-up son of a duke or peer and this charming boy who so recently had been in the iron clutches of poverty here in Paris. His beauty and his youth were capable of masking profound gulfs, as with so many young men who want to play a role in Paris without possessing the necessary capital, and who every day risk all in a bid to win all, worshippers of the most adored god of this royal city, Chance. Nevertheless, his appearance and his manners were irreproachable as he paced the classic floors of the Opéra as if he had always belonged there. Haven't we all noticed that here, just as in every other place in Paris, the way you act reveals what you are, what you do, where you are from, and what you are after?

"That splendid young man! If we stand just here, we can turn and watch him," said a masked woman, recognized by regulars as a respectable woman.

"Don't you remember him?" asked the young man escorting her. "Madame du Châtelet introduced him to you. . . ."

"What! You mean that's the pharmacist's son she was involved with, the one who turned into a journalist, the one who was Coralie's lover?"[3]

"I would have thought he had fallen too far to ever climb back up to this height again, and I really can't understand how he dares show his face again in Parisian society," said Comte Sixte du Châtelet.

"He acts like a prince," said the mask, "and he didn't learn that from his little actress. My cousin had him all figured out, but couldn't get him out of his troubles. I'd like to meet the mistress of this Sargine.[4] Tell me something about her so I'll have something that will let me get his attention."

This couple, who whispered together as they followed behind the young man, were carefully observed by the masked man with the broad shoulders.

"Dear Monsieur Chardon," said the prefect of the Charente as he took the young dandy by the arm, "allow me to introduce a lady who would like to renew her acquaintance with you."

"My dear Comte Châtelet," the young man replied, "this lady is the one who taught me the absurdity of that name. An ordinance from the king has restored to me the name of my ancestors on my mother's side, the Rubemprés. It was published in the newspapers, but it concerns such an unimportant person that I do not blush to remind my friends of it, nor my enemies, nor those indifferent to me: you may place yourself in whichever of those three categories you prefer, but I am quite certain you cannot possibly disapprove of a measure that your wife herself counseled me to take, back when she was still Madame de Bargeton." (This clever little phrase made the marquise smile but made the prefect start nervously.) "You might inform her," said Lucien, "that now I bear *gules*, with a raging *argent* bull on a meadow *vert*."

"The bull is presumably raging after money then," replied Châtelet.[5]

"*Madame la marquise* here can explain it to you, if you don't know already, how this ancient coat of arms ranks higher than the chamberlain's key and the golden bees of the Empire that feature in yours, no doubt to the great despair of Madame Châtelet, née Nègrepelisse d'Espard," said Lucien in a sharp tone.[6]

"Since you have apparently recognized me, I have lost all my mystery and fascination, but I can hardly tell you how mysterious and fascinating you are to me," said the Marquise d'Espard quietly, entirely dumbfounded by the impertinence and the assurance of this man she had formerly despised.

"Permit me then, madame, to preserve my only chance of occupying your thoughts by remaining within that mysterious twilight," he said, with the smile of a man who does not want to risk losing a sure thing.

The marquise could not help but start a little at that, feeling that—to use the English expression—she had been cut dead by Lucien.

"Allow me to compliment you on your change of position," said the Comte du Châtelet to Lucien.

"I receive your compliment in the same spirit you give it," replied Lucien, bowing to the marquise with infinite grace.

"That conceited little ass!" the count exclaimed quietly to Madame d'Espard. "He has managed to acquire ancestors."

"With these young men, that kind of conceit, when they aim it at us, always arises out of their having some highly placed lover—among men such as you, on the other hand, it always arises out of bad luck. I'd love to know which of our friends has taken this pretty little bird under her protection; this could be matter for some amusement tonight. The anonymous letter I received must have been part of a scheme by a rival, because it did mention that young man;—he was impertinent because he was told to be. Keep your eye on him. I'll be with the Duc de Navarreins, so you'll know where to find me."

As Madame d'Espard went off to meet her relative, the mysterious masked man interposed himself between her and the duc. He whispered in her ear: "Lucien loves you. He's the author of the letter. But your prefect over there is his greatest enemy, so how could he possibly explain himself in front of him?"

With that, the unknown man was gone, leaving Madame d'Espard doubly surprised. The Marquise knew of no one who could possibly play the role of the man in the mask; she suspected some kind of trap was being laid, so she sat down out of sight. Meanwhile, the Comte Sixte du Châtelet, whose ambitious *du* Lucien had slashed off with an affected ease that suggested a long-planned vengeance, now followed the marvelous dandy at a distance, soon encountering a young man with whom he could speak openly.

"Well, Rastignac, have you seen Lucien? He's apparently shed his old skin and grown a new one."

"If I were as good-looking as he is, I'd be even richer than he is," replied the elegant young man lightly, but with an undertone that suggested an Attic wit.

"No," said a voice close to his ear. It was the heavy man in the mask, putting such a weight on that monosyllable that it would have dissipated a thousand clever remarks.

Rastignac was not the kind of man to accept an insult, but he stood there as if thunderstruck, and, feeling a hand of steel on his arm, allowed himself to be led over to a window seat, knowing it would be impossible to escape that grip.

"My little rooster from Mama Vauquer's barnyard,[7] you're the one who lost his nerve when it came to getting your hands on Papa Taillefer's millions, even though all the hard work had already been done, and right now the one thing you need to know, for your personal safety, is that if you don't treat Lucien like a brother you dearly love, well, you'll be in our hands. Keep your mouth shut and be devoted to him, or I'll come to your roost and pluck your feathers. Lucien de Rubempré is protected by the greatest power there is today, the Church. Choose, then: life or death. What's your answer?"

Rastignac was dizzy with fear, like a man who had fallen asleep in a forest and awoke to find a hungry lion beside him.[8] He was afraid, but there were no witnesses present, and in such circumstances sometimes the bravest of men will surrender completely to their fear.

"The only one who could know would be *him* . . . the only one who would dare . . ." he said, as if talking to himself.

The man in the mask shook his hand and, as if to save him the trouble of completing his sentence, said: "Then you'd better act as if it were really *him*."

Other Masks

At that, Rastignac reacted the way a millionaire on the highway would upon finding a pistol pointed at his head: he surrendered.

He returned to Châtelet, saying, "My dear count, if you value your position, you must treat Lucien de Rubempré like a man you expect to find placed much higher than you are one day."

The man in the mask made an almost imperceptible nod of satisfaction, then turned away to follow Lucien once more.

"My friend, you've changed your opinion of him very suddenly," said the astonished prefect.

"Yes, a rapid change, the sort we see when someone from the Center suddenly votes with the Right," Rastignac said to the prefect and député whose votes had not aligned with the Ministry for some days.

"What's that—are there still opinions these days? I thought there were only interests," said des Lupeaulx, who had heard their last exchange. "What's the issue you're talking about?"

"The issue is Monsieur de Rubempré, a man Rastignac wants me to see as someone of importance," said the député to the secretary-general.

"My dear count," des Lupeaulx said with a suddenly serious tone, "Monsieur de Rubempré is a young man of the greatest merit, and he is a man so powerfully supported that I would consider myself very fortunate to renew my acquaintance with him."

"Well, I see him over there, about to step into that hornets' nest of the young rogues of the day," said Rastignac.

The three of them turned toward a corner of the room where several clever and elegant young men were gathered, all of them more or less notorious. They were exchanging observations, witty remarks, and gossip, seeking to amuse themselves until something better turned up. Among this strangely composed group were some people with whom Lucien had had some relations in the past, relations that were friendly on the surface but secretly malicious.

"Ah, Lucien, old boy, my friend, here we are all reupholstered, eh, all patched back up. Where are we coming from, eh? It would appear we have clambered back up on the horse's back, with a little help from some gifts sent your way from Florine's boudoir.[9] Well done, my boy!" said Blondet, letting go of Finot's arm to seize Lucien around the waist and embrace him.

Andoche Finot was the proprietor of a review for which Lucien had worked practically gratis, and which Blondet had enriched through his collaboration, his wit, his advice, and the depths of his cunning. Finot and Blondet could have been Bertrand and Raton,[10] with the difference that in La Fontaine's fable the cat eventually realized he was being duped, whereas Blondet went right on serving Finot. That brilliant *condottiere* of the pen had long become effectively a slave. Behind his unimpressive appearance Finot concealed a brutal willpower, masking that ruthless will with an impertinent stupidity, like a workingman who rubs his crust of bread with garlic. He knew how to stockpile what he gleaned, the little ideas and pennies' worth of thoughts dropped along the edges of the fields of life by men of letters and politicians. Blondet had entered into bondage, unfortunately for him, in order to support his vices and his laziness. Always surprised by need, he belonged to that tribe of men who do everything to make the fortune of another without being able to do anything for their own, Aladdins who let others borrow their lamps. Such men are marvelous advisers and counselors, so long as their own interests are not at stake. Such men work with their heads, while their arms remain idle. From this arises the disorder of their lives; from this arises the disdain of lesser men. Blondet would share his purse with the man he had insulted the day before; he would dine with, drink with, lodge with the man whose throat he would cut the next day. He would justify everything with some clever paradox. Accepting that the world was essentially a joke, he had no desire himself to be taken seriously. Young, beloved, almost famous, and happy, he did not bother to do as Finot did and seek to heap up a sufficient fortune to keep him when he grew older. The most difficult courage, perhaps, is precisely the kind Lucien needed now: he needed the courage to cut Blondet the way he had just cut Madame d'Espard and Châtelet. Unfortunately, though, in Lucien's case the pleasure afforded by vanity took precedence over the exercise of real pride—and the latter is no doubt the basis for many great things. In the preceding encounter, his vanity had triumphed: he showed himself rich, happy, and disdainful of the two people who had previously been disdainful of him when he was poor and miserable. But can anyone expect a poet to do as a seasoned diplomat would have done, to openly break with two so-called friends, men who had welcomed him in his poverty, men in whose homes he had taken shelter during the days of distress? Finot, Blondet, and he had degraded themselves in each other's company; they had wallowed together in orgies where more than their creditors' money had been consumed. Like those soldiers who do not know where to exercise their courage, Lucien did what most young men of Paris would have done, and he compromised his character anew, accepting Finot's handshake and not pulling back from Blondet's embrace. Anyone who has steeped, or is steeping, himself in the world of journalism lives with the cruel necessity of bowing to men he despises, of smiling on his worst enemy, of coming to terms with the vilest acts, of soiling his fingers by paying his aggressors back in their own coin. Such a man grows accustomed to seeing evil done, and he lets it go; he begins by condoning it, and ends by committing it. Eventually the soul, stained day after day by constant shameful acts, begins to shrink, and the springs of noble thoughts begin to rust over and the hinges of banality swing ever more readily. An Alceste becomes a Philinte,[11] character begins to waver and dissipate, talents atrophy, and faith in beautiful works flees. He who wanted to take pride in the pages he produced wastes himself in pathetic articles that, sooner or later, his conscience tells him were really only so many debased acts. Such men come to Paris—like Lousteau, like Vernou—to be great writers, and one day they find that they have become impotent scribblers. This is why there is no honor too great for those whose character rises to the level of their talent, those like d'Arthez who know how to navigate safely through the difficult reefs of the literary life. Lucien could find no reply to Blondet's hypocrisies, though the man's intellectual powers were still incredibly seductive to him, which meant that Blondet retained the status of a kind of corruptor and Lucien that of his pupil. Moreover, Blondet's relationship with the Comtesse de Montcornet was no trivial fact either.

"Did an uncle die and leave you something?" Finot asked teasingly.

Lucien replied in the same tone, "Well, like you I've been able to squeeze a little profit out of some fools."

"Has monsieur managed to acquire a review or a paper then?" replied Andoche Finot with that impertinent directness that an exploiter always uses with those he exploits.

"Oh, better than that," said Lucien, his vanity wounded by the superior tone the editor-in-chief took with him, and he struggled to regain his new position.

"What is it, old friend?"

"I have a party."[12]

Vernou smiled at this. "So there's a Lucien party now?"

"Finot, I warned you that this boy would surpass you. Lucien has talent, and you didn't respect it; you just used him up. Repent, repent, you old boor!" said Blondet.

Blondet's sharp nose had sniffed out that there was more than one secret behind the accent, the gestures, the air of Lucien tonight; he softened his words and tone in order to get a firmer hold on the bridle and to tighten up the bit. He wanted to find out what was behind Lucien's return to Paris, what his plans were, and on whose money he was living.

"On your knees before a superior man, the kind you'll never be, even if you are Finot!" he continued. "Admit, monsieur, and at once, that this is the kind of man to whom the future belongs—and he's one of ours! Clever and handsome as he is, don't you agree that his success is guaranteed, *quibuscumque viis*?[13] Look at him there in his fine Milanese armor, his splendid dagger already half out of its sheath, and his pennant flying! Good God! Where on earth did you manage to steal that superb waistcoat from, Lucien? It must be love; only love knows how to acquire such material. So, do we have a place to stay? At the moment I need to know all the addresses of all my friends, because I've got no place to sleep. Finot kicked me out for tonight, on the vulgar pretext that he has a piece of good fortune coming over later."

"My dear friend," replied Lucien, "I've taken to following a certain axiom, guaranteed to lead to a tranquil life—*fuge, late, tace!*[14] I have to leave you now."

"But I'm not leaving you—not till you pay that sacred debt you owe, our little supper, eh?" said Blondet, who was a little too addicted to good cheer and liked to be treated when he was short on money.

"What supper?" asked Lucien, letting his impatience show a little.

"You don't remember? Ah, that's the sure sign of a friend who's come into prosperity—he loses his memory."

"Oh, he knows what he owes us. I'll vouch for his heart," said Finot, joining in with Blondet's pleasantry.

"Rastignac," said Blondet, taking hold of that elegant young gentleman's arm as he was passing by the column at the end of the room where the so-called friends were conversing, "there's going to be a supper, and you have to join us. . . . Unless," he said, adopting a grave tone, "this gentleman persists in denying his debt of honor, and he might."

"Ah, I assure you that Monsieur de Rubempré is incapable of such a thing," said Rastignac, who was in no mood for joking.

"Look, there's Bixiou!" cried Blondet. "He'll come too—it wouldn't be complete without him. Without him, champagne merely coats the tongue, and I begin to find everything boring, even witty conversation."

"My friends," said Bixiou, "I can see that you're all assembled here surrounding the wonder of our day. Our dear Lucien has started a new chapter for Ovid's *Metamorphoses.* Just as the gods changed themselves into different kinds of plants and vegetables to seduce women, so has he changed Chardon into a gentleman, and all for the purposes of seduction—of—whom? Charles X! Ah, my dear little Lucien," he said, taking him by the buttonhole of his lapel, "a journalist metamorphosing into a great aristocrat deserves a real charivari![15] If I were them," the merciless wit went on, indicating Finot and Vernou, "I'd try to get you into my newspapers; you'd bring in a hundred francs for sure, ten columns of clever little sayings."

"Bixiou," said Blondet, "an Amphitryon is a sacred personage to us for twenty-four hours before and twelve hours after a feast: our illustrious friend is throwing us a supper."

"What's that! What?" exclaimed Bixiou. "But that means we must do everything we can to preserve this great name from oblivion, to bestow a man of true talent upon our supine aristocracy. Lucien, the press adores you, for you were its finest ornament, and we shall not forsake you. Finot, a paragraph on every page one! Blondet, a clever little anecdote on your page four! We must announce the publication of the most beautiful book of our era, *The Archer of Charles IX*! We must beg Dauriat to publish, without delay, the *Marguerites,* those divine sonnets of our French Petrarch! Let us hoist up our friend on the shield of stamped paper, upon which reputations are made and unmade!"

"Look, if you want a meal," said Lucien quietly to Blondet in order to get free of the throng that threatened to grow even larger, "you didn't need to use all that phony rhetoric with an old friend, as if I were some simpleton new in town." Then, for all to hear, he said, "Tomorrow, then, at Lointier's,"[16] and as he said so, he caught sight of a woman; he hurried off toward her.

"Oh—oh—oh!" exclaimed Bixiou in three descending notes, apparently recognizing the masked woman Lucien was running after. "Now this is going to require verification."

La Torpille

And he set off after the handsome couple, looked them over with a shrewd glance, and returned at once, to the great satisfaction of the envious group, who were all anxious to learn the origins of Lucien's fortune.

"My friends," Bixiou announced to them, "you've all known the source of my lord de Rubempré's fortune for a long time. That woman is none other than the old *rat* of des Lupeaulx!"

A particular perversity forgotten these days but well known in the century's early years was the luxury known as rats. A rat—the term is completely obsolete today—was a child of, say, ten or eleven, a hanger-on at one of the theaters, notably the Opéra, whom the débauchés of the era groomed for a life of vice and iniquity. A rat was a sort of page from Hell, a female waif allowed to get away with anything. The rat could take anything it wanted; but you had to regard it as a dangerous animal, though it did introduce a certain gaiety into life, like the Scapins, Sgnarelles, or the Frontins of old comedies. A rat was expensive; it brought you neither honor, profit, nor pleasure; the fashion for rats has so completely died out that hardly anyone today remembered this intimate detail of elegant life before the Restoration until some recent writers took up the subject of rats.

"What," said Blondet. "Lucien had Coralie shot out from under him, so now he takes up with La Torpille?"[17]

The powerfully built man in the mask heard that name and made an involuntary start, which Rastignac observed.

"No, it isn't possible!" said Finot. "La Torpille doesn't have a sou to give him; Nathan told me she borrowed a thousand francs from Florine."

"Come now, gentlemen, gentlemen," said Rastignac, trying to defend Lucien from such foul insinuations.

"No, come on, yourself," cried Vernou, "if you think the man who was essentially kept by Coralie is suddenly some kind of prude."

"Yes," said Bixiou, "I think the thousand francs proves that Lucien is living with La Torpille."

"Ah, what an irrecoverable loss to the higher realms of literature, science, art, and politics!" exclaimed Blondet. "La Torpille is the only whore who has what it takes to be a true courtesan—she hasn't been spoiled by any education, for the girl can't read or write, or she would have understood us. We could have endowed our era with one of those grand Aspasian figures—without which no century can truly be great.[18] Consider how Dubarry perfectly fit the eighteenth century, Ninon de Lenclos the seventeenth, Marion de Lorme the sixteenth, Imperia the fifteenth, and Flora the Roman republic—to which she left her fortune, and which as a result was able to pay off its public debt! What would Horace have been without Lydia, Tibullus without Delia, Catullus without Lesbia, Propertius without Cynthia, or Demetrius without Lamia, who in fact made his reputation?"[19]

"Blondet, talking about Demetrius in the Opéra foyer strikes me as just a little too *Débats*," Bixiou whispered in his ear.[20]

But Blondet continued. "And without these queens, what would have become of the Caesars' empire? Laïs and Rhodope define Greece and Egypt. They are the very poetry of the eras in which they lived. That poetry, which Napoleon lacked, incidentally, because the widow of his *grand armée* is a barracks-room joke—but it wasn't lacking with the

Revolution, which had Madame Tallien![21] And now, just when thrones in France are back in fashion, one particular throne is vacant! We, you and I, could have created a queen. Now, if it were up to me, I would come up with an aunt for La Torpille, because her mother is all too well known to have met her end upon the field of dishonor. Du Tillet would have paid for an apartment for her, Lousteau a carriage, Rastignac a set of lackeys, des Lupeaulx a chef, and Finot—hats." (Finot could not repress a start at being the target of this dig.)[22] "Vernou would have provided advertisements for her, and Bixiou would have fashioned clever things for her to say! The aristocracy would have come to amuse itself at the salon of our Ninon, which would be well stocked with artists who would attend or else be subject to withering articles by us! Ninon II would have displayed a magnificent impertinence and a positively overwhelming luxury. She would have been a woman of opinions. Her home would be the sort of place you might go to read some banned theatrical work, which would turn out to have been written for her. Of course she would not have been a liberal; any courtesan is a monarchist at heart. Ah, what a loss! She should have embraced the entire century, and instead there she is, enamored of that little man! Lucien will turn her into a hunting dog."

"But none of the female notables you mention ever walked the streets," said Finot, "and this pretty little rat has wallowed in the gutters."

"Just like the seed in a compost heap that eventually becomes a lily," replied Vernou, "she was nourished there, and she flowered from there. That's exactly where her superiority lies. She had to know all, didn't she, in order to be able to give happiness and joy to all?"

"He has a point," said Lousteau, who had listened without speaking until now. "La Torpille knows how to laugh and how to make others laugh too. That skill, so sought after by great authors and great actors, belongs to those who have penetrated to the lowest social depths. At eighteen years of age that girl has already experienced the highest levels of opulence, the lowest depths of poverty, and men at every stage along the way. She has a magic wand, so to speak, and she can use it to unleash the animal instincts in men who otherwise keep them violently repressed, men in politics, in science, in literature, in art. There's no other woman in Paris who can be so effective in saying to the Animal, 'Come out of your cage!' And the Animal comes out, and he rolls and wallows in excess; she leads you to the table, up to your chin, and she helps you to a drink, a cigar. That woman is the salt that Rabelais wrote about, the salt that, when it's sprinkled across matter, animates it, raises it up into the great and marvelous regions of Art.[23] Her dress exudes hitherto unknown splendors, her fingers drip with jewels, and her mouth is equally generous with its smiles. She gives a sense of occasion to every little thing she touches, her talk sparkles and glitters, she understands the secret of onomatopoeias, the most highly colored, the most coloring, she . . ."

"You just wasted a hundred sous worth of copy," Bixiou said, interrupting Lousteau. "La Torpille is infinitely better than all that. You've all, more or less, been her lovers, but none of you has had her for a mistress—she can always have you, but you'll never have her. You force open her door, burst in, there's a service you want to ask of her . . ."

"Oh, she's more generous than a bandit chief with a pile of loot, and more devoted than your dearest school friend," said Blondet. "You can trust her with your money and with your secrets. But what makes me want to elect her queen is her Bourbonian indifference to a fallen favorite."

"She's like her mother, much too expensive," said des Lupeaulx. "That beautiful Hollander would have swallowed up the revenues of the archbishop of Toledo, and in fact she did devour two different notaries. . . ."[24]

"She also fed Maxime de Trailles when he was just a page," said Bixiou.

"La Torpille is too expensive—like Raphael, like Carême, like Taglioni, like Lawrence, like Boulle—like all artists of genius, all of them too expensive. . . ." said Blondet.[25]

Then Rastignac said, pointing to the masked woman on Lucien's arm, "No, Esther never had that look about her, that respectability. I'm betting it's Madame de Sérisy."

"Yes, no doubt about it," said du Châtelet, "and that gives us a perfect explanation for Monsieur de Rubempré's sudden wealth."

"Oh, the Church knows how to choose its Levites," quipped des Lupeaulx. "What a pretty little ambassador's secretary he'll make!"

"All the more because Lucien is a man of talent," replied Rastignac. "These gentlemen have had more than one proof of that," he added, looking at Blondet, Finot, and Lousteau.

"Yes, the boy is built to go far," said Lousteau, feeling overwhelmed with jealousy, "and all the more because he's what we like to call an independent thinker. . . ."

"But you're the one who formed him," said Vernou.

"All right," said Bixiou, looking at des Lupeaulx. "I humbly request monsieur the secretary-general and master of requests to deploy his memory in settling this—that woman in the mask is La Torpille, and I'll wager a supper for us all on it. . . ."

"I'll take that bet," said Châtelet, interested in learning the truth.

"Let's go, des Lupeaulx," said Finot. "Come along and see if you can identify your former rat by her ears."

"No need to violate the laws of the mask," said Bixiou. "La Torpille and Lucien will be passing by us as they go through the foyer, and I promise to prove that it's her."

"So our friend Lucien is back upon the waters," said Nathan as he joined the group. "I thought he'd spend the rest of his days in Angoulême. Has he discovered some secret method of outwitting the English?"[26]

"He's done the very thing you will never be in a hurry to do: he's paid off his debts," said Rastignac.

The burly man in the mask nodded in assent.

"A man who can settle down at his age is a man who's lost all his dash and audacity," Nathan insisted.

"Oh, that one will always be the lordly gentleman—he'll always have the kind of ideas that separate him from a great many men who think they're superior," replied Rastignac.

At that, all of them—journalists, dandies, loafers—all stood and stared at the delicious object of their wager, like so many horse dealers appraising a mare. These judges, all old hands in the knowledge of Parisian depravities, all of them of superior intelligence in their various ways and métiers, all equally corrupt, all equally corrupting, all consumed with insatiable ambition, accustomed to assuming anything, to getting below the surface of anything—all of them had their eyes fixed on a masked woman, a woman only they could decode. Only they, and a few other habitués of the Opéra Ball, were capable of distinguishing what lay beneath that long black domino shroud, beneath the hood, beneath the ruff that trails down from the neck in such a way as to raise the question of whether it was even a woman, the roundedness of the figure, the little particularities of manner and walk, the movement of the hips and waist, the way the head was held, all the things an ordinary observer would miss entirely but all things they could make out clearly. And despite her draped and formless exterior, they were all able to recognize the most moving of all spectacles, that of a woman animated by genuine love. Whether it was La Torpille, the Duchesse de Maufrigneuse, or Madame de Sérisy, the highest or the lowest rung on the social ladder, such a creature is a stunning sight, like a flash of the special light we see in dreams. These aged young men, as well as the youthful old men, all felt so vivid a pang at the sight that they all envied Lucien the sublime privilege of escorting that metamorphosis, that transformation of woman into goddess. As for the woman in the mask, she may as well have been alone with Lucien; for her, there was no longer a crowd of thousands around her, no heavy, dusty atmosphere around them; no, she was all alone with him under the celestial vault of Love, like the Madonnas of Raphael beneath their threadlike oval aureoles. She felt no longer the elbowings of the crowd. The flame of her gaze burst through the eyeholes of her mask and, meeting Lucien's eyes, was reignited there; the tremblings she felt in her body seemed to originate in, and respond to, the movements of her lover. Where does it come from, that light that glows all around a woman in love and sets her off from all the others? Where does that sylphlike movement come from, making a woman seem to defy the laws of gravity? Is it the soul, escaping for a moment? Does happiness cause physical changes? The domino enclosed beneath it the simplicity of a virgin, the graces of a child. Although they walked along separately, the two beings resembled those statuary groupings of Flora and Zephyr, cleverly intertwined by the hand of the most cunning sculptor. But Lucien and his pretty domino not only put the onlooker in mind of sculpture, the greatest of the arts: they also recalled those angels busy with flowers or birds as painted by Giovanni Bellini accompanying his depictions of the Virgin Mother[27]; Lucien and the woman belonged to Fantasy, a higher realm than Art, just as Cause is ranked higher than Effect.

When this woman, who had forgotten everything else in the world, passed close by the group of men, Bixiou called out: "Esther?" The unfortunate woman quickly turned her head, as a person does upon hearing herself called; she immediately recognized the malicious individual, and lowered her head like someone in the throes of death. Loud laughter broke out, and the group dispersed, melting into the crowd like so many frightened field mice rushing off from the roadside to seek their holes. Only Rastignac stood his ground, moving only as far as he needed to in order to avoid looking as if he were fleeing Lucien's furious gaze, and from where he stood he was able to see and wonder at two equally profound, though veiled, sorrows: the first was the poor Torpille, looking as if she had been struck by a bolt of lightning, and the other was the mysterious man in the mask, the only one of the group who had not moved away at all. Esther said something in Lucien's ear just as her knees grew weak, and Lucien, supporting her, swept her away with him. Rastignac continued to follow the beautiful couple with his eyes, seeming lost in thought.

"Where did this nickname La Torpille come from?"[28] asked a somber voice that struck fear deep in Rastignac, for the voice no longer attempted to disguise itself.

"It's really him . . . he's escaped again. . . ." he said to himself.

"Keep quiet or I'll slit your throat," the mask said, this time using a different voice. "I'm satisfied with you—you kept your word, so there is more than one who will be willing to aid you. But now, you stay as silent as the grave—but first, answer my question."

"Yes—well, that woman is so attractive that she would have stunned the Emperor Napoleon, and she could stun one much harder to seduce—you!" Rastignac said, trying to slip away.

"Just a minute," said the mask. "I'm going to show you that you could not possibly have seen me, anywhere."

With that, he pulled off his mask, and Rastignac stood there uncertain, finding no resemblance between this man and the one he had known when he stayed at the Maison Vauquer.

"The Devil has given you the power of changing your appearance, but you can't change those eyes—I'll never forget them," he said.

The man's steel grip on his arm tightened, as if to remind him to stay silent about this forever.

At three in the morning, des Lupeaulx and Finot found the elegant Rastignac standing in the same spot, leaning against the column where the terrifying man in the mask had left him. Rastignac had been to confession with himself: he had been priest and penitent, judge and accused. Now he meekly allowed himself to be led off to breakfast, and when he returned home he was quite drunk, but still silent.

A Parisian Landscape

The Rue de Langlade, as well as the adjacent streets, runs between the Palais-Royal and the Rue de Rivoli.[29] This area, which is part of one of the most splendid neighborhoods in Paris, will long retain the foul contamination it received from the dungheaps of old Paris, atop which windmills were erected. These streets, narrow, dark, and muddy, where the kind of businesses that don't care much about appearances are carried on, at nighttime take on a mysterious physiognomy, marked by many contrasts. If a man who did not know Paris at night were to leave the brilliantly lit Rue Saint-Honoré, the Rue Neuve-des-Petits-Champs, and the Rue de Richelieu, where the masterworks of Industry, Fashion, and the Arts are displayed to their busy crowds, and if he were to plunge into this network of dark, tiny streets surrounding bright urban light that even the sky reflects, he would be seized with sorrow, and with fear. From that torrent of gaslight, he would have plunged into thick darkness. Here and there in the distance an oil lamp gives off a wavering, smoky gleam, failing to give any light at all to some of the dark passageways and dead ends. Passersby are rare; they walk by swiftly. Most shops are closed, and the ones that are open are of a sordid type: a filthy wine-shop, a shop selling linen and eau de cologne. An unhealthy chill wraps its damp shawl around your shoulders. Few carriages pass. Sinister corners lurk everywhere, among them the entrance to the Rue de Langlade, the opening of the Saint-Guillaume passageway, and the turnings of various other streets. The Municipal Council has never found a way to clean up this leper house; prostitution long ago established its headquarters here. And perhaps it is better for Parisian society that these alleyways be allowed to retain their foul character. Passing through during the day-time, no one would guess how the place is transfigured at night: then it streams with bizarre creatures that belong to no world; half-nude white shapes line the walls, and the shadows teem with movement. Females, or rather dresses, sweep between the passerby and the walls, chatting and talking among themselves. From certain half-open doorways, sudden laughter bursts out. The kind of words Rabelais called "frozen" now fall and melt around one's ears.[30] Ritornellos arise from the paving stones. All these sounds are not vague; they mean something. A hoarse one is a human voice, but if one sounds like a song, it is no longer human, only a kind of whistling sound. In fact, whistle blasts are often heard. The sound of heels on the pavement has something aggressive, some-thing mocking about it. The whole ensemble of sounds engenders a kind of vertigo. The weather itself is inverted there: winter nights are hot, and summer ones cool. But the nature of this strange world is the same, whatever the weather: this is the fantastic world of Hoffmann the Berliner. The most mathematical of accountants would find nothing of the real here after making his twisting way into this dark region from respectable streets where there are passersby, shops, and modern oil lamps. Whether more disdainful or more ashamed than the kings and queens of earlier times, who were not timid when it came to courtesans, modern politicians and administrators dare not look directly upon this plague of capital cities. Granted, mores change with the times, and those that touch upon the individual and his freedoms are delicate; but surely someone could be bold enough to try to improve basic material condi-tions involving air, light, and building construction. The moralist, the artist, and the wise administrator must miss the old Wooden Galleries near the Palais-Royal where the little lambs that walk the streets flocked together. And wouldn't it be better if they were in one place, where those who were seeking them could find them? Instead, what has happened? Today even the most brilliant stretches of the boulevards, which ought to be the most enchanting promenade, are places one dare not take the family at night. The police have failed to find a way to make use of the passages in order to spare the public streets.[31]

The girl who had been crushed by a word at the Opéra Ball had lived here, in the Rue de Langlade, for the last month or two, in an ignoble-looking house. Stuck up against the wall of an enormous house, this badly plastered construction, incredibly tall but with no depth, getting its little light only from the street, towers and totters like a parrot's perch. Every floor consists of a two-room apartment. A narrow staircase clings to the outer wall, lit in a bizarre manner by the windows it passes, and on every landing stands a sink, one of the most horrible of Paris's peculiarities.[32] At that time the shop and the mezzanine floor above it belonged to a tinsmith, while the owner lived on the floor above that; the other four floors were occupied by very respectable working girls who received many indulgences from the owner and caretaker because of the difficulty of renting such an oddly constructed and situated building. The neighborhood is marked by a great many buildings such as this, the kind of places for which Commerce has no use, and therefore it could only be exploited by forsaken, precarious, or undignified trades.

An Interior Familiar to Some but Unknown to Others

At three in the afternoon, the caretaker, who had seen Mademoiselle Esther brought home half dead by a young man at two in the morning, had just been talking with a tenant lodging on the top floor who, before getting up into a carriage and heading off to some party or other, had confided her concern about Esther: she hadn't heard a sound from her. Esther was no doubt still sleeping, but that sleep was not normal. Alone now in her own room, the caretaker wished she were able to go up to the fourth floor where Esther lived. But just when she had decided to leave her porter's lodge—which was little more than a niche off the landing to the tinsmith's mezzanine—a carriage came to a stop. A man in a long mantle that cloaked him from head to toe, clearly intended to conceal his identity, got out and asked for Mademoiselle Esther. This reassured the caretaker completely; it seemed to explain perfectly Esther's quietness and her tranquility. As the visitor climbed the exterior stairs and passed her lodge, the caretaker noticed the silver buckles that adorned his shoes, and she thought she could make out the black fringe of the sash that is worn over a cassock; she went out and questioned the cab driver, who replied quite clearly without saying a word, and the caretaker now understood everything. The priest knocked, heard no response, and then heard what sounded like sighs coming from inside; he burst the door open with his shoulder and a vigor that was no doubt the sign of holy charity, though in any other man it might simply signal a habitual way of doing things. He rushed into the second room and there discovered Esther half kneeling and half collapsed before a painted plaster Holy Virgin, her hands clasped in prayer. The girl was dying. Burnt charcoal in the grate told the tale of that dreadful morning. The cape and mantle from her domino costume were strewn on the floor. The bed had not been slept in. The poor creature, suffering from a mortal wound to the heart, had come up with the plan to asphyxiate herself, no doubt, upon her return from the ball. A candlewick, trailing from the candle sconce, showed how completely Esther had been absorbed in her final reflections. A handkerchief wet with tears proved the sincerity of the Magdalene, whose classic pose was that of the godless courtesan. Her profound repentance made the priest smile. Inexpert in suicide, Esther had left the door open, without realizing that the air in the two rooms would require a great deal more charcoal to become really unbreathable; the fumes had merely left her dazed; cooler air from the stairs now brought her back, by degrees, to a renewed awareness of her misery. The priest remained standing, lost in his own meditations, untouched by the beauty of the girl, simply observing her first movements as if she had been some kind of animal. His eyes traveled from the crumpled body to other objects in the room in complete indifference. He examined the furnishings of the room, whose cold and much-worn red tile floor was only partly hidden beneath a filthy and threadbare carpet. A day bed of painted wood, old-fashioned, enclosed by yellow curtains with red roses; a single armchair and two painted wooden chairs, all covered with the same calico that served as curtains for the windows; wallpaper with a gray background, dotted with flowers but blackened by time and greasy smoke; a fireplace strewn with the vilest kitchen utensils; two bundles of firewood; a worktable of mahogany; a mantel of stone, upon which were scattered a few glass knickknacks; a dirty pincushion, some perfumed white gloves, a pretty hat tossed on a water jug, a Ternaux shawl plugging a hole in the window, and an elegant dress hanging from a nail; a hard little sofa lacking cushions; ugly broken clogs and pretty slippers, a pair of boots a queen might envy; some chipped porcelain plates of the common variety, upon which could be seen the remains of the last meal, and some nickel knives and forks (the silver of the Parisian poor); a basket filled with potatoes and laundry, on top of which perched a clean lace bonnet; a foul-looking mirrored armoire, its doors open, its shelves exposed, empty except for some pawnshop tickets: such was the ensemble of things both dreary and cheerful, impoverished and luxurious, that struck the observer's eye. Those vestiges of luxury amid the broken fragments, that way of life so appropriate to the bohemian life of the girl kneeling there, her garments unbuttoned, looking like a horse that had died in harness between the broken shafts of the cart, all tangled up now in the reins—what thoughts did the strange spectacle arouse in the priest? Did he say to himself that at least the poor lost creature must have been selfless to go on living in such squalor while in love with a rich young man? Did he think the disorder of her apartment mirrored the disorder in her life? Did he feel any pity, any fear? Was his sense of charity moved at all? Anyone who saw him, his arms crossed, forehead creased, lips tightly closed, his eyes bitter, would have thought the man was entangled in somber, even hateful emotions, conflicted thoughts, sinister projects. Certainly he was entirely unmoved by the sight of the sensuously rounded breasts flattened beneath the weight of the torso in the delicious pose of the crouching Venus, visible beneath the black slip—so intensely coiled up was the dying woman; the drooped head offered from behind a view of the white, slender, lithe neck, the beautiful, well-developed shoulders, but none of this moved him; he did not step forward and raise Esther up, and he didn't even seem to hear the painful, difficult breathing that indicated her slow return to life: a terrible sob and a frightened glance were necessary to get him to raise her up and carry her to her bed with an ease that revealed prodigious strength.

"Lucien!" she murmured.

"If love returns, the woman won't be far behind," said the priest with a bitterness in his voice.

The victim of Parisian depravity then, seeing the clothes her rescuer wore, smiled like a child who held in her hand some long-desired object and said, "So, I won't die without being reconciled with the Lord!"

"You'll have a chance to expiate your sins," said the priest, wiping her forehead with a damp cloth and holding under her nose a bottle of vinegar that he had found in a corner.

"I feel life flowing back into me instead of leaving," she said after accepting the priest's attentions and expressing her gratitude in mute, natural gestures.

And that attractive pantomime, which the Graces themselves might have used for purposes of seduction, justified perfectly the nickname the girl bore.

"Are you feeling better?" asked the cleric, handing her a glass of sugar water.

The man seemed to know places like this one intimately, for he knew where everything was. He made himself at home. The privilege of being at home everywhere is reserved for kings, courtesans, and thieves.

A Rat's Confession

"When you feel like yourself again," said the singular priest after a pause, "you'll tell me the reasons that led you to commit this new sin, this attempted suicide."

"My story is very simple, Father," she replied. "Three months ago I was living in the state of disorder that I was born into. I was the lowest, the most wicked of creatures, but now I'm only the most miserable. Please don't make me tell you about my poor mother, who died at the hands of a murderer. . . ."

"Yes, at the hands of a captain, and it happened in a brothel," the priest said, interrupting his penitent. "I know about your origins, and I also know that if any person of your sex could ever be excused for living a shameful life, it would be you, for no one ever gave you a good example."

"Oh, Father—I've never been baptized, and I've never been taught the basics of any religion."

"All that can still be remedied," said the priest, "provided that your faith, your repentance are sincere and without any reservations."

"Lucien and God fill my heart," she exclaimed with a touching ingenuousness.

"You should say God and Lucien," replied the priest with a smile. "You've reminded me of the purpose of this visit. Tell me everything, and omit nothing, regarding this young man."

"You came because of him?" she asked with so tender, so loving an expression that it would have melted the heart of any other priest. "Oh, he must have been afraid I'd really do it!"

"No," he said; "it's not your dying that concerns me, but your living. Go on, tell me about your relations with him."

"I'll be brief," she said.

The poor girl trembled at the cleric's brusque tone, but as a woman does who has long ceased to be surprised at brutality.

"Lucien is Lucien," she said, "the most handsome young man, and the best creature living; if you knew him, my love for him would seem perfectly natural to you. I met him by chance, three months ago, at the Porte Saint-Martin,[35] where I had gone on my day off—because in Madame Meynardie's house, we only got one day a week off. Well, you won't be surprised to hear that I slipped away the very next day, without permission. Love had come into my heart, and it changed me so completely that when I came home from the theater I no longer even recognized myself: I contemplated myself with horror. Lucien never knew anything about it. Instead of telling him where I really lived, I gave him the address where one of my friends was living; she was kind enough to let me do it. I swear to you on my word of honor . . ."

"Don't swear."

"Is that swearing, to give your sacred word? All right—ever since that day I've been working here in this room, like some lost soul, sewing shirts for twenty sous apiece, trying to make an honest living. For the last month, I haven't eaten anything but potatoes, in order to stay good and worthy of Lucien, because he loves me and respects me as if I were the most virtuous of all possible women. I made my formal declaration to the police in order to get my rights back, and I agreed to two years' surveillance. Oh, they manage to move quickly enough when it's a matter of putting your name on the list of infamy, but they somehow find it awfully difficult to erase it afterward. All I ask of God is to help me keep my resolution. I'll be nineteen in April—at that age, there's still hope. But somehow I feel as if I were born just three months ago. . . . I pray to our Good Lord every morning, begging him to keep Lucien from finding out about my past life. I bought this Virgin you see there; I pray to her in my own way, since I never learned any prayers; I can't read or write, and I've never been in a church; I've only seen our Good Lord in processions, out of curiosity."

"And what do you say to the Virgin?"

"I speak to her the way I speak to Lucien, when I speak from the depths of my soul and make him cry."

"Ah! He cries?"

"But from joy!" she exclaimed. "The poor little thing! We understand each other so well—it's as if we had just one soul between us! He says he's a poet, but I say he's my God. . . . I'm sorry! But you priests, you don't know what love is. And it takes someone like me, someone who knows men as well as I do, to appreciate a Lucien. You see, a Lucien is as rare as a woman without sin, and when you meet one, you can't help loving him and only him—and that's the truth. But a man like that needs a woman like that, and I want to be worthy of being loved by my Lucien. That's where my misery came from. Last night at the Opéra Ball, I was recognized by some young men who have no more heart, no more pity than tigers do—worse, really, because I could manage a real tiger! My veil of innocence was ripped right off, and their laughter went right to my brain, right to my heart. So don't think you've saved me; I believe I still might die of grief."

"Your veil of innocence?" asked the priest. "You mean you haven't, well, indulged Lucien?"

"Oh, Father, you know him, so how could you ask that!" she replied with a brilliant, delighted smile. "You don't resist a God."

"Don't blaspheme," said the cleric, but with a gentle tone. "No one can resemble God; this exaggeration doesn't suit with real love, and your love for your idol hasn't been a pure and true one. If you had really felt the change you boast of, you would have acquired the virtues that are the accompaniment of adolescence—you would have known the delights of chastity, the delicacies of modesty, the two chief glories of a young girl. You don't love him."

Esther started with horror, a movement that the priest observed but seemed in no way to affect his imperturbable confessor's demeanor.

"Yes, you love him for yourself and not for him, for the temporal pleasures that have fascinated you, and not for the sake of love itself; if you've got such a hold on him, you clearly haven't felt that holy trembling that inspires a being upon whom God has set the seal of the most adorable perfections. Didn't it occur to you that your past impurity would be degrading him, that you were in the process of corrupting a child with those frightful pleasures that led to your nickname, to your infamy? You've been illogical with yourself and with your passing infatuation...."

"Passing infatuation!" she said, raising her eyes to his.

"How else would you describe a love that is not eternal, which won't unite us, even in the next life, with the one we love?"

"Oh, I want to be a Catholic!" she cried in a voice that welled up out of her so violently that it would have won the grace of Our Savior Himself.

"Could a girl who has received neither the baptism of the Church nor that of ordinary education, who can't read, can't write, can't pray, can't take a single step without the paving stones themselves rising up to accuse her, a girl remarkable only for a fleeting beauty that might be torn away tomorrow by disease, could that creature, so soiled, so degraded, and knowing her own degradation perfectly well—if you had been ignorant of it and less amorous you might have been more excusable—could that creature, the future prey of suicide and denizen of Hell, possibly become the wife of Lucien de Rubempré?"

Every phrase was a dagger thrust deep in her heart. At every phrase, her sobs intensified, and the abundant tears of the despairing girl were testimony to how powerfully light had penetrated into her mind, as pure as a savage's, and into her soul, finally awakened, and into her nature, upon which depravity had placed a layer of dirty ice, melting now in the sun of her faith.

"Oh, why aren't I dead!" was the sole thought she expressed out of the torrent of thoughts that streamed painfully through her mind, leaving it ravaged.

"My daughter," said the terrible judge, "there is a love that remains unconfessed before men, but which is seen by the angels, and upon which they smile with happiness."

"What love do you mean?"

"I mean the love without hope, when it inspires one's life, when it becomes the motive behind all devotions, when it ennobles every act by the thought of reaching an ideal perfection. Yes, the angels approve such a love, because it leads to the knowledge of God. Perfecting yourself always in order to become worthy of the beloved, making a thousand secret sacrifices for him, adoring him from afar, giving him your very blood drop by drop, eradicating all self-love for his sake, never feeling pride, never feeling anger, always sparing him even the knowledge of the fearful jealousies that he ignites within your heart, giving him everything he wants, even if it harms you, keeping your gaze always upon him so as to follow him without his knowing it—a love like that would have been pardonable from religion's point of view, for it offends neither human nor divine laws and leads you into a path safe from that of your filthy sensual pleasures."

Listening to this horrible verdict, expressed in few words—but what words! And spoken in what voice!—Esther felt a distrust grow within her. The verdict was like a thunderclap announcing a coming storm. She looked at the priest and she felt that gripping sensation inside that even the bravest cannot help but feel when faced with sudden, imminent danger. No gaze could have deciphered what that man was thinking, but the boldest would have seen more to tremble at than to hope for in those eyes that once had been as clear and yellow as a tiger's, but over which austerity and privations had placed a veil like the haze we see on the horizon on the hottest days of August: the earth is hot, luminous, but that mist renders it indistinct, vaporous, almost invisible. A perfectly Spanish gravity and the deep wrinkles that the thousand scars of small-pox had raked into his face rendered it hideous, like furrows in a field, crisscrossing the olive-skinned, sun-darkened face. The severity of his physiognomy was all the more striking for the hair that made a frame around it, the dried-up wig of a priest who no longer takes any care for his appearance, a wig that was black but looked rusted in the light. His athletic chest, his hands like those of an old soldier, his muscular build, his broad shoulders were like those of the caryatids that the medieval architects built into some Italian palaces, and which recall, somewhat, those of the façade of the Théâtre Saint-Martin. The most insightful observer would have thought that either the most powerful passions or some very unusual events must have driven this man into the bosom of the Church; certainly, changing him in any way would have taken the most tremendous thunderbolts, if indeed a nature like his was even susceptible to change.

Anatomy of the Whore

Women who have lived the life that Esther had now so violently repudiated eventually arrive at a state of complete indifference regarding the appearance of a man. In several respects they resemble modern literary critics, who arrive ultimately at a profound indifference to artistry: they've read so many books, seen so many come and go, have become so accustomed to the printed page, seen so many plots through to their resolutions, watched so many dramas, produced so many articles without ever saying what they really thought, betrayed the cause of art so often to serve the cause of friendships and enmities, that they develop a disgust with everything, though they continue nonetheless to make their critical evaluations. It would take a miracle for writers like these to produce real work, just as it takes a miracle for pure and noble love to blossom in the heart of a courtesan. The tone and the manner of this priest, who seemed to have stepped right out of a painting by Zurbarán,[34] seemed so hostile to the poor girl—to whom form had no importance at all— that she felt she was less the object of solicitude than the target of some kind of scheme. Incapable of distinguishing between the rhetoric that masked pure self-interest and that of true charity—for one needs to be on guard at all times to recognize the counterfeit coin palmed off on one by a friend—she felt as if she had been caught up in the talons of some fierce, monstrous bird that had swooped down upon her after long hovering, and in her terror she exclaimed: "I thought priests were supposed to console us, but you're here to murder me!"

At that cry of innocence, the cleric made an involuntary gesture and paused; he reflected before replying. For a moment these two people, so strangely brought together, observed each other. The priest understood the girl, but the girl could not understand the priest. He apparently abandoned some plan that would have been a threat to poor Esther and reverted to his original ideas.

"We are the physicians of the soul," he said gently, "and we know which remedies suit which maladies."

"Poverty must excuse many sins," Esther said.

She felt she had been wrong about him, and she slid down from the foot of the bed to prostrate herself at his feet, kissing the hem of his cassock with a deep humility; she turned her tear-filled eyes up to him.

"I thought I had managed to do a lot," she said.

"Listen, my child: your unwholesome reputation has plunged Lucien's family into grief; they fear, and rightly so, that you'll only lead him into dissipation, into one folly after another . . ."

"It's true—I'm the one who brought him to the ball, hoping to attach him to me."

"You're beautiful enough that he wants to have his triumph in society through you, to show you off proudly, like a prize thoroughbred horse. If it were only a matter of the money he'd be spending! But he'll also be spending his time, his powers—he'll begin to lose his taste for the magnificent future that his supporters have been planning for him. Instead of ultimately becoming an ambassador, rich, widely admired, celebrated, he will end up like so many of the debauched young men who get trapped in the Paris mud—simply the lover of a degraded woman. And as for you, after having risen up into the sphere of elegance for a moment, you'll soon sink back down into the life you led before, because you lack the strength that a good education would have given you to resist vice and to consider the future. You won't be able to break away from your old friends any more effectively than you were able to break away from those men who shamed you at the Opéra this morning. Lucien's real friends, alarmed at the love you've inspired in him, have been following him, and they've learned the whole story. Highly concerned, they sent me to you to sound out your intentions and decide your fate; but while they are powerful enough to clear any stumbling block out of the young man's way, they are merciful too. Understand this, my girl: someone loved by Lucien has rights in their eyes, just as a true Christian can adore a spot of mud in which, for some reason, the divine light shines. I've come to you as the instrument of their benevolent purpose, but if I had found you utterly perverse, armed with effrontery and cunning, corrupt right down to your bones, deaf to the call to repentance, I would have abandoned you to their fury. Now, that civil, political release that is so difficult to obtain, that the police wisely withhold for a time in the interests of society as a whole, and that I heard you hoping for with all the passion of a real pentitent—here it is," said the priest, pulling out a piece of paper that had the look of a formal document. "You saw them yesterday, and this letter is dated today: you can easily see, therefore, how powerful they are, these people supporting Lucien."

The sight of that piece of paper so convulsed Esther by bringing her to the heights of an unhoped-for happiness that, in her naïve joy, she smiled fixedly like a madwoman. The priest paused a moment, watching the girl to see if, once delivered from the horrible strength that their corruption gives to the corrupt, and now returned to her fragile, delicate original nature, she would continue to be open to influence. If she remained a deceitful whore, Esther would have slipped into playing a role; but if she had truly returned to innocence and sincerity, she might die, like a blind man who, restored to sight by a successful operation, goes blind again, unable to bear so much light. At this moment, thus, the priest saw human nature all the way down to its depths, but he remained calm, with a terrible fixedness: he was a cold, granite-flanked Alp, white with snow, neighbor to the sky, unalterable, remote, yet benevolent nevertheless. Whores are essentially creatures of incessant change, capable of slipping, for no reason, from a state of uncertainty and suspicion into one of complete trust. In this respect they are lower than the animals. Extreme in everything, their joys and their despairs, their religiosity and their atheisms, most of them would end up mad if the particular mortality that hovers over them did not take so many of them so early, and if unpredictable bursts of good luck did not raise some of them up and out of the gutters in which they live. To understand the depths of misery that mark this horrible life, one would only have had to observe how deeply into madness one of these creatures can go without remaining there, and one would have had to marvel at the violent ecstasies of La Torpille kneeling before this priest. The poor girl stared at the document giving her her release with an expression on her face that Dante forgot to paint, one that would have surpassed the inventions of his Inferno. But the reaction was accompanied by tears. Esther rose up, throwing her arms around the priest and laying her head against his breast, her tears streaming, and she kissed the rough material that covered up his heart of steel, as if she wanted to penetrate through to it. She held him tightly, covered his hands with kisses; she employed all the little endearments she could think of, called him all the sweetest names she could, but in a holy outpouring of gratitude, and amid all those murmured phrases, continued to say, "Give it to me!" over and over, with varying kinds of intonation; she enveloped him with little tendernesses, swathed him in rapid glances that ought to have rendered him utterly defenseless, and ultimately she did succeed in calming his anger at her. The priest now understood how the girl had earned that nickname; he understood how difficult it was to resist such a charming creature, and he now understood Lucien's love for her, and how she must have seduced the poet. A passion like that conceals, amid its many attractions, a hook that is especially effective with exalted souls like those of artists. Such passions, inexplicable to the mass of people, are perfectly explained by that thirst for the beautiful and the ideal that is so typical of creative souls. For aren't we something like the angels, whose task it is to bring us back from our guilty pleasures to higher things, when we purify such a being as Esther—indeed, in doing so, are we not ourselves creators? How tantalizing it is, to try to unite moral and physical beauty! What an orgy of pride if we succeed at it! How noble the task, its sole instrument being love! Liaisons such as this—well illustrated through history by the examples of Aristotle, Socrates, Plato, Alcibiades, Cethegus, and Pompey,[35] and yet seen by the vulgar as so monstrous—are founded on the same emotion that moved Louis XIV to build Versailles, and that hurls other men into ruinous enterprises, like converting the fetid miasma of a marsh into a mound of perfumes moated by living waters, or placing a lake on the heights of a hill, as did the Prince de Conti at Nointel, or reproducing Swiss landscapes at Cassan, as Farmer-General Bergeret did. It is the eruption of art, in short, into the moral realm.

The priest, ashamed at having given in to such a feeling, pushed Esther violently away; she sat down and felt shame as well when he said, "You're always the whore." And with that he took the document back, tucking it into his ceinture. Like a child who only wants one thing, Esther could not tear her eyes away from the spot where he had tucked away the paper.

The Rat Becomes a Magdalene

After a pause, the priest continued, saying, "My child, your mother was a Jew, and you've never been baptized, nor have you ever been taken to synagogue. You're in the same state of limbo as little babies. . . ."

"Babies!" she repeated in a soft, wistful voice.

"Likewise, in the files of the police, you're a number, with no social identity," continued the impassive priest. "If love came to you as a runaway three months ago and made you feel you were born anew, you must now therefore be in a state of childhood. You must conduct yourself as a child; you must change yourself completely, and I will take it upon myself to render you unrecognizable. And first of all, you must forget Lucien."

The girl felt her heart breaking at those words; she raised her eyes up toward the priest and shook her head; she was incapable of speaking, finding, again, her savior turning into her executioner.

"You will, in any case, not see him," he said. "I'll take you to a convent where girls from the best families are educated: you'll become a Catholic, you'll learn all about Christian practices, and you'll learn religion; you'll leave that place as an accomplished, chaste, pure, well-brought-up young girl, if . . ."

He paused and raised one finger .

"If," he continued, "you feel that you have the strength to leave La Torpille behind you, here."

"Oh!" cried the girl, for whom each word was like the music that opens the gates of Paradise. "Oh! If only I could do that, pour out all my blood here and replace it with new! . . ."

"Listen to me."

She was silent.

"Your future depends on your ability to forget. Think about the extent of the obligations you'll be taking on. One word, one gesture that recalls La Torpille will be the death of Lucien's wife; one word murmured in sleep, one involuntary thought, one immodest gaze, one impatient motion, one recollection of degradation, one omission, one single nod of the head that reveals what you know, or what, sadly, you have known . . ."

"Oh, Father, Father," said the girl, rapt in a saintly exaltation, "I could walk in shoes of red-hot iron and keep smiling, or live in a corset with iron spikes and maintain the grace of a dancer, or eat bread sprinkled with ashes, or drink wormwood—all that would be sweet to me; all that would be easy!"

She fell back down to her knees, kissing the priest's shoes, wetting them with her tears, embracing his knees and then clinging to them, muttering inarticulate words through her tears of joy. Her splendid, beautiful hair streamed down, forming a kind of carpet for the feet of her heavenly messenger, whose expression, however, upon looking up she saw to be somber and hard.

"How have I offended you?" she asked, frightened. "I heard once about a woman like me who bathed the feet of Jesus Christ with perfumes. But you see, virtue has left me so poor that tears are all I can offer."

"Haven't you been listening to me?" he said in a cruel voice. "I'm telling you that when you leave the house to which I'll be taking you, you'll be so completely changed both physically and morally that none of the men or women you've known will be able to call out "Esther!" to you and make you turn your head. Yesterday, your love proved inadequate to burying forever the whore that you were, and today she makes her appearance again in this act of adoration, which ought to be reserved solely for God."

"Didn't He send you to me?" she asked.

But he continued: "If, during the course of your education, you should so much as catch sight of Lucien, everything will be lost."

"Who will console him?" she asked.

"What was it that you consoled him for?" asked the priest in a voice that, for the first time in their scene together, betrayed a nervous tremor.

"I don't know, but he was often sad."

"Sad?" asked the priest. "Did he tell you why?"

"Never," she said.

"He was sad about being in love with a girl like you," he cried.

"Oh, and he had reason for it," she said in profound humility. "I'm the most detestable creature of my sex, and the only way I could find grace in his eyes was through the power of my love."

"That love is going to have to give you the strength to give me your total obedience. If I were to take you off to begin your education today, everyone around here would tell Lucien that you had gone off with a priest, and he might be able to find where you went. So, in a week, when the caretaker hasn't seen me return, she'll take me for something other than what I am. One week from tonight, then, at seven o'clock, you'll leave quietly and get into a cab that will be waiting for you at the corner of the Rue des Frondeurs. During this coming week, avoid Lucien altogether; find some excuses to keep him from coming up, and when he does come, slip into a friend's room; I'll know if you've seen him, and in that case everything is off, and you'll never see me again. You'll need this week to get some decent clothes and to get rid of that whorish look of yours," he said, putting money on the mantel. "There's something in your air, in your clothes, something that Parisians will recognize in you and make them take you for what you've been. You've encountered, haven't you, out on the streets or the boulevards, a modest, virtuous young girl walking along with her mother?"

"Yes, I have, to my sorrow. The sight of a mother and daughter is one of our greatest tortures—it brings back all the remorse we've tried to hide away deep in our hearts, and it devours us! . . . I know what I'm lacking. I know it all too well."

"Well, then, you know how you need to look next Sunday," said the priest, rising to leave.

"Oh, but wait," she said. "Please teach me a prayer, a real one, before you leave, a real prayer I can pray to God."

It was a moving sight, the priest teaching the girl the Ave Maria and the Paternoster in French.

"So beautiful!" said Esther, when she had managed to repeat without any mistakes those two magnificent and popular expressions of the Catholic faith.

"What is your name?" she asked the priest when he said good-bye.

"Carlos Herrera. I'm from Spain, but I'm exiled from my country."

Esther took his hand and kissed it. She was no longer a courtesan but an angel, recovering from a fall.

A Portrait Titian Would Have Liked to Paint

In a house that was famed for the aristocratic and religious education that was provided there, one Monday morning in March of that year, the young ladies in residence saw their number augmented by one, a newcomer whose beauty unquestionably outshone not only each of theirs but the finest traits of each of them as well. In France it is extremely rare, not to say impossible, to encounter all thirty of the famous perfections described in Persian verse and inscribed, they say, in the seraglio, which are necessary for a woman to be perfectly beautiful. In France, if that ensemble is lacking, there are nevertheless many ravishing individual traits. But as for that imposing combination of traits that statuary both seeks to depict and has given us some examples, like the Diana and the Callipygian Venus, that is the possession of Greece and Asia Minor. Now Esther's roots were in that region, the cradle of the human race and the capital of beauty: her mother had been a Jew. The Jews, though thinned and diluted by their contact with other races, still offer among their numerous tribes strains in which that sublime Asiatic beauty is preserved. When they are not repulsively ugly, they present the magnificent character of Armenian beauty. Esther would have been the prize of the seraglio, for in her were combined, harmoniously, all thirty beauties. The strange life she had lived, far from wearing down the fine edges of her charms, had instead instilled some indefinable quality of womanhood: no longer the close, smooth texture of green fruit but not yet the warm tones of maturity—the scent of the flower still lingered. Had she spent a little more time in her dissolute life, she would have begun to thicken around her waist. That rich, full health, that animal perfection in a creature for whom voluptuousness had taken the place of thought would make a rare study for the physiologist. Through some unusual circumstance, not to say an impossible one among very young girls, her hands were of an incomparably aristocratic appearance; and they were soft and transparently white like the hands of women giving birth to their second child. Her feet and her hair were exactly those of the celebrated Duchesse de Barri, hair no coiffeur could tame, so abundant was it and so long, forming ringlets as it fell to the floor, for Esther was of that medium height that allows a woman to be made a sort of toy, to be picked up and set back down, to be carried without fatigue. Her skin, as fine as Chinese rice-paper, had tints of warm amber, given nuance by her pink veins; it had a sheen that was warm without being dry, soft without being moist. Her constitution was strong, though she gave the appearance of fragility, and she often caught an onlooker's attention by a trait we see in the faces Raphael painted to perfection—for Raphael, of all painters, is the one who best studied and best captured Jewish beauty. That marvelous trait and its dramatic effect are the result of the depth of the arch beneath which the eye turns, as though it were freed from its setting, its curve delineated as sharply as the groining of a vault. When youth embellishes that fine arch with its pure, diaphanous tints and outlines it with finely drawn eyebrows; when light slips into the half-circle below it and lingers there with a light pink hue—there the lover finds the treasures of tenderness that comprise his happiness, and there the painter finds his despair. Nature's finest efforts are in those luminous folds, where the shadows have a golden tint, and in that tissue, as fine as a nerve and as flexible as the most delicate membrane. The eye, reposing within, is like a miraculous egg laid in a nest of silken threads. But that marvel, that eye, takes on, as time goes by, a terrible melancholy, when the passions have burned and darkened those delicate contours, and when sorrows have wrinkled that network of fine fibers. Esther's origins could be read in that Asiatic formation of her eyes with their Turkish lids, their color a slate gray that, in sunlight, contracted into the dark blue sheen we see on the black wings of the raven. The fire of those eyes was only tamed by the excessive tenderness in her gaze. It is only with those races whose origins are in the desert that we find such eyes, with the power to fascinate everyone who encounters them (for any woman, of course, can always fascinate one or two). Their eyes no doubt retain something of that infinity they are used to contemplating. Has Nature, in her foresight, armed their retinas with some reflective surface, something that allows them to endure the mirage of the sands, the torrents of sunlight, and the burning cobalt of the sky? Or do human beings, like other creatures, retain something of the environments in which they lived and developed, and do those qualities stay with them for centuries afterward? The great solution to the conundrum of race perhaps lies in the question itself. The instincts are living facts whose origin lies in some necessity that had to be met. And the diversity of animal species is the result of exercising those instincts. To convince yourself of this long-sought truth, you only need to observe the herd of humankind the same way herds of Spanish and English sheep were recently observed. In the meadows where the grass is abundant and thick, each flock stays close together and feeds side by side, but on the mountains, where the grass is sparse, they separate and feed apart. Now, when the two flocks are taken from their native lands and transferred to Switzerland or France, the mountain sheep will continue to feed apart even in a meadow with abundant grass, and the sheep used to the meadow will stay close together even when moved to the mountainside with its sparse grass. Eliminating such acquired and transmitted instincts will take many generations. Even after a hundred years, the spirit of the mountainside will continue to appear in a refractory lamb, just as, after eighteen hundred years of exile, the Orient shone in the eyes and the features of Esther.[36] But her gaze did not cause fearful fascination; on the contrary, it generated a gentle warmth, melting hearts without any surprise, and softening the harshest wills by that same warmth. Esther had prevailed over hatred, and astonished the decadent rakes of Paris; her gaze and the splendor of her flesh had earned her the frightening nickname that had so recently led her to the edge of her grave. Everything about her seemed suited to a Peri of the burning sands. Her forehead was strong and proud. Her nose, like that of Arabs, was thin, the nostrils oval, well placed, and turned up at the edges. Her mouth, red and fresh, was a rose unmarked by any flaw or any trace from her orgies. Her chin, contoured as if some amorous sculptor had polished it, was as white as milk. One thing only, which she had not had time to remedy, betrayed the courtesan fallen so low: her chipped and cracked nails would need more time to recover their shape, so abused had they been by household tasks. The other boarders began by feeling jealousy about all those miracles of beauty, but eventually they came to admire them instead. In less than a week they had all grown attached to the naïve Esther, for they were intrigued by what must have been the secret misfortunes of an eighteen-year-old girl who could neither read nor write, and to whom all knowledge, all instruction were new, and who was bringing the archbishop the triumph of converting a Jew to Catholicism and the convent a fête for her baptism. They found it easier to pardon her beauty when they found themselves so much her superior in education. Esther soon took on their manners and the gentleness of their voices, as well as the bearing and the attitudes of those highly distinguished girls; she was finally recovering her original nature. The change was so complete that Herrera was surprised when he made his first visit—he whom nothing in the world seemed to surprise—and the sisters complimented him on his pupil. The women had never, in their careers as teachers, encountered a nature more charming, a Christianity more delicate, a modesty more genuine, nor a greater desire to learn. When a girl has undergone as much misery as this poor new boarder had, and who expects the reward some day that the Spaniard promised Esther, it is hard to believe that she won't reproduce those miracles that were common in the early days of the Church, the kind the Jesuits have so recently witnessed in Paraguay.[37]

"She is an edification," said the mother superior, giving her a kiss on the forehead.

That word—such a Catholic word!—says it all.

Nostalgia

During their recreation times, Esther discreetly questioned her fellow students about the simplest things in the world, though they were like an infant's first surprises in life to her. When she learned that she would be dressed all in white on the day of her baptism and first communion, that she would wear a white satin band in her hair, white ribbons, white shoes, and white gloves, and that she would have white rosettes in her hair—she burst into tears, right in the midst of her astonished companions. It was the opposite of the scene of Jephthah's daughter on the mountain.[38] The courtesan was afraid of being found out, so she dissembled and attributed what was actually a horrible melancholy to the joy that the prospect made her feel. There is every bit as wide a gulf between the way of life she was leaving behind and the one upon which she was embarking as there is between savagery and civilization, and she had the grace, the innocence, and the depth that characterize the marvelous heroine of *The Prairie*.[39] She had something else, too, though she did not know it: a love that was eating her heart away, a strange love, a more violent desire than any virgin can know, for she knew all and the virgin knows none, though the two might be experiencing the same desire and might share a similar object. During the first months, the novelty of her reclusive life, the surprising things she was being taught, the work she was learning to do, the religious practices, the fervor of a holy resolution and the sweetness of the feelings it inspired in her, and the exercise of her reawakened intelligence all combined to keep her memories quieted, even the efforts she was making to create new memories, for she had as much to unlearn as she had to learn. We are creatures with more than one kind of memory: body and soul each have their own, and nostalgia is an example of a malady of the bodily memory. During the third month, the violent impulses of that virgin soul, stretching its wings to take flight to Heaven, were thus not exactly tamed, but blocked by some heavy resistance whose origin Esther herself could not identify. Like the Scottish sheep, she wanted to pasture alone; she could not overcome the instincts that had been developed during her life of debauchery. Was it the muddy Parisian streets that kept reminding her of the life she had abjured? Was it the chains of those horrific habits she had renounced that were attaching themselves to her, tightly, as if with strong but forgotten bolts? And did she continue to sense their presence the way, physicians tell us, old soldiers continue to feel pains in limbs they have lost? Had the vices, and their excesses, so deeply penetrated into her marrow that even holy water could not reach the demon lurking there? Was the sight of him for whom she was making all these angelic efforts necessary to this girl, whom God must forgive for mingling together human and divine love? One had led to the other. Was it a matter of some kind of displacement taking place within her that was causing this suffering? Everything is doubtful, everything shadowy in such a situation, one that science has not deigned to examine, deeming the subject too immoral, too compromising—as if doctors and writers, priests and politicians, were above suspicion. There was one doctor, however, who did have the courage to begin such a study, though an early death left his work incomplete.[40] Perhaps the black melancholy that preyed upon Esther, darkening what ought to have been her happy life, was the result of all these causes; and unable to divine their nature, perhaps she suffered in the same way sick people do who know nothing about medicine or surgery. The fact is strange. A wholesome and abundant diet replacing an inflammatory one did not sustain Esther. A pure and well-regulated life, alternating between periods of moderate work and periods of recreation, replacing a disordered life in which the pleasures were as horrific as the pains, exhausted the young boarder. The freshest sleep, the calmest nights, replacing crushing fatigues and the cruelest agitations, gave her a running fever, the symptoms of which escaped the eye and touch of the nurse. In short, a happy life succeeding a wretched one and a state of security succeeding anxiety were as lethal to Esther as her past miseries would have been to her young companions. Planted in a bed of corruption, she had grown up in it. The infernal land of her birth continued to exercise its empire over her, despite the commands of a sovereign will. What she hated was life to her; what she loved was death. Her faith was so ardent that her piety was a joy to witness. She loved to pray. She had opened up her soul, letting in the light of true religion, and she welcomed it without effort, without doubts. The priest who acted as her spiritual director was delighted, but her body rebelled against her soul at every moment. Madame de Maintenon once took a notion to have some carp removed from their muddy pool and placed in a marble tank with clean, clear water; she fed them with scraps from the royal table. The carp all died. Animals are capable of devotion, but no human has ever been able to infect them with the disease of flattery. In those days at Versailles, a courtier remarked on the fish's mute resistance. "They are like me," said the secret queen; "they miss their native mud."[41] The phrase explains Esther's whole life. There were times when the poor girl succumbed to an impulse to run madly through the convent's magnificent gardens, rushing from tree to tree, throwing herself desperately into the darkest corners, seeking—what? She did not know, but she was in the grip of the demon; she flirted with the trees, murmuring unspoken words to them. There were times in the evenings when she would creep along the walls like a snake, wearing no shawl, shoulders bared. Often, in the chapel during Mass, she kept her eyes fixed upon the crucifix, tears in her eyes, and the others admired her for it; but her tears were tears of rage: instead of the holy images that she wanted to gaze upon, there rose up before her flaming nights in which she conducted the orgy—conducted the orgy as Habeneck at the Conservatory[42] conducts Beethoven—those wild, lascivious nights with their frenetic activities, their inextinguishable laughter, rising up again before her now, disheveled, furious, animalistic. On the outside she was as smooth and delicate as a virgin held to the earth only by her feminine body—but on the inside raged an imperial Messalina. No one else knew anything about this endless battle between angel and demon; when the mother superior lightly chided her for paying more attention to her hair than the convent's rules called for, she changed her hair style with an adorably prompt obedience; she would have cut all hair off at once if the mother had told her to. This nostalgia was a grievous thing for the girl, who would rather have died than have to return to the country of impurity. She grew pale, she changed, she thinned out. The mother superior lightened her assignments, and called the interesting creature in to question her. Esther was happy; she was infinitely delighted with her companions; she felt no pain or discomfort in any of her vital parts—and yet her vitality was somehow being undermined. There was nothing she regretted, nothing she wished for. The mother superior was surprised by her pensioner's responses; she didn't know what to think, seeing the girl becoming a prey to some all-devouring lassitude. When her state became ever more serious, the doctor was called, but he knew nothing of Esther's previous life and could not even suspect what it had been like; he found her to be healthy in every part, and in pain nowhere. The invalid's responses undid every hypothesis he tried. The learned physician was struck by a fearful suspicion, and there remained only one way to clear that up; but Esther vehemently refused to allow him to examine her. In this crisis the mother superior called upon Abbé Herrera. The Spaniard came, saw Esther's desperate state, and called the doctor aside to talk with him. After hearing those confidences, the man of science declared to the man of faith that the only remedy was a voyage to Italy. But the abbé did not want that trip to take place before Esther's baptism and first communion.

"How much more time will that take?" asked the doctor.

"Another month," said the mother superior.

"She'll be dead," replied the doctor.

"Yes, but in a state of grace, and she will be saved," said the abbé.

In Spain religious questions dominate every other kind of question, whether political, civil, or related to life and death; the doctor therefore made no reply to the Spaniard, turning instead to look at the mother superior, but the terrible priest gripped him by the arm and stopped him.

"Not one word, monsieur!" he said.

The doctor, though he was a Church and Monarchy man,[45] cast a glance of tender pity toward Esther. She was as beautiful as a lily drooping on its stem.

"Then it's up to the grace of God!" he cried, and left.

On the same day as that consultation, Esther's protector took her to Rocher-de-Cancale,[44] for his desire to save her had suggested the oddest possible expedients to the priest. He thought of trying two different forms of excess: an excellent dinner, which might remind the poor girl of her past sensualities, and the Opéra, which would present her with the imagery of worldly luxury. It took the full weight of his overwhelming authority to convince the young saint to partake of those profanations. Herrera disguised himself so perfectly as a military man that Esther could scarcely recognize him; he took care that his companion would be veiled, and he got her a seat in a box where she would be hidden from view. But this treatment, which was entirely without danger for a person of her rediscovered innocence, was promptly abandoned. The young boarder felt disgusted at the dinners given her by her protector, and felt a religious repulsion for the theater, and she sank back into her melancholy. "She is dying of love for Lucien," Herrera said to himself, and he decided to sound the depths of that soul of hers to learn how much it could take. A moment soon came when the poor girl was supported only by her sheer moral will, her body on the verge of surrendering. The priest calculated this moment with the kind of hideous scientific wisdom that executioners use in their art of putting the body to the question.[45] He found his young pupil in the garden, seated on a bench by a trellis upon which the April sun cast gentle rays; she looked as if she were cold and trying to warm herself; her fellow boarders looked with interest upon her pallor, so like withered grass, her eyes like those of a dying gazelle, her melancholic pose. Esther arose to approach the Spaniard with a movement that revealed how little life there was left in her, as well as, we must add, how little taste for life she still had. The poor Bohemian, the wild, wounded swallow aroused, for the second time, a feeling of pity in Carlos Herrera. This somber minister—who was likely to be of use to God only as an instrument of His vengeance—greeted the invalid with a smile that was half bitter and half gentle, equal parts vengeful and charitable. Esther, well versed in meditation, having turned in upon herself during this quasi-monastic life she was living, felt for the second time an upwelling of distrust at the sight of her protector; but, as with the first time, she was immediately reassured by his words.

"Well, now, my dear," he said, "why haven't you ever spoken to me about Lucien?"

"I promised you," she said, shuddering with a sudden convulsion from head to foot; "I swore to you that I'd never mention his name."

"But you haven't stopped thinking about him."

"That, monsieur, is my only sin. I think about him all the time, and just now when you came in, I was saying his name to myself."

"And his absence is killing you?"

Esther's only response was to lower her head, in the manner of invalids who are already breathing the air of the tomb.

"And seeing him again? . . ." he asked.

"That would be life," she replied.

"Are you thinking about him only with your soul?"

"Oh, monsieur—love can't be divided like that."

"Daughter of an accursed race! I've done everything to save you, but now I'll abandon you to your fate—you'll see him again!"

"But why are you insulting my happiness? I can love Lucien and live a virtuous life, can't I? And I love that life as much as I love him. I'm ready to die for it here, aren't I, just the same way I'd be ready to die for him?

Aren't I dying for those two fanaticisms—for the virtue that would make me worthy of him, and for him who threw me into the embrace of virtue? Yes, I'm ready to die without ever seeing him again, and I'm ready to live by seeing him. God will judge me."

Color had returned to her face; her pallor had taken on a golden tint. Her charm had returned.

"The day after you're washed in the waters of baptism, you'll see Lucien again, and if you think you can live a virtuous life by living for him, you won't be separated again."

The priest was obliged to lift Esther up, her knees having given way. The poor girl had fallen as though the earth had slipped out from under her feet; the abbé helped her onto the bench, and when she was able to speak, she said, "Why not today?"

"Do you want to rob Monseigneur of the triumph of baptizing and converting you? You're too close to Lucien, and too far from God."

"Yes—I wasn't thinking of anything else."

"You'll never have any religion," said the priest with profound irony.

"God is good," she said. "He can read what's in my heart."

Entirely vanquished by the delicious naïveté in her voice, her facial expression, her gestures, and her carriage, Herrera bent and kissed her on the forehead for the first time.

"The libertines named you well: you could seduce God the Father. Just a few more days now—it has to be—and you two will be free."

"'You two'!" she exclaimed in an ecstasy of joy.

This scene, viewed from a distance, was a striking one for the boarders and the sisters, who felt they were observing some magical operation, comparing Esther now to how she had been just a moment before. The girl had changed completely. She now took on her true nature, loving, sweet, coquettish, provocative, cheerful—in short, she was resurrected!

A Number of Reflections

Herrera lived on the Rue Cassette, near Saint-Sulpice, a church to which he had attached himself. That church, with its hard, dry style, well suited the Spaniard, whose religion was of the Dominican variety. A lost son committed to the astute political machinations of Ferdinand VII, he served the constitutional cause knowing that his devotion would not be rewarded until the restoration of the *Rey netto*.[46] And Carlos Herrera had devoted himself body and soul to the *camarilla* at a time when the Cortes seemed likely to survive.[47] Such conduct, in the eyes of the world, seemed to proclaim a superior soul. The Duc d'Angoulême's expedition had taken place, Ferdinand reigned as king, and yet Carlos Herrera did not return to Madrid to claim the reward for his services.[48] His defense against curiosity was a diplomat's silence; he explained that his reason for remaining in Paris was his affection for Lucien de Rubempré, and the young man owed to that affection the French king's ordinance giving him the right to use the name de Rubempré. Herrera lived, moreover, the way priests on secret missions always live—obscurely. He carried out his religious duties at Saint-Sulpice and only went out on business, and then only at night and in a closed carriage. His days were occupied by the Spanish siesta, which calls for sleep between the two meals, falling squarely during the time when Paris is most tumultuous and busy. The Spanish cigar also played its role, burning up time as much as it did tobacco. Laziness, though, can be a mask, the same as solemnity, which is in fact a kind of laziness. Herrera lived in one wing of the house, on the second floor, and Lucien occupied the other wing. The two apartments were separate but linked by a large reception room whose antique magnificence suited both the grave cleric and the poet. There was a gloomy courtyard, and the garden was darkened by the shade of tall, thick trees. Silence and discretion always meet in the habitations priests choose. Herrera's lodgings can be described in two words: a cell. Lucien's, on the other hand, brimming with luxuries and furnished with all the niceties of comfort, brought together everything required for the elegant life of a dandy, a poet, a writer, ambitious and oriented toward vice, prideful, vain, utterly negligent but desirous of order, one of those geniuses who have a certain amount of power when it comes to desire, to conceive (which may be the same thing), but are entirely impotent when it comes to execution. Lucien and Herrera, if combined, would constitute a politician. And that, no doubt, was the secret of this alliance. Old men for whom the life of action has been narrowed to the sphere of self-interest often feel the need for some handsome instrument, some young, passionate actor, to accomplish their projects. Richelieu waited too long to find a fine and fair, mustachioed face to present to the women he needed to amuse. Misunderstood by stupid young men, he found it necessary to banish his master's mother and terrorize the queen, after having tried and failed to make himself loved by the one and the other, not possessing the kind of qualities that please queens. However he approaches his object, an ambitious man will eventually come up against a woman, just when such an encounter is least expected. And however powerful such a politician might be, he needs a woman to confront a woman, just as the Dutch use diamonds to cut diamonds. At its moment of power, Rome bowed to this same necessity. Note how the Italian cardinal, Mazarin, was so much more dominating than was Richelieu, the French one. Richelieu finds himself opposed by the great lords, and he reacts by taking an axe to their roots; he died at the height of his power, worn out by his long duel with only a Capuchin monk for a second. Mazarin is opposed by both the united bourgeoisie and nobility, who together were sometimes victorious, putting royalty itself to flight; but the servant of Anne of Austria causes no one to be beheaded, finds a way to seduce the whole of France, and oversees the formation of Louis XIV, who completes Richelieu's work by strangling the nobility with gilded cords in the great seraglio of Versailles. Madame de Pompadour died, and Choiseul was lost. Was Herrera tutored by these great examples? Had he come to know himself at an earlier age than Richelieu had? Had he chosen Lucien to be his Cinq-Mars, but a faithful Cinq-Mars?[49] Nobody could answer these questions, nor could anyone take the measure of the Spaniard's ambition, and still less could anyone see what his goal was. When people managed to get a glimpse of the alliance, so long kept secret, the solution to the mystery that they inferred was horrific, and Lucien had only heard about it a few days previous. Carlos was ambitious for the two of them, and this seemed clear evidence to such observers that Lucien was the priest's natural son.

Fifteen months after Lucien's appearance at the Opéra Ball, which had thrust him into the thick of high society before the abbé had had time to arm him fully for it, Lucien now had three splendid horses in his stable, a carriage for the evenings, and both a cabriolet and a tilbury for the mornings. He ate out. Herrera's predictions were correct: his pupil threw himself entirely into dissipation; the priest thought it was necessary in order to divert the young man from the mad love for Esther that still reigned in his heart. Even after burning through some forty thousand francs, each of his escapades only ended up bringing Lucien to a renewed obsession with La Torpille; he looked everywhere for her, and, unable to find her, she became what game is to the hunter. Could Herrera really understand what love is to a poet? Once such a feeling gets established in the mind of one of these little geniuses, along with his heart and his senses, the poet comes to believe himself as superior to all humanity by virtue of that love as he feels himself to be by virtue of his imagination. Owing to some caprice in his intellectual composition, he has the rare faculty of being able to express nature through imagery in which both feeling and thought combine, and he gives to his love the wings upon which his mind soars: he feels, he describes, he struggles and reflects, he multiplies his sensations by his thought, and he triples his present bliss by means of his hopes for the future along with his memories of the past; he mingles his love with the exquisite pleasures of his soul, and this makes him the prince of artists. Thus the passion of a poet becomes in itself a great poem that far surpasses human dimensions. But is it not also true that the poet ends up placing his mistress up much higher than she would like? He transforms—like the sublime knight of La Mancha—a country girl into a princess. He uses that wand, with which he touches everything and makes it a thing of marvel, for his own purposes, and he thereby transfigures and transplants sensual pleasures into the realm of the adorable ideal. Such a love is therefore the real essence of passion: it is excessive in every respect, in its hopes and its despairs, in its rages and its melancholies, and in its joys; it soars, it leaps, it crawls, resembling nothing like what ordinary men feel; it is to the love of a bourgeois what the eternal torrent of the Alps is to a stream on the plains. These splendid geniuses are so rarely understood that they exhaust themselves with false hopes; they consume themselves in the quest for the ideal mistress, and they die almost always like those beautiful insects ostentatiously designed by some great natural poet and adorned for veritable feasts of love—but that meet their death while still in their virginity, crushed under the boot of some passerby. And there is yet another danger! When they do encounter the bodily form that seems to suit their idea, and which often turns out to belong to a baker's wife, they do as Raphael did, and die in the embrace of their Fornarina.[50] This was the state to which Lucien had arrived. His poetic nature, extreme in all things by its nature, had divined the angel in the prostitute, only brushed by corruption, not actually corrupted: he saw her always white and winged, pure and mysterious—just as she had fashioned herself for him, knowing this is what he wanted.

A Friend

Toward the end of May 1825, all Lucien's vivacity had abandoned him; he no longer went out, instead dining in with Herrera; he seemed always pensive, and he worked, reading volumes on diplomatic topics, sitting cross-legged like a Turk on his divan and smoking three or four hookahs a day. His groom spent more time cleaning and scenting the tubes of that superb instrument than he did brushing the horses' coats or bedecking their manes with roses for a drive in the Bois. The day the Spaniard observed how pale Lucien looked, perceiving what appeared to be signs of illness beneath the absurd excesses of frustrated love, he decided to sound the heart of this man with whom he had bound up his own life.

One fine evening Lucien was sitting in an armchair, absently watching the setting sun through the trees in the garden, exhaling scented smoke in slow, langorous puffs, the way preoccupied smokers tend to do, when his reverie was interrupted by the sound of a heavy sigh. He turned and saw the abbé looking at him with arms crossed.

"Ah, you're there, are you?" said the poet.

"Yes, for quite a long while," the priest replied. "My thoughts have been following yours on their upward path . . ."

Lucien understood what he meant.

"I never pretended that I had a nature of bronze like yours. Life is either heaven or hell for me; but when it's neither the one nor the other, it bores me, and I am bored. . . ."

"How could anyone with such magnificent hopes before him be bored?"

"Well, when one no longer believes in those hopes, or when they're so hidden behind veils . . ."

"Let's stop the nonsense!" said the priest. "Opening your heart to me would be more worthy of you, and of me. There's something standing between us that should never be there—a secret! That secret has been there for the last sixteen months. You're in love with a woman."

"And so?"

"A foul prostitute named La Torpille."

"And so?"

"Look, my child, I've given you permission to take a mistress, but it should be a woman of the Court, someone young and beautiful, someone influential, someone who is at least a countess. I chose Madame d'Espard for you, and without any scruples about it because she would have served as an instrument for making your fortune—and she would certainly never have perverted your heart; she would have left you free. . . . But to love a prostitute, and the lowest kind, when you're not like a king with the power to ennoble her, this is a serious error."

"And would I have been the first one to turn my back on ambition and give myself up to wild, passionate love?"

"All right," said the priest, picking up the *bocchettino* of the hookah[51] that Lucien had allowed to fall onto the floor and handing it to him. "I get your point. But can't you combine ambition and love together? Child, you have in old Herrera a mother whose devotion to you is absolute."

"I know it, old friend," said Lucien, taking his hand and shaking it.

"You wanted the toys that go with wealth, and you have them. You want to stand out, so I open doors and show you the way to power, I kiss some very dirty hands to help you get ahead—and you get ahead. In only a little while you'll have everything that charms both men and women. You're womanly in your capriciousness but masculine in your mind— I've thought of everything for you, and I forgive you everything. You have only to speak to have your passing desires met. I've enlarged your life by inserting into it the thing that the greatest number of people adore, the cachet of political influence and power. You will be as great one day as you are small today—but one thing you must not do, and that is break down the machine with which we coin our money. I permit you every- thing, but not the stupid mistakes that could one day put an end to your future. When I open up the doors of the salons in the Faubourg Saint- Germain for you, I positively forbid you to stay outside and wallow in the gutters! Lucien! I'll be like a staff of iron supporting your interests, and I'll put up with everything from you, for you. And to begin with, I've transformed your awkwardness at the game of life into the finesse of a winner. . . ."

At this, Lucien abruptly and angrily raised his head.

"I've removed La Torpille!"

"You?" cried Lucien.

In a fit of animal rage, the poet got up and threw the bejeweled gold *bocchettino* into the priest's face, powerfully enough to knock the Span- iard down, strong as he was.

"You do this to me!" exclaimed the Spaniard, rising to his feet with a terrible solemnity.

The black wig had fallen off. The skull, smooth as a death's head, revealed the man's true physiognomy: it was terrifying. Lucien remained on his divan, his arms dangling, overwhelmed, staring stupidly at the priest.

"I took her away," said the priest.

"What have you done with her? You took her away, then, the morning after the masked ball. . . ."

"Yes, the day after I observed a person attached to you being insulted by a pack of fools I wouldn't even bother to kick in the . . ."

"Fools," interrupted Lucien. "No, monsters—compared with them, the people who end up guillotined are angels. Do you know what that poor La Torpille did for three of those men? One of them had been her lover for two months, when she was poor and had to seek her bread in the gutters; he didn't have a sou to his name, just like me when you met me, getting closer to the river every day; this character would get up in the middle of the night and go to her cupboard to find whatever was left from her meal, and eat it. Eventually, she figured out the shameful thing he was doing, and she took care to leave more for him, and she was happy—she told me all this in the cab on the way home from the Opéra Ball. The second one was a thief, he'd stolen some money, and she was able to put together a large enough sum for him to cover the theft—for which he never bothered to repay her. As for the third one, she made his fortune by playing out a role worthy of the genius of Figaro—she pretended to be his wife and became the mistress of a very powerful man who thought she was the most honest and respectable bourgeois possible. Life for one, honor for the other, fortune for the third—which he still has! And you saw for yourself the reward they give her."

There was a tear in Herrera's eye. He asked, "Do you want them to die?"

"Oh, come on—that's just like you, isn't it?"

"Well, my angry poet, you need to know the whole story," said the priest. "La Torpille no longer exists. . . ."

Lucien threw himself at Herrera so violently, seizing him by the throat, that any other man would have fallen again; but the Spaniard's strong arm took hold of the poet.

"Listen to the whole story," he said coldly. "I've made her into a chaste, pure, well-raised, devout woman, the kind of woman who is all she should be. She is currently taking instruction. She can become—she must become, with the power of your love—a Ninon, a Marion de Lorme, a Dubarry, as the journalist said at the Opéra. You can openly avow her as your mistress, or you can remain behind the curtains and watch your creation perform, which would be the wiser course. But either way will serve your profit and your pride, your pleasure, and your progress— but if you're as good a politician as you are a poet, Esther will simply remain a whore for you, because later on she might do us both a lot of good—she's worth her weight in gold. Drink, then, but don't get drunk. If I hadn't come along and reined in your passion, where would you be today? You'd be wallowing with your Torpille in the same mud I pulled you out of. Take this—read it," said Herrera with all the simplicity of Talma playing Manlius (which he had never seen).[52]

A piece of paper dropped into the poet's lap, for he sat stunned at this startling, ecstatic news, and he now was roused out of it. He picked up, and read, the very first letter ever written by Mademoiselle Esther.

To Monsieur l'abbé Carlos Herrera

My dear protector, please accept this proof that my gratitude takes precedence over my love, for my first attempt at expressing my thoughts through writing is addressed to you, rather than devoting that first attempt to describing my love, which Lucien has perhaps forgotten. But I can say things to you, as a man of God, that I could not say to him who still walks upon this earth, to my great happiness. The ceremony yesterday poured out the treasures of grace upon me, and I again put my destiny in your hands. If I must die far from my well-beloved, I will die purified like Magdalene, and my soul will go on to rival his guardian angel. Will I ever forget yesterday's festival? How could I ever wish to abdicate the glorious throne I was set upon? Yesterday, all my sins were washed away in the waters of baptism, and I received the sacred body of our Savior; I have become one of His tabernacles. At that moment I heard the singing of the angels, I was no longer a woman, I was born anew into a world of light amid the acclamations of the earth, admired by the world in an intoxicating cloud of incense and prayers, adorned like a virgin bride for a celestial spouse. Finding myself to be what I never hoped to be, that is, worthy of Lucien, I have renounced all impure love, and I never want to walk in any path but that of virtue. If my body is weaker than my soul, may it perish. Be the arbiter of my destiny, and if I die, tell Lucien that I died to him while being born to God.

This Sunday evening

Lucien stood up and faced the abbé, his eyes wet with tears.

"You know the apartment where fat Caroline Bellefeuille lives, on the Rue Taitbout," said the Spaniard.[53] "The girl was abandoned by her magistrate lover and found herself in a terrible fix, with creditors closing in; I bought her house with everything in it, and she's gone, taking only her clothes. Esther, the angel who wants to ascend to Heaven, has descended there, where she awaits you."

At that moment Lucien could hear his horses pawing the ground outside in the courtyard; he lacked the strength to express the admiration he felt at such devotion, a devotion only he could truly appreciate. He threw himself into the arms of the man he had just assaulted, making amends for everything by the expression on his face and his mute overflow of feeling; he then raced down the stairs, called out Esther's address to his tiger,[54] and the horses rushed off as if their master's passion had animated their limbs.

In Which We Learn That There Is No Priest
in the Abbé Herrera

The next day a man, whose clothes would have suggested to a passerby a policeman in disguise, was walking back and forth along the Rue Taitbout, across the street from a house that he seemed to be watching, waiting for someone to emerge; the way he walked suggested that he was somewhat agitated. You will often encounter, in Paris, people walking in just this way—real policemen hunting down some National Guardsman who's gone missing, bailiffs preparing an arrest, creditors meditating some means of extorting a little money from a debtor in hiding, lovers and husbands in the throes of suspicion and jealousy, friends standing watch to help out a friend; but you will very rarely encounter a face like this one, with wild, rude ideas animating it, or anything like the somber athlete who was pacing back and forth beneath Mademoiselle Esther's windows with the single-minded intensity of a caged bear. At noon a window opened, and through it came the hand of a maidservant, pushing back the padded shutters. Shortly after that, Esther appeared at the window in her dressing gown to breathe in the air; she was leaning on Lucien's shoulder; anyone seeing them might have taken them for the original of a pretty English vignette. But then Esther saw the basilisk eyes of the Spanish priest, and the poor creature jumped as if she had been struck by a bullet, giving a little cry of fright.

"It's that terrible priest," she said, pointing him out to Lucien.

"Him!" he said with a smile. "He's no more a priest than you are. . . ."

"Well, what is he then?" she asked, frightened.

"Oh, he's just an old rogue who only believes in the Devil," said Lucien.

Anyone less devoted than Esther seizing upon this piece of information about the false priest might have led to Lucien's permanent downfall. The two lovers left their bedroom window and walked toward the dining room, where their breakfast was being served, but on the way they encountered Carlos Herrera.

"What are you doing here?" Lucien asked brusquely.

"I've come to give you my blessing," said the boundlessly audacious character, blocking the couple's way and forcing them to stay in the apartment's little drawing room. "Now listen to me, little lovebirds! Have fun, be happy, everything is fine. Happiness above everything else, that's my motto. But you," he said to Esther, "the one I pulled up out of the gutter and washed clean, body and soul, you don't have the gall to think you can stand in Lucien's way? . . . And as for you, my little friend," he continued, looking now at Lucien, "I trust you're not going to be such a poet as to let yourself run after a new Coralie. We're making prose now, not poetry. What great future awaits the lover of Esther? None. Could Esther become Madame de Rubempré? No. Well, then, little one," he said, taking hold of Esther's hand, which shuddered as if a serpent had wrapped itself around it, "society must never know you're alive, and it must certainly never know that Mademoiselle Esther loves Lucien, and that Lucien is infatuated with her. . . . This apartment is going to be your prison, little one. If you want to leave, if your health requires it, you can go out after nightfall, at an hour when no one can possibly catch sight of you—because your beauty, your youth, and the distinction you've acquired at the convent would be all too quickly noticed in Paris. The day when anyone—and I mean anyone," he said in a frightening voice and with the most terrifying expression on his face, "learns that Lucien is your lover or that you are his mistress, that day will be the second to the last one of your life. I've managed to get an ordinance permitting that young man to take the name of his maternal ancestors. And that's not the end of it: the title of marquis was not yet given; to obtain that, he must marry the daughter of a good family, a girl for whose sake the king will grant this favor. That alliance will place Lucien in the social world of the Court. That boy, the one I've turned into a man, will begin by being an ambassador's secretary; later on, he'll be a minister posted to some small court in Germany, and with God's help—or rather, with mine, which is more to the point—he will take his seat on the benches of the peers of France. . . ."

"Either that or the benches of the galleys."

"Be quiet," cried Carlos, covering Lucien's mouth with his large hand. "Would you reveal secrets like that in front of some woman?"

"'Some woman'—Esther?" exclaimed the author of the *Marguerites*.

"Oh, more sonnets!" said the Spaniard. "Gibberish. All angels revert to just women sooner or later, and every woman has her moments when she's an ape, a child! Two beings we laugh at, but at our own peril. Esther, my jewel," he said to the terrified young boarder, "I've found a personal maid for you, a woman as closely bound to me as my own daughter. And for a cook you'll have a mulatto, which will give the place a nice tone. With Europe and Asia, you can live here like a queen—a stage queen, anyway— for a thousand francs a month, and that covers everything. Europe has been a dressmaker, a seamstress, and a stage extra. Asia has cooked for a gourmet gentleman. The two of them will be like good fairies to you."

Seeing Lucien shrink into a little boy before this being who was guilty of, at the least, sacrilege and impersonation, the young woman, consecrated by her love, felt a terror deep within her heart. Saying nothing, she drew Lucien with her into the bedroom, where she asked, "Is he the Devil?"

"No, he's worse—for me!" he said vehemently. "But if you love me, try your best to match that man's devotion and obey him, on pain of death."

"Of death?" she said, even more terrified.

"Of death," replied Lucien. "Oh, my little darling, no death could compare to what would befall me if . . ."

Esther grew pale as she waited for him to finish his sentence; the words seem to stick in his throat.

"Well?" thundered the sacrilegious imposter. "Have you both had enough time to sniff your marguerites?"

Esther and Lucien came back out, and Esther said, not daring to meet the eyes of the mysterious man, "You will be obeyed, monsieur, exactly as if you were God Himself."

"Good!" he said. "Now you will be quite happy, for a while, and . . . you'll only need clothes for going out at nighttime, which will be very economical."

Two Extraordinary Watchdogs

At that, the two lovers turned to proceed to their dining room; but Lucien's protector made a gesture to stop them. "I've just described a couple of people to you, my child, and now you need to meet them both."

The Spaniard rang twice. The two women, whom he had called Europe and Asia, appeared, and indeed it was easy to see how they'd acquired those names.

Asia, who looked as if she had been born on the island of Java, offered to the observer that copper-colored face typical of Malays, a frightening face, one flat as a board, one where the nose seemed to have been driven inward by some powerful, violent force. The strange formation of the maxillary bones made the lower part of her face resemble that of the great apes. The forehead was low, but it nonetheless suggested a cunning intelligence. Two small, fiery eyes were calm, like those of the tiger, but the gaze was averted. It was as if Asia were afraid of scaring people. Her lips, a very pale bluish color, parted to reveal twisted but bright white teeth. The general impression this animal physiognomy suggested was guileful treachery. The hair, oily and gleaming, like the skin of her face, parted into two black bands, was edged by a very rich headscarf. Her ears were quite pretty, ornamented with two great dark pearl earrings. Petite, short, and squat, Asia looked like one of those bizarre creatures the Chinese like to paint on screens, or, more precisely, like those Hindu idols that surely cannot exist in nature but which travelers nonetheless seem always to run across. Upon seeing this monster, wearing a white apron over a cloth dress, Esther shuddered.

"Asia!" said the Spaniard, and the woman raised her head exactly the way a dog does when looking up at its master: "This is your mistress. . . ."

And he pointed to Esther in her dressing gown. Asia looked at the young fairy with an expression almost sorrowful; but at the same time, a gleam flashed from between those compressed eyelids and shot like a flaming arrow toward Lucien, who was dressed in a splendid robe that hung open, revealing beneath it a fine Holland linen shirt and red trousers, a Turkish-style cap on his head from which escaped his thick blond curls; he looked like a god. The Italian genius, perhaps, can invent and tell the tale of Othello; the English genius can animate it and put it on the stage; but only nature herself has the power to create that expression of jealousy, surpassing anything Italy or England could have imagined. Esther caught sight of it, and she clutched the Spaniard's arm, digging her fingernails into it like a cat digging in its claws to avoid falling into some bottomless pit. The Spaniard then spoke some three or four words in an unknown language to the Asiatic monster, who stepped forward and knelt at Esther's feet, bending forward and kissing them.

"This," said the Spaniard to Esther, "is no ordinary cook, but a chef who would make Carême go mad with jealousy.[55] Asia can do anything in the kitchen. She can prepare a simple dish of beans for you, and you'll wonder if angels haven't come down from Heaven with some celestial herbs. She goes to Les Halles herself every morning, and she'll battle like a demon to get the best prices; she is discreet, and the curious get nothing out of her. You're going to pass for having lived in the Indies, and Asia will help you a great deal in making that fable credible, for she is one of those Parisians who can claim to be any nationality she wishes. But my advice would be for you not to pretend to be a foreigner. . . . Europe, what do you think?"

Europe was a perfect contrast to Asia, for she was the sweetest lady's maid that Monrose could ever wish to be playing opposite him on the stage.[56] Slim and seemingly somewhat scatterbrained, with a weasel's face and sharp nose, Europe looked like a person worn down by the corruptions of Parisian life; she looked like someone who had been nourished on nothing more than sour apples; she was lymphatic, sinewy, soft yet tenacious. Her foot thrust forward, her hands in her apron pocket, she gave the impression of restless movement even when she was standing still. Both grisette and stagehand, she had already pursued many careers. As perverse as all the Madelonnettes together, she seemed the type who might have robbed her parents and hobnobbed with her peers on police station benches.[57] Asia inspired great fear, but one felt one understood her immediately: she was a direct descendant of the tribe of Locusta.[58] Europe, on the other hand, inspired a disquiet, which inevitably worsened the longer one was around her; her corruption seemed boundless; she could, as the saying goes, stir up serious trouble.

"Madame might come from Valenciennes," said Europe in a quiet, dry tone. "That's where I'm from. Would monsieur," she said to Lucien with something of a schoolteacher's tone, "kindly let us know the name he would like madame to be called?"

"Madame Van Bogseck," replied the Spaniard, inverting Esther's real name.[59] "Madame is a Jew originally from Holland, the widow of a merchant and ill with a liver malady contracted in Java. . . . Doesn't have a large fortune—not enough to excite curiosity."

"Enough to live on," said Europe. "Six thousand francs a year, and we'll complain about her being stingy."

"That's it," nodded the Spaniard. "You two devils!" he exclaimed in his terrible voice, having detected Asia and Europe exchanging a look that displeased him: "Have you forgotten what I told you? You're serving a queen, and you're going to give her the respect that a queen deserves—you're going to cherish her the way you'd cherish some vengeance, and you're going to be as devoted to her as you are to me. Neither the porter, nor the neighbors, nor the other tenants—nobody on earth is to know what happens here. Your job is to deflect all curiosity, if any arises. And madame," he said, gripping Esther's arm with his big, hairy hand, "madame must not commit the slightest imprudence, and you'll stop her if she's about to—but always respectfully. Europe, you'll go out for anything concerning madame's clothes and needs, and you'll sew for her here, to be thrifty. Finally, no one, not even the most insignificant person in the world, is ever to set foot in this apartment. You two will have to do everything that needs to be done. Now, my little beauty," he said to Esther, "when you want to go out, you'll go in a carriage, and you'll tell Europe, so that she can go round up your people—for you'll have a man-servant, someone who belongs to me, just like these two slaves."

Esther and Lucien said not a word, listening to the Spaniard and staring at the two precious specimens to whom he was giving orders. What did he have on them to ensure that absolute submission, that devotion that was so clearly written on both their faces? He could tell what Esther and Lucien were thinking, standing there stunned like Paul and Virginie faced with two horrible serpents,[60] and he said to them more quietly, in his more pleasant voice, "You can count on them as completely as you do on me. Have no secrets from them—that will flatter them. You, my little Asia," he said to the cook, "go to your work; and you, my little pretty one, set a place," he said to Europe. "The least the children can do is give Papa some breakfast."

When the two women had closed the door and the Spaniard could hear Europe going to and fro in the next room, he said to Lucien and the girl, spreading wide his large hand: "I own them!" he said with a gesture that made them shudder.

"Where did you find them?" cried Lucien.

"Well, by God, I can tell you I did not find them on thrones! Europe comes from the gutter, and is afraid of ending up there again.... Threaten them with *monsieur l'abbé* whenever they aren't satisfactory, and you'll see them tremble like a mouse who hears talk about a cat. I'm good at taming wild animals," he added with a smile.

"You seem like a demon to me!" exclaimed Esther, quite attractively, as she clung even more tightly to Lucien.

"My child, I've tried to give you to Heaven, but the reformed whore will always be a mystery for the Church—if it found one and took her to Paradise, she'd turn whore again there.... You've succeeded in forgetting who you were and in becoming respectable, because what you've learned there you never could have learned in the foul life you'd been living.... No, you don't owe me anything," he said, observing the charming expression of gratitude coming over Esther's face. "I did it all for him," and with that he indicated Lucien. "You're a whore and you'll always remain one; you'll die a whore, because despite the seductive theories of people who keep wild animals, in this life you can't be anything other than what you are. The man who feels the bumps is right. You have the bump of love."[61]

The Spaniard was, as one can see, a fatalist, just like Napoleon, Mohammed, and many other great politicians. It is a strange fact that nearly all men of action are inclined to fatalism, just as most thinkers incline toward a belief in Providence.

"I don't know what it is that I am," replied Esther with an angelic sweetness, "but I love Lucien, and I'll die adoring him."

"Come on and let's have our breakfast," said the Spaniard brusquely. "And pray to God that Lucien doesn't get married very soon, because you won't see him again after that."

"His marriage will be my death," she said.

She let the false priest pass first in order to reach up to Lucien's ear without being seen, and whisper to him.

"Is it what you want," she said, "that I remain in the power of that man, who's going to have me guarded by those two hyenas?"

Lucien nodded. The poor girl suppressed her sorrow and put on a joyful demeanor, but inwardly she felt painfully oppressed. It would take more than a year of constant, devoted service for her to get used to those two terrible creatures, called by Herrera "the two watchdogs."

A Tedious Chapter, Explaining Four Years of Happiness

Lucien's conduct, since his return to Paris, was marked by a political skill so profound that it inevitably invited the jealousy of all his old friends, toward whom he exercised no further vengeance than enraging them by his success, his irreproachable behavior, and his new habit of keeping people at a distance. The poet who had been so open, so expansive, now turned cold and reserved. De Marsay, taken by the youth of Paris as the very model of behavior, was no more measured in his discourse and in his actions than Lucien. As for his intelligence, the journalist had already given proof of that. People began comparing de Marsay and Lucien to the latter's advantage, and de Marsay was petty enough to get angry about it. Lucien, very much in favor among the men who secretly held the power,[62] so thoroughly turned his back on all thoughts of literary glory that he was uninterested in the success of his novel, republished now under its original title, *The Archer of Charles IX,* and to the public stir caused by his collection of sonnets, the *Marguerites*—and that book, printed at last by Dauriat, sold out in under a week. "It's a posthumous success," he said with a smile when he was complimented on it by Mademoiselle des Touches. The terrible Spaniard used his arm of steel to keep his creature firmly on the path leading to the glory and spoils that await the politician who remains patient. Lucien took over Beaudenord's apartment on the Quai Malaquais,[63] so as to be closer to the Rue Taitbout, and his mentor took lodgings in the same building, on the fourth floor.[64] Lucien now kept only a saddle horse and a small cabriolet, along with one manservant and one groom. When he did not dine in town, he dined with Esther. Carlos Herrera kept such a close eye on the people in the Quai Malaquais house that Lucien spent no more than ten thousand francs a year. And ten thousand francs was adequate for Esther, due to the constant, inexplicable devotion of Europe and Asia. Lucien took the most elaborate and careful precautions both in going to the Rue Taitbout and in coming back from it. He always went there by cab, keeping the blinds drawn, and he made the driver pull into the courtyard. Thus his passion for Esther and the very existence of the household at the Rue Taitbout, completely unknown to anyone in society, did no harm to any of his enterprises or his relationships; no indiscreet word about any of it ever fell from his lips. The errors of that type that he made during his first sojourn in Paris, with Coralie, had been a valuable experience. His life now showed the kind of regularity and good form behind which any number of mysteries can remain concealed: he stayed out in society every evening until one in the morning; you could find him always at home between ten in the morning and one in the afternoon; at that time he went to the Bois du Boulogne and paid visits until five. He was rarely seen on foot, which allowed him to evade his old acquaintances. When some journalist or one of his old friends did hail him, he responded with a nod of the head, polite enough that no one could take offense, but with just a hint of disdain, enough to discourage French familiarity.[65] He was thus able to shed very quickly those people he no longer wanted to know. A longstanding hatred kept him from visiting Madame d'Espard, though she had wanted to have him there a number of times; but when he met her at the homes of the Duchesse de Maufrigneuse or of Mademoiselle des Touches, he always maintained an impeccable politeness with her. That hatred, which was fully reciprocated by Madame d'Espard, obliged Lucien to use prudence, for, as we will see, he allowed himself a certain act of revenge that ended up costing him a strong rebuke from Carlos Herrera: "You're not powerful enough yet to take your revenge on anybody," the Spaniard said. "When you're walking under a hot sun, you don't stop to pick even the choicest flower." Lucien had too fine a future ahead of him, and too much real superiority, for the young men not to wish him ill, the same young men who were shocked and annoyed to see him return to Paris. Knowing he had many enemies, Lucien was well aware of how his friends were disposed toward him. And so the abbé was admirable in the way he took care of his adoptive son, putting him on his guard against the treachery of society and the imprudences that can prove fatal to a young man's chances. Lucien was expected to narrate, and in fact did narrate, all the day's events to the abbé, including the most seemingly inconsequential. Thanks to his mentor's advice, he deflected even the shrewdest curiosity, that of higher society. Guarding himself by adopting an English gravity of manner, and erecting around himself impenetrable walls of circumspection worthy of a diplomat, he gave no person the right or the opportunity to catch a glimpse of his affairs. His youthful, beautiful face, when in society, had become as impassive as that of a princess at a ceremony. Around the middle of 1829 there was talk of his marriage to the eldest daughter of the Duchesse de Grandlieu, who at the moment had no fewer than four daughters to get settled. No one doubted that, if this alliance took place, the king would confer upon Lucien the title of marquis. The marriage was going to decide Lucien's political future; he would probably be named minister to some court in Germany. Certainly, for the past three years his life had been conducted with an irreproachable sagacity; even de Marsay was heard to say about him, "That fellow must have some real power behind him." Lucien was on the verge of becoming someone of importance. His passion for Esther had actually helped him play the role of the solemn gentleman. A habit of that sort keeps an ambitious man well clear of any number of stupid acts; caring for no other woman, he was in no danger of letting physical needs undermine his plans. The happiness Lucien was now enjoying was that of the penniless poet, dreaming his dreams in a garret. Esther, the ideal of the courtesan in love, naturally reminded Lucien of the actress Coralie with whom he had lived for a year, but Esther entirely eclipsed her. Every woman in love, every devoted woman, seeks seclusion, incognito, the life of the pearl in the depths of the sea; but with most of them, it is only a charming whim, a conversation topic, a proof of love that they dream of giving but never really do; Esther, on the other hand, still as on the morning of her first happiness, as on the first day she felt the warmth of Lucien's loving gaze, had never in these four years had the slightest bit of curiosity. She deployed all the resources of her mind to remain carefully within the terms of the program traced for her by the lethal hand of the Spaniard. And more! She never, amid all these intoxicating raptures, took advantage of the power that a beloved woman gets from her lover's reviving desire to ask Lucien anything more about Herrera, who continued to terrify her: she dared not let herself think about him. The shrewd benefits that mysterious person had bestowed on her, the education at the convent school, the ways of a respectable woman, her spiritual regeneration—all these seemed to the poor girl to be only loans from Hell. "I'm going to have to pay for this someday," she told herself with a shudder. On nights when the weather was fine, she went out in a hired carriage. The driver took her, with a rapidity that had no doubt been ordered by the abbé, to one of those charming wooded areas around the outskirts of Paris, at Boulogne, Vincennes, Romainville, or Ville-d'Avray, sometimes accompanied by Lucien, sometimes only with Europe. She could get out and walk without fear, for when Lucien was not with her, she was accompanied by a big serving man dressed like a huntsman, armed with a real knife, a man whose features and build suggested a powerful athlete. This other guardian was equipped in the English style with a long stick called a "quarterstaff," the kind known to singlestick players, with which they can hold off multiple assailants. In obedience to the abbé's command, Esther never addressed a single word to this guardian. When madame was ready to return, Europe would call out and the huntsman would whistle to the coachman, who was never very far away. When Lucien was with Esther, Europe and the huntsman would stay a hundred paces back, like those infernal pages we read about in the *Arabian Nights,* given by the enchanter to those he protects. Most Parisians, especially Parisian women, never get to learn the charms of a walk in the woods on a fine night. The silence, the moonlight, the solitude all have the calming effects of a bath. Normally, Esther would leave at ten o'clock, walk from midnight to one, and be back home by two-thirty. She was never up before eleven in the morning. She bathed, and then proceeded to a lengthy, elaborate process of dressing and readying herself that most Parisian women never have the time to undertake; it is practiced only by prostitutes, courtesans, and great ladies who have their whole day to themselves. She was never ready until Lucien arrived, and then she offered herself to him like a newly opened flower. Her only care was for her poet's happiness; she was like a thing that belonged to him, that is, she gave him complete liberty. She never cast a glance outside the sphere in which she shone; the abbé had ordered this, for it was part of that deep politician's plan that Lucien would have some other romantic adventures. Happiness carries no story with it, and the storytellers of all lands have understood this so well that the phrase "they were happy" is the conclusion to every love story. Thus we can only detail the ways and means of this particular, fantastical happiness right in the heart of Paris. It was happiness in its finest form, a poem, a symphony composed of four years! Every woman will say, "That's a lot!" Neither Esther nor Lucien said, "It's too much." And so that phrase, "they were happy," was even more exactly true than it is in fairy tales, for "they had no children." And so Lucien could go on flirting with the world, abandoning himself to his poet's caprices and, let us add, to the exigencies of his position. During this time when he was slowly clearing his path, he secretly did some services for certain political men who needed some assistance. He assiduously cultivated the society of Madame de Sérisy, for whom, to use the phrase they use in the salons, he did everything.[66] Madame de Sérisy had stolen him away from the Duchesse de Maufrigneuse, who, they said, no longer wanted him, though that is the kind of phrase women use to avenge themselves on a happiness that they envy. Lucien was, so to speak, in the very bosom of the Grand Chaplaincy,[67] and on intimate terms with a number of women who were friends with the archbishop of Paris. Modest and discreet, he waited patiently. Thus what de Marsay said about Lucien showed more than a little insight, de Marsay himself having married by now and making his wife lead the kind of retired life Esther led. But the perils that were lurking below the surface of Lucien's position will become clear in the course of this tale.

How a Lynx Met a Rat, and What Ensued

Such was the situation when, one fine August night, Baron Nucingen returned to Paris from the country estate of a foreign banker now established in France, where he had dined. That estate lies eight leagues from Paris, in the midst of the Brie region. Now, since the baron's driver had said he could drive the baron there and back with the same set of horses, when night fell he moderated his pace. Upon entering the woods of Vincennes, the situation of the animals, the men, and the master was as follows. Liberally steeped in wine while in the kitchen of that aristocrat of the stock exchange, the coachman was now completely drunk and had fallen asleep, but his hands still gripped the reins, so as to put on a respectable show for any passersby. The footman, seated behind him, was snoring like one of those toy tops they make in Germany, the land of little wooden figures, *Reinganum,* and humming tops.[68] The baron wanted to think, but ever since they passed the Gournay bridge, the gentle somnolence of digestion had closed his eyes. The horses, feeling how slackly the reins were being held, understood the condition of the coachman; they could hear the basso continuo of the footman seated at his lookout post in the rear; and they took advantage of this little quarter hour of liberty to wander along just as they liked. Intelligent slaves, they were offering to any nearby thieves the opportunity to fleece one of France's wealthiest capitalists, the most profoundly capable of those who have come to be called "lynxes."[69] Finding themselves to be the masters, and drawn by the kind of curiosity we often see in domestic animals, they came to a crossing and stopped in front of some other horses, to whom they no doubt said, in the language of horses, "To whom do you belong? What are you up to? Are you happy?" But now that the coach had stopped moving, the sleepy baron awoke. At first he thought they had not yet left the estate of his colleague, but then he was startled by a celestial vision, which broke upon him defenseless, without his customary weapon of self-interested calculation. The light of the moon was so bright one could have read even a newspaper by it. There, in the silence of the woods and in that pure radiance, the baron saw a woman walking alone to her carriage;

mounting up into it, she looked wonderingly at the spectacle of another, apparently sleeping, carriage. At the sight of that angel, Baron Nucingen felt something like an inner illumination. But seeing that she was being admired, the young woman hurriedly lowered her veil with a frightened gesture. A huntsman let out a vigorous cry, the meaning of which the driver clearly understood, for the coach shot off like an arrow. The old banker experienced a terrifying emotion: his blood seemed on fire as it rushed from his feet to his head, and his head shot flames back down into his heart; he felt his throat tighten. The poor man feared an attack of indigestion, but despite that supreme fear, he rose up onto his feet.

"Make ze horses go gallop! Sleeping you are! Follow zat coach!" he cried. "Hunnert francs if you catch!"[70]

Hearing the words "hundred francs," the coachman shook himself awake, and the footman at the back no doubt heard it in his sleep. The baron repeated the command, and the coachman whipped the horses into a full gallop, and eventually, at the Trône tollgate, succeeded in catching up with a carriage very similar to the one in which Nucingen had seen his divine mystery woman, but in this one there was only the head clerk of some big department store with a "perfectly respectable" woman from the Rue Vivienne.[71] This mistake infuriated the baron.

"If I had prought Shorge inshtead of you, fat dummy, he vood haff found zat voman!" he said to the coachman, while the toll collectors came up to the carriage.

"Oh, *monsieur le baron,* it was the Devil himself, I believe it, and I think he must've taken the shape of a heyduck, and switched this carriage for his own."[72]

"Ze Debbil duss not eggsist!" said the baron.

Baron de Nucingen was sixty years old, and he had always been perfectly indifferent to women, and to his wife even more so. He prided himself on never having experienced the kind of love that drove men to mad deeds. He felt it was something of a triumph to have reached the stage where he was through with women, of whom he liked to say quite freely that the most angelic of them weren't worth what they cost, even when they gave themselves for free. He appeared to be so completely blasé that he no longer felt it necessary to spend a couple thousand francs a month for the pleasure of being deceived. From his box at the Opéra, his cold gaze was cast serenely down at the ballet corps. There were no little glances shooting back and forth between the capitalist and that formidable swarm of aging girls and youthful old women, the very elite of Parisian pleasures. Natural love, artificial and narcissistic love, vain love, respectable love, rational-style love,[73] decent and conjugal love, eccentric love: the baron had bought them all, known them all—all except real love. And the latter had just swooped down upon him like an eagle upon its prey, as it had swooped down upon Gentz, the confidant of His Highness Prince Metternich.[74] We know all the foolishness the aging diplomat got involved with over Fanny Elssler, and how he paid closer attention to her rehearsals than to European political interests. The woman who had just overwhelmed that double-locked, impenetrable safe known as Nucingen appeared to him to be unique in her generation. Indeed, it is not certain that the mistress of Titian, that Leonardo's Mona Lisa, that Raphael's Fornarina were as beautiful as the sublime Esther, in whom even the most practiced Parisian eye could not have detected the least vestige of the courtesan. The baron was stunned by the air of nobility, the air of a truly great lady, that Esther, beloved, surrounded by luxury, elegance, and love, possessed in the highest degree. Happy, contented love is the Holy Ampulla of women, for with it they all become as proud as empresses.[75] Over the next week the baron returned every night to the woods of Vincennes, then to those of Boulogne, then those of Ville-d'Avray, then to those of Meudon, and then to all the outskirts of Paris, but without ever encountering Esther. That sublime Jewish face of hers—which he described as "a face of ze people"—was always before his eyes. After two weeks he lost all his appetite. Delphine de Nucingen and her daughter Augusta, whose coming-out the baroness was supervising, did not at first notice the changes in the baron. Mother and daughter only saw Monsieur de Nucingen in the morning for breakfast and again in the evening for dinner on those evenings when they all dined at home, and those evenings only took place when Delphine was having company. But at the end of two months, consumed by a feverish impatience and something not unlike nostalgia, the baron, surprised at the impotence of his millions, began to lose weight and appeared so markedly weakened that Delphine began secretly to hope she might be a widow soon. In her hypocrisy she began to make a show of pitying her husband, and she began keeping her daughter at home. She assailed her husband with questions, to which he responded like a splenetic Englishman—that is, hardly at all. Delphine de Nucingen gave large dinner parties every Sunday. She had chosen that day after noticing that in higher society no one went to the theater then, and so there was usually nothing to do on Sunday evenings. The invasion of the merchant class and the bourgeois makes Sunday almost as annoying in Paris as it is boring in London. The baroness therefore invited the famous Desplein to dinner in order to have a consultation with him—despite the invalid himself, who insisted that he had never felt better. Keller, Rastignac, de Marsay, du Tillet, all the friends of the house had made it clear to the baroness that a man like Nucingen must not be allowed to die unexpectedly; his enormous business affairs required careful planning; it must be absolutely clear exactly where everything stood. These gentlemen were invited to the dinner, as well as the Comte de Gondreville, father-in-law to François Keller, the Chevalier d'Espard, des Lupeaulx, Bianchon the physician—the pupil Desplein loved the best—as well as Beaudenord and his wife, the Comte and Comtesse de Montcornet, Blondet, Mademoiselle des Touches and Conti, and, finally, Lucien de Rubempré, for whom Rastignac, over the past five years, had developed a warm friendship—by special order, as they say in the advertisements.

Cashbox in Despair

"It's not going to be easy to get rid of that one," Blondet said to Rastignac when he saw Lucien entering the salon, more handsome than ever and perfectly dressed.

"Better to be his friend, because he's formidable," said Rastignac.

"Him?" said de Marsay. "The only man I'd call formidable is one whose position is perfectly clear, and this one is not so much unassailed as unassailable! Look! What does he live on? Where does his money come from? He must have—I'm sure of it—at least sixty thousand in debts."

"He's found a protector, and a very wealthy one, a Spanish priest, who wants to see him succeed," said Rastignac.

"He's marrying Mademoiselle de Grandlieu, the eldest daughter," said Mademoiselle des Touches.

"Yes, but," said the Chevalier d'Espard, "they want him to buy an estate with revenue of thirty thousand a year as security for his future bride, and that will cost him a million. There won't be a million in any Spaniard's pockets."

"It's an expensive proposition, because Clotilde is downright ugly," said the baroness. Madame de Nucingen liked to call Mademoiselle de Grandlieu by her first name—as if she, née Goriot, had been born on such a social level herself.[76]

"No," said du Tillet; "the daughter of a duchess is never ugly in the eyes of others, and especially not when she brings with her the title of marquis and a diplomatic post; but the greatest obstacle to this marriage is the insane love of Madame de Sérisy for Lucien. She must give him a lot of money."

"I'm not surprised then to see Lucien looking so solemn, because Madame de Sérisy will surely not give him a million so he can marry

Mademoiselle de Grandlieu. Probably he doesn't know how to extricate himself from that situation," de Marsay said.

"Yes, but Mademoiselle de Grandlieu adores him," said the Comtesse de Montcornet, "and with the help of that young person, the conditions might turn out to be easier to meet."

"What will he do with his sister and brother-in-law in Angoulême?" asked the Chevalier d'Espard.

"But his sister is rich," said Rastignac, "and nowadays he calls her Madame Séchard de Marsac."

"Well, even if there are any troubles, still, he's a good-looking fellow," said Bianchon as he got up to greet Lucien.

"Hello, my good friend," said Rastignac, shaking Lucien's hand warmly.

De Marsay greeted him coolly, after waiting for Lucien to greet him first. Before the dinner, Desplein and Bianchon chatted in a cheerful way with Nucingen while discreetly examining him, and they came to the conclusion that his malady must be an entirely nervous one; yet nobody could guess the cause, so impossible did it seem that the great politician of the stock exchange could be in love. When Bianchon, finally concluding that only love could explain the banker's pathology, said as much to Delphine de Nucingen, she smiled like a woman who has known her husband very well for a long time. After dinner, however, when everyone stepped out into the garden, the most intimate habitués of the house surrounded the banker, attempting to get clarity on the matter after hearing Bianchon say that Nucingen must be in love.

"Baron, are you aware," said de Marsay, "that you've grown quite a bit thinner recently? And that people are beginning to suspect that you've broken the laws of a banker's nature?"

"Neffer!" said the baron.

"Oh, yes," replied de Marsay. "People are claiming that you've fallen in love."

"Ach, zat's true," Nucingen replied pitifully. "I fall in luff vit somebody I don't know who she is."

"You, in love? You? Come on—you're joking!" said the Chevalier d'Espard.

"Beink in luff at mine age, ja, zere is nussing could be more ridiculous. But vat can I do? Zere it iss!"

"Is it a lady in society?" asked Lucien.

"But," said de Marsay, "the baron could only be losing weight like this over a hopeless love, and he has enough money to buy all the women who want to or could possibly sell themselves."

"I don't know who she iss," said the baron. "Und I can tell you zis becauss Madame de Nucingen iss in de drawink room, but till now, I never know vat iss luff. Vat iss luff? I tink maybe it means you lose veight."

"Where did you meet her, this young innocent?" asked Rastignac.

"In a carriage, at midnight, out in ze voods by Vincennes."

"What was she like?" asked de Marsay.

"Ach, she vore a hat of vite gaze, rose-colored dress, a vite scarf, a vite veil . . . a face like sometink out of ze Pible! Ze eyes like fire, skin like from ze Orient."

"You were dreaming!" said Lucien with a smile.

"Vell, yess, I vas shleeping like a cow full uff food," he said, "becauss I vas cominck back home after dinner vit mine friend in ze country. . . ."

"Was she alone?" asked du Tillet, interrupting the lynx.

"Yess," said the baron in a doleful voice, "hexcept for ein heyduck on ze back und ein meddshervent . . ."

"Lucien looks like he knows her!" exclaimed Rastignac, noticing a smile on the face of Esther's lover.

"Of course! Who doesn't know the women who wander out at midnight in order to run into Nucingen?" he said, trying to turn away.

"Well, it must not be a woman who goes out into society," said the Chevalier d'Espard, "because otherwise the baron would have recognized the heyduck."

"I haff not seen her anywhere," replied the baron, "und now it's forty dayss dat I'm making ze police hunt for her but zey find nothing."

"You'd be better off if she cost you a few hundred thousand francs than costing you your life, because at your age a passion without any nourishment is dangerous," said Desplein; "you might die of it."

"Yess," Nucingen said to Desplein, "vat I eat is givink me no nourishment, chust breathing air seems dangerous to me. I go beck to Vincennes voods, place vhere I saw her! Yess, zis iss my life! I can't bozzer about ze last loan—I haff to ask my bartners to haff pity on me. I giff a million to meet zat woman, und I make profit, because I stop goink to stock exchange. . . . You ask du Tillet."

"That's right," said du Tillet. "He's lost his taste for business affairs. He's changed—it must be a sign of approaching death."

"Sign uff death, sign uff luff—same ting, for me," said Nucingen.

The simple openness of the old man, no longer the lynx, and his having perceived for the first time in his life that there might be something more sacred, more holy than gold, moved the little circle of worldly men: some exchanged smiles, while others looked at Nucingen, their expressions revealing their thoughts: "If a man that strong can come to this!"

They all went back into the drawing room talking about it. It was a freak of nature, something to wonder at. Madame de Nucingen laughed when Lucien told her the banker's secret; but when the baron heard his wife's mocking laugh, he took her by the arm and led her to the recess of a window.

"Matame," he said to her quietly, "haff you effer heard a vord of mockery from me about your passions? Vhy do you mock mine? A good vife, she vood try to help her hussband and mek him get his health back, not mek fun uff him. . . ."

Lucien realized that the old banker's description must refer to Esther. Deeply irritated that his smile had been noticed and commented upon, he benefited from the busy turn the conversation had taken while coffee was being served to disappear.

"What happened to Monsieur de Rubempré?" asked the Baroness de Nucingen.

"He's being faithful to the family motto, '*Quid me continebit,*'" said Rastignac.

"Which means either 'who can hold me back,' or 'I am untamable'"—take your choice," said de Marsay.

"When the baron was talking about his mystery woman, a little smile escaped Lucien, and it made me think that maybe he knows who she is," said Horace Bianchon, not realizing the danger of making such a remark.

"Goot!" exclaimed the lynx to himself. Like all desperately sick men, he grasped at anything that seemed to hold out hope, and he promised himself to have Lucien spied upon by someone better than Louchard, the most capable Garde du Commerce in Paris, who had turned up nothing during the past two weeks.[77]

The Abyss beneath Esther's Happiness

Before going to Esther, Lucien had to pay a call at the Grandlieu home for a couple of hours, which made Mademoiselle Clotilde-Frédérique de Grandlieu the happiest girl in the Faubourg Saint-Germain. The ambitious young man's conduct was governed by a prudence that told him he needed to inform Carlos Herrera immediately of the effect of the smile that escaped from him at the baron's description of Esther. But the baron's love for Esther as well as his setting the police on the trail of his beautiful mystery woman were events important enough to get communicated to the man who had sought, under a cassock, the sanctuary that criminals formerly sought in churches. From the Rue Saint-Lazare, where the banker then lived, to the Rue Saint-Dominique, where the

Grandlieus lived, Lucien's path took him past his own place on the Quai Malaquais. Lucien found his frightening friend smoking his breviary, that is, having a pipe before going to bed. The man, more strange than foreign,[78] had recently given up Spanish cigars, which he found too mild.

"Things are getting serious," said the Spaniard when Lucien had finished his tale. "The baron, employing Louchard to find the little one, might very well have the intelligence to put a tail on you, and then everything would come out. The remainder of tonight and tomorrow morning will give me time to prepare the hand I want to play against this baron, and above all I need to demonstrate to him that the police are useless. When our lynx abandons all hope of finding the little lost lamb, then I'll take over, and sell her to him for what he thinks she's worth."

"Sell Esther?" cried Lucien, whose first reactions were always excellent.

"Have you forgotten our situation?" snapped Carlos Herrera.

Lucien lowered his head.

"No money left, and sixty thousand francs' worth of debts!" the Spaniard continued. "If you want to marry Clotilde de Grandlieu, you need to buy an estate worth a million to ensure security for your ugly duckling's settlement. Well, Esther will be the piece of meat I'll use to lure that lynx and get us our million. Anyway, it's my business. . . ."

"Esther will never agree."

"That's my concern."

"She'll die if you do it."

"That's the concern of the undertaker. And anyway, what of it?" cried the savage, cutting off Lucien's elegies by the stance he was taking. "How many generals died in the flower of their prime for the emperor Napoleon?" he asked Lucien after a moment's pause. "There will always be more women! In 1821, for you, Coralie could never be equaled, but nevertheless you did find Esther. And after her, who will it be? The as yet unknown woman! And you see, out of all women, that's the finest one, and you'll go seeking her in that foreign capital where the Duc de Grandlieu's son-in-law will be minister representing the king of France. . . . And then tell me, dear little boy, will Esther die of that? And anyway, can the husband of Mademoiselle de Grandlieu keep Esther? Just leave it to me; don't bother trying to think it all through; that's my job. But don't go to Esther's for a week or two, though you'll still go to the Rue Taitbout. Meantime, go on, do your billing and cooing with the girl who's going to be your lifeline—slip Clotilde the overheated note you wrote her this morning, and bring me back an equally warm one from her! The girl consoles herself for all her sorrows by writing, and that suits me fine!

You'll find Esther a little sad, but tell her she needs to be obedient. We have to wear our livery of virtue, our cassocks of respectability, the outfits behind which great people hide all their infamies. It's a matter of presenting my best me; you must never come under any suspicion. Well, chance has been kinder to us than my own brain has, flailing about in the void these last couple of months."

Tossing off these terrible sentiments one by one like pistol shots, Carlos Herrera got dressed and ready to leave.

"Your glee is obvious," cried Lucien. "You've never cared for poor Esther, and you're delighted now at the thought of getting rid of her."

"You've never got tired of loving her, have you? Well, I've never got tired of detesting her. But haven't I always acted as though I were sincerely attached to the girl—I who, through Asia, hold her very life in my hands! A few bad mushrooms in a ragout, and it's all over—and yet Mademoiselle Esther lives on! . . . She's happy! . . . Do you know why? Because you love her! Don't pretend to be a child. For four years now we've been waiting for chance to turn something up, either something that works for us or the opposite, and, let me tell you, it's going to take more than ordinary skill to wash the vegetables fate has tossed our way today—this spin of the wheel has both good and bad in it, as usual. Do you know what I was thinking about when you came in?"

"No."

"Of trying to make myself the heir, as I did in Barcelona, of some aged churchgoing female, with Asia's help. . . ."

"You mean a crime?"

"I didn't think I had any other options open to me to keep you on the path to success. The creditors are sniffing around. What would we do if the bailiffs entered the picture and hunted you down at the Grandlieus' place? That would have been the Devil demanding his due."

Carlos Herrera pantomimed a desperate man committing suicide by jumping in the river; then he stopped and fixed upon Lucien one of those steady, penetrating stares by which the will of the strong man enters into the soul of the weak. That fascinating stare, the effect of which was to evaporate all resistance, made it clear that not only were there secrets of life and death between these two men, but also feelings as high above ordinary feelings as this man was superior to the baseness of his position.

Constrained to live outside the world, the law having banned him from ever returning to it, worn out by vice and by furious, terrible struggles but endowed with a power in his soul that always gnawed away at him, this ignoble and grand, obscure and famous personality, consumed with the fever of life itself, was reborn in the elegant body of Lucien, whose soul had become his. He was represented in the life of society by this poet, to whom he had given his unwavering determination and his iron will. For him Lucien was more than a son, more than a beloved woman, more than a family, more than his own life: he was his vengeance; and thus, because strong souls cling more firmly to a feeling than they do to existence, he had bound the poet to him by indissoluble ties.

After he had bought Lucien's life when the poet, in despair, was on his way to committing suicide, he had proposed to him one of those hellish pacts that one only sees in novels, but the terrifying possibility of which has often enough been seen in famous courtroom dramas. By lavishing upon Lucien all the delights Parisian life can offer, and by showing him that he could still create a fine future for himself, he had made Lucien his. No sacrifice was too great for this strange man, for it was a matter of serving his second self. But in the very exercise of his power, he was so weak when it came to the caprices of his creature that he had confided his secrets to him. Could this have been yet another bond between them, this moral complicity? From the day on which La Torpille had been carried off, Lucien was aware of the frightful base upon which his happiness was founded.

The cassock of this Spanish priest concealed Jacques Collin, a famous inhabitant of the penal world who, ten years before, had been living under the bourgeois name of Vautrin in the Vauquer boardinghouse, where Rastignac and Bianchon were as well. Jacques Collin, known as Deathcheater, had escaped from Rochefort almost as soon as he had been returned there, profiting from the famous example of the Comte de Saint-Hélène, but with some improvement on Coignard's scheme.[79] To assume the role of an honest man while continuing criminal enterprises is a proposition whose terms are so contradictory that they are bound to lead to disaster, especially in Paris; when a convict tries to establish himself in a family, he multiplies the chances of danger. To be safely hidden from all pursuers, wouldn't it be best for a man to try to place himself in a position well above the level of ordinary life? A man of the world is subject to dangers that would rarely bother a person who cuts off contact with the world. And thus the cassock is the surest of disguises, as long as one can combine it with a truly exemplary, solitary, and nonactive life. "Therefore, I'll be a priest," said this man who was legally dead but determined to resuscitate himself and to live in the social world under some other form, and to satisfy those passions that were as strange as he was. The civil war caused by the Constitution of 1812 in Spain, where our energetic man had fled, gave him the opportunity of secretly killing the real Carlos Herrera in an ambush. The bastard son of a great lord, long abandoned by his father and ignorant of who his mother might be, this priest had been charged with a political mission in France by King Ferdinand VII, having been recommended by a bishop. That bishop, the only man who took an interest in Carlos Herrera, died while this lost child of the Church was making his journey from Cádiz to Madrid and from Madrid to France. Pleased to have found this much-desired identity, and under such perfect conditions, Jacques Collin cut into the flesh of his back in order to remove the fateful letters[80] and altered his face with the aid of chemical reagents. He performed this metamorphosis next to the body of the dead priest, before burying it, so as to achieve some similarity of appearance with his doppelgänger. To complete this transmutation, almost as marvelous as the one in the Arabian tale in which the old dervish is able to enter into a youthful body by the use of some magical incantations,[81] the convict, who spoke Spanish, now learned as much Latin as an Andalusian priest would be likely to know. The banker for all three penal colonies,[82] Collin was wealthy with the money that had been freely entrusted to him, for he had a reputation of honesty— sometimes enforced honesty, because any error in accounting among such men would result in a dagger's thrust. To these funds he added the money the bishop had given to Carlos Herrera. Before leaving Spain, he was able to make off with a large sum of money from a repentant woman in Barcelona to whom he gave absolution, promising that he would make restitution of the money she had got hold of through a murder. Having turned himself into a priest, charged with a secret mission that would provide him with powerful recommendations in Paris, Jacques Collin resolved to do nothing that would compromise the character he had assumed, had abandoned himself to whatever chance might bring him— and that is when he encountered Lucien on the road from Angoulême to Paris. That boy immediately struck the false priest as being a marvelous instrument of power; he saved him from suicide, saying, "Give yourself completely to a man of God the same way others give themselves to the Devil, and you'll have every chance of a new fate. Your life will be like a dream, and the worst awakening will only be the death you were already going to give yourself. . . ." The alliance of these two beings, making them as one, was founded on the power inherent in such reasoning, which Carlos Herrera further cemented by ingeniously leading Lucien into complicity. Endowed with a genius for corruption, he undermined Lucien's morality by plunging him into cruel necessities, from which he would extricate him only after gaining tacit consent to shoddy or evil acts that left him always pure, loyal, and noble in the eyes of the world. Lucien was to be the social splendor, in the shadow of which the forger intended to live. "I am the author, and you are the play; if you aren't a success, I'm the one they'll hiss," he said to Lucien on the day he confessed the truth about his sacrilegious disguise. From there Carlos moved along from confession to confession, measuring the degree of horror in his revelations to the progress and needs of Lucien. Thus, Deathcheater reserved his ultimate secret for the moment when the habit of Parisian pleasures, social success, and vanity had fully enslaved the body and soul of the all-too-weak poet Lucien. Where Rastignac had resisted the demon, Lucien succumbed, having been more expertly manipulated, more cunningly compromised, and finally conquered by the pleasure of seeing himself having achieved an eminent position. Evil, the poetic fabulation of which is called the Devil, used its most seductive attractions on this half-woman man, asking so little of him at first while giving so very much. Carlos's strongest argument was that eternal secret that Tartuffe promised to Elmire. The reiterated proofs of absolute devotion, like the devotion of Seid for Mahomet,[83] put the finishing touches on the complete subjugation of Lucien by a Jacques Collin. At the present moment, not only had Esther and Lucien spent all the money that had been entrusted to the banker of the penal colonies, which exposed them to the eventuality of a hideous reckoning, but the dandy, the forger, and the courtesan were also deeply in debt. Just when Lucien was so close to succeeding, the slightest pebble beneath the foot of any one of them would be enough to bring the whole fantastical edifice of their audaciously acquired fortune crashing down upon their heads. At the Opéra Ball Rastignac had recognized Vautrin from the Vauquer boardinghouse, but he knew he was a dead man if he said anything, so Madame de Nucingen's lover and Lucien exchanged nervous glances, their fear barely concealed behind the semblance of friendship. If the critical moment arose, Rastignac would have gladly furnished the carriage to drive Deathcheater to the scaffold. Everyone can now understand fully the solemn joy that Carlos felt upon learning of Baron Nucingen's infatuation, instantly seeing all the profit that a man of his type might be able to get out of poor Esther.

"Go on," he said to Lucien. "The Devil will protect his chaplain."

"You're smoking a cigar on a powder keg."

"*Incedo par ignes!*"[84] replied Carlos with a smile. "It's my profession."

With the Grandlieus

The Grandlieu house was divided into two branches around the middle of the past century: the ducal branch is destined to come to an end, as the present duke has only daughters; the other branch is that of the vicomtes, and they will inherit the title and the arms of the senior branch. The ducal branch bears *gules, in a fess three battle-axes or,* with the famous motto *Caveo non timeo,*[85] which epitomizes the house.

The coat of arms of the viscounts is the same, quartered with that of the Navarreins, which is *gules, a fess or* surmounted by a knight's helmet, with the motto *Grands faits, grand lieu.* The current viscountess, a widow since 1813, has one son and one daughter. Though she was almost ruined upon her return from exile, through the devoted work of a lawyer, Derville, she recovered a considerable fortune.[86]

When the Duc and Duchesse de Grandlieu returned in 1804, they were wooed by the emperor; he not only received them at Court but got much of their property restored to them, worth some forty thousand a year. Of all the great aristocrats of the Faubourg Saint-Germain who allowed themselves to be seduced by Napoleon, only the duke and the duchess (she was an Ajuda of the senior branch, allied with the Braganzas) never disowned him or rejected his benefactions. The Faubourg Saint-Germain considered this a crime, but Louis XVIII respected them for it; perhaps, however, the king only wanted to annoy MONSIEUR.[87] It seemed probable that the young Vicomte de Grandlieu would marry Marie-Athénaïs, the duke's youngest daughter, who was then just nine years old. Sabine, the second youngest, would marry the Baron du Guénic, following the July Revolution. Joséphine, the third youngest, became Madame Ajuda-Pinto when the marquis lost his first wife. The eldest had taken the veil in 1822. The second eldest, Mademoiselle Clotilde-Frédérique, twenty-seven years old, was deeply in love with Lucien de Rubempré.

It would be pointless to ask whether the Grandlieu *hôtel,* one of the most beautiful on the Rue Saint-Dominique, exerted a powerful spell over Lucien's imagination; every time the great doors turned on their hinges to admit his tilbury, he felt the balm to his vanity of which Mirabeau has spoken. "My father was only a pharmacist in l'Houmeau, and yet here I am, entering this place. . . ." Such were his thoughts. And he would have committed far greater crimes than associating with a known criminal for the pleasure of walking up those steps and hearing the words announced—"Monsieur de Rubempré!"—and hearing them announced in the great Louis XIV salon, constructed during that era and modeled on the salons in Versailles where the very cream of Paris society were to be found, called then *le petit Château.*

The noble Portuguese lady, one of those women who least enjoy leaving their own homes, was most often surrounded by her neighbors, the Chaulieus, the Navarreins, and the Lenoncourts. Often, the pretty Baroness de Macumer (née Chaulieu), the Duchesse de Maufrigneuse, Madame d'Espard, Madame de Camps, and Mademoiselle des Touches, who was allied to the Brittany Grandlieus, also came to visit her, either on their way to a ball or on their way back from the Opéra. The Vicomte de Grandlieu, the Duc de Rhétoré, the Marquis de Chaulieu (who would one day become the Duc de Lenoncourt-Chaulieu), his wife, Madeleine de Mortsauf (granddaughter to the Duc de Lenoncourt), the Marquis d'Ajuda-Pinto, the Prince de Blamont-Chauvry, the Marquis de Beauséant, the Vidame de Pamiers, the Vandenesses, the aging Prince de Cadignan and his son the Duc de Maufrigneuse: these were the usual visitors to the grandiose salon, where one breathed the air of the Royal Court, where manners, tone, and wit were in harmony with the grandeur of the owners, whose grand aristocratic style eventually caused their bondage to Napoleon to be forgotten.

The old Duchesse d'Uxelles, mother of the Duchesse de Maufrigneuse, was the oracle of the salon, to which Madame de Sérisy had never gained admittance, even though née Ronquerolles.

Lucien had been brought here by Madame de Maufrigneuse, who had urged her mother to act on Lucien's behalf; she had been infatuated with him for two years, and the appealing poet maintained his position there thanks to the influence of the high chaplain of France, and with the help of the archbishop of Paris. However, he was not admitted until he had received the royal ordinance allowing him to use the name and bear the arms of the house of de Rubempré. The Duc de Rhétoré, the Chevalier d'Espard, and a few others, resentful of Lucien, from time to time stirred up the Duc de Grandlieu against him by repeating anecdotes concerning his antecedents; but the pious duchesse, the highest dignitaries of the Church, and Clotilde de Grandlieu all supported him. Lucien understood these enmities as having arisen from his adventure with Madame d'Espard's cousin, Madame de Bargeton, now the Comtesse du Châtelet. Then, sensing the necessity of being adopted by such a powerful family, and motivated by his intimate counselor to seduce Clotilde, Lucien found within himself the boldness of the social climber: he came to the house five days out of the week, gracefully swallowed insults from the resentful, tolerated impertinent glares, and made witty responses to mockery. His persistence, the charm of his manners, and his unflappability eventually neutralized scruples and lowered obstacles. Always in favor at the Duchesse de Maufrigneuse's home (her passionate letters, written when her infatuation was at its peak, were kept by Carlos Herrera), the idol of Madame de Sérisy, well thought of by Mademoiselle des Touches, Lucien, pleased to be welcomed at all three places, learned from his Spaniard the need to conduct his relations with the greatest reserve.

"You can't devote yourself to several houses at the same time," said his personal counselor. "A person who goes everywhere will be of interest nowhere. The great ones only protect those who become part of the furniture, those they see every day, who become necessary to them, like a divan they sit on."

Accustomed to seeing the Grandlieu salon as his personal field of battle, Lucien held back his wit, his clever anecdotes, his news and his courtier's graces for the evening hours he spent there. Insinuating, flattering, warned in advance by Clotilde which dangerous reefs to avoid, he found ways to praise all the little interests and passions of Monsieur de Grandlieu. After first envying the bliss the Duchesse de Maufrigneuse must have enjoyed, Clotilde fell madly in love herself with Lucien.

Quickly perceiving all the advantages such an alliance would have, Lucien played his role of lover as perfectly as Armand, the young star of the Comédie-Française, would have done.[88] He wrote letters to Clotilde that qualified as literary masterpieces of the first order, and Clotilde replied in a kind of competition of genius, giving her love furious expression on paper, for that was the only way she knew to love. Lucien went to Mass at the church of Saint-Thomas-d'Aquin every Sunday, presenting himself as a fervent Catholic, delivering himself of monarchist and religious pronouncements that were a marvel. Moreover, he wrote, for the papers that supported the Congrégation, extremely remarkable articles, refusing payment for them, and signing them only L. He wrote political pamphlets, requested either by Charles X or by the king's chaplain, without expecting the slightest payment: "The king," he would say, "has done so much for me that I owe him my very blood." For a few days there was talk of attaching Lucien to the office of the prime minister as his personal secretary, but Madame d'Espard stirred up so many people to campaign against him that in the end the king's Maître Jacques had to hesitate.[89] Lucien's position was not really clear, and the question on everyone's lips—"What does he live on?"—demanded an answer; both benevolent curiosity and the malicious kind led from investigation to investigation, and more than one chink in the ambitious young man's armor was detected. Clotilde de Grandlieu served, unwittingly, as a spy in the service of her father and mother. A few days earlier she had led Lucien to a window seat and informed him about her family's objections. "Get an estate of a million, and you'll have my hand—that's what my mother said," Clotilde had told him. "Later on they'll want to know where your money came from," Carlos had said to Lucien when he heard this. "My brother-in-law must be worth a lot," Lucien suggested, "so we could use him for our answer." Carlos exclaimed, "Right—all we need now is the million. I'll get to work on it."

To clarify Lucien's position within the Grandlieu household, we must point out that he had never actually dined there. Neither Clotilde, nor the Duchesse d'Uxelles, nor Madame de Maufrigneuse, who was always on Lucien's side, could obtain that favor for him from the old duke; that gentleman retained a strong distrust of the man he called "the Sire de Rubempré." The nuance in that phrase, noticed by everyone in the salon, inflicted serious wounds on Lucien's self-esteem, for he could tell he was only just tolerated. Of course, society has the right to be suspicious: it is so often deceived! To try to be someone significant in Paris without having any known fortune, without having any acknowledged livelihood, is an untenable position, no matter how much artifice one deploys. Thus Lucien's rise in the world gave ever greater weight to the question "What does he live on?" He had been forced to say to Madame de Sérisy, who had procured for him the support of Attorney-General Granville and of a minister of state, Comte Octave de Bauvan, president of the court of appeal: "I'm horribly in debt."

When he entered the courtyard of that home that could deliver full legitimation to all his vanities, he said to himself bitterly, thinking of Deathcheater's grand plans, "I can feel the earth cracking beneath my feet!" He loved Esther, and he wanted Mademoiselle de Grandlieu for his wife. A strange situation! To have one, the other would have to be sold. Only one man could manage this exchange without damage to Lucien's honor, and that man was the false Spaniard: were not the two of them bound together, each requiring discretion from the other? Life affords few examples of pacts in which both parties are, in turn, dominator and dominated.

Lucien drove away the clouds that had darkened his brow, and he stepped into the salons of the *hôtel* Grandlieu radiant, smiling.

The Daughter of a Fine House

Just at that moment, the windows were opened, allowing the scents from the garden to waft in and perfume the drawing room; a flower stand in the middle drew the eye to its pyramid of flowers. The duchess, seating in a corner on a sofa, was conversing with the Duchesse de Chaulieu. Several women composed a grouping that was remarkable for the varied attitudes of feigned grief on display. In the world of society, nobody is really interested in sorrow or suffering; everything is just talk. The men walked about the room or out into the garden. Clotilde and Joséphine were busy with the tea table. The Vidame de Pamiers, the Duc de Grandlieu, the Marquis d'Ajuda-Pinto, and the Duc de Maufrigneuse were playing their game of whist over in one corner. When Lucien was announced, he walked across the room to greet the duchess, asking her what the reason was for the affliction her face revealed.

"Madame de Chaulieu has just received some terrible news: her son-in-law, the Baron de Macumer, formerly Duc de Soria, has just died.[90] The young Duc de Soria and his wife, who had gone to Chantepleurs to care for their brother, wrote to give her this sad news. Louise is simply overcome."

"A woman is never loved twice in her life the way Louise was by her husband," said Madeleine de Mortsauf.

"She'll be a rich widow," said the old Duchesse d'Uxelles, looking at Lucien, whose face remained impassive.

"Poor Louise," said Madame d'Espard. "I know how she feels, and I pity her."

The Marquise d'Espard assumed the pose of a pensive, soulful, feeling woman. Although Sabine de Grandlieu was only ten years old, she shot her mother an intelligent and mocking expression, which was immediately suppressed by the mother's subtle glance in response. This is known as bringing one's children up properly.

"If my daughter can survive this blow," said Madame de Chaulieu with the most maternal air, "I'll be worried for her future. Louise is quite the romantic."

"I cannot understand," said the old Duchesse d'Uxelles, "where our daughters picked that sort of thing up."

"It is not easy," said an elderly cardinal, "nowadays to reconcile the heart with the proprieties."

Lucien could find nothing to say, so he made his way over toward the tea table to pay his compliments to the Grandlieu daughters. When the poet had moved a few feet away from the group of women, the Marquise d'Espard leaned over to whisper in the ear of the Duchesse de Grandlieu.

"Do you think that boy truly loves your dear Clotilde?" she asked.

The treachery of such a question can only be understood fully after we have given a sketch of Clotilde. This young person, aged twenty-seven, was standing up at the moment. That pose allowed the mocking gaze of the Marquise d'Espard to take in Clotilde's thin, narrow figure, resembling nothing so much as a stalk of asparagus. The chest of the poor girl was too flat to allow the use of those colonial resources that the dressmakers call *fichus menteurs*.[91] But Clotilde was quite aware that her name alone carried sufficient advantages, and so, far from taking the trouble of disguising her lack, she heroically put it on full display. Wrapped tightly in her gowns, she resembled the effect that medieval sculptors sought with their rigid, thin statuettes, placed so as to seem to stand forth from their niches in cathedrals. Clotilde stood five feet four in height. If we may be permitted the use of a term that is rather common but does have the merit of conveying the point vividly, she was all legs. Her complexion rather dark, her hair black and stiff, eyebrows quite thick, eyes quite fiery and set within orbits that had already darkened as well, her profile like that of the moon in its first quarter and her brow jutting, she seemed to be a caricature of her mother, who had been one of the most beautiful women in Portugal. Nature enjoys playing little tricks like that. One often sees in families a daughter of surprising beauty whose traits are repeated in a brother who, however, is downright ugly. Clotilde's mouth, which was quite sunken in, wore a perpetual expression of disdain. Therefore her lips were what revealed her secret thoughts and feelings, because affection changed that expression into something charming, which was even more remarkable considering that her cheeks were too dark to redden, and her black, always hard eyes never gave anything away. But despite all these disadvantages, despite her resemblance to a wooden plank, her birth and education had given her an air of grandeur, a proud countenance, in short, all that we refer to as a *je ne sais quoi*, aided perhaps by the simplicity of her dress, which denoted her as a daughter of a proud family. Her hair—thick and long—helped too, for with it she could pass for beautiful. Her voice, which she had carefully cultivated, had a charming effect. She sang ravishingly. She was the kind of girl of whom people would say, "She has lovely eyes," or "What a charming personality!" If someone addressed her in the English fashion as "Your Grace," she would reply, "Call me Your Thinness."

"Why wouldn't someone love my poor Clotilde?" the duchess replied to the marquise. "Do you know what she said to me the other day? 'Even if he only loves me out of ambition, I'm going to make him love me for myself.' She's clever and ambitious, and there are men who appreciate those two qualities. As for him, well, my dear, he's gorgeous as a dream; and if he's able to buy back the de Rubempré estate, the king will give him—out of his regard for us—the title of marquis. After all, his mother is the last of the Rubempré line. . . ."

"But the poor boy—where is he going to get a million?" asked the marquise.

"That's his business," said the duchess, "but I'm quite sure he's not likely to steal it. . . . Anyway, we wouldn't give Clotilde to a schemer or a dishonest man, even if he was gorgeous, a poet, and young like Monsieur de Rubempré."

"You're arriving late," said Clotilde, casting an infinitely gracious smile on Lucien.

"Yes—I ate in town."

"You've been out socializing quite a lot for several days now," she said, hiding her jealousy and her anxiety behind a smile.

"Socializing?" said Lucien. "No, it's just by an odd chance that I've been dining with bankers every evening this week. Today it was Nucingen, yesterday du Tillet, and the day before the Kellers."

The reader will notice that Lucien had picked up the tone of witty impertinence used by the great lords.

"You have a great many enemies," Clotilde said to him while passing him (with such grace!) a cup of tea. "My father has just been told that you owe sixty thousand francs, and that it won't be long till Sainte-Pélagie will be your new residence.[92] And if you only knew what all these calumnies cost me. . . . It all comes down on me. I don't want to talk about the pain it causes me (my father has a glare that makes me feel I've been crucified), but of the pain you must feel if any of this, even a little of it, is true. . . ."

"Don't bother yourself with absurdities like that. Love me the way I love you, and give me a few months' grace period," replied Lucien, setting his emptied cup down on the engraved silver tray.

"Keep away from my father; he'll just deliver himself of some impertinence to you, and because you won't be able to tolerate it, we'll be done for. . . . That wicked Marquise d'Espard told him that your mother was a midwife, and your sister worked in a laundry . . ."

"We lived in the deepest poverty," replied Lucien, tears starting in his eyes. "What she said wasn't calumny, just nasty gossip. Today my sister is worth over a million, and my mother has been dead for two years. . . . I've been keeping those bits of information for the moment when I was close to success here."

"But whatever did you do to Madame d'Espard?"

"I was imprudent enough to tell, at Madame de Sérisy's, and in front of Messieurs de Bauvan and de Granville, the amusing story of the trial she was trying to set up involving an injunction against the Marquis d'Espard, her husband, which I had heard about from Bianchon.[93] Monsieur de Granville's opinion, which was supported by Bauvan and Sérisy, influenced that of the keeper of the seals. Both were afraid of the *Gazette des tribunaux* and of a scandal,[94] and the marquise got a slap on the wrist when the judgment was finally given on the whole awful affair. So while

Monsieur de Sérisy may have committed an indiscretion that resulted in the marquise becoming a mortal enemy of mine, I also gained his protection, the attorney-general's, and that of Comte Octave de Bauvan, for Madame de Sérisy told him about the peril in which they had placed me by letting her guess the source of their information. And the Marquis d'Espard had the clumsiness to actually come and call on me, seeing me as the cause of his winning out in that dreadful legal mess."

"I'm going to rid us of Madame d'Espard," said Clotilde.

"What? How?" cried Lucien.

"My mother will invite the d'Espard children here; they're quite charming, and already nearly grown. The father and the two sons will sing your praises, and we'll be sure never to see their mother again."

"Oh, Clotilde, you're adorable! If I didn't love you for yourself, I'd love you for your cleverness."

"It's not cleverness," she said, putting all the love she felt into her smile. "Farewell. Don't come visit for a few days. When you see me wearing a pink scarf at Saint-Thomas-d'Aquin, you'll know my father's mood has changed. There's a note stuck to the back of the chair you're in, which might be some consolation for not seeing us. . . . Put the letter you've brought me in my handkerchief."

Clearly, the young lady was older than her twenty-seven years.

The House of a Fine Daughter

Lucien took a cab to the Rue de la Planche. He got out on the street, and then took another near the Madeleine, instructing the driver to take him to the Rue Taitbout.

Entering Esther's apartment at eleven, he found her in tears but dressed as if she were in the most festive mood. She awaited her Lucien reclining on a divan of white satin, brocaded with yellow flowers, wearing a lovely peignoir of India muslin with cherry-colored bows, uncorseted, her hair twisted up simply on her head, her feet in pretty velour slippers lined with cherry-colored satin, all the candles lit and the hookah at the ready; but she was not smoking hers, which remained unlit next to her, like a hint of her emotional state. Upon hearing the doors open, she wiped away her tears, leaped up like a gazelle and wrapped her arms around Lucien like tissue picked up by the wind and hurled against a tree.

"Separated!" she said. "Is it true?"

"Oh, but only for a few days," replied Lucien.

Esther let go and fell back onto the divan as if she were dead. In situations like this, most women will fall to babbling like parrots. Ah, they love you! . . . Even after five years, it's as if it's only the morning after the first happy day; they simply can't leave you, and their indignation, their despair, the depth of their love, their rage, their regrets, their fears, their chagrin, their presentiments of doom—how sublime they are! It's all as pretty as a scene in Shakespeare. But the important thing to understand is this: such women are not really in love. When they truly are all that they say they are, when they are truly in love, they do as Esther did, as children do, as real love does; Esther said not a word, lying there with her face in the cushions and weeping hot tears. Lucien, for his part, tried to raise her up and speak to her.

"But, my little one, we aren't really separated . . . How is it that after four years of happiness together, you can't endure an absence? Oh, what is it I've done to all these girls?" he added to himself, thinking of how similarly Coralie had loved him.

"Ah, monsieur, you are looking so handsome," said Europe.

The senses have their own ideals. When such seductive looks are combined with the sweet nature and the poetry that distinguished Lucien, one can imagine the mad passion felt by such sensual creatures for the external gifts nature bestows, and one can imagine the naïve sincerity of their admiration. Esther continued to sob quietly, still the picture of utter grief.

"But, my little fool," said Lucien, "haven't they explained that it's a matter of my life being at stake!"

At that word, Esther raised herself up like a woodland animal, her disheveled hair trailing over her sublime features like foliage. She looked intently at Lucien.

"Your life at stake!" she cried, raising her arms and then lowering them again in a gesture typical of women in danger. "But of course—that beast said something about things being that serious."

She drew a tattered scrap of paper from her sash, but then she caught sight of Europe and said, "Leave us now, girl." After Europe had closed the door: "Here, look at what *he* wrote," she said, handing Lucien the note that Carlos had just sent, and that Lucien now read aloud.

> You'll leave tomorrow at five in the morning, and you'll be taken
> to a watchman's lodge deep in the Saint-Germain forest, where
> you'll be given a room on the second floor. Do not leave this
> room without my permission. You'll be given everything you
> need. The watchman and his wife can be trusted. Do not write
> to Lucien. Do not stand near the window during the day, but you

may take walks at nighttime with the protection of the watch-
man, if you feel you'd like to do so. Keep the blinds down on the
coach while you're on the road: Lucien's life is at stake.

Lucien will come this evening to say good-bye. Burn this letter in front of him.

Lucien immediately burned the note with a candle's flame.

"Listen, Lucien," said Esther, after she had listened to the contents
of the note like a criminal who has just heard her death sentence pronounced. "I'm not going to tell you that I love you; that would just be
stupid. . . . For these last five years, loving you has been like breath to
me, like life. Even on the very first day of my happiness, under the protection of that inexplicable man who has put me here like some strange
little animal in a cage, I knew that you would have to marry. Marriage is
a necessary element in your destiny, and God forbid that I should ever
stand in the way of your progress toward your fortune. But this marriage
will be my death. I'm not going to bore you with this; I'm not going to act
like one of those girls who kill themselves with the help of a charcoal
stove, because I've tried that once, and as Mariette says, the second time
it's disgusting. No, I'll leave instead and go far away, far from France. Asia
is an adept at the secrets of her country, and she promised to show me
gentler ways of dying. You just prick yourself, and poof!—it's all over. I
only ask one single thing, my dear angel, and that's not to be lied to. I've
been doing an accounting of my life—since the day I first saw you in 1824
up until today, I've had more happiness than any two women living a so-
called happy life could ever achieve. So take me for what I am—a woman
who is just as strong as she is weak. Say it to me: 'I'm getting married.'
All I'll ask of you is a tender good-bye, and after that you'll never hear
anyone speak of me again. . . ." A moment of silence followed upon this
declaration, as sincere as it was simple in its tone of voice and its gestures. "So, is it your marriage?" she asked, looking so directly into Lucien's eyes that her gaze penetrated his blue eyes like the point of a blade.

"We've been working on this marriage for a year and a half, and it's
still not settled," said Lucien. "And I don't know when it will be. But no,
my little one, it's not related to that. . . . No, it's more a matter of the abbé,
of me, of you. . . . There's a serious threat. . . . Nucingen has seen you."

"Yes," she said, "at Vincennes. Did he recognize me?"

"No," said Lucien, "but he's fallen in love with you, to the point of
spending everything he has. After dinner, when he described you, I
couldn't help but let a little smile escape me, which was highly imprudent, being in the middle of a group as savage as some enemy tribe intent

on trapping me. Carlos, who does the thinking for me, finds this situation very dangerous, and he's taking it upon himself to break Nucingen if Nucingen tries to spy on us—something the baron is perfectly likely to do, since he already told me that he found the police incompetent. You've managed to start a fire in a very old chimney, caked with soot. . . ."

"And just what does your Spaniard have in mind?" Esther asked quietly.

"I don't know anything about it. He told me I should sleep soundly," replied Lucien, unable to meet her eyes.

"All right. If that's the way it is, I'll obey, with that canine submission I'm so good at," said Esther, putting her arm in Lucien's and leading him into the bedroom. She continued, "And did you dine well there, Lulu?"

"Asia's cuisine is so good that nothing else seems good, no matter how celebrated the chef might be where I'm dining, but Carême prepared the dinner the same way as every other Sunday."

Involuntarily, Lucien compared Esther with Clotilde. The mistress was so beautiful and so endlessly charming that the most feared monster—Satiety, who devours even the most robust loves—had never yet come near them. "What a pity," he said to himself, "to find your perfect woman in two separate volumes! On the one hand, poetry, sensuality, love, devotion, beauty, tenderness . . ." Esther was singing, fluttering here and there like a butterfly, as women preparing for bed will do, coming and going around the room. You would have taken her for a hummingbird. "And on the other, an aristocratic name, family, honors, rank, knowledge of the world! And no way to unite them within a single person!" Lucien exclaimed to himself.

The next day, at seven in the morning, awakening in that charming pink and white bedroom, the poet found himself alone. When he rang, the fantastical Europe came in.

"What would monsieur like?"

"Esther!"

"Madame left at about four forty-five. On the orders of *monsieur l'abbé*, I have admitted a new face in the house, paid upon delivery."

"A woman?"

"Oh, no—she's from England. One of those who do their day's work at night, and we have been ordered to treat her as if she were madame . . . But what does monsieur want with an old nag like that? Oh, poor madame, how she cried when she got up into the carriage: 'Enough—it has to be!' she cried. 'I left that poor darling sleeping,' she said, wiping her tears. 'Europe, if he had just looked at me or spoken my name, I would have stayed, I would have died with him. . . .' You see, monsieur,

I like madame so much that I didn't let her see her substitute, and I can tell you there are plenty of ladies' maids who would have never been so thoughtful, and would have broken their ladies' hearts too."

"So the new woman, the unknown, is here?"

"Monsieur, yes, she came in the carriage that took madame away. I hid her in my room, as per instructions."

"Is she all right?"

"She'll do well enough in a pinch. She'll play her role well enough, as long as monsieur plays his," said Europe, going off to fetch the false Esther.

Monsieur de Nucingen at Work

The night before, just before he went to bed, the all-powerful banker gave orders to his valet, who now, at seven in the morning, introduced the famous Louchard, the most capable agent of the Gardes du Commerce, into a little drawing room, into which the baron shuffled in bathrobe and slippers.

"Chew magging fun of me!" he said in response to the *garde*'s greeting.

"There was no other way, baron. I stick to doing what my duty calls for, and I simply had the honor of informing you that I could not get mixed up in some affair that falls outside the functions of my position. What did I promise you? That I would put you in contact with the agent of ours who seemed to me to be the one best suited to helping you out. But *monsieur le baron* must understand the boundaries that exist between men of different occupations. When you're building a house, you don't ask the carpenter to do what the locksmith does. Well, then. There are two different police units—the Political Police and the Judicial Police. The men working for the Judicial Police don't mix in the affairs of the men working for the Political Police, and vice versa. If you applied to the chief of the Political Police, he would need to get authorization from the Ministry to take up your affairs, and you wouldn't dare tell the director general of the police of the kingdom about it.[95] Any agent who used his police status for his own purposes would be fired. Now, the Judicial Police are just as circumspect as the Political Police. This means that no one, whether he's from the Ministry of the Interior or the prefecture, takes any steps except in the interests of the State and the interests of justice. If it were a matter of some plot or a crime, good God, the various chiefs of police would be at your service immediately—but, *monsieur le baron,* you surely must see that they have plenty of cats to skin without running around getting involved in the fifty thousand love affairs going on in Paris. As for gardes like myself, we're only supposed to arrest debtors, and the minute it's a matter of something else, we're exposing ourselves to real trouble if we disturb anybody. I sent you one of my men, but with the understanding that I take no responsibility—you told him to find you a woman in Paris. Contenson pinched a nice fee of a thousand francs from you without doing a thing for it. Look, you might as well go hunting for a needle in a haystack as hunt around Paris to find a woman who frequents the Bois de Vincennes, the description of whom fits every other pretty woman in Paris."

"Zat Condenzon [he meant Contenson]," said the baron, "why he no tell me troof, inzted of binching zat tousand francs?"

"Listen, *monsieur le baron*," said Louchard, "if you want to give me a thousand écus, I'll give you—I mean, I'll sell you some advice."

"Ziss advice, it gost me tousand écus?" asked Nucingen.

"I'm not going to be trapped, *monsieur le baron*," said Louchard. "You're in love, and you want to find the object of your desire, and it's drying you up like a lettuce without water. Your valet tells me that you had two doctors here yesterday warning you that your health is in danger. I can put you in touch—and I'm the only one who can—with a capable man. But, what the hell! If your life isn't worth a thousand écus . . ."

"Giff me ze name of ziss capable man, und depend on my cheneros-ity!"

Louchard picked up his hat, bowed, and walked to the door.

"Deffil of a man!" cried Nucingen. "Come. Take."

"Let's be clear," said Louchard before accepting the money. "I'm selling you a reference, pure and simple. I give you a name and the address of a man who will be able to serve you, but this man is a master . . ."

"Go on vit chew!" exclaimed Nucingen. "Only name is vort tousand écus iss name of Rothschild, und zen only venn name is on bottom of bill. I giff you tousand francs."

Louchard, a little nobody who'd never been able to finagle a position for himself as lawyer, notary, bailiff, or legal adviser, stared at the baron intently.

"No. For you, it's a thousand écus or nothing. You'll make that much on the stock exchange in a few seconds," he said.

"I say tousand francs!" the baron repeated.

"You'd haggle if I were offering you a gold mine!" said Louchard, bowing and turning away.

"I get zat address for fiff hunnerd francs!" cried the baron, telling his valet to send in his secretary.

There are no more Turcarets today.[96] Today the greatest banker is just like the smallest one, exercising business acumen over the smallest details; he'll haggle over the arts, good deeds, love; he'll bargain with the Pope for an absolution. And so it was that Nucingen, listening to Louchard, had rapidly calculated that Contenson, as the right hand of the Garde du Commerce, would surely know the address of that master of espionage. Contenson would sell him for five hundred francs what Louchard had wanted to sell for a thousand écus. That rapid calculation gives vivid proof that if the heart of our banker had been invaded by Love, his head remained that of a lynx.

"Go now, munzeer," said the baron to his secretary, "to zis Condenzon, who iss spy for Lichard, ze Garde uff ze Commerce, und quick, take a cab, und bring man here right away. I wait! By garten gate. Take key, becauss most ideal ting is for nobody zey see zat man here vit me. Brink him to ze paffilion. Try doink all zis mit intelligence, eh?"

People had come to talk business with Nucingen, but he was awaiting Contenson and dreaming of Esther, saying to himself that very soon he would see that woman again, that woman who had raised such powerful and unexpected emotions in him. Soon he sent everyone away with vague statements and ambiguous promises. Contenson seemed to him to be the most important man in Paris; he constantly went to look out into his garden. Finally, after giving orders to admit no one else, he had his meal served in the pavilion that stood in a corner of the garden. Back in the office, the behavior, the hesitations of this, the most cunning, most insightful, most politic of all the bankers in Paris, seemed inexplicable.

"What's the trouble with the boss?" a stockbroker asked one of the chief clerks.

"Nobody knows—it looks as if people are getting nervous about his health. Yesterday, *madame la baronne* had both doctors, Desplein and Bianchon, over. . . ."

One day a group of foreigners who had come to see Newton arrived just when he was in the process of giving some medicine to one of his dogs, named Beauty, who, as is well known, caused him a great deal of trouble (Beauty was a bitch), though he said nothing more than "Ah, Beauty, you don't know how much harm you've done. . . ." The foreigners, respecting the great man's work, went away. There is a little bitch like Beauty in the lives of all great people. When the Maréchal de Richelieu arrived to congratulate Louis XV on the battle of Mahon, one of the greatest feats of arms in the whole eighteenth century, the king said to him, "Have you heard the news? My poor Lansmatt is dead!" Lansmatt was a mere doorkeeper, a man who had to be thoroughly up to date with all the king's love affairs.[97] The bankers of Paris never learned how much they owed to Contenson. That spy was the cause for Nucingen's allowing a large business deal to go through without him. The great lynx could train his artillery of stock-market speculation every day upon profits, but the man was now in the service of happiness.

Contenson

The distinguished banker took some tea, and was nibbling at some bread and butter like a man whose teeth had not been sharpened by appetite for a long while, when he heard a carriage stop outside his garden gate. Nucingen's secretary came in, introducing Contenson to him; he had finally found him in a café near Sainte-Pélagie, where the agent was lunching, thanks to the money paid him as a tip by a recently incarcerated debtor for certain privileges that need to be paid for. This Contenson, let me tell you, reader, was poetry, real Parisian poetry. The look of him alone would have convinced you that the Figaro of Beaumarchais, the Mascarillo of Molière, the Frontin of Marivaux, and the Lafleur of Dancourt—all those great expressions of audacity and scamming, of plotting and intriguing arising up out of the ashes of disaster— all of them were mediocre compared to this colossus of cleverness and poverty. When, in Paris, you encounter not a man but a type, it's a true spectacle! It's no longer just a moment in life, but a whole life, multiple lives! If you bake a plaster bust three times in a furnace, you get a kind of bastard imitation of Florentine bronze; well, in just the same way the thunderbolts of innumerable misfortunes, the cruel necessities of terrible situations had bronzed the head of Contenson as though sweating in a furnace, three times over, had tinted his face. The tight wrinkles of his face could never again be smoothed out; they formed eternal furrows, white at the bottom. The yellowed face had grown all wrinkles. The skull, reminiscent in shape of Voltaire's, looked as unfeeling as a death's head; if it had not been for a few hairs growing at the back, nobody would have taken it for the skull of a living man. Beneath his motionless brow, betraying nothing behind it, darted the eyes of a Chinaman, but as if seen through the glass window of a tea shop, and though those eyes moved, they were always expressionless, conveying nothing at all. The nose, flat as that of a death's head, seemed to sniff at Fate, and the mouth, thin-lipped as a miser's, was always open but saying nothing, like the slot of a letterbox. As calm as a savage, with weathered hands, Contenson, a small, thin, dry man, had that Diogenes-like attitude of indifference that can never quite bend itself into anything resembling respect. And what commentaries on his life and habits were presented by his clothes, for those who know how to decode clothing! The trousers, to begin with. The kind of thing a bailiff's assistant wears, black and shiny with age, looking like the material called *voile*, the stuff they make lawyers' gowns out of! . . . A waistcoat purchased in the Temple, but with lapels, and embroidered! . . . An overcoat of black, turning rusty! . . . All of it brushed and more or less clean, ornamented by a watch on an ormolu chain. Contenson's shirt front was visible, yellow and pleated, sporting a false diamond pin! . . . The velour collar resembled a yoke, and the folds of his flesh spilled over it, making him look like a Carib. The silk hat shone like satin, but you could have got enough oil out of its lining to fuel two small lamps, if some grocer had bought it and boiled it down. But enumerating these accessories is one thing, while painting the extraordinary air of importance that Contenson seemed to imprint upon them is something quite different. There was some little *je ne sais quoi* of the gallant about the coat collar, about the gleamingly waxed boots with their gaping soles, that no French expression can possibly render. Ultimately, an intelligent observer trying to make sense of all these details of Contenson's appearance would have seen that if, instead of being a police spy, he had been a thief, all these rags would have aroused fear rather than amusement. Gazing upon this outfit, the observer would have said, "Now there's a man who looks as if he's up to no good; he drinks, he gambles, he has vices, but he doesn't let himself get drunk, he doesn't cheat, and he's not a thief or a murderer." And he was truly indefinable; one would never know what to make of him— until the word "spy" came into one's thoughts. The man had already followed as many unknown trades as there are known ones. The thin smile on his pale lips, the gleam in his greenish eyes, the little twitch his brownish nose made showed that he was not a man who lacked intelligence. His face reminded you of tin plate, and his soul was surely just like his face. Any movements in his physiognomy were extracted from him by the demands of politeness rather than by any interior movement. He would have struck fear into you, if he hadn't already made you laugh. Contenson, one of the most curious products of the froth that bubbles to the surface from the great Parisian cistern, in which everything is in constant fermentation, piqued himself particularly on being a philosopher. He would say, without any bitterness, "I have great talents, but they get me nowhere—I might as well be a cretin." And he would blame himself rather than other men. Just try to find some other spies who have as little bile as Contenson! "Circumstances are against us," he would say to his chiefs. "We might be crystal, but we remain grains of sand, nothing more." His apathy about his clothes was meaningful:

he cared no more about his appearance than actors do about theirs; he excelled in disguise, in makeup; he could have given lessons to Frédérick Lemaître, for he could transform into the dandy when he needed to.[98] When he was young, he must have belonged to that unkempt social class associated with what are called the *petites maisons*.[99] He showed a deep contempt for the Judicial Police, because during the days of the Empire, he had worked for the police under Fouché, whom he regarded as a great man.[100] Since the suppression of the Ministry of Police,[101] he had taken on the work of pursuing commercial cases; but his abilities and skills were well known, and he was useful many times to the mysterious heads of the Political Police, who kept his name handy. Contenson, like his colleagues, only played minor roles in the drama; the leading parts went to his superiors when political intrigue was afoot.

Where Passion Leads

"Go on, leef us now," said Nucingen, dismissing his secretary with a gesture.

"Why is it this man's living in a mansion while I'm in a furnished room," Contenson said to himself. "He's been the ruin of his creditors three different times,[102] he's a thief, and me, I've never stolen so much as a sou. . . . And I've got more talent than he does. . . ."

"Condenzon, my frenn," said the baron, "chew haff tricked me out of tousand francs . . ."

"Well, my mistress owed money everywhere, from God to the Devil . . ."

"Chew hass a mistress?" cried Nucingen, looking at Contenson with an expression of mingled admiration and envy.

"I'm only sixty-six," said Contenson, a man Vice had kept young, so as to serve as a fatal example to others.

"Und vat doss she do?"

"She helps me," said Contenson. "When a man's a thief and an honest woman loves him, either she turns thief too, or he turns honest. Me, I'm a police spy. Always have been."

"Ja, but chew need money, all de time, ja?"

"All the time," said Contenson with a smile. "That's my nature, to want money and not get it, just like it's your nature to get it. Maybe we should get together: you make the money and I'll spend it. You can be the well, and I'll be the bucket. . . ."

"Vould chew like to make fiff hundred francs?"

"What a question! But what am I, some kind of fool? You aren't making the offer to compensate me for life's injustices, are you?"

"No. I add it to ze tousand francs you take from me already; zat make fifteen hundred francs you get from me."

"Ah, I see. You give me the thousand I already got, and then you add five hundred to that."

"Hexactly," said Nucingen, nodding his head.

"Still, that only gets me five hundred francs," said Contenson, imperturbably.

"To giff?"

"To take. Well, what is it *monsieur le baron* wishes to buy with that money?"

"Zey tell me chew know ze man in Paris who can find woman I luff, and chew know man's haddress . . . Zis man, he master spy?"

"Yes, he is."

"Hokay. You giff me haddress, I giff you five hundred francs."

"Where are they?" said Contenson quickly.

"Here zey are," said the baron, pulling a note from his pocket.

"All right. Let's have it," said Contenson, holding out his hand.

"Chust a minute. We go see zis man, and chew get money. Chew could giff me any old haddress chust to get money."

Contenson laughed.

"Well, I guess you have the right to think that low of me," he said as if chastising himself. "The dirtier our business, the more important honesty becomes. But look here, *monsieur le baron*: you give me six hundred francs, and I'll give you some good advice."

"Giff ze advice, und depend on my chenerosity. . . ."

"I'll risk it," said Contenson, "but I'm playing a dangerous game. With the police, you see, you need to know exactly where you stand. You can give the order—'All right, let's go!'—because you're rich, and for you money solves everything. And sure, money is important. But with money, as the three or four smartest folks I know like to say, you've only bought men. And there are other things, things you haven't thought of, things that you can't just buy! . . . You can't bribe luck. Besides, this isn't how you do good policework. Do you really want to be seen up in a cab with me? People will see us. And luck is just as likely to be for us as against us."

"Iss true?" said the baron.

"Of course, monsieur! Remember, it was a fallen horseshoe found in the street that led the prefect of police to find the infernal machine.[103] Well, if you and I were to take a cab tonight and go see Monsieur de Saint-Germain, I don't think he'd want to see you walking in there any more than you'd want to be seen."

"Ja, ja," said the baron.

"All right. This man is the best of the best, the second to the famous Corentin,[104] right arm to Fouché; some people say he's Fouché's natural son, from when he was a priest, but that's nonsense: Fouché knew what he had to do to be a priest, same as he knew what he had to do to be minister of police.[105] And listen, you're not going to get that man to work for you for anything less than ten thousand francs, so think about it.... But if you do you'll get results, and you'll get them fast. Unseen and unheard, as they say. I'll go tell Monsieur de Saint-Germain about this, and he'll set up a meeting somewhere that nobody can see or hear anything, because he'll be running a risk in using police powers for an individual like this. But what can you do? He's a good man, the king of men, a man who's had to put up with real persecutions, and all for having been the savior of France! Like me, like all of us who've saved her!"

"Hokay," said the baron, "chew write me and tell me when is happy day," and he smiled at his own little joke.

"But surely *monsieur le baron* would like to grease my palm?" said Contenson in a tone that was both humble and threatening.

"Chan," the baron called to his gardener. "Go ask Georges for twenty francs, and bring to me."

"But still, if *monsieur le baron* has no further detail or information beyond what he's told me, I fear that even the master spy will come up empty."

"Oh, I haff more!" said the baron with a shrewd air.

"I have the honor, then, of bidding you good day," said Contenson, taking the twenty-franc piece, "and I'll have the further honor of coming back and telling Georges where monsieur should go this evening, because in such policework you never write anything down."

"Iss funny, ze way zese hrascals operate," the baron thought. "With police, iss chust like with businessmen."

Father des Canquoëlles

When he left the baron, Contenson proceeded tranquilly down the Rue Saint-Lazare to the Rue Saint-Honoré, until he reached the Café David; he looked in through the window and saw an old man sitting there who went by the name of Father Canquoëlle.

The Café David, situated on the corner of the Rue Saint-Honoré and the Rue de la Monnaie, enjoyed, during the first thirty years of our century, a sort of celebrity, though it was limited to the neighborhood called the Bourdonnais.[106] The place attracted a number of retired merchants as well as some wholesalers still in the game: the Camusots, the Lebas, the

Pilleraults, the Popinots, and some shopkeepers like little old Molineux. From time to time old man Guillaume would drop in from the Rue de Colombier.[107] They talked politics among themselves, but prudently, for the Café David was liberal. They gossiped about all the little events in the neighborhood—for men do so enjoy mocking their fellow man! This café, like all the cafés of that era, had its own resident eccentric in this same Father Canquoëlle, who began frequenting the place back in 1811, and who appeared to be in such perfect harmony with the others that they all talked politics freely around him. Now and then the good old man, whose simplicity was cause for quite a few little jokes among the other regulars, would disappear for a month or two; but these absences, always attributed to the infirmity of his advanced age—for he appeared to have already passed sixty in 1811—were surprising to no one.

"What's happened to Father Canquoëlle?" someone would ask the woman at the counter.

"I wouldn't be surprised," she would reply, "that one of these days we'll read in the *Petites-Affiches* that he's died."[108]

Father Canquoëlle gave away his origins by the odd way he pronounced certain words: he referred to an "estatue," and to "the peoble," and instead of "Turk" he said "Turg." His name derived from a small estate called Les Canquoëlles, a word that signifies a kind of beetle in a number of the provinces, situated in the Vaucluse Département, where he was born. People had taken to calling him Canquoëlle rather than des Canquoëlles, though this never bothered him, for as far as he was concerned, the aristocracy had died in 1793; and, anyway, the estate of Les Canquoëlles didn't belong to him, because he was the younger son of a junior branch of the family. The clothes Father Canquoëlle wore would appear strange to us today, but they would not have surprised anyone between 1811 and 1820. The old man wore shoes with faceted steel buckles, silk stockings with alternating blue and white stripes, and heavy silk knee breeches with oval buckles that matched the ones on his shoes. A white embroidered waistcoat beneath an old coat, maroon and green, with metal buttons, and a ruffled shirt with pleated frills completed the outfit. Amid the shirt's frills a gold locket gleamed, which revealed, behind glass, a lock of hair shaped into a tiny church, one of those charming little trinkets that men wear to reassure themselves. Most men, just like animals, are either frightened or reassured by trifles. Father Canquoëlle's breeches were held up by a button that, in the style favored in the preceding century, fit tightly right across the middle of his abdomen. From the belt hung two parallel steel chains, each composed of numerous smaller chains, terminating in a bunch of trinkets. His white cravat was fastened in the back by a little gold buckle. Finally, atop his snowy and powdered hair perched the tricorner municipal hat that Monsieur Try, the president of the Tribunal, used to wear. Father Canquoëlle, feeling he had to make some sacrifices to keep up with the times, had recently replaced this hat, which he liked very much, with one of those round, ignoble hats that nobody can object to. A short pigtail, tied up with a ribbon, had traced a little half-circle on the back of his coat, but this was disguised by the fine rain of powder that trailed down from his hair. If your observation went no further than the most outstanding feature of his face, a nose so peppered with red protuberances that it could have taken its place in a plate of truffles, you might conclude that this was an easygoing, good-natured, rather foolish old man, but you would have been wrong, just like everybody else at the Café David, where no one had ever noticed the thoughtful forehead, the sardonic cast of the mouth, and the cold gaze of this old man steeped in vices, as serene as a Vitellius from whose imperial womb he would appear to have emerged, as it were, via palingenesis.[109] In 1816 a young traveling salesman named Gaudissart, a regular at the Café David, got drunk one night between eleven and twelve with a soldier on half pay. He was imprudent enough to talk about a plot that was being hatched against the Bourbons, a serious one that was just about to explode. There was nobody else in the café except old Canquoëlle, who seemed to have nodded off, two other men who were asleep, and the woman at the counter. Within the next twenty-four hours, Gaudissart was arrested and the conspiracy was unmasked. Two men went to their deaths on the scaffold. Neither Gaudissart nor anyone else ever suspected good old Father Canquoëlle of having been the informant. The waiters were fired, and everybody was under suspicion for a year, all of them living in fear of the police, as was Father Canquoëlle, who even talked about giving up going to the Café David, he was so afraid of the police.

Contenson walked into the café, ordered a small glass of brandy, and did not so much as glance at Father Canquoëlle, who was busy reading the papers; but when he had gulped down his brandy, he took the baron's gold coin and called the waiter, thumping it loudly on the table three times. The woman at the counter and the waiter examined the gold piece with the kind of care that seemed insulting to Contenson; but their distrust was justified by the surprise that Contenson's appearance had caused to all the regulars. "How did he get that gold piece: was it theft, or murder?" That was the thought that went through the minds of a number of intelligent customers who looked Contenson over from behind their reading glasses while pretending to be absorbed by the newspapers. Contenson, who missed, and was surprised by, nothing, wiped his lips with a handkerchief that had been sewn back together a mere three times, got his change, and slipped every single sou into his waistcoat's side pocket, the once-white lining of which was now as black as his trousers, leaving nothing at all for the waiter.

"That one's on his way to the scaffold one of these days," said Father Canquoëlle to his neighbor, Monsieur Pillerault.

"Not at all!" exclaimed Monsieur Camusot to the café at large; he had been the only one to feel no surprise at the man's behavior, and he added, "That's Contenson, Louchard's right-hand man, our Garde du Commerce. Those clowns must have been tracking somebody in the neighborhood."

Fifteen minutes later, good old Canquoëlle got up, picked up his umbrella, and calmly went on his way.

But it's really necessary, isn't it, to explain what kind of terrible and complicated man lived beneath the costume of Father Canquoëlle, the way the Abbé Carlos hid Vautrin beneath his? This southerner, born at Canquoëlle, the only property his perfectly respectable family owned, was in fact named Peyrade. He belonged to the junior branch of the La Peyrade line, an old but impoverished family from Comtat, still in possession of the small La Peyrade estate. The seventh child, he had come on foot to Paris in 1772, at seventeen years of age, with two six-franc pieces in his pocket, impelled there by the vices of his ardent temperament and by the brutal desire to succeed that attracts so many southerners to the capital when they realize that their fathers' houses will never net them enough income nor satisfy their passions. The reader will know all that is necessary to know about Peyrade's youth when I mention that, in 1782, he had the trust of the lieutenant-generals of police and was even their hero, held in the highest esteem by Messieurs Lenoir and d'Albert, the last two lieutenant-generals.[110] When the Revolution broke out, there was no police force; none was needed. Spying was universally practiced, and was called doing one's civic duty. Under the Directory, the government, which was a little more stable than that of the Committee for Public Safety, was obliged to reconstitute a police force, and the first consul instituted a prefect of police along with a general Ministry of Police.[111] Peyrade, a man with a history of policework, put the force together along with a man named Corentin, a much more powerful man, though younger, and a man known for his genius only in the subterranean world of policing. In 1808 Peyrade was rewarded for his enormous services by being posted as general commissioner in Antwerp. As Napoleon saw it, a post like this was the equivalent of a police prefecture overseeing all Holland. But after the 1809 campaign, Peyrade was removed from Antwerp by order of the emperor's cabinet, brought swiftly back to Paris between two gendarmes, and thrown right into La Force.[112] Two months later he was released on the word of his friend Corentin, but not before undergoing three different six-hour interrogations in the office of the police prefecture. Had Peyrade owed his disgrace to the miraculous activity with which he had supported Fouché in the defense of the French coasts, attacked in what was then called the Walcheren expedition, in which the Duc d'Otrante showed a capacity that put the fear into the emperor?[113] Even then, Fouché thought this was the case, but today everybody knows what went on in that Council of Ministers called by Cambacérès.[114] Stunned by the news of the British attempt, which was in retaliation for Napoleon's Boulogne expedition, and surprised when the master himself was absent on the island of Lobau, where all Europe believed he was defeated forever, the ministers didn't know which way to turn. The general opinion was to send a courier off to the emperor, but Fouché came up with a military plan by himself, which he proceeded to put into action. "Do as you see fit," said Cambacérès to him, "but as for me, I prefer keeping my head attached to my shoulders, and I'm rushing a report to the emperor." Everyone knows the absurd pretext the emperor adopted upon his return for dismissing his minister publicly in the Council of State and punishing him for having saved France without Napoleon. From that day forward the emperor had to contend with the enmity of Talleyrand and the Duc d'Otrante, the only two great politicians to come out of the Revolution and the only two who might have been able to save him in 1813. The pretext for dismissing Peyrade was the old, vulgar standby of accusing him of misappropriation: he had been guilty of looking the other way with smugglers and sharing his profits with high-level financiers. This was harsh treatment for a man who had earned the maréchal's baton for his great services to the police force. The man, who had been steeped in intrigue, knew all the secrets of every government since 1775, when he first entered the service of the lieutenant-general of police. The emperor Napoleon thought he was so powerful that he could create the men he needed, and thus took no further note of a man considered one of the surest, most capable, sharpest, and most reliable of those unknown and unsung geniuses upon whom depends the security of states. Napoleon thought he could replace Peyrade with Contenson; but Contenson by then was already in the service of Corentin, for his own benefit. Peyrade's situation was all the crueler because the man was both a libertine and a gourmand; his relations with women were like those of a pastry cook with confections. His vices had become second nature to him; he could no longer get along without dining well, gambling, and generally leading the life of a great lord (though a nonostentatious one) as all men with powerful talents tend to do when they have made their exorbitant distractions essential to their lives. Till now he had lived on this grand scale without ever having to account for his expenditures— neither he nor his friend Corentin. A cynic and a wit, he liked things the way they were; he was a philosopher. Now, a spy, no matter on what level of the machinery of policework he operates, soon reaches a state like that of the convict, unable ever to return to any respectable or honorable profession. Once marked, once matriculated, spies and convicts take on, like deacons, an indelible imprint. There are beings upon whom the Social State inscribes a fatal destiny. Peyrade, unfortunately, very much loved a pretty little girl, a child of his (he was sure of it) by an actress, a woman for whom he had done some service and who went on to show her gratitude for some three months. Peyrade brought the child back with him from Antwerp and now found himself in Paris with no resources beyond an annual pension of twelve hundred francs that the Prefecture of Police had settled upon the old disciple of Lenoir. He rented a five-room apartment in the Rue des Moineaux, on the fourth floor, for two hundred and fifty francs.

The Mysteries of the Police

If any man should be expected to know well the utility, the sweetness of friendship, is not that man the one the crowd calls a spy, the people call a snitch, and the government calls an agent? Peyrade and Corentin were as close as Orestes and Pylades. Peyrade had created Corentin, the way Vien created David.[115] But the pupil soon outstripped the master. They had worked together on more than one adventure (see *Une ténébreuse affaire*).[116] Peyrade, delighted at having discovered such a talent in Corentin, arranged for his career to be launched with a success: he compelled his pupil to make use of a mistress who had scorned him as bait to catch a man (see *Les Chouans*).[117] And Corentin at the time was barely twenty-five! . . . Corentin, remaining one of the generals under the minister of police, still held as high a position under the Duc de Rovigo as he had under the Duc d'Otrante.[118] Now, in those days the General Police and the Judicial Police operated along similar lines. When a significant, large-scale case came up, it was put on the account, so to speak, of the three, four, or five most capable agents. The minister, having heard of some plot, warned about some intrigue, no matter what, would say to one of his police colonels: "How much do you need to achieve such and such a result?" Corentin or Contenson would reflect sagely for a moment and then reply, "Twenty, thirty, forty thousand francs." Then, once the go-ahead had been given, the entire choice of methods and men to be used would be left up to the judgment of Corentin or the designated agent. The Judicial Police operated in the same way in solving crimes under the famous Vidocq.[119]

Both the Political Police and the Judicial chose their men primarily from the group of already known agents, men who had, so to speak, already matriculated, the men who are like soldiers in a secret army that is utterly indispensable to governments, despite the denunciations of moralists and do-gooders. But the absolute confidence that was placed in the two or three generals at the level of Peyrade and Corentin allowed them to choose unknown men if they saw fit to do so, though they would always be accountable to the minister in serious cases. Now the experience and the finesse of Peyrade were simply too precious to Corentin, and thus once the little trouble of 1810 was safely in the past, he soon employed his old friend, constantly consulted him, and took care of most of his needs. Peyrade, on his side, rendered tremendous services to Corentin. In 1816 Corentin, following on the discovery of the conspiracy involving the Bonapartist Gaudissart, tried to get Peyrade officially taken back into the police force, but some unknown force seemed to be working against Peyrade. This is the reason. In their desire to make themselves necessary, Peyrade, Corentin, and Contenson, following the suggestion of the Duc d'Otrante, had organized a kind of counterpolice for the private use of Louis XVIII, a force consisting of the very best agents. Louis XVIII died, in possession of secrets that will remain secrets despite the efforts of the most informed historians. The struggles between the General Police of the Kingdom and this counterpolice force gave rise to a number of horrific affairs, the secrets of which have been sealed by the gallows. This is neither the place nor the time to go into more detail on the subject, for these are Scenes of Parisian Life after all, and not Scenes of Political Life; but enough has been said already to make it clear how the man known as good old Canquoëlle at the Café David made his living, and what sort of thread tied him to the terrible and mysterious powers of the police. From 1817 to 1822, Corentin, Contenson, Peyrade, and their agents were often given the mission of spying on the minister of police himself. This might very well explain why the minister refused to employ Peyrade and Contenson; Corentin managed, without their knowing it, to cast suspicion upon the two of them in order to be able to make use of his old friend himself once it was clear he would never be accepted back into the force. The ministers did have faith in Corentin, and they tasked him with keeping tabs on Peyrade, which must have made Louis XVIII smile. Corentin and Peyrade thus remained masters of the field. Contenson, affiliated for a long time now with Peyrade, continued to help him. He had gone into the Gardes du Commerce on the orders of Corentin and Peyrade. Out of that species of wild enthusiasm that the love for one's profession can lead to, those two generals loved to get their most able soldiers placed in the kind of positions where information is most likely to abound. Moreover, Contenson's vices, his depraved habits, had led him to fall lower than his two friends, and those habits required a great deal of money, which meant he had need of a great deal of work. Contenson, without committing the slightest of indiscretions, had told Louchard that he knew the only man capable of getting results for the Baron de Nucingen. Peyrade in fact was the only agent who could with impunity take on police-level work on behalf of an individual. Louis XVIII being dead, Peyrade had lost not only his importance but all the profits of being His Majesty's official spy. Believing himself to be indispensable, he had continued with his way of life. Women, dining well, and the Cercle des Étrangers[120] had combined to keep the good old man from saving any of his money; and like all such men with such vices, he had an iron constitution. But from 1826 to 1829, having reached the age of seventy-four, Peyrade began to slow down a little, to use his expression; he had begun to see his health diminishing from year to year. He attended funerals for acquaintances in the police, and he watched with chagrin the government of Charles X abandoning the grand traditions. At every session the legislature pared back the estimates of what was necessary for the continued existence of the police force, out of hatred for that instrument of power and a desire to make the institution more moral. "It's as if they want to cook while wearing white gloves," Peyrade said to Corentin. Corentin and Peyrade had foreseen the events of 1830 as far back as 1822. They knew the deep hatred Louis XVIII felt for his successor, which explains his attitude toward the younger branch, and without which the politics of his reign would be entirely enigmatic.

As he aged, Peyrade's love for his natural daughter grew even stronger. For her sake he had adopted a respectable bourgeois lifestyle, hoping to get Lydie married to some good young man. And thus for the last three years he had tried especially hard to land some position within the Prefecture of Police or within the General Police of the Kingdom—some open, avowable position. He ended up inventing a position, the necessity of which, he told Corentin, would sooner or later become obvious. His idea was to set up what he would call an information bureau at the Prefecture of Police, a clearinghouse or intermediary among the Paris police, the Judicial Police, and the Police of the Kingdom so that the general director could profit from the various work of all the subsidiaries. Peyrade was the only one who could, at his age and after fifty-five years of discretion, serve as the ring that could connect the three police forces, the archivist to whom both the Political and the Judicial people could come to clarify certain details. Peyrade hoped that with this plan he would be able to put together a dowry and find a good husband for his little Lydie. Corentin had already spoken of it to the director-general of the Police of the Kingdom, without mentioning Peyrade's name, and the director-general, also a southerner, thought an idea like this ought to originate from the prefecture.

At the moment Contenson rapped three times with his gold coin on the café table, a signal that denoted "I need to talk to you," the lifelong man of the police was wondering, "Who can I get, or what can I do to get the prefect to move on the idea?" To the untrained eye, he looked like an imbecile studying his *Courrier français*.[121]

"Poor old Fouché!" he said to himself as he passed along the Rue Saint-Honoré. "The great man is dead! All the people who were our intermediaries with Louis XVIII are in disgrace! And anyway, like Corentin said the other day, nobody puts any faith in the agility and intelligence of a seventy-year-old anymore. . . . Oh, why did I make it such a habit to dine at Véry's, to drink the finest wines . . . to sing 'Mère Godichon'[122] . . . to gamble money away when I had it! . . . To land a position, it's not enough to have intelligence, as Corentin says; you've also got to know how to handle yourself! That nice Monsieur Lenoir predicted my fate after that necklace affair: when he learned that I didn't stay put under Olivia's bed, he exclaimed, 'You'll never amount to anything!'"[123]

A Spy at Home

If the venerable Father Canquoëlle (and he was called Father Canquoëlle in his house) continued to live in the apartment on the fourth floor on the Rue des Moineaux, you can bet that he had found details there that were favorable to the practice of his frightful profession. Situated on the corner of the Rue Neuve-Saint-Roch, his house had no neighbor on one side. The staircase divided the building in two, which meant that on each floor there were two completely isolated rooms. These two rooms were on the Rue Neuve-Saint-Roch side. Above the fourth floor were garret rooms, one of them a kitchen and the other the apartment of Father Canquoëlle's only servant, a Flemish woman named Katt who had been Lydie's wet-nurse. Father Canquoëlle had divided his bedroom

in two, one serving as his study. A thick shared wall kept the office private and isolated from the other apartment. The window that opened
onto the Rue des Moineaux faced a blank, windowless wall. Now, because
the whole width of the bedroom separated the office from the staircase, the two friends needed to fear no gaze, no listening ear, when they
spoke of their affairs in the study, a room designed expressly for their
dreadful profession. Out of further precaution, Peyrade had installed a
straw bed, a carpet of felt, and a thick rug in the Fleming's room, on the
pretext of keeping his child's nurse content. Moreover, he had plugged
up the chimney, making use of a stove for warmth, putting a pipe for it
through the wall on the Rue Saint-Roch side. Finally, he had laid several
carpets on his floor, to keep anyone on a lower level from being able to
hear any sounds. Expert in the procedures of espionage, he sounded the
shared wall, the ceiling, and the floor once a week, examining them as if
he were in search of invasive insects. The certainty of being there with
no witnesses and no listeners made Corentin choose this study for his
deliberations when his own was unavailable. The only people who knew
where Corentin lived were the director-general of the Police of the Kingdom and Peyrade; he received there any personages whom the minister
or the Palais used for intermediaries in affairs of unusual importance;
but no other agent, no subordinate ever went there, and when it came to
professional plans, he always came to Peyrade's. In this modest, anonymous room plans were laid, resolutions taken that would furnish material for strange annals and curious dramas if the walls could talk. There,
between 1816 and 1826, very great interests were discussed. There, events
were foreseen that would eventually come to weigh heavily upon France.
There, in 1819, Peyrade and Corentin, just as foresighted as but even better informed than Bellart, the attorney-general, asked themselves: "If
Louis XVIII doesn't want to strike such and such a blow, do away with
such and such a prince, is it because he hates his brother? Does he want
him to inherit a revolution?"[124]

Upon Peyrade's door hung a slate, and upon that slate he would
often discover strange notations scrawled in chalk. This infernal alge-
bra was perfectly clear to initiates. Facing Peyrade's scruffy apartment
was Lydie's, which consisted of an anteroom, a little drawing room, a
bedroom, and a dressing room. Lydie's door, like that of Peyrade's room,
was sheet iron, four layers thick, placed between two strong oak boards,
and armed with locks and a system of weights that would make the door
as difficult to force as one in a prison. And thus, even though there was
a public passageway outside her apartment, with a shop below and no

caretaker, Lydie lived there with nothing to fear. Her dining room, her little drawing room, her bedroom all had windowboxes, and all were luxurious, models of Flemish cleanliness. The Flemish nurse had never left Lydie, referring to her as her daughter. The two of them went to church with such regularity that the Royalist grocer downstairs developed an excellent opinion of old Canquoëlle; his shop was on the corner of the Rue des Moineaux and the Rue Neuve-Saint-Roch, and his family, his kitchen, and his employees were all on the first floor and the entresol. On the second floor lived the building's owner, and the third had been rented for the last twenty years to a lapidary. Each tenant had a key to the main door. The grocer cheerfully accepted packages and letters addressed to the other three, peaceable tenants, for his shop was furnished with a box for letters. Without such details, foreigners and even those who know Paris could not understand the privacy, the quiet, the isolation, and the security of this unusual Parisian house. After midnight Father Canquoëlle could hatch plots, receive spies and ministers, women and harlots, without anyone in the world knowing a thing about it. The Flemish woman said of Peyrade to the grocer's cook, "He wouldn't hurt a fly!" And Peyrade passed for the very best of men. He spared nothing for his daughter. Lydie, having been taught music by Schmucke, was now a musician herself and did some composing.[125] She knew how to "wash" a "sepia," and could paint with watercolors. Peyrade dined every Sunday with his daughter. On that day the man was entirely father. Religious but not pious, Lydie performed all her Easter duties and went to confession every month. Nevertheless, she enjoyed the occasional play, and she strolled in the Tuileries when the weather was fine, but those were her only pleasures, for she led a very sedentary existence. Lydie, who adored her father, knew nothing whatsoever about his sinister capabilities and his shadowy doings. No desire had yet troubled the life of that so pure girl. Slim and beautiful like her mother, gifted with a beautiful voice and a sweet face framed by lovely blond hair, she resembled a type of angel, the more mystical than real-looking type that painters sometimes pose in the background of their Holy Family pictures. A glance from her blue eyes seemed to cast a ray of heaven itself upon the person favored with a look from her. Her chaste style of dress, avoiding any sort of exaggeration, seemed to breathe the charming perfume of the bourgeoisie. Picture an aging Satan, father to an angel, continually purifying himself by that divine contact, and you'll have some idea of Peyrade and his daughter. If anyone had dared to stain that perfect diamond, her father would have invented a means of swallowing him up, one of those terrifying traps in use during the Restoration for wretches who would go on to lose their heads on the scaffold. A thousand écus were sufficient for Lydie and Katt, whom she referred to as her nurse.

As he turned onto the Rue des Moineaux, Peyrade caught sight of Contenson; he passed him by and went up the stairs first, hearing the steps of his agent following later, and he got him inside before the Fleming could show her nose at her kitchen door. There was a bell that was set off down at the gate, ringing up on the third and fourth floors to let the resident know someone was on their way up. Needless to say, every midnight Peyrade would muffle the bell.

"What's so important, Philosopher?"

Philosopher was the nickname Peyrade had given Contenson, one that this Epictetus of Snitches had well earned. The name Contenson hid within it, shameful though it is to admit, one of the oldest names of Norman feudalism (see *Les Frères de la Consolation*).[126]

"Well, there are ten thousand francs in it."

"What kind of thing? Political?"

"No, an absurdity! The Baron Nucingen—you know him, that certified thief—is sniffing after some woman he saw in the Vincennes forest, and he just has to find her or else he's going to die of love. . . . They had doctors in to examine him the other day, his valet tells me. I've already squeezed a thousand francs out of him by pretending to look for the girl."

Contenson went on to describe the encounter between Nucingen and Esther, adding that the baron evidently had some additional clues to offer.

"All right," said Peyrade; "we'll find this Dulcinea. Tell the baron to come in a carriage tonight to the Champs-Élysées, by the Avenue Gabriel and the Allée de Marigny."

Peyrade walked Contenson to the door and then went to knock on his daughter's door, for he always knocked before going in. He came in feeling joyful, chance having at last tossed him the means of gaining the position he had wanted. He plumped himself down in a Voltaire-style armchair after having kissed Lydie on the forehead and saying, "Play something for me."

Lydie played a piano piece by Beethoven.

"Well played, my little doe," he exclaimed, taking Lydie onto his knees. "Do you realize that we're twenty-one? We need to get married, because our father is over seventy. . . ."

"I'm happy just as I am," she replied.

"You love only me—a man so ugly, and so old?" asked Peyrade.

"But who am I supposed to love?"

"I'll dine with you, little doe; let Katt know. I'm thinking of getting us set up, finding a place and finding a husband worthy of you . . . some good young man, full of talent, someone of whom you can be proud one day. . . ."

"I haven't seen anybody I liked enough to marry, except for one."

"You have seen one?"

"Yes, at the Tuileries," said Lydie. "He went walking past me, with the Comtesse de Sérisy on his arm."

"Did you find out his name?"

"Lucien de Rubempré! I was sitting under a lime tree with Katt, not thinking about anything in particular. A couple of women were sitting next to me, saying to each other: 'Look, there's Madame de Sérisy and the gorgeous Lucien de Rubempré.' So I looked to see the couple they were looking at. 'Ah, my dear,' one of them said to the other, 'some women are so lucky! That one can get away with anything, because she was born a Ronquerolles, and her husband is a powerful man.' The other one said to her, 'But you know, my dear, Lucien costs her a great deal. . . .' What did she mean, Papa?"

"That's just the kind of nonsense they talk in high society," Peyrade said to his daughter in a friendly tone. "Maybe they were making some allusion to politics."

"Well, you asked me, and I told you. If you want me to get married, find me a man who looks like that one."

"Child!" cried the father. "Beauty in a man is not always a sign of goodness. Young men endowed with an attractive exterior never encounter any difficulties in getting started in life, they never have to use any talent, they become corrupted by the advances society makes to them, and sooner or later they pay up the interest on what they've only borrowed! . . . I'd rather find for you the kind of man the bourgeois, the wealthy, and the imbeciles abandon without any help, any protection . . ."

"But who, father?"

"A man of undiscovered talents. . . . But let's leave it for now, my dear child; I have my methods, I know how to comb through all the garrets in Paris and find someone who will meet your standard, a man just as good looking as the bad sort you just described to me, but one with a real future, one of those men destined for glory and fortune. . . . Oh, why didn't I think of this! I have a whole flock of nephews, and there just might be one among them worthy of you! I'll write, or have somebody write, down to Provence!"

A strange coincidence: at that very moment a young man, half dead from hunger and fatigue, just arrived on foot from the Département of

Vaucluse, a nephew to Father Canquoëlle, was entering Paris through the Barrière d'Italie, in search of his uncle. In the fantasies of a family to whom their unknown uncle, Peyrade, offered a text of boundless hope, they dreamed that he had returned from the Indies with millions! Stimulated by these fictions by the fireside, the great-nephew, whose name was Théodose, had undertaken a voyage of circumnavigation to seek his fantastic uncle.

Three Men Begin to Circle Each Other

After having savored the pleasures of fatherhood for several hours, Peyrade, his hair washed and dyed (the powdering was a disguise), dressed in a heavy blue frock coat buttoned all the way up to the chin, covered up in a black cloak, wearing heavy boots with thick soles, carrying a specially made map, was walking slowly along the Avenue Gabriel where Contenson, disguised as an old woman street vendor, met him outside the Élysée-Bourbon gardens.

"Monsieur de Saint-Germain," Contenson said, using his old boss's nom de guerre, "you've put me in the way of making five hundred *faces* [i.e., francs], but the reason I'm here is I want to let you know that the damnable baron, before he gave them to me, went looking for information at the house [i.e., the prefecture]."[127]

"I'll probably need you," said Peyrade. "Look up agents seven, ten, and twenty-one; we can employ them without either the police or the prefecture knowing it."

Contenson went and stood again next to the carriage in which Monsieur de Nucingen was awaiting Peyrade.

"I am Monsieur de Saint-Germain," the southerner said to the baron, raising himself up to the level of the carriage window.

"Iss goot; get in wiz me," said the baron, giving the order to drive toward the Arc de Triomphe.

"You went to the prefecture, *monsieur le baron*? That's not so good. . . . May I ask what you said to *monsieur le préfet*, and what he said to you?" asked Peyrade.

"Vell, beforr I giff fiff hundred francs to a clown like zis Contenson, I vant to know if he really hass earned zem. So I only say to Ze prefect zat I vant to employ an achent by name of Peyrade, und iss zis goot man for ze job, und can I trust him. Ze Prefect he say you wass one of ze most cleverest and most honestest of men. Zat is ze whole story."

"All right. Now that *monsieur le baron* has shown that he knows my real name, will he please go on to tell me what this is all about?"

When the baron had explained at great, tedious length in his hideous Polish Jew's[128] accent the story of his encounter with Esther, the cry of the footman at the back of the carriage, and all his vain efforts, he concluded by narrating what had taken place the evening before at his house, the little smile that slipped out of Lucien de Rubempré, and the guess of Bianchon and several dandies that the young man had some acquaintance with the unknown woman.

"Listen, *monsieur le baron*: you'll be giving me ten thousand francs in advance for expenses because this business for you is a matter of life or death; and because your life is an important one in the business world, we must leave no stone unturned in our search for this woman. Ah, you're smitten, aren't you!"

"Ja, shmitten, ja . . ."

"If I need anything more from you, baron, I'll let you know; meanwhile, trust me," said Peyrade. "I'm not just a spy, as you might think. . . . In 1807, I was general commissioner in Antwerp, and now that Louis XVIII is dead, I can confide that I was his director of counterpolice for seven years . . . so people don't haggle with me. You understand, *monsieur le baron*, that no one can know how much a person's confidence will cost us, before we learn more about this affair. And don't think that I'm going to be satisfied simply with a sum of money—there's something else I want for my recompense."

"So long as zis is not a kinkdom, ja. . . ."

"For you, it's less than nothing."

"Zis I like!"

"You know the Kellers?"

"Uff course."

"François Keller is son-in-law to the Comte de Gondreville, and the Comte de Gondreville dined at your house yesterday with his son-in-law."

"Ze Debbil muss tell you zis!" cried the baron. "Or maybe it's Georges talk too much."

Peyrade laughed. As he looked at the man's smile, the banker began to conceive some strange suspicions concerning his domestic.

"The Comte de Gondreville is perfectly situated to get me the position I want at the Prefecture of Police, and within forty-eight hours the prefect will understand how important it is to create such a position," Peyrade continued. "Ask for this position for me, get the Comte de Gondreville to involve himself in the matter, and with zeal, too. That will be sufficient recompense for the service I'm about to render you. I only want your word on it—because if you fail me, sooner or later you will curse the day you were born. . . . I swear to it."

"I giff my vort of honor I do vat iss possible to do."

"If I only do 'what's possible' for you, it won't be enough."

"Okay. I vill act frankly."

"Frankly. . . . All right: that's all I ask," said Peyrade. "Frankness is the only new thing we can offer each other."

"Frankly," the baron repeated. "Vere chew vant I put you down?"

"At the end of the Pont Louis XVI."[129]

"To ze bont de la Jambre," the baron said to his footman when he came up to the door.

"Zo, I get zis voman finally, I haff her. . . ," the baron said to himself as they drove along.

"How bizarre!" Peyrade said to himself as he walked toward the Palais-Royal, where he thought he might try to triple his ten thousand francs in order to get a decent dowry for Lydie. "Here I am, having to investigate the little affairs of the young man who bewitched my daughter. I imagine he's the type who has 'an eye for the ladies,'" he continued, using the particular phrasing that had become part of his own language with which his observations, and those of Corentin, could be quickly communicated, for even if their language violated proper usage, it was energetic and picturesque.

Returning home, the Baron Nucingen seemed transformed; he surprised the guests and his wife by showing them a lively expression and a face that had got its color back.

"The stockholders better look out!" said du Tillet to Rastignac.

They were all taking tea just then in Delphine de Nucingen's salon, having returned from the Opéra.

"Ja!" said the baron with a smile, overhearing du Tillet's little joke. "I am in ze mood to do some business!"

"So you've seen your mystery woman?" asked Madame de Nucingen.

"No," he replied, "but I haff hopes now to find her."

"Does any man ever love his wife this way?" cried Madame de Nucingen, expressing a little jealousy—or perhaps feigning it.

"When you finally have her to yourself," du Tillet said to the baron, "you have to invite us to dinner with her, because I'm awfully anxious to get a look at the creature who's put you into such a youthful state."

"Ziss voman—she iss a masterpiece of greation!" exclaimed the old banker.

"He's going to get taken like a greenhorn," Rastignac whispered to Delphine.

"Ah, no matter—he makes enough money to . . ."

"To give a little of it back, eh?" said du Tillet, interrupting the baroness.

Nucingen was walking around the salon as if his legs were bothering him.

"This is the moment to get him to pay off your debts," Rastignac whispered in the ear of the baroness.

At that same moment, Carlos, coming back from the Rue Taitbout, where he had been giving his final instructions to Europe, who was to play the main role in the comedy being devised to trick Baron Nucingen, was walking along in a state of high hopes. Lucien was accompanying him as far as the Boulevard, and he was disquieted by the presence of this demon who could disguise himself so perfectly that he could only be recognized by his voice.

"Where the devil did you manage to find a woman more beautiful than Esther?" he asked his corrupter.

"Ah, my young friend, you don't find them in Paris. Coloring like that is not manufactured in France."

"I mean, I'm still stunned—the Callipygian Venus doesn't have a body that perfect! A man would sell his soul for her. . . . But where did you get her?"

"The most beautiful woman in London. Drunk on gin, she killed her lover in a fit of jealousy. The lover was just some miserable lowlife whom the London police were glad to be rid of, and the creature was sent over to Paris to let the whole thing blow over. . . . The funny thing is that she was brought up very well, daughter of a preacher, speaks French like it's her mother tongue. She doesn't know, and she never will know, what she's doing here. She's been told that if you like her, she might get her hands on your millions, but you're jealous as a tiger—and they haven't told her anything about Esther. She doesn't know your name."

"But what if Nucingen prefers her to Esther. . . ."

"Ha! So you're already there!" cried Carlos. "Today you're afraid the thing won't happen, the very same thing that had you so worked up yesterday! Relax. This one is blonde, pale, blue-eyed, just the opposite of the beautiful Jew, and only Esther's eyes will be able to move a man as decayed as Nucingen. No one would believe you were hiding some ugly duckling, after all! Once this little doll has played her role, I'll send her on, with some escort I can trust, to Rome maybe, or Madrid, where she can inflame the passions of other men."

"Well, since we're only going to have her around for a little while," said Lucien, "maybe I'll go back there now. . . ."

"Go, my boy, enjoy yourself. Tomorrow you'll be another day older. Meantime, I have to wait for somebody I've hired to find out what's going on at the Baron de Nucingen's."

"Who's that?"

"His valet's mistress, because you have to keep up with the movements of the enemy."

At midnight Paccard, Esther's manservant, found Carlos on the Pont des Arts, the best place in Paris to exchange a few words with no danger of being overheard. As they spoke, the servant continued to face one direction, while his master faced the other.

"The baron went to the police prefecture first thing this morning," said the servant, "and this evening he boasted that he was about to find the woman he saw in the Bois de Vincennes, somebody promised him ..."

"So we're being watched! But by whom?" said Carlos.

"He's already hired Louchard, the one from the Gardes du Commerce."

"That would be like child's play," said Carlos. "We only have to fear the Security Brigade and the Judicial Police, and as long as they're not moving, we can!"

"There's something else."

"What?"

"The 'boys from the fields.' I ran into La Pouraille ... he knocked off some pair of lovebirds and walked away with ten thousand alms in five-ballers—gold!"[130]

"They'll catch him," said Jacques Collin; "those are the Rue Boucher murders."

"What are my orders?" asked Paccard, with an air as respectful as that of a maréchal of France seeking the command from Louis XVIII.

"Go out every evening at ten," Carlos replied, "and get to the Bois de Vincennes quickly, by way of the woods around Meudon and Ville-d'Avray. If somebody observes you, let them; be sociable, chatty, corruptible. Talk about the jealousy of de Rubempré, who's absolutely wild about madame, and above all that nobody should ever know he has a mistress like that."

"Got it. Should I be armed?"

"No—never!" Carlos exclaimed. "Armed? What for? It only causes trouble. Don't pull out that hunting knife of yours. And you know you can break the legs of the strongest man by that trick I taught you! And when you know you can beat back three armed wardens, having two of them laid out flat before they can even get their sabers out, what's to fear? You've got a cane, right?"

"That's right!" said the manservant.

Paccard, variously known as Old Guard, the Rabbit, or Just Right, a man with a leg of iron, an arm of steel, Italian-featured, with an artist's hair and a fireman's beard, a face as pale and impassive as Contenson's, kept his restless energy hidden and carried himself as stiffly as a drum major, which deflected suspicion. An escaped convict from Passy or Melun doesn't show this kind of smug seriousness, this kind of belief in his own merit. Playing Jafar to the Haroun Al-Rashid of the penal colonies, he exhibited the same friendly admiration for him that Peyrade felt for Corentin. This colossus was thin, without much of a chest or much flesh on his bones, and he strode along on his two long pins with a grave air. The right leg never moved without the right eye investigating the surrounding circumstances with the rapidity peculiar to the thief and the spy. The left eye imitated the right one. One step, one careful look! Skinny, agile, ready for anything at any time, if it weren't for that too-familiar enemy known as *liqueur des braves*,[151] Paccard would have been perfect, as Jacques often said, for he possessed all the talents needed by a man at war with society; but the master had succeeded in convincing the slave to "keep his powder dry" and not to drink until the evenings. When he returned home at night, Paccard absorbed his liquid gold by means of little glasses filled from a large stone jar from Gdansk.

"I'll keep my eyes open," Paccard said, putting his splendid feathered cap back on after bidding the man he called his "confessor" good evening.

And this is what led three men, each of them strong in their own spheres—Jacques Collin, Peyrade, and Corentin—to close in on each other on the same terrain, and to make use of their wits in a struggle in which each was fighting for his own passion or his own interest. It was to be one of those unsung but terrible battles in which the powers that might lead to a fortune instead are expended in hatred, in irritation, in moves and countermoves, broils and stratagems.

Nucingen, Closing In on His Bliss, Readies Himself

Peyrade kept his men and methods secret, with his friend Corentin supporting his efforts, both of them thinking the whole thing was an absurd trifle. And so history must be mute on the subject, just as she is mute on the real causes of most revolutions. But here is how it worked out.

Five days after the interview between Monsieur de Nucingen and Peyrade on the Champs-Élysées, in the morning, a man of about fifty, with that leaden complexion that society life imparts to diplomats, dressed in blue cloth and elegantly turned out, descended, with an air almost like that of a minister of state, from a splendid cabriolet, tossing the reins to his manservant. He asked a footman, sitting on a bench in the large columned entrance hall, who stood up respectfully and opened the glass doors, if the Baron de Nucingen was receiving.

"And monsieur's name . . . ?" the servant asked.

"Tell *monsieur le baron* that I've come from the Avenue Gabriel," replied Corentin. "If there are others there, be careful not to say that name out loud, or they'll have you thrown out."

A moment later the valet returned and conducted Corentin into the baron's study by way of inner apartments.

Corentin and the banker looked at each other, both of them with impenetrable expressions, and they exchanged a polite greeting.

"*Monsieur le baron*," said Corentin, "I come to you in the name of Peyrade. . . ."

"Goot!" exclaimed the baron, rushing around the room and making sure both doors were bolted.

"The mistress of Monsieur de Rubempré lives on the Rue Taitbout, in the apartment that once belonged to Mademoiselle de Bellefeuille, who was once the mistress of Monsieur de Granville, the attorney-general."

"Ah, she liffs so near to me!" cried the baron. "Iss so strange!"

"It's easy for me to believe that you're mad about that magnificent woman; it was a pleasure to me just to see her," said Corentin. "Lucien is so jealous that he has forbidden her to show herself; and she must love him very much, because over the last four years since she took over Bellefeuille's place, and her situation as well, nobody—not her neighbors, not the doorman, not the other tenants in the building—has ever laid eyes on her. The girl only goes out at night. And when she does, the cab's curtains are lowered and madame is veiled. Now, Lucien has reasons beyond just jealousy for keeping this woman so well hidden: he plans to marry Clotilde de Grandlieu, and he is currently the intimate favorite of Madame de Sérisy. Naturally, he wishes to keep both his mistress and his fiancée. This puts you in an excellent position. Lucien will sacrifice his pleasures in favor of his self-interest and his vanity. You are wealthy, and this will probably be your final affair, so be generous. You'll achieve your goals via the maid. Give her twelve thousand francs, and she'll hide you in her mistress's bedroom; and for you the price will be a bargain!"

Rhetoric affords no figure for describing the sheer eloquence of Corentin, its straightforwardness, its clarity, its absolute assurance; the baron could not hold in an expression of surprise at it, bursting through the façade of impassivity he had cultivated till now.

"I've come to ask for five thousand francs for my friend, who managed to misplace five of your banknotes . . . just a little slip!" Corentin continued, in his practiced tone of command. "Peyrade knows Paris too well to put any money into putting up posters advertising the search, and he's counting on you. But this isn't the important thing," said Corentin, changing his tone from one of command to one of gravity. "If you don't want to spend your last years in misery, get Peyrade that position he asked you for. You can do it easily. The director-general of the Police of the Kingdom will have received a note about this yesterday. The only thing that needs to be done is for you to get Gondreville to talk to the prefect of police about it. And, in fact, you should say to Malin, Comte de Gondreville, that it's a matter of doing a little favor for the people who got rid of those Simeuse people for him, and that should do it. . . ."[152]

"Here, monsieur," said the baron, handing five thousand-franc bills to Corentin.

"The lady's maid has a good friend, a big manservant named Paccard, who lives on the Rue de Provence, in the house of a carriage maker, and who rents himself out to anyone who gives himself princely airs. You'll make contact with Madame Van Bogseck's maid by means of Paccard, a big Piedmontese oddball who loves his vermouth a little too much."

Apparently this last piece of information, elegantly tossed off like a kind of postscript, was what cost the five thousand francs. The baron tried to guess what sort of man Corentin was, for his information suggested he was not so much a spy as a man who managed spies; but Corentin remained for him what an inscription lacking three-quarters of its letters is for an archaeologist.

"Und ze name of ziss lady's maid?" he asked.

"Her name is Eugénie," replied Corentin, bowing to the baron and taking his leave.

Baron Nucingen in a transport of joy abandoned the day's business and his office, going back home in that thrilling state that a young man of twenty experiences when he's about to have his first meeting with his first mistress. The baron collected all the thousand-franc notes in his personal cash drawer—a sum with which he could have changed the lives of a whole village of people, some fifty-five thousand francs!—and he stuffed them into his pocket. But the prodigality of millionaires cannot compete with their love of gain. If it's a matter of some whim or some passion, money means nothing to these Croesuses, but in truth it's harder for them to even have a whim than it is to pile up gold. Sensual bliss is the greatest rarity in these oversated lives, too stuffed with the emotions that Speculation arouses in them, the only emotion on which their dried-out hearts still feed. To take an example: one of the wealthiest of Parisian capitalists, well known for his eccentricities, happens to encounter one day, on the boulevards, a terribly pretty little working girl. Accompanied by her mother, the grisette is walking on the arm of a young man of questionable character, one who walks with a kind of strut in his hips. The millionaire falls in love at his first sight of the pretty Parisienne; he follows her to her house, he goes in, he hears the story of a life dotted with dances at Mabille's,[133] of days without bread, of plays and of work; he takes an interest, leaving five thousand-franc notes under a five-franc coin: a dishonorable gesture of generosity. The next day the famous interior decorator, Braschon,[134] comes to take mademoiselle's orders and furnishes the apartment she has chosen, running up a bill of some twenty thousand francs. The working girl abandons herself to all sorts of fantastic hopes: she buys a new wardrobe for her mother, is sure she'll be able to get her ex-lover a position in one of the life insurance companies. She waits . . . one day, two days . . . then one week, two weeks. She feels obliged to remain faithful; she runs up debts. Meanwhile, the capitalist has been called away to Holland, where he entirely forgets the working girl; he never visits, not even once, the paradise in which he placed her, and from which she will fall as far and as hard as it's possible to fall in Paris. To return to Nucingen: he didn't gamble, didn't patronize the arts, had no hobbies, and thus he flung himself headlong into his passion for Esther, and did so with the blindness upon which Carlos Herrera was counting.

After his luncheon, the baron called for his personal servant, Georges, and told him to go to the Rue Taitbout and ask to see Mademoiselle Eugénie, the maidservant to Madame Van Bogseck, and tell her to come to his office for some important business.

"Vatch for her," he said, "und bring her up to my room, und tell her she iss on her way to her fortune."

Georges had much difficulty in persuading Europe/Eugénie to come. "But madame," she told him, "never lets me go out; I might lose my job," etc., etc. Georges was obliged to sing her praises to the baron, who gave him ten *louis*.[135]

"If madame goes out tonight without her," Georges said to his master, whose eyes were glowing like carbuncles, "she will come to you tonight at ten."

"Goot! Chew come dress me at nine . . . do my hair. Becuss I vant to look as goot as bossible . . . I tink I going to see my mistress, or else money not vork like it should."

From noon to one the baron had his hair and whiskers dyed. At nine the baron, who had bathed before dinner, now readied himself like a bridegroom, scenting himself, adorning himself, beautifying himself. Madame de Nucingen, hearing about this metamorphosis, gave herself the pleasure of coming in to get a look at her husband.

"My God!" she said, "how ridiculous you are! Put a black satin cravat on, not that white thing that makes your whiskers stick out so badly. Besides, the whole look is so Empire; you look like a nice little old man, like some old counselor from parlement. And don't wear those diamond studs; they're worth a hundred thousand francs, and this little monkey of yours will ask you for them, and you'll give her them. If you're going to just give them away to a slut, you might as well let me have them for earrings."

The poor banker, struck by the intelligence of his wife's comments, obeyed, but sullenly.

"Ritickulous! Ritickulous! Never I say you are ritickulous ven you are mekking yourself all looking your best for zat liddle Monsieur Rastignac."

"Yes, and I assume that's because you never saw me looking ridiculous. Am I the kind of woman who would make these kinds of basic spelling errors in getting myself dressed? Come on now, turn around! . . . Button your coat, all the way up, the way the Duc de Maufrigneuse does, but leave the top two buttons undone. And for heaven's sake, try to act young."

"Monsieur," said Georges, "here is Mademoiselle Eugénie."

"Gootbye, madame," cried the banker. He led his wife quickly to the farthest corner of their respective apartments, to ensure that she wouldn't be able to hear the conversation.

Disappointments

Coming back into the room, the baron took Europe by the hand and brought her into another room, with a respectful air that had just a touch of irony in it.

"Vell, my little one, chew are lucky girl, beink maid to beautifullest woman in whole universe. . . . Und now your fortune is made, if you talk to her for me, help me vit her."

"Oh," cried Europe, "I wouldn't do such a thing for ten thousand francs! You must understand, *monsieur le baron*, that I am an honest girl above all else. . . ."

"Ja, ja. Und I pay you good for your honesty. In ze business vorld, is vat ve call a rarity."

"But that's not all," said Europe. "If madame didn't take a liking to monsieur—and anything is possible!—she would be angry, I would be fired, and this job is worth a thousand francs a year."

"Ze cabbidal chew need for t'ousand is twenty t'ousand, und zis I giff you. Chew don't lose nothing."

"Well, heavens, if that's how you're willing to operate, the whole thing gets a lot easier. Now, where *is* that money? . . ."

"Iss right here!" said the baron, counting out the bank notes one by one.

He noticed that every bill caused Europe's eyes to flash, and he recognized in that the greed he was depending on.

"All right, you've paid for my job, but what about my honesty, my conscience?" asked Europe, lifting up her shrewd face and looking at him with a *seria buffa* expression.

"Conscience, zis not cost so much as job, but maybe we say is worth five t'ousand," he said, counting out another five thousand-franc notes.

"Oh no: it's twenty thousand for the conscience, and five for the job, if I do end up losing it . . ."

"As you like . . ." he said, adding the five notes to the twenty. "But chew haff to earn zem, by hiding me in your mistress's bedroom in ze night, ven she iss all alone. . . ."

"If you'll assure me that you'll never say who let you in, I'm willing. But I better warn you: madame is as strong as a Turk, she loves Monsieur de Rubempré madly, and you could put a million francs in an account for her without her agreeing to be unfaithful. . . . It's crazy, but that's the way she is when she's in love—she's worse than an honest woman, I tell you! When she goes out for a stroll in the woods with monsieur, he usually doesn't stay with her that night; she's gone out this evening, and I could hide you in my room. If madame comes back alone, I'll come get you; you can stay in the drawing room, I won't lock the door to her bedroom, and the rest—well!—the rest is up to you. So get yourself ready."

"I giff you the twenty-five t'ousand ven I am in ze drawing room. I giff, I giff . . ."

"Really?" said Europe. "You're not any more distrustful than that? I mean, excuse me, but . . ."

"Oh, iff you vant to cheat me, you vill haff many chances. Ve goink to be friends. . . ."

"Well, then, be at the Rue Taitbout at midnight. But better bring thirty thousand with you. The honor of a chambermaid costs more after midnight, just like taxis."

"I be careful, so I brink a form for cash order for bank. . . ."

"No, no," said Europe. "Cash only, or there's no deal."

At one in the morning, the Baron de Nucingen was hiding in the attic room where Europe slept, a prey to all the anxieties a man on the verge of happiness can feel. He was alive, his blood pounded in his ears, and his head felt ready to explode like an overheated machine.

"I had more than hundred t'ousand écus' vort of plessure," he exclaimed to du Tillet later, telling him about the adventure. He listened closely to every little sound coming up from the street, and at two o'clock he heard the cab of his mistress outside on the boulevard. His heart was beating hard enough to wear the silk off his waistcoat when he heard the gate turning on its hinges: at last he was going to see it again, the celestial, the sublime face of Esther! . . . He heard the sounds of the carriage steps being lowered and its door slamming shut, echoing in his heart. Waiting now for the supreme moment agitated him more than the thought of losing his entire fortune.

"Ja!" he exclaimed. "Zat was really being alive! Too much alive even—I neffer be able to hexplain it."

"Madame is alone, go on downstairs," said Europe, coming up into her room. "But don't make a sound, you big elephant!"

"Big helephant!" he repeated with a laugh, walking downstairs as if over hot coals.

Europe went down ahead of him, a candle in her hand.

"Here it iss; count it," said the baron, handing the sheaf of bills to Europe when they reached the drawing room.

Europe took the thirty bills with a serious air and left, shutting the banker in. Nucingen made his way directly to the bedroom, where he found the beautiful Englishwoman, who was saying, "Is that you, Lucien?"

"No, beautiful child," cried Nucingen, stopping dead.

He stood there stupidly, seeing before him a woman who was the very opposite of Esther: blonde where she had been brunette, slim and petite where she had been strong and forceful. It was a gentle night in Brittany, not an Arabian day in the burning sun.

"What? Where did you come from? Who are you? What do you want?" said the Englishwoman, ringing the bell, which, however, made no sound.

"I haff had ze bells muffled, but bleeze don't be afraid—I go away now," he said. "T'irty t'ousand francs tossed in ze ocean. But chew—chew are really ze mistress of Monsieur Lucien de Rubempré?"

"That's the way it looks, sonny," said the Englishwoman, whose French was excellent. "But who iss chew?" she said, imitating Nucingen's mode of speech.

"I am a man zat hass been tricked," he said pitifully.

"A man he iss tricked ven he stands in front of a pyootiful voman?" she said, joking with him.

"Allow me, madame, to send chew tomorrow a nice gift to remind you of ze Baron de Nucingen."

"Ziss name iss one I do not know!" she said, bursting into laughter; "but gifts are always appreciated, my fine big burglar."

"Chew vill make his acquaintance. Farewell, madame. Chew are a morsel fit for a king; but I am only poor sixty-year-old banker, und chew haff made me see how much power ze voman I love hass over me, because eefen your superhuman beauty hass not made me to forget hers."

"Well, ziss vat you say to me iss very pretty," said the Englishwoman.

"Not so pretty as ze one who inspires me to say it."

"You said something about t'irty thousand francs, though. . . . To whom did you give all that?"

"To zat no-good maid of yours."

The Englishwoman called; Europe was close by.

"Oh!" cried Europe. "A man in madame's chamber, and he is not Monsieur Lucien! How horrible!"

"He gave you thirty thousand francs to get him in here?"

"No, madame—heavens, the both of us aren't worth that kind of money. . . ."

And at that Europe began to cry, "Thief!" so loudly and so insistently that the terrified banker found his way to the door, and Europe followed, knocking him down the stairs.

"You dirty scoundrel," she cried, "telling on me to my mistress! Thief! Thief!"

The lovesick baron in despair managed without any more damage to make it to his carriage, which was standing and waiting for him on the boulevard; but now he didn't know which of his spies he could trust.

"Now, would madame, by any chance, be thinking of skimming off some of my profits?" said Europe, turning like a Fury on the Englishwoman.

"I am unaware of how they do things like this in France," said the Englishwoman.

"Well, all I need to do is say the word to monsieur and he'll turn madame out of the door tomorrow," Europe said insolently.

"Zat damm chambermaid," said the baron to Georges, who naturally asked his master if he was happy, "cheated me out of t'irty t'ousand francs—but iss my fault, my great great fault!"

"And so all the care we put into dressing monsieur did no good. My heavens! Well, I would remind monsieur that he should not take those amber pills without . . ."[136]

"Georges, I goink to die of despair . . . I feel cold . . . I feel like ice in my heart. Ah, no more of Esther, my friend."

Georges was always the "friend" of his master in moments of catastrophe.

The Abbé Wins the First Round

Two days after this scene, when young Europe had just finished narrating the tale more amusingly than we can here, due to her gift for mimicry, Carlos was eating lunch alone with Lucien.

"We can't let the police or anyone else, my little one, start poking their noses into our affairs," he said quietly, lighting his cigar from the tip of Lucien's. "It's not healthy. I've thought of something a little audacious but guaranteed to work at keeping our baron and his agents quiet. You're going to go visit Madame de Sérisy, and you're going to be very nice to her. In the course of your conversation, you'll mention to her that you've been doing a favor to Rastignac, who, for some time now, has been tiring of Madame de Nucingen, so you've agreed to serve as a kind of cloak for him to conceal his other mistress. Meanwhile, Monsieur de Nucingen has fallen in love with the woman Rastignac is hiding—this will make her laugh—and he's taken it upon himself to hire some policemen to spy on you, who are completely innocent in all your friend's tricks; you're concerned now that your reputation with the Grandlieus might be compromised. You'll plead with the comtesse to use her influence on her husband, who's a minister of state, to take you to the Prefecture of Police. When you get there, in the presence of the prefect you complain, but in the way that a clever young man who's about to enter into the machinery of the State as one of its most important pistons would do. Being a man of the State yourself, you understand the police, you admire them, including especially the prefect. But even the most practiced machinists let some oil drop or spill onto the floor. Don't overdo your anger. You have no complaint at all about *monsieur le préfet,* but you would suggest he keep an eye on his people, and you feel sorry for him at having to call them on the carpet. The quieter and the more gentlemanly you are, the more terrible the prefect will be with his agents. From then on we'll be left alone, and we can even call Esther back—she must be bellowing like a fallow deer out there in the forest."

The man who was prefect at the time had previously been a magistrate. Former magistrates become prefects at too young an age. Imbued with the importance of the Law, sticklers for legalities, they are too slow to employ the necessary improvisation that is so often necessary in a critical situation, the kind of moment when the prefect needs to act rather like a fireman putting out a fire. Now, in the presence of the vice president of the Council of State, the prefect enumerated more difficulties in policework than there really were, deplored abuses, and then remembered a certain visit from the Baron de Nucingen, who had been asking for information about Peyrade. The prefect, promising to put an end to the excesses to which his agents had been prone of late, thanked Lucien for having come directly to him, promised to keep his secret, and seemed to understand the whole business. Some splendid rhetoric was bandied back and forth about individuals' liberty and the inviolability of the home between the vice president and the prefect, to whom Monsieur de Sérisy observed that while the larger interests of the nation sometimes required secret, illegal methods, the real crime began only when those State-level methods were applied to private interests. The next day, just when Peyrade was about to go to his beloved Café David, where he enjoyed watching the bourgeois the way an artist enjoys watching flowers bloom, a gendarme in plain clothes stopped him on the street.

"I was on my way to your place," he said quietly. "I have orders to bring you to the prefecture."

Peyrade made no response, but he hailed a cab and he and the gendarme got in.

The prefect of police treated Peyrade as if he were the lowest of the guards in the lowest prison, walking with him down a little alley in the small garden behind the prefecture, which, in those days, stretched out along the Quai des Orfèvres.

"Monsieur, there are good reasons you've never been given a place in the Administration. . . . Don't you understand what you're exposing me to, and what you're exposing yourself to?"

This harangue ended with an explosion. The prefect announced to poor Peyrade that not only was his annual pension being terminated, but that henceforth he himself would be the object of special surveillance. The old man took this torrent of bad news with perfect calmness. Indeed, there is nothing more impassive and impenetrable than the face of a man who has just been struck by lightning. Peyrade had gambled and lost every sou. Lydie's father had been counting on the new position, and he saw himself now reduced to hoping for alms from his friend Corentin.

"I was once a prefect of police, and I grant that you are quite right," said the old man calmly to the functionary, who, currently invested with judicial majesty, gave a significant start at this. "But permit me, without in any way excusing myself, to observe simply that you do not know me," Peyrade continued, glancing shrewdly at the prefect. "What you've just said is either too harsh for the former commissioner of police in Holland, or not harsh enough for a simple spy. However, monsieur," Peyrade added after a pause, seeing that the prefect remained silent, "remember what I have the honor of being about to tell you. Without being mixed up in any way with *your police,* nor with any intent of justifying myself, some day you will understand that, in this affair, someone is being duped. Today it's me, yours truly, but a little later you may find yourself saying, 'It was me.'"

With that he bowed to the prefect, who stood there pensively, trying to conceal his astonishment. Peyrade went back home, every inch of his body consumed with weariness, and filled with a cold rage against the Baron de Nucingen. It could only have been that thick-skulled banker who betrayed the secret that had been confined to Contenson, Peyrade, and Corentin. The old man accused the banker of trying to get out of making a payment now that he'd achieved his goal. Yes, just one interview was all it took to see how astute that man, the most astute of bankers, really was. "He sells everybody out, including us, but I'll get my revenge," he said to himself. "I've never asked anything of Corentin, but now I'll ask him to help me avenge myself on this imbecile cashbox. Damnable baron! You'll learn who you're dealing with one fine morning when you wake up to find your daughter dishonored. . . . But does he even love his daughter?"

On the evening of the day that dashed the old man's hopes, he felt he had aged ten years. Talking about it with his friend Corentin, he interrupted his tale with tears, drawn out of him by the prospect of the sad future he'd be leaving his daughter, his idol, his pearl, his peace offering to God.

"We'll get to the bottom of this," said Corentin. "First we need to find out if the baron is really your informant. Were we wise in relying on Gondreville? He's sly enough to figure out how much he owes us and try to sink us; so I've started surveillance on his son-in-law, Keller, a political dimwit who's perfectly capable of getting himself mixed up in some wild plot to overthrow the elder branch by the younger. I'll know by tomorrow what's going on with Nucingen, whether he got to see his mistress and who it was who pulled back on our reins like this. . . . Don't be too worried. For one thing, prefects are changed out constantly. These are revolutionary times, and revolutions always roil the waters up."

A recognizable whistle sounded in the street.

"That's Contenson," said Peyrade, who had put a light in the window. "He's got something for me."

A moment later the faithful Contenson appeared before the two police gnomes, who, to him, were men on the level of geniuses.

"What is it?" asked Corentin.

"News! I was coming out of one thirteen, having lost everything I had.[137] And who did I see there in the Galleries? Georges! He'd just been fired by the baron, who suspected him of having been a traitor."

"Ah, now there you have the effect of a smile I let slip out once," said Peyrade.

"Oh, the disasters I've seen result from somebody smiling!" said Corentin.

"Not to mention the disasters a riding crop can cause," said Peyrade, alluding to the Simeuse affair. (See *Une ténébreuse affaire*.) "But go on, Contenson, what happened next?"

"I'll tell you what happened," said Contenson. "I managed to get Georges talking by buying him a series of little drinks in a whole rainbow of colors, and he's still drunk; as for me, I'm carrying around enough to fill a barrel. Well, our baron went to the Rue Taitbout, fortified by the amber pills they use in the harems. There he found the lovely lady you know about. But here's the joke—that Englishwoman isn't his 'meesterie voman'! And he spent thirty thousand francs to bribe the chambermaid. Idiot. He thinks he's hot because he can use his big sums for little purposes—but you just turn that around and you see the kind of problem that needs a genius to solve. The baron is back in his pitiful state. So the next day Georges, that little hypocrite, he says to his master, 'Why does monsieur get mixed up with these cloak-and-dagger people? If monsieur would simply trust in me, I would find his mystery woman for him, because the description monsieur has already given me is all I need, and I'll turn Paris upside down till I find her.' And to that the baron says, 'Do it, and I'll pay you very well!' Georges told me all this, along with all sorts of absurd details. But . . . the rain rains on us all! Next day the baron receives an anonymous letter saying something along the lines of 'Monsieur de Nucingen is dying of love for a mystery woman, and he's already wasted a great deal of money. But if he'd like to be at the end of the Pont de Neuilly at midnight tonight, and if he'll get up into a carriage, on the back of which he'll see the servant he saw in the Bois de Vincennes, and if he'll allow himself to be blindfolded, he'll get to see the woman he loves. . . . And because his wealth may make him suspicious of the purity of our intentions, *monsieur le baron* will be permitted to take along his faithful Georges. There will be no one else in the carriage.' So the baron goes there, needless to say with Georges, but without saying anything about it all to Georges. They both allow themselves to be blindfolded and hooded. The baron recognizes the manservant. Two hours later the carriage, rolling along like one of Louis XVIII's—God bless him! Now that was a king who understood policework—comes to a halt in the middle of the woods. The baron's blindfold is removed, and he sees, sitting in another parked carriage, the mystery woman, who—poof!—disappears immediately. So now the carriage—the same Louis XVIII pace—brings him back to the Pont de Neuilly, where he finds his own carriage. Someone has placed a note in Georges' hand, saying, 'How many one thousand franc notes is monsieur le baron willing to pay to be put in contact with the mystery woman?' Georges hands the little note to his master, and the baron, convinced that Georges is in cahoots either with me or with you, Monsieur Peyrade, seizes on all this and fires Georges. That imbecile of a banker! He shouldn't have let Georges go until he'd got on top of his 'meesterie voman'!"[138]

"Georges saw the woman?" asked Corentin.

"Yes," said Contenson.

"Well, then," cried Peyrade, "what's she like?"

"Oh," replied Contenson, "he only used one phrase for her: 'beautiful as the sun.'"

"'We've been tricked by some jokers—they've outwitted us!" exclaimed Peyrade. "Those dogs are planning on selling their girl to the baron at the highest price they can get."

"Ja, mein Herr!" said Contenson. "So, since I heard they showered you with roses at the prefecture, I made it a point to make Georges talk."

"I just wish I knew who it is who's playing us," said Peyrade. "Then we'd see who's smarter."

"Need to get inside the walls," said Contenson.

"Right," said Peyrade. "We need to slip inside the cracks, be quiet, wait, listen. . . ."

"We'll get into all that," cried Corentin, "but for the moment I don't see anything I can do. Be smart, Peyrade! Let's all obey our beloved prefect in everything we do."

"Monsieur de Nucingen needs a good bleeding," Contenson suggested. "He has too many thousand-franc notes running through his veins."

"And that was exactly where I hoped to find Lydie's dowry!" Peyrade whispered to Corentin.

"Contenson, come along—let's let the old man get some sleep. So . . . till . . . to . . . morrow. . . ."

"Monsieur," Contenson said to Corentin when they got outside, "what an odd little piece of commercial exchange our friend had in mind! . . . Think of it—marry off your daughter with the money you got from. . . . Oh, listen, this would make a terrific play, one with a nice little moral to it, and we could title it *A Young Girl's Dowry*."

"Well trained, aren't you—very good at overhearing things!" said Corentin to Contenson. "Social Nature—I see it now—Social Nature arms every one of its species with all the qualities they need to perform the services expected of them! Society is another Nature!"

"Very philosophical of you," cried Contenson. "A professor would get a book out of it."

"Stay on top of things," replied Corentin with a smile, as he and the spy walked along the streets, "especially what's happening at Monsieur de Nucingen's regarding the mystery woman—basically, I mean—don't get too elaborate."

"I'll watch to see if there's smoke coming out of the chimneys!" said Contenson.

"A man like the Baron de Nucingen can't have anything good happen without people knowing," Corentin went on. "And then remember—we're the ones who play people like they're cards, so we can't let them play us!"

"Exactly! It would be like the convict having fun by cutting off the executioner's head," said Contenson.

"You've always got a clever way of putting it," said Corentin, unable to repress a smile breaking out across the plaster mask that was his face.

This affair was extremely important both in itself and in its aftereffects. If the baron had not been the one who went to the prefect of police and betrayed Peyrade, who could it have been? Corentin decided he'd better find out if someone among his own people was false. As he went to sleep that night, he was having the same thoughts Peyrade was having: "Who went to the prefect? And whose woman is that, really?" And so it was that, despite them being ignorant of the others, Jacques Collin, Peyrade, and Corentin were all drawing closer together without knowing it; and poor Esther, Nucingen, and Lucien were being drawn inexorably into a battle that had already begun, and that the self-esteem peculiar to men of the police would turn into something terrible.

False Abbé, False Notes, False Debts, False Love

Thanks to the cleverness and skills of Europe, the most threatening part of the sixty thousand francs of debt that weighed on Esther and Lucien was paid off. Their creditors' confidence in them was firm again. Lucien and his corrupter could each breathe freely for a moment. They were like two hunted animals who stopped to lap the water at the edges of a marsh, able again to make their way along the precipices, where the strong man was leading the weak one, either to the scaffold or to a fortune.

"Today," Carlos announced to his creature, "we're going to bet everything in order to win everything—but, fortunately, the cards are marked and the other players are green!"

For some time now Lucien, on the orders of his terrible mentor, had been assiduously seeing Madame de Sérisy. In fact it was indispensable that no one suspect Lucien was keeping a woman as his mistress. And in any case he found in the pleasure of being loved, and in the delights of life among high society, a force sufficient to deaden his feelings. He obeyed Mademoiselle Clotilde de Grandlieu and saw her only in the Bois or on the Champs-Élysées.

The day after Esther had been shut up in the gamekeeper's house, the being who was for her so problematic, so terrible, such a weight on her heart, arrived and asked her to sign three stamped pieces of paper with these tormenting words on them: "Accepted for sixty thousand francs," said the first; "Accepted for one hundred and twenty thousand francs," said the second; and "Accepted for one hundred and twenty thousand francs," said the third. Three hundred thousand francs in acceptances. When you use the words "good for," you're making a simple note. But the word "accepted" makes it a letter of exchange, leaving you open to being arrested for debt. The word can cost the person who signs it five years in prison, though that sentence is rarely passed in police courts, and even at assize courts it is only passed upon known criminals. The law concerning bodily arrest is a holdover from the days of barbarism, one that combines stupidity with futility, since it never captures the real criminals. (See *Lost Illusions*.)

"Doing this is necessary," the Spaniard said to Esther, "to get Lucien out of a tangle. We have sixty thousand francs in debt, and with three hundred thousand we can perhaps stay out of trouble."

After antedating the letters of exchange by six months, Carlos had them drawn on Esther by "a man unknown to the police," one whose adventures, despite all the noise they once made, have been forgotten, lost, drowned out by the great symphony of July 1830.

This young man, one of our most dauntless knights of the financial world, the son of a bailiff from Boulogne near Paris,[139] was named Georges-Marie Destourny.[140] His father had been obliged to sell off his position for little return, and around 1824 he left his son with no resources apart from the brilliant education he had given the boy (a common mania among the petit-bourgeois). Twenty-three years old, the young and promising law student had already denied his father by having his name engraved on business cards in this form:

GEORGES D'ESTOURNY

The card gave him a little whiff of aristocracy. Setting up as a man of fashion, he had the boldness to set himself up with a tilbury and a groom, and he began frequenting clubs. This is readily explained: he speculated on the stock exchange with money entrusted to him by various kept women. Eventually the police picked him up and accused him of playing with a little too much luck. He had accomplices, some young men he had corrupted, his faithful henchmen, all witnesses to his elegance and his credit. Obliged to flee, he neglected to pay his debts on the stock exchange. All Paris—the lynxes, the clubs, the boulevards, the businessmen—still trembled over this double swindle.

In the days of his splendor, Georges d'Estourny, a good-looking, good-natured fellow, generous as a bandit chief, had kept La Torpille for a few months. The false Spaniard based his own speculation on the connection between Esther and this famous crook, the kind of connection common among women of that class.

Georges d'Estourny's ambitions were only emboldened by his success, and he had taken under his tutelage a man up from the provinces to make his way as a businessman in Paris, one the Liberal party wanted to see recompensed for difficulties he had bravely endured in attacking the government of Charles X, though the persecution had lightened somewhat under Martignac's ministry.[141] A pardon had been granted to the fine Cérizet, that excellent manager, who had been given the nickname Courageous Cérizet.[142]

Now, Cérizet, still being patronized by the leading lights of the Left but only for form's sake, had established a firm that was a combination of general business agency, bank, and commission agency. The place was reminiscent of one of those advertisements unemployed domestics take out in the *Petites-Affiches,* offering themselves as capable of doing anything and everything.

Esther, somewhat as in the anecdote told about Ninon,[143] could pass for being the faithful guardian of a part of Georges d'Estourny's fortune. A blank acceptance signed "Georges d'Estourny" made Carlos Herrera the master of the money that he had created. This forgery courted no danger so long as either Mademoiselle Esther or someone else acting on her behalf would or could meet the bills. Having investigated the firm of

Cérizet, Carlos saw that this was one of those men determined to make a fortune, but . . . legally.

Cérizet, who was the real depositary for d'Estourny's money, was the security for major sums of money being bet on the markets rising, which allowed Cérizet to call himself a banker. Things like this happen in Paris; a man may be despised, but never his money.

Carlos came to see Cérizet, intending to play him the way he did others, because he had, by chance, discovered all the secrets of this worthy associate of d'Estourny's.

Courageous Cérizet lived in an entresol on the Rue du Gros-Chenet, and Carlos, who had himself mysteriously announced as having come on the part of Georges d'Estourny, came in to see the self-styled banker having turned pale from that announcement. Carlos saw in that modest office a man with fair, thinning hair who perfectly fit the description Lucien had given of him, the man who had played Judas to David Séchard.

"May we speak here with no fear of being overheard?" said the Spaniard, currently metamorphosed into an Englishman with red hair and blue spectacles, just as neat and trim as a puritan on his way to a prayer service.

"Why do you ask, monsieur?" asked Cérizet. "And who are you?"

"My name is William Barker, and I'm a creditor of Monsieur d'Estourny's, but since you ask, I will explain to you why we should keep your doors closed. We know, monsieur, about your relations with Petit-Claud, the Cointets, and the Séchards in Angoulême. . . ."[144]

At that, Cérizet hurried across the room to close the door, then crossed to the other door, which opened onto his bedroom, and bolted it; then he said to the stranger, "Keep your voice down, monsieur!" He looked the false Englishman over carefully and said, "What do you want with me?"

"Good heavens!" said William Barker, "it's every man for himself in this world. You're in charge of that wretched d'Estourny's money. . . . I assure you, though, I haven't come to ask for it, but at my request that deadbeat who deserves hanging has given me—this is just between ourselves, now—certain securities, telling me that there was some chance of turning them into money, and because I didn't want to use my own name, he told me that you would not refuse the use of your own."

Cérizet looked at the letter of exchange and said, "But he's not in Frankfort any longer. . . ."

"I know that," said Barker, "but he might have been when he put these dates on."

"But I don't want to take the responsibility," said Cérizet.

"Oh, I'm not asking you to make any sacrifice here," Barker replied.

"You might end up being ordered to receive them. Endorse them, and I'll see to recovering the money."

"I'm surprised d'Estourny has so little trust in me," said Cérizet.

"Well, in his position you'd want to put your eggs in different baskets too," said Barker.

"And do you think . . ." asked the little businessman, handing the duly endorsed bills back to the Englishman.

"Oh, I know—you'll continue to oversee his funds," said Barker. "I'm sure of it! They're already in play at the stock exchange."

"My own fortune depends on . . ."

"On their apparently showing a loss," said Barker.

"Monsieur!" Cérizet exclaimed.

"Look, my dear Monsieur Cérizet," Barker said coldly, interrupting Cérizet, "you would be doing me a service by facilitating this payment. Please be so kind as to write me a letter in which you tell me that you are giving me these bills backed by d'Estourny's account, and that the officer or bailiff should consider the bearer of the letter as the possessor of the three notes."

"Tell me your full name."

"No names!" said the English capitalist. "Put down 'the bearer of this letter and the notes. . . .' You'll be well paid for your cooperation."

"How?" asked Cérizet.

"By a piece of information. You'll be remaining in France, won't you?"

"Yes, monsieur."

"Well, then—Georges d'Estourny will never be coming back."

"And why is that?"

"I personally know of more than five individuals who will murder him, and he knows it."

"Now I see why he's asking me for this, to help pack up his bags for the Indies!" exclaimed Cérizet. "And unfortunately he's forced me to put everything into government bonds. We're already in debt to the du Tillet firm. I'm just living from day to day."

"Take your money out!"

"Oh, if only I'd known about this sooner!" cried Cérizet. "I could have made a fortune."

"One last thing," said Barker. "Discretion! You're capable of it, I know. Even more important is fidelity! We'll meet again, and I'll see to it that you make that fortune."

Having tossed a scrap of hope to that mud-trapped soul, knowing it would assure his discretion for a long while, Carlos, still in the guise of

Barker, went to a bailiff he knew and trusted, telling him to get a court order against Esther.

"It will all be paid up," he told the bailiff. "It's just an affair of honor, and we want everything to be done by the book."

Barker employed an attorney to represent Esther at the commercial court, so that judgment would be given after hearing both parties. The bailiff, who was instructed to act respectfully, went himself to seize the furniture in the Rue Taitbout apartment, where he was admitted by Europe. Esther was now apparently liable for three hundred thousand francs of undisputed debt. All this did not put Carlos's powers of invention to much of a test. The vaudeville of false debts is performed often in Paris. There are sub-Gobsecks, and sub-Gigonnets, who will be party to such little tricks for only a small fee, seeing the whole thing as a joke. Everything in France is done with a laugh, even crimes. By such means recalcitrant parents are bled dry, as are stingy lovers; all are made to comply, whether through gross necessity or the threat of dishonor. Maxime de Trailles frequently used similar stratagems, the kind of thing old comedies were full of. But Carlos Herrera, wishing to preserve the honor of his cassock as well as that of Lucien, was making use of a plan without much danger, the kind of forgery that had grown so common that the Law was beginning to take notice of it. There was a thriving trade in such forgeries; people said that you could get a signature in the neighborhood of the Palais-Royal for three francs.

Before getting into the question of the hundred thousand écus that would function as a kind of sentry at the bedroom door, Carlos came up with a plan to pay another hundred thousand francs to Monsieur de Nucingen. Here is how he did it.

On his orders, Asia went to the amorous baron disguised as an old woman who was well informed on matters concerning the beautiful mystery woman. Up until now, all the others who have striven to depict society and its ways have shown us many male usurers, but so far no one else has brought a female Madame Resource on the stage, an extremely curious character type who can often be found using the title of "wardrobe merchant," a type the ferocious Asia could readily play, considering the two establishments she operated, one near the Temple and the other on the Rue Neuve-Saint-Marc—both of them run by women in her employ.

"I want you to call yourself Madame de Saint-Estève,"[145] Herrera told her. He wanted to see Asia in the right costume for the role. The phony procuress arrived in a dress of flowered damask, which had spent its earlier life as curtains in some repossessed apartment, on top of which rode one of those worn, unsalable old cashmere shawls that often end up on the shoulders of such women. She wore a collar that had once been magnificent lace, but was now frayed, and a hideous hat; but she also wore boots of Irish leather, over which the fat of her bulging, black-stockinged legs rolled.

"And look at this buckle on my belt!" she said, showing a piece of dubious gold that held back her cook's belly. "What a thing, eh? And then this belt. . . . God, it makes me ugly! Oh, mother Nourisson did a job on me, all right."

"Be very gentle and sweet at first," Carlos told her. "In fact, act almost as if you're fearful, mistrustful, like a cat; and make the baron feel ashamed of having used police, without letting on that you'd be trembling in front of police agents. And be sure to make it perfectly clear that as a practical matter you defy all the policemen in the world to learn where the beauty is stashed. Be careful to cover your tracks . . . and when the baron finally gets to the point where you can poke him in the belly and call him 'dirty old man,' then go ahead and turn insolent, and order him around like a lackey."

Threatened with never again seeing the procuress if he set any kind of spy on her, Nucingen watched Asia go on foot from the stock exchange to, mysteriously, a miserable little entresol on the Rue Neuve-Saint-Marc. Those muddy walkways—how many millionaires have trod along them, and with what inner ecstasies! All the pavements of Paris know them. Madame de Saint-Estève so expertly led the baron along that he, tossed back and forth between hope and despair, came to the point of wanting to know anything at all concerning his mysterious beloved, and to know it *at any price.*

At the same time the bailiff got to work, and all the better because, meeting no resistance at Esther's, he was able to fulfill all the legalities within twenty-four hours.

Lucien was able to visit his recluse at Saint-Germain five or six times, always brought there by his counselor. His fierce conductor judged these conjugal visits necessary to keep Esther from withering, for her beauty was essentially capital for him. When it was time to leave the gamekeeper's house, he escorted Lucien and the poor courtesan to a lonely footpath, a place from which the city of Paris could be seen in the distance and where no one could hear them. All three sat down on the trunk of a felled poplar, looking off at that view, one of the finest in the world, one that takes in the Seine, Montmartre, Paris, even Saint-Denis.

"My children," said Carlos, "your dream is over. You, my little one, will never see Lucien again—or if you do, you must pretend to have only known him just briefly some five years ago."

"Then my death has come!" she said, without shedding a tear.

"Oh, you've been ill for five years now," replied Herrera. "Think of yourself as tubercular, and just die without boring us all with your elegies. But you're going to see that in fact you're about to live again, and to live very, very well! . . . Leave us now, Lucien, go gather some *sonnets*," he said, pointing to a meadow nearby.

Lucien cast a pleading look at Esther, one of those looks common with weak and greedy men, a look filled with the tenderness of the heart and the cowardice of the soul. Esther made a sign with her head that implied, "I'm going to sit here and listen to my executioner in order to learn how to pose my head beneath the axe, and I will have the courage to die a good death." Her look was so gracious but at the same time so horrifying that the poet stood and began to weep. Esther ran to him, holding him tightly in her arms, and said to him, "Don't worry!"—the kind of thing one says with gestures and with the eyes, the kind of thing the voice says in a kind of delirium.

Carlos began to explain with perfect clarity, with no ambiguity, and with sometimes brutal language, the critical situation Lucien was in, his status with the Grandlieu family, the fine life he would have if he succeeded, and, finally, why it was so necessary for Esther to sacrifice herself for that magnificent future.

"What do I have to do?" she asked frantically.

"Obey me blindly," said Carlos. "And what do you have to complain about? It's up to you to shape a good destiny for yourself. You're going to be the same thing that Tullia, Florine, Mariette, and the Val-Noble woman were, all your old friends—the mistress of a rich man you will not love. Once we get our schemes concluded, your lover is rich enough to make you very happy. . . ."

"Happy!" she exclaimed, casting her eyes up to the sky.

"You've had four whole years in your paradise," he replied. "Hasn't that time created enough memories for you to live on?"

"I'll obey you," she said, wiping a tear from the corner of her eye. "And don't worry about the rest! You said it yourself—my love is a mortal sickness."

"Well, that's not all," Carlos continued. "You need to stay beautiful. You're twenty-two and a half, and you're at the peak of your beauty, thanks to the happiness you've had. So now, the important thing is that you need to become La Torpille again. Be kittenish, spend like mad, be cunning, and be ruthless with the millionaire I'm going to send you. Listen—this man is a great thief from the stock exchange, he's never had an ounce of pity for anybody, and he's grown fat on money he's extracted from widows and orphans—you will be their avenger! . . . Asia will come get you in a coach, and you'll be back in Paris tonight. If you let anyone so much as suspect your relations with Lucien these past four years, you might as well take a pistol and blow his brains out. People will ask where you've been. You'll tell them you've been off on a trip with a very jealous Englishman. In the old days you were clever enough to spin believable tales—revive that old talent now."

Have you ever seen a glittering kite, one of those giant butterfly-like toys children love, all spangled with gold, gliding high up in the sky? The children forget about the string for just a moment, and a passerby inadvertently breaks it, and what was a gaudy meteor suddenly goes bottom up, as the schoolboys say, and now it hurtles to the earth with a startling speed. So Esther, listening to Carlos.

II ✦

WHAT LOVE COSTS
AN OLD MAN

A Hundred Thousand Francs Invested in Asia

Almost every day for the past week, Nucingen had been going to the shop on the Rue Neuve-Saint-Marc to carry on negotiations for the delivery of the woman he loved. There, high on a throne, sat Asia, sometimes using the name Saint-Estève, sometimes that of her creature, Madame Nourisson, surrounded by what had once been the most beautiful gowns but now hovered in a state midway between dresses and rags. Such shops are among the most sinister of Parisian oddities, so the setting was in perfect harmony with the looks of the woman. In these places you can find dresses plucked away from their owners by the bony hand of Death, and you can just hear the rasping breath of consumption beneath a shawl, or the death rattle of poverty from within a gown spangled with gold. In a swatch of fine lace you may read a hideous debate between Luxury and Hunger. Gazing upon an abandoned turban with nodding plumes, you can reconstruct from it all the details of a queen's physiognomy, and reconstruct from it the pose, almost the very face of its absent owner. Pretty things conceal horrors within them! Juvenal's lash, wielded by the official hands of the appraiser, scatters the threadbare muffs, the withered furs of desperate whores.[1] The place is a dunghill of flowers upon which you can find the occasional rose, cut just yesterday and worn for but an hour, being sniffed at now by an old hag, first cousin to Usury: the bald and toothless Secondhand, always ready to sell, always used to selling, whether the garment or what it once covered, the gown without woman, or the woman without gown! And there perched Asia, like a guard in a prison, like a vulture among corpses, its beak blood-reddened, fully, completely in her element, more hideous than the sight that made passersby shudder when they looked in through the dirty window and saw one of their memories from unspoiled youth now hanging before the grimacing visage of that Saint-Estève.

One irritation followed another; one ten-thousand franc demand followed another, and the banker finally reached the point of offering sixty thousand francs to Madame de Saint-Estève, who refused with a grimace fit for a macaque. But after one more sleepless night, after realizing what disorder his passion for Esther had brought into his life, and after having made an unexpected killing on the stock market, he came to the shop one morning, intending to agree to the hundred thousand francs Asia asked for but also determined to get a great deal of information out of her for it.

"So you've made up your mind, have you, my old haggler?" she said, patting him on the shoulder.

Such dishonorable familiarities constitute the first tax that these kinds of women like to impose on the wild passions or the sufferings of the men who put their trust in them; they never rise up and try to meet the client on his own level, but rather drag him down to squat next to them on their little heap of filth. Asia, as we can see, was obeying her master to perfection.

"Vat must be, must be," said Nucingen.

"And you've paid the right price," replied Asia. "People have sold women for more than this, relatively speaking. There are women, and then there are women! De Marsay gave sixty thousand for the late Coralie. The one you're after cost a hundred thousand new—but for me, you understand, you old rake, it's a matter of convenience."

"But vhere iss she?"

"Ah, you'll see. I'm just like you, you see: if you want something, you give something. Look, my sweetie, your *passion* has led you into some follies. Now these young girls, they aren't reasonable. Your little princess at this moment is what we call a fly-by-night. . . ."

"A vly by vat?"

"Oh come on, are you going to play the innocent? She's got Louchard on her heels, and I had to lend her—me, personally—fifty thousand francs. . . ."

"Fifty t'ousand! Diss I don't believe!"

"Oh yes, well, twenty-five for fifty, goes without saying," said Asia. "But that woman, I have to say, she's the soul of honesty! She had nothing, not a thing, and she says to me, 'Oh my dearest Madame Saint-Estève, I'm being hunted down, and you're the only one who can help me, so give me twenty thousand francs, and you'll have my heart for security. . . .' And, oh, what a heart it is! I'm the only one who knows where she is. Be a little indiscreet, and I lose twenty thousand francs. She did use to live in the Rue Taitbout. That was before she moved out of there . . . they seized all her belongings! Those bailiffs are thieves! But you know that, a big stock market man like you. Well, she's no fool, so she rents the place for two months to an Englishwoman, a real beauty who had that pretty boy . . . Rubempré, that's his name . . . for her lover, and he was so jealous he told her she could only go out at night. But now that they're going to sell off all the furnishings, the Englishwoman has skipped town, because anyway she cost way too much for a little grasshopper like that Lucien. . . ."

"So you play ze banker too," said Nucingen.

"Seems natural enough, eh?" said Asia. "I lend to pretty women, because then I've got two assets at once."

Asia was having fun, hamming it up, imitating the way certain women are who are just as bitter-natured as the Malay but who smooth it over with hypocritical talk and justify it with high-sounding motives.[2] Asia posed as a person who lost all her illusions along with five different lovers and a number of children, and who had been "ripped off" by everyone she knew, despite her experience. From time to time she would pull out a pawn ticket and brandish it to prove just how much bad luck her business dragged her into. She played the role of the destitute, deep in debts. Ultimately she came across as so nakedly hideous that the baron ended up believing in the persona she was putting on.

"Vell, so I giff ze hundred t'ousand, und zen vere do I get to see her?" he asked with the gesture of a man prepared to make any sacrifice necessary.

"Oh, any time. This evening you could take a cab and come, and stop right across from the Gymnase.[3] It's on your way," said Asia. "Stop at the corner of the Rue Sainte-Barbe. I'll be there waiting, and we'll go off together to find my little raven-tressed asset . . . and oh, does my little asset have beautiful hair! When Esther lets it down, it covers her like a tent. Now you may know your numbers, but you strike me as not too sharp when it comes to anything else, so I'm going to advise you to keep this little girl very well hidden, or otherwise they'll come and whisk her away to Sainte-Pélagie, and right away, the next day, if they find her . . . and . . . they're looking for her."

"But can I not somehow be allowed to see ze bills?" asked the incorrigible lynx.

"The bailiff has them. . . . No, no way. Our girl flew into a rage and ate up the deposit they left with her, and now they want it back. Damn, a girl's spirit at twenty-two—it's a funny thing!"

"Hokay, hokay—I vill arrange efferyt'ing," said Nucingen, trying to sound knowing. "Iss understood zat I be her protector."

"Well, you big dummy, all you need to do is make her love you, and you've got enough cash to buy something that'll look pretty close to love, and might actually be even better. I'm going to put my princess in your hands; she's been told she needs to go with you, and I'm not worried about anything beyond that . . . But remember, she's used to having the best, and I mean the best. Oh, my boy! This is a real lady . . . hell, if she hadn't been, would I have given her fifteen thousand francs?"

"Hokay, iss all set! Ziss evening!"

The baron went through the same prenuptial grooming and adorning process he had before, but this time the certainty of success led him to double the dose of amber pills. At nine o'clock he found the horrible woman waiting for him at the arranged spot, and he invited her up into his carriage.

"Vere?" asked the baron.

"Where?" said Asia. "Rue de la Perle, in the Marais, a temporary place—because your little pearl has dropped down into the mud, but you'll pluck her up and clean her off!" When they had arrived, the false Madame Saint-Estève said to Nucingen, with a hideous smile, "We're going to go on foot for a little way. I'm not stupid enough to have given you the real address."

"You t'ink of efferyt'ing," Nucingen replied.

"It's my job," she said.

Asia led Nucingen to the Rue Barbette, to a furnished house belonging to an upholsterer from the neighborhood, and they went up to the fourth floor. When he entered the shabbily furnished room and caught sight of Esther sitting and working on some embroidery, the millionaire went pale. And even after some fifteen minutes, during which Asia seemed to be deep in a whispered conversation with Esther, the newly youthful old man could hardly speak.

"Matemoiselle," he finally managed to say to the poor girl, "vood you haff ze goodness to accept me as your protector?"

"Evidently I must, monsieur," said Esther, two big tears escaping from her eyes.

"Do not cry! I vant to make you ze happiest of all vomen. . . . Let me chust luff you, und you see."

"Now, little one, monsieur is reasonable," Asia said. "He knows that he's past sixty-six, and he's going to be very indulgent. You see, my angel, it's like a father I've found for you. . . ." Turning to the annoyed banker, she whispered, "I have to say that. You don't catch a swallow by shooting a pistol at it. Come in here," she added, leading Nucingen into the next room. "You know what we need to do now, don't you, sweetheart?"

Nucingen took out his billfold and counted out the hundred thousand francs, which Carlos—concealed in an adjoining study—was anxiously awaiting, and which the cook promptly handed over to him.

"That's a hundred thousand francs our man has invested in Asia— now let's get him to invest in Europe too," said Carlos to his accomplice when they were together on the staircase.

He disappeared after giving some instructions to the Malay, who came back in the apartment to find Esther weeping bitterly. The child, like a criminal condemned to death, had been living in hopes of a fairy-tale ending, but now the fatal hour had struck.

"Well, my dear children," said Asia, "where would you like to go? Because the Baron de Nucingen . . ."

Esther looked at the famous banker and made an admirably played gesture of astonishment.

"Yess, my child, I am ze Baron de Nushingenn."

"The Baron de Nucingen cannot, must not, remain in a hovel like this. I have an idea! That maid you used to have, Eugénie . . ."

"Eugénie! From ze Rue Taitbout!" exclaimed the baron.

"Well, yes, she's the trustee they put in charge of the furnishings there," Asia continued, "and she's the one who rented it to that lovely Englishwoman."

"Oh, now I unnerstand!" said the baron.

"Madame's previous chambermaid," Asia said respectfully, nodding toward Esther, "would be pleased to welcome you there this evening, and the Garde du Commerce would never think of coming to look for her in her old apartment, which she left three months ago. . . ."

"Iss berfect! Berfect!" cried the baron. "Bezides, I know zese Gardes du Commerce peoples, und I know ze t'ings to say to keep zem gone for good."

Asia said, "You'll find Eugénie to be a clever one; I'm the one who found her for madame."

"I know zis!" exclaimed the millionaire with a laugh. "Zat Eugénie, she get t'irty t'ousand francs out of me!" At that, Esther executed a splendid gesture of horror that would, in itself, have led a wealthy man to hand over his fortune to her. "Oh, ze t'ing vass my fault," the baron went on. "I vass searching for you. . . ." And he went on to recount the tale of the confusion that had resulted from her renting the apartment to an Englishwoman.

"Well, do you see, madame?" said Asia. "Eugénie never told you any of this, the sly fox! But madame is used to the girl," she said to the baron, "so keep her on all the same." Asia took Nucingen aside and said to him: "With five hundred francs a month for Eugénie, who's taking good care of her own interests, you'll always know everything that madame does, so be sure to keep her on as the maid. Eugénie will be all the better for you, since she's already swindled you. Women get very attached to men they swindle. But keep Eugénie on a tight leash: she'll do anything for money, that girl. She's just horrible!"

"Und you?"

"Me?" said Asia. "Oh, I'm just making sure I get reimbursed."

Nucingen, shrewd as he was, might as well have been wearing a blindfold; he let himself be led along like a child. The sight of that innocent, adorable Esther wiping her eyes and stitching away at her embroidery with all the modesty of a young virgin aroused in the amorous old man those same powerful sensations he had felt when he first caught sight of her in the Bois de Vincennes. He would have given her the key to his cashbox! He felt young again, his heart filled with adoration, and he waited for Asia to be gone so he could go down upon his knees before this Madonna out of Raphael. This sudden flowering of youth in the heart of a lynx, and an old man, is one of those social phenomena that Physiology is best equipped to explain. Weighted down by business concerns, stifled by continual calculations, by the perpetual preoccupations of the quest for millions, adolescence with all its sublime illusions is born anew, springing up and bursting into bloom like some long-forgotten cause, like a sown but forgotten seed whose splendid blossoming is the result of sheer chance, of a sun that happens to shine, awakening it and bringing it forth. A clerk at the age of twelve in the old firm of Aldrigger in Strasbourg, the baron had never set foot in the country of the sentiments. And so now, as he stood there gazing upon his idol, trying to pick one of the thousand phrases that were whirling through his brain but finding that none would come to his lips, he turned to obey the brutal desire that burned within the sixty-six-year-old man:

"Do you vant to go to ze Rue Taitbout?" he asked.

"Wherever you like, monsieur," said Esther, getting up.

"Vere I like?" he repeated, enraptured. "You are an anchel coming down from ze sky, und I am luffing you chust like young man, efen t'ough I am gray in ze hair. . . ."

"Oh, I'd say more white than gray. Your hair is too fine a black to be just gray," said Asia.

"Get hout of here, you file merchant uff human flesh! You has your money—go, und do not be drooling upon zis flower uff luff!" cried the banker, reimbursing himself somewhat with this savage attack for all the indignities she had visited upon him.

"You old goat! I'll make you pay for that," said Asia, threatening the banker with an obscene gesture,[4] at which he only shrugged. "Between the mouth of the bottle and the mouth of the boozer there's room for a viper, and you're going to find that out!" she went on, infuriated by Nucingen's disdain.

Millionaires—whose money is guarded by the Bank of France, whose homes are guarded by squadrons of valets, whose person has between it and the street a rapid carriage pulled by English horses—fear no misfortune; and so the baron merely glared coldly at Asia, as a man who had just given her a hundred thousand francs. And that majesty had its effect. Asia went into retreat down the stairs, grumbling as she went, using the language of revolution and making mention of the guillotine.

"What did you say to her?" innocently inquired the Embroidering Virgin. "She's a good-hearted woman."

"She hass solt you off, she hass robbed you. . . ."

"But when you've fallen into poverty," she said, in a tone worthy of melting the heart of a diplomat, "who will give you money, who will care about you?"

"My liddle one!" said Nucingen. "Stay not one minute more in zis place!"

A First Night

Nucingen gave Esther his arm and led her out, just as she was, helping her up into his carriage with more respect and care, probably, than he would have shown to the Duchesse de Maufrigneuse.

"I giff you fine carriage, prettiest in Paris," said Nucingen as they drove along. "Effry kind of luxury, zis will be all around you. Not efen ze queens be richer than you. You get all ze respect zey giff to bride of Cherman man—I vant you to be free. . . . Oh, not to cry, please! Listen: I luff you vit ze purest luff. Effry tear you cry is painful to me."

"But can a man truly love a woman he's bought?" the poor girl asked, in the most delicious voice.

"Vell, Joseph, he vas solt by hiss brothers because he vas goot-looking. Iss in ze Bible. Besides, in ze Orient, zey buy ze vomen—iss legal."

When they arrived at the Rue Taitbout, Esther could not help but grieve at revisiting the scene of her former happiness. She remained sitting on a divan, wiping away her tears one by one without taking in a word of the absurdities the banker kept jabbering, even when he got down on his knee; she let him stay there without saying a thing, letting him take hold of her hands, not even aware, so to speak, of the sex of the creature who was now chafing her feet, which Nucingen found cold. This scene, with hot tears falling from time to time on the baron's head and with her icy feet being warmed by him, went on from midnight till two in the morning.

"Eugénie," the baron eventually called out to Europe, "ask your miztress if she vill go to bed now. . . ."

"No!" exclaimed Esther, rearing up on her legs like a frightened horse. "Never in this place!"

"Don't worry, monsieur, I know madame very well, and she's as gentle and sweet as a lamb," said Europe, "but you mustn't startle her—you've got to go round about with her, you see? She was so miserable here! You see? Look how worn the furniture is. Give her some time and let her think her way through things. Maybe set her up somewhere nicer, some new place, someplace pretty, and then maybe in new surroundings she'd feel a little lost, and then she might think you're even nicer than you are, and she might just be as sweet as an angel to you. . . . Oh, madame is one of a kind! And you can pride yourself on your excellent acquisition—a good heart, fine manners, the prettiest ankle, skin like a rose. . . . Ah, and clever enough to make a man on death row laugh. . . . Madame has a tendency to become very *attached* . . . and how she dresses! Well, it may be expensive, but a man gets his money's worth, as they say. . . . But all her dresses here have been seized, so she's three months behind the style. . . . But madame is so good, you know, that I just love her, and she's my mistress! But seriously, imagine it, a woman like that here among seized furnishings! And what for? For a little crook who went and ruined her. . . . Poor little thing! She's not herself anymore."

"Esther, Esther," said the baron, "go on to bed, my anchel! And, you see, if it's me you are afraid uff, look, I stay here on zis sofa . . ." He said all this while positively enflamed with the purest love, gazing on Esther, who continued to weep gently.

"All right, then," said Esther, taking the baron's hand and kissing it with a kind of gratitude that brought something that seemed almost to resemble a tear to the eye of the old lynx. "I thank you."

And with that she took flight, locking herself in her bedroom.

"Iss somet'ing I cannot explain," Nucingen said to himself, agitated by the amber pills he had taken. "Vat vould zey say at my house?"

He got up and looked out the window. "My carriage is still zere. Iss almost ze dawn!"

He walked slowly around the room. "How Matame de Nucingen vould laugh at me if she effer found out how I spent zis night."

He put his ear up to the bedroom door, feeling how absurd it was for him to be sleeping out here like this. "Oh, Esther!"

No response.

"Heffens, she still veeps!" he said, returning to the sofa and stretching out.

About ten minutes past sunrise, Baron Nucingen, who was sleeping an uneasy sleep in an uncomfortable position, on a strange sofa, was startled awake by Europe, in the middle of one of those dreams that awkward physical positions engender in us, dreams whose rapidly escalating complications are one of the insoluble phenomena of medical physiology.

"Oh heavens, madame! Madame!" she was crying. "Soldiers! The law, the police! They want to arrest you!"

When Esther opened her bedroom door and stood there, only half covered by her nightgown, her bare feet in slippers, her hair disordered, she would have been the damnation of the angel Raphael, while the drawing room was suddenly flooded by the human equivalent of mud, all of it rolling on its ten feet toward that celestial girl who was posed there like an angel in a Flemish religious painting. One man separated from the crowd and advanced. Contenson, the terrifying Contenson, reached out and put his hand on Esther's soft, moist shoulder.

"You are Mademoiselle Esther Van . . ." he asked.

Europe applied a backhand so dexterously to Contenson's face that he fell, measuring out his full length on the carpet as if he were about to go to sleep there, and she encouraged the latter by distributing a number of kicks to his leg of the kind known to those who follow the sport as *savate*.

"Get back!" she screamed. "Don't you dare touch my mistress!"

"She's broken my leg!" cried Contenson, getting back onto his feet. "Somebody's going to pay for this. . . ."

Out of the group of underlings, all wearing standard underling uniforms, all keeping their hideous hats perched up on top of their even more hideous heads, with faces like veined mahogany from which squinting eyes protruded, some of them minus noses, and with grimacing mouths—out of that mass stepped Louchard, dressed better than his men but with his hat also still on his head, wearing an expression that was sweet yet mocking.

"Mademoiselle," he said to Esther, "I am here to arrest you. And as for you, my girl," he added, turning to Europe, "any resistance will be punished, and it's pointless anyway."

The clatter of the rifles as their butt ends were set down on the tiled floor, a sound that announced that the garde had come with a garde of his own, gave authority to what he said.

"But why am I being arrested?" asked Esther, innocently.

"Could it be because of our little debts?" replied Louchard.

"Ah, yes, that's right," cried Esther. "Let me get dressed."

"Unfortunately, mademoiselle, I must make sure that your room affords you no means of escape," said Louchard.

All of this happened so quickly that the baron had had no time to intervene.

"Now am I a 'file merchant uff human flesh,' Baron Nucingen?" exclaimed the terrible Asia, slipping through the wall of underlings and over to the sofa, where she pretended to discover the banker.

"Och, you wretched beesht!" cried Nucingen, getting up onto his feet and drawing himself up in all his bankerly majesty.

And he threw himself between Esther and Louchard, who immediately doffed his cap when he heard Contenson's exclamation:

"Monsieur le Baron Nucingen!"

Louchard made a gesture and all the underlings trooped out of the apartment, now removing their caps in a sign of respect. Contenson alone remained.

"Is *monsieur le baron* going to pay . . . ?" the garde asked, hat in hand.

"Ja, I pay," he replied, "but shtill I need to know how much it iss."

"Three hundred thousand francs and some centimes, cash in hand, but the cost of the arrest is separate."

"T'ree hundred t'ousand francs!" cried the baron. "All zis is a bit too much for a man who spends night on a sofa," he added in a whisper to Europe.

Now Europe turned to Louchard and asked, "Is this man really the Baron de Nucingen?" and accompanied her expression of doubt by a gesture that Mademoiselle Dupont, the latest starlet at the Théâtre-Français, would have envied.[5]

"Yes, mademoiselle," said Louchard.

"Yes," added Contenson.

"I vill be responsible for her," said the baron, annoyed at Europe's doubt. "Let me haff a vord vit her."

Esther and her aging lover went together into the bedroom, upon the door of which Louchard found it prudent to apply his ear.

"I luff you more zan my life, Esther, but vhy should ve giff your creditors ze money zat vould be better in your purse? Let zem take you prison; I buy back zis hundred t'ousand vit hundred t'ousand, und you keep two hundred t'ousand for yourself . . ."

"That won't work," cried Louchard. "The creditor isn't likely to be in love with mademoiselle, don't you understand? And he's going to want it all, now that he knows you're so crazy about her."

"File spy!" Nucingen shouted to Louchard, opening the door and pulling him into the bedroom. "You don't know vat you say! I giff to you, chust to you, tventy percent if you fix zis business."

"Impossible, *monsieur le baron.*"

"What, monsieur?" said Europe, interrupting. "You could find it in your heart to let my mistress go to prison? . . . Oh, madame, will you take my savings, my wages? Please take it all madame—I have forty thousand francs. . . ."

"Oh, my poor dear," cried Esther, "I never really knew you!" And she threw her arms around Europe.

At that, Europe broke into tears.

"I pay," said the baron piteously, pulling out a pocket book, from which he drew one of those little square, imprinted papers that the Bank of France gives to bankers; all they have to do is write down the amount, both in figures and spelled out in words, to make them into bills payable to the bearer.

"Don't bother, *monsieur le baron,*" said Louchard. "I have orders not to accept any form of payment except gold or silver. But because it's you, I'll accept bank notes."

"Damn it!" cried the baron. "Giff me ze papers."

Contenson presented three documents folded in blue paper; the baron took them, looking at him and whispering, "You vould have done better if you had come to varn me."

"Well, how could I know you were going to be here, *monsieur le baron?*" said the spy out loud, unconcerned as to whether Louchard heard or not. "You've incurred a real loss by withdrawing your trust in me. Yes," the deep philosopher added with a shrug, "you're getting taken now."

"Iss true," the baron said to himself. "Ah, my little one!" he exclaimed, addressing Esther while looking at the bills of exchange. "You haff been ze victim uff a real crook! A real t'ief!"

"I'm afraid that's so," said poor Esther, "but he loved me so!"

"Iff I had known . . . I vould haff protested ze bills und I vould haff taken all zis off your hands."

"You're getting carried away, *monsieur le baron*," said Louchard. "There's a third endorser."

"Ach, yes," he said, "zere iss a t'ird . . . Cérizet! A man of ze Opposition!"

"Misfortune is making you witty," said Contenson with a smile. "He's opposed, all right."

"Will *monsieur le baron* please write a note to his cashier?" said Louchard with a smile. "I'll send Contenson and dismiss the others. It's getting later, and soon everybody will be talking about this, . . ."

"Go zen, Contenson!" cried Nucingen. "My cashier iss at ze corner of ze Rue des Madurins und ze Rue de l'Argate. Here iss note telling him to go see du Tillet or ze Kellers, in case ve no haff ze hundred t'ousand écus on hand, because ve keep our money at ze bank . . . Und you, mine anchel," he added, turning to Esther, "go ahead und get dressed. You are free now." Then, gazing over toward Asia, he added, "I learn zat old vomen are bigger danger zan ze young . . ."

"I'll be off then, and give your creditor a good laugh," Asia said to him, "and I imagine he'll give me a pretty good tip for all this. So goot-bye, *monsewer le barown*," added Madame Saint-Estève, making a grotesquely exaggerated bow to him.

Louchard took the deeds back from the baron, and he stayed there alone with him for half an hour until the cashier arrived, followed by Contenson. At the same time Esther emerged, dressed and made up beautifully, though she had had to improvise a bit. Once Louchard had counted the money, the baron wanted to look the deeds over, but Esther swept them away, as quick as a cat, and locked them in her desk.

"Any tip for the lower classes?" Contenson said to Nucingen.

"You haff not shown me much consideration," said the baron.

"And besides, my leg!" Contenson cried.

"Luchard, giff to Contenson hundred francs from ze change from ze t'ousand . . ."

"Zat iss beautiful voman," said the cashier to Baron du Nucingen as they left the Rue Taitbout, "but she iss costing monsieur much money!"

"Keep all zis secret," said the baron, who had also asked Contenson and Louchard to keep it secret.

Louchard had left, followed by Contenson, but out on the boulevard Asia had been watching for the Garde du Commerce to come out.

"The bailiff and the creditor are right over there in that cab," she said to him, "and they'd both like a drink, and you've got some cash."

While Louchard counted out the money, Contenson looked the clients over. He took note of Carlos's eyes as well as the shape of the forehead beneath the wig, and he thought to himself that the wig itself looked suspicious; he took down the number of the cab, all while seeming completely oblivious to what was going on, but he found both Asia and Europe extremely interesting. He thought that the baron had fallen victim to some extraordinarily skillful people, and all the more so because of the secretive way Louchard had enlisted him. The kick Europe had given him made an impression on more than his leg. "That kick had a Saint-Lazare flavor to it!" he had said to himself as he got up.[6]

Carlos paid the bailiff handsomely and then dismissed him, telling the driver: "Palais-Royal, the Steps!"

"Ah, clever!" thought Contenson, who heard the order. "Something's up."

Carlos arrived at the Palais-Royal too quickly to fear that he had been followed. But to be sure, he followed his usual procedure, walking through the Galleries and getting into another cab on the other side by the Château d'Eau, telling the driver: "Passage de l'Opéra, on the Rue Pinon side." Fifteen minutes after that, he entered the apartment on the Rue Taitbout.

Seeing him, Esther said, "Here they are, the fatal documents."

Carlos took the deeds and looked them over carefully; then he went into the kitchen and burned them.

"We did it!" he cried, pulling out the three hundred and ten thousand francs in a roll from the pocket of his jacket. "This, plus the hundred thousand Asia got, will be enough for us to move forward."

"My God, my God!" cried poor Esther.

"Oh, you little imbecile," said the ferocious con artist, "just pretend to be Nucingen's mistress, and you'll get to see Lucien. He's a friend of Nucingen, and I'm not forbidding you to go on feeling your passion for him!"

Esther thought she could see a feeble ray of light in the shadows that were her life, and she took a deep breath.

Some Gleams of Light

"Europe, my girl," said Carlos, taking the creature over to a corner of the bedroom where no one would be able to overhear them, "I'm very pleased with you."

Europe raised up her face and looked at the man with an expression that so transfigured her withered face that the one witness to the scene—Asia, who watched from the doorway—wondered whether the hold Carlos had on Europe might be even deeper than the hold he had on her.

"That's not all, my girl. Four hundred thousand francs are nothing compared to what we need. . . . Paccard will give you an invoice that comes to thirty thousand francs, which has been accounted for, but our goldsmith, Biddin, has gone to some expense for us, and he's behind the seizure of the furniture, which will no doubt go up for sale tomorrow. Go see Biddin. He lives on the Rue de l'Arbre-Sec, and he'll give you pawn tickets for ten thousand francs. You understand, now: Esther has ordered some silverware, she hasn't paid, she's pawned it, and she'll be threatened with an action for fraud. So we need to give thirty thousand francs to the goldsmith and ten thousand to the pawnshop to get the silverware back. That's a total of forty-three thousand francs, with fees. Now that silver is largely alloy. The baron will get her a new set, and we can pinch a few thousand more out of him over that. And you owe—how much, for two years' worth at the dressmaker's?"

"Call it six thousand francs," said Europe.

"All right. If Madame Auguste wants to be paid, and to stay in business, she'll have to make out a bill for us of thirty thousand francs over four years. Same with the milliner. The jeweler, Samuel Frisch, a Jew on the Rue Sainte-Avoie, will give you some pawn tickets, and we've got to 'owe' him twenty-five thousand francs, and we'll claim that we had six thousand francs in pawned jewelry. We'll give the jewels back to the jeweler, half of which will be fake, but the baron won't examine them. So, you'll be able to get our mark to fork out fifty thousand francs by a week from today."

"Madame is going to have to help me a little," said Europe. "You talk to her, because she just stands there like a mute and I have to come up with more lines than three authors writing a play."

"If Esther starts turning prudish, let me know," said Carlos. "Nucingen owes her a carriage and horses, which she'll pick out and buy herself. Choose the horse dealer and coachmaker Paccard knows. We'll get some superb horses at a very high price, and they'll go lame within a month, so we'll need new ones."

"We could probably get a six thousand franc bill from a perfumer," said Europe.

"Well," he said, nodding, "we need to proceed carefully, from one vendor to another. So far we've only got Nucingen's arm caught in the machine, and we need to get his head trapped in it. Beyond all this, I need to come up with five hundred thousand francs."

"You'll be able to get it," said Europe. "Madame will begin to soften toward the fat imbecile when we get close to six hundred thousand, and then she can ask for another four hundred to love him right."

"Listen to this, my girl," said Carlos. "The day I get my hands on the final hundred thousand francs, there'll be twenty thousand for you."

"What good will that do me?" she said, throwing up her hands in a gesture of hopelessness.

"You'll be able to return to Valenciennes, buy a nice shop, and turn honest woman, if that's what you want. There are all sorts of tastes out there—that's what Paccard dreams about sometimes. He's got nothing hanging over his head, and almost nothing on his conscience. You two could come to an agreement," said Carlos.

"Return to Valenciennes! . . . Why would you say that, monsieur?" exclaimed the frightened Europe.

Born in Valenciennes, the daughter of very poor weavers, when Europe was seven she was sent to a spinning mill where the demands of Modern Industry damaged her physically, just as Vice had depraved her too prematurely as well. Corrupted by age twelve, a mother at thirteen, she found herself living among the most degraded creatures. At sixteen she was in court as a witness to murder. At that age she still retained traces of truthfulness, and in the presence of the terror that the Law represented, she testified, and the result was that the accused was convicted and sentenced to twenty years' hard labor. The criminal, one of those well known to the courts and one known for exacting terrible vengeance, said to the child right in the courtroom: "In ten years, as sure as today is today, Prudence [for that was Europe's real name, Prudence Servien], I'll be back and I'll put you underground, even if they guillotine me for it." The president of the court did all he could to reassure Prudence Servien, promising to protect her in the interests of Justice, but the poor child was so terrified that she fell ill and spent a whole year in the hospital. Now, Justice is a kind of abstract creature, represented by a collection of individuals that is constantly changing, and its good intentions, along with its memory, are always changing too. The courts and tribunals cannot prevent crimes—they were invented to punish them after the fact. In this respect, a preventive police force would be a great advantage to a country, but the very word "police" so frightens the legislators that they can no longer distinguish among the terms "governor," "administrator," and "lawmaker." The legislator absorbs everything into the State, as if the State were capable of acting. The convict thinks every day about his victim, while Justice forgets completely about both of them. Prudence understood all this instinctively, if vaguely, so she left Valenciennes at seventeen and came to Paris to hide. She followed four different trades there, the best of them acting as an assistant in a little theater. There she met Paccard, to whom she told all her woes. Paccard, the right-hand man, the primary henchman to Jacques Collin, spoke to his master about Prudence, and when the master needed a slave, he said to her: "If you're willing to serve me as absolutely as you would the Devil, I'll take care of Durut for you." Durut was the name of the convict, the sword of Damocles hovering over the head of Prudence Servien. Without knowing all these details, some critical readers might have found Europe's attachment a little hard to believe. But nobody could have known the great announcement that Carlos, like a stage manager, was about to make.

"Yes, my dear girl, you can return to Valenciennes. . . . Here, read this." And he handed her a newspaper from the day before, his finger pointing to one particular article: "Toulon. Yesterday, the execution of Jean-François Durut took place. . . . Early in the morning . . . the garrison . . ." and so on.

Prudence dropped the newspaper; her legs gave way beneath her; she was given a new life, for she had never, as she put it, enjoyed so much as the taste of bread since Durut made his threat.

"You see, I kept my word. It took four years to trap Durut so that his head would roll. . . . Well, so now you can go ahead and finish the job here for me, and you'll find yourself running a little shop back in your hometown, with twenty thousand francs, wife to Paccard, and as for him, I'm going to allow him to retire to a life of virtue."

Europe picked the paper up and read it again, this time eagerly soaking up all the details given in the paper—because for the last twenty years, newspapers have never tired of giving all the details concerning executions of convicts: the imposing spectacle of the thing, the chaplain accompanying the condemned man, the old criminal exhorting his former colleagues to repent, the artillery prepared to fire, the criminals down on their knees; and then the banal comments, which never lead to any change at all in how the prisons are run, continuing to serve as the hive swarming with eighteen thousand crimes.

"We need to get Asia back into the household," said Carlos.

Asia came forward, having understood nothing of Europe's pantomime.

"In order to get her rehired as chef here, you'll have to start by giving the baron a dinner like nothing he's ever tasted before," he went on. "Then you'll tell him that Asia lost all her money gambling and has gone back into domestic service. We won't need a porter. Paccard will be our coachman. Coachmen stay put up on their boxes where they're not as conspicuous, so the spies will miss him. Madame will have him wearing a powdered wig, and on top of that we'll put a tricorner hat with braided felt. That'll change his look, and, besides, I'll disguise him with some makeup."

"Will we have any servants here with us?" asked Asia, squinting.

"Of course—all honest men," said Carlos.

"All dimwits!" laughed the mulatto.

"If the baron rents a house, Paccard has a friend we can pass off as caretaker," Carlos continued. "In that case, all we'd need would be a footman and a woman for the kitchen, and you could manage a couple of strangers."

When Carlos was about to leave, Paccard came in.

"Wait a bit—there's a crowd in the street," the manservant said.

Such a statement was disturbing. Carlos went up into Europe's room, staying there until Paccard had come back to pick him up with a rented carriage down in the courtyard. Carlos lowered the coach's blinds, and they drove off at a speed calculated to discourage pursuit. When they got to the Faubourg Saint-Antoine, he got out a little distance from the spot where the cabs stopped, and went on foot to the Quai Malaquais, avoiding any curious glances.

"Look here, my boy," he said to Lucien, showing him the bills for four hundred thousand francs. "This, I hope, will work as a down payment on the Rubempré estate. We'll speculate elsewhere with one hundred thousand. They've just introduced this Omnibus idea in Paris,[7] and the Parisians are going to love it—we should triple our investment in three months. I understand the business side—they'll give out a very nice dividend in order to make the shares seem more attractive and to get the whole thing on a solid footing. Nucingen has started using the idea too. We can get the Rubempré estate without putting down all the price at once. You need to go find des Lupeaulx, and ask him to give you a recommendation for a lawyer named Desroches, a clever crook you'll meet in his office; tell him to go to Rubempré and examine the place, and promise him twenty thousand francs for his fee if he can buy up the lands around the château for eight hundred thousand, so as to guarantee you an annual income of thirty thousand."

"Too fast! You're going too fast!"

"Yes, but at least I'm going somewhere. No more joking now. Go put a hundred thousand écus in Treasury bonds, so as not to lose any interest—you can let Desroches handle that, because he's honest enough, even if he is cunning. . . . Once that's done, get right down to Angoulême and talk your sister and brother-in-law into telling an innocent little lie: they can say they've given you six hundred thousand francs to help with your marriage to Clotilde de Grandlieu—nothing dishonorable in that."

"Yes! We're saved!" exclaimed an astonished Lucien.

"You are, yes!" said Carlos. "But not completely—not until you're walking out of Saint-Thomas-d'Aquin with Clotilde as your wife. . . ."

"You're afraid of something. What is it?" asked Lucien, plainly concerned for his mentor.

"I've got someone on my tail. . . . I need to go back to acting like a real priest, and that's damned annoying! The Devil might stop being my friend if he sees me with a breviary under my arm."

At that same moment the Baron de Nucingen, along with his cashier, was just reaching the front door of his home.

Profits and Losses

"Ach, I am afraid," said the baron as they went in, "zat mebbe I haff made a bad bargain. . . . Bah! Ve shall get our own back."

His worthy German colleague, concerned primarily with decorum, replied, "Ze bad t'ing iss dat *monsieur ze baron* hass done all ziz publicly."

"Ja, my mistress should be in a position zat iss vorzsy uff me," responded our Louis XIV of the cash drawer.

Sure of getting Esther sooner or later, the baron returned now to being the grand financier that he was. He took up his affairs again so adroitly that his cashier, coming in to find him the next day hard at work in his office at six in the morning, rubbed his hands together in delight.

"Iss no doubt, *monsieur ze baron* hass saved plenty of money overnight," he exclaimed with a German smile, half shrewd, half vacuous.

If wealthy men on the level of the Baron de Nucingen have more occasions than other men for losing money, they also have more occasions for making it, even when they give themselves up to their follies. While the financial policy of the famous Maison Nucingen can be found detailed elsewhere, it may be worthwhile to observe that, amid the commercial, political, and industrial revolutions of our epoch, fortunes of this size are not acquired, not constituted, not enlarged, and not retained without there being immense losses of capital from, or, if you like, levies imposed upon, the fortunes of other individuals. There is very rarely any truly new wealth created in the common treasury of the world. Every profit made represents some new inequality appearing somewhere in the general distribution. What the State demands, it gives back; but what the Maison Nucingen takes, it keeps. When it betrays or swindles somebody, there are no legal ramifications, for the simple reason that if there were, Frederick the Great would have been a Jacques Collin or a Mandrin[8] if, instead of plying his interests across whole countries by means of battles, he had worked with contraband or with liquid securities. When it comes to the grand politics of making money, forcing the states of Europe to borrow at twenty or ten percent and then make up that twenty or ten percent by taking it out of public funds, by shaking industry down on a vast scale by buying up raw materials, throwing out a lifeline to some drowning financier while taking over his drowning business—this is the great warfare of the highest finance, fought with armies of écus. Of course, for the banker, just as for the military conqueror, there are risks; but there are so few people in a position to compete in such contests that the sheep have no idea what's going on. Such large-scale events take place only among the shepherds. When people are knocked flat—to use the kind of terminology they use on the stock exchange—it's because they were guilty of trying to make too much money too quickly, and there aren't very many of us who can get very worked up about the goings-on in firms like that of Nucingen. One speculator blows his brains out, another one flees the country, another one steals the savings of a hundred families, which is frankly worse than murder: all these catastrophes, entirely forgotten in Paris within a few months, are soon absorbed into the great tidal flow, so to speak, of that grand city. The colossal fortunes of a Jacques Coeur, of the Medicis, the Angots of Dieppe, the Auffredis of La Rochelle, the Fuggers, the Tiepolos, the Corners—all these were more or less honestly accumulated through privileges built upon the people's ignorance of the source of the various precious commodities; but today geographical realities have been so well communicated to the masses, and competition has made profit margins so much narrower, that every rapidly acquired fortune is either the result of chance or some new discovery—or of some legal theft. Scandalous examples have perverted even the more modest levels of commerce, which have begun to imitate the worst practices of the higher levels, especially over the last ten years, by adulterating raw materials. Thus, every place that chemistry is practiced, wine is no longer wine, and so the wine industry continues to decline. Artificial salt is sold, so as to avoid taxes. This widespread lack of integrity horrifies the tribunals. We have reached the point where French business practices have become suspect the world over, and those of England are not far behind. In our country, the evil has its roots in politics. The Charter has proclaimed the supreme reign of money, and in an atheistic era success justifies everything. Thus the corruption rampant at the highest levels, despite all its attempted dazzle and feeble rationalizations, is infinitely more disgusting than the ignoble, merely personal corruption found in the lower spheres, some details of which often provide matter for comedy, though not of the most pleasant kind, on our great Stage. The Government, always frightened of any new idea, has banned any comedy that truly reflects contemporary life from the theaters. The bourgeoisie, currently less progressive than Louis XIV, trembles at the thought of seeing its own *Marriage of Figaro* on the stage, forbids the staging of political Tartuffes, and, above all, will never consent to presenting *Turcaret* these days, for Turcaret has become the true sovereign. From now on, therefore, comedy is confined to the Book, which is the poet's only weapon now—a less immediate weapon, but a surer one.

All that morning the comings and goings, grantings of audiences, placing of orders, very brief consultations, all made Nucingen's office into a kind of financier's waiting room. One of his agents came to tell him of the disappearance of a member of the company, one of the most skillful, Jacques Falleix, brother to Martin Falleix, and successor to a man called Jules Desmarets. Jacques Falleix was the agent in charge of title changes for the Nucingen firm. Together with du Tillet and the Kellers, the baron had coldly brought about the ruin of the man, as if he had been a lamb to be slaughtered for Easter dinner.

"Ze man vas veak," the baron now responded, calmly.

Jacques Falleix had rendered enormous service to the field of stockjobbing. A few months previous, during a crisis, he had "kept all their heads above water" by bold maneuvering. But to expect recognition or gratitude from lynxes—well, isn't that about the same as counting on the tender feelings of a wolf in the Ukraine?

"Poor man!" replied the agent. "He had no idea this was coming. He'd recently furnished a little house on the Rue Saint-Georges for his mistress; he'd spent a hundred and fifty thousand francs on paintings, on furniture. And how he loved Madame du Val-Noble! The poor woman has no choice now but to clear out, because nothing's paid for."

"Ah, goot, goot!" said Nucingen to himself. "Zis is ze way I get my money back from last night." Turning to the stockbroker, he asked, "Und you say not'ing is paid for?"

"Well, of course," said the agent. "Is there any interior decorator in Paris who wouldn't have given Jacques Falleix all the credit he asked for? I hear the cellar is exceptional. By the way, the house is up for sale—he was planning to buy it. The lease is in his name. How stupid, really! Silver, furniture, wines, carriages, horses—it'll all be sold in a single lot, and how much will the creditors realize out of that?"

"Come back tomorrow," said Nucingen, "und by zen I vill haff gone to see it all, und if zere is no legal bankruptcy issue, und it can all be arranged nice and friendly, I send you for to offer reasonable price for ze place, und I take over ze lease. . . ."

"There'll be no trouble at all," said the stockbroker. "Go on over this morning, and you'll find one of Falleix's associates there with the

WHAT LOVE COSTS AN OLD MAN | 149

contractors, because they want to put in for a preferential claim, but that Val-Noble woman has all the invoices in Falleix's name."

Baron de Nucingen immediately sent a clerk to his notary. Jacques Falleix had told him about the house, which was worth sixty thousand francs at most, and he wanted to become the owner at once in order to avail himself of tenant's privileges.

The cashier (an honest man!) came to ask if his master had lost anything in the ruin of Falleix.

"On ze contrary, old Volfgang, I am about to make a hundred t'ousand francs."

"Ja? But how is zat?"

"Ha! I get holt of zis little house zat poor deffil Falleix has been making ready for his mistress for a whole year. I get efferyt'ing by offering fifty t'ousand francs to ze creditors, und Gartod, my notary, vill haff my orders for ze house, becauss ze proprietor iss in trouble. . . . All zat I already knew, but I t'ought nozzing about it. Now, in little while my diffine Esther going to liff in a leetle palace. . . . All t'anks to Falleix—iss a marfel, und nice and close to here. . . . Ah, it all fits me like gluff!"

The ruin of Falleix meant that the baron had to go to the Bourse, but he found it impossible to go there without passing by the Rue Taitbout; he was already suffering at having spent several hours away from Esther, and he wanted to be close to her again. The profit he knew he would make out of his employee's ruin would make the loss of that four hundred thousand francs a mere trifle. Enchanted with the thought of announcing to his "anchel" that she would be translated soon from the Rue Taitbout to the Rue Saint-Georges, where she would have "a leetle palace" to herself, a place with no unfortunate memories to interfere with their happiness, the very paving stones felt soft and light beneath his feet, and he strode along like a young man dreaming the dreams of young men. When he turned the corner of the Rue des Trois-Frères, right in the middle of his dream, and right in the middle of that soft pavement, the baron saw Europe heading directly toward him, looking as if something were very wrong.

"Vere are you going?" he asked.

"Oh, monsieur! I was heading to your place. You were so right yesterday! Now I understand that it would have been better for madame to have gone to prison for a few days. But what do women know about financial matters? When madame's creditors heard that she had come back home, the whole gang of them descended upon her like some kind of prey. . . . Yesterday, monsieur, at seven in the evening, they came and put horrible stickers all over the furniture. But that's not the worst . . .

madame, as you know, is all heart, and she only wanted to do a favor to that monster of a man!"

"Vat monster?"

"Oh, the one she was in love with, that d'Estourny. Oh, he was a charmer! But he gambled, and that's all that mattered."

"Zat man, he gamble vit marked cards!"

"Well, yes, but don't you?" said Europe. "Isn't that what you do on the stock market? But let me tell the story. One day, in order to keep Georges from doing what he said he would do, blow his brains out, she went to the pawnshop and pawned all her silver, along with some jewels that hadn't been paid for. But when they heard that she had 'given something to another creditor,' they all rushed in and made a scene. They're threatening to take her to court. Imagine it— your angel, in that courtroom! It's enough to make a wig stand on end, isn't it? . . . She broke down in tears, and now she's talking about going to throw herself in the river —and oh, she might do it!"

"Ach, if I come vit you, I miss ze Bourse!" cried Nucingen. "Und I haff to go, because I make money for her today. You go make her nice and calm. . . . I vill pay her debts, und I come see her at four o'clock. But, Eugénie, tell me, do you t'ink she luff me a little?"

"A little? Oh, monsieur, a lot! Let me tell you, monsieur, there's nothing like generosity if you want to win a woman's heart. Now, you definitely would have saved around a hundred thousand francs by letting her go to prison, but you never would have won her heart. . . . In fact, she even said to me, 'Eugénie, what a good man, what a generous man— he's got a noble soul!'"

"She say zis to you, Eugénie?" exclaimed the baron.

"Oh yes, monsieur, she said it to me directly."

"Ach, ach—here iss ten écus. . . ."

"Why, thank you. . . . But right now, she's over there crying; she's cried as much, this last day, as a weeping Magdalene would in a month. . . . The woman you love is in despair, and it's all over some debts that aren't even hers! Oh, men! They devour women, the same way women devour older men—imagine!"

"Zey are all like zat! Zey commit too much! No, no, you should not commit so fast! She should never sign nothing. Nothing. I pay, yes, but if she go and sign somet'ing else . . . if she do zat . . ."

"What will you do?" said Europe, standing back.

"Ach, mine Gott! I haff no powers ofer her. I going to take charge of her business problems. . . . Go now, go console her, und tell her in only one mont' she going to be liffing in her own leetle palace."

"*Monsieur le baron,* you have made investments in the heart of that woman that are going to pay you big dividends! Look . . . you're becoming more youthful already—I know, I'm only a chambermaid, but I've seen this phenomenon so many times . . . it's happiness, that's what it is . . . and happiness makes a difference in a person. If you've had a few expenses, don't let it bother you . . . you'll see how it's going to pay off. And I said to madame: she'd be the lowest of the low, the worst kind of whore, if she didn't return your love, because you've snatched her right up out of hell. You'll see it once she's finally free of her worries. And just between us, I can tell you . . . the night she was crying so much . . . how can I say it? You see, a woman feels esteem for the man who's helping her . . . well, she didn't want to tell you all this. She wanted just to run away."

"Run avay!" cried the baron, terrified at the thought. "But ze Bourse, ze Bourse . . . go, go, I vill not come in right now, but maybe I could see her at ze vindow. Ze sight uff her vould giff me courage."

Esther smiled at Monsieur de Nucingen as he passed the front of the house, and he clomped along, saying to himself, "She iss an anchel." Now, the following explains how Europe succeeded in obtaining that impossible result.

Necessary Explanations

Around two-thirty Esther had finished dressing the way she used to when she was awaiting Lucien, and she looked exquisite. Prudence noticed how she looked, and standing by the window, she exclaimed, "There's monsieur!" The poor girl rushed over, expecting to see Lucien, and instead saw Nucingen.

"Oh, that was cruel!" she said.

"Well, how else am I going to get you to look like you're paying attention to the poor old man who wants to pay off your debts?" replied Europe. "Because in fact they're all going to be paid."

"What debts?" asked the girl, always thinking only of trying to retain her love, though terrible hands were busy trying to wrench it from her.

"The ones that Monsieur Carlos incurred for madame."

"What! There are nearly four hundred thousand francs right here!" cried Esther.

"Yes, and then there's an additional hundred and fifty—but he took it all very well, our baron. He's going to get you out of here, and put you in a 'leetle palace.' . . . Good lord, you're not exactly unlucky, you know! If I were in your shoes, since you've got that man wrapped around your little finger, once you've done everything Carlos wants, I'd be sure to get myself set up with a house and a proper income. Madame is certainly the most beautiful woman I've ever seen, and the most charming too, but when the ugliness comes, it comes fast! I was once young and pretty, and look at me now. I'm twenty-three, just about madame's age, but I look at least ten years older. . . . One illness is all it takes. But see, when you've got a house of your own in Paris and an income, you don't have to worry about ending up on the streets. . . ."

Esther had stopped listening to Europe/Eugénie/Prudence Servien. The power of that man's will—that man who was a genius in corruption—had plunged Esther back down into the mud with the same strength he had used to pull her up out of it. Those who have come to know love in its infinitude understand that you cannot experience its pleasures without experiencing its virtues. Since the scene in that slum in the Rue de Langlade, Esther had completely forgotten her former life. She had lived virtuously, cloistered within her passion. Thus, to avoid running into any obstacles, the shrewd corruptor had so planned things that the poor girl, entirely motivated by her devotion, could not but consent to participating in scams and cheats that had already been consummated or were about to be so. The corruptor's methods, showing how supreme he was in the intricacy of his schemes, were similar to those he used in obtaining the complete subjugation of Lucien. Create a terrible situation: prepare the mine—fill it with gunpowder—and then, at the critical moment, say to the accomplice, "Just nod your head, and it'll go off." Esther in the past had been steeped in the morality peculiar to courtesans, and she had found little touches like these so natural that her opinions of her rivals were entirely based on how much money they could get a man to spend. Ruined fortunes are notches in the belts of such creatures. Carlos counted on Esther's memories, and he was not mistaken. These wartime stratagems, these tactics put into practice a thousand times over, and not only by women but by the money-dispensing men as well, never troubled Esther. The poor girl only felt her own degradation. She loved Lucien, and now she was, at least nominally, the mistress of the Baron Nucingen; that summed it all up for her. That the false Spaniard should keep the money as a deposit, that Lucien's future was to be built upon the tomb of Esther, that a single night of pleasure would cost the aging banker so many thousand francs more or less, that Europe should find more or less clever ways of extracting a hundred francs here or there, none of that really mattered to the girl in love; but there was one cancer that was eating away at her heart. For five years she had seen herself as white and unstained as an angel! She loved, and she was happy, and she never committed the slightest infidelity. And now that beautiful love was about to be defiled. She did not think consciously about the contrast between that beautiful, secret life and the vile life of her near future. There was neither calculation nor poeticizing: instead, she simply felt an indefinable sensation and an infinite power. From the white, she was passing to the black; from the pure, to the impure; from the noble, to the ignoble. She was ermine-pure through the sheer power of her own will, and this moral defilement seemed intolerable to her. And so, when the baron appeared and his passion began to threaten her, she seriously thought of throwing herself out the window. Lucien, in short, had been loved absolutely, and in a way that women very rarely love a man. Women who say they love, even the ones who believe they love more than others, dance and waltz and flirt with other men, adorn themselves for others to look at, and hope to reap a harvest of lustful glances; but Esther had accomplished, without having to make any sacrifices, a miracle of true love. For six years she had loved Lucien the way actresses and courtesans do who, mired in filth and impurity, thirst after the nobility and the devotion of real love, and who therefore practice *exclusivity* (we need a word like that, don't we, one to denote something that rarely exists). The bygone nations of Greece, of Rome, of the Orient always sequestered their women, but the woman who truly loves should sequester herself. The reader can therefore understand how Esther, descending from that fantastic castle in which such a fête, such a poem was lived out, would feel a mortal sickness coming over her upon contemplating the "leetle palace" that a cold old man was offering. Manipulated and pushed along by an iron hand, she now found herself immersed waist-deep in infamy before she could even realize what was happening; but the past two days she had reflected upon it all, and her heart was gripped by a mortal chill.

At the words "ending up on the streets," she abruptly stood and said, "End up on the streets? No, in the Seine . . ."

"In the Seine? And what about Monsieur Lucien?" asked Europe.

The name alone made Esther sit back down in her chair, and there she stared down at a rosette on the carpet, forcing her tears to remain unshed. At four o'clock, Nucingen arrived to find his angel plunged deep in that ocean of reflections and resolutions upon which the female mind floats, emerging only to speak in a way that would be incomprehensible to anyone who had not been upon the same waters.

"You must stop vit zis frowning, my luffly girl," the baron said, seating himself next to her. "You vill haff no more debts. . . . I vill arrange t'ings vit Eugénie, und in chust vun mont' you vill quit zis apartment und move into your leetle palace. . . . Ach, such a pretty hand! Giff it me so I may kiss it." Esther presented her hand to him like a dog presenting its paw. "Ach, you giff me ze hand, but not ze heart . . . und iss ze heart zat I luff. . . ."

This was said with such truth in it that poor Esther turned her eyes upon the old man with an expression of such pity that it nearly drove him mad. Lovers, like martyrs, know torture so well! Nothing in the world creates such a sense of brotherhood as sharing similar sorrows.

"Poor man," she said. "He's in love."

Hearing the word but not quite understanding how she was using it, the baron went pale, the blood raced in his veins, and he breathed in the air of paradise. At his age, millionaires will pay as much for that kind of sensation as a woman cares to charge.

"I luff you like I luff mine daughter," he said. "Und I feel zis luff right here," he added, placing his hand over his heart, "zo much zat I cannot bear to see you unhappy."

"If you only wanted to be a father to me, I would love you deeply, I would never leave you, and I would make you see that I am not a wicked woman, or venal, or self-interested, like I must seem to you now. . . ."

"You haff committed some little follies," said the baron, "like all pretty women—zat is all. Ve say no more about it. Right now, ve need to make some money for you. . . . Be happy—I vill be like ze vather for you zese next few days, because I understand zat you need time to get used to my poor old carcass."

"Do you really mean it?" she cried, arising and sitting on Nucingen's lap, putting her arm around him and pulling him close.

"Ja! I mean it!" he said, forcing himself to smile.

She kissed his forehead, believing that the impossible was going to be possible after all: she would be able to remain pure, and see Lucien. . . . She coaxed and wheedled the banker so well that La Torpille made a new appearance. She enchanted the old man, who promised to remain fatherly for forty days. Those forty days were necessary for the purchase of and arrangements regarding the Rue Saint-Georges house. Once he was out in the street and on his way back home, the baron said to himself, "I am a fool!" And in fact, while he may have acted like a child in Esther's presence, now that he was out of it he turned back into the lynx, just like Regnard's gambler, who falls back in love with Angélique as soon as he's broke.[9]

Twenty days later he was saying to himself, "Haff a million, und I haffn't efen seen her legs. Iss too stupid. But nobody knows, und zat is ze good t'ing." And now he would make firm resolutions to be done with a woman who had cost him so much for so little—but then, when he was in Esther's presence, he spent all his time making up for the brutality of his initial approach. However, by the end of a month he was saying to himself, "I cannot go on being ze Eternal Fazzer!"

Two Great Loves: Conflict

Around the end of the month of December 1829, on the day before installing Esther in the Rue Saint-Georges house, the baron asked du Tillet to take Florine there to see if everything was right for a man of Nucingen's status, and if those words "leetle palace" had in fact been realized by the contractors charged with making the nest worthy of the bird. All the innovations of pre-1830 luxury came together to make this house the very model of good taste. The architect Grindot[10] had turned the place into a masterpiece of his decorative genius. The staircase, redone in marble, the moldings, the materials, the subtle use of gilding—from the smallest details up to the grandest effects, the place outshone everything like it that the era of Louis XV had left in Paris.

"This place is my ideal! Well, this plus virtue," said Florine with a smile. "And you've incurred all this expense for whom?" she asked Nucingen. "Some virgin who just tumbled down out of Heaven?"

"Ha—iss a voman who belongs dere," replied the baron.

"So you're playing the role of Jupiter," said the actress. "And when may one get a look at her?"

"Oh, on the day of the housewarming," cried du Tillet.

"Und not before," said the baron.

"Well, then, we'll just have to get ourselves all brushed up, put together, and gilded," said Florine. "Oh, the headaches all the women will be giving their dressmakers and hairdressers on *that* day! . . . And when is it?"

"I am not ze master."

"What a woman she must be!" exclaimed Florine. "I can't wait to see her!"

"Ja, me too," said the baron ingenuously.

"Oh, my—the house, the woman, the furnishings, everything brand new?"

"Even the banker," said du Tillet, "because my friend seems much younger these days."

"Well, we need to work him all the way down to twenty, at least for a moment or two," said Florine.

During the early days of 1830, everyone in Paris society was talking about Nucingen's passion and the extreme luxury of his house. The poor baron, on display and universally mocked, was possessed by a rage that is easy to imagine, for it combined the willpower of the financier with the furious passion storming in his heart. He wanted to make the night of the housewarming the night he put off the noble-father costume, the night he finally got his hands on the great reward for all his sacrifices. Constantly outwitted by La Torpille, he resolved to settle the marriage question by means of correspondence in order to get an agreement and her signature on it. Bankers have faith in firm documentation only. Thus the lynx arose early on one of those early days in the new year, closeted himself in his study, and began composing the following letter, written in good French—for, if his pronunciation was dreadful, his spelling was quite good.

Dear Esther,

flower of my thoughts and sole happiness of my life, when I told you that I loved you the way I love my daughter, I misled you, and I misled myself. I only put it that way because I wanted to express the holiness of my feelings, which do not resemble the ones most men ordinarily feel, in the first place because I am an old man, and in the second because I have never been in love before. I love you so much that even if you cost me my entire fortune, I would not love you any the less. Be fair: few men would have seen the angel in you, as I did; and I never once cast so much as a glance at your past. I love you as I love my daughter Augusta, my only child, and as I would love my wife if she had been capable of loving me. Since achieving happiness is the only justification for an old man in love, ask yourself if I have not been playing something of a ridiculous role. I have made you into the consolation and the sole joy of my late years. You know that until my death you will live in as fine a state as any woman could have, and you also know that after my death you will have the kind of wealth that will make you the envy of a great many other women. In all the business I have done since I first had the pleasure of speaking with you, you have been a part of it, and you have an account with the Maison Nucingen. In a few days you will move into a house that will sooner or later be your own, if it pleases you. Come now, will I still be your father when I meet you, or will I finally be made a happy man? . . . Forgive me for writing so bluntly, but when I am near you I lack the courage, and I sense only too well that you are in control. I have no intention of offending you; I only want to tell you how much I suffer, and how cruel it is at my age to have to wait, when every day that passes plucks away my hopes and my pleasures. In any case, the delicacy of my behavior has surely been a guarantor

of the sincerity of my intentions. Have I ever behaved like a creditor? You are like a citadel, and I am not a young man. You respond to my complaints that this is a matter of life and death for you, and you make me believe it when I am with you and listening to you; but when I am alone I fall back into black melancholy, and I experience doubts that are dishonorable to you and to me. You have always seemed just as good and as candid with me as you are beautiful, but you seem intent on destroying my convictions. Judge for yourself! You tell me you have a passion in your heart, a pitiless one, and you refuse to confide in me the name of the man you love . . . is this natural? You have taken a man of considerable strength and reduced him to a weakling. . . . This is the state I've come to: after five months, I have to ask, what future is there for my love? So, again, I need to ask you what role I am to play when we have the housewarming for your new home. Money is no object for me when it comes to you; I am not fool enough to think that my contempt for money will impress you, but if my love is limitless, my fortune is not, and it matters to me only for you. Well then, if by giving you everything that I possess I could, an entirely impoverished man, obtain your affection, I would rather be poor and loved by you than wealthy and disdained. You've changed me so much, dear Esther, that people don't recognize me anymore: I paid Joseph Bridau ten thousand francs for a painting because you told me he was a man of talent and insufficiently recognized. Every time I encounter a poor person now, I give him five francs, in your name. Well, what is it this poor old man wants, the man who sees himself as your debtor every time you do him the honor of accepting anything from him? He only wants hope—and what a hope, great God! Isn't it, rather, a certainty of never having anything from you except what my passion elicits? But the flame burning in my heart will always help you in your cruel deceptions. You see me before you, ready to submit to any and every condition you place upon my happiness, my rare pleasures; but at least tell me that on the day when you take possession of your house, you will accept the heart and the servitude of the man who calls himself, for the remainder of his days,
　　Your slave,

Frédéric de Nucingen

　　"Oh, what a bore he is, this old moneybox!" cried Esther, all courtesan again.

　　She picked up a piece of paper and wrote in letters big enough to cover the entire page, the phrase made proverbial by Scribe: "Take my bear."[11]

Fifteen minutes later, in the grip of remorse, Esther wrote him the following letter:

> Monsieur le Baron,
>
> Please pay no attention to the letter you just received from me; I had slipped back into the madness of my youth. Please pardon, Monsieur, a girl who deserves to be nothing more than a slave. I never felt the degradation of my position more powerfully than on the day I was sold to you. You have paid for me, and you should own me. There is nothing more sacred than a dishonorable debt. I have no right to try to "pay it off" by throwing myself into the Seine. But a debt can always be discharged by paying in that frightful money that is only of value to the creditor: you will therefore find me ready at your command. I wish to pay, in a single night, all the sums mortgaged for that fatal moment, and I am sure that an hour with me is worth millions, for the very good reason that it will be the sole one, and the last. After that I will be quit, and I'll be free to leave this life. An honest woman always has the possibility of rebounding from a fall, but we others, we've fallen too far. My resolution on this is firmly fixed, and I ask you to keep this letter; it will testify as to the cause of death of the woman who calls herself, for one day only,
>
> Your servant,
>
> *Esther*

But once that letter had been sent, Esther regretted it. So ten minutes later she wrote the third letter, which follows.

> Forgive me, dear Baron, but it's me yet again. I did not want to mock you, nor did I want to hurt you; I simply want to make you reflect on this simple logic: if we remain in our relationship of father and daughter, you will have a weak pleasure, but a durable one; if, on the other hand, you insist on fulfilling the terms of the contract, you will be mourning me. I don't want to bore you: the day you choose pleasure over happiness will be my final day.
>
> Your daughter,
>
> *Esther*

At the first letter, the baron flew into one of those icy rages that are sometimes the death of a millionaire; he looked at himself in the mirror, and he rang for his servant. "Draw me a bath for my foots!" he shouted at the new valet. While he was taking the foot bath, the second letter came; he read it, and he fell down unconscious. The domestics carried the millionaire to his bed. When the financier had come to, Madame de Nucingen was sitting at the foot of his bed.

"The little whore is right!" she said to him. "Why are you trying to buy love? Do they sell it on the market? Let me see your letter!"

The baron gave her the various drafts he had made, and Madame de Nucingen read them with a smile. Then the third letter arrived.

"What an original she is!" cried the baroness after reading it.

"Vhat shall I do, matame?" the baron asked his wife.

"Wait."

"Vait?" he replied. "But ze needs of nature iss vit'out pity. . . ."

"Wait, my dear," said the baroness. "You've turned out to be excellent for me, and I want to give you good advice."

"Ach, you are good voman!" he said. "Go ahead and make ze debts—I pay zem for you."

"The way you reacted to this slut's letters will move a woman more than spending millions on her, and more than all the letters you could write, no matter how beautifully worded. Make sure she learns about it, but indirectly, and you might have her yet! And by the way, don't feel any scruples—it's not going to kill her," she said, looking her husband over and weighing him up.

But Madame de Nucingen knew nothing of the courtesan's nature.

Peace Treaty between Asia and the Nucingen Firm

"How intellichent iss Matame de Nucingen!" the baron thought when his wife left the room. But the more the banker admired the shrewdness of the baroness's advice, the less he could think of how to put it into practice; he not only felt stupid, but he told himself he was.

The stupidity of financiers, though it may have become proverbial, is really only relative. Our mental faculties are like our bodily ones. The dancer's strength resides in his feet, and the blacksmith's in his arms; the delivery man gets exercise by toting weighty parcels, the singer works his larynx, and the pianist works his wrist. A banker is accustomed to bringing business deals together, studying them, and knowing how to manipulate the various interests, just as a vaudeville writer is accustomed to bringing situations together, studying the characters, and moving the actors through their paces. One should no more demand witty conversation from someone like Baron de Nucingen than one should demand a mathematician produce poetic images. How many times in a single era does one encounter poets who are equally good with prose, or as witty in the affairs of daily life as Madame Cornuel?[12] Buffon was dull, Newton unloved, Lord Byron loved no one but himself, Rousseau was gloomy and half crazy, La Fontaine was absent-minded. Human energy, when equally distributed, produces fools or universal mediocrity; but unequally distributed, it gives rise to the ones we name "geniuses"—a quality that, if it were visible to the eye, we would call a deformity. And the same law applies to the body: perfect beauty is almost always accompanied by coldness or stupidity. That Pascal was both a great geometrician and a great writer, that Beaumarchais was an excellent businessman, that Zamet[13] was a superb courtier: these rare exceptions confirm the principle of the specialization of intelligences. Within the sphere of financial speculation, the banker deploys as much intelligence, know-how, and finesse as a highly capable diplomat does with national interests. But if, once he stepped out of his office, a banker continued to be remarkable, he would be a great man. Nucingen multiplied by the Prince de Ligne, by Mazarin, or by Diderot is a practically impossible human formula, but it has existed nonetheless, and it bore the names of Pericles, Aristotle, Voltaire, and Napoleon. The rays of the imperial sun should not dazzle us into making an error about the private man, for the emperor had charm, he was cultivated and intelligent. Monsieur de Nucingen was entirely a banker, with no invention or original thought outside of his sphere of calculation, and like most bankers he believed in nothing but safe, solid securities. In matters of expertise—when it was a matter of buying a house, taking care of his health, or buying up some curiosity or some estate—he had the good sense of turning, cash in hand, to experts in whatever field it was, choosing the best architect, the best surgeon, the subtlest connoisseur of paintings or statues, the shrewdest lawyer. But since there is no expert to whom one can turn for help with a love affair or a grand passion, a banker handles things quite badly when he falls in love, and always bungles his relations with women. Thus, Nucingen could think of no better plan than to keep doing what he had been doing: giving money to some Frontinus[14] or other, male or female, to act or think in his place. Madame de Saint-Estève was the only one who could possibly put the baroness's idea into practice. Now the banker bitterly regretted having quarreled with the despicable secondhand clothing merchant. Nonetheless, confident in the charisma and charm that his cashbox possessed and in the soothing, sedative qualities of papers bearing Garat's signature,[15] he called for his valet and told him to go to the Rue Neuve-Saint-Marc and see if the loathsome widow would agree to come see him. In Paris it is the passions that bring the extremes together. Vice there is always busily welding together rich and poor, great and small. The empress consults Mademoiselle Lenormand. The great lord, from one century to the next, always has his Ramponneau.[16]

The new valet returned two hours later.

"*Monsieur le baron,*" he said, "Madame Saint-Estève is bankrupt."

"Oh, all ze better!" said the banker joyfully. "I haff her now!"

"The good woman is apparently given to gambling," the valet continued. "And she seems to be under the thumb of a second-class actor from the suburban theaters who, out of a sense of decorum, she passes off as her godson. They say she's an excellent cook, and she's looking for a job."

"Zese damned geniuses of ze lower classes always find ten vays to make money, und twelve vays to spend it," said the baron, unaware that Panurge thought something similar.[17]

He sent the valet off to track Madame Saint-Estève down, and she finally arrived the next day. Asia had interrogated the valet, and the female spy had learned all about the terrible reaction the baron had had to the letters his mistress had sent him.

"Monsieur must really love that woman," said the valet, "because he nearly died. Personally, I advised him not to go back to her, because he'd only get swindled. A woman who's cost *monsieur le baron* five hundred thousand francs already," he continued, "not to mention what he's just spent on that little house on the Rue Saint-Georges! But that woman is after money, and only money. When she was coming out of his rooms, *madame la baronne* laughed and said, 'If this goes on, that slut will make me a widow.'"

"Damn!" exclaimed Asia. "You never kill the goose that lays the golden eggs."

"*Monsieur le baron* is pinning all his hopes on you," said the valet.

"Ah, yes—that's because I know how to manage women!"

"Well, go on in," said the valet, bowing to this woman of such occult powers.

"Well, now," said the false Saint-Estève, entering the sick man's rooms with a humble air, "*monsieur le baron* is experiencing some little difficulties? What can I say—everybody has their troubles. Me too, I've hit a rough patch. The wheel of fortune sure has turned for me these last couple of months! Here I am, looking for a job . . . and you know, neither one of us was being reasonable. If *monsieur le baron* wants to hire me as a chef for Madame Esther, he'd find me the most devoted of the devoted, and I can be pretty useful too when it comes to keeping an eye on Eugénie and madame."

"Zat's not vhat I vant," said the baron. "I haff not succeeded in becoming ze master, und I am being treated like . . ."

"A top, a child's toy," said Asia. "You want to make the others all spin for you, Papa, but now the little one has the upper hand, and she's being naughty with you. . . . Ah, Heaven is just after all!"

"Chust?" exclaimed the baron. "I did not ask you to come here for to hear you preach at me."

"Come on, my boy, a little preaching never hurt anybody. It's like a little spice for people like us, the way sin is for the pious types. Now, let's get to it. Have you been generous? You've paid off her debts. . . ."

"Ja!" said the baron, piteously.

"Good. And you got all her belongings back, which is even better. But look, it's not enough—you've made it so she can eat, and that's fine, but creatures like her, they want so much money they can just *burn* it. . . ."

"I am making for her a nice surprise, over on ze Rue Saint-Georges. . . . She knows about it," said the baron. "But I do not vant to be made a fool!"

"Drop her, then."

"But I am affrate she vould let me," cried the baron.

"And we want to get a little something for our money, don't we," said Asia. "Let's see—I hear we've bilked millions from the general public, isn't that right, my little friend? I hear twenty-five million." At this, the baron could not repress a smile. "Well, you're going to have to let go of one. . . ."

"I'd be glat to," said the baron, "but soon as I giff one, I vill be asked for a second!"

"Yes, I see," said Asia. "You don't want to go to point B for fear you'll have to go on all the way to point Z. But Esther is basically honest. . . ."

"Ach yes, very honest girl!" cried the banker. "Und she is ready to do ze duty, but she sees it only as paying off ein debt."

"So, in short, she doesn't want to be your mistress; the idea is repugnant to her. Well, I can understand it, because she's a girl who's always had all her whims catered to, and when all your life you've only known charming young men, you're bound to balk a little around an old man. . . . And you're not handsome, you're fat as Louis XVIII, and you're not the wittiest either, just like all the others who've spent their lives chasing money instead of women. Well, if you're willing to put up six hundred thousand francs," said Asia, "I'll see to it that she turns into everything you want her to be."

"Six hundred t'ousand francs!" exclaimed the baron, taking a step backward. "Esther hass already cost me a million!"

"Isn't happiness worth *sixteen* hundred thousand, you old rake? You know other men right now, in these times, who've certainly gone through one or two millions with their mistresses. I even know women who've cost men their lives, women for whom men were ready and willing to let their heads thump down into the basket. . . . You heard of that doctor who poisoned his friend? He needed to get his hands on serious money to make his woman happy."[18]

"Ja, I know zat, but zo I am a man in luff, I am not stupid—at least, I do smart t'ing, alvays giff her my vallet. . . ."

"Listen, *monsieur le baron,*" said Asia, striking a Semiramis-style pose,[19] "you've already been swindled enough. As sure as my name's Saint-Estève, I'm going to be on your side in this business we're starting."

"Goot! Und I vill pay you."

"I know you will, because I've already shown you that I know how to get revenge when I want to. Another thing you need to know, Papa," she said, giving him a terrifying look, "is that I know how to see to it that Esther is snuffed out just as easy as snuffing out a candle. And I know this woman! Once the little slut finally lets you have it, she's going to be even more necessary to you than she is now. You've paid up, and you've been led around a little by the nose, but you did finally cough up. You know me: I live up to my agreements, don't I? Well, listen closely then, because I'm going to make a deal with you."

"I listen."

"You get me the job as cook for madame, you hire me for ten years and I get a thousand francs a year in salary, you'll pay the last five years' worth in advance—just a little something to show your good faith, eh? Once I'm moved back in with madame, I'll get her to make certain concessions. For instance, you have delivered to her, say, some splendid outfit from Madame Auguste, who knows all madame's tastes and fashions, and you give orders for the new coach to be at the door and ready at four o'clock. After the Bourse, you get up in there with her, and the two of you go make the circuit in the Bois de Boulogne. Well, doing that is her telling the world that she's your mistress, for all Paris to see and know about. . . . A hundred thousand francs. . . . You come and dine with her—and don't worry, I know how to put on a dinner like that—and afterward you take her to a play, to the Variétés, in a prominent box, and next thing you know, everyone in Paris is saying, 'Look at that old crook Nucingen with his mistress. . . .' Which is pretty flattering, yes? All those benefits are included for that hundred thousand francs, and I'm good for it . . . In a week, if you do it my way, you'll be making good progress."

"Yes, but it cost me hundred t'ousand francs . . ."

"Now, in the second week," Asia continued, seeming not to have heard that pitiful exclamation, "madame will decide, encouraged by these preliminaries, to leave her little apartment and move into the house you're offering. Your Esther has been back among society again, she's seen some of her old friends, and she wants to shine, and she'll be able to do it up proud in your little palace! Perfectly natural. . . . Another hundred thousand francs! Damn. . . . But now you're comfortable, at home, and Esther is compromised—she belongs to you. That leaves just one little thing, just one trifle, though for you it's the main thing, you old elephant! (Oh look, the big fat monster—that made him open his eyes!) Well, just leave it to me; I'll take care of it. Four hundred thousand . . . but you don't have to pay for that till the day after, old boy. How's that for honesty? . . . I've got more trust in you than you do in me. If I can get madame willing to show herself in public as your mistress, to compromise herself, to show she's taking everything you're offering, and maybe even today, then you'll trust me to show you the way into the Great Saint Bernard Pass. It's not easy, either! . . . If you want to get your artillery through, you're going to have work harder than the first consul did going over the Alps."[20]

"Vhy is so hard?"

"Her heart is just filled up with love, *rasibus*—as you'd say, you people who know Latin," said Asia. "She thinks she's the Queen of Sheba because she's been bathing herself in all the great sacrifices she's made for her lover . . . women like her get ideas like that in their heads. But then, my little friend, we have to do her justice; it's a nice thought, eh? I wouldn't be surprised if the poor clown did die of grief once she finally was your mistress, but then, you know what I personally find reassuring, and I say this to encourage you, is that there's still plenty of whore in that girl."

"I t'ink," said the baron, who was listening quietly and admiringly to everything Asia said, "dat you haff ze genius for corruption, like I haff ze knack uff ze bank."

"So are we agreed, my little pup?" asked Asia.

"I say ja to fifty t'ousand francs, but not to hundred! . . . Und I giff you five hundred t'ousand ze morning after my victory."

"All right. I'm going to go get to work," said Asia. "Oh, and you can come over any time you like!" she added in an exaggeratedly respectful tone. "Monsieur will find madame as sweet as a kitten, and perhaps disposed to be nice to him."

"Go zen, go, my good voman," said the banker, rubbing his hands together. And after giving a big smile to the hideous mulatto, he thought, "How smart I am, to haff lots uff money!"

And with that, he hopped out of bed, headed off to his office, and took up the management again of all his immense business affairs, all with a light heart.

An Abdication

Nothing could have been more deadly for Esther than the plan Nucingen had just adopted. In defending herself against infidelity, the poor courtesan was fighting for her life. Carlos called this entirely natural self-defense "prudishness." Now Asia, taking all the necessary precautions, went quickly to inform Carlos of the conversation she had just had with the baron, and the profit she had got out of it. His fury was as terrible as the man himself: he immediately got into a cab, had the blinds lowered, and went directly to Esther's, pulling off the street and into the courtyard. Still almost white with anger, the double forger went in to the poor girl; she had been standing up when he entered, but now she crumpled down into a chair, her legs giving way.

"What's the matter, monsieur?" she asked, trembling all over.

"Leave us alone, Europe," he said to the chambermaid.

Esther looked up at her like a baby seeking its mother when an assassin, murder in his heart, has come between them..

When he was alone with Esther, Carlos said, "Do you know where you're sending Lucien?"

"Where?" she asked, her voice weak, daring only a glance at her executioner.

"The place I came from, my little jewel."

Esther felt everything was turning red as she looked at him.

"To the penal colonies," he added, in a low voice.

Esther's eyes closed; her legs stretched out before her, and her arms went limp; she turned white. The man rang, and Prudence returned.

"Get her conscious again," he said coldly. "I'm not done with her."

He paced back and forth while he waited. Prudence/Europe was obliged to come and ask monsieur to carry Esther to her bed; he picked her up with an ease that suggested his athletic strength. They had to send to the pharmacy for the strongest resources they could supply to bring Esther back to the consciousness of her ills. An hour later the poor girl was finally in a condition to listen to the living nightmare seated at the foot of her bed and staring at her with a fixed intensity, his eyes like molten lead.

"Well, little one," he went on, "Lucien finds himself at a crossroads, between a splendid life, a life of honors and happiness, a worthy life, and the dirty pond full of mud and rocks into which he was about to jump when I found him. The Grandlieu people are demanding that our dear boy own a million-franc estate before being given the title of marquis and before they will give him the hand of that tall broomstick named Clotilde, with the aid of whom he will rise to power. Thanks to the two of us, Lucien has just acquired his maternal manor, the old Rubempré château, for a song, only thirty thousand francs, but his lawyer, negotiating excellently well, managed to buy up an additional million in adjoining properties, and we've paid three hundred thousand down on that. The château, the fees, the money paid out to the people who helped us conceal the nature of the purchase from the locals ate up the rest. Now it's true that we have a hundred thousand invested, and within a few months we'll double or triple that, but even so there'll still be four hundred thousand needed. . . . And in three days Lucien will return from Angoulême, because we mustn't let people think he came into this money by finding it in your mattress. . . ."

"Oh, no!" she said, lifting up her eyes with a sublime effort.

"So I ask you, Is this the time to be scaring the baron off?" he asked quietly. "You almost killed him the other day! He fainted like a woman when he read your second letter. You have a fine writing style, and I offer you my compliments on it. But if the baron had died, what would become of us? When Lucien walks out of Saint-Thomas-d'Aquin, son-in-law to the Duc de Grandlieu, then if you want to go slip into the Seine . . . well, come on, my love, I offer you my hand—we can jump in together. It's one way to end. But think just a little! Wouldn't it be better to live on, saying to yourself every single hour of the day, 'That brilliant fortune, that happy family' . . . because of course he'll have children . . . children! Have you ever thought about what a pleasure it would be to run your fingers through his children's hair?"

Esther closed her eyes and shuddered a little.

"Well, imagine looking on at that great edifice of happiness and being able to say, 'That's *my* work!'"

He paused, and the two of them looked at each other.

"This is what I've been trying to build, from the despair I encountered when he was about to throw himself in the water," Carlos continued. "Does that make me an egotist? Look, look how a person can love! People only feel this kind of devotion for kings; but I have a sacred king, my Lucien! They could rivet me for the rest of my days back into my chains, but I think I'd be able to accept it happily, saying to myself, '*He's* at the ball, *he's* at Court.' My soul and my mind would triumph while this old rag of a body was thrown to the cops! You're just a miserable female, and you love the way females do! But love, for a courtesan, like any other degraded creature, ought to be a way to become a mother, despite the wretched nature that renders you sterile! If they ever stripped away the covering of the abbé Carlos Herrera to find the convict I was before, do you know what I'd do to avoid compromising Lucien?"

Esther waited for him to go on, in a kind of anxiety.

"Well," he said after a pause, "I'd die the way the blacks do, by swallowing my tongue. And you, with your little theatrics, you're helping them track me down! And what have I asked of you? To put the guise of La Torpille back on for six months, for six weeks, and use it to help us twist a million out of him. . . . Lucien will never forget you! Men don't forget a person who's reawakened in their memory by the very happiness they feel each morning, awakening to find themselves wealthy. Lucien is worth more than you are. He began by falling in love with Coralie, and she died—fine. But when he didn't have even enough money to bury her, he didn't do like you just now, he didn't faint, even if he is a poet. He wrote six racy drinking songs, and that got him three hundred francs, with which he could pay for Coralie's funeral. I have those songs; I know them by heart. All right, then—write your own songs, be gay, be mad! Be irresistible and . . . insatiable! Do you understand me? Don't make me come here and have to talk like this again. Now, kiss your papa. Farewell. . . ."

Half an hour later, when Europe came into her mistress's room, she found her kneeling before a crucifix in that pose that the most devout of painters have given to Moses before the burning bush, trying to convey his most profound and complete adoration of Jehovah. After having said her last prayers, Esther renounced her beautiful life and the honor she had been constructing for herself along with her reputation, and her virtues, and her love. She stood up.

"Oh, madame! You will never be as beautiful again as you are right now!" cried Prudence Servien, astounded at the sublimity of her mistress.

And she quickly turned the tall dressing mirror so the poor girl could see herself. Her eyes still revealed a little of that soul that had just taken heavenly flight. Her Jewish coloring seemed aglow. Damp with the tears that her fiery prayer had nearly burned away, her eyelashes resembled foliage after a summer rain, the sun of pure love shining in them for the last time. Her lips retained something of her last invocation to the angels, from whom no doubt she had borrowed the martyr's crown while offering up her spotless life. She had, in short, the majesty that shone from Mary, Queen of Scots, at the moment she said farewell to her crown, to the earth, and to love.

"I would have liked for Lucien to see me like this," she said, stifling a sigh. "But now," she continued in a vibrant voice, "let's have ourselves some *fun*. . . ."

The word stunned Europe; it was as if she'd just heard an angel blaspheme.

"What? You're looking at me as if I've got cloves in my mouth instead of teeth. From now on I'm nothing but an infamous and filthy creature, a *thief*, and now I'm awaiting my lord and master. So get a warm bath ready for me, and lay out my things. It's noon, and the baron will undoubtedly come after the market closes; I'm going to let him know that I'm waiting for him, and I want Asia to prepare a meal that's a bit special—I plan to make this man wild. . . . So let's go, go, my girl. We're going to have a laugh—that is, we're going to *work*."

She sat down at her table, and wrote the following letter:

> My friend, if the cook you sent me hadn't already been in service to me before, I would have thought your purpose was to remind me how many times you fainted the other day when you got my three little notes. (But what can I say? I had an attack of nerves that day, and I kept going over memories from my miserable past life.) But I know Asia's sincerity. And I will cease repenting having caused you such trouble, since it served to prove how much I really mean to you. That's the way we poor creatures are: real affection moves us more than spending wild amounts on us does. And I've always feared being something like the rack on which you'd hang your vanities. It frustrated me to think I was nothing more to you than that. Yes, despite all your fine protests to the contrary, I believed that you really saw me as nothing more than a bought item. Well, now that will change, and you'll find me behaving like a good girl—but on the condition that you agree always to obey me a little. If this letter does you more good than one of your prescriptions, you can prove it by coming to see me after the Bourse closes. If you do, you will find, fully armed and wearing your gifts, the one who calls herself, for the rest of her life, your pleasure machine,
>
> *Esther*

At the Bourse, Baron Nucingen was so witty, so pleased, so easy-going, so ready to allow himself to make little jokes, that du Tillet and the Kellers couldn't help but ask him what the reason was.

"I am luffed . . . und ve vill soon haff zat housevarming," he added to du Tillet.

"How much did it cost you?" asked François Keller brusquely, for people said that Madame Colleville had cost him twenty-five thousand francs a year.

"Neffer zis voman, an anchel! Neffer zis voman she ask me for efen two sous."

"Of course—they never do," said du Tillet. "It's precisely in order to ask for nothing themselves that women provide themselves with aunts or mothers."

Esther Resurfaces in Paris

Between the Bourse and the Rue Taitbout the baron called out seven times to his driver, "Ve aren't moofing! Put ze vip to ze horse!"

He climbed the stairs lightly, and for the first time found his mistress as beautiful as those women whose sole occupation is caring for their clothes and their beauty. Just out of the bath, the flower was fresh enough to arouse desires in a Robert d'Arbrissel.[21] Esther was dressed informally but exquisitely. A jacket of black rep trimmed with pink silk opened to reveal a gray satin dress, the same outfit that would later be worn by the lovely Amigo in *I Puritani*.[22] A lace kerchief fell across her shoulders, and the sleeves of her dress were banded by piping, which had the effect of dividing the billows of the sleeve, a fashion women had recently adopted, the enormous leg-of-lamb sleeves of the past having come to be seen as monstrosities. Esther had fixed, upon her magnificent hair, a bonnet in the style called *à la folle*,[23] which hovered on the edge of falling off but did not fall off, making her coiffure seem a little disorderly, a little uncombed, but at the same time the observer could not fail to see the white furrow of her scalp, revealing the truth that this was perfectly and carefully parted hair.

"Isn't it a crime to see madame looking so beautiful in a drawing room as passé as this one?" said Europe to the baron, opening the door onto the room.

"Ja. Vell, let's go Rue Saint-Georges!" said the baron, stopping short, stunned, looking like a hunting dog spotting a partridge. "Ze vezzer iss maknifichent, ve can stroll down Champs-Élysées, und Madame Saint-Estève und Eugénie vill dransbord all your clozzing, your linen, und efen our dinner to ze Rue Saint-Georges!"

"I'll do anything you wish," said Esther, "if you'll do me the pleasure of calling my cook Asia and Eugénie, Europe. I've given nicknames to all my women servants in the past, all the way back to the first two I had, and I hate changing . . ."

"Ja. Asia. Europe." The baron repeated the names, with a laugh. "You are funny. You haff big imagination. . . . I vould haff eaten many dinners before I call a cook Asia."

"That's just the way we are, having our little jokes. After all, can't a poor girl like me be fed by Asia and dressed by Europe, when you live off everybody? Is it just a myth, or is it true that some girls want the whole world? Well, I'm only asking for half."

"Oh, zat Madame Saint-Estève! Vot a voman she iss!" thought the baron, delighted with the change in Esther.

"Dear Europe, I need a hat," said Esther. "I should wear the black satin one, the one with the pink lining and the lace trim."

"Madame Thomas hasn't sent it yet. . . . Come on, baron, let's move along! Get those paws up in the air! You're about to begin your servitude, or in other words, you're about to be very happy. But happiness takes labor! . . . You have your coach here, so go to the shop of Madame Thomas," Europe said to the baron. "You can have your manservant go in and ask for the bonnet for Madame Van Bogseck. . . . And above all," she went on in a whisper, "bring back the finest bouquet Paris has ever seen. It's winter here, so try to get some tropical flowers."

The baron went down and said to his servant, "Go to ze shop uff Madame Thomas." The coachman took them to the shop of a famous pastry cook. "No, iss place zey sell fashions, not cakes," said the baron, going off himself to the Palais-Royal, where, at Madame Prévôt's, he had them put together a bouquet costing five louis, while his servant went off to the modist's shop.

The casual observer making his way around Paris might ask himself who they are, the fools who buy the kind of outlandish flowers displayed in the shop window of the illustrious florist, or who buy the early fruits and vegetables at Chevet's, the only place other than the Rocher-de-Cancale that offers a true, and quite delicious, Review of Two Worlds.[24] A hundred and one passions just like that of the baron awaken every morning in Paris, impelling men to prove themselves by offering their beloveds the kind of gifts that even queens dare not indulge in—and they offer them to the kind of whores who, as Asia would say, like to *shine* a little. Without a grasp on that particular detail, an honest bourgeois wife would never understand how a whole fortune can slip through the hands of these creatures whose social function, according to the Fourier system, is perhaps to rectify the havoc wreaked by Avarice and Cupidity. Dissipations like these perhaps are, to the Body Social, what the lancet is to the plethoric body. In two months Nucingen had showered more than two hundred thousand francs on the business.

When the aging lover returned, night was falling and the bouquet was useless. The time one goes down the Champs-Élysées, during the winter months, is from two to four. Still, the carriage would be useful in moving Esther from the Rue Taitbout to the Rue Saint-Georges, where she took possession of her "leetle palace." Never, we must say, had Esther been the object of quite such worship nor of quite this level of profusion, and she was surprised; but she kept it hidden, refusing, the way ungrateful royalty always does, to show the slightest surprise. When you enter into Saint Peter's in Rome, in order to help you appreciate the extent and the height of this queen of all cathedrals, they draw your attention to the little finger on a statue of I don't know what length, and it seems to you just like a real little finger. Now, there have been so many criticisms of the kind of descriptions that are nonetheless necessary to anyone writing the history of our era that we must in this case imitate the Roman guide. So, as they entered the dining room, the baron could not keep from having Esther feel the material of the window curtains, draped in regal abundance, lined with white silk moiré and decorated with a braid worthy of a Portuguese princess's corsage. The material was a kind of silk purchased in Canton, where Chinese patience had learned how to depict Asian birds with a perfection unmatched anywhere else, unless it is in the tapestries of the Middle Ages or in the prayerbook of Charles V, the pride of the Imperial Library of Vienna.

"Ziss cost two t'ousand francs per ell, bought by a lord who took it back vith him all ze way from India."

"Quite nice. Charming! What a pleasure it will be to drink champagne here," said Esther. "The foam won't get on the windows!"

"But oh, madame," said Europe, "just look at this carpet. . . ."

Nucingen said, "Ziss carpet vass designed for ze Duc de Torlonia, friend of mine, who t'ought it too expensive, so I buy it for you, becauss you are a queen!"[25]

By chance this carpet, the product of one of our most ingenious designers, fit in well with the whimsicalities of the Chinese curtains. The walls, painted by Schinner and Léon de Lora, portrayed sensual scenes thrown into relief by sculpted ebony; having been bought from Sommerard for much gold, they formed panels, between which narrow filets of gold subtly caught the light.[26] From this you may judge of the rest.

"You did well bringing me here," said Esther. "It'll take me at least a week to get used to my house, and not to feel like some kind of social climber in it. . . ."

"'Mine house'!" the baron repeated joyfully. "So you vill accept it?"

"But of course—yes, a thousand times yes, you stupid animal," she said with a smile.

"'Hanimal' vould haff been enough. . . ."

"Well, 'stupid' is there just like a kind of caress," she said, looking at him.

The poor lynx took Esther's hand and placed it against his heart: he was animal enough to feel, but too stupid to find a thing to say.

"Look, see how it beats . . . it beats chust for leetle vord of tenderness. . . ." he said. And with that he led his goddess (which sounded more like "coddess") into her bedroom.

"Oh, madame!" exclaimed Eugénie. "I can't stay in here. I couldn't possibly keep from getting into that bed."

"Well, I guess I'd better pay you for this at once. . . . Come on, you big elephant, after dinner we'll go to the theater together. I've got a yen to see a play."

It had been exactly five years since Esther had been in a theater. Just then, all Paris was streaming to the Porte-Saint-Martin to see one of those plays where the actors convey a powerful impression of reality, *Richard d'Arlington*.[27] Like all artless souls, Esther enjoyed being made to shiver with fear as much as being brought to tears. "We're going to see Frédérick Lemaître," she said. "I adore his acting!"

"Ach, zat iss bad play," said Nucingen, who felt he was being forced to go out and be seen in public.

But the baron sent his manservant to get tickets for one of the two stage-level boxes. Now, this is another originality you find in Paris! When Success, with its feet of clay, fills a theater's auditorium, there is always a box at stage level available ten minutes before the curtain rises; the directors reserve it for themselves when it's not taken by some infatuated type like Nucingen. That box is just like those early fruits you can get at Chevet's, a tax levied upon the Olympian fantasies in which Paris abounds.

It is pointless to describe the tableware. Nucingen had combined three services: the daily, the special, and the very best. The dessert service from the very best set was—all of it, plates and serving dishes alike—sculpted silver. The banker, to avoid appearing to overwhelm the table with gold and silver, had combined each service with Meissen porcelain of the most charming fragility, which in fact cost more than the silverware. As for the linen, the products of England, Flanders, and France all competed for perfection with their flowered damask.

At dinner, it was the baron's turn to be surprised when he tasted the cuisine of Asia.

"Now I unnerstand," he said, "vhy you vant to call her Asia—zis cuisine, iss Asiatic."

"Ah, I'm beginning to think maybe he does love me," Esther said to Europe. "He just said something that actually sounded like a word."

"Vords! I know many vords!" he said.

"My, he's even more of a Turcaret than they told me," cried the courtesan, laughing at that response, worthy of the naïve sayings for which the banker was famous.

The dinner was prepared using the kind of spices that would give the baron indigestion and send him home early, and it was, therefore, the only pleasure he enjoyed on that first night with Esther. At the play he had to drink an enormous number of glasses of sugared water, leaving Esther alone during the intervals. By a chance that was after all too predictable to be really called chance, Tullia, Mariette, and Madame du Val-Noble were also attending the play that night. *Richard d'Arlington* was a real hit, and deserved to be, the kind of phenomenon only seen in Paris. Watching this play, all the men entertained the thought that one could throw one's legitimate wife out a window, while all the women enjoyed seeing themselves depicted as being unjustly oppressed. The women thought, "It's awful, the way they push us. . . . But it does happen often enough!" Now, a creature of beauty like Esther's, and dressed as Esther was, cannot *glow* like that with impunity in the stage-level box of the Porte-Saint-Martin. And so, by the second act, the box where the two dancers were sitting was in an uproar, caused by the realization that the beautiful unknown was in fact La Torpille.

"Where did she come from?" Mariette said to Madame du Val-Noble. "I thought she'd drowned ages ago. . . ."

"Is that her? She looks thirty-seven times younger and more beautiful than she did six years ago."

"Maybe she conserved herself by having herself packed in ice, like Madame d'Espard and Madame Zayonchek," said the Comte de Brambourg, who had escorted the three women to the play and was now with them in their orchestra-level box. "Isn't she the rat you were going to send me to try to hoodwink my uncle?" he asked Tullia.

"Exactly," Tullia said to the other dancer. "Du Bruel, go closer and see if it's really her."

"Isn't she all high and mighty!" cried Madame du Val-Noble, making use of an admirable expression drawn from the vocabulary of whores.

"Oh, she's got a right to be," said the Comte de Brambourg; "because she's with a friend of mine, the Baron de Nucingen. I'll go."

"Can that be the great Joan of Arc who's conquered Nucingen, the one they've been boring us with for three months?" asked Mariette.

"Good evening, my dear baron," said Philippe Bridau, walking into Nucingen's box. "So, have you and Mademoiselle Esther got married? . . . Mademoiselle, I'm the poor officer you once helped out of a jam, at Issoudun . . . Philippe Bridau."

"Never heard of you," said Esther, training her opera glasses on the house.

"Vell, mademoiselle," said the baron, "is not to be called Esther now. She hass taken ze name of Champy, for a leetle estate I haff bought her. . . ."

"While you do arrange things so very well, these ladies are saying that Madame de Champy is 'all high and mighty.' . . . If you choose not to remember me, do deign to recognize Mariette, Tullia, and Madame du Val-Noble," said the upstart, whose climb had been facilitated by the Duc de Maufrigneuse speaking favorably of him to the dauphin.[28]

"If those ladies are polite to me, I'm disposed to be the same to them," Madame de Champy replied dryly.

"Excellent!" said Philippe. "They're very good—in fact, they called you Joan of Arc."

"Vell, if zese laties vill keep you company," said Nucingen, "I'll go home, becauss I haff eat too much. Ze carriage vill be zere for you und your people. . . . Oh, damn zat Asia!"

"You're leaving me alone, and it's our first time out together!" cried Esther. "No you don't. You need to go down with the ship. I need my man with me when I leave. What if I were insulted by someone—I'd look for help, and who'd be there for me?"

The egoism of the aged millionaire had to yield to the obligations of the lover. The baron suffered, and he stayed on. Esther had her reasons for hanging on to "her man." If her old friends showed up, they wouldn't dare question her as closely if he were present as they would if she were alone. Philippe Bridau hurried over to the dancers' box to update them on the situation.

"Ah, so she's inherited *my* place on the Rue Saint-Georges!" said Madame du Val-Noble bitterly, for nowadays she found herself "on foot," as the saying goes.

"Probably," said the colonel. "Du Tillet told me that the baron spent three times what your poor Falleix did on the place."

"Let's go see her!" said Tullia.

"Oh no," replied Mariette. "She's looking too beautiful—I'll wait and see her at her place."

"I think I look good enough to risk it," Tullia replied.

The hardy first dancer went forth, therefore, during the interval, and renewed acquaintance with Esther, who spoke only in generalities.

"But where have you been, my dear girl?" the dancer asked, overcome by curiosity.

"Oh, I stayed five years in a château up in the Alps with an English-man who was jealous as a tiger or a nabob[29]—in fact I called him my 'nabot,' because he was as short as the Bailli de Ferrette.[30] Then I landed with a banker—from a savage to a sap, as Florine might say. Anyway, now that I'm back in Paris, I plan to have a real carnival of fun. I'll be keeping open house. I have to make up for five years of solitude, and I'm starting now. Five years of English—it's too much. The posters promise you can pick it up in six weeks."

"Was it the baron who gave you that lace?"

"No, that's left over from the nabob . . . Oh, what a time I had of it! He was thin as the smile of a friend when you've had a success, and I thought surely he'd be dead in ten months. But oh, no—he was strong as one of those Alps. Don't believe anyone who says he's got a liver problem. . . . But look, I don't want to talk about livers. I believed in the proverbs too much. . . . That nabob robbed me. He died without a will, and the family tossed me out the door as if I had the plague. That's why I said to fatso here, 'Pay for two!' You've got good reason to call me Joan of Arc—I lose England! And I might end up burned at the stake."

"Burned with love!" said Tullia.

The word made Esther pause, dreamily. "And alive!" she quickly added.

The baron laughed at all this crude joking, but without really under-standing all of it, so his little bursts of laughter went off like forgotten squibs after a fireworks show.

We all live in one kind of sphere or another, and the inhabitants of all the various spheres are endowed with an equal dose of curiosity. The next day, at the Opéra, the saga of Esther's return was the talk of the backstages. The next morning, between two and four o'clock, everyone in the world of Champs-Élysées Paris knew about La Torpille, and knew as well that she had been the object of Baron de Nucingen's passion.

"Do you realize," Blondet said to de Marsay as the two stood in the foyer of the Opéra, "that La Torpille disappeared the morning after we recognized her here as the mistress of our little Rubempré?"

Paris is just like provincial towns in this: everybody knows every-thing. The police on the Rue de Jérusalem[31] are not as efficient as Soci-ety is, for there everyone is unknowingly spying on everyone else. This is why Carlos so quickly understood the danger of Lucien's position during and after the Rue Taitbout.

A Woman on Foot

There is no situation more terrible than the one in which Madame du Val-Noble now found herself, and the phrase "on foot" renders it perfectly. Women like her have a certain insouciance, coupled with an eagerness to spend money, and these two traits combine to keep them from thinking about their future. In their extraordinary world—much more comical and witty than you might expect—women who are not endowed with that positive beauty, the kind that is always the same and impossible to miss, women who only attract lovers out of caprice, are the only ones who do think about their old age and lay up a fortune for themselves. But the more beautiful they are, the less careful they are. "Are you afraid of turning ugly? Is that why you've started saving?" said Florine to Mariette, and this may suggest one motive of their prodigality. In the kind of case where a stockbroker kills himself, or a big spender comes to the bottom of his money bags, these women fall, with frightening rapidity, from the heights of opulence to the most abject poverty. Then it is that they throw themselves into the arms of the secondhand merchant, selling off at pathetic prices their finest jewelry; then it is that they run up debts, especially if by doing so they can return to the luxury they've had to abandon—a little cashbox to draw on. These heights and depths in their lives explain why an affair with them is so expensive, and why it is, in reality, almost always "fixed up" (another term from their vocabulary), as Asia had fixed Nucingen up with Esther. And thus those who know their Paris will understand the reality of the situation at once when they see, on that busy, noisy bazaar called the Champs-Élysées, a certain woman in a hired cab who, six months before, was riding in a stunningly luxurious carriage. "When you've come down to Sainte-Pélagie, you need to know how to bounce back up into the Bois de Boulogne," Florine said, laughing together with Blondet over the little Vicomte de Portenduère.[52] Some shrewd women will never risk the contrast. They bury themselves in hideous furnished rooms in boarding-houses, or they seek to expiate their profusion by the kind of privations travelers lost in some Sahara might undergo; but they never acquire the slightest taste for thrift. They risk going out to masked balls, or take a trip into the provinces, or, on fine days, show themselves by going for a stroll on the boulevards. Sometimes they find a certain devotion and

kindness among themselves, of the sort often found among the pro-
scribed classes. For a woman in a good situation, there's no cost in helping out someone else, for she can say to herself, "That could be me by
next Sunday." But the most effective help is the kind given by the secondhand wardrobe dealer. When that usurer finds herself the creditor, she
busies herself and works on the heartstrings of old men in favor of the
indebted creature in thin boots and a hat. Unable to foresee the disaster
that befell one of the richest, cleverest stockbrokers around, Madame du
Val-Noble was thrown into utter confusion. She had made use of Falleix's
money for all her whims, and counted entirely on him for practicalities
and for her future. "How on earth," she said to Mariette, "could I have
expected something like that from a man who seemed such a good sort?"
In nearly every social class, the "good sort" is the generous man, the one
who hands around a few écus here and there without expecting any
repayment, who conducts himself at all times according to the rules of a
certain delicacy, above and beyond any vulgar, constrained, ordinary
morality. Some men who are thought to be virtuous and trustworthy, like
Nucingen, have turned out to ruin their benefactors, while some men
who have come out of the correctional institutions behave with complete
integrity toward a woman. Complete virtue, the kind of thing Molière's
Alceste dreamed of, is extremely rare, and yet one does meet with it
everywhere, even in Paris. Being a "good sort" is the product of a certain
grace in one's character, but it proves nothing. A man may be like that
the way a cat may have smooth fur, the way a slipper fits on a foot. Thus,
given the way the "good sort" is conceived among kept women, Falleix
ought to have warned his mistress of what was coming, and he ought to
have left her something to live on. D'Estourny, that gallant crook, was a
"good sort"; he cheated at cards, but he put aside thirty thousand francs
for his mistress. When people made accusations against him at extrava-
gant suppers, women replied, "That doesn't matter at all! . . . You can say
whatever you like, but Georges was a good sort, with good manners, and
he deserved better luck!" Whores couldn't care less about the law, but
they adore a certain kind of delicacy; they know how to sell themselves,
as Esther did, for a secret ideal, which is religion to them. After saving,
with great difficulty, one or two pieces of jewelry from the general wreck,
Madame du Val-Noble now had to endure the terrible weight of the accusation: "She was the ruin of Falleix!" She had reached the age of thirty,
and though she was still in the full flower of her beauty, she could nonetheless easily be taken for older, for in such a crisis all a woman's rivals
now turn against her. Mariette, Florine, and Tullia certainly continued

to invite their friend to dinner with them, and gave her what help they could; but not knowing how big her debts were, they dared not sound the depths of that abyss. The space of six years now separating La Torpille from Madame du Val-Noble was too large a gap in the fluctuating tides of Parisian life for the woman "on foot" to approach the woman in the carriage; but Val-Noble also knew that Esther was too generous not to think, from time to time, about what she had "inherited" from her, and thus she hoped to run into her in a way that would seem to be mere chance, no matter how stage-managed it actually might be. In order to help that chance meeting along, Madame du Val-Noble dressed every day most respectably and went strolling along the Champs-Élysées on the arm of Théodore Gaillard, the man she would later marry and who, in her present distress, was conducting himself very admirably with his old mistress, giving her theater tickets and inviting her to all the *parties*.[33] She told herself that one of these days she would surely run into Esther, and they would find themselves face to face at last. Esther had Paccard as her driver, for over the last five days the house had been organized by Asia, Europe, and Paccard, following the instructions of Carlos, in such a way as to make the Rue Saint-Georges home a virtually impregnable fortress. Peyrade, for his part, seething with a deep hatred and desire for vengeance, and moved above all by the desire to get his dear daughter Lydie well set up, took to strolling also along the Champs-Élysées, when he heard from Contenson that Nucingen's mistress had finally emerged into the light. Peyrade disguised himself perfectly as an Englishman, and could imitate the kind of French that adds those babbling sounds the English introduce into our language; he knew English so well, and so perfectly understood the affairs of that country, that the Paris police had sent him, in 1779 and 1786, to London, where he maintained his English guise among the ambassadors there without ever arousing any suspicions. Peyrade had a lot in common with Musson, the famous hoaxer,[34] and could disguise himself so artfully that one day even Contenson did not recognize him. Accompanied by Contenson, who had disguised himself as a mulatto, Peyrade examined, with that eye that always seemed inattentive but in fact never missed a thing, Esther and her people. He naturally therefore found himself on the side path where the people in the carriages get out to stroll when the weather is fine and dry, on the very day that Esther ran into Madame du Val-Noble there. Peyrade, followed by his mulatto in livery, was walking along without any affectation, like a genuine nabob thinking only of himself, on the same path as the two women, and close enough to be able to catch a few words from their conversation.

"Well, my dear friend," Esther was saying to Madame du Val-Noble, "come and visit me. Nucingen owes it to himself not to leave a little something for the mistress of the man who was his chief agent. . . ."

"All the more because they say he's the one who ruined him," said Théodore Gaillard, "so we might even consider a little *blackmail*. . . ."

"He's dining with me tomorrow. Come, my friend," said Esther. Then she whispered, "I can do whatever I like—he hasn't been able to get any yet." With that, she put her gloved forefinger behind the prettiest of her teeth, and made that clicking gesture that signifies, in the most vivid way, not one bit of it!

"Ah, you've got him then. . . ."

"So far, my dear, he's only paid my debts."

"You're in his pockets!" cried Suzanne du Val-Noble.

"Oh!" exclaimed Esther, "my debts were enough to shake a minister of finances. Now, before midnight tonight, I plan to get him to commit to thirty thousand a year. . . . Oh, he's charming enough, so I really can't complain. . . . It's going well. In a week we'll have the housewarming party, and you'll be there. The morning after that, he'll give me the deed to the Rue Saint-Georges house, and you can't live in a house like that without your own income of thirty thousand, money you can get hold of if some trouble comes up. I've known poverty, and I don't want any more of it. It's like one of those acquaintances you drop as soon as you can."

"You're the one who used to say, 'I'm all the fortune I need!' How you've changed!" Suzanne cried.

"Well, maybe it was the Swiss air; it makes you a little thrifty. . . . But look, why don't you try it! Find yourself a Swiss, and maybe you can turn him into a husband! Because they don't know about women like us. . . . In any case, you'd come back home in love with income, the kind you track in a big ledger book, and that's an honest, good sort of love! Goodbye for now."

Esther got back up into her fine carriage, pulled by the most magnificent pair of dappled gray horses there were to be seen anywhere in Paris.

"The woman who got into the carriage," Peyrade then said in English to Contenson, "is good-looking, but I'm especially attracted to the one who's walking. Go follow her and find out who she is."

"Let me tell you what that Englishman just said," Théodore Gaillard said, translating for Madame du Val-Noble.

Before taking the risk of speaking English, Peyrade had dropped a word or two in that language and noticed a little reaction on Théodore Gaillard's face, indicating that the journalist did in fact know the language. Now Madame du Val-Noble proceeded very slowly toward her home on the Rue Louis-le-Grand, furnished rooms in a decent house, keeping an eye out to ensure that the mulatto was still following her. The house belonged to a certain Madame Gérard to whom Madame du Val-Noble had, in her days of splendor, done some kindnesses, and Madame Gérard now paid her back by providing her with a suitable home. The good woman, a respectable, virtuous, even pious bourgeois, took the courtesan in as if she were a woman of a superior order; she still saw her as she had been in her days of luxury, and now she saw her as a fallen queen; she trusted her daughters with her, and what is more natural than one might think, the courtesan was as scrupulous about taking them to the theater as a mother would be; the two Gérard girls adored Madame du Val-Noble. This fine, worthy landlady was like those sublime priests who always see a soul to save and a person to love in women who have lived outside the law. Madame du Val-Noble respected her honest qualities, often expressing envy of her during evening conversations and deploring her own misfortunes. "You're still beautiful, and you can still end up having a happy life," Madame Gérard assured her. And Madame du Val-Noble was only relatively impoverished. The wardrobe of that big-spending, elegant woman was still sufficiently stocked to allow her to appear in full glory from time to time, as she had done at the performance of *Richard d'Arlington* at the Porte-Saint-Martin. Madame Gérard continued to pay, graciously, for the carriages needed for the woman on foot when she had to dine somewhere or attend the theater.

"Guess what, dear Madame Gérard," Madame du Val-Noble said to the worthy mother. "My luck is about to change, I believe. . . ."

"Wonderful, madame, but be smart about it, think about the future . . . no more debts. It's such trouble getting rid of those people who come here looking for you!"

"Ah, never mind those dogs—they've all bled enormous sums out of me. But look, here are tickets to the Variétés for your daughters, a good box on the second tier. If someone asks for me this evening and I'm not back yet, let them go on up anyway. Adèle, who used to be my maid, will be there; I'll send her to you."

Madame du Val-Noble, who had neither aunt nor mother, had no recourse but to turn to her old maid (who was also on foot!) to play the Saint-Estève role with this unknown man, the conquest of whom was going to let her reassume her rank. She went to dine with Théodore Gaillard, who, that evening, had a *party*—that is, a dinner being thrown by Nathan, who was paying off a debt—one of those debauches whose guests are invited with the words "There will be women."

Peyrade the Nabob

Peyrade had had powerful reasons to let himself get involved in this web of intrigue. But his curiosity, like that of Corentin, had been so powerfully stimulated that even if there had been no reasons, he might well have entered into the drama. At just this moment the political plans of Charles X had reached their fruition. After giving the helm to his chosen ministers, the king was preparing the conquest of Algiers, in the hope that such a glorious achievement would serve as justification for what some called his coup d'état.[35] There were no internal conspiracies simmering at the time, and Charles believed he had no more enemies. In politics as at sea, there are quiet moments that are deceptive. Corentin now found himself slumped in a state of complete idleness. In such a situation, a real hunter seeks to find some way to keep his hand in, and so he will "kill blackbirds for lack of thrushes." Domitian killed flies for lack of Christians. Having witnessed the arrest of Esther, Contenson, with the exquisite sensitivities of the spy, had quickly understood the operation. The odd man, as we saw, did not even bother to conceal his opinion of Baron Nucingen. "Who's making money from the banker's infatuation?" was the first question the two friends discussed. Having recognized Asia as having some role in the play, Contenson hoped that through her he might discover the author; but she slipped through his hands like an eel and went underground somewhere in the muddy depths of Paris, and when she popped up again as the cook at Esther's, the role of the mulatress seemed inexplicable to him. For the first time, the two espionage artists had encountered an indecipherable text, but one that hinted in a shadowy way at some kind of story. Even after three successive, and bold, attacks on the Rue Taitbout house, Contenson encountered only stubborn muteness. As long as Esther continued to live there, the porter seemed possessed by some profound fear. Perhaps Asia had promised to cook up poisoned meatballs for the whole family if there were any indiscretion. But two days after Esther had moved out, Contenson found the porter a little more reasonable; he missed the little lady a great deal, he said, for she had passed on leftovers from her table to him. Contenson, disguised as a commercial broker, tried negotiating for the apartment, and he listened to the porter's complaints with a false skepticism, affecting to doubt everything the man said: "Oh, is that really possible?" "Yes, monsieur, the little lady lived here for five years without ever going out, and on top of that her lover, always jealous even though she was above reproach, took the greatest precautions whenever he came or left. Besides, he was a very good-looking young man." Lucien was still in Marsac with his sister, Madame Séchard; but as soon as he got back, Contenson sent the porter over to the Quai Malaquais to ask Monsieur Rubempré if he would consent to selling the furniture left in the apartment Madame Van Bogseck had vacated. The porter then confirmed that Lucien was the mysterious lover of the young widow, and that was all Contenson needed to know. The reader can imagine the astonishment felt by Lucien and Carlos, though of course they concealed it well, and they pretended to think the porter must be mad; they tried to persuade him of his error.

Within twenty-four hours Carlos had organized an antipolice force, which quickly caught Contenson red-handed in the act of espionage. Contenson, disguised as a porter from the food market, had twice already delivered provisions that morning that had been ordered by Asia, and twice he had stood inside the house on the Rue Saint-Georges. Corentin for his part was not idle; but the reality of a person named Carlos Herrera stopped him short, for he quickly learned that the abbé was a secret envoy from Ferdinand VII, and that he had come to Paris toward the end of the year 1823. Nevertheless, Corentin needed to examine the possible reasons that might have led this Spaniard to become the protector of Lucien de Rubempré. Corentin soon learned that Esther had been Lucien's mistress for five years. Therefore, the substitution of the Englishwoman for Esther had been done in the interests of that dandy. Now, Lucien had no means whatsoever, he had been stymied in his suit for Mademoiselle de Grandlieu, and yet he had just bought the Rubempré estate for a million. Corentin talked the director-general of the Police of the Kingdom into making discreet inquiries of the prefect of police, and he learned that the trouble Peyrade had got into was the result of a visit from the Comte de Sérisy and Lucien de Rubempré.

"Now we've got it!" Peyrade and Corentin exclaimed.

The two friends sketched out a plan in no time.

"This whore has had relationships, and she's had friends. Maybe one of the friends is in bad straits; one of us can play the role of a rich foreigner who'll take her up; we'll be sure the two friends see each other. These types always have need of each other to carry on their little love games, and that will lead us to the truth of the situation." Peyrade naturally thought he'd reprise his role as an Englishman. The debauched life he would have to lead appealed to him, as did getting to the bottom of this plot that had already made him a victim. Corentin, his work having aged him, and being naturally somewhat lazy, wanted nothing to do with this. As a mulatto, Contenson readily shook off the antipolice of Carlos.

Three days prior to the meeting of Peyrade and Madame du Val-Noble on the Champs-Élysées, the agents of the firm of Sartine and Lenoir,[36] both with passports in good order, had checked into the Hôtel Mirabeau on the Rue de la Paix, having come from the colonies via Le Havre in a small coach so mud-spattered when it arrived that no one would have believed that it had only traveled from Saint-Denis to Paris.

Meanwhile, Carlos Herrera went to the Spanish embassy for his visa, and then back to the Quai Malaquais to prepare for a trip to Madrid. This is why. In just a few days, Esther would officially be the owner of the house on the Rue Saint-Georges, and she would have the necessary documents for her annual income of thirty thousand francs; Europe and Asia were clever enough to get her to sell the documents and quietly pass the money on to Lucien. Lucien, seeming wealthy due to the generosity of his sister, could now make the final payment on the Rubempré estate. No one could object to any of this except Esther, and she would rather have died than so much as raise an eyebrow. Clotilde wrapped a little pink kerchief around her great storklike neck, indicating that the point had been won at the Grandlieu home. The Omnibus shares had already tripled in value. Carlos could evade all suspicion by disappearing for a few days. Human prudence had foreseen everything; nothing could go wrong. The false Spaniard was set to depart the day after Peyrade had encountered Madame du Val-Noble on the Champs-Élysées. But that night, at two in the morning, Asia arrived by cab at the Quai Malaquais and found the stoker of this grand machine sitting and smoking quietly in his room, going over the details of the plan we have just summarized, like an author combing over his manuscript to root out any remaining faults. A man like this was not the type to allow a slip like that of the Rue Taitbout porter to take place a second time.

"Yesterday," Asia began in an urgent whisper, "at about two-thirty, on the Champs-Élysées, Paccard recognized Contenson, disguised as a mulatto, a servant to an Englishman who had been seen walking the Champs-Élysées looking for Esther. Paccard recognized him then the same way I did when he claimed to be a delivery man from Les Halles, by his eyes. Paccard brought the girl back home in such a way as to keep an eye on our little friend. He's at the Hôtel Mirabeau, but since he clearly was exchanging signs with the Englishman, it's impossible, Paccard says, that the Englishman is really an Englishman."

"We've got a horsefly buzzing around us," said Carlos. "I won't leave till the day after tomorrow. This Contenson is the one who tossed that Rue Taitbout porter our way; I need to find out if the false Englishman is our enemy."

At noon the mulatto who worked for Monsieur Samuel Johnson was, with great gravity, serving his master lunch; the master ate too much lunch, by design. Peyrade wanted to pass for an Englishman of the Big Drinker variety; he always drank plenty of wine before going out. He wore black gaiters that reached up to his knees, padded to make his legs look thicker; his trousers were thickened by a great mass of fustian; he wore his jacket buttoned up to his chin; his blue cravat encircled his neck up to his cheeks; he wore a small red wig that covered part of his forehead; he had managed to give himself an additional three inches in height; in short, even the most regular of all the regulars of the Café David would have been unable to recognize him. His square-cut, black cloth overcoat would lead a passerby to take him for an English millionaire. Contenson affected the chilly insolence of a nabob's personal valet, mute, abrupt, contemptuous, noncommunicative, and to all this he added the occasional bizarre gesture and ferocious outburst. Peyrade was finishing his second bottle when one of the hotel's waiters brought in without ceremony a man whom Peyrade and Contenson both recognized as a plainclothes police officer.

"Monsieur Peyrade," the gendarme whispered to the nabob, "I have orders to take you to the prefecture." Peyrade made no reaction but got up and picked up his hat. "You'll find a cab at the door," said the gendarme as they descended the stairs. "The prefect wanted to have you arrested, but he's settled for demanding an explanation of your conduct—you're to explain yourself to the officer you will find in the cab."[37]

"Should I stay with you?" asked the gendarme to the officer when Peyrade had got in.

"No," he replied. "Tell the driver, quietly, to take us to the prefecture."

Peyrade and Carlos thus found themselves seated together in the same coach. Carlos had a dagger at the ready. The cab was driven by a trusted coachman, capable of letting Carlos out quickly and unobtrusively, and capable of handling the situation if, upon arriving at his destination, he were to find a dead body in his cab. When a spy is found dead, no one raises any fuss. The law almost always lets such murders go unsolved and unpunished, so difficult is it to learn the truth about them.

A Duel in a Cab

Peyrade cast his expert spy's eye on the officer the prefect had sent to him. Carlos looked right enough: a bald head, furrowed with deep wrinkles at the back, powdered hair; a pair of very light, very bureaucratic gold spectacles with double lenses, tinted green, over red-rimmed eyes that probably needed more care than they received, for they seemed to testify to some ignoble malady. A cotton shirt with its pleated frills ironed flat, a worn waistcoat of black satin, the trousers of a man of the law, black spun-silk stockings, shoes tied with ribbons, a long black frock coat, a forty-sou pair of gloves, black and clearly worn for ten days straight, a chain with a gold watch: he was neither more nor less than that low-grade official paradoxically named an *officier de paix*.

"My dear Monsieur Peyrade, I find it regrettable that a man like you should be under surveillance, and even more regrettable that you make a point of deserving it. Your disguise is not to *monsieur le préfet*'s taste. If you thought you could escape our vigilance, you were mistaken. You no doubt began your journey from England at Beaumont-sur-Oise?"

"At Beaumont-sur-Oise," replied Peyrade.

"Or at Saint-Denis?" said the false officer.

This rattled Peyrade. The new question required a response. But any reply could be a dangerous one. Saying yes would sound like sarcasm; saying no, if this man knew the truth, would be worse. "He's sharp," thought Peyrade. He tried gazing at the officer with a smile, allowing his smile to be his reply. The smile was accepted without protest.

"What is your objective with this disguise, with taking rooms at the Hôtel Mirabeau, and with disguising Contenson as a mulatto?" the officer asked.

"*Monsieur le préfet* can do with me as he wishes, but I don't need to account for my acts to anybody but my superiors," said Peyrade with dignity.

"If you're suggesting that you are operating on behalf of the General Police of the Kingdom," the false officer said dryly, "we'll change direction and go to the Rue de Grenelle rather than the Rue de Jérusalem.[38] My orders regarding you are perfectly clear. But be very careful! You haven't attracted too much negative attention, so what you say could make things worse for you. Personally, I don't have any ill will toward you . . . but come on! Tell me the truth."

"The truth? Here it is," said Peyrade, casting a shrewd glance at the reddened eyes of his Cerberus.

The false officer said nothing, his expression impassive; he was only doing his job, and all truths were the same to him; he looked as if he might suspect the prefect of some caprice in the matter. Prefects do have their whims.

"I've fallen in love, madly, with a woman, the mistress of that stockbroker who flew the coop for his own pleasure and the displeasure of his creditors, Falleix."

"Madame du Val-Noble," said the officer.

"Yes," Peyrade replied. "To be able to keep her for a month will cost me about a thousand écus, so I've got myself dressed up as a nabob, and I got Contenson to play my servant. That's the truth, monsieur, and so entirely true that if you'd like to leave me here in this cab and go, on the word of a former commissioner-general of police, into the hotel and question Contenson, you'll find that not only will Contenson confirm what I've had the honor of telling you, but you'll also see Madame du Val-Noble's maid arriving, for she's about to come this morning and tell us either that her mistress has agreed to my proposition brings us new conditions of her own. An old ape knows what tricks to perform: I've offered her a thousand francs a month and a carriage, which makes fifteen hundred, plus another five hundred in presents, and that much again on parties, dinners, and shows; so you can see my math is right when I say a thousand écus. There's nothing wrong with a man my age spending a thousand écus on his last fantasy."

"Oh, Papa Peyrade, you still desire women, but for . . . what? But you've got me—I'm sixty, and I get along without it just fine. . . . But, I suppose, if things are the way you say, I can see that in order to pursue this fantasy you've got yourself up as a foreigner."

"You must understand that neither Peyrade nor Father Canquoëlle of the Rue des Moineaux would have had any chance . . ."

"No, neither of them would have suited Madame du Val-Noble," said Carlos, delighted to have learned the address of Father Canquoëlle. "Before the Revolution, I had a woman for a mistress," he said, "who had been kept by the high executioner, popularly known as the Hangman. One evening, in the theater, she inadvertently pricked her finger with a pin, and she exclaimed, 'Hang it!' Her neighbor turned and said, 'So, is that what it feels like?' Well, my dear Peyrade, she left the man over that little joke. I'm sure you don't want to expose yourself to a similar snub. . . . Madame du Val-Noble is a woman fit for the best kind of men. I saw her once at the Opéra, and I thought she was quite beautiful. . . . Let's turn our carriage back to the Rue de la Paix, my dear Peyrade—I want to go up into your rooms with you and see things for myself. A verbal report will suffice, no doubt, for the prefect."

Carlos took from his pocket a black snuffbox lined with silver gilt, opened it, and offered it to Peyrade in the friendliest way. Peyrade was saying to himself, "So this is the quality of their agents! Good God! If Monsieur Lenoir or Monsieur Sartine were to come back to life, what would they say?"

"I'm quite sure you've told me some part of the truth, but not all of it, my dear friend," said the false officer, going casually on as he finished taking his snuff. "You've mixed yourself up in the love affair of Baron de Nucingen, and you're no doubt hoping to catch him in some kind of trap; you missed with your pistol, and now you're pulling out the big cannon. Madame du Val-Noble is a friend of Madame de Champy...."

"Damn it! I need to be very careful!" Peyrade thought. "He's smarter than I thought. He's playing me—he talks about letting me go, but he's still forcing me to talk."

"Well, then," said Carlos with a magisterial air.

"Monsieur, it is true that I was wrong in agreeing to look for a woman Monsieur de Nucingen had got himself infatuated with. That's the cause of the disgrace I find myself in, because it would appear that I accidentally stepped on some important toes." The false officer remained impassive. "But I know the police well enough after fifty-two years of service," Peyrade continued, "to get myself completely clear of that tangle, after the prefect told me off the way he did, and of course he was right to do so...."

"You'd give up this little affair of yours if *monsieur le préfet* asked you to? That, I believe, would be the best proof that what you've told me is sincere."

"Look how he works! How he works!" thought Peyrade. "My God—the agents today are just as good as they were in Lenoir's day."

"Give it up?" said Peyrade. "I'll wait for the prefect's orders.... But if you want to come up, here we are at the hotel."

"Where do you find the money?" Carlos asked point-blank, a shrewd expression on his face.

"Monsieur, I have a friend ..." said Peyrade.

"Tell that to the examining magistrate!" said Carlos.

The plan for this audacious scene was so simple that it could only have sprung from the head of a man like him. He had sent Lucien early in the day to the Comtesse de Sérisy. Lucien asked the count's private secretary—as if the request were coming from the count himself—to go to the prefect and ask for information concerning an agent who had recently been employed by Baron de Nucingen. The secretary returned with a note on Peyrade, a copy of the summary in his dossier:

> With the Police since 1778, came from Avignon to Paris two years before.
>
> Has neither money nor morality, but knows some State secrets.

> Lives on the Rue des Moineux under the name of Canquoëlle,
> the name of a small holding where his family lived, in the Vau-
> cluse, the family otherwise honorable.
>
> Was recently asked about by one of his grandnephews, named
> Théodore de la Peyrade. (See agent's report, Document 37)

"That must be the Englishman, to whom Contenson is playing the mulatto," Carlos cried when Lucien reported what he'd heard orally, apart from the note.

Within three hours this man, with a scope and capability for action comparable to those of a general, had found in Paccard a seemingly innocent accomplice who could play the role of a plainclothes policeman and had disguised himself as an *officier de paix*. Three times he was on the verge of killing Peyrade in the cab, but since he had made it a rule never to kill anyone himself, he promised himself that he would get rid of Peyrade by pointing him out as a millionaire to a few ex-convicts.

Peyrade and his mentor could hear Contenson talking with Madame du Val-Noble's chambermaid. Peyrade signed to Carlos that he should remain in the outer room, as if he were saying to him, "Now you'll see that I was telling the truth."

"Madame agrees to everything," Adèle said. "Right now madame is with a friend of hers, Madame de Champy, who has a fully furnished apartment for the next year on the Rue Taitbout, and she'll no doubt give it to madame. Madame will be better situated there for receiving Monsieur Johnson, because the furnishings are all still in fine condition, and monsieur can arrange to buy it for madame from Madame de Champy."

"Good, my girl. If we haven't quite got our hands on the carrot, we've at least got the leaves of one," the mulatto declared to the stupefied girl. "We can share the profits."

"Just like a colored man!" cried Mademoiselle Adèle. "If your nabob is really a nabob, he can just give the furniture to madame. The lease ends in April 1830, and your nabob can renew it if he likes the place."

"I am veddy content with all this!" replied Peyrade, who made his entrance tapping the chambermaid on the shoulder.

And he made a sign to Carlos, who responded with his own sign, implying that he understood the nabob had to remain in character. But the whole scene altered suddenly with the entrance of a new character, one over whom neither Carlos nor the prefect had any power. Corentin walked in unexpectedly. Passing by, he had seen the door open, and he came in to see how his old friend Peyrade was doing with his nabob role.

Corentin Wins Round Two

"The prefect is getting in the way again!" said Peyrade in a whisper to Corentin. "He's found out about me as nabob."

"We're going to take care of the prefect," Corentin whispered back.

Then, after making a chilly bow to the false officer, he proceeded to look the man over closely.

"Stay here till I return; I'm going to the prefecture," said Carlos. "If you don't see me, assume that your little fantasy may proceed."

He said these words privately to Peyrade so as not to undo his persona in front of the maid, and then Carlos left, wishing to avoid the intense gaze of the newcomer, in whom he recognized one of those blond, blue-eyed, and terrifyingly ice-cold natures.

"That's the officer the prefect sent to me."

"Him!" exclaimed Corentin. "You should have thrown him out. That man has three decks of cards in his shoes; you can tell by the way the foot sits in the shoe; and no *officier de paix* has any need to disguise himself!"

Corentin went down rapidly to confirm his suspicions. Carlos was getting into a cab.

"Oh, *monsieur l'abbé*, is that you?" Corentin called out.

Carlos turned his head, saw Corentin, and got into the cab. But as the door closed Corentin had time to say, "That's all I needed to know."

"To Quai Malaquais!" Corentin called out to the driver, with diabolical mockery in both voice and expression.

"All right," Jacques Collin said to himself, "they're on to me, so now I'll need to move even more quickly—I especially need to know what they're after."

Corentin had seen the abbé Carlos Herrera, a man whose looks you didn't forget, five or six times. Corentin had first noticed the square shoulders, then the scars on the face and the trick of adding three inches to his height.

"Ah, my old friend, he got you, didn't he!" Corentin said, seeing that only he, Peyrade, and Contenson were still in the room.

"Who is he?" cried Peyrade in a harsh, metallic voice. "I'll spend my last days finding him, putting him on a grill, and turning him over it."

"He's the abbé Carlos Herrera, probably the Corentin of Spain. This explains everything. The Spaniard is a crook of the worst kind, and he wants to make a fortune for that little young man by beating money out of a pretty whore. . . . It's up to you if you want to joust with a diplomat who seems damned clever to me."

"Oh!" cried Contenson. "He's the one who took the three hundred thousand francs the day of Esther's arrest—he was the one in the cab! Now I remember those eyes of his, and the forehead, and the pockmarks."

"Ah, what a dowry my little Lydie might have had!" said Peyrade.

"You can stay on as nabob," said Corentin. "If we're going to keep an eye on Esther, we need to get her linked up with Val-Noble—Esther was Lucien's real mistress."

"They've already swindled more than five hundred thousand francs out of Nucingen," said Contenson.

"They need as much again," Corentin continued. "The Rubempré estate costs a million. Papa," he said, tapping Peyrade on the shoulder, "you're going to have a hundred thousand for Lydie's dowry."

"Don't tell me that, Corentin. If your plan fails, I don't know what I might do. . . ."

"You might even have it tomorrow! The abbé, my friend, is shrewd, and we need to remember that; he's a devil of one of the superior orders; but I've got him now, he's no fool, and he'll give in. Just try to be as dense as a nabob, and don't worry about a thing."

On the evening of that day in which the true adversaries had met face to face on level ground, Lucien attended a gathering at the Grandlieu house. The guests were numerous. In front of her guests, the duchess kept Lucien at her side for some time and behaved kindly toward him.

"I understand you took a short trip recently?" she said to him.

"Yes, *madame la duchesse*. My sister, in an effort to help facilitate my marriage, has made some major sacrifices, and I've been able to purchase the Rubempré estate and to rejoin the lands around it. But my agent here in Paris is a shrewd man, and he's been able to keep me clear of the claims the owners might have made if they had known who the purchaser was."

"Is there a château?" asked Clotilde, smiling too much.

"There's something like a château, but the wisest course would be to tear it down and use the materials to build a more modern house."

Clotilde's eyes were positively shooting out flames of happiness, accompanied by smiles of contentment.

"You can make up a *rubber* at whist with my father tonight," she said. "In a couple of weeks, I expect to be inviting you to dinner."

"Well, my dear monsieur," the Duc de Grandlieu said to him, "they say you've bought the Rubempré estate; my compliments on that. It's a response to those who claim you have debts. People at my level, we can, like France and England, have some public debt; but, you see, people without a fortune, beginners, can't have that privilege. . . ."

"Oh, *monsieur le duc,* I still owe five hundred thousand on my estate."

"In that case, you need to marry a girl who will give the sum to you; but you'll find it difficult to turn up somebody with that kind of money in our faubourg, for typically we give our daughters small dowries."

"But they bring their name, and that is enough," replied Lucien.

"We have only three whist players tonight—Maufrigneuse, d'Espard, and me," said the duke. "Would you like to be our fourth?" he asked Lucien, guiding him toward the table.

Clotilde came over to watch her father play.

"She wants me to think she's come over here for me," the duke said, patting his daughter's hand, and taking a sideways glance at Lucien, who was quiet.

Lucien, partnered with Monsieur d'Espard, lost twenty louis.

Clotilde went to the duchess and told her, "Oh dear mother, he was clever enough to lose!"

At eleven, after exchanging a few words of love with Mademoiselle de Grandlieu, Lucien went home and got into bed, thinking of the complete triumph that would be his in a month, for he had no doubts about being accepted as Clotilde's fiancé and being married before Lent of 1830.

The next day, after luncheon, as Lucien was smoking cigarettes in the company of Carlos, who was worried, a visitor was announced: Monsieur de Saint-Estève (what a name!) had come to speak with either the abbé Carlos Herrera or Monsieur Lucien de Rubempré.

"Did they tell him that I'd gone?" asked the abbé.

"Yes, monsieur," the groom replied.

"All right. Receive the man," he said to Lucien, "but not a single compromising word, not a single gesture of surprise—this is the enemy."

"You'll be able to hear me," said Lucien.

Carlos hid in the adjoining room, and through a vent in the door he was able to see Corentin come in, though he only recognized him by his voice, so well could the great man transform himself. And just now Corentin was in the guise of on elderly division chief in the Ministry of Finance.

"I do not have the honor of being acquainted with you, monsieur," Corentin began, "but . . ."

"Excuse me for interrupting, monsieur," said Lucien, "but . . ."

"But it's a matter concerning your marriage with Mademoiselle de Grandlieu, which will not be taking place," Corentin said vigorously.

Lucien sat down, and made no reply.

"You are in the grip of a man who has the power, the will, and the ability to prove to the Duc de Grandlieu that the Rubempré estate will be paid for with the money a dupe paid you for your mistress, Mademoi-selle Esther," Corentin continued. "It will be easy to turn up the details of the judgments pursued against Mademoiselle Esther, and there are ways of ensuring that d'Estourny will talk. Those very clever stratagems used against the Baron de Nucingen will be brought out into the light of day . . . But all this can be arranged quickly. Give me the sum of one hundred thousand francs and you'll be left in peace. . . . None of this has anything to do with me. I am simply an agent working for those who've conceived this *blackmail*—that's all."

Corentin could have spoken for an hour. Lucien continued to smoke his cigarette in the most untroubled manner.

There was a pause, during which Lucien's gaze met the catlike stare that Corentin fixed upon him.

"Either you are basing all this on complete falsehoods, in which case I need pay you no further attention, or you're right, and in that case, by giving you a hundred thousand francs I leave you free to come back and demand the same amount as many times as there are Saint-Estèves. . . . But to conclude this splendid negotiation of yours, let me explain that I, Lucien de Rubempré, fear no one. And I have nothing to do with this rigamarole you've spoken of. If the Grandlieus make difficulties, there are many other noble young ladies to marry. In fact, perhaps I really ought to remain single, so I can concentrate on the white slavery busi-ness I am so good at."

"If *monsieur l'abbé* Carlos Herrera . . ."

"Monsieur," Lucien interrupted, "the abbé Carlos Herrera is at this moment on the road toward Spain; he has nothing to do with my mar-riage, nor with anything that concerns me. That State councillor has indeed aided me with his advice for some time now, but he has business to attend to with the king of Spain. If you have anything to say to him, I suggest you go to Madrid."

"Monsieur," Corentin said sharply, "you will never be the husband of Mademoiselle Clotilde de Grandlieu."

"Too bad for her then," said Lucien, pushing Corentin to the door with impatience.

"Are you sure about this?" Corentin asked coldly.

"Monsieur, I don't see that you have any right to meddle in my affairs—or even to make me waste a cigarette," said Lucien, tossing aside his cigarette, which had gone out.

"Farewell, monsieur," said Corentin. "We will not see each other again. . . . But a moment will come when you'll wish you could give half your fortune to call me back from this staircase."

In response to that threat, Carlos made a gesture like that of cutting off a head.

The Music Old Men Sometimes Hear at the Italiens

"Back to work now!" Carlos cried, seeing Lucien going pale after that terrifying conversation.

If among the (admittedly small) number of readers who care about the moral and philosophical aspects of a book there could be found just one capable of believing that Baron de Nucingen was satisfied, that one person would prove how difficult it is to map the heart of a whore using any physiological formula. Esther had resolved to make her poor millionaire pay dearly for what he called his "day uff fictory." Now, at the beginning of February 1830, no housewarming party had yet taken place at the "leetle palace."

"But," said Esther confidentially to her friends, who in turn repeated it to the baron, "at Carnival I'm going to make my man as *happy as a plaster rooster.*"

That phrase became proverbial in the world of courtesans. The baron now began to indulge in lamentations. Like other married men he became quite absurd, complaining to his intimates, and his dissatisfaction was widely known. But Esther assiduously kept up her role, playing Pompadour to this Prince of Speculation. She had already hosted two or three parties solely in order to get Lucien in the house. Lousteau, Rastignac, du Tillet, Bixiou, Nathan, the Comte de Brambourg, the very flowers of the roué set, all became regular guests at her house. And to act the female roles in her play, Esther accepted Tullia, Florentine, Fanny-Beaupré, Florine—two actresses and two dancers—and Madame du Val-Noble. Nothing is duller than a house of courtesans without some rivalry, competition in dress, and changing faces. In six weeks Esther had become the wittiest, the most amusing, the most beautiful, and the most elegant of the class of kept women. Placed up on her proper pedestal, she savored all the enjoyments of vanity that will seduce the ordinary woman, but in her case she added a secret thought that ranked her up above all others of her kind. She maintained within her heart an image of herself that at the same time glorified her and made her ashamed; the hour of her abdication was always present to her, and so it was that she played a double role, and she pitied herself. Her sarcasms had an extra sting in that they arose from the profound contempt that the angel of love, who lived within the courtesan, felt for the foul, odious role acted by the body, in the very presence of the soul. Both spectator and actor, judge and accused, she embodied the marvelous idea in the Arabian tales where a sublime being is almost always hidden beneath a degraded exterior, or in the book of books, the Bible, where the type is found in the story of Nebuchadnezzar. Having fixed the terminus of her life as the day after the infidelity, the victim felt free to amuse herself with her executioner. Moreover, having caught some glimpses of the secret, shameful methods the baron had employed to build up his colossal fortune, Esther could imagine herself playing the role of the goddess Ate, Vengeance, in Carlos's phrase. Thus she shuttled back and forth between being perfectly charming and perfectly detestable to that millionaire who lived only for her. When the baron had been made to suffer so much that he wanted to leave her, Esther would pull him back to her with a scene of tenderness.

Herrera, making a great show of having gone to Spain, had actually gone to Tours. From there he sent his carriage on to Bordeaux, carrying a servant who had been charged with pretending to be the master, and told to wait for him in a hotel there. Then he returned by public transportation, disguised as a traveling salesman, and had himself secretly installed in Esther's house, where, along with Asia, Europe, and Paccard, he would carefully direct all his schemes while keeping a close eye on everyone, especially Peyrade.

A couple of weeks before the day she had chosen for her party, which would be the day after the first Opéra Ball of the season, the courtesan, whose clever tongue had begun to make her formidable, found herself in a box in the Italiens, the baron having been forced to buy her her own box at stage level in an effort to conceal his mistress and not be seen in public with her, just a few yards away from Madame de Nucingen. Esther had chosen this box in order to be able to see into that of Madame de Sérisy, whom Lucien almost always accompanied. The poor courtesan's whole happiness now depended on being able to gaze at Lucien on Tuesdays, Thursdays, and Saturdays, sitting beside Madame de Sérisy. About nine-thirty Esther saw Lucien enter the box of the countess looking worried and pale, his features drawn and haggard. No one but Esther perceived these signs of his inner desolation. A woman who loves a man can read his face the way a sailor reads the sea. "My God, what's wrong with him? What's happened? Could it be that he needs to talk to the evil angel, his personal guardian angel, who lives hidden in an attic room between those of Europe and Asia?" Occupied with such painful thoughts, Esther scarcely heard the music. The reader will easily believe that she didn't hear a word from the baron, who sat there holding one of his "anchel's" hands in his, nattering away in his Polish Jew's patois, the singularities of which must cause just as much trouble to those who read them as they did to those who had to hear them.

"Mine Esther," he said, letting go of her hand and giving it a bad-tempered push, "you do not lizzen to me!"

"Oh, look, baron, you mangle love as badly as you mangle French."

"Ach, ze deffil!"

"I am not at home in my boudoir; I am here at the Italiens. If you were not one of those safes manufactured by Huret or Fichet[39] and metamorphosed into a man by some weird trick of Nature, you wouldn't make so much racket in the box of a woman who loves music. You're completely right to say I'm not listening to you! There you are, paddling around in my gown like a beetle in a paper bag, and you make me laugh at you, you're so pitiful. You're always saying to me, 'You are zo briddy, I could chust eat you hup!' You old fool! If I were to respond by saying, 'You displease me less tonight than yesterday, let's go back home.' Well, from the way you're breathing—and if I don't listen to you, I can always feel you there—I can tell you've had a huge dinner and your digestion process has begun. Believe me—and I cost you enough that I'll throw in some advice from time to time, a little something extra for your money—believe me, my dear, when a person has the kind of digestive problems you do, you really shouldn't let yourself say at any time you feel like it, 'You are zo briddy. . . .' An old soldier dropped dead of that sort of thing, 'in the arms of Religion,' as Blondet put it.[40] It's ten o'clock now, and you finished dining with your current pigeon, the Comte de Brambourg, at nine, so now you have both millions and truffles to digest. Come back tomorrow at ten."

"Ach, you are zo gruel!" cried the baron, who nevertheless recognized the justness of her medical diagnosis.

"Cruel?" said Esther, her eyes remaining fixed on Lucien. "Haven't you consulted Bianchon, Desplein, old Haudry?[41] . . . You know, ever since you've become obsessed with this ultimate joy of yours, do you know what you remind me of?"

"Vhat?"

"You make me picture a little old man all wrapped up in flannel who keeps getting up from his armchair and making his way to the window, to check and see if the thermometer is still at *silkworms*, the temperature his physician prescribed . . ."

"Ach, such an ingrade you are!" exclaimed the baron, dismayed at having to listen to music of the kind that, unfortunately, old men in love often do have to hear at the Italiens.

"Ingrate!" said Esther. "And exactly what have you given me so far?

A lot of irritation, that's what. Come on, Papa! Can I possibly be proud of you? You're proud of me, and yes, I'm wearing your braid and your livery very nicely. You've paid off my debts! Fine. But you've swindled enough millions—oh, don't you make that face at me, remember our agreement—so that didn't even make a dent. And that's your great claim to fame. . . . Whore and thief—they go together so well. You've built a magnificent cage for the parrot that took your fancy. . . . Go ask some Brazilian macaw if he feels grateful for the golden cage they've put him in. . . . Don't look at me like that—you look like an old Buddha. You want to show your macaw off all over Paris. You say, 'Ah, is there anyone in Paris with a parrot like mine?' And ah, how it talks! Look how it picks just the right word to say! If du Tillet comes along, it'll say, 'Bonjour, you little crook!' But you're as happy as a Dutchman with a tulip nobody else has ever owned, or like some retired nabob on a pension from England, wandering through Asia, excited to have bought from some traveling salesman the first snuffbox that can play three different overtures. And you want to win my heart! Well, pay attention, because I'm going to show you how to do it."

"Yes, say ziss, tell me! I vill do anyt'ink for you . . . I efen luff it vhen you make zese chokes on me!"

"Be young. Be handsome. Be like Lucien de Rubempré, who's right over there with your wife, and you'll obtain, for free, everything you couldn't buy for all your millions!"

"Hokay—I leef you. Ach, you are zo unbleazant tonight . . ." said the lynx, with a long face.

"Ah, fine, good evening then," said Esther. "Remember to tell 'Chorche' to prop up your pillows and keep your feet well down; you look a little apoplectic this evening. Dear, you certainly can't say I don't take any interest in your health."

The baron was standing up, his hand on the door handle.

"Nucingen! Come here!" said Esther with a haughty gesture.

The baron approached and bent down to her with canine servility.

"Do you want me to be nice and take you to my house for some glasses of sugar water and some petting for 'ze old doggie'?"

"You preak mine heart . . ."

"I'll break your heart, all right—I'll beat it till it breaks!" she said, mocking him. "Come now—go fetch Lucien, so I can invite him to our great Balthazar's feast, because I want to be sure he comes. If you succeed in that little business matter, I'll say that I love you, my fat Frédéric, so well that you'll believe I mean it. . . ."

"You are ein enchandress," said the baron, kissing Esther's gloved hand. "I vould gonzent to listen to zese insults for hours, so long as I get nice caress at ze end."

"Go then—if you don't obey me, I'll . . ." she said, wagging a threatening finger at him the way one does with a child.

The baron nodded his head, looking like a bird in a trap gazing imploringly at the hunter.

"Good God, what can be wrong with Lucien?" she thought when she was alone and she could not prevent tears from falling. "He's never looked so sad!"

Next, we'll learn what had befallen Lucien on that same evening.

How Much One Can Suffer in a Doorway

At nine o'clock Lucien had gone out, as he did every evening, in his coupé and driven to the Grandlieu home. Only using his saddle horse and his cabriolet in the mornings, like all the other young men, he had rented a coupé for winter evenings; he had gone to the best firm for renting one, and he had picked out one of their very best, along with two magnificent horses. For the last month everything had been going his way: he had dined with the Grandlieus three times, the duke behaving charmingly to him; he had sold his Omnibus shares for three hundred thousand francs, allowing him to pay off another third on the price of his estate; Clotilde de Grandlieu, who dressed superbly, was wearing ten pots of makeup on her face whenever he entered the drawing room, and, moreover, was openly avowing her passion for him. A few highly placed personages were speaking of the marriage of Lucien and Mademoiselle de Grandlieu as a likely event. The Duc de Chaulieu, former ambassador to Spain and, for a time, foreign minister,[42] had promised the Duchesse de Grandlieu to ask the king to grant Lucien the title of marquis. And so that evening, after dining with Madame de Sérisy, Lucien had gone from the Rue de la Chaussée-d'Antin to the Faubourg Saint-Germain for his usual daily visit. He arrives. His driver asks for the gate to be opened. It opens, and the coupé comes to a stop at the steps. Lucien, stepping down, sees four other coaches there. One of the footmen, who had been busily opening and closing the doorway to the interior, seeing Monsieur de Rubempré, hurries over to the steps and stations himself in front of the door like a soldier returning to his post. "His Lordship is not at home!" he says. "*Madame la duchesse* is receiving guests," Lucien says to the valet. "*Madame la duchesse* is out," the footman announces solemnly. "Mademoiselle Clotilde . . ." "I do not believe that Mademoiselle Clotilde will receive monsieur in the absence of the duchesse . . ." "But—but—there are other guests here," says Lucien, stunned. "I don't know about that," says the footman, trying to seem both immovable and respectful. Nothing is more formidable than Etiquette to those who have adopted it as Society's most powerful law. Lucien readily understood the meaning of this scene, so horrific to him: the duke and the duchess did not want to admit him; he could sense the spinal fluid freezing over in his vertebrae, and a few pearls of cold sweat appeared on his forehead. The interchange had taken place in front of his own valet, who was standing there with his hand still on the carriage door, uncertain whether to close it; Lucien made a sign to him that they should leave; but as he got in, he heard the sounds of people coming down the inner staircase, and the footman announced, "The attendants of Monsieur le Duc de Chaulieu! . . . The attendants of Madame la Vicomtesse de Grandlieu!" Lucien turned to his servant and said: "Quickly! To the Italiens!" But despite his attempt to hurry, the unfortunate dandy was unable to avoid the Duc de Chaulieu and his son, the Duc de Rhétoré, with whom he was forced to exchange a bow of greeting, for they didn't say a word to him. Some great catastrophe at the Royal Court, the fall of some powerful favorite, is often consummated at the doorway of a private room by similar words from a servant with a face expressionless as a plaster cast. "How can I get word of this disaster to my adviser?" Lucien asked himself on his way to the Italiens. "What's going on?" He was lost in conjecture. But here is what had happened. That same morning, at eleven, the Duc de Grandlieu said, as he entered the little room where the family was breakfasting, to Clotilde, after having kissed her: "My child, until I tell you differently, you are to give no more thought to that Rubempré." Then he took the duchess by the hand and led her to a little window nook in order to tell her a few things quietly, while poor Clotilde was changing color. Mademoiselle de Grandlieu observed her mother as she listened to the duke, and she observed the look of sudden surprise on her face. "Jean," the duke said to one of the domestics, "here, take this little note to Monsieur le Duc de Chaulieu, and ask him for a yes or no answer. . . ." And turning to his wife, he explained, "I'm asking him to dine with us today." The meal was a deeply gloomy one. The duchess seemed pensive, the duke seemed annoyed with himself, and Clotilde could barely keep her tears in. "Child, your father is right; obey him," the mother said in a tender voice to her daughter. "I can't say, the way he did, 'give no more thought to Lucien!' No, I understand what you're feeling. At that, Clotilde bent and kissed her mother's hand. "But I will say this, my angel: 'Wait, and do nothing; suffer in silence, because you love him, but trust in your parents' concern for your well-being.' Great ladies, you know, my dear, are great because they know how to do their duty in every kind of situation, and they do it nobly . . ." "But what's the problem?" Clotilde asked, pale as a lily. "It involves things too serious to tell you about, my dear," the duchess replied; "because if they turn out to be false, your thoughts would have been needlessly sullied, and if they turn out to be true, you should not know of them."

At six, the Duc de Chaulieu came to the Duc de Grandlieu's study, where he was awaited. "Tell me, Henri . . ." (These two dukes were on the most familiar terms, calling each other by their first names. This is one of the inventions that serve to mark degrees of intimacy, an attempt to hold back the tide of easy familiarity that was invading French life, and to rein in other people's conceit.) "Tell me, Henri: I'm in such an awkward mess that the only one I can turn to for advice is someone who knows the world as well as you do. My daughter Clotilde is in love, as you know, with that little Rubempré, and they've almost pushed me into promising her to him. I've always been against this marriage; but Madame de Grandlieu can't hold out against Clotilde's feelings. When this boy purchased his estate, when he'd paid for three-fourths of the price, there could be no more objections on my part. But look at this, yesterday evening I received an anonymous letter—and you know how much weight to give to such things—in which the writer asserts that the boy's money comes from some tainted source, and that he's lying when he tells us his sister gave him the funds he needed for the purchase. The letter insists that, in the name of my daughter's happiness and the honor of my family, I make inquiries, and it lays out the means of doing so. Here, read it." After he had read it, the Duc de Chaulieu said, "I share your opinion of anonymous letters, my dear Ferdinand, but even though I detest them, I feel one needs to make use of them. A letter like this needs to be treated the same way you'd treat a spy. Close your door to the boy, and we'll look into it. . . . Ah, I've got it! Your lawyer, Derville, is a man we can trust. He knows the secrets of a great many families—he'll know how to handle this. He's a man of integrity, a careful man, an honorable man, and he's a shrewd one too—but he's only shrewd about business and money matters, and therefore you can use him to collect solid, trustworthy evidence. Now, at the Ministry for Foreign Affairs, in the Royal Police, we have a man uniquely suited to ferreting out secrets of State, and we often send him on missions. Tell Derville that for this affair he'll have a kind of lieutenant under him. Our spy is a gentleman, who'll show up wearing the cross of the Legion of Honor—he looks like a diplomat. This rogue will be our real hunter, and Derville will simply join the hunt. Your lawyer will be able to tell you whether we've got a mountain or a molehill, and whether you need to break off with the little Rubempré. In a week, you'll know enough to be able to make a decision." The Duc de Grandlieu replied, "The young man isn't marquis enough yet to demand a formal explanation if he finds me not at home when he calls for the next week." The former minister said, "And especially if you're going to be giving him your daughter. If this anonymous letter is right, it doesn't matter at all! You can send Clotilde off on a trip with my daughter-in-law Madeleine—she wants to go to Italy anyway. . . ." "Ah, you're saving me so much anxiety! I don't know how I can thank you." "Well, let's wait and see how it all turns out." "Wait," cried the Duc de Grandlieu, "what's the name of the gentleman? I'll need to tell Derville. Send him here tomorrow, at four o'clock—I'll have Derville here, and get the two to start working together." The former minister replied, "His real name is, I believe, Corentin—and that's a name you should not have heard—but the gentleman will come to your house decked out in his ministerial name. He goes by the name of Monsieur de Saint-something-or-other. . . . Oh, Saint-Yves! Or, no, Saint-Valère—one or the other. You can trust him—Louis XVIII trusted him implicitly."

After this conversation, the steward was given orders that the door was to be closed to Monsieur de Rubempré—which was done.

The Scene Is Played Out in the Boxes

Lucien walked through the foyer of the Italiens like a drunken man. He imagined that everyone in Paris was talking about him. He had, in the Duc de Rhétoré, one of those enemies upon whom one can only smile, for vengeance is impossible, their attacks always being in perfect conformity with society's laws. The Duc de Rhétoré knew what had just taken place on the steps of the Grandlieu house. Lucien felt it crucial to communicate this disaster to his personal, private privy counselor immediately, but he feared compromising himself if he were to go to Esther's, where he might run into other people. He forgot that Esther was here, so confused was his thinking; and in the midst of all this perplexity, he found that he had to make small talk with Rastignac, who, knowing nothing of the recent event, congratulated him on his forthcoming marriage. Just at that moment, Nucingen arrived, approaching Lucien with a big smile and saying to him, "Vould you do me ze great bleasure of gomming und seeing Madame de Champy, who vants to infite you to ze housevarmink ve are haffing. . . ."

"Of course, baron," Lucien replied, seeing the financier now as a kind of angel of salvation.

"Leave us alone," said Esther to Monsieur de Nucingen when she saw him coming back with Lucien. "Go see Madame du Val-Noble: I see her over there in a box on the third level with her nabob. . . ." And turning to Lucien, she said, "These nabobs shoot up like weeds in India."

"Yes, and that one," Lucien said with a smile, "looks a lot like yours."

"Also," Esther said, indicating to Lucien that she was addressing the baron, "bring her back here along with her nabob; he really wants to meet you, and they say he's ridiculously rich. The poor lady has already sung me so many sad songs about the way her nabob never leaves her alone that maybe you could help things along: if you were to extract some of his money, it might make him lighter on his feet."

"You tink ve are all t'ieves," said the baron.

As soon as the door to their box had closed, Esther whispered, "What's the matter, Lucien," in her friend's ear, her lips fluttering lightly against it.

"I'm finished! They just refused to let me come in the Grandlieus', on the pretext that no one was home, even though the duke and the duchess were both there, and there were five carriages sitting in the courtyard. . . ."

"What—the marriage is off!" said Esther, her voice revealing how moved she was, for she thought she might be catching a glimpse of a possible paradise.

"I don't know yet what kind of trap they're laying for me. . . ."

"My Lucien," she replied, her voice adorably soft and persuasive, "why let it bother you? You'll make a fine marriage later on. . . . I'll be able to buy you two estates. . . ."

"Give a supper party tonight, so I can speak secretly with Carlos, and by all means invite the phony Englishman and Val-Noble. That nabob is behind all this, he's our enemy, we'll get him, and we'll . . ." Lucien interrupted himself, making a despairing gesture.

"What is it?" asked the poor girl, who felt as if she were being burned at the stake.

"Oh, Madame de Sérisy sees me!" cried Lucien, "and as if that's not bad enough, she's with the Duc de Rhétoré, who witnessed my humiliation."

And in fact at the same moment, the Duc de Rhétoré was busy worsening Madame de Sérisy's grief.

"You allow Lucien to be seen in Mademoiselle Esther's box," said the young duke, pointing across to them. "You take an interest in him, so you'd better tell him that kind of thing isn't done. A man might dine with her, a man might even . . . with her, but really, now I'm not surprised at the sudden coldness of the Grandlieus toward that boy; I've just seen him being refused entry, on the steps. . . ."

"Girls of that kind are dangerous," said Madame de Sérisy, gazing at Esther through her lorgnette.

"Yes," said the duke, "as much for what they can do as for what they want. . . ."

"She'll ruin him!" said Madame de Sérisy. "I've heard they cost you just as much when you don't pay them as when you do."

"Oh, but not in his case!" said the young duke, making a gesture of astonishment. "Far from costing him money, they actually give it to him when he needs it; they all run after him."

A little nervous twitch could be seen around the countess's lips, a movement no one would confuse with a smile.

"Well, then," said Esther, "come to supper at midnight. Bring Blondet and Rastignac. Let's have at least two amusing people, and we'll keep the number to nine."

"We need to find some way of having the baron go look for Europe, on the pretext of giving Asia advance notice, and you can tell him what just happened to me, so that Carlos will be informed before he gets the nabob in his grip."

"I'll see to it," said Esther.

Peyrade was, therefore, without knowing it, about to find himself under the same roof with his adversary. The tiger was walking into the lion's den—and the lion was well guarded.

When Lucien returned to Madame de Sérisy's box, instead of turning and smiling to him and arranging her gown so as to make room for him next to her, she affected to pay no attention to his entrance, continuing to look around the auditorium through her lorgnette; but Lucien observed a slight trembling of the lorgnette, suggesting the countess was in the grip of one of those powerful agitations that are the currency with which we pay for our illicit joys. He stayed back from her, sitting in the opposite corner of the box, leaving a wide space between them; he leaned on the edge of the box on his right elbow, holding his chin in his gloved hand; he sat like that, in three-quarters profile, waiting for her to speak first. But by the middle of the act the countess had still not said a word to him, nor cast a glance his way.

"I don't know," she said now, "why you're here—your place is over there in the box with Mademoiselle Esther. . . ."

"I'll go there," said Lucien, getting up and leaving without looking at her.

"Ah, my dear," said Madame du Val-Noble as she entered Esther's box with Peyrade, the baron not recognizing him, "I'm delighted to introduce to you Monsieur Samuel Johnson; he's an admirer of the talents of Monsieur de Nucingen."

"Is that so, monsieur," said Esther, giving Peyrade a smile.

"Deah me yes, veddy much," said Peyrade.

"Ah! Well, baron, here's somebody speaking French the way you do, or at least the way Breton French is like Burgundian. It ought to be quite amusing listening to you two talk finance . . . Do you know what I'd like to ask of you in return for introducing you to my baron, dear Monsieur Nabob?" she asked with a smile.

"Oh deah, I rally do thenk you, do introduce me to Sir Baron."

"Very well," she said. "But you must give me the pleasure of coming to dine with us this evening. There's no sealing wax quite like champagne for binding two men together; it seals every business deal, especially the kind where you lose your shirt. Come this evening, and you'll find wonderful company! And as for you, my little Frédéric," she said in the baron's ear, "you have your carriage here, so rush over to the Rue Saint-Georges and bring Europe to me; I need to tell her a couple of things about the supper. I got Lucien to agree to come, and he'll bring along a couple of witty friends. . . ." Then, whispering to Madame du Val-Noble, "We're going to have a little fun with your Englishman."

Peyrade and the baron left the two women to themselves.

When Pleasures Turn Disagreeable

"Ah, my dear, if you can have any fun with that beast, you're smarter than the rest of us," said Val-Noble.

"If all else fails, you can lend him to me for a week," said Esther with a laugh.

"No, you wouldn't get through half a day with him," replied Madame du Val-Noble; "it's tough bread I've got to eat, and I'm breaking my teeth on it. I hope for the rest of my life I never again have to be in charge of entertaining an Englishman. . . . They're all cold egotists, just pigs dressed up in men's clothing."

"But surely there's some consideration?" asked Esther, smiling.

"On the contrary, my dear—that monster still hasn't even begun calling me *tu!*"

"Not even in . . . any situation?" asked Esther.

"The lout always refers to me as *madame,* and he's always completely impassive just when other men are more or less nice. Love, for him, I swear, it's like shaving. He wipes off his razor, puts it back in its case, looks at himself in the mirror, and says, 'Well, I managed not to cut myself.' Then he treats me with so much respect it would drive a woman mad. This damned Lord Stay-at-Home amuses himself by hiding poor Théodore, having him left standing in my dressing room half the day. And he seems determined to undermine me in every way. And stingy . . . God, he's like Gobseck and Gigonnet combined. He asks me out for dinner, and then he doesn't pay for the cab that brings me, if by chance I didn't use my own."

"Well, what do you get in return for all this?" asked Esther.

"Absolutely nothing. Five hundred francs cold cash a month, and the rent on the carriage. And that carriage, do you know what it is? It's the kind that grocers rent on their wedding day, to take them to the Town Hall, the church, and the Cadran-Bleu . . .[43] He drives me crazy with his respect. If my nerves are giving me trouble and I'm a little nasty, he doesn't get upset. He just says, 'I meahly wish milady to do as she likes, for nothing could be as detestable—cehtainly no rill gentlmn would say such a thing to a nice lady—as, don't you know, "You're a fine bale of cotton, a fine piece of merchandise." Tee-hee! No, I belong to the Temperance Society, and I am antislavery!' And my fool sits there pale and ice cold, giving me to understand that he has an equal amount of respect for me and a negro, and it's not because he feels anything, but because he's got abolitionist opinions."

"What could be worse!" said Esther. "But I'd empty those cashboxes of his, our little Chinaman."

"Empty his cashboxes?" said Madame du Val-Noble. "He'd have to be in love first. But even you, you wouldn't dare ask him for two sous. He'd listen to you solemnly and then pronounce, in that British tone that makes you feel you'd rather he just came right out and slapped you in the face, that he's already been paying you plenty 'consid'ring what a small role love plays in my humble existence.'"

"To think that, in our situation, we have to put up with men like that!" exclaimed Esther.

"Ah, you've been lucky, you know! . . . But watch out for your Nucingen."

"Oh, he has some scheme, your nabob?"

"That's what Adèle thinks," said Madame du Val-Noble.

"The more I think about it, my dear, the more I think that man must have set out deliberately to make himself hated by women, and to get sent packing when the time is right."

"Yes, or else he wants to do some business with Nucingen and he took me on only because he knew we were connected—again, that's what

Adèle thinks," Madame du Val-Noble replied. "That's why I introduced him to you tonight. Ah, if I could be sure of what scheme he's plotting, how prettily I could come to an understanding with you and Nucingen!"

"Don't you ever lose your temper and tell him off once in a while?" asked Esther.

"You'd try it, you're sharp enough . . . but no matter how nice you were to him, he'd still kill you off with those icy smiles of his. 'I'm evah so antislavery, you know, and deah me, you are quite free. . . .' You could say the most amusing things to him, and he'd look at you and say, 'Oh, veddy good!' And you'd realize that in his eyes you're nothing more than a puppet."

"Don't you get angry?"

"Oh, it's the same thing! It's like a little play for him to watch. A surgeon could operate on him on his left side, below his breast, and it wouldn't do him the slightest harm; his insides are all made of tin. I said that to him. He replied, 'I'm rathah pleased to have such a physical cawnstitution. . . .' And always, always polite. I swear, his soul wears gloves. . . . I'll go on enduring this martyrdom for a few more days, just to satisfy my curiosity. Otherwise, I would have had my man Philippe give Milord a slap in the face by now, because Philippe has no peer when it comes to the sword. . . ."

"I was going to suggest that!" cried Esther. "But you'd better find out first if he knows how to box, because these old Englishmen, my dear, can be bottomless pits of malice."

"There aren't any more like this one! . . . No, if you could see him coming to me to get his orders, and at what hours he duly presents himself in order to surprise me (of course), and the way he uses the formulas of respect that the English consider *gentlemanly,* you'd say, 'There's a woman whose man adores her.' And any other woman would say so too . . ."

"But you know, they envy us, my dear," said Esther.

"Yes, well!" cried Madame du Val-Noble. "Look, we've all had occasion in our lives to see just how little we matter to them; but my dear, I've never been so cruelly, so profoundly, so completely scorned by any brutal man as I have been by the respect I get from this fat sack of Porto. When he's drunk he goes away, 'so as not to be unpleasant,' he said to Adèle, and not to be under the influence of two *temptations* at once— women and wine. He actually makes more use of my carriage than I do . . . Oh, if we could manage to drink him under the table tonight . . . But he can drink ten bottles and not be drunk: his eyes get bleary, but he still sees everything."

"Just like people who let their windows stay dirty on the outside while they can still see everything perfectly from inside," said Esther. "I know some men like that—du Tillet is an excellent example."

"Try to get du Tillet working together with Nucingen—the two of them could pull one of their fancy schemes on him, and at least I'd feel avenged! They'd reduce him to begging! Oh, my dear, to have fallen into the hands of this hypocrite Protestant, and after my poor Falleix, who was so funny, such a good sort, such a *wit*! Oh, the laughs we had. . . . People say stockbrokers are all dullards . . . well, this one was dull-witted only once."

"When he left you without a sou, he taught you how pleasure can have its disagreeable side."

Europe, brought in by Nucingen, stuck her viperlike head in the door; and after listening to a few words whispered to her by her mistress, she disappeared.

Vipers' Tangle

At eleven-thirty that night, five coaches came to a halt on the Rue Saint-Georges, in front of the home of our illustrious courtesan. One contained Lucien with Rastignac, Blondet, and Bixiou, another was du Tillet's, another the baron's, another the nabob's, and the last was Florine's, she having been recruited by du Tillet. The fact that the windows were still boarded up was disguised by thick Chinese curtains that fell in magnificent folds. The supper was to be served at one, the candles glowed, and the drawing room and dining room displayed their sumptuous furnishings. This promised to be one of those debauched nights that only these three women and these men knew how to resist. There was gambling first, because a couple of hours had to be passed somehow.

"Will you play, milord?" du Tillet asked Peyrade.

"I deah say. You know, I've played with O'Connel, Pitt, Fox, Canning, Lord Brougham, Lord . . ."

"Oh, just say 'an infinity of lords,'" said Bixiou.

"Lord Fitz-William, Lord Ellenborough, Lord Herfort, Lord . . ."

Bixiou was staring at Peyrade's shoes, and he bent down to examine them.

"What are you looking for?" Blondet asked.

"The switch you use to turn this machine off," said Florine.

"Shall we play for twenty francs a trick?" asked Lucien.

"I say, we sh'll play for whatever amount you'd cah to lose. . . ."

"He's good, isn't he?" Esther said to Lucien. "They all take him for an Englishman."

Du Tillet, Nucingen, Peyrade, and Rastignac all sat down to play whist. Florine, Madame du Val-Noble, Esther, Blondet, and Bixiou stood around the fireplace chatting. Lucien passed the time paging through a superb volume of engravings.

"Madame is served," announced Paccard, outfitted in splendid livery.

Peyrade was put on the left of Florine, with Bixiou on his other side, the latter having been coaxed by Esther into challenging the nabob to drink as much as he possibly could. Bixiou himself possessed the ability of being able to drink endless amounts. Never in his life had Peyrade seen such splendor, nor tasted such magnificent cuisine, nor seen such beautiful women.

"This evening is worth all the money Val-Noble has cost me," he thought, "and besides, I've just won a thousand francs from them."

"Now this is an example other men ought to follow," Madame du Val-Noble exclaimed to Lucien, making a sweeping gesture around at all the luxurious furnishings of the dining room.

Esther had seated Lucien next to her, and she kept his foot between hers below the table.

"Did you hear me?" Val-Noble said to Peyrade, who was playing blind. "This is how you ought to decorate my house! When a man comes back from the Indies with millions and he wants to do some business with the Nucingens, he ought to get himself up on the same level."

"You see, I belong, don't you know, to the temperance society. . . ."

"Then you'd better drink up, because it's hot over there in the Indies, old Uncle!" said Bixiou.

Bixiou maintained a running joke all through the dinner that Peyrade was an uncle of his, just back from the Indies.

"Madame du Val-Noble tellss me zat you haff some ideas. . . ." Nucingen said, looking Peyrade over.

"This is what I wanted to hear," said du Tillet to Rastignac, "the two kinds of gibberish together."

"They'll end up understanding each other," said Bixiou, who guessed what du Tillet had just said to Rastignac.

"Sir Baron, I've devised just the teeniest little speculation scheme, and I do say, quite the comfortable scheme it is, with a fine prospect of profits. . . ."

"Just wait," Blondet said to du Tillet, "he won't be able to go a whole minute without bringing in Parliament or the English government."

"Naow, to be in China, you see, for the opium . . ."

"Ach, ja, I know zis," said Nucingen, a man who practically owned global trade, "but ze Henglich gufferment hass ze planss for using zis opium for hopening hup zis China, und zey vill neffer permit us . . ."

"Ah—Nucingen scooped him on the government reference," du Tillet said to Blondet.

"I see now—you're involved in the opium business," cried Madame du Val-Noble. "That explains why you have such a stupefying effect—you must have absorbed it into your heart. . . ."

"Chust look at zat!" said the baron to the so-called opium merchant, pointing to Madame du Val-Noble. "You are chust like me—ve millionaires, ve neffer get luffed by ze ladies."

"Oh, rathah, indeed, I'm quite the one for love, I am, my deah lady" said Peyrade.

"But always in the cause of temperance," said Bixiou, who had just got Peyrade to ingest his third bottle of Bordeaux, and who was now opening a bottle of Porto wine.

"I say!" exclaimed Peyrade. "Very fine, this Portugal wine from England."

Blondet, du Tillet, and Bixiou exchanged a smile. Peyrade had the ability to parody everything, even wit. Few Englishmen will fail to insist that the gold and silver in England are better than that found elsewhere. The chickens and the eggs we export from Normandy for sale in the London markets authorize the English to claim that the chickens and eggs of London are superior (*very fines*)[44] to those of Paris, though they come from the same place. Esther and Lucien sat there astounded at this perfect imitation of costume, language, and prejudice. The drinking and the eating went on, accompanied by so much laughter and conversation that it was now four in the morning. Bixiou thought he had managed to bring off one of the sort of triumphs that Brillat-Savarin so pleasantly describes.[45] But just as he was saying to himself, pouring a drink for his uncle, "I've conquered England," Peyrade responded with "Fill it up, my boy." Only Bixiou heard this slip into colloquial French.

"Well, now! He's no more English than I am! My uncle is a Gascon! Perfectly natural, I suppose!"

Bixiou was alone with Peyrade, and nobody else heard this revelation. Peyrade fell from his chair onto the floor. Paccard immediately appeared, picking Peyrade up and carrying him up into an attic room, where he remained in a deep sleep.

At six o'clock the next evening, the nabob was awakened by feeling a wet cloth being applied to his face, and he found he was lying on a rough trestle bed, face to face with Asia, who was wearing a domino mask.

"Hello, Papa Peyrade. It's just the two of us, eh?" she said.

"Where am I?" he asked, looking around the room.

"Just listen to me; it'll sober you up," Asia replied. "Now, even though you don't really love Madame du Val-Noble, you do love your daughter, don't you?"

"My daughter?"

"Yes, Mademoiselle Lydie."

"Ah. Well."

"Well. She's not at your home on the Rue des Moineaux anymore. She's been taken away."

Peyrade let out the kind of sigh wounded soldiers sigh on a battlefield when they're dying of a mortal wound.

"While you were counterfeiting an Englishman, they were counterfeiting Peyrade. Your little Lydie believed she was going off with her father. She's in a safe place . . . but oh, you'll never find her! At least not unless you make up for the damage you've done."

"What damage?"

"Yesterday, the Duc de Grandlieu refused Lucien de Rubempré entrance to his house. This is the result of your intrigues—you and the man you work with. Shut your mouth. Listen to me!" said Asia, seeing Peyrade about to speak. "You'll never see your girl again, pure and unstained," Asia continued, emphasizing every word to be crystal clear to him, "until the day after Monsieur Lucien de Rubempré walks out of Saint-Thomas-d'Aquin, the husband of Mademoiselle Clotilde. If, within ten days, Lucien de Rubempré is not received again as he was in the past at the home of the Grandlieus, you will die a most violent death, from which no power on earth can protect you. . . . And then, when you feel yourself dying, you'll be given just enough time to absorb the thought, 'My daughter will be a prostitute till the end of her days!' You were stupid enough to let us get our claws into that little prize, but you still have enough intelligence to reflect on this communication from our government. Don't go barking around; don't say a word; go to Contenson's, change your clothes, and then go home. Katt will tell you that Lydie received word from you, she went out and hasn't returned. If you make a complaint, take any steps, your little Lydie will begin where I told you she'd finish—she's been *promised* to de Marsay. We don't need to say any soft, soothing words to old Papa Canquoëlle now, do we? We don't need to wear mittens, eh? . . . All right—go now, and think carefully before you meddle in our affairs again."

Asia left Peyrade in a pitiable state; every word had struck him like a hammer. There were two tears in the spy's eyes, and two more at the bottom of his cheeks, both pairs joined by trails of moisture.

"We're expecting Monsieur Johnson for dinner," said Europe, poking her head in the door a moment later.

Peyrade made no reply, instead making his way down the stairs and into the street, coming to a cab stand; he then hurried to change his clothes at Contenson's, saying not a word to him, resuming his guise of Father Canquoëlle, and he was home by eight. He ascended the stairs, his heart pounding. When the Fleming heard her master coming, she said innocently, "Oh, where is mademoiselle?" At those words, the old spy had to lean against the wall. The blow was too much for him. He went into his daughter's room, ultimately fainting with grief when he saw it was empty, and heard Katt describe the circumstances of her taking, as cleverly pulled off as anything he could have done himself. "All right," he said to himself, "I'll have to bend with it; I'll get my revenge later, but right now, let's head to Corentin's. . . . This is the first time we've met real adversaries. Corentin will let the fine young man marry empresses, if that's what he wants! . . . Oh, now I understand—my daughter loved him at first sight. . . . The Spanish priest knows his business. . . . Courage, Papa Peyrade—disgorge your prey!" But the poor father could not imagine the hideous blow that yet awaited him.

Once arrived at Corentin's, Bruno, a trusted servant who knew Peyrade, told him, "Monsieur has left. . . ."

"For how long?"

"Ten days!"

"Where?"

"I don't know!"

"Good God, I'm getting stupid," he exclaimed to himself. "I asked him where—as if we ever told them."

At the Belle-Étoile

A few hours before Peyrade would be awakened in the attic room on the Rue Saint-Georges, Corentin, coming in from Passy, presented himself at the home of the Duc de Grandlieu, dressed like the valet of some good house. The ribbon of the Legion of Honor decorated his black suit. He had made himself into a very wrinkled little old man with powdered hair, very pale. His eyes were veiled by tortoise-shell spectacles. He looked very much like an old bureaucrat. When he announced his name (Monsieur de Saint-Denis), he was conducted into the study of the Duc de Grandlieu, where he found Derville reading the letter he had himself dictated to one of his agents, the one who was a handwriting expert. The duke took Corentin aside to explain to him everything that Corentin already knew. Monsieur de Saint-Denis listened coldly, respectfully, amusing himself by observing the great aristocrat, penetrating to the bedrock below the velvet, seeing that this man's entire life, now and for always, was dedicated to whist and the status of the Grandlieu family. Great lords are so naïve with their inferiors that Corentin did not need to pose many questions to Monsieur de Grandlieu to get the condescensions flowing.

"Please believe me, monsieur," Corentin said to Derville after having been properly introduced, "we really should leave this very evening for Angoulême via the Bordeaux diligence, which gets there just as quickly as the mail coach, and we shouldn't need to stay there any more than six hours to pick up all the information *monsieur le duc* wants. It is simply a matter—if I have understood Your Lordship—of learning whether the sister and brother-in-law of Monsieur de Rubempré are able to have given him twelve hundred thousand francs?" he asked, looking to the Duc.

"Perfectly understood," said the peer of France.

"We can be back here in four days," Corentin said, looking at Derville, "and neither of us will have been gone long enough for our affairs to have suffered."

"That was the sole objection I had to make to His Lordship," said Derville. "It's four o'clock; I'll go say a word or two to my chief clerk, pack my bag, and, after dinner, by eight o'clock, I'll . . . But will there be seats open on the diligence?"

"I'll see to that," said Corentin. "Be at the courtyard of the Messageries du Grand-Bureau at eight o'clock. If there aren't any seats, I'll see to it that some will be made for us—after all, that's the way Monsieur le Duc de Grandlieu deserves to be treated. . . ."

"Messieurs," the duke said with infinite grace, "I can never thank you enough . . ."

Corentin and the lawyer, understanding that phrase to mean that they were dismissed, bowed and took their leave. At the moment when Peyrade was questioning Corentin's servant, Monsieur de Saint-Denis and Derville, seated in the Bordeaux diligence, were silent as they departed Paris. The next morning, between Orléans and Tours, Derville became bored and started chatting, and Corentin deigned to humor him; but he kept his distance, letting him think he belonged to the diplomatic corps and was hoping to achieve a consul-generalship through the offices of the

Duc de Grandlieu. Two days after their departure from Paris, Corentin and Derville stopped at Mansle, to the great surprise of the lawyer, who thought they were going to Angoulême.

"We'll get some good details in this little town," Corentin explained, "concerning Madame Séchard."

"You know her?" asked Derville, surprised to find Corentin seeming to be so well informed.

"I got the driver talking when I realized he was from Angoulême. He told me Madame Séchard lives in Marsac, and Marsac is only one league from Mansle. I thought we'd be better off here than Angoulême for finding out the facts."

"Well, anyway," Derville said to himself, "I'm only here, as *monsieur le duc* said, to act as a witness to the inquiries this confidential agent carries out."

The inn at Mansle, called the Belle-Étoile, was run by one of those huge, fat men that one assumes will no longer be living if one returns on a future visit and yet that are still there, ten years later, standing in the doorway, sporting the same surplus quantity of flesh, the same greasy hair, the same triple chin that novelists from the immortal Cervantes to the immortal Walter Scott have depicted to the point of sterotype. Don't they all brag up their cuisine, and then end up serving you a skinny chicken with vegetables drenched in rancid butter? And they boast about their fine wines, and then force you to drink the local ones. But since he was quite young, Corentin had learned how to coax things more essential than dubious dishes and apocryphal wines out of innkeepers. Thus he acted the part of a man easy to please, one who was prepared to rely entirely on the recommendations of the best cook in Mansle—as he told the fat man.

"It isn't hard to be the best, when you're the only one," replied the host.

"Serve us in the side room," said Corentin, giving Derville a wink, "and above all don't be afraid to give us a good fire; we need to thaw out our frostbite."

"It was not warm in that coach," said Derville.

"Is it far from here to Marsac?" Corentin asked the innkeeper's wife, who had come down from the upper regions of the house when she learned the diligence had left two travelers who would be spending the night.

"Are you going to Marsac, monsieur?" the hostess asked.

"I'm not sure," he replied, a little sharply. "But the distance from here to there—is it considerable?" Corentin reasked the question after giving the hostess time to get a glimpse of his red ribbon.

"By cabriolet it's about half an hour," the innkeeper's wife said.

"Do you know if Monsieur and Madame Séchard are there in the winter?"

"Of course. They live there all year round. . . ."

"It's five o'clock now. I assume we'd find them still up if we got there at nine."

"Oh, until ten. They have company every evening—the curé, Monsieur Marron, the doctor."

"Good people, eh!" said Derville.

"Oh, monsieur, the cream of the crop!" replied the innkeeper's wife. "Honest, decent—and not a bit ambitious! Monsieur Séchard is comfortable enough, but he could have had millions, people say, except he let his invention for papermaking be stolen from him, and now it makes all that money for the Cointet brothers. . . ."[46]

"Ah, yes, the Cointet brothers!" said Corentin.

"That's enough of that now," said the innkeeper. "Why should these gentlemen care if Monsieur Séchard does or doesn't hold the patent on the papermaking procedure? These gentlemen aren't paper merchants. . . . If you plan to spend the night with me here—at the Belle-Étoile," said the innkeeper, addressing the two travelers, "here is the book, and I ask you to please sign your names. We have a local policeman here with nothing better to do than to harass us. . . ."

"Well, damn it, I was under the impression that the Séchards were very wealthy," said Corentin while Derville signed them both in, also writing down his position as lawyer connected to the Tribunal of the First Instance of the Seine.[47]

"Some people," the innkeeper said, "say they're millionaires, but then, trying to stop tongues from talking is like trying to stop rivers from flowing. Séchard's father left two hundred thousand francs in property, they say, and that's plenty for a man who started life as a laborer. I wouldn't be surprised to hear he had that much again in savings . . . because toward the end, he was making ten or twelve thousand out of his land. So, let's suppose he was fool enough to just let his money sit for ten years, then that would be the whole of it. But you put three hundred thousand francs out for interest, which is what people think he did, and you can figure it out for yourself. Five hundred thousand francs—that's pretty well shy of a million. Let me have the difference, and you wouldn't see me here at the Belle-Étoile for long."

"So," said Corentin, "Monsieur David Séchard and his wife do not have two or three million. . . ."

"You see," interjected the innkeeper's wife, "that's what they gave to the Cointets, the ones who stole his invention, and they didn't pay him any more than twenty thousand for it. . . . So where are honest, decent people going to get their hands on millions? They had a hard enough time of it during the old man's lifetime. Without Kolb, their manager, and Madame Kolb, who's just as devoted to them as her husband is, they'd have had a hard time just surviving. What did they have, with La Verberie? A thousand écus in income!"[48]

Corentin took Derville aside, saying to him, "So, *in vino veritas*! If you want the truth, look under the *buchons*.[49] In my view, the local inn is the real civic center—the notary himself knows less than the innkeeper about what goes on in a small town. . . . Look how they expect us to know all about the Cointets, the Kolbs, and all the rest of it. An innkeeper is like a living record of everything that happens—he outpolices the police. A government needs to employ a couple of hundred spies at most, because in a country like France, there are ten million honest informers. But we don't have to believe this report completely, even though, in this little town, people would have heard about twelve hundred thousand francs going to purchase the Rubempré estate. . . . We won't stay here long. . . ."

"I certainly hope not," said Derville.

"This is why," Corentin continued, "I've come up with the most natural method for getting the truth right from the Séchards themselves. I'm going to count on you, in your role as lawyer, to support me in a little ruse I'm going to use to get them to give us a clear and complete account of their finances. After dinner, we'll leave to go see Monsieur Séchard," said Corentin to the innkeeper's wife, "so please prepare our beds for us; we'd each like our own room. There's always plenty of room to sleep *à la Belle-Étoile*."

"Oh, monsieur, we didn't name the place; it was already called that when we came."

"Oh, no, that pun works all over France; you don't have a monopoly on it."[50]

"Dinner is ready, messieurs," said the innkeeper.

"Well, where the devil did that young man get his money? . . . Was the anonymous letter right? Could he have got the money from some pretty girl's earnings?" said Derville to Corentin as they settled down at the table.

"Now that's a subject for a different inquiry," said Corentin. "Lucien de

Rubempré lived, the Duc de Chaulieu told me, with a converted Jewess who passed herself off as coming from Holland, by the name of Esther Van Bogseck."

"What a coincidence!" exclaimed the lawyer. "I've been looking for the heiress of a Dutchman named Gobseck—which is the same name, only with a couple of consonants turned around . . ."

"Well, I can find more information on the connection for you when I get back to Paris."

An hour later, the two agents of the house of Grandlieu left for La Verberie, the home of Monsieur and Madame Séchard.

One of Corentin's Thousand Traps

Lucien had never felt emotions as deep as those that seized him at La Verberie when he compared his fate with that of his brother-in-law. And now the two Parisians were about to encounter the same spectacle that a few days earlier had so powerfully struck Lucien. There everything breathed calm and abundance. At the hour the two strangers were to arrive, the drawing room of La Verberie was occupied by five people: the curé de Marsac, a young priest of twenty-five who, at the request of Madame Séchard, was tutor to her son Lucien; the local doctor, whose name was Monsieur Marron; the mayor of the commune; and an old retired colonel who grew roses on a little plot across the road from La Verberie. Every evening during winter this same group met to play an innocent game of Boston, at one centime per trick, to have a look at the newspapers, or to report what they had read. When Monsieur and Madame Séchard bought La Verberie—a pretty little house, limestone, with a slate roof—it included a pleasant garden area of some two acres. As time passed, Madame Séchard, by devoting her savings to the project, had extended her garden as far as a little stream, cutting down the vines she had bought and converting the area into lawn and flowerbeds, so that, by now, La Verberie, surrounded by a little park of around twenty acres and enclosed by walls, passed for the most important property in the region. The house that had belonged to old Séchard, as well as its various outbuildings, was now used only for the twenty-some acres of vines he had left, as well as five small farms that produced around six thousand francs a year in income, and ten acres of meadow, situated on the other side of the little stream, facing the park of La Verberie; thus Madame Séchard was hoping to add them the next year. La Verberie was frequently being referred to these days as a château, and people had taken to calling Ève Séchard the Lady of Marsac. It gratified

Lucien's vanity to imitate the local peasants and wine-growers in this. Courtois, who owned a mill that was picturesquely located a couple of rifle shots from La Verberie, was—people said—in negotiations with Madame Séchard to sell the mill. That likely acquisition would make La Verberie into one of the finest estates in the Département. Madame Séchard, who did a great deal of good, and did it with as much intelligence as generosity, was widely esteemed and loved. Her beauty had blossomed magnificently and was now approaching its highest point of fullness. Although she was about twenty-six, she still enjoyed the freshness of youth while rejoicing in the peace and abundance of country life. She was still in love with her husband, respecting in him both the man of talent and the man modest enough to turn his back on a life of fame; to give her portrait in its essence, perhaps nothing more need be said beyond this: never had a single throb of her heart been inspired by anyone other than her children and her husband. The tax that misfortune levies on us was, in her case, the sorrow that Lucien's mode of living had caused them, and Ève Séchard had presentiments of something mysterious and worse when, during his most recent visit, Lucien waved off all their questions by saying that an ambitious man owes an account of himself and his actions only to himself. In the last six years Lucien had seen his sister only three times, and had written her no more than six letters. His first visit to La Verberie had been to attend his mother's funeral, and the most recent had been to ask her to do him the favor of telling a lie that was critical to his plans. This was between Monsieur Séchard, madame, and her brother, and the scene had been a painful one that had left a hideous lurking fear in the heart of this otherwise sweet and noble existence.

The interior of the house had been changed as much as the surroundings had, and it now spoke of comfort without luxury, which was evident from casting a rapid glance around the drawing room where the company had now gathered. A pretty Aubusson carpet,[51] hangings of gray cotton twill bound with green silk braid, painting that created the impression of Spa woodwork, furniture of carved mahogany upholstered in gray and green as well, flower stands loaded with flowers no matter the season—all this created an ensemble to charm the eye. The window curtains were green silk, and the ornaments above the fireplace, the frames around the mirrors, all were exempt from that false taste so common in the provinces. The smallest details were elegant and clean, providing a space in which soul and eyes could rest, a space marked by the poetry with which a loving, intelligent woman can and should suffuse her home.

Madame Séchard, still wearing mourning for her father-in-law, was working near the fire on a piece of tapestry, aided by Madame Kolb, the housekeeper, to whom she entrusted all the details of the household. At the moment the cabriolet was reaching the first houses in Marsac, the regular company of La Verberie was being augmented by the presence of the miller, Courtois, a widower, who was hoping to retire from business and who was also hoping he could get *"the best price"* for his property, which Madame Séchard clearly wanted very much, and Courtois knew why.

"Look—a cabriolet is stopping here!" said Courtois, hearing the noise of the vehicle. "And from the way the metal sounds, it must be local. . . ."

"It's probably Postel and his wife, coming to see me," said the doctor.

"No," said Courtois, "it's coming from the Mansle side."

"Matame," said Kolb, a big, fat Alsatian, "here iss lawyer from Baris who vants to speak vit monsieur."

"A lawyer!" cried Séchard. "The word gives me the colic."

"Thank you very much," said the mayor of Marsac, a man named Cachan, a lawyer for some twenty years in Angoulême, and who had, at one time, been given the task of pursuing David Séchard.

Ève smiled, and said, "Ah, my poor David will never change! He'll always be absent-minded."

"A lawyer from Paris," said Courtois. "So you have some business in Paris?"

"No," said Ève.

"Well, you have a brother there," Courtois said with a smile.

"Let's just hope it's got nothing to do with the old man's inheritance," said Cachan. "He was involved in some shady dealings."

Upon entering, Corentin and Derville, after having introduced themselves to the company, asked to speak privately with Madame Séchard and her husband.

"Of course," said Séchard. "But is it a matter of business?"

"It's only a matter involving the inheritance from your father," Corentin replied.

"In that case, permit monsieur the mayor to join us—he's a former lawyer from Angoulême."

"You are Monsieur Derville?" Cachan said, looking at Corentin.

"No, monsieur; monsieur here is Derville," indicating his colleague, who bowed.

"But," Séchard said, "we're all family here—we have nothing to hide from our neighbors, so there's no need to go into the study, where there's no fire anyway. . . . Our lives are an open book."

"The life of monsieur your father," said Corentin, "may involve some mysteries that, perhaps, you would not want widely known."

"Is it something that will embarrass us?" asked Ève, suddenly afraid.

"Oh, no—just a peccadillo from the years of his youth," said Corentin, beginning to deploy, in the calmest possible way, one of his thousand traps. "Monsieur your father has given you an older brother. . . ."

"Oh, the old Bear!" cried Courtois. "He never much liked you, Monsieur Séchard, and he kept this a secret, the sneak. . . . Ah! Now I understand what he meant one day when he said, 'When I'm in the ground, then you'll hear some fine things!'"

"Don't be alarmed, monsieur," said Corentin to Séchard, while studying Ève with a sidelong glance.

"A brother!" cried the doctor. "But that means your inheritance will need to be shared."

Derville pretended to be looking at the engravings, proof sheets, that were hung on the room's paneled walls.

"Oh, don't worry, madame," said Corentin, seeing the surprise on Madame Séchard's beautiful face, "it's only a matter of a natural child. A natural child does not have the same rights as a legitimate one. This boy is living in terrible poverty, and he is entitled to a sum based on the whole inheritance . . . the millions left by your father. . . ."

At that word, "millions," a cry of surprise rose up in unison from the entire company in the drawing room. Now Derville was no longer studying the engravings.

"Old Séchard, millions?" said fat Courtois. "Who on earth told you that? Must have been some peasant."

"Monsieur," said Cachan, "you're not from the taxation office, so we can tell you how things truly stand. . . ."

"Rest assured," said Corentin; "I give you my word of honor that we are not employed by the Treasury."

Cachan made a sign for everyone else to be still, and he looked satisfied.

"Monsieur," continued Corentin, "even if there had only been one million, the natural child would be very well situated. We haven't come to start any lawsuit. On the contrary, we've come to propose that you simply give us one hundred thousand francs, and we'll be on our way—"

"A hundred thousand francs!" cried Cachan, interrupting Corentin. "But, monsieur, old Séchard left twenty acres of vineyard, five little farms, and ten acres near Marsac, and not a single sou with it. . . ."

"Monsieur Cachan, I won't tell a lie for anything in the world," cried David Séchard, intervening, "and especially when it concerns someone else's interest. . . . Monsieur," he said to Corentin and Derville, "my father left us, in addition to his property—"at this, Courtois and Cachan vainly signaled him to be quiet—"three hundred thousand francs, which brings the total of the inheritance to about five hundred thousand."

"Monsieur Cachan," said Ève Séchard, "what does the law say a natural child is owed?"

"Madame," said Corentin, "we are not Turks. We will simply ask you to swear to us, in front of these gentlemen, that you have received no more than one hundred thousand écus in money from your father-in-law, and that will be good enough for us. . . ."

"Give me first your word of honor," the former lawyer of Angoulême said to Derville, "that you are truly a lawyer."

"Here is my passport," Derville said to Cachan, handing him a paper folded in four, "and my colleague here is not an inspector from the Treasury, so rest assured on that point," Derville added. "Our only aim is to find out the truth about the Séchard inheritance, and now we know it." Derville took Madame Ève's hand and led her very courteously to the other side of the drawing room. "Madame," he said to her in a low voice, "if the honor and the future of the house of Grandlieu were not at stake in this issue, I would never have agreed to the stratagem of that decorated gentleman. . . . But you must pardon him, for it's a matter of discovering the lie that allowed your brother to get access to that family's sanctuary. Be very careful now, and do not let it be said that you have given twelve hundred thousand francs to monsieur your brother to purchase the Rubempré estate. . . ."

"Twelve hundred thousand francs!" exclaimed Madame Séchard, going pale. "But where did he get it then, the poor man?"

"Ah," said Derville, "I fear that the source of that money is tainted."

Ève had tears in her eyes, which her friends perceived.

"We have, I think, done you a great favor," Derville said to her, "by preventing you from getting mixed up in a lie that could have some very dangerous consequences."

Derville left Madame Séchard seated there, pale, tears on her face, and bowed to the company.

"To Mansle!" said Corentin to the boy driving the cabriolet.

The diligence going at night from Bordeaux to Paris had only one seat available: Derville begged Corentin to let him have it, saying he had important business to attend to; but deep down he distrusted his traveling companion, whose diplomatic dexterity and cold-bloodedness looked too much like they were habitual with him. Corentin stayed on in Mansle three days without finding a way to get back; at last he had to write to Bordeaux and reserve a place for the Paris diligence; he did not get back home until nine days from his departure.

During that time, Peyrade went looking for him every morning—to his place in Passy, to his place in Paris—to find out if he had returned. On the eighth day he left a letter in code at each place, explaining to his colleague the death threat he was under, the kidnapping of Lydie, and the hideous fate his enemies had promised him.

Mene, Tekel, Upharsin

Under attack now, as he had so often attacked others, Peyrade, deprived of Corentin but still aided by Contenson, continued to wear his nabob disguise. Even though his invisible enemies had found him out, he thought it would be wise to remain on the field of battle. Contenson had set all the people he knew on the trail of Lydie, hoping to discover the house where she was being held; but as each day passed, the impossibility of learning even the smallest fact became clearer, and every hour added to Peyrade's despair. The old spy surrounded himself with a sort of guard, consisting of some twelve to fifteen of the most capable agents, each of whom was assigned a code number. They kept up surveillance on the Rue des Moineaux and the Rue Taitbout, where he lived, as nabob, with Madame du Val-Noble. During the last three days of the fatal period that Asia had allowed Peyrade to get Lucien reestablished with the Grandlieus, Contenson never left the old veteran, the former lieutenant-general of police. That poetic terror that warring tribes spread throughout the forests of America, of such benefit to Cooper, was likewise being spread throughout Parisian life. Pedestrians passing by, shops, cabs, a person standing at a corner, all presented the same potentially profound interest to the agents tasked with defending Peyrade's life as, in the novels of Cooper, do a tree trunk, a beaver dam, the skin of a bison, a motionless canoe, or a leaf drifting on the water.

"If the Spaniard is gone, you have nothing left to fear," Contenson said to Peyrade, pointing out how quiet everything around them was.

"And if he's not gone?" replied Peyrade.

"He took one of my men along in his wake, but at Blois my man was forced to get down off the coach, and wasn't able to get back on."

One morning, five days after Derville's return, Lucien was visited by Rastignac.

"My friend, I feel terrible having to bring this news to you; I was given the task because of our friendship. Your marriage is broken off, and there's no hope of reviving it. Never set foot again in the Grandlieu home. To marry Clotilde, you'd have to wait for her father to die, and he's too much of a narcissist to go any time soon. These old whist players hang on forever—hang on to the edge of the card table. . . . Clotilde is headed to Italy with Madeleine de Lenoncourt-Chaulieu. The poor girl was so much in love with you, my friend, that they've had to keep watch over her—she wanted to come see you, she'd made an escape plan. . . . I thought knowing that might be some consolation in your misfortune."

Lucien said nothing, instead simply looking at Rastignac.

"But after all, is it such a disaster?" his compatriot said. "You can easily find another girl just as noble as, and more beautiful than, Clotilde! . . . Madame de Sérisy would find you a wife out of vengeance; she detests the Grandlieus, because they've never invited her. And she has a niece, little Clémence du Rouvre. . . ."

"My friend, since that last supper we had, I'm not on good terms with Madame de Sérisy. She saw me in Esther's box, she started making a scene, and I just let her do it."

"A woman of forty won't stay angry long at a man as good-looking as you," said Rastignac. "I'm familiar with these little sunsets. . . . They last ten minutes on the horizon, and ten years in a woman's heart."

"I've waited all week for a letter from her."

"Go over there!"

"Now I suppose I have to."

"Are you coming, anyway, to Val-Noble's? Her nabob is giving a dinner for Nucingen, to repay the one he had."

"Yes, I am, and I will," Lucien said gloomily.

The day following this confirmation of his fall from grace, the facts of which were quickly passed on to Carlos by Asia, Lucien went along with Rastignac and Nucingen to the home of the phony nabob.

At midnight the dining room that used to be Esther's reunited nearly all the characters in this drama, the underlying truths of which were known only to Esther, Lucien, Peyrade, the mulatto Contenson, and Paccard, who was there as servant to Esther. Unbeknownst to Peyrade and Contenson, Madame du Val-Noble had asked Asia to come and help her cook. When they all came to the table, Peyrade—who had given Madame du Val-Noble five hundred francs to be sure things were done well—found folded up in his napkin a slip of paper, on which the following words were written in pencil: *The ten days are up the minute you sit down at the table.* Peyrade passed the paper to Contenson, who was standing behind him, saying to him in English, "Was it you who put that in there?" Contenson read, by the light of the candles, that *Mene, Tekel, Upharsin* and put the paper in his pocket, but he knew how hard it was to tell anything from pencil, and above all from a phrase written in all capitals, which might be called having mathematical spacing, since capital letters are composed entirely of curves and straight lines, so it is impossible to divine from them the habits of an individual's hand, the way one can with the style we call cursive.

The supper was entirely cheerless. Peyrade's preoccupation was obvious. The only young men of the type who know how to liven up a dinner were Lucien and Rastignac. Lucien was sad and absorbed in his own thoughts. Rastignac had, just before the dinner, lost two thousand francs, and now he ate and drank thinking only of recouping them later. The three women were all affected by the chill and could only stare at each other. The general boredom rendered all the dishes bland and tasteless. There are some dinner parties like this, just as there are plays and books like it too; all are subject to chance. At the dinner's end they were served the ice cream desserts known as *plombières.* As everyone knows, these ices contain tiny, delicate preserved fruits and are served in small glasses, in which they take on a kind of pyramidal form. Madame du Val-Noble had ordered these desserts from Tortoni's, whose celebrated establishment is found on the corner of the Rue Taitbout and the boulevard. The cook called the mulatto out to the kitchen to pay the ice-cream vendor's bill. Contenson thought the urgency of this seemed odd, and he went downstairs, saying to the boy, "Aren't you from Tortoni's, then?" And with that he hurried back upstairs. But Paccard had already taken advantage of his absence to distribute the desserts to all. The mulatto had almost reached the door of the apartment when one of the agents surveilling the Rue des Moineaux called up the staircase to him: "Number twenty-seven."

"What is it?" said Contenson, racing back down the stairs as quickly as he could.

"Tell the old man his daughter is back, but in what a state! For God's sake, tell him to hurry—she may be dying."

When Contenson came back into the dining room, old Peyrade, who had drunk quite a lot, was just eating the cherry from the top of his dessert. They were about to drink to Madame du Val-Noble's health, and the nabob filled his glass with Constantia wine and drank it down. Even though Contenson was greatly concerned about the news he was about to tell Peyrade, he could not help noticing the profound attention with which Paccard was watching the nabob. The eyes of Madame de Champy's valet looked like two fixed flames. This observation, important as it was, did not slow the mulatto, who bent down to his master just as Peyrade set his empty glass on the table.

"Lydie is back at the house," said Contenson, "and she's in bad shape."

Peyrade loosed the most French of all French curse words with so evident a southern accent that a look of utter shock descended upon all the guests. Recognizing his slip, Peyrade dropped the disguise altogether, saying to Contenson in perfect French:

"Get me a cab! I'm going right now."

Everyone got up from the table.

"Who are you then?" cried Lucien.

"Ja! Who?" asked the baron.

"Bixiou told me you could be more English than the English, and I didn't want to believe him," said Rastignac.

"This must be some disguised bankrupt," said du Tillet in a loud voice. "I always suspected him!"

"What a strange place Paris is!" said Madame du Val-Noble. "After he goes bust in his own neighborhood, a businessman dresses up like a nabob or a dandy and walks right down the Champs-Élysées with impunity! Oh, this is just my luck—I seem to attract bankrupts like flies."

"They say every flower has its insects," Esther said calmly. "Mine is more like Cleopatra's—an asp."

"You want to know who I am?" said Peyrade from the doorway. "Ah, you'll all find out, because even if I die, I'll come back from the grave to torment you every night of your lives!"

As he said these last words, he was looking at Esther and Lucien; then he took advantage of the general astonishment to disappear with extraordinary agility, for he planned to run home without waiting for a cab. Out in the street, as he left by the carriage entrance, Asia grabbed his arm; her head was covered by one of those black shawls women in those days used to carry when they were returning from a ball.

"Better send for the sacraments, Papa Peyrade," she said, in that same voice that had prophesied his disaster.

A cab was standing there. Asia got up into it, and the cab disappeared as if carried by the wind. There had been five vehicles there; Peyrade's men couldn't tell one from the other.

The Terrible Oath of Corentin

When he returned to his country house, in one of the quietest and most pleasant streets in the little town of Passy, the Rue des Vignes, Corentin, who passed for a businessman who was a gardening enthusiast, found the coded message from his friend Peyrade. Instead of resting, he got right back into the cab that had brought him home and headed straight for the Rue des Moineaux, where he found nobody except Katt. The

Fleming told him about Lydie's disappearance, and as he listened he was astonished at the lack of foresight both he and Peyrade had been guilty of.

"*They* still don't know me," he thought. "These people are capable of anything, so I need to find out whether they're going to kill Peyrade, and if they are, I need to remain unknown."

The more disreputable a man's life is, the more fiercely he clings to it, turning every moment into one of protest or revenge. Corentin went back home and disguised himself as a sickly little old man, putting on a frock coat so worn it was turning green and a cheap wig; he then returned on foot, motivated by his friendship for Peyrade. He wanted to give orders to the most dedicated and most capable of his agents. Walking along the Rue Saint-Honoré to get from the Place Vendôme to the Rue Saint-Roch, he found himself behind a girl wearing slippers, dressed in what appeared to be nightclothes. The girl, who had on a white jacket and a nightcap, from time to time emitted little sobs intermixed with involuntary groans; Corentin passed her and then, after a few steps, turned back and recognize Lydie.

"I'm a friend of your father's, Monsieur Canquoëlle," he said, in his own, natural voice.

"Ah! Someone I can trust...." she said.

"Act as if you don't know me," Corentin continued, "because we're being hunted by cruel enemies, and we're forced to go in disguise. But tell me what's happened to you...."

"Oh, monsieur," said the poor girl, "I can give you the facts, but not the story.... I've been dishonored, lost, and I can't even say how it happened!"

"Where were you?"

"I don't know, monsieur! I escaped so hurriedly, and I've run through so many streets, taken so many detours, afraid I was being followed.... And when I encountered some respectable person, I asked the way to the boulevards, in order to get to the Rue de la Paix! Now, I've been walking for ... what time is it?"

"Eleven-thirty," said Corentin.

"I got away just when night was falling, so I've been walking for five hours now!" cried Lydie.

"Well, come along—you'll have some rest now, and you'll get to see your good old Katt again...."

"Oh, monsieur, there'll be no more rest for me! The only rest I want is in the grave, and I plan to await it in a convent—that is, if they'll think I'm worthy to enter...."

"You poor little thing! You must have resisted as much as you could?"

"Yes, monsieur. Oh, if you only knew the kind of place and the kind of creatures they put me with. . . ."

"They probably put you to sleep? . . .

"Ah, yes, that must have been it. Just a little farther and I'll be home. I feel weaker, and my thinking isn't right. . . . Just now I thought I was in a garden . . ."

Corentin picked Lydie up and carried her in his arms, where she lost consciousness, and he carried her up the stairs.

"Katt!" he called.

Katt appeared, and she shouted for joy.

"Don't rejoice yet," Corentin said solemnly. "This girl is very sick."

When they got Lydie into her bed and when, by the light of two candles that Katt had lit, she recognized her own room, she became delirious. She sang refrains from pretty songs, interspersed with some of the disgusting phrases she had heard! Her lovely face was mottled with purple. She intermixed memories of her life of purity with memories of her days of foulness. Katt wept. Corentin paced back and forth in the bedroom, stopping now and then to examine Lydie.

"She's paying for her father!" he said. "Is there really a Providence? Oh, I was wise not to have a family! A child . . . a child is, word of honor, just like some philosopher said, a hostage we give to fortune. . . ."

"Oh!" exclaimed the poor child, sitting up, her beautiful hair loosed and falling down, "instead of lying here, Katt, I ought to be lying in the sand at the bottom of the Seine. . . ."

"Katt, don't just weep and stare at your child; that isn't going to cure her; go find a doctor—try the one at the Town Hall first, and then Messieurs Desplein and Bianchon. We need to save this innocent creature. . . ."

And Corentin wrote down the addresses of the two celebrated doctors. Just then they heard familiar steps on the staircase, and a man made his way into the apartment. Peyrade, soaked in sweat, his face purple, his eyes bloodshot, panting like a porpoise, rushed to Lydie's door, crying out, "Where is my daughter?"

He saw Corentin's sad gesture, his eyes following the finger that pointed to Lydie. The only way to describe Lydie is to compare her to a flower, lovingly cultivated by a botanist, fallen from its stem and crushed underfoot by the iron clogs of a peasant. Implant that image in the heart of Fatherhood, and you'll begin to understand the blow Peyrade now received, as his eyes filled with heavy tears.

"Someone's crying—it's my father," said the child.

Lydie could still recognize her father; she got out of the bed and went down on her knees before the old man, just as he collapsed into an armchair.

"Forgive me, Papa!" she said in a voice that pierced Peyrade's heart at the very moment he was feeling as if his skull had just been clubbed in.

"I'm dying . . . oh, the beasts!" These were his last words.

Corentin rushed over to help his old friend and received his last breath.

"Poisoned!" thought Corentin. "Good, here's the doctor," he cried, hearing a coach pulling up outside.

Contenson came in, without his mulatto disguise, and he stood there like a bronze statue as he listened to Lydie saying, "Then you don't forgive me, Father? . . . But it wasn't my fault!" She did not see that her father was dead. "Oh! The way he looks at me!" said the poor mad girl. . . .

"We need to close his eyes," said Contenson. "Let's carry him to his room. His daughter is half mad already, and she'll won't be able to take it if she knows he's dead. She'll believe she caused his death."

Seeing them carry her father out of the room, Lydie stood still as if dazed.

"He was my only friend!" said Corentin, seeming to be moved when they had Peyrade laid out on his bed in his own room. "In his whole life, he never had a single impulse of greed, except for his daughter! . . . Let this be a lesson, Contenson. Every station in life has its own code of honor. Peyrade was wrong to get mixed up in the affairs of private individuals—we should always stick to public matters. But whatever happens, I swear," he said with a tone, an expression, and a gesture that struck fear into Contenson, "to avenge my poor Peyrade! I'll find out the people responsible for his death and the dishonor of his daughter! . . . And for the sake of my own self-respect, and for the few years left to me, which I will risk for this vengeance, every one of them will end his days at four o'clock, in good health, and will be given a final shave on the Place de Grève!"[52]

"And I'll help you!" Contenson said with emotion.

Nothing is more moving, in fact, than the spectacle of passion appearing in a cold, collected, methodical man, one who for twenty years had never betrayed the slightest hint of sensibility. It is like seeing the iron bar begin to melt, and melting everything it touches. There was a kind of revolution underway within Contenson.

"Poor old Papa Canquoëlle," he continued, looking at Corentin. "He stood me drinks and dinners so many times. . . . And now look—it takes a vicious man to do something like this. . . . And he used to give me ten francs to go gamble with. . . ."

After that funeral oration, Peyrade's two avengers went to Lydie's room, hearing Katt and the Town Hall doctor on the stairs.

"Go to the police commissioner," said Corentin. "The king's prosecutor won't find anything here to justify an inquiry, but still we're going to make a report to the prefecture, and that might turn out to be of some use."

Turning to the Town Hall doctor, Corentin said: "Monsieur, you'll find a dead man in that room; I do not believe he died a natural death, so therefore you will carry out an autopsy in the presence of the police commissioner, who, when I invite him, will be here soon. Try to discover any traces of poison—you'll be getting assistance from Messieurs Desplein and Bianchon, whom I've asked to come and examine the daughter of that man, my best friend. Her condition is just as bad as the father's, though he's already dead. . . ."

"I do not need," the Town Hall doctor said, "any assistance from those gentlemen to do my job. . . ."

"Well, good," thought Corentin. Then aloud he said, "Monsieur, we won't argue. Let me give you my opinion straight—those who've just killed the father have also dishonored the daughter."

When dawn came, Lydie finally surrendered to her fatigue; she was sleeping when the celebrated surgeon and the young doctor arrived. The doctor tasked with determining the cause of Peyrade's death had by then opened up the corpse for his examination.

"While we're waiting for the girl to wake up," Corentin said to the two famous doctors, "would you be willing to help one of your colleagues in a determination that will surely be of interest to us? Your own thoughts on the matter will be welcome in the police report too."

"The man died of apoplexy," said the doctor. "There are symptoms present of a terrible cerebral congestion. . . ."

"Please have a look, messieurs," said Corentin, "and see if toxicology doesn't tell us about some poisons that could have a similar effect."

"The stomach," said the doctor, "was very full with any number of matters; but short of doing a chemical analysis, I see no trace whatsoever of poison."

"If the traits associated with cerebral congestion are clearly present, then, given the age of the subject, that is a sufficient cause of death," said Desplein, indicating the enormous amount of food in the stomach.

"Did he eat here?" asked Bianchon.

"No," said Corentin. "He rushed here from the boulevard to find his daughter had been raped."

"Well, there's the real poison, if he loved his daughter," said Bianchon.

"But what sort of poison could produce an effect like this?" said Corentin, unwilling to give up his hypothesis.

"There's only one," said Desplein, after having looked everything over carefully. "It's a poison that comes from the archipelago of Java, derived from a shrub we don't know much about. It's in the family we call *Strychnos,* and is applied to those lethal weapons—the *krisses* of the Malays. Anyway, that's what people say. . . ."

The police commissioner arrived, and Corentin filled him in on his suspicions, asking him to include the house where Peyrade had dined, and the people who were there, in his report. He also told him about the plot against Peyrade's life and the causes for Lydie's condition. After that, Corentin went into the poor girl's rooms, where Desplein and Bianchon were examining her. He met them at the door.

"Well, then!" Corentin said.

"Put the girl into a clinic, and if she doesn't recover her sanity following childbirth—that is, if she turns out to be pregnant—she'll spend the rest of her days in melancholic madness. There's no other cure, no other hope but in maternal feeling, if in fact it ever awakens in her. . . ."

Corentin gave each doctor forty francs in gold and then turned to the police commissioner, who was pulling at his sleeve.

"The doctor says it's a natural death," said the functionary, "and it's even harder for me to file a report, considering it involves Canquoëlle; he's had a history of meddling in so many affairs that we could never begin to guess who might have been the one to attack him. . . . People like him get killed *by contract.* . . ."

"My name is Corentin," Corentin said in the commissioner's ear.

The commissioner gave a little start of surprise.

"So," Corentin continued, "make a note—it'll be useful later—and only pass it on under the category of confidential. Crime can't be proven, and I know that the investigation could be called off right from the start. . . . But one day I'll be bringing the guilty parties in—I'm going to put them under surveillance, and I'll catch them red-handed in some crime."

The police commissioner bowed and departed.

"Monsieur," said Katt, "Mademoiselle won't do anything but sing and dance. What should I do?"

"Why—has something happened?"

"She's found out that her father just died."

"Get her into a cab and send her at once to Charenton;⁵³ I'm going to write a note to the director-general of the Police of the Kingdom to see to it that she's given good accommodations there. The daughter in Charenton, the father in a common grave . . ." said Corentin. "Contenson, arrange for the hearse for the poor. . . . And now it's you and me, Don Carlos Herrera!"

"Carlos!" said Contenson. "But he's in Spain."

"He's in Paris!" Corentin said peremptorily. "I sense a little of the Spanish genius in all this, something from the era of Philip II—but I have traps for everybody, and that includes kings."

The Trap Snares a Rat

Five days after the nabob's disappearance, Madame du Val-Noble was sitting, at nine in the morning, at Esther's bedside, and she was weeping, for she sensed that she was about to slip down the slope of poverty.

"If only I had, say, a hundred louis' income! With that, my dear, a person can retire to some little town, and maybe find a husband. . . ."

"I could get you that money," said Esther.

"How?" cried Madame du Val-Noble.

"Nothing easier. Listen. You're about to kill yourself—play that kind of role, and play it well. Send for Asia, and make her an offer of ten thousand francs for two black pearls in very thin glass, containing a poison that kills instantly. Bring me the pearls, and I'll give you fifty thousand francs. . . ."

"But why not just ask for them yourself?" said Madame du Val-Noble.

"Asia would never sell them to me."

"It's not for you? . . ." asked Madame du Val-Noble.

"Maybe."

"You! You, living in the midst of pleasure and luxury, and with your own house! And just before a celebration people will be talking about for a decade! And one that's costing Nucingen twenty thousand francs. They say you'll be eating strawberries in February, asparagus, grapes . . . melons. . . . There'll be a thousand écus' worth of flowers in the various rooms."

"Oh, what are you saying? There'll be a thousand écus' worth of flowers just on the staircase."

"People say your clothes for the night cost ten thousand francs."

"Yes, the dress is Brussels lace, and Nucingen's wife, Delphine, is furious. But I wanted to be dressed like a bride."

"Where are the ten thousand francs?" asked Madame du Val-Noble.

"This is all the cash I've got," said Esther with a smile. "Look in my dressing table, under my curling papers. . . ."

"People who talk about killing themselves almost never do it," said Madame du Val-Noble. "Now, if you were going to use this to commit—"

"A crime! Come on!" said Esther, finishing the sentence her friend left dangling. "Rest easy," Esther continued. "I'm not going to kill anybody. I had a friend, she was very happy, she's dead now, and I'm going to follow her . . . that's all."

"But that's stupid!"

"What can I say? We made a promise to each other."

"That's a debt I'd recommend defaulting on," her friend said with a smile.

"Well, do as I say, and get going now. I hear a carriage outside, and it's Nucingen, the man who's about to go wild with happiness! He loves me, that one. . . . Why is it we don't love the ones who love us? They do so much to make us like them. . . ."

"Ah, yes," said Madame du Val-Noble, "it's the same old story all over again, about the herring, the most fascinating of all the fishes. . . ."

"Why?"

"Well, you see, no one's ever been able to figure that out."[54]

"All right—away with you, my little doe! I need to put in a request for your fifty thousand francs."

"Very well then, good-bye."

Over the previous three days, Esther's behavior toward Nucingen had undergone a radical change. The monkey had turned into a kitten, and the kitten into a woman. Esther heaped affection and charm on the old man. Her conversation was stripped of all its malice and acidity, and now became charged with tender hints, all of which combined to create a sense of certainty in the banker's mind: she began calling him Fritz; he felt loved.

"My poor Fritz, I've put you through quite a trial," she said, "and a great deal of misery, but you've been sublimely patient; you love me, I see it now, and I'm going to compensate you. I like you now; I don't know how it's come about, but I actually prefer you to a younger man. Maybe it's the result of experience. Eventually we come to realize that pleasure is like the money of the soul, and that being loved for the pleasure one gives is just as unflattering as being loved for one's money. . . . And then young men are such egoists, thinking more of themselves than of us, whereas you think only of me. I'm your whole life. So I'm not going to ask for anything more from you—I want to prove to you that I'm disinterested."

"Oh! I haff giffen you not'ing, not'ing at all!" replied the enchanted baron. "Tomorrow I come und bring you t'irty t'ousand francs ingome. . . . Ziss vill be mine vedding present."

Esther embraced him so sweetly that Nucingen went pale, even without taking any pills.

"Oh," she said, "don't think that the thirty thousand francs are the reason I'm like this with you. No, it's because now . . . I love you, my big fat Frédéric. . . ."

"Oh! Mine Gott! Vhy you had to put me t'rough so much—I could haff been happy for ze last t'ree mont's. . . ."

"Did you put it in the three percent funds or the five, my little doe?" asked Esther, toying with Nucingen's hair, arranging it to suit her whim.

"In ze t'ree. . . . I had many of zem."

The baron had that morning brought her the documentation for her annual income; he had come to have lunch with his sweet little girl and to get his orders for the next day, the famous Saturday—the great day!

"Zere it iss, mine leetle voman, mine only vife," the banker declared joyfully, his face radiant with happiness. "Ziss vill pay your household hexpenses till ze hend uff your days. . . ."

Esther took the piece of paper without the slightest emotion; she folded it and put it away in her dressing table.

"Look at you, all happy, you sinful monster," she said, giving Nucingen a little tap on the cheek, "at seeing me accept something from you. I can't speak any more bitter truths to you, now that I've shared in the fruits of what you call your labors. But it's not a present, my poor boy, it's a restitution. . . . Oh come on, don't give me your stock exchange face. You know perfectly well that I love you."

"Mine beaudiful Esther, mine anchel of luff," said the banker, "don't speak to me like zat. . . . Ach, I don't care if ze whole vorld t'inks I am a t'ief, zo long as you zee me as honest man. I luff you alvays, und more und more."

"That's just what I intend," said Esther. "And so I won't ever say anything to hurt you, my big pet elephant, because I can see you've become as honest and open as a little child. . . . But for heaven's sake, you scoundrel, you never had any innocence—the tiny bit you were born with needed coaxing to surface eventually, but it was pushed down so far inside you that it's only appearing now, at sixty-six years of age, and only hooked and fished up by love. This phenomenon can be observed in the very old . . . and that's why I've come to love you—you're young, very, very young. . . . And I'm the only one who's ever met this Frédéric—only me! Because you were a banker already at fifteen—at school I bet you'd lend out a bill to your friends and expect to get two back. . . ." Here she jumped up on his lap when she saw him laughing. "All right, you'll get to do whatever you want! Good Lord, plundering men . . . go on, I'll help you with it. Men aren't worth the trouble of trying to love them—Napoleon killed them like flies. What's the difference if they pay taxes to the government or to you! . . . You can't make love with the government and— how does it go?—oh yes, it's in the Gospel according to Béranger, 'shear my sheep.'[55] . . . Give your Ezder a kiss. . . . Oh yes, give all the furnishings from the Rue Taitbout apartment to that poor Val-Noble! And then, tomorrow, give her fifty thousand francs . . . that will set her up nicely, my little cat. You murdered Falleix, and now the posse is after you. . . . But if you show her that kind of generosity, it'll seem almost Babylonian, and all the women will be talking about you. Oh, you'll be the only grand, noble man in all Paris, and then everybody will forget all about Falleix. So, you see, it'll be money spent for a good cause!"

"Ja, you are right, mine anchel, you know ze vorld so vell. . . ." he said. "I use you for my perzonal adviser."

"Well," she replied, "you see how carefully I think about my man's affairs, about what's in his best interests, and about his honor. Go now, go, and find the fifty thousand francs. . . ."

She wanted to get rid of Monsieur Nucingen so she could have a broker come and sell off her bond by that very evening.

"But vhy so hurried?" he asked.

"Heavens, my little kitten, the francs need to be presented to her in a nice little satin envelope, wrapped around a fan. And you must say, 'Here, madame, is a fan that I hope will bring you pleasure. . . .' People think you're a Turcaret now, but after this they'll be comparing you to Beaujon!"[56]

"Charmink! Charmink!" cried the baron. "I vill be a vitty man now, eh! Ja, I repeat zese chokes you tell!"

Just when Esther was sitting down, exhausted after playing this role, Europe came in.

"Madame," she said, "there's a messenger here, sent from the Quai Malaquais by Célestin, Monsieur Lucien's valet. . . ."

"Have him come in! . . . No, wait: I'll go out to the foyer."

"He has a letter from Célestin for madame."

Esther hurried out to the foyer, looked the messenger over, and decided he was nothing but a messenger.

"Tell *him* to come down!" said Esther in a feeble voice, falling back into a chair after having read the letter. "Lucien means to kill himself. . . ." she added in a whisper to Europe. "Take the letter upstairs to *him*."

Carlos Herrera, still in his disguise as a traveling salesman, came downstairs quickly, immediately catching sight of the messenger, surprised to see a stranger in the room. "You told me there was nobody here," he whispered to Europe. And out of an excess of prudence he went immediately into the drawing room after having looked the messenger over. Deathcheater didn't know that for some time now the celebrated head of the detective bureau who had arrested him at the Vauquer boardinghouse had a rival who had been designated as his replacement. This rival was the messenger.

"You're right," said the false messenger to Contenson, who had been waiting for him down in the street. "The man you described is up in that house, but he's not a Spaniard, and I'd bet my right hand that the man we're looking for is under that cassock."

"He's no more priest than he is Spaniard," said Contenson.

"No doubt about it," said the police agent.

"Oh, but if only we could be certain!" said Contenson.

Lucien had been absent for two days, and they took advantage of his absence to lay this trap; but he came back that very evening, and Esther's anxieties were calmed.

A Farewell

The next morning, at the hour when the courtesan emerged from her bath and returned to her bed, her friend arrived.

"I got the two pearls!" said Val-Noble.

"Can I see them?" asked Esther, sitting up and propping her pretty elbow on a pillow trimmed in lace.

Madame du Val-Noble handed her friend what looked like two black currants. The baron had given Esther two whippets of a special breed, the kind that would come to bear the name of the great contemporary poet who made them fashionable.[57] The courtesan was very proud of them, and she gave them names that belonged to their parents, Romeo and Juliet. No one could overpraise the sweet natures, the whiteness, the grace of such animals, bred for apartment life and, in their manner, suggestive of something like English discretion. Esther called Romeo, and Romeo hurried over on his slender, flexible legs, so firm and muscular a person might think they were stems of steel, and he gazed up at his mistress. Esther pretended to throw him one of the two pearls in order to get his attention.

"His name destines him to death too!" said Esther, tossing the pearl, which the dog broke between his teeth.

The dog made no sound but turned over and lay rigid and dead, even before Esther was done speaking that funereal sentence.

"My God!" exclaimed Madame du Val-Noble.

"You have a carriage; take the late Romeo away with you," said Esther. "His death would cause a scene here—say I gave him to you, say he ran away, say you've put out advertisements. Hurry, because tonight you'll have your fifty thousand francs."

The courtesan said this so calmly, and with such perfect impassibility, that Madame du Val-Noble exclaimed, "You really are our queen!"

"Come early, and make yourself beautiful. . . ."

At five o'clock Esther had herself dressed like a bride. She wore her lace gown over a white satin skirt, a white sash, and slippers of white satin, while her lovely shoulders were draped with a shawl of English point. She wore white camellias in her hair, in imitation of a young virgin's hair style. Upon her breast she wore a pearl necklace that Nucingen had bought for her for thirty thousand francs. Even though she was finished dressing by six, she closed her door to everyone, even Nucingen. Europe knew that Lucien was to be brought into the bedroom. At seven Lucien arrived, and Europe found a way to slip him into madame's room without anyone else knowing he had come.

Gazing upon Esther, Lucien thought, "Why not go live with her at Rubempré, far from the world, and never return to Paris! . . . I've put down five years' deposit on that woman's life, and she's not the type who would ever deny it! . . . And where would I ever find a masterpiece to match this?"

"My friend, whom I've made my god," said Esther, kneeling before him on a cushion, "give me your blessing. . . ."

Lucien tried to pull Esther up and embrace her, saying, "What kind of a joke is this, my love?" He tried to put his arms around her, but she pulled away with a sudden movement that suggested both respect and horror.

"I'm no longer worthy of you, Lucien," she said, letting the tears fall from her eyes; "I beg you, bless me, and swear to me that you'll endow two beds at the Hôtel-Dieu[58] . . . because prayers said in church would only earn me God's forgiveness if I went there and prayed them myself. . . . I've loved you too much, my friend. But now, tell me that I've made you happy, and that you'll think of me from time to time . . . please, say it."

Lucien realized that Esther was speaking in solemn good faith, and he stood there thinking.

"You plan to kill yourself!" he said at last, in a voice that suggested deep reflection.

"No, my friend, but today, you see, is the day a pure, chaste woman who loved you is to die . . . and I'm afraid that the grief of it will kill me."

"Poor child—just be patient!" said Lucien. "Over these last two days I've made real efforts, and I've succeeded in seeing Clotilde."

"Always Clotilde!" said Esther in a voice of concentrated rage.

"Yes. You see, we've written to each other. . . . Tuesday morning she's leaving for Italy, but I've set up a meeting with her on her route, at Fontainebleau."

"Ah, what is it you men want your women to be? Stepping-stones!"[59] cried poor Esther. "Look, if I had seven or eight million, wouldn't you marry me?"

"Child! What I was about to say was that, if I'm finished, I don't want any other woman but you. . . ."

Esther lowered her head to hide her sudden pallor and the tears that she was brushing away.

"You love me?" she said, looking up at Lucien with profound sorrow. "Well, then, that's my blessing. Be careful not to compromise yourself— leave by the secret door, and act as if you've gone straight from the foyer to the drawing room. Kiss my forehead," she said. She held Lucien tightly against her heart with rage, saying to him, "Leave! Leave . . . or I'll live."

When the doomed woman made her entrance in the drawing room, there was a cry of admiration. Esther's eyes seemed expressive of infinity; gazing upon those eyes, the soul lost itself. The camellias stood out against the rich blue-black of her hair. In short, all the effects the sublime whore had aimed at were achieved. She had no rivals. She seemed to be the supreme expression of the unbridled luxury that surrounded her. Her wit sparkled too. She reigned over the orgy with the icy, calm power that Habeneck deploys at the Conservatory during those concerts in which the finest musicians of Europe reach the heights of sublimity as they interpret Mozart and Beethoven.[60] She did observe, however, with some trepidation, that Nucingen was eating little, not drinking at all, and acting as if he were the master of the house. By midnight all of the guests had left their reason behind. They broke their glasses, to ensure they'd never be used again. Two Peking curtains had gotten torn. Bixiou was drunk, for the first time in his life. Because nobody was capable of remaining upright, and the women were nodding off on the sofas, the guests had to abandon the joke they had planned in advance of leading Esther and Nucingen to the bedroom, standing in two lines holding candles in their hands and singing the "Buona Sera" from *The Barber of Seville*. Nucingen, alone, gave his hand to Esther; drunk as he was, Bixiou saw them and had just enough strength to say, like Rivarol at the Duc de Richelieu's last marriage, "Somebody ought to call the police, because this will lead to no good. . . ."[61] The wit thought he was joking, but he was prophetic.

The Lamentations of Nucingen

Monsieur de Nucingen didn't appear at his house that Monday until around noon, but at one o'clock one of his brokers told him that Mademoiselle Esther Van Gobseck had sold her thirty thousand–franc bond already on the Friday, and that she had just been paid.

"But, *monsieur le baron*," he said, "the head clerk of Maître Derville came by just when I was making the transfer, and when he saw me writing down Mademoiselle Esther's name, he realized what her real name was, and told me she had inherited a seven million–franc fortune."

"Bah!"

"Yes, she was the sole heir to the old discounter Gobseck . . . Derville will verify everything. If the mother of your mistress is the one they call *la belle Hollandaise,* she'll inherit . . ."

"Ja, ziss iss correct," said the banker; "she hass told me ze story uff her life . . . I vill chust write a note to Derville!"

The baron went to his desk, wrote a short note to Derville, and had one of his domestics deliver it. Then at three, when the stock exchange had closed, he returned to Esther's.

"Madame has ordered us not to awaken her no matter what; she's in bed and asleep."

"Ach, ze deffil!" exclaimed the baron. "Europe, she vould like to know zat she iss rich voman. . . . She inherits seffen millions. Ze old Gobseck iss dead, und leafs her zese seffen millions—ja, your mistress is ze sole heir, her modder vas Gobseck's niece, und ja, ze man hass left a vill. . . . But I vould neffer haff suspegded millionaire like zat man vould leaf Esther benniless."

"Well, well! That's the end of your reign then, you old clown!" said Europe, giving the baron a look of sheer effrontery worthy of a servant in Molière. "Ha, ha, you old Alsatian crow! . . . She loves you about as much as she loves the plague! . . . God on top of God—millions! Oh, but now she can marry the man she loves! Oh, how happy she's going to be!"

And Prudence Servien left Baron de Nucingen standing there, thunderstruck, to go announce the news—she would be the first one to tell her mistress about this twist of fate! But the old man, intoxicated by superhuman sensual bliss and believing in his happiness, had suddenly had his love doused with cold water, at just the moment when it had reached the state of incandescence.

"She vass cheating on me!" he cried, tears starting from his eyes. "Cheating! Oh, Esther. . . . Oh, mine life. . . . Fool dat I vass! Flowers like zese, no, zey neffer grow for ze old men. . . . I can buy efferyt'ing, but not ze youth! Oh, mine Gott! . . . Vot shoult I do? Vot vill I become? Ach, zat Europe, she iss right. . . . Esther is rich, und she vill escape from me. . . . Shoult I go hang mineself? Ach, vat iss ze life vit'out ze difine flame of ze pleasure zat I haff tasted. . . . Mine Gott. . . ."

And now the old lynx tore off the toupée he had been wearing for the last three months. But then a piercing shriek from Europe made Nucingen shudder right down to his very innards. The poor banker got up and paced around unsteadily, his legs weakened by the cup of Disenchantment he had just emptied, for nothing makes us drunk faster than misery. Through the open door of the bedroom, he could see Esther lying rigid on her bed, her skin made blue from the poison, and dead. . . . He went to the bed and fell down on his knees.

"You vass right—she said she vould do it! She iss dead of me. . . ."

Paccard, Asia, the whole household came running. It was a spectacle, a surprise, but not a desolation. Everyone seemed a little uncertain. But then the baron became the banker again: he was suspicious, and he was imprudent enough to ask where the seven hundred and fifty thousand francs' income had gone. Paccard, Asia, and Europe all looked at each other in so peculiar a manner that Monsieur de Nucingen quickly left, believing both theft and murder had been committed. Europe, who had discovered a soft packet, suggesting that bank notes were inside it, beneath her mistress's pillow, turned to the task of laying the dead woman out, she said.

"Go tell monsieur, Asia! . . . To die before knowing she was getting seven million! Gobseck was our deceased madame's uncle!" she cried.

Paccard saw what Europe was up to. When Asia turned her back, Europe had opened up the packet, on which the poor courtesan had written: "To be given to Monsieur Lucien de Rubempré!" Seven hundred and fifty bills of a thousand francs gleamed in the eyes of Prudence Servien, who exclaimed: "Couldn't a body live happily and honestly on that for the rest of her life!"

Paccard said nothing; his essential nature as thief was stronger in him than his loyalty to Deathcheater.

"Durut is dead," he replied, taking the bills in his hand; "my shoulder has never been branded; let's run off together, and divvy up the money so we don't have all our eggs in one basket, and then let's get married."

"But where do we hide?" asked Prudence.

"Right in Paris," replied Paccard.

Prudence and Paccard hurried down the stairs with the alacrity of two honest people who had just turned thieves.

"My child," Deathcheater said to the Malay when she had given him a brief version of events, "find me a letter from Esther while I write up a will in proper form, and then you take the will and the letter to Girard, but hurry, because we need to slip the will under Esther's pillow before they come to put seals on."

And he quickly sketched the following will:

> Having never loved anyone in the world aside from Monsieur Lucien Chardon de Rubempré, and having resolved to put an end to my life rather than slip back into vice and the foul way of life from which charity rescued me, I give and bequeath to the said Lucien Chardon de Rubempré everything I possess on the day of my death, on the condition that he arrange for a Mass to be said in the parish of Saint-Roch for the repose of she who gives him everything, even her final thoughts.
>
> *Esther Gobseck*

"That's pretty much her style," Deathcheater thought.

At seven in the evening the will, formally written out and sealed, was placed by Asia beneath Esther's pillow.

"Jacques," she said, having rushed back upstairs, "just when I was leaving the bedroom, in came the law—"

"You mean an *officier de paix.*"

"No, my boy—yes, there was an *officier de paix* there, but there were gendarmes with him as well. The prosecutor and the examining magistrate are there too, and the doors are under guard."

"This death has caused quite a commotion, and fast too," said Collin.

"And there's something else—Europe and Paccard haven't come back, and I fear they've made off with the seven hundred and fifty thousand francs," Asia said.

"Oh, those rats!" exclaimed Deathcheater. "Their little swindle is going to end up hanging us!"

Corentin's Revenge Gets Under Way

Human justice, and justice as it's done in Paris—which is to say the most mistrustful, the cleverest, the most capable, the best informed of all justices—perhaps even too clever, for it is in the habit of interpreting the law in passing, right on the spot—had finally reached its hand out to grasp the perpetrators of this horrific scheme. Baron de Nucingen, recognizing the effects of poison, and failing to find the seven hundred and fifty thousand francs, assumed that Paccard or Europe—the two odious characters he most disliked—were guilty of the crime. In his first fit of rage, he went directly to the Prefecture of Police. This was like a tolling bell that called together all Corentin's agents. The prefecture, the prosecutor's office, the chief of police, the *officiers du paix,* the examining magistrates, all swung into action. At nine o'clock in the evening, three doctors had been summoned and were busy performing an autopsy on the body of poor Esther, and the searches were underway. Deathcheater, warned by Asia, cried: "No one knows I'm here, so I can get some fresh air!" And with that he pulled himself up through the skylight and, with an unparalleled agility, was quickly standing upright on the roof, from which he was able to examine the surroundings with all the calm assurance of a roofer. "Good," he thought, looking down and seeing, five houses away, on the Rue de Provence, a garden; "that's where I'll head!"

"You're under arrest, Deathcheater!" said Contenson, suddenly coming out from behind a chimney. "You can explain to Monsieur Camusot what sort of Mass you're holding up here on the roof, *monsieur l'abbé,* and, even more important, you can also tell him why you were running away. . . ."

"I have enemies in Spain," said Carlos Herrera.

"Let's go to Spain together—back down through your attic," said Contenson.

The false Spaniard looked as if he were going to obey, but after bracing himself against the skylight, he took hold of Contenson and hurled him with such force that the spy fell all the way down to the gutter on the Rue Saint-Georges. Contenson died on the field of battle. Jacques Collin slipped calmly back down into his attic, where he proceeded to get into bed.

"Give me something that will make me genuinely sick without killing me," he said to Asia. "I need to be deathly ill so that I can't respond to any questions from *the curious.* . . .[62] Don't worry—I'm a priest, and I'll remain a priest. I just managed to rid myself, and in a perfect, natural way too, of one of the people trying to unmask me."

On the previous evening, at seven o'clock, Lucien had taken his cabriolet and left Paris with a passport he had taken out that morning for Fontainebleau, spending the night at the last inn on the Nemours side. Around six the next morning he set off alone, and on foot, into the forest, walking as far as Bourron.[63]

"It was there, at that fatal spot," he said to himself, sitting down on one of the rocks from which one can gaze out on the fine landscape of Bourron, "where Napoleon hoped to make one last gigantic effort, two days before his abdication."

At daybreak he heard the sounds of a coach approaching, and soon he saw a britska[64] pass by; seated within it were the servants of the young Duchesse de Lenoncourt-Chaulieu and the chambermaid of Clotilde de Grandlieu.

"There they are," Lucien thought. "Let's go now, and act out this little comedy well—if I do, I'm saved, and I'll be the son-in-law to the duke despite his wishes in the matter."

One hour later he heard and easily recognized the sound of a berline,[65] in which two women were riding. They had asked for the carriage to stop on the hill outside Bourron, and the valet who was riding behind stopped the vehicle. And at that moment, Lucien stepped forward.

"Clotilde!" he called, rapping on the window.

"No!" the young duchess said to her friend; "he cannot be allowed in the carriage, and we cannot allow ourselves to be alone with him, my dear. Have one last conversation with him—I won't object to that—but it will have to be on the road ahead, where we'll go on foot, with Baptiste behind us. . . . It's a fine day, we're dressed well enough, and we're not afraid of the chill. The coach will follow along behind us. . . ."

With that, the two women got down.

"Baptiste," called the young duchess, "the postilion can drive along slowly; we want to walk for a while, and you should accompany us."

Madeleine de Mortsauf took Clotilde's arm and allowed Lucien to speak with her. They walked along in this manner until they were close to the little village of Grez. By then it was eight o'clock, and there Clotilde dismissed Lucien.

"Well, my friend," she said, putting an end to that long conversation, "I will never marry anyone but you. I'd rather believe in you than in what others say, or my father or my mother. . . . No one can give a more complete proof of attachment than that, can they? . . . So now, try to clear away the fatal obstacles that stand in your way. . . ."

They could hear the galloping of many horses, and suddenly, to the great astonishment of the two women, a group of gendarmes was surrounding the little assemblage.

"What do you want?" asked Lucien, with all the insolence of a dandy.

"Are you Monsieur Lucien Chardon de Rubempré?" asked the Fontainebleau king's prosecutor.

"Yes, monsieur."

"You're going to be sleeping tonight at La Force," he replied. "I have a warrant here for your arrest."

"Who are these ladies?" cried the head gendarme.

"Ah yes—your pardon, ladies, but I must see your passports. For Monsieur Lucien here, according to the information I've been given, is known to consort with women who are capable of . . ."

"Do you take the Duchesse de Lenoncourt-Chaulieu for a whore?" said Madeleine, fixing the icy stare of a duchess upon the king's prosecutor.

"You're certainly pretty enough for it," was the magistrate's clever reply.

The duchess smiled and called out, "Baptiste, show him our passports."

"And of what crime is monsieur being accused?" asked Clotilde, though the duchess wanted them to get back up into the coach.

"Of complicity in a theft and a murder," replied the head gendarme.

Baptiste picked up Mademoiselle de Grandlieu, who had fainted dead away, and put her back into the berline.

At midnight Lucien was taken to La Force, a prison situated between the Rue Payenne and the Rue des Ballets, and put in solitary confinement; the abbé Carlos Herrera had been arrested and was already there.

III ❧

WHERE EVIL PATHWAYS LEAD

The Salad Basket

The next day, at six, two carriages, the sort that are called, in the energetic language of the people, "salad baskets," both with postilions, came riding out of La Force and headed to the Conciergerie and the Palais de Justice.

Just about every Parisian flâneur will have come across this sort of rolling prison; but while most books are written solely for Parisians, foreigners would no doubt appreciate a little description here of this formidable instance of our criminal justice. And after all, who knows but that the police forces of Russia, Germany, or Austria, and the magistrates of other salad basket–deprived countries might benefit from it; certainly, in many foreign countries, an imitation of this mode of transport would be an improvement for the prisoners.

This squalid vehicle has a yellow body mounted up on two wheels and lined with sheet metal; it is divided into two compartments. In front there is a bench with leather cushions and a splashguard. This is the free section of the salad basket, designed for a bailiff and a gendarme. A strong iron grate like a trellis separates—from top to bottom and side to side—this part of the vehicle from the second half, where two wooden benches are placed, as on an omnibus, on facing sides of the body and upon which the prisoners are seated. The prisoners are put in by means of wooden steps and a windowless door at the back of the vehicle. The "salad basket" nickname derives from earlier versions that were open on the sides, and the prisoners could be seen shaking about within just like salad ingredients. For even more security, and in case of an accident, the vehicle is followed by a gendarme on horseback, especially when it is carrying condemned prisoners on the way to their executions. Thus, escape is impossible. The vehicle is lined with sheet metal, and no tool can cut through it. The prisoners, scrupulously searched at the time of arrest or admittance to prison, could have at most something like a watch spring, useful for sawing through a bar but useless on a plane surface. And so the salad basket, perfected by the genius of the Paris police, has come to serve as a model for the compartmentalized van[1] that transports convicts to the penal colony, and it has come to replace the horrible cart, shame of previous civilizations, the kind Manon Lescaut made famous.[2]

Prisoners are sent by salad basket from the various prisons in the capital to the Palais de Justice, where they are interrogated by an examining judge. In prison argot, this is called "going to the judge." When it is only a question of a misdemeanor, the accused are also taken from their prison to this same Palais de Justice to receive their sentence; but then, when it is a question of a major crime, they are taken to the Département of the Seine. Finally, those who are sentenced to death are taken by salad basket from the Bicêtre to the Barrière Saint-Jacques, which, since the July Revolution, has been used for executions. Thanks to philanthropists, these unfortunates no longer have to undergo the torment of the old system, in which they would have been transported from the Conciergerie to the Place de la Grève in an open cart, exactly like the kind used by firewood vendors. Such carts nowadays are only used to transport the scaffold itself. Without this explanation, we would be unable to appreciate the jest made by a famous murderer to his accomplice as they were getting up into the salad basket: "Now it's all up to the horses!" In short, one could not possibly go to one's final torment in greater comfort than one does in Paris.

The Two Patients

At that particular moment, the two salad baskets departing so early in the morning were being used in a rather unusual manner, for transporting two accused persons from La Force to the Conciergerie, and each person had a salad basket all to himself.

Nine out of ten readers—and nine out of ten of that tenth—are undoubtedly ignorant of the important differences among these terms: *inculpé, prévenu, accusé, détenu, maison d'arrêt, maison de justice,* or *maison de détention*; and ten out of ten might be surprised to learn that the differences are essential to an understanding of our criminal Law, but they will be given a succinct, clear account of all this presently, as much for their instruction as for ensuring the clarity of the rest of our story. In any case, reader, when you hear that the first salad basket contained Jacques Collin and the second Lucien, who within a matter of only a few hours had fallen from the grandest level of society to a prison cell, your curiosity will already be sufficiently awakened. The attitude taken by the two accomplices was typical of them. Lucien de Rubempré hid himself to avoid the gaze that passersby would cast at the grill of the sinister, fatal vehicle on its route via the Rue Saint-Antoine toward the quays by the Rue du Martroi, and then through the Arcade Saint-Jean in order to cross the Place de l'Hôtel de Ville. Today that arcade forms the entrance to the Préfecture de la Seine within the sprawling municipal palace. The convict, audacious and unrattled, pressed his face up against the grill that separated the vehicle's two compartments, between the heads of the bailiff and the gendarme, both of whom, fully confident in their salad basket, chatted away together.

The days of July 1830, and the great storm that burst forth from them, created so much noise that they've drowned out the memory of what preceded them; the last six months of that year went on to absorb so much political interest that hardly anyone today recalls, or barely recalls, strange as they were, the private, judicial, and financial catastrophes (the usual annual meal served up for Parisian curiosity) that so preoccupied them during the first six months. This makes it necessary for us to note how momentarily fascinated all Paris was by the news of a Spanish priest being found in the home of a courtesan and arrested, and by news of the elegant Lucien de Rubempré, the future husband of Mademoiselle de Grandlieu, being picked up on the main road to Italy, at the little village of Grez, and both of them being involved in a murder that was worth seven million francs—for the trial publicized such a scandal that it effectively overshadowed, for several days, the great interest everyone took in the final elections under Charles X.

To begin with, the criminal trial was due in part to a complaint brought by the Baron de Nucingen. Moreover, the arrest of Lucien, and on the eve of his being appointed personal secretary to the prime minister, was the talk of the highest levels of Parisian society. Every salon in Paris had young men who could remember envying Lucien when he had been favored by the beautiful Duchesse de Maufrigneuse, and all the women were quite aware of the interest Madame de Sérisy, the wife of one of the most important men in the Government, took in him. And, finally, the sheer beauty of the victim had been famous throughout all the different worlds that compose Paris: in high society, in the world of finance, in the world of the courtesans, in the world of the young, in the literary world. The examining magistrate in whose lap the case fell, Monsieur Camusot, saw it as a chance for personal advancement, and in order to bring about this eventuality as quickly as possible, he had ordered the two accused men to be transferred from La Force to the Conciergerie as soon as Lucien de Rubempré had arrived from Fontainebleau. The abbé Carlos and Lucien had spent, respectively, only twelve hours and half a night in La Force, and therefore no great description is necessary of that prison, which has since undergone a great deal of change; and as for the details of their commitment there, any description would be a mere repetition of what was about to happen at the Conciergerie.

Criminal Law Made Plain for Ordinary People

But before we enter into the terrible drama that is a criminal inquiry, it is indispensable, as was just said, to explain the normal course of events in a trial such as this; for, first, its diverse phases will be better understood, both in France and elsewhere; and second, those who are unfamiliar with the subject will be able to appreciate how economical criminal Law is, as it was conceived by our legislators under Napoleon.

A crime is committed; now, if it is flagrant, the suspects (the *inculpés*) are brought to the nearest guardhouse and put in the cell they call the "violin," no doubt because music is made there: there is screaming, and there is weeping. From there the suspects are taken before the police commissioner, who proceeds to a basic examination and who is empowered to release them if he finds there has been some kind of error; otherwise, the suspects are transported to the police station of the prefecture, where the police hold them according to the disposition of the king's prosecutor and the examining magistrate, who, depending on the gravity of the case, are notified more or less swiftly, arrive, and interrogate the individuals, who are now in a state of provisional arrest. According to the nature of his presumptions, the examining magistrate issues a warrant for imprisonment and orders the suspects to one of the three *maisons d'arrêt* in Paris: Sainte-Pélagie, La Force, or Les Madelonnettes.

Note the term "suspect," or *inculpé*. Our Code lays out three essential distinctions in criminality: *inculpation*, or the first level; *prévention*, the state of being detained while under interrogation; and *accusation*, the level reached where the accused is committed for trial. As long as the warrant for arrest has not been signed, the presumed perpetrators of a serious crime are considered suspect, or *inculpé*. But with such a warrant they fall into the category of *prévenu*, and they remain in this category as long as the investigation proceeds. Then, once the Royal Court has determined, at the request of the prosecutor, that there are sufficient grounds to indict them and bring them to trial, they fall into the third category of *accusés*. Thus, people suspected of having committed a crime pass through three different kinds of status, and are weighed and sifted three different times before standing before what is called the justice of the Nation. In the first category, innocent people have many routes by which they can clear themselves: via the public, via the town guard, via the police. In the second category, they appear before a magistrate, are confronted by witnesses, and are judged by a Paris chamber of tribunal, or a similar tribunal in the various provinces. In the third, they appear before twelve counselors, and the accused may, in case of any error or failure to follow proper procedure, be deferred to the court of appeal, or *cour de cassation*. The jury does not know what a slap in the face they are giving to the people's, administrative, and judicial authorities when they acquit an *accusé*. Thus, as we see it, in Paris—we say nothing about other jurisdictions—it is very difficult for a truly innocent person to find himself on the bench in a court of assize.

Now, the *détenu* is the person who has been convicted and sentenced. Our criminal justice system has set up three kinds of places for holding suspects and perpetrators—*maisons d'arrêt, maisons de justice,* and *maisons de détention*—each corresponding to the stages of the *prévenu*, the *accusé*, and the *condamné*. Imprisonment, or jailing, is only a minor punishment, used for minor crimes, but detention is far more punishing, and in certain cases it may also involve degrading and painful hard labor. Thus, those people today who advocate a uniform penitentiary system would end up overthrowing an admirable system of criminal law with graduated punishments, and they would end up treating minor offenses in nearly the same way as major ones. One might compare, in the sequence titled *Scenes from Political Life* (especially *A Murky Business*), the curious differences between the Criminal Code of Brumaire, Year IV, and the Napoleonic code that replaced it.[5]

In most cases involving serious crimes, like this one, the suspects very quickly become *prévenus*. A warrant for arrest and detention is immediately issued. Most commonly, of course, the suspects are either already in flight or they are caught in the act. And as we have seen, the police, the only instrument for executing the law, and Justice itself had descended with the rapidity of a thunderbolt upon Esther's house. Even if Corentin had not whispered in the ear of the police, there had also been a report of the theft of seven hundred and fifty thousand francs, made by the Baron Nucingen.

The Machiavelli of the Penal Colony

As the first vehicle, the one carrying Jacques Collin, was passing through the Arcade Saint-Jean, a dark and narrow passage, something caused the postilion to stop right under the arcade. The eyes of the prévenu gleamed through the grill like two gems, despite the appearance of mortal illness, which had made the warden of La Force, the night before, think it necessary to call in a doctor. Those flamboyant eyes were free to gleam at the moment, for neither the gendarme nor the bailiff turned around to look at their "customer," but if they had, they would have seen eyes speaking a clear and vivid language, one that would have instantly led a clever examining magistrate—like Monsieur Popinot, for example—to recognize the convict beneath the sacrilegious cassock. And in fact Jacques Collin, from the very moment the salad basket departed La Force, had been carefully examining every detail of their journey. Despite the rapidity of the vehicle, his avid and careful gaze scanned every house they passed, from the top story to the ground floor. He saw every single passerby, analyzing each one. God does not have a better grasp on the means and ends of His creation than this man had as he assessed the minutest differences in the things and people they passed. Armed only with hope, as the last of the Horatii was armed only with his sword, he awaited some form of help. For anyone other than this Machiavelli of the penal colony, such a hope would have appeared so impossible that he would have allowed himself to sink into a machine-like apathy, as the guilty always do. None of them would dream of trying to resist the situation into which the justice system and the Paris police plunge the *prévenus* and, above all, those who had been kept in solitary, as both Lucien and Jacques Collin had. It is hard to imagine what the sudden immersion into complete isolation for a *prévenu* is like: the gendarmes who arrest him, the guards who conduct him to what in literature is termed "the dungeon," those who take him by the arms to force him into the salad basket, indeed every being who has surrounded him from the first moment of his arrest is entirely mute, or else taking notes on anything he might say so as to present them to the police or the magistrate. This absolute isolation, so easy to engineer between the *prévenu* and everyone else, completely overwhelms his faculties and prostrates his mind, especially in a man who has never become familiar with the ways of the justice system. The duel between the criminal and the judge is thus all the more terrifying because of the allies that the justice system has on its side: the silence of the walls, and the incorruptible indifference of its agents.

But Jacques Collin, or Carlos Herrera (it will be necessary to use one or the other name depending on the needs of the situation), knew all about the methods of the police, the jails, and the justice system. That colossus of subterfuge and corruption had therefore put to work all his cunning and all his mimicry to play the role of a surprised, foolish, innocent man, at the same time ensuring that his interrogators saw how terribly ill he was. As we have seen, Asia, that shrewd Locusta, had given him a poison concocted in such a way as to make him appear to be mortally ill. All the plans of Monsieur Camusot, of the police commissioner, and of the prosecutor were defeated by what looked like an apoplectic stroke.

"He's poisoned himself!" exclaimed Monsieur Camusot, startled by the agony the so-called priest was clearly enduring when he was brought down from the attic in convulsions.

Four agents had a difficult time in conveying the abbé Carlos down the stairs and into Esther's bedroom, where all the magistrates and gendarmes had gathered.

"Well, if he's guilty, it was the smartest thing he could do," replied the prosecutor.

"What—do you think he's really sick?" asked the police commissioner.

The police are skeptical about everything. The three magistrates went on to discuss the matter—in whispers, as one might imagine—but Jacques Collin could read what they were saying from the looks on their faces, and he took advantage of it by ensuring that the preliminary interrogation would be impossible or, at best, meaningless; he stammered out Spanish and French in such a mixed-up way that he seemed to be speaking nonsense.

At La Force, the farce turned out to be even more successful because of the chance fact that the head of the Sûreté (the word abbreviates the full title, Head of the Brigade of the Guardians of Public Security), Bibi-Lupin,[4] who had once arrested Jacques Collin at the *pension* of Madame Vauquer, was away in the provinces on a mission, and the agent serving as his successor did not know the convict.

Bibi-Lupin, a former convict and companion of Jacques Collin in the penal colonies, was his personal enemy. This enmity had its source in some squabbles, in which Jacques Collin always came out the winner, and in the supremacy over his fellow prisoners that Deathcheater always assumed. And for the last ten years Jacques Collin had acted as the benign Providence for escaped convicts, their chief, their counselor in Paris, their banker—and as a result the antagonist of Bibi-Lupin.

A Victory over Solitary Confinement

And so it was that, even though he was in solitary confinement, he continued to count on the intelligent and absolute devotion of Asia, his right hand, and perhaps also on Paccard, his left hand, whom, he told himself hopefully, would return to his master once he had hidden away his seven hundred and fifty thousand francs. This is why he paid such careful, focused attention to every detail along their route. And strange as it may sound, his hopes were about to be abundantly fulfilled.

The two enormous walls of the Arcade Saint-Jean were permanently smeared with mud up to a height of about six feet, the result of splashing from the gutters; pedestrians in those days had no protection from being spattered by passing coaches except a series of posts, most of which had been nicked and beaten down over the years by the great hubs of the wheels. More than once, some inattentive pedestrian had been crushed in this very archway. Many areas in Paris were like this for a long time. This detail may help the reader understand the narrowness of the Arcade Saint-Jean, and how easy it would have been to cause some blockage. If a cab were to come in from the Place de la Grève side while a woman pushing her vendor's cart full of apples came in from the Rue de Martroi, a third vehicle trying to come in would block the place up. Frightened pedestrians hurried through, trying to reach a post to be behind when the hub of a coach wheel was approaching; those hubs projected out so ridiculously far that laws had to be passed to shorten them. When the salad basket arrived, the arcade was blocked by one of those fruit-selling women whose survival in Paris is so remarkable, considering how many grocers' shops have been opened. This woman was so utterly typical of her kind that some town sergeant upon catching sight of her would have let her pass on without needing to show her permit, despite that sinister physiognomy which positively sweated crime. Her head was tied up in a ragged, cheap cotton kerchief, bristling with rebellious locks of her unkempt hair, resembling the tufts of hair on a wild boar. Her neck, reddened and wrinkled, was hideous, and her shawl failed to conceal skin darkened from the sun, the dust, and the mud. Her dress looked like it had been patched together. Her shoes seemed to grimace, as if they were mocking the woman's face, as full of pockmark holes as her dress. And what she wore around her stomach! An old bandage would have been less filthy. From ten feet away, a delicate passerby's nose would have been assaulted by this walking heap of rags. Those hands had been through a hundred bouts of ragpicking! The woman had either come straight from some German witches' Sabbath, or straight from a beggar's asylum. And what looks she cast around her! What audacious intelligence, what hidden vitality when the magnetic rays of her eyes and those of Jacques Collin joined together to communicate an idea.

"Out of the way, lice breeder!" shouted the postilion.

"Don't you crush me, guillotine-boy," she replied. "The goods you're hauling aren't worth as much as mine are."

And as she tried to squeeze herself between two posts in order to make room, the vendor blocked the path for just long enough to accomplish her aim.

"Oh, Asia!" Jacques Collin thought, recognizing his accomplice immediately. "Everything's going to be fine."

The postilion continued to exchange courteous remarks with Asia, while other vehicles were backing up on the Rue du Martroi.

"Ah! Pecare fermata! Souni la. Vedrem!" shouted old Asia, with the kind of Indian intonations[5] peculiar to street merchants, who so twist the pronunciation of their words that they become just so many onomatopoeias, comprehensible only to Parisians.

In the brouhaha of the streets and the exclamations of all the shouting coach drivers, no one paid any attention to this savage cry from the street vendor. But what sounded like mere noise to them was perfectly distinct to Jacques Collin, a jargon they had established that mixed together pidgin Italian and corrupt Provençal, the meaning of which was this terrible bit of news:

"Your poor little boy has been arrested, but I'm going to be there for both of you. You'll see me again. . . ."

Along with the infinite joy that this triumph over the justice system gave him—for now he could expect to be in contact with the outside world—Jacques Collin was overwhelmed by an emotional reaction so powerful that it would have killed anyone else.

"Lucien arrested!" he said to himself. He almost fainted. This news was more horrible to him than news of the rejection of his own appeal would have been if he had been sentenced to death.

Historical, Archaeological, Biographical, Anecdotal, and Physiological History of the Palais de Justice

Now that the two salad baskets are rolling their way along the quays, our story requires us to say a few words concerning the Conciergerie during the time it takes them to get there. The Conciergerie, a historical name, a terrifying word, and a thing even more terrifying, is closely involved with the revolutions of France, and those of Paris even more. It has seen most of the worst criminals. It may be the most interesting of all Parisian monuments, but it is also the least well known . . . at least to people in the upper reaches of society. But despite the immense interest there is in this historical digression, we will make it just as rapid as the journey of the salad baskets themselves.

Is there any Parisian—or foreigner or provincial, for that matter, who has spent at least two days in Paris—who has failed to notice the black walls flanked by three great pepper-pot towers, two of them almost conjoined, those somber, mysterious ornaments of the quay called des Lunettes? This quay begins at the Pont au Change and stretches almost to the Pont-Neuf. One square tower, the Tour de l'Horloge (from which the signal for Saint Bartholomew was given[6]), is nearly as tall as the tower of Saint-Jacques-la-Boucherie; it shows where the Palais de Justice is, and it forms the corner of the quay. These four towers and the walls wear the shroud of black that every north-facing edifice in Paris wears. Toward the middle of the quay, at a blank archway, begin those private establishments that date from the construction of the Pont-Neuf during the reign of Henri IV. The Place Royale was meant to duplicate the Place Dauphine, using the same architectural style, with brick framed by hewn stone. This arcade and the Rue de Harlay mark the limits of the Palais to the west. The police prefecture, along with the hôtel where the presidents of the *parlement* resided, used to be attached to the Palais. The Court of Audit (Cour des Comptes) and the Board of Excise (Cour des Aides) completed the supreme justice system, that of the Sovereign. The reader can see that before the Revolution, the Palais enjoyed an isolation that some today are trying to restore to it.

This block, this island of houses and monuments, among them the Sainte-Chapelle, the most magnificent gem in the great jewel box of Saint Louis,[7] is the sanctuary of Paris; it is the sacred space, the Holy Ark. Originally, of course, this was the whole of the city, for the site of the Place Dauphine was an open field attached to the royal grounds, with a mill there for striking coins. This is why the street was named Rue de

Monnaie, running down to the Pont Neuf. This is also why the second of the two round towers is named the Tour d'Argent, which seems to prove that it was initially erected as a site for minting money. The famous mill, which can be found on old maps of Paris, was most likely built after the period in which money was coined in the palace itself, and probably involved some improvements in the art of coining money. The first tower, the one practically conjoined with the Tour d'Argent, is called the Tour de Montgommery. The third one, the smallest but the best preserved of the three, with its battlements still in place, is called the Tour Bonbec. The Sainte-Chapelle and these four towers (including the Tour de l'Horloge) precisely mark off the shape, or the perimeter, as the real-estate surveyors would say, of the Palais, dating back from the time of the Merovingians to that of the Valois; but for us today, because of the many changes the place has undergone, it especially seems to belong to the era of Saint Louis.

Charles V was the one who ceded the Palais to the *parlement*,[8] which was a newly created institution, and under the protection of the Bastille he went to live in the famous Hôtel Saint-Pol, which was soon thereafter attached to the Palais de Tournelles. Then, under the last Valois monarchs, royalty returned from the Bastille to the Louvre, which had been its original *bastille*.[9] The first home of the kings of France, the Palais de Saint Louis, known today simply as the Palais, as a way of signifying the supreme palace, is now entirely buried under the Palais de Justice; it forms the cellars, for it was built, like the cathedral, down into the Seine, but with such skill and care that the river at its highest stage only covers the very first steps. The Quai de l'Horloge sits about twenty feet above those thousand-year-old constructions. Carriages today roll along at about the height of the capitals of the pillars that support those towers; their appearance, in former times, must have harmonized with the elegance of the Palais, and they must have made for a picturesque effect on the water, for even today the towers are as tall as the tallest monuments in Paris. When you contemplate this great capital from the *lanterne* of the Panthéon,[10] the Palais and Sainte-Chapelle stand out as the most monumental among the very many monuments. This palace of our kings, above which you can walk when you walk across the waiting room, the great hall of the Pas-Perdus, was an architectural marvel, and it still is to the sensitive eyes of the poet who studies it while exploring the Conciergerie. Alas, the Conciergerie itself invaded the palace of the kings. The heart bleeds to see the way that jail cells, miserable lodgings, corridors, rooms with neither light nor air, were quarried out of this magnificent building, in which the Byzantine, the Roman, the Gothic—the three faces of ancient art—were all united in the architecture of the twelfth century. This palace is to the monumental history of France of the first era what the château of Blois is to the next one. Just as with Blois (see the *Étude sur Catherine de Médicis,* in the *Études philosophiques*[11]), where from one courtyard you can admire the château of the Comtes de Blois, that of Louis XII, that of François I, and that of Gaston—so, at the Conciergerie, you can see, within the same stretch of ground, the traces of the earliest inhabitants, and in the Sainte-Chapelle the architecture of Saint Louis. And so, Municipal Council, if you are going to be spending millions, add one or two poets to your team of architects if you want to preserve the very cradle of Paris and the cradle of kings, as you go about endowing Paris and the Royal Court with a palace truly worthy of our France! It's a question worth reflecting on for several years before beginning the work. Erect one or two more prisons like La Roquette, and the Palais de Saint Louis will be saved.[12]

The Same Subject, Continued

Today we can see many wounds inflicted on this gigantic monument, buried beneath the Palais and below the quay, like one of those antediluvian animals represented by plaster casts in Montmartre; but the worst injury of all was having to become the Conciergerie! The word needs some explanation. During the early years of the monarchy, important criminals, both *villeins* (retaining this spelling is important, as it reminds us that the word suggests roughly what "peasant" does) and bourgeois, whether they fell under urban or manorial jurisdictions, whether the possessors of great or small fiefs, were brought to the king and kept in the Conciergerie. Since there were relatively few important criminals, the Conciergerie was sufficient for the king's justice. It is difficult to determine precisely where the original Conciergerie was located. But since the kitchens from the time of Saint Louis still exist, forming part of what we now call the Mousetrap,[13] it is worth assuming that the original Conciergerie was situated in the same place where, before 1825, the judicial Conciergerie of the *parlement* existed, beneath the arcade on the right of the great external staircase that leads up to the Royal Court. Up until 1825, the condemned would proceed from there to their place of punishment; from there emerged all the important criminals, all the political victims—the Maréchale d'Ancre as well as the queen of France, Semblançay as well as Malesherbes, Damien as well as Danton, Desrues as well as Castaing.[14] The office of Fouquier-Tinville,[15] occupied today by the king's prosecutor, was situated so that from it the public prosecutor could see prisoners who had been condemned by the revolutionary tribunal filing out and into the carts that would take them away. That man—more lethal weapon than man—could thus cast one last glance on his latest batch.

But after 1825, under the ministry of Monsieur de Peyronnet,[16] a great change took place in the Palais. The old intake wicket of the Conciergerie where all the ceremonies of registration and barbering took place was closed and moved to the place it occupies today, between the Tour de l'Horloge and the Tour Montgommery, in an inner courtyard through an arcade. To the left is the Mousetrap, and to the right, the intake wicket. The salad baskets drive right into this irregularly shaped courtyard, where they may park or, if need be, turn around easily, and in the case of a prison riot, they will be protected by the strong grillwork closing off the arcade; before this change, they had great difficulty in maneuvering in the narrow space separating the great external staircase from the right wing of the Palais. Today the Conciergerie is scarcely big enough to hold the *accusés*—there would have to be enough space for three hundred people, both men and women—so it takes in neither the suspects nor the convicted, except on rare occasions like the one that brought Jacques Collin and Lucien there. Everyone who is a prisoner there must appear before a court of assize. The magistrate may grant an exception for offenders who come from the higher realms of society, who, having already been dishonored simply by virtue of receiving a sentence in the court, would suffer unusually harsh punishment if they were to serve their sentence at Melun or Poissy. Ouvrard preferred his time in the Conciergerie to that in Sainte-Pélagie.[17] At present the notary Lehon and the Prince de Bergues are both serving their sentences there, the result of an arbitrary but humane dispensation.[18]

How All This Is Put to Use

Generally, people who have been arrested and indicted, whether they are—in the special jargon of the Palais—"going to the schoolroom" or going before a lower court, are taken by salad basket directly to the Mousetrap. The Mousetrap, directly opposite the intake wicket, is composed of a number of cells built out of the kitchens of Saint Louis, and this is where the *prévenus,* brought from their prisons, are put to wait either for their court or for their examining magistrate to be ready for them. The Mousetrap extends on the north to the quay, on the east to the headquarters of the Municipal Guard, on the west to the Conciergerie courtyard, and on the south to an immense vaulted room (probably once a banquet hall) that is currently unused. Above the Mousetrap extends an inner guardroom, looking out over the Conciergerie's courtyard, staffed by departmental gendarmes; the staircase ends there. When the hour of their trial sounds, the bailiffs call the names of the *prévenus,* and the gendarmes descend, as many gendarmes as there are prisoners being called, and each gendarme takes a *prévenu* by the arm; and paired off in this manner, they ascend the staircase, crossing the guardroom and arriving, via corridors, at the famous Sixth Chamber of the Tribunal, which is where the lower court hearings are held. This path is the same one taken by prisoners on their way from the Conciergerie to the court of assize, and they return the same way.

In the waiting room, between the door to the First Chamber of the Tribunal and the steps that lead up to the Sixth, you cannot help but notice, your first time walking through, a doorless entryway, devoid of any architectural flourish or detail, simply a squared-off, ugly hole. This is where the judges and the lawyers enter, heading into the corridors and then the guardroom, down into the Mousetrap and out to the intake wicket of the Conciergerie. All the magistrates' offices are located on various floors in that part of the Palais. You reach them by frightening stairways, a labyrinth in which anyone who doesn't work there is bound to get lost. The windows of those offices look out, some of them, onto the quay, and some onto the Conciergerie courtyard. In 1830 a number of offices for examining magistrates looked out onto the Rue de la Barillerie.

Thus, when a salad basket turns left in the Conciergerie courtyard, it brings *prévenus* to the Mousetrap; but when it turns right, it brings *accusés* to the Conciergerie. So it was on this side that the salad basket carrying Jacques Collin was directed, depositing him at the wicket. Nothing could be more foreboding. Criminals and visitors here first see two grates of wrought iron, separated by a space of about six feet, which are swung open one after the other, and everything at this point is so rigorously examined that people with a visitor's permit have to pass it through before the key grinds in the lock. The examining magistrates, including those from the public prosecutor's office themselves, are not allowed to enter until they have been formally recognized. So, go ahead, talk all you like about the possibilities for passing clandestine messages, or of escaping! The director of the Conciergerie will have on his lips the kind of icy smile that will discourage even the boldest novelist from sinning against probability. In the annals of the Conciergerie there is only the tale of Lavalette's escape; but the certainty of connivance on the part of people very high up, now fully proven, diminished, if not the wife's devotion, at least the risk of failure.[19] Thus, even the most ardent devotees of the marvelous, casting an eye around at all these obstacles, must admit that they were, and are, insurmountable. Words cannot describe the strength of these walls, these vaulted ceilings: they must be seen. The courtyard's paving is below the level of the quay, but, even so, when you pass through the wicket you must descend several steps lower in order to arrive in an immense, vaulted room whose thick, powerful walls are supported by magnificent columns, flanked on one side by the Tour Montgommery, which houses the sleeping quarters of the Conciergerie's warden, and on the other by the Tour d'Argent, which houses those of the jailers, guards, or turnkeys—whatever term you like. Their number is smaller than you might imagine (they are twenty); their sleeping quarters are no different from the cells called the *pistoles*.[20] The name no doubt originates in the old custom of the prisoner paying one pistole a week for such a cell, the bareness of which is reminiscent of the cold garrets where future great men live in poverty as they begin their lives in Paris.[21] On the left in this great entrance hall is the administrative registry of the Conciergerie, a kind of office formed of large windows behind which sit the warden and his secretary, and here the record books are stored. In this entrance hall the *prévenu* and the *accusé* are registered, described, and searched. Here the decision is made as to their housing, which depends entirely upon their ability to pay. Facing the wicket of this room one sees a glass door to a room in which relatives and lawyers communicate with the prisoner through a double grating of wood. This room gets its light from the prison yard, an interior area where the *accusés* are allowed to walk and breathe in the fresh air at certain predetermined hours.

The great entrance hall only gets light from those two gratings, because the only window that looks out on the courtyard is within the record office, which entirely surrounds it, and the result is an atmosphere and a quality of light that perfectly fits what one might imagine in such a place. The atmosphere is all the more fearful in that you can see, parallel to the Montgommery and d'Argent towers, mysterious, vaulted, forbidding, unlit crypts that wind away behind the inner room and off to the cells that held the queen and Madame Élisabeth[22] as well as the ones called only "secret cells." This labyrinth of hewn stone has become the underground world of the Palais de Justice, though it once saw royal festivals. From 1825 to 1832 it was in this enormous room, between a large open stove and the first of the two gratings, that condemned men were given their last preparations for execution. One can only shudder, when walking across these stone floors, to think of what terror, what last confidences, what last looks these stones have heard and seen.

The Committal Process

In order to get out of his dreadful vehicle, the dying man needed the assistance of two gendarmes, each of whom took one of his arms, lifted him up, and carried him, evidently fainted away, to the registration counter. Being dragged along in that way, the dying man lifted his eyes to heaven, looking like Jesus brought down from the cross. There is no painting showing Jesus looking more cadaverous, more broken down than the way the phony Spaniard looked now; he appeared to be ready to draw his last breath. When finally seated in the registration office, he repeated in a failing voice the same things he'd been saying to everyone since his arrest: "I demand to see His Excellency the Spanish ambassador. . . ."

"You can tell that," the warden replied, "to your examining magistrate."

"Oh, Jesus!" sighed Jacques Collin. "May I not even have a breviary? Will you continue to refuse to let me see a doctor? . . . I have less than two hours to live."

Carlos Herrera was to be placed in solitary confinement, and thus there was no point in asking him whether he wanted to pay for the advantages of a *pistole*—that is, if he wanted the right to be taken to one of those cells in which one could enjoy the only comforts that the Justice system allowed. Those cells are located at the far end of the prison yard; our story will return to them later. Meanwhile, the bailiff and the clerk impassively continued with the formalities of committal.

"Monsieur warden," Jacques Collin began, in his badly pronounced French, "I am dying, as you can see. Tell this, if you can, tell this as quickly as possible to monsieur the judge; tell him that I ask as a favor something that a real criminal would most fear, that is, to appear before him as soon as he arrives, because my sufferings are truly intolerable, and when I see him, all these mistakes will be cleared up."

It is a general rule that prisoners always talk about "mistakes." Go into one of the penal colonies and question the convicts there, and you'll learn that just about every single one is there because of a mistake made by the justice system. Therefore, the word always brings a slight smile to the lips of those who come in contact with the *prévenus,* the *accusés,* and the convicted.

"I can tell the judge about your request," the warden replied.

"Oh, I bless you for that, monsieur!" replied the Spaniard, lifting his eyes up to heaven.

Once his committal paperwork was complete, Carlos Herrera was taken up under the arms by two municipal guards, and then, accompanied by a turnkey, to whom the warden explained where the prisoner was to be taken, he was escorted through the subterranean labyrinth of the Conciergerie to a solitary cell that was quite clean (despite what certain philanthropists claim) but without any possible means of communication.

When he was gone, the guards, the prison's warden, the clerk, and even the bailiff all looked at each other like people seeking each other's opinion, and indeed doubts seemed present on every face; but when they got a look at the second *prévenu,* they all returned to their habitual skepticism hidden behind a mask of indifference. It takes very unusual circumstances to get the Conciergerie employees to feel much curiosity, criminals being to them what customers are to a barber. And thus all the formalities that so disturb one's imagination are accomplished with even more simplicity than a simple business transaction, and often with even more politeness. Lucien presented them with the look of a guilty and defeated man, doing only what was asked of him, and doing that mechanically. Since the Fontainebleau arrest, the poet had been contemplating his ruin, saying to himself that the hour of expiation had struck. Pale and disheveled, ignorant of what had happened at Esther's since his absence, he knew that he was the intimate friend of an escaped convict, a situation that was enough in itself for him to foresee catastrophes worse than death. When his mind turned to thoughts of what to do, suicide seemed the only option. He wanted to escape, at any price, the ignominy he foresaw like the fantasy of a nightmare.

Jacques Collin was held, being considered the more dangerous of the two, in a cell of hewn stone; the only light came from one of the smaller interior courtyards that are scattered here and there around the grounds of the Palais, this one situated in the wing where the prosecutor-general has his office. This little courtyard is used as an exercise space for women inmates. Lucien was brought along the same pathway, but, the examining magistrate having given orders that he should be treated with some kindness, was taken to a cell next to the *pistoles.*

How the Two Prisoners React to Their Troubles

People who have never gotten entangled with the law usually have very grim ideas of what solitary confinement must be like. When they think about criminal justice, they think about medieval-style torture, the unhealthiness of prisons, the cold, dank stone walls that seem to sweat tears, the crudity of the jailers and of the food, all the required accoutrements of stage plays; but it may not be out of place here to say that such exaggerations really only exist in the theaters, and they make magistrates, lawyers, and those who visit or study the prisons smile. True, for a long time prison was horrible. And it is true that accused persons under the old *parlements,* in the centuries of Louis XIII and Louis XIV, were thrown haphazardly into a single big room above the current reception room. The prisons were themselves one of the crimes of the Revolution of 1789, and it is enough to see the cells where the queen and Madame Élisabeth were held to feel a profound horror at the old judicial system. But today philanthropy, though it may have done irreparable harm to society, has done some good for individuals. To Napoleon we owe our Criminal Code, which, even more than our Civil Code, which is still in need of some urgent reforms, will stand as one of the greatest achievements of that so-brief reign. The new criminal law system did away with a whole mountain of abuses. And while one might argue that when people of the higher classes of society fall into the hands of the law, their moral sufferings are very great indeed, still the powers of the law are executed in a simpler, even milder manner than might have been expected. Suspects and *prévenus* are certainly not made as comfortable as they were at home, but the necessities of life are present in the prisons of Paris. Moreover, the pressure of unaccustomed emotions removes the importance of the little details that had made up their ordinary home life. It is never the body that suffers. The mind is in so violent a state that every kind of discomfort, every brutality, when encountered in this new environment, is easily endured. And it is important to note that anyone who is innocent, in Paris especially, will be quickly set at liberty.

Lucien, upon entering his cell, found there a faithful replica of the first room he had rented in Paris, in the Hôtel Cluny. A bed just like those found in the poorest furnished rooms in the Latin Quarter, a couple of straw-bottomed chairs, a table, and a few utensils comprised the furniture of one of these rooms, where often two prisoners would be housed, so long as they seemed mild-mannered enough and their two crimes were of the reassuring type, like forgery and bankruptcy, for example. The strong resemblance between the point where he started and that to which he had now arrived, the lowest level of shame and degradation, was so fully grasped by one last effort of his poetic nature that the miserable young man burst into tears. He continued weeping for four hours, and though to an observer he looked as unfeeling as a stone statue, inwardly he was tormented by the wreckage of all his hopes, wounded by the destruction of all his social vanity, all his pride annihilated, grieving for the deaths of all those selves of his: the man of ambition, the lover, the happy man, the dandy, the Parisian, the poet, the sensualist, and the privileged. Everything he had been came crashing to earth in this Icarus-like fall.

But Carlos Herrera paced around his cell, once he had been left alone there, like the polar bear in the Jardin des Plantes in his cage. He examined the door in detail, assuring himself that, apart from the Judas hole, no other spyhole had been made in it. He sounded the walls, looked up at the hood that let in a little, feeble light, and said to himself, "I'm secure, all right!" He sat down in a corner where an observer looking through the hole could not see him. Then he removed his wig and quickly took out a piece of paper he had stuck inside. The side of the paper that contacted his head was so filthy that it looked as if it were part of the inner wig. If Bibi-Lupin had been there, and had had the idea of removing the wig to see if the Spaniard was indeed Jacques Collin, he would never have found this slip of paper, so fully a part of the wigmaker's art it seemed. The other side of the slip of paper was still white and clean enough for a few lines to be written on it. The difficult, painstaking process of unsticking it had begun in La Force; two hours would not have been enough time; he had spent half the previous day working on it. The *prévenu* began by trimming the precious slip of paper so as to produce a strip four or five lines wide, which he then divided into several pieces; then he replaced his little piece of paper back in its strange repository, making it stick by moistening the bit of gum arabic that allowed him to keep it in place. He searched in his hair for one of those tiny pencils, thin as a pin, that Susse had begun to manufacture[23] and which he had also kept in place with gum. He broke off a piece that was just long enough to write with, but small enough to be concealed behind his ear. Quickly finishing up these preliminaries with the nimble touch of old, experienced convicts, who are in fact as agile as monkeys, Jacques Collin sat on the edge of his bed and began to think over the instructions he would give to Asia, feeling certain she would cross his path again, so highly did he trust the woman's cleverness.

"In my first interrogation," he thought, "I made the Spaniard speak bad French, demand to see his ambassador, claim diplomatic privilege, and fail to understand what was said to him, and I salted in lots of groans and sighs and faints, all the little hallmarks of a dying man. Let's stay the course. My papers are in order. Asia and I will devour this Monsieur Camusot—he's a weakling. So let's think about Lucien. We need to boost his morale, we need to get to the boy no matter what it costs, give him a plan of conduct—otherwise he'll give himself away, give me away, and we'll lose everything! . . . It'll need to be drummed into him before his interrogation. And I need to have witnesses to attest to my priestliness!"

Such was the mental and physical condition of our two *prévenus*, whose fate depended at the moment upon Monsieur Camusot, the examining magistrate of the Tribunal of First Instance for the prefecture of the Seine and, for the time allowed to him by the Criminal Code, the sovereign judge over them and the smallest details of their existences, for he, and he alone, could decide whether to allow the chaplain, the Conciergerie doctor, or anyone else to communicate with them.

Explaining the Functions of an Examining Magistrate

No human power—not the king, not the keeper of the seals, not the prime minister—can impinge upon the powers of an examining magistrate; no one can stop him, and no one can give him orders. He is sovereign, subject only to his own conscience and the law. In our time, when philosophers, philanthropes, and publicists are incessantly calling for the diminution of all social authorities, the rights that our laws grant to examining magistrates have become the target of the fiercest attacks, and justifiably so, for those rights are exorbitant. Nevertheless, anyone who thinks it through clearly must conclude that those rights must remain intact; in certain cases, the powers can be softened somewhat by a liberal exercise of caution; but society, already damaged by the stupidity and weaknesses of juries (an august and supreme magistrature that should be confided only to carefully selected and qualified people), would be threatened with outright ruin if we broke down this column that supports our entire criminal justice system. Preventive arrest is one of the terrible but necessary powers whose social danger is balanced by its great importance. Sowing distrust of the magistracy is the beginning of social dissolution. Go ahead and destroy the institution, and rebuild it on other bases; insist, as was the case before the Revolution, that all magistrates be wealthy men; but believe in it; don't turn it into an image of society in order to mock it. Today the magistrate is paid like a civil servant, and he is most often a poor man; today's magistrates have traded away their dignity for an arrogance that is intolerable to people on an equal level with them; for arrogance is a dignity with no real foundation. From this springs the weakness of the institution as it is today. If France were to be divided into ten jurisdictions, the magistracy could be improved by conferring it only on wealthy men, but this is impossible with twenty-six jurisdictions. The only real improvement worth insisting upon with regard to the powers of the examining magistrates involves the rehabilitation of the prisons we call *maisons d'arrêt*. There need be no change in the daily lives of the *prévenus* housed in them. The *maisons d'arrêt* in Paris should be constructed, furnished, and organized so as to make the public feel more confident about the conditions there. The law is good, and it's necessary, but its execution is bad, and it is the custom to judge the laws by the manner in which they are executed. Public opinion in France tends to condemn the person who is arrested but then turns and sympathizes with the situation of those who come up for trial. This is perhaps the result of an essentially rebellious strain in the French national character. This illogic of the Parisian public will be one of the factors leading to the catastrophe of our drama; indeed, it was to be one of the most powerful ones. To understand the terrible scenes acted out in the offices of the examining magistrates—to understand the respective positions of the *prévenu* and the representative of Justice, and how the two struggle over the secrets of the former, the magistrate's curiosity determined to ferret it out (and, indeed, in prison slang the magistrate is simply referred to as "the curious")—to understand this, we must never forget that the person kept in solitary confinement has no idea of what the seven or eight different groups we call "the public" have been saying, nor does he know what is already known by the police and others in the judicial system, and even what the newspapers have been saying concerning the circumstances of the crime. Thus, to have been given the little bit of information that Jacques Collin received from Asia concerning the arrest of Lucien was comparable to a drowning man having been thrown a lifeline. It made all the difference in outwitting a plot, as we shall see, that otherwise would certainly have led to the convict's downfall. Having explained all this in general terms, those readers who are not the most sensitive and most easily moved will nonetheless probably experience the terror that results from the three chief causes: isolation, silence, and remorse.

The Examining Magistrate in a Difficult Situation

Monsieur Camusot, son-in-law to one of the clerks in the Royal Cabinet, is already too well known for us to explain his connections and position.[24] But at the present moment he found himself nearly as perplexed as Carlos Herrera was, with regard to the inquiry that had been entrusted to him. He had formerly presided over a court in the provinces, and he had been plucked from that position to become a magistrate in Paris, one of the most coveted of positions, which he owed to the influence of the well-known Duchesse de Maufrigneuse, whose husband was an attendant of the dauphin, colonel of a cavalry regiment of the Royal Guard, and as much in the king's favor as his wife was in Madame's. For a favor—a very small one, but a very important one to the duchess—when a charge of forgery had been lodged against the young Comte d'Esgrignon by an Alençon banker (see *Le Cabinet des antiques* in the series *Scenes of Provincial Life*), the simple provincial magistrate was made president and then examining magistrate in Paris. For the preceding eighteen months, during which time he sat on the most important tribunal in the kingdom, he had, on the recommendation of the Duchesse de Maufrigneuse, attempted to help a no less powerful lady, the Marquise d'Espard, but in this he had failed. (See *L'Interdiction*.[25]) Now, as we saw at the beginning of our story, Lucien had avenged himself on Madame d'Espard by bringing the matter to the attention of the prosecutor-general and the Comte de Sérisy. These two powerful personages united to support their friend the Marquis d'Espard, and the wife only escaped further consequences from the court because of her husband's mercy. When, the day before, Madame d'Espard heard of Lucien's arrest, she sent her brother-in-law, the Chevalier d'Espard, to see Madame Camusot. Madame Camusot had sped right back to see the illustrious marquise in person. When she returned home, at dinnertime, she took her husband into her bedroom.

"If you can send that little social climber Lucien de Rubempré to the court of assize for trial, and if you can get him condemned there," she whispered to him, "you'll be made counselor at the Royal Court. . . ."

"How so?"

"Madame d'Espard wants that young man's head. I had chills down my back when I heard that pretty woman spewing such hatred."

"Don't get mixed up in Palais matters," Camusot said to his wife.

"What—me 'get mixed up'? Look, a third party could have overheard our entire conversation without having a clue as to what it was about. The marquise and I were both just as splendidly hypocritical with each other as you're being with me right now. She wanted to thank me for your efforts with her suit, and she said that even though it failed, she appreciates all you did. She spoke about the terrible mission that the law entrusts to you now. 'It's horrible to have to send a man to the scaffold, but this one! It's only simple justice!' And so on. She deplored the fact that such a handsome young man, who had been brought to Paris by her cousin, Madame du Châtelet, turned out so badly. 'This is where it leads,' she said, 'consorting with awful women like that Coralie and that Esther, who entice young men into sharing their criminal profits with them!' And then there were fine tirades on charity, and on religion! Madame du Châtelet told her that Lucien deserved to die a thousand times over for having nearly been the death of his sister and his mother.... She spoke, too, about a vacancy at the Royal Court—she knows the keeper of the seals. She ended by saying, 'Your husband, madame, is in an excellent position to distinguish himself!' There—now you have it."

"We distinguish ourselves every day, by doing our duty," said Camusot.

"Oh, you're going to go far if you act the magistrate everywhere, even with your wife!" cried Madame Camusot. "My, my ... I thought perhaps you were a little thick, but today, I'm full of admiration...."

A smile played across the magistrate's lips, a kind of smile that only they shared, like the secret smile that dancers give each other.

"Madame, may I enter?" asked the chambermaid.

"What is it?" her mistress asked.

"Madame, the first maid of Madame la Duchesse de Maufrigneuse came while madame was out, and she begs madame, on her mistress's behalf, to come at once to the Hôtel de Cadignan, regardless of anything else madame might be doing."

"Tell them dinner will have to be late," the judge's wife said, realizing that the coachman who had brought her home was still outside and waiting to be paid.

She put her hat back on, climbed back up into the cab, and in twenty minutes she was at the Hôtel Cadignan. Madame Camusot was brought in by a private entrance, and then waited ten minutes in a boudoir adjoining the bedroom of the duchess until the latter finally appeared, resplendent, for she was on her way to Saint-Cloud, having been invited by the Court.

"My friend, between us, a few words will suffice."

"Of course, *madame la duchesse.*"

"Lucien de Rubempré has been arrested, your husband has been assigned the inquiry, and I now want to guarantee the poor boy's innocence; I want him freed within forty-eight hours. And that's not all. Someone wants to see Lucien tomorrow in prison; your husband may be present if he wishes, so long as he is not seen.... I'm loyal to people who do me favors, and you know it. The king has high hopes for the courage of his magistrates in the solemn circumstances in which they are about to find themselves. I will put your husband forward—I will recommend him as a man devoted to the king, a man willing to risk his life for him if need be. Our Camusot will be a counselor first, and then president of some court, it doesn't matter where. Now farewell—they're waiting for me, so you'll pardon me, won't you? You'll be obliging not only the prosecutor-general, who cannot say anything on this matter. You'll also be saving the life of a woman who'll die otherwise, I mean Madame de

Sérisy. As you can see, you will not lack for support. Come now, I trust you, and I needn't suggest . . . well, you know!"

She put one finger to her lips and disappeared.

"And here I didn't even have a minute to tell her that the Marquise d'Espard wants Lucien executed!" thought the magistrate's wife as she got back into her cab.

When she got home, her anxiety was so obvious that her husband asked, "Amélie, what's the matter?"

"We're caught, trapped between two fires. . . ."

She spoke softly as she told her husband about her meeting with the duchess, fearing that the chambermaid might be listening at the door.

"Which one is the more powerful?" she asked, when she came to the end of her story. "The marquise almost got you compromised in that ridiculous business of having her husband committed, and we owe everything to the duchess. The one made me vague promises, but the other one said, 'You'll be counselor first, and then president afterward!' God forbid I should give you advice, because I never 'get myself mixed up in Palais matters,' but I really do need to report faithfully what they're saying at the Court, and what they're planning there. . . ."

"You don't know, do you, Amélie, what the prefect of police sent me this morning, and by whom? By one of the most important men from the Police of the Kingdom, the Bibi-Lupin of the political wing, who told me that the State has secret interests in this trial. Let's have our dinner, and then go to the Variétés . . . we'll continue talking about all this later, in the privacy of my study, because I'm going to need the help of your intellect—that of the magistrate alone isn't going to be sufficient."

The Way a Bedroom Can Sometimes Be a Council Chamber

Nine out of every ten magistrates would deny that their wives had such influence over them in this kind of a situation; but even if this case is all that exceptional, we must nevertheless insist that it is true. The magistrate is like the priest—in Paris especially, where the elite of the magistrature are to be found—in that he rarely speaks about his Palais cases, except perhaps those that have been settled and are done with. The wives of the magistrates not only pretend to know nothing about it, but they have a sound enough sense of what is appropriate to be able to see that they would be doing harm to their husbands if, having been entrusted with some secret, they let that secret get out. Nevertheless, on those important occasions when career advancement depends on taking this side or that, many wives, like Amélie, have helped their husbands in their deliberations. Such exceptions, which are all the more easily deniable because nobody knows, really, what went on, depend entirely on the manner in which the ongoing battles between husband and wife are carried out in the particular household. Now, Madame Camusot dominated her husband completely. That evening, when everyone was sleeping, the magistrate and his wife sat together at his desk, upon which the magistrate had already spread out the basic documents in the case.

"Here are the notes that the prefect of police sent me—at my request, by the way," said Camusot.

> The abbé Carlos Herrera
>
> This individual is certainly the man named Jacques Collin, also called Deathcheater, whose last arrest was in 1819, at the home of a certain Madame Vauquer, who ran a boardinghouse on the Rue Neuve-Sainte-Geneviève, and where he was living under the name of Vautrin.

In the margin, the prefect of police had written a note: "Orders have been telegraphed to Bibi-Lupin, head of the Sûreté, to return immediately to aid in the investigation, because he personally knows Jacques Collin, having been the one who arrested him in 1819 with the help of a Mademoiselle Mochonneau."

> The other inhabitants of the Vauquer boardinghouse are still alive and can be used to establish his identity.
>
> The so-called Carlos Herrera is the intimate friend and counselor of Monsieur Lucien de Rubempré, to whom, for the past three years, he has been giving significant funds, apparently the proceeds from robberies.
>
> This close connection, if we are able to establish that the so-called Spaniard is in fact Jacques Collin, will serve to condemn Monsieur Lucien de Rubempré.
>
> The sudden death of the agent Peyrade is due to poisoning carried out by Jacques Collin, and by Rubempré or their associates. The reason for the murder is that the agent had, for a long while, been on the trail of these two clever criminals.

In the margin, the magistrate pointed to the following sentence, written by the prefect of police himself: "This is something I happen to know personally, and I am certain that this Monsieur Lucien de Rubempré has dishonorably mistreated His Lordship the Comte de Sérisy as well as the prosecutor-general."

"What do you think, Amélie?"

"It's terrifying!" said the magistrate's wife. "But keep going!"

> The substitution of a Spanish priest for the convict Collin is the result of some crime more cleverly pulled off than the one that made Cogniard the Comte de Sainte-Hélène.[26]

> Lucien de Rubempré:

> Lucien Chardon, son of an Angoulême pharmacist whose wife was from the de Rubempré family, received a charter from the King authorizing him to use the name de Rubempré. This charter was given in response to formal request by Madame la Duchesse de Maufrigneuse and Monsieur le Comte de Sérisy.

> In 182 . . . this young man came to Paris with no means of making a living, following Madame la Comtesse Sixte du Châtelet, who was then Madame de Bargeton, cousin to Madame d'Espard.

> An ingrate toward Madame de Bargeton, he lived as man and wife with a Mademoiselle Coralie, deceased, an actress at the Gymnase, who, in order to be with him, had left Monsieur Camusot, a silk merchant living on the Rue des Bourdonnais.

> Soon having been plunged into the depths of poverty, finding the money the actress gave him insufficient, he proceeded to gravely compromise his honorable brother-in-law, a printer in Angoulême, by issuing forged bills, leading to the arrest of David Séchard during a brief stay the said Lucien made in Angoulême.

> This affair led to de Rubempré's flight, and his subsequent resurfacing in Paris with the abbé Carlos Herrera.

> With no known means of livelihood, this Monsieur Lucien somehow managed to spend, during the first three years of his second sojourn in Paris, around three hundred thousand francs, which he could only have got from the abbé, but how and why?

> Moreover, he has recently spent over a million in purchasing the de Rubempré estate, thus meeting one of the conditions set for his marriage to Mademoiselle Clotilde de Grandlieu. This marriage was broken off when the Grandlieu family, to whom Monsieur Lucien had said that the money came from his brother-in-law and his sister, were given information concerning the respectable Séchard couple by the lawyer Derville—that not only were they unaware of that purchase, but they still believed Lucien to be in extreme debt.

Also, the estate that the Séchards inherited consisted of buildings; their available money, according to their own declaration, amounted to less than two hundred thousand francs.

Lucien lived secretly with Esther Gobseck, and therefore it is certain that all the profuse gifts given her by Baron de Nucingen went directly to the said Lucien.

Lucien and his companion the convict succeeded in their plans longer than Coignard did, making use of the resources afforded them by the prostitution of the said Esther, who had formerly been a registered prostitute.

Concerning the Police and Their Files

Despite the fact that these notes repeat matters already covered in our narrative, it was necessary to provide them here so the reader could have a better idea of how the Paris police operate. As we have already seen from the case of the note requested on Peyrade, the police keep files, almost always very reliable ones, on all those individuals who have come under suspicion or whose acts have been reprehensible. These files omit nothing; every deviation, everything that is out of the ordinary will be recorded. This great, universal account book, the registry of consciences, is as carefully tended as the ledgers in the Bank of France that record fortunes. Just as the bank makes note of the slightest delay in payment, oversees all credits, evaluates all capitalists, and keeps a close eye on their operations, so the police keep these files concerning citizens' reputations. In this regard, as with the operations of the Palais, innocence has nothing to fear, for this activity is only concerned with crimes. No matter how highly placed a family might be, it needs this social providence. Its discretion is just as important as the extent of its reach. This immense quantity of police logs, reports, notes, dossiers, this ocean of information sleeps, immobile, deep, calm as the sea itself. If some accident, some incident breaks out, some public disorder or some crime, Justice turns to the police; and at once appears a file on the suspects, and the magistrate informs himself from it. These dossiers, in which the background of the incidents has been set down for analysis, are only so much information that lies immobile behind the walls of the Palais; Justice can make no legal use of it but can simply use it for clarification, for enlightenment—nothing more. These files are like the threads one can observe on the reverse side of a tapestry—in this case the tapestry of crimes, their initial causes—and they are almost always kept secret. Juries would put no credence in them; indeed, the whole country would arise in indignation if they were to be introduced during a trial in the court of assize. These files are the truth, condemned to remain deep down in their well, as truth is always and everywhere. No magistrate could, after working for a dozen years in Paris, remain ignorant of the fact that the courts and the police conceal the half of all these infamous acts, which are like the seedbed on which crime slowly germinates; nor could any magistrate fail to learn that Justice does not punish the half of the criminal acts committed. If the public could only realize how extremely discreet the police agents are, and how long their memories are, they would reverence those brave people as much as they do people like Cheverus.[27] People think of the police as being cunning, Machiavellian, when in fact they are extraordinarily benign; all they do is listen to the paroxysms of passions, take note of what is said, and keep careful records. They're only frightening when viewed from one particular angle. What they do for the interest of Justice they also do for political interests, and in political matters they are as cruel and as partial as the late Inquisition.

"Let's leave all that," said the magistrate, putting the notes back in the folder. "It's a secret known only to the police and the law. Monsieur and Madame Camusot know nothing about it."

"As if you need to remind me of that," said Madame Camusot.

"Lucien is guilty," the magistrate continued, "but of what?"

"A man who's loved by the Duchesse de Maufrigneuse, by the Comtesse de Sérisy, by Clotilde de Grandlieu, is simply not guilty," replied Amélie. "The other man *must* have done it all."

"But Lucien was his accomplice!" cried Camusot.

"May I tell you what I suggest?" asked Amélie. "Give this priest back to the diplomatic world of which he is the finest ornament, declare the young one innocent, and go find other criminals. . . ."

"Oh, how you talk!" replied the magistrate with a smile.

"But," Amélie continued, "whether he's a diplomat or a convict, the abbé Carlos can finger somebody who'll let you ease out of this affair."

"I feel like I'm just a cap, and you're the head," Camusot said to his wife.

"Well, then, our deliberations are closed. Come kiss your 'Mélie; it's one o'clock. . . ."

And Madame Camusot went off to bed, leaving her husband to put his papers and his thoughts in order for the inquiry that would begin the next day for the two *prévenus*.

A Product of the Palais

And so, while the salad baskets were bringing Jacques Collin and Lucien to the Conciergerie, the examining magistrate, after a hearty breakfast, set off on foot across Paris, in keeping with the simplicity practiced by the Parisian magistrates, walking to his office, where all the documents had already been delivered. This is how.

All the examining magistrates have a clerk, a kind of sworn judicial private secretary, a race that continues to perpetuate itself without any perks or even encouragement, one that is always producing excellent specimens, among whom discretion is natural and absolute. No one in the Palais has ever heard, going back to the days of the early *parlements* and forward to the present, of a case in which one of these clerks committed an indiscretion. Gentil sold the acquittance that Louise of Savoy had given to Semblançay, and a War Office clerk sold the plan of the Russian campaign to Czernicheff; such traitors typically end up more or less wealthy.[28] The prospect of a position at the Palais and the conscience that comes with a professional career have been sufficient to make the magistrates' personal clerks close-lipped enough to rival the grave itself (though graves have been giving up secrets lately, with developments in forensic science). An employee such as this functions as the very pen of the examining magistrate. Everyone can understand how a person might be content to be the main shaft of a machine, but can a person remain content simply being one of the bolts? Perhaps the bolt is afraid of the machine? . . . Camusot's private clerk was a young man of twenty-two named Coquart; he had come in that morning to pick up all the documents and all the magistrate's notes, and he had already arranged everything in the office while the magistrate was strolling along the quays, looking at the curiosities in the shop windows, and asking himself, "How do I approach someone like this Jacques Collin, assuming it really is him? The head of the Sûreté will recognize him, so I just need to look like I'm doing my job, even if only for the benefit of the police! All the options I can see are impossible—the best of which would be to meet with both the marquise and the duchess and let them read the police files, and then I could avenge my father for having his Coralie stolen away by Lucien! If I can tear the masks off a couple of genuinely wicked criminals like these, I'll get the reputation of being really sharp, and Lucien will be abandoned by all his friends. Well, enough—the interrogation will show me where I need to go."

He strolled into a shop, attracted by a Boulle clock.[29]

Influence Applied

"Hanging on to my own integrity while serving the interests of both those great ladies—that's the great challenge, the real masterpiece," thought Camusot. "Oh, *monsieur le procureur générale,* you're here too!" he exclaimed. "I see you're looking at medals!"

"Oh, yes," said the Comte de Granville, laughing. "All of us in the Justice community are interested in medals, and even more in the reverse side of the medal!"[30]

Then, after having looked around the shop a bit longer, as if he were completing his examination of the place, he escorted Camusot out along the quay so smoothly that Camusot would have to assume this had been a chance encounter.

"You're going to be questioning a certain Monsieur de Rubempré this morning," said the prosecutor-general. "Poor young man—I always liked him. . . ."

"There are serious charges against him," said Camusot.

"Yes, I've read the police files, but those files are partly based on the word of a man who doesn't work for the prefecture, the famous Corentin, a man who's gotten the heads chopped off more innocent men than you'll ever convict guilty ones, and . . . But we have no control over that character. Without wanting to influence the thinking of a magistrate such as yourself, I can't help but mention to you that if you could somehow convince yourself that Lucien knew nothing at all about that whore's will, you would then see that he had nothing to gain from her death, and in fact she did bequeath him a great deal of money!"

"We're certain of his absence when the poisoning of this Esther took place," said Camusot. "He was in Fontainebleau, watching and waiting for Mademoiselle de Grandlieu and the Duchesse de Lenoncourt to pass by."

"Oh!" exclaimed the prosecutor-general. "He had such hopes for that marriage with Mademoiselle de Grandlieu—and I know that from the Duchesse de Grandlieu herself—that it's impossible to believe such a clever young man would compromise all that by some pointless crime."

"I agree," said Camusot, "and especially if this Esther was giving him everything she earned. . . ."

"Derville and Nucingen say that she died ignorant of the inheritance, which could have come to her long before," added the prosecutor-general.

"But who do you suspect, then?" asked Camusot. "Because clearly something did go on."

"It was a crime committed by domestics," replied the prosecutor-general.

"Well, unfortunately," Camusot observed, "it would be perfectly in keeping with the ways of Jacques Collin, because the Spanish priest is no doubt that same escaped convict, to make off with the seven hundred and fifty thousand francs from the sale of the income certificate that Nucingen had given her."

"You go ahead and weigh everything carefully, dear Camusot, and be prudent. The abbé Carlos Herrera is claiming diplomatic privilege... but an ambassador who commits a crime would not be immune to prosecution. Is he or is he not the abbé Carlos Herrera—that's the most important question. . . ."

Monsieur de Granville bowed a farewell like a man who did not want a reply.

"So he wants Lucien saved too?" thought Camusot, who walked on following the Quai des Lunettes, while the prosecutor went into the Palais by way of the de Harlay courtyard.

A Trap for a Convict

When he entered the courtyard of the Conciergerie, Camusot went to the office of the prison's warden and took him aside, out to the middle of the paved courtyard, to talk privately.

"My dear sir, please do me the favor of going over to La Force and ask your colleague there if he has any inmates who were imprisoned in the Toulon penal colony between 1810 and 1815, and see also if you have any like that here. We could arrange to transfer the ones from La Force here for a few days, and you could let me know if any of them recognize the so-called Spanish priest as Jacques Collin, also known as Deathcheater."

"Very well, Monsieur Camusot, but Bibi-Lupin is back. . . ."

"Ah! Already?" cried the magistrate.

"He was in Melun. When they told him it might be Deathcheater, he grinned with pleasure, and right now he's awaiting your orders. . . ."

"Send him to me."

The Conciergerie warden then proceeded to pass on Jacques Collin's request to the examining magistrate, along with a description of his pitiful condition.

"I planned to question him first," replied the magistrate, "but not because of his health. This morning I received a note from the warden of La Force. Apparently this man, who's been practically at the point of death for the last twenty-four hours, slept so soundly in his cell at La Force that he didn't even hear the doctor enter, so the doctor didn't even bother taking his pulse, just let him go on sleeping—and this would seem to prove that both his conscience and his health are in good shape. I'll act as if I believe in this illness of his in order to figure out what his game is," said Monsieur Camusot with a smile.

"You learn something new every day with these *prévenus* and *accusés*," said the Conciergerie warden.

The police prefecture is connected to the Conciergerie, and the magistrates, just like the warden, can move from one to the other with extraordinary quickness, by virtue of being acquainted with the subterranean passageways. This explains the miraculous speed with which the public ministry and the judges in the courtrooms can get the information they need. And so when Monsieur Camusot got to the top of the stairs leading to his office, he found Bibi-Lupin rushing toward him from the hall of the Pas-Perdus.

"Such zeal!" exclaimed the magistrate with a smile.

"Oh, but if it's really him!" replied the chief of the Sûreté. "Then you'll see some real dancing out in the prison yard, especially if there are any of the *old nags* [a slang term for recidivists and old-time convicts] here."[31]

"Why do you say that?"

"Deathcheater has eaten up their loot, and I happen to know they've sworn to kill him for it."

The "they" referred to the convicts who had entrusted their funds to Deathcheater over the preceding twenty years—funds he had used up in supporting Lucien, as we have seen.

"Do you think you could find any witnesses to his last arrest?"

"Give me two summonses, and I'll have them for you today."

"Coquart," said the magistrate, removing his gloves and putting his cane and his hat in their corner spot, "make out two summonses according to monsieur's directions."

He examined himself in the mirror atop the mantelpiece; instead of a clock there were a basin and a water jug, with a bottle of water and a glass on one side and a lamp on the other. The magistrate rang. His usher came in a few moments later.

"Are there people waiting?" he asked the usher, who was in charge of receiving witnesses, verifying their summonses, and arranging them in order of arrival.

"Yes, monsieur."

"Get the names and bring me the list."

The examining magistrates, misers when it comes to their time, are sometimes obliged to conduct several different inquests at the same time. This is the reason for the long wait that witnesses need to endure, being seated by the ushers and waiting to hear the magistrate's bell ringing.

"After that," Camusot added to his usher, "go and find the abbé Carlos Herrera."

The chief of the Sûreté exclaimed, "Ah, so he's Spanish? And a priest too, I hear. Bah—it's just the old Collet trick all over again, Monsieur Camusot."[32]

"There's never anything really new," replied Camusot. The magistrate went on to sign two summonses, those ominous documents that disturb anyone receiving one, even the most innocent witnesses commanded by the Law to appear and testify, or else face grave penalties.

Jacques Collin, in Solitary, Gets Things Moving

Just then, Jacques Collin had concluded his half hour or so of profound deliberations, and he now felt fully armed. The best way to depict this man of the people in rebellion against the laws is to show the few lines he had written on his greasy little slips of paper.

The gist of the first one is given here rather than the original, for it was written in a language understood only by Asia and him, a kind of slang derived from slang, encrypted commands.

> Go to the Duchesse de Maufrigneuse or Madame de Sérisy, so that one or the other sees Lucien before his questioning, and have her be sure to give him the slip enclosed here. Then you need to find Europe and Paccard, so that the two thieves will be available to me, to play the role I'll tell them to.
>
> Hurry to Rastignac, and tell him on the part of the individual he recently encountered at the Opéra Ball to come and testify that the abbé Carlos Herrera does not look at all like the Jacques Collin who was once arrested at the Vauquer boarding-house.
>
> Get the same from the doctor Bianchon.
>
> Get those two women of Lucien's working toward this goal.

Upon the enclosed slip of paper he had written, in good French:

> Lucien, don't admit to anything about me. I must remain the abbé Carlos Herrera to you. Not only will this keep you from being declared guilty, but if you simply hold on a bit, you're going to have seven million francs, not to mention an unsullied reputation.

The two slips of paper were stuck together on the writing side with the aim of making them look like a single slip, and they were then rolled with the art peculiar to those who, in the penal colonies, have dreamed of finding a way to freedom. The whole thing had the form and the consistency of a little ball of muck, about the same size as those little balls of wax that frugal housewives press onto needles when the eye has been broken.

"If I'm interrogated first we're going to be fine, but if they start with the little one, it's all over," he thought as he waited.

The moment of waiting was so cruel that this man, strong as he was, felt his face bathed in a cold sweat. Within his own sphere—the sphere of crime—his grip on the truth was as certain as was Molière's on dramatic poetry or Cuvier's on the vestiges of an extinct world. Genius, in all things, is an intuition. At levels lower than genius, all remarkable works are the products of talent. This is what separates men of the first order from men of the second. And crime too has its men of genius. Jacques Collin, at bay now, was entirely focused, like Madame Camusot focused on her ambition, or Madame de Sérisy focused on her passionate love, which had been reanimated when she heard about the terrible catastrophe that had befallen Lucien. Such was the supreme effort of human intelligence rallying against the steel armor of the Law.

Hearing the screech of the heavy iron locks and bolts, Jacques Collin put his dying-man's mask back on, and in this he was aided by the intoxicating feeling of pleasure that the sound of the guard's footsteps in the hallway aroused in him. He didn't know how Asia would manage to get to him, but he was certain he would find her on his passage to the interrogation, especially after the promise she had made him in the Saint-Jean arcade.

Asia's Maneuvers

After that lucky encounter, Asia had gone down to the Place du Grève. Before 1830 the name la Grève had a sense that is lost today.[33] That whole stretch of the quayside, from the Pont d'Arcole to the Pont Louis-Philippe, was still just as nature had made it, the only exception being the paved footpath at the top of the bank. So, when the water was high a person could go by boat all along the houses and into the streets that sloped down toward the river. Along this shoreline, most of the houses were raised up by a few steps. When the river rose up to the feet of the houses, vehicles had to go by the dreadful Rue de la Mortellerie, which has since been completely torn up to make room for an expansion of the Hôtel de Ville. Thus it was easy for the counterfeit street vendor to push her cart rapidly down to the edge of the quay and stash it there until its owner, the real vendor—who, incidentally, was drinking up the price of renting it out in one of the wretched taverns on the Rue de la Mortellerie—came to take possession of it again, at the very spot the borrower had agreed to leave it. At that time there was construction work going on to expand the Quai Pelletier, and the entry to the site was being guarded by a disabled soldier, so the cart was safely entrusted to him.

Asia quickly got into a cab on the Place de l'Hôtel de Ville and said to the driver, "To the Temple! Make it fast, and you'll get a tip."

A woman dressed as Asia was could easily, without arousing the slightest curiosity, lose herself in the vast market where all the rags in Paris are heaped up, where a thousand peddlers are wandering around, and where the voices of two hundred shouting women mingle, all trying to sell their used clothing. The two *prévenus* were barely admitted to the prison before she was putting on a new set of clothes in a low, damp room just above one of those horrible shops where all sorts of remnants stolen by tailors and dressmakers are sold, this one run by an old woman called La Romette, short for her real name, Jéromette. La Romette was to the other used-clothes dealers what they—nicknamed Mesdames de la Resource—were to gentlewomen in difficulties, that is to say, usurers, whose interest rate was one hundred percent.

"Hey, girl!" called Asia. "I need to get decked out. I have to look like at least a baroness from the Faubourg Saint-Germain. And let's make it fast too," she continued, "because they've got my feet in hot oil! You know the kind of dress that'll do me. Break out your rouge pot, and find me some high-class lace! And get me some nice, shiny baubles too. . . . Send the young one out to get me a cab, and have it wait for me at the back door."

"Yes, madame," replied the old girl, with all the submissiveness and the anxious dispatch of a servant aiding her mistress.

If anyone had witnessed the scene, he would have readily understood that the woman concealed behind the name of Asia was in her own element here.

"I've been offered some diamonds!" said La Romette, as she did Asia's hair.

"Stolen?"

"I think so."

"Well, no matter how good a deal it is, my friend, you'll have to pass on it. We're going to have lots of the *curious* around for a while."

All this should help to explain how Asia was seen in the great hall of the Pas-Perdus inside the Palais de Justice, a summons in her hand, making her way down the corridors and staircases leading to the offices of the examining magistrates, asking to see Monsieur Camusot some fifteen minutes before the magistrate arrived.

A View of the Pas-Perdus

Asia was no longer recognizable. After having washed off, like an actress, her old woman's face, and after adding some rouge and some powder, she covered her head with a splendid blonde wig. Dressed and looking exactly like a woman from the Faubourg Saint-Germain in search of a lost dog, she seemed to be about forty, for she had hidden her face behind a superb veil of black lace. Her thick cook's midsection was held in mercilessly by a corset. Gloved in just the right way, sporting a rather large bustle, she exuded the scent of face powder, exactly like the wife of a *maréchal*. She toyed with a handbag sporting gold trim as she divided her attention between the great walls of the Palais, where she hoped it would appear she had never been before, and a leash which perhaps ought to have been attached to a pretty little King Charles spaniel. A dowager such as this was immediately noted by the black-robed population of the Pas-Perdus hall.

In addition to the lawyers without brief who keep the floor of the great hall swept with their gowns, and who refer to the great lawyers by their first names, the way great lords speak of each other, to pretend that they belong to the aristocracy of the Order, one also often sees patient young men who are attached to the lawyers, standing around in the hopes that some one case, even one of the least importance, might fall to them if the assigned lawyers cannot make it. It would be an interesting painting, if one could depict all the differences among the black robes that stalk back and forth across this immense hall, three by three, sometimes four by four, their conversations producing an extraordinary buzzing sound that booms throughout the hall, so well named,[34] since all the walking wears the lawyers out as much as their prodigalities of speech do; but such a depiction will find its place in a future study dedicated to the lawyers of Paris.[35] Asia had counted on the presence of these flâneurs of the legal world, and she laughed up her sleeve at some of the witticisms she heard from them as she finally attracted the attention of Massol,[36] a young law probationer more interested in the *Gazette des tribunaux* than in his clients and who laughed and offered to place himself at the service of a woman so well perfumed and so richly dressed.

Asia assumed a delicate little voice to explain to this most obliging gentleman that she was in search of a magistrate, named Camusot. . . .

"Ah—for the Rubempré case."

The case had a name already!

"Oh, it doesn't involve me, but my maid, a girl who's nicknamed Europe, who I'd only had for twenty-four hours and who simply ran away the minute she saw my servant bringing in a formal document."

Then, exactly like all older women whose lives are passed away in chats by the fireside, and being egged on by Massol, she rattled on, piling parenthesis upon parenthesis, about her troubles with her first husband, one of the three directors of the provincial banks. She consulted the young lawyer as to whether she ought to initiate a suit against her son-in-law, Comte Gross-Narp, who was causing her daughter some real unhappiness, and whether the law gave her permission to do what she wished with her fortune. Massol could not get it clear whether the summons had been for the maid or the mistress. At first he had merely glanced at the small legal form, copies of which he had seen many times; for, in the interests of efficiency, they are printed up in advance, and the clerks of the examining magistrates only have to fill in the blanks for the names and addresses of witnesses, the hour they are to appear, etc. Asia was asking him to explain the workings of the Palais, which she knew much better than the young lawyer did; eventually, she asked him at what time Monsieur Camusot would arrive.

"Well, in general the examining magistrates start their inquests around ten."

"It's just a quarter to ten," she said, glancing down at a pretty little watch, a true masterpiece of the jeweler's art, which roused a thought in Massol: "I wonder what she's going to be doing with that fortune of hers. . . ."

Massol Dreams of Marriage

Just then Asia arrived at the dark room that looks out on the Conciergerie courtyard, where the ushers keep watch. Seeing the wicket, she cried out: "What are those enormous walls?"

"That's the Conciergerie."

"Oh, the Conciergerie, where our poor queen . . . Oh, I'd so like to be able to see her cell!"

"I'm afraid that's impossible, *madame la baronne*," the young lawyer replied, offering his arm to the dowager. "You need special permission, and it's very difficult to obtain."

"I've been told," she continued, "that Louis XVIII himself wrote an inscription for the cell of Marie-Antoinette."

"Yes, *madame la baronne.*"

"Oh, I wish I knew Latin, so I could study the words of that inscription!" she replied. "Do you think Monsieur Camusot could give me the permission . . ."

"That's not up to him, but he could accompany you."

"But what about his prisoners?"

"Oh!" exclaimed Massol. "The *prévenus* can wait."

"Oh yes, they're *prévenus*, that's correct!" Asia said naïvely. "But you see, I know Monsieur de Granville, your prosecutor-general. . . ."

That statement produced a magical effect on both bailiffs and lawyer.

"Ah, you know *monsieur le procureur-général*," said Massol, who was thinking of how to ask the name and address of the client that chance had dropped in his lap.

"I see him often at the home of his good friend, Monsieur de Sérisy. Madame de Sérisy is my relation via the Ronquerolles. . . ."

"But if madame would like to go down into the Conciergerie," said an usher, "she . . ."

"Yes," said Massol.

And with that the ushers allowed the lawyer and the baroness to descend; they soon found themselves in the little guardroom next to the staircase that leads to the Mousetrap, an area that Asia knew well, and that forms, as we have seen, a kind of observation post between the Mousetrap and the Sixth Chamber, a spot through which everyone must pass.

"Ask these gentlemen if Monsieur Camusot has arrived yet," she said, observing the gendarmes who were busy playing cards.

"Yes, madame—he just went up into the Mousetrap."

"The Mousetrap!" she said. "Now, what is that. . . . Oh, how silly of me—I should have gone straight to the Comte de Granville. . . . But I don't have time now. Please take me, monsieur, to see Monsieur Camusot, before he gets busy."

"Oh, madame, you have plenty of time to see Monsieur Camusot," said Massol. "Just have them send your card in—that'll save you the awkwardness of having to wait in the outer room with all the witnesses. . . . You see, here at the Palais we show proper respect to a lady like yourself. . . . Now, you do have a card? . . ."

A Use for Massol, and One for the Spaniel

At that moment Asia and her lawyer found themselves right in front of the guardroom window, from which the gendarmes could keep an eye on any movement around the wicket of the Conciergerie. The gendarmes, raised to have respect for the defenders of widows and orphans, and also aware of the privileges of the lawyer's gown, tolerated for a time the presence of this baroness and her lawyer. Asia let the young lawyer talk about the dreadful things associated with the wicket. She simply refused to believe that men condemned to death had their heads shaved before execution right behind that grill he was pointing to; but the sergeant-at-arms affirmed it.

"How I'd like to see that!" she said.

She stood there flirting with the sergeant and her lawyer until she saw Jacques Collin coming through the wicket, supported by two gendarmes and preceded by an usher from Monsieur Camusot's office.

"Oh, look—that must be the prison chaplain coming to make some poor unfortunate ready to face his fate. . . ."

"No, no, madame," replied the gendarme. "That's a *prévenu* being taken for his questioning."

"What is he accused of doing?"

"He's involved in that poisoning case."

"Oh, I'd love to get a look at him!"

"You can't stay here," said the gendarme, "because he's in solitary, and he has to pass through our guardroom. Here, madame, this door leads to the stairway. . . ."

"Thank you, officer," said the baroness, turning toward the doorway and stepping onto the stairs; but then she suddenly cried out, "Oh, where am I?"

That raised voice came to the ears of Jacques Collin, and it was intended to let him know he should prepare himself for seeing her. The sergeant rushed in after the baroness, picked her up by the waist, and carried her as if she weighed no more than a feather into the midst of five gendarmes who had stood up as one—for in this area no one trusts anyone. It was sudden and arbitrary, but sometimes sudden arbitrariness is called for. The lawyer himself was shouting, "Madame! Madame!" terrified at the thought he might be compromised.

The abbé Carlos Herrera, seeming to faint, dropped into a chair in the guardroom.

"Poor man!" said the baroness. "Is he guilty?"

Those words, though spoken almost in a whisper to the young lawyer, were heard by everyone, for the guardroom was as silent as death. It does sometimes happen that privileged people are given permission to come have a look at famous criminals when they pass through the guardroom or the corridors, so the usher and gendarmes escorting Carlos Herrera said nothing about it. Moreover, thanks to the quick thinking of the sergeant who had grabbed the baroness, he ensured, to eliminate any possibility of communication between the *prévenu* from solitary confinement and any strangers, that there was a safe space between them.

"All right—let's proceed," said Jacques Collin, making an effort to stand up.

At the same moment, the tiny ball of paper fell out of his sleeve, and the baroness made a mental note of the exact spot it fell, for her veil covered her face so that no one could see where she was looking. Moist and sticky, the little ball didn't roll; these apparently indifferent little things had been in fact carefully calculated by Jacques Collin to ensure maximum success. While the *prévenu* was being led up the stairway, Asia quite naturally dropped her bag and hurriedly bent to pick it up; but in bending down she was able to snatch the ball, its color identical to that of the mere dust and grit on the floor, and no one saw it.

"Well, that just sends a chill to my heart . . . he's a dying man. . . ."

"Or so it appears," replied the sergeant.

"Monsieur," said Asia to the lawyer, "please bring me right up to Monsieur Camusot now. This is the very case I've come for, and he might appreciate the chance to talk to me before he begins his questioning of that poor abbé."

The lawyer and the baroness left the guardroom with its greasy, sooty walls; but when they reached the top of the staircase, she exclaimed: "My dog! . . . Oh, monsieur, my poor little dog!"

And with that she rushed like a madwoman back into the hall of the Pas-Perdus, asking everyone if they'd seen her dog. When she reached the Galerie Marchande and was hurrying toward a staircase, she called out, "There he is!"

This staircase was the one that leads to the Harlay courtyard, and from there the little stage play ended. Asia threw herself into one of the cabs stationed on the Quai des Orfèvres, and she disappeared with the summons ordering Europe to reappear, though her real names were still unknown to the police and the Law.

Asia on Fine Terms with the Duchess

"Rue Neuve-Saint-Marc," Asia called out to the driver.

She could count on the inviolable discretion of the secondhand-clothing merchant who was known as Madame Nourisson, though she also called herself Madame Saint-Estève; this is the woman who lent not only her shop but one of her names to Asia—and her shop was the place where Nucingen had made his deal for the purchase and delivery of Esther. Asia was quite at home there, for she had a room of her own in Madame Nourisson's place. She paid the cab driver and went upstairs to her room, passing Madame Nourisson with a gesture that meant she had no time to talk.

Once she was sure she was alone, Asia began to unfold the papers, using the level of care that a scholar will use in unrolling a palimpsest. After reading her instructions, she thought it would be best to transcribe from that paper the lines addressed to Lucien; then she went downstairs to Madame Nourisson, keeping her talking just long enough for the little shop girl to have gone out and hailed her a cab from the Rue des Italiens. Asia needed Madame Nourisson to give her the addresses of two women with whose chambermaids she had had dealings, the Duchesse de Maufrigneuse and Madame de Sérisy.

These tasks and all their attendant details ended up taking about two hours. The Duchesse de Maufrigneuse, whose home was at the farthest end of the Faubourg Saint-Germain, kept Madame Saint-Estève waiting an hour, even though her maid had knocked on her door and passed in a card upon which Asia had written, "Came concerning urgent matters relating to Lucien."

Her first glance at the face of the duchess made Asia understand how badly she had timed her visit, so she hurried to apologize for having disturbed the repose of Madame la Duchesse about this business of the peril in which Lucien stood.

"Who are you?" asked the duchess with no pretense of politeness, looking Asia up and down; Asia might have been taken for a baroness by Maître Massol in the hall of the Pas-Perdus, but here, on the carpet of the little drawing room in the Hôtel de Cadignan, she created the effect of a grease stain on a white satin gown.[37]

"I deal in secondhand clothing, *madame la duchesse,* and in situations like this a person turns to women whose profession is founded on absolute discretion. I have never betrayed the confidence of a soul, and God knows how many great ladies have entrusted me with their diamonds for a month, asking for false jewelry that looked exactly like their own. . . ."

"Do you have another name?" asked the duchess, smiling at the memory this evoked for her.

"Yes, *madame la duchesse*—I am Madame Saint-Estève on important occasions, but the name I use in business dealings is Madame Nourisson."

"Ah, yes—fine," the duchess replied, changing her tone.

"I can," Asia continued, "do important services, for we know the husbands' secrets as well as the wives'. Now, I've had a number of dealings with Monsieur de Marsay, whom *madame la duchesse*—"

"Enough! Enough!" cried the duchess. "Let's focus on Lucien."

"If *madame la duchesse* would like to save him, she must be brave and lose no time in dressing, but in any case *madame la duchesse* could not possibly appear any more beautiful than she does at this moment. You look good enough to eat, word of honor from an old lady! But please don't bother having your carriage brought around, but instead just get in the cab with me. . . . Come along to Madame de Sérisy's, if you want to avoid misfortunes worse than the death of that little cherubim. . . ."

"All right—I'm with you," said the duchess after just a moment's hesitation. "The two of us together will have to give Léontine strength. . . ."

A Fine Sorrow

Despite the truly infernal activity of this Dorine[38] of the penal colonies, it was already two o'clock when she and the Duchesse de Maufrigneuse entered the home of Madame de Sérisy, who lived on the Rue de la Chaussée-d'Antin. But once there, thanks to the duchess, not a moment was lost. The two of them were taken in to see the countess, who was lying stretched out on a divan in the miniature chalet in the middle of her garden, amid the fragrance of the rarest flowers.

"This will do fine," said Asia, looking around. "No one can eavesdrop here."

"Ah, my dear! I'm dying over all this! Come, Diane—what have you done?" cried the countess, leaping up like a fawn, grasping the duchess around the shoulders and bursting into tears.

"Now, Léontine, there are moments when women like us must not weep but act," said the duchess, forcing the countess to sit back down with her on the divan.

Asia studied this countess with the gaze peculiar to old débauchées like herself, a gaze that penetrated into the woman's soul like the scalpel of a surgeon searching a wound. The accomplice of Jacques Collin could recognize in her the signs of the rarest feeling in the women of high society: genuine grief, the kind of grief that traces permanent furrows in the heart and on the face. And not the slightest trace of vanity in what she wore! The countess had counted forty-five springtimes, and the wrinkled muslin peignoir opened to reveal her bosom, bare, uncorseted! . . . Black rings circled her eyes, and the mottled color of her cheeks testified to she shedding of bitter tears. No sash around the peignoir. The embroidered borders of her shift and petticoat were rumpled. Her hair was gathered up under her lace bonnet, and, innocent of comb or brush for the last twenty-four hours, revealed the thin poverty of her plait and loose curls. Léontine had forgotten to put on her false braids.

"You're in love for the first time in your life. . . ." said Asia, solemnly.

Léontine now noticed Asia, and she started back in fright.

"Who is that, dear Diane?" she said to the Duchesse de Maufrigneuse.

"Who do you think I'd bring you, if not a woman devoted to Lucien and ready to help us?"

A Type of Parisian Woman

Asia had divined the truth. Madame de Sérisy, long regarded as one of the women least encumbered by sober virtue, had had a ten-year attachment to the Marquis d'Aiglemont. After his departure for the colonies, she became madly infatuated with Lucien and managed to detach him from the Duchesse de Maufrigneuse, being ignorant (as was all Paris) of Lucien's love for Esther. In the highest levels of society, an open attachment does more harm to a woman's reputation than ten secret ones, and two open attachments only make things that much worse. Nevertheless, since no one made an official count with Madame de Sérisy, the historian cannot guarantee that the porcelain of her virtue had only been chipped twice. She was blonde, of medium height, and well preserved the way blondes are when they keep in shape—that is, she looked no more than thirty; she was slender but not skinny, fair-complected, with a silvery tint in her hair; her feet, her hands, her body were all aristocratically fine; she was witty as befitted the Ronquerolles family, and thus just as wicked toward women as she was kind toward men. Her great fortune had always been her salvation, along with the elevated rank of her husband and that of her brother the Marquis de Ronquerolles, all of which helped support her through the kind of romantic setbacks that would have overwhelmed any other woman. She had one great merit: she had always been frank and open in her debauchery, avowing her taste for Regency mores. And now, at forty-two, this woman for whom men had been pleasant playthings to whom—and this was a strange thing—she had given so much, seeing love only as a sacrifice she had to make in order to dominate them—this woman saw Lucien's face and was overcome by a love, just like Baron de Nucingen and Esther. And she was in love then, as Asia had just said, for the first time in her life. Such sudden reversions to youth are more common among Parisian women, especially great ladies, than people might think, and they lead to those inexplicable downfalls of virtuous women, just when they are about to reach the calm port of their forties. The Duchesse de Maufrigneuse was the only one who knew about this terrible, absolute passion whose moments of bliss—from childlike sensations all the way to gigantic gusts of voluptuousness—rendered Léontine half mad and entirely insatiable.

Real love, as we know, is pitiless. When she learned of the existence of an Esther, she broke off with him angrily, with the kind of rage that can lead women to murder; but that was followed by a period of weaknesses, the kind to which sincere love surrenders with such delight. Thus, for a month now the countess would have given ten years of her life to see Lucien again for just one week. Ultimately she reached the point where she accepted Esther as a rival, but this paroxysm of affection took place just when the news broke out, like the trumpet of the last judgment, announcing Lucien's arrest. The countess almost died; her husband nursed her himself in her bed, afraid of what revelations might arise from her delirium; and for the last twenty-four hours she had been living with a dagger in her heart. In her feverish state, she had said to her husband, "Free Lucien, and I'll live for no one but you alone!"

Asia, Peasant from the Danube

"It doesn't help for you to sit there making eyes like a dead goat, as *madame la duchesse* says," cried the terrible Asia, shaking the countess by the arm. "If you want to save him, there's not a minute to lose. He's innocent—I swear it on the bones of my mother!"

"Oh! Yes, yes of course . . ." exclaimed the countess, looking with kindness at the dreadful old woman.

"But," Asia went on, "if Monsieur Camusot gives him a *rough interrogation,* he can turn him into a guilty man with two sentences. And if you have the power to make the Conciergerie let you in to speak with him, go at once, and hand him this paper. . . . And then tomorrow he'll be free, I guarantee it. . . . Get him out of there, because it's you who put him in. . . ."

"Me!"

"Yes, you! All you great ladies, you never have a sou with you, even if you're worth millions. When I gave myself the luxury of having kids, I made sure their pockets were always stuffed with gold! It did me good to see them happy. It's a good thing, being mother and mistress at the same time! But you others, you'd let men die of hunger without ever asking about their business. Esther now, she didn't just talk fine phrases; no, she gave, even though it meant the damnation of her body and soul, and she got Lucien that million that he needed, and that's what got him into the situation he's in. . . ."

"That poor girl! She did that! Oh, I like her!" said Léontine.

"Well, high time," said Asia with glacial irony.

The duchess spoke in an undertone to Léontine, saying, "Yes, she was quite beautiful, but now you're much more beautiful than she . . . and the plan for Lucien to marry Clotilde is so thoroughly broken off that nothing can put it back together again."

Such a reflection, and such a calculation, immediately had so powerful an impact on the countess that her suffering ended altogether; she passed her hands over her face once, and then she was young again.

"Very good, my little one—paws up now, and off we go!" said Asia, observing the metamorphosis and comprehending its cause.

"But," said Madame de Maufrigneuse, "if we want to prevent Monsieur Camusot from interrogating Lucien, we can have your valet deliver him a quick note at the Palais, Léontine."

"Let's go back to my room," said Madame de Sérisy.

Meanwhile, while Lucien's two protectresses were busy obeying the orders of Jacques Collin, this is what was happening at the Palais.

Observations

The gendarmes transported the dying man to a chair that was placed so as to face the window in Monsieur Camusot's office; Camusot himself was sitting in his chair behind his desk. Coquart, pen in hand, occupied a small table a few feet away from the examining magistrate.

The way these examining magistrates laid out their offices is not a trivial matter, and even if they didn't always consciously choose the pattern, the lady Chance has always favored her sister Law. These magistrates are like painters, in that they need the even, pure light that comes from the north, for the face of a criminal is itself a painting requiring careful study. And so it is that most examining magistrates arrange their offices like Camusot's, so that the interrogators' backs are to the light and the faces of the people being questioned are fully illuminated. There's not a one of them who, after six months' experience, will fail to put on a pair of spectacles or a distracted, indifferent air during an interrogation, no matter how long it lasts. This method, which makes it possible to detect a sudden change of expression in the prisoner's face, following an abrupt, direct question, led to uncovering Castaing's crime, and just when the magistrate was about to set him free, after a long consultation with the prosecuting attorney, for lack of evidence.[39] A tiny detail such as this might give pause to the reader who has not thought about the matter, and might suggest how intense, fascinating, strange, dramatic, and terrible is the duel between prisoner and questioner in a criminal interrogation, a duel without witnesses, but one that is written down and recorded as it takes place. God only knows what remains on the page of these scenes that are both icy and ardent, where the eyes, the tone of voice, a little tremor in the face, the slightest reddening brought on by a hidden feeling, in fact everything functions as the kind of sign that Savages closely read in order to seek out and kill each other.[40] And the written report—it is merely the ashes after the fire is out.

"What are your real names?" Camusot asked Jacques Collin.

"Don Carlos Herrera, canon of the Royal Chapter of Toledo, and secret envoy for His Majesty Ferdinand VII."

We must note here that Jacques Collin was speaking French like a Spanish cow, jabbering in such a way as to make his answers nearly unintelligible, requiring Camusot to ask him frequently to repeat for clarity's sake. The Germanisms of Monsieur de Nucingen have already so sufficiently ornamented this narrative that no further difficulties need be placed in the reader's way, because doing so would only slow down the pace of things as they rush toward their denouement.

The Convict Proves He Is a Man of Note

"You have the papers that will prove the titles you claim?" asked the magistrate.

"Yes, monsieur—my passport as well as a letter from His Catholic Majesty authorizing my mission. . . . In short, you may immediately send a note, which I'll write in front of you, to the Spanish Embassy, and they will claim me. Then, if you require further proofs, I can write to His Eminence the high chaplain of France, and he will send his personal secretary right over to you."

"You continue to claim that you're dying?" asked Camusot. "If you really felt as miserable as you've been claiming ever since your arrest, you would surely have been dead by now," he added with irony.

"You're putting the courage and temperamental strength of an innocent man on trial!" replied the prisoner gently.

"Coquart, ring and have the Conciergerie doctor and his assistant come up," continued Camusot. "We're going to have to ask you to remove your jacket so we can verify the mark on your shoulder."

"I am in your hands, monsieur."

The prisoner then asked if the magistrate would be good enough to explain what sort of mark he was referring to, and why he would be looking for it on his shoulder. The magistrate was expecting the question.

"You're suspected of being Jacques Collin, an escaped convict of such audacity that he quails at nothing, not even sacrilege!" the magistrate said forcefully, staring directly into the eyes of the *prévenu.*

Jacques Collin neither trembled nor reddened; he remained calm, and assumed a naïvely curious air, looking back at Camusot.

"Me, monsieur? A convict? May the Order to which I belong and may the Good Lord pardon you for an error like that! Please, tell me what I must do to keep you from persisting in so grave an insult to the rights of men, to the Church, and to the king, my master."

The magistrate did not reply directly, but he explained to the prisoner that if he had submitted to the branding then required by the laws governing men sentenced to hard labor, slapping him on the shoulder would make the brand immediately reappear.

"Ah, monsieur," said Jacques Collin, "it would be most unfortunate if my devotion to the royal cause now were to do me harm."

"Explain yourself," said the magistrate; "that's what you're here for."

"Well, monsieur, I imagine I do have quite a few scars on my back, for I was shot from behind as a traitor to my country, for the crime of being faithful to my king, by the Constitutionalists who left me there for dead."

"You were shot in the back, and yet here you are, alive!" said Camusot.

"I had made an arrangement with several of the soldiers, men to whom certain pious individuals had sent a little money, and they stood me up far enough away from them that the only shot that reached me was nearly spent, and they aimed only at my back. This fact will be sworn to by His Excellency the ambassador."

"This devil of a man has an answer for everything. But that's so much the better," thought Camusot, who was only putting on an air of severity to satisfy the Law and the police.

An Admirable Invention by Jacques Collin

"How could a man of your character be picked up in the house of Baron Nucingen's mistress—and what a mistress! A longtime prostitute!"

"I'll explain to you how they came to find me in the house of a courtesan, monsieur," said Jacques Collin. "But before getting into what brought me there, I must first tell you that the very moment I stepped across the threshold and put one foot on the stairs, I suffered an attack of my illness, and I never had the chance to speak to that girl. I had been told about Mademoiselle Esther's plan to kill herself, and since this had implications for the interests of young Lucien de Rubempré, for whom I have a very strong affection, the motives of which are quite sacred, I was going to try to keep the poor creature from taking the path down which her despair was leading her: I wanted to tell her that Lucien was not going to succeed in his final attempt regarding Mademoiselle Clotilde; and I wanted to tell her about her inheritance of seven million francs, which I hoped would give her the courage to go on living. I am certain, monsieur, that I am the victim now of the secrets that had been confided to me. When I recall how dramatically, how instantly I fell ill, I suspect that I must have been poisoned that morning, but I was saved by the strength of my constitution. I know that a man from the political police has been following me for some time, seeking to get me entangled in some sort of wicked business. . . . If, as I asked at the time of my arrest, you had sent a doctor to examine me, you would have been given all the proof you needed of the state of my health. Believe me, monsieur, when I say that there are some people, more highly placed than ourselves, who have a powerful motive for making others confuse me with some criminal, in order to do away with me. Being servant to a king is not all gain, you know; there is sometimes mean-spiritedness. Only the Church is perfect."

It is impossible to render the play of facial expression Jacques Collin deployed during the ten minutes or so this tirade went on, phrase by phrase; it was all so credible, and especially the allusion to Corentin, that the magistrate was unnerved.

"Can you tell me the reasons you have this affection for Monsieur Lucien de Rubempré—"

"Can't you guess? I'm sixty years old, monsieur. You, I beg you, don't write this down. . . . It's . . . must I answer?"

"It's in your own interest, and certainly in that of Lucien de Rubempré, to explain everything," replied the magistrate.

"Very well! It's . . . O, my God! . . . He's my son!" he added in a murmur. And he fainted dead away.

"Don't write that down, Coquart," Camusot said quietly.

Coquart got up to fetch a little vial of four-thieves vinegar.[41]

"If this really is Jacques Collin, he's a tremendous actor!" thought Camusot.

Coquart got the old convict to breathe in the vinegar while the judge observed him with the keen eye of a lynx—or a magistrate.

Cunning Meets Cunning, and Well Met, Too[42]

"We need to get him to take off his wig," said Camusot as he waited for Jacques Collin to regain consciousness.

The old convict heard this and trembled with fear, for he knew the ignoble quality his face would take on without it.

"If you don't have the strength to take off your wig yourself . . . yes, Coquart, go ahead and take it off," said the magistrate to his clerk.

Jacques Collin leaned his head forward to the clerk with an admirable resignation, but once that head had been despoiled of its ornament it was a frightful thing to see. The spectacle of it plunged Camusot into a deep uncertainty. While waiting for the doctor and his assistant to arrive, he turned to classifying and arranging all the papers and other objects that had been seized at Lucien's home. After having worked through the Rue Saint-Georges, Esther's house, the Law had turned its attention to the Rue Malaquais and carried out a search there.

"I see you're holding some letters from the Comtesse de Sérisy," said Carlos Herrera; "but I can't see why you've taken practically all of Lucien's papers," he added, with a startlingly ironic smile, to the magistrate.

Seeing that smile, Camusot realized the importance of that word "practically"!

"Lucien de Rubempré is suspected of having been your accomplice, and he's been arrested," he replied, interested to see what effect this piece of information would have on his *prévenu*.

"You've done a great wrong then, because he's just as innocent as I am," said the false Spaniard, without showing the slightest emotion.

"We'll see, but right now we're concerned with determining your identity," said Camusot, surprised at how calmly his *prévenu* took the news. "If you are really Don Carlos Herrera, that would immediately alter the situation for Lucien Chardon."

"Yes, yes, it was Madame Chardon, Mademoiselle de Rubempré!" murmured Carlos. "Ah! It was one of the greatest sins of my life!"

He raised his eyes to the heavens, and from the way he silently moved his lips, he appeared to be saying a fervent prayer.

"But if you are Jacques Collin, and if he was knowingly the companion of an escaped convict, of a man of sacrilege, then all the crimes that the Law currently suspects him to be guilty of would become more than probable."

Carlos might as well have been made of bronze as he listened to the magistrate's shrewdly worded statement, and at the words "knowingly" and "escaped convict" he raised up his hands in a gesture both noble and doleful.

"*Monsieur l'abbé,*" the magistrate went on in a tone of exaggerated politeness, "if you are Don Carlos Herrera, you will forgive us for all that we are obliged to do in the interests of justice and the truth. . . ."

Jacques Collin sniffed out the trap that the magistrate was laying for him by the way he had enunciated *monsieur l'abbé*, and he remained expressionless. Camusot was waiting to detect a little movement of joy, which would have served as the first indicator of the man's convict nature, that ineffable delight of the criminal who deludes his interrogator; but he found our hero of the penal colonies armed with the most Machiavellian powers of dissimulation.

"I am a diplomat, and I belong to an order that requires vows of the utmost austerity," replied Jacques Collin with apostolic sweetness. "I understand it all, and am accustomed to suffering. I would already be free if you would have discovered, in your search of my home, the place I hide my papers. I see, instead, that you've only taken insignificant papers."

This was a death blow to Camusot. Jacques Collin had already counteracted, by his air of ease and simplicity, all the suspicions to which the sight of his bare head had given rise.

"Where are these papers?"

"I'll tell you the place if you'll agree to having your deputy accompanied by a secretary from the legation of the Spanish embassy, who will take the papers, and who will be answerable to you for them, for this is a matter that involves my State—there are diplomatic items and secrets that would compromise the memory of the late King Louis XVIII. Oh, monsieur! It would be so much better . . . but then, you are a magistrate! In any case, the ambassador, to whom I appeal in all this, will understand."

The Sign Erased

Just then, the doctor and assistant came in, the usher announcing them.

"Good day, Monsieur Lebrun," said Camusot to the doctor. "I need you to have a look at this *prévenu* and make a pronouncement on his condition. He says he has been poisoned, and he claims that he nearly died over the last couple of days. Please see if there is any danger in undressing him so that we can verify whether the mark is there."

Doctor Lebrun took Jacques Collin's hand and checked his pulse, told him to stick out his tongue, and looked him over very carefully. The examination took about ten minutes.

"The prisoner," said the doctor, "has clearly suffered a great deal, but now he enjoys a tremendous strength. . . ."

"That strength is only apparent, monsieur, and it's due to the nervous excitement I feel at having been placed in this strange situation," said Jacques Collin, with all the dignity of a bishop.

"That may well be," said Doctor Lebrun.

At a sign from the magistrate, the *prévenu* was undressed and his shirt removed, though he was allowed to keep his trousers on; and then everyone gaped at a hairy torso of Cyclopean power. It was the Farnese Hercules from Naples without its colossal exaggeration.

"What end did Nature have in mind, creating a man like this?" the doctor asked Camusot.

The usher reappeared, carrying that kind of small ebony baton that, since time immemorial, has been the badge of the office, and that is known as "the rod"; he slapped it, several times, against the spot where the executioner would have branded the fatal letters. Seventeen different depressions then appeared, distributed all over the skin in the area; but despite the great care they took in examining the spot, nothing that looked like letters could be distinguished. The usher did opine that the top bar of a T might have been present once, for there were two depressions that might have been the two serifs at the ends of the bar, and there was another depression that might once have been the very bottom of the vertical line.

"Still, that's hardly conclusive," said Camusot, seeing doubt on the face of the Conciergerie doctor.

Carlos asked if they would perform the same operation on his other shoulder, and on the middle section of his back. Some fifteen additional scarlike depressions now appeared, which the doctor proceeded to study at the Spaniard's request, and he declared that the back had been so deeply plowed by wounds that the branding could not possibly be seen, assuming that the executioner had put it there.

Thrusts and Parries

At that moment, a boy from the office of the police prefecture came in, handed a letter to Monsieur Camusot, and waited for a reply. After reading it, the magistrate went aside to speak with Coquart, but so quietly that none of them could hear him. But from a glance that Camusot shot at him, Jacques Collin guessed that it was something new concerning him from the prefect of police.

"I've still got that friend of Peyrade's on my heels," thought Collin. "If I knew who he was, I'd get rid of him the way I did with Contenson. I wonder if I could see Asia again?"

After having signed the paper that Coquart had just written up, the magistrate put it in an envelope and handed it back to the boy from the delegations office.

The Office of Delegations is an indispensable arm of the Justice system. This office, presided over by an ad hoc police commissioner, is composed of officers who execute—coordinating with other police officials from each neighborhood—the search for and the arrest of persons suspected of crimes or of complicity. These "delegates" operate on judicial authority, and they save the examining magistrates in charge of an investigation a great deal of precious time.

At a sign from the magistrate, Doctor Lebrun and his assistant helped the prisoner get his clothes back on, and they then left, along with the usher. Camusot sat at his desk and toyed with his pen.

Abruptly, he addressed Jacques Collin: "You have an aunt."

"An aunt," Don Carlos Herrera repeated with surprise. "But, monsieur, I have no relatives. I am the unacknowledged illegitimate child of the deceased Duc d'Ossuna."

But to himself he exclaimed, "They're getting warm!"—a phrase from the children's game of hide-and-seek, and indeed, that is a fitting metaphor for this terrible struggle between the Law and the criminal.

"Bah!" said Camusot. "Come on—you still have your aunt, Mademoiselle Jacqueline Collin, and you've given her the bizarre name of Asia in getting her placed as a cook in the household of Mademoiselle Esther."

Jacques Collin gave an indifferent shrug of the shoulders, perfectly in harmony with the expression of curiosity with which he awaited hearing more from the magistrate, the latter looking at him with a kind of sneer.

"Be careful," Camusot continued. "Listen to me carefully."

"I'm listening, monsieur."

Asia's Résumé

"Your aunt is a merchant on the Rue du Temple; her business is run by a certain Mademoiselle Paccard, sister of a convict, though herself a perfectly honest woman, who goes by the name La Romette. The Law has been tracking your aunt, and in a few hours we will be in possession of decisive proofs. The woman is quite devoted to you. . . ."

"Please go on, monsieur," said Jacques Collin tranquilly when Camusot paused. "I'm listening."

"Your aunt, who is about five years older than you, was the mistress of Marat, he of odious memory. And that was the bloody source from which her fortune sprang. . . . From the information I've been given, it appears that she is a very accomplished fence for stolen goods, though we have no proofs of it. After Marat's death, she was kept by, according to the report I have here in my hands, a chemist who was sentenced to death in the Year XII, for the crime of counterfeiting. She appeared as a witness at his trial. The relationship with him is where she developed her skills in toxicology. She was a merchant selling clothes from the Year XII of the Republic until 1810. She spent two years in prison, in 1812 and 1816, for having been a pimp for minors. . . . At that time you had already been convicted of forgery, having left the bank where your aunt had got you a place as a clerk, thanks to the education you had been given and the protection from individuals your aunt provided with victims. All this, prisoner, doesn't sound very much like the grandeur of the Duc d'Ossuna. . . . And now, will you persist in denying it?"

Jacques Collin listened to Monsieur Camusot while thinking back to his happy childhood at the Oratorians' school he had attended, a meditation that lent his face an expression of real surprise. But despite the skillful rhetoric of Camusot's interrogation, he could not discern any movement or reaction on that placid countenance.

"If you faithfully wrote down the explanation I gave you when we started, you can simply reread that," said Jacques Collin. "I can't change it. I did not succeed in going inside the courtesan's house, so how could I possibly know who her cook was. All these people you're talking about are complete strangers to me."

"We're going to proceed, despite your denials, to some confrontations that might shake your assurance a bit."

"A man who has already been shot once is a man who can tolerate anything," said Jacques Collin in a gentle voice.

Camusot turned back to the confiscated papers, waiting for the return of the head of the Sûreté; the diligence of the latter was extreme, for it was now eleven-thirty, the interrogation having begun at ten-thirty, and the usher came in to notify the magistrate, in a very low voice, that Bibi-Lupin had arrived.

"Have him come in!" said Monsieur Camusot.

Reacquainting Old Acquaintances

When he entered the room, everyone expected Bibi-Lupin to exclaim, "It's him, all right!" But instead he stood there, looking surprised. He could no longer recognize the face of his old prisoner in this one, pitted from smallpox. His hesitation struck the magistrate.

"It's definitely his size and shape," said the agent. "Oh, it is you, Jacques Collin," he continued, looking now at his eyes, the slant of his forehead, his ears . . . some things simply can't be disguised! . . . It's definitely him, Monsieur Camusot. . . . Jacques had a knife scar on his left arm; get him to remove his jacket, and you'll see it."

Again Jacques Collin was forced to remove his jacket. Bibi-Lupin pulled up the shirt sleeve and pointed to the scar.

"It's from a gunshot," said Don Carlos Herrera. "See—here are plenty of other scars."

"Oh, yes—that's his voice all right!" cried Bibi-Lupin.

"Your certainty," said the magistrate, "is just one piece of data—it's not proof."

"I know that," said Bibi-Lupin humbly, "but I'll find you witnesses. Already we've got one of the people who lived in the Vauquer pension outside . . ." he said, looking at Collin.

Collin's imperturbable expression never changed.

"Have that person come in," said Camusot peremptorily, his irritation showing despite his apparent indifference in the matter.

That little flicker was noticed by Jacques Collin, who had not counted on any sympathy from his examining magistrate, and he now assumed a complete apathy to mask an urgent, desperate train of thought, seeking what might account for this. The usher now introduced Madame Poiret, an unexpected sight that occasioned a slight shudder in the convict, though this was not observed by the magistrate, whose mind seemed already made up.

"What is your name?" asked the magistrate, proceeding immediately to the formalities that always preface every kind of deposition and interrogation.

Madame Poiret, a pale little woman, her skin wrinkled like veal sweetbread, dressed in a dark blue silk dress, declared her name to be Christine-Michelle Michonneau, spouse of Monsieur Poiret, aged fifty-one, born in Paris, residing on the corner of the Rue des Poules and the Rue des Postes, earning her living by keeping a boardinghouse.

"You resided, madame," said the magistrate, "in a bourgeois pension in the years 1818–19, run by a Madame Vauquer."

"Yes, monsieur, and that's the place I met Monsieur Poiret, a retired clerk who became my husband and who, for the past year, has had to stay in bed . . . poor man! He's very ill. So I really shouldn't be away from home for too long."

"Now, in that pension there also resided a certain Vautrin. . . ." said the magistrate.

"Oh, monsieur, what a story that is! He was a frightful convict. . . ."

"You helped in his arrest."

"That's not true, monsieur."

"You're standing before the Law here, so be very careful!" Monsieur Camusot said with severity.

Madame Poiret remained silent.

"Think back!" said Camusot. "You remember that man very well! . . . Would you recognize him?"

"I think so."

"Is this the man?" the magistrate asked.

Madame Poiret put on her spectacles and gazed at the abbé Carlos Herrera.

"That's the same build, the same size, but . . . no . . . if . . . monsieur magistrate, if I could see his bare chest, I'd recognize him at once." (See *Père Goriot.*)

The magistrate and his clerk could not help laughing, despite the gravity of their offices. Jacques Collin shared in their hilarity, though more moderately. The *prévenu* had not yet put his arms into the sleeves of the jacket that Bibi-Lupin had just taken off him; and at a sign from the magistrate, he cooperatively opened his shirt front.

"That's his *palatine,* I'm sure of it.[45] But it's gone gray, Monsieur Vautrin!" cried Madame Poiret.

The Prisoner's Audacity

"What do you say to that?" asked the magistrate.

"The poor woman is mad!" said Jacques Collin.

"Oh, my heavens, if I had any doubts they're gone now—he doesn't have the same face, but that voice would be enough for me to recognize him. This is definitely the man who threatened me. . . . Oh! That's his glare!"

"The Sûreté agent and this woman," the magistrate continued, addressing Jacques Collin, "could not have conspired to say this, because neither had the chance to see each other. So, how would you explain it?"

"Well, the Law has committed worse errors than taking the word of a woman who recognizes a man by his chest hair and trusting the suspicions of a police agent," replied Jacques Collin. "They find a resemblance in my voice, my way of looking at them, my size with some great criminal, but that's all pretty vague. As for the reminiscence that would prove some intimate relations between madame and my doppelgänger, though it does not cause her to blush, it did make both of you burst out laughing. If, monsieur, in the interests of discovering the truth—which I am just as anxious to do as you could possibly be for the sake of the Law—please ask this woman, Foi—"

"Poiret."

"Poiret. Pardon—I'm Spanish. Ask if she can remember the people who lived at this . . . what did you call the place . . ."

"A bourgeois pension," said Madame Poiret.

"I'm not sure what that is!" said Jacques Collin.

"It's a boardinghouse, a place where you eat your meals by subscription."

"That's right," cried Camusot, making a gesture that seemed favorable to Jacques Collin, as if he were suddenly struck with the evident good faith with which the latter was suggesting ways of getting results. "Try to remember the people who were living in the pension at the time of Jacques Collin's arrest."

"There was Monsieur de Rastignac, Doctor Bianchon, old Goriot . . . Mademoiselle Taillefer . . ."

"Good," said the magistrate, who had not ceased observing the unchanging countenance of Jacques Collin. "Very well. This old Goriot . . ."

"He's dead," said Madame Poiret.

"Monsieur," said Jacques Collin, "I have often met a Monsieur de Rastignac at the home of Lucien—he was connected, I believe, with Madame de Nucingen and, if this is the man in question, he certainly never took me for the convict they're trying to claim I am. . . ."

"Monsieur de Rastignac and Doctor Bianchon," said the magistrate, "both occupy the kind of social position that, if their testimony were favorable to you, nothing further would be needed for your release. Coquart, prepare two summonses."

In a few minutes the formalities of the deposition of Madame Poiret were complete, Coquart read her the record of the testimony she had just given, and she signed it; but the prisoner refused to sign, claiming ignorance as to the formalities of the French justice system.

An Incident

"That will be enough for today," Monsieur Camusot said. "You must be in need of some food—I'll have you escorted back to the Conciergerie."

"Unfortunately, I'm not well enough to eat," said Jacques Collin.

Camusot wanted to time Jacques Collin's return to coincide with the hour the prisoners took their exercise in the prison yard, but since he wanted to hear a reply from the warden of the Conciergerie to the order he'd given that morning, he rang for his usher to have him go get it. The usher came and said the woman porter at the Quai Malaquais house had given him an important document relating to Monsieur Lucien de Rubempré. This news was so important that Camusot forgot his intentions.

"Have her come in!" he said.

"Excuse me, pardon me, monsieur," said the woman, bowing in turn to the magistrate and the abbé Carlos. "We got ourselves into such a state, my husband and me, by the Law people, the two times they've come to our place, that we forgot we had this letter, addressed to Monsieur Lucien, in our drawer, and you see we had to pay ten sous for it, even though it only came from Paris, because it's so heavy. Will you please reimburse me for the postage due? God only knows when we might see our tenants again!"

"The postman brought you this letter?" asked Camusot when he had examined the envelope very closely.

"Yes, monsieur."

"Coquart, you're to write up this deposition. Come along, my good woman. We'll start with your name, your occupation. . . ."

Camusot had the woman sworn in, and then proceeded to dictate the report.

While these formalities were being taken care of, he verified the postal stamp, which showed the hours of pickup and delivery as well as the date. Now, this letter, delivered to Lucien's home the day after Esther's death, had no doubt been written and put in the mailbox on the day of the catastrophe.

The reader may now gauge the stupefaction of Monsieur Camusot in reading the letter, written and signed by the person the Law had been considering as the victim of a crime.

Enough

Esther to Lucien
Monday, May 13, 1830
(My Last Day, at Ten in the Morning)

My Lucien,

I have less than an hour to live. By eleven o'clock I'll be dead, and I'll die without the slightest sorrow. I've paid fifty thousand francs for a pretty little black currant containing a poison that kills with lightning speed. So, my lamb, you'll be able to say: "My little Esther didn't suffer." No, my only suffering will be in writing these pages.

The monster who bought me at such a high price, knowing that the day I truly had to regard myself as his would be my last day—Nucingen has just left, drunk as a bear who got into the liquor. For the first, and the last, time in my life, I've been able to compare my old life as a whore with the life of love, to set them side by side, the one marked by a tenderness that blossoms out into the infinite, and the other that feels horror at its duties, so eager to annihilate itself that it will not even leave room for a kiss. This disgust is necessary, in order to make death seem a delight. . . . I've taken a bath; I wish I could have had my old confessor from the convent come and bathe my soul. But there's already been enough prostitution; it would be profaning the sacrament, and anyway I feel I've been washed in the waters of sincere repentance. God will do with me as He likes.

But enough whining; I want to be your Esther for you right up to the last moment, not bore you with my death, with the future, with the good God—who would not be so good if He tortured me in the next life, when I've had to endure so much misery in this one . . .

I have that delicious portrait Madame de Mirbel made of you in front of me right now.[44] This little ivory panel consoled me in your absence, and as I look at it now, writing my last thoughts, describing for you my last heartbeats, it intoxicates me all over again. I'll enclose it with this letter, because I don't want anyone to steal it or to sell it. It's like another death, imagining it ending up in a shop window among ladies and officers of the Empire, or Chinese curiosities. My sweetheart, take this portrait and either keep it or have it erased, but do not give it to anyone else . . . well, unless giving it as a gift would win you the hand of that walking stick in women's garments, that Clotilde de Grandlieu, who will turn you black and blue if you sleep with her, her bones are so pointy. . . . Yes, I consent to that, because then I'll still be good for something for you, as I was when I was alive. Oh, if it would have given you some pleasure, or even if it would only have given you a laugh, I would have stood in the fire with an apple in my mouth to roast it for you! So my death will still be useful to you . . . I would have only caused trouble for your married life. . . . Oh, that Clotilde—I do not understand her! To be your wife, to carry your name, to stay with you day and night, to be with you—and with all that in her future, to cause you so many difficulties! You have to be born to the Faubourg

Saint-Germain for that! And to have less than ten pounds of flesh on your bones . . .

Poor Lucien, my dear, disappointed, ambitious one, I dream of your future! Go on: you're going to miss your poor old faithful dog now and then, that good girl who stole for you, who'd have let herself be dragged into criminal court if it aided your happiness, whose sole occupation was to think about your pleasures, to invent more of them for you, whose love for you was so complete it was even in her hair, her feet, her ears—or maybe your ballerina, whose every glance was a blessing upon you; who, for six years, thought only of you, who was so entirely yours that I was never more than an emanation of your soul, the way light is an emanation of the sun. But in the end, having neither money nor respectability, alas, I could not be your wife. . . . I've always provided for your future by giving you everything I had . . . Come here right away, as soon as you get this letter, and take what I've put beneath my pillow, because I don't trust the domestics in this house . . .

You see, I want to look beautiful in death, so I'll go to bed, stretch out in a pose (why not?), and then I'll crush the little currant against my palate; I won't be disfigured by any convulsions or any ridiculous posture.

I know that you and Madame Sérisy have quarreled because of me; but my little one, when she hears that I'm dead she'll forgive you, and you'll cultivate the relationship, and she'll get you well married if the Grandlieus persist in their refusal.

My dear one, I don't want you to make a great fuss when I'm dead. In the first place, I remind you that eleven o'clock on May 13 is only the termination of a long illness that began on the day when, on the terrace at Saint-Germain, you turned me back toward my old career . . . A person can be sick in the soul as well as in the body. But the soul won't simply let itself suffer stupidly the way the body does—the body doesn't help the soul, the way the soul helps the body—and the soul has at its disposal a cure, in thinking of the bag of charcoal that the seamstresses use. You offered me a whole life the other day when you told me that if Clotilde refused you, you'd marry me. That would have been a disaster for us, and I would have died of that, so to speak; there are even more bitter deaths, after all. Society would never have accepted us.

I've been thinking things over seriously for two months now—really seriously! A poor whore is stuck down in the mud, the way I was before I entered the convent; men think she's pretty, and they make her serve their pleasure without any thought for her, they make her walk home after getting a carriage for themselves, and if they don't literally spit right in her face, it's only because her beauty preserves her from that particular outrage, but in a moral sense they do even worse things to her. But now, let's imagine that the same girl inherits five or six million—now she'll be sought out by princes, people will bow out of respect when she passes them in her carriage, and she'll have the choice of all the finest, oldest family names in France and Navarre. This same society that would have shouted raca at us,[45] at two fine creatures united and happy, consistently bowed before Madame de Staël, despite the wild life she led, just because she had an income of two hundred thousand. Society puts Money ahead of Glory, and it will not bow down either to happiness or virtue; because I would have done good . . . Oh, how many tears I could have dried! As many as I've shed! Oh yes, I would have liked to live only for you, and only to do works of charity.

Well, it's thinking thoughts like these that has made death so attractive to me. So don't let yourself go into any grand lamentations, my good little pet! Say to yourself, often: there have been two good whores, two beautiful creatures, both of them dead for me without asking anything from me, both of them adoring me; and build up in your heart the memory of Coralie and of Esther, and then continue on your way! Remember the day you pointed out to me an old woman who had been the mistress of a poet before the Revolution? She was all shriveled, wearing a green bonnet the color of a melon, and a puce quilted shawl, with black grease stains all over it; she looked cold even though she was sitting in the sun there in the Tuileries, getting all angry with her little pug dog, a really nasty looking pug at that. And you know, this is a woman who had had lackeys, carriages, a fine house! I said to you then, "It's better to die at thirty!" Well, that day you found me pensive, and you played all sorts of tricks to distract me; and between two kisses, I abruptly said: "Every day you can see women who walk out of the theater before the play is over!" And that's really all . . . I just don't want to stay for the last act.

You're thinking that I'm rambling—but it's my last ramble. I'm writing to you the same way I'd talk to you, and I want to talk cheerfully to you. The dressmakers who make those long laments have always horrified me; you know that I really did try to kill myself decently once already, when I got home from that fatal Opéra Ball, where people told you that I'd been a whore!

But no, my dear one, don't ever give that portrait away—if you only knew the waves of love I felt just now, like going down underwater, as I gazed into your eyes, just intoxicated with them, and I paused in my writing . . . if you could find a way to feel the love I've just lavished on this piece of ivory, you'd see that the soul of the one you loved is overlaid on it.

A dead woman asking for alms—something comic about that! . . . No, no, she'll have to learn how to rest quietly in her tomb.

You can't imagine how some imbeciles would call my death heroic simply because last night Nucingen offered me two million francs if I would be willing to love him the way I love you. He's going to feel he's been robbed all right, and then some, when he finds that I kept my word and died of him. I tried everything to be able to go on breathing the same air you breathe. I said to the old fat thief: "If you really want to be loved in the way you say, I'll promise never to see Lucien again. . . ." At that he asked, "What do I have to do?" And I said, "Give me two million to give him up!" But oh, no, if you could only have seen the grimace on his face! Oh, I would have burst out laughing if it hadn't been so tragic. "You're trying so hard not to say no," I said to him. "But I can see it: you think more highly of the two million than you do of me. It's always good for a woman to know exactly what she's worth," I said, turning my back to him.

In an hour or two, the old rogue will know I wasn't joking.

How will you find anyone to part your hair as well as I could? Bah! I don't want to think about life any more. I've only got five minutes left, and I want to give them to God; don't be jealous, my dear angel: I want to speak to Him about you, and ask him to give you happiness in return for my death and my punishments in the next world. I hate the thought of going to Hell; I'd so like to see the angels, to see if they look like you . . .

Farewell, my darling, farewell! I bless you, from all my miseries. Even in the tomb I'll remain

YOUR ESTHER . . .

The clock is striking eleven. I've said my last prayer, and now I'm going to bed to die. Once more, farewell! I wish the warmth of my hand could retain my soul there, as I put one last kiss on it, and now I want, just one last time, to call you my sweet pet, even though you are the cause of the death of your

ESTHER

In Which We See That the Law Is and Must Be Heartless

The magistrate's heart contracted a little with a feeling of jealousy as he finished reading the suicide's letter, the only one he had ever read that was so gay, though its gaiety was feverish, the final effort of a blind tenderness.

"What is it about him that he could have been loved like that!" he thought, repeating the same thing men always say when they themselves have never had the gift of being pleasing to women.

The magistrate turned to Jacques Collin, saying: "If you can prove not only that you are not Jacques Collin, an ex-convict, but also that you are really Don Carlos Herrera, canon of Toledo and secret envoy of His Majesty Ferdinand VII, you'll be set free, because the impartiality demanded of a magistrate compels me to inform you that I've just received a letter written by Mademoiselle Esther Gobseck, in which she declares her intention of killing herself, and in which she expresses suspicions about her domestics, suspicions that lead one to think they may well have been the ones who stole the seven hundred and fifty thousand francs."

While he was saying this, Monsieur Camusot was comparing the handwriting of the letter with that of the will, and it was clear to him that the letter was indeed written by the same person who had made the will.

"Monsieur, you were too quick to believe in a murder. Do not turn around now and be too quick to believe in a theft."

"Oh?" asked Camusot, casting a magistrate's eye on the prisoner.

"Don't think that I'm compromising myself in saying that this sum of money may be recoverable," Jacques Collin continued, letting the judge know he understood his suspicion. "Those servants loved that poor girl, and if I were free, I would take it upon myself to find that money, which right now belongs to the creature I love best in all the world, Lucien! . . . If you'd have the goodness to allow me to read that letter, it would be most helpful— it's the proof of the innocence of my dear child. . . . You don't need to fear that I will destroy it . . . nor that I'll tell anyone about it—I'm in solitary confinement."

"In solitary confinement!" cried the magistrate. "Well, you won't be any longer. . . . Indeed, I'm the one who urges you to establish your true identity as quickly as possible, and you may have recourse to your ambassador if you wish."

And he handed the letter over to Jacques Collin. Camusot was happy to get out of this entanglement and to satisfy the general prosecutor and both Madame de Maufrigneuse and Madame de Sérisy. But still he continued, with coolness and curiosity, to examine the face of the *prévenu* as he read the courtesan's letter, and despite the sincerity of the feelings he could see there, he said to himself, "All the same, it's the kind of face you see in the penal colonies."

"Look how she loved him!" said Jacques Collin, handing the letter back, letting Camusot see his face bathed in tears. "If you only knew him!" he went on. "He's such a young, fresh soul, with such splendid beauty—a child, a poet. . . . People feel an irresistible urge to sacrifice for him, to find a way to satisfy his every desire. And when he's affectionate, that dear Lucien is so captivating . . ."

"All right," said the magistrate, making another effort to get at the truth, "you can't possibly be Jacques Collin. . . ."

"No, monsieur," replied the convict.

And Jacques Collin was now, more than ever, Don Carlos Herrera. In his desire to bring things to a conclusion, he walked over to the magistrate and led him to the window nook, putting on the manners of a prince of the Church and adopting a confidential tone.

"I love that boy so much, monsieur, that if I had to become a criminal in order to remove some obstacle to the happiness of my heart's idol, I would accuse myself," he said quietly. "I'd imitate that poor prostitute who killed herself to benefit him. And so, monsieur, I beg you to grant me the favor of setting Lucien free right away. . . ."

"My duty will not allow it," said Camusot in a friendly way, "but if Heaven has its accommodations, the Law too can make its compromises, and if you can give me good reasons. . . . Go ahead and speak—this won't be written down."

"Well," began Jacques Collin, duped by Camusot's friendly tone, "I know how much the poor child is suffering right now—he's capable even of ending his life, seeing himself in prison. . . ."

"Oh, as for that . . ." said Camusot, with a shrug.

"You don't know who you're obliging when you oblige me," added Jacques Collin, trying to pluck a different chord. "You'd be rendering a service to an Order more powerful than the Sérisy comtesses or the Maufrigneuse duchesses, who won't forgive you for having their letters in your office," he said, pointing to two scented stacks of envelopes. "My Order has a long memory."

"Monsieur," said Camusot, "enough! Find some other reasons for me. I owe a duty to the prisoner as well as to public justice."

"Well, then, believe me, I know Lucien. He has a woman's soul, he's a poet, he's a southerner, entirely inconstant, with no willpower," Jacques

Collin continued, thinking that the magistrate had come over to his side. "You're already certain of this young man's innocence, so don't torture him, don't even interrogate him—give him this letter, tell him he's Esther's heir, and set him free. . . . If you take any other course, you'll plunge him into despair, but if you simply relax your hold on him, I'll explain to you, tomorrow—and meanwhile you can keep me locked up here, in solitary confinement—or this evening, everything that still seems mysterious to you about this whole affair, and the reasons why certain people are fiendishly persecuting me—although I'll be risking my head, which they've been after for the last five years. But with Lucien free, rich, and married to Clotilde de Grandlieu, my task here below is complete, and I will no longer defend my own skin. . . . My persecutor is a spy in the service of your former king. . . ."

"Ah! Corentin!"

"Ah, his name is Corentin . . . I thank you. Well, monsieur, will you promise to do what I've asked of you?"

"A magistrate cannot, and must not, make promises. Coquart! Tell the usher and the gendarmes to conduct the prisoner back to the Conciergerie . . . I'll give orders for you to be moved to the *pistoles* cells this evening," he added gently, giving the prisoner a slight nod of the head.

The Magistrate Back on Top

Camusot now felt all his distrust returning, struck as he was by what Jacques Collin had just said to him and remembering how he had insisted on being questioned first, pleading his illness. Allowing his suspicions free rein, he now watched the so-called dying man walking out like a Hercules, no longer putting on any of those little stage-play touches he had deployed so carefully when he came in.

"Monsieur?"

Jacques Collin turned around.

"My clerk will read to you his report on the interrogation, despite your refusal to sign it."

The prisoner now seemed to be in excellent health; the way he moved as he sat down beside the clerk was like another ray of illumination for the magistrate.

"You've been fully cured?" asked Camusot.

"I'm caught now," thought Jacques Collin. Then he said aloud, "Joy, monsieur, is the real panacea in this life. This letter, the proof of the innocence I myself never doubted . . . this is the great remedy."

The magistrate watched his prisoner with a thoughtful gaze as the usher and the gendarmes moved in around him; then he shook himself, like a man trying to wake up, and he tossed Esther's letter onto the desk of his clerk.

"Coquart, copy out that letter!"

The Melancholy Peculiar to Examining Magistrates

It is natural for us to distrust something we are begged to do when the thing being asked for is contrary to our interests or our duty, even though we may be indifferent about the matter ourselves, but feeling such a distrust is practically an inborn law when it comes to an examining magistrate. The more the prisoner—whose identity was still not established—saw dark clouds on the horizon if Lucien were to be interrogated, the more that interrogation seemed essential to Camusot. This formality would not have been required, according to the Code and to usual practices, but it became crucial because of the question of the identity of the abbé Carlos. There is some form of professional conscience in virtually every kind of career. If only out of curiosity, Camusot would have questioned Lucien just as he had questioned Jacques Collin, and he would have deployed all the little ruses that a magistrate of integrity would have used. Doing a favor for others, or contributing to his own advancement—all this was less important to Camusot than finding out the truth, getting the answer, even if he could never share it. He drummed on the windowpanes with his fingertips, surrendering himself to the flow of his conjectures, for in such moments thought is like a river that streams through a thousand countries. Lovers of truth, magistrates are like jealous women, giving themselves up to endless suppositions and poking around in them with the dagger of suspicion, like the ancient priest on the sacrificial altar, disemboweling his victims; and then they—magistrates and jealous women—do not stop at the true but rather at the probable, and so they end up catching a glimpse of the truth. A woman will interrogate a man the way a magistrate does a criminal. And in such depositions a little flash, a word, an inflection in the voice, a hesitation will suffice to point toward the fact, the betrayal, the hidden crime.

"The way he just now described his devotion to his son—if he is his son—makes me think that he was in that whore's house in order to keep an eye on things, and, not knowing there was a will under the dead woman's pillow, he would have snatched up the seven hundred and fifty thousand francs for his son *just in case!* . . . And that's why he said he could recover the money. Monsieur de Rubempré owes it to himself, and to the Law too, to clarify his father's social position. . . . And then to

promise me the protection of his Order—his Order!—if I don't interrogate Lucien! . . ."

He continued to think about this.

As we have just witnessed, an examining magistrate may run an interrogation as he sees fit. It's up to him to proceed shrewdly or plainly. An
interrogation is nothing—and it's everything. And therein lies the chance
to do the favor. Camusot rang, and the usher came back in. He ordered
him to go and find Monsieur Lucien de Rubempré, but to be sure he has
no communication with anyone else along the way. It was now two in
the afternoon.

"There is some kind of secret here," said the magistrate to himself,
"and that secret must be very important. The reasoning that my amphib-
ious prisoner used, he who is neither priest nor lay, neither convict nor
Spaniard, but who is anxious that some terrible word not be allowed to
pass the lips of his young protégé, is this: 'The poet is weak, he's feminine, not like me, the Hercules of diplomacy, and therefore you will easily get the secret out of him!' Well, let's learn everything we can from
this innocent!"

He continued tapping the edge of his table with his ivory paper knife,
while his clerk continued copying Esther's letter. How oddly we use
our faculties! Camusot suspected any and every crime to be possible in
the case, but he passed right by the one that was actually committed,
the forged will in Lucien's favor. Let anyone who feels like criticizing the
position of the examining magistrate consider carefully this life passed
in constant suspicion, the torment these people inflict on their own
minds—for civil cases are no simpler than criminal ones, and the critic
might well come to believe that the priest and the magistrate do their
work in equally heavy harnesses, both of which are well furnished with
sharp spikes in their inner lining. Every profession has its own particular hair shirts, its own particular Chinese puzzles.

The Dangers an Innocent Man Faces at the Palais

Around two o'clock Monsieur Camusot saw Lucien de Rubempré come
in the office, pale, defeated, his eyes red and swollen, in a state of such
complete collapse that the magistrate had the opportunity to study the
difference between nature and art, the stage-play dying man and the real
one. Walking the route from the Conciergerie to the magistrate's office,
supported by two gendarmes, an usher leading the way ahead of them,
had brought Lucien to the very depths of despair. It's natural for a poet
to prefer torture to judgment. Observing how this man's nature was so

utterly devoid of moral courage, the kind of courage the previous prisoner had so powerfully demonstrated, gave the magistrate pause; Monsieur Camusot felt only pity at this too-easy victory, and contempt at realizing how easily he would be able to land his decisive blows, leaving him sole master of the field, as clearheaded and at ease as a marksman picking off dolls at a shooting range.

"Take heart, Monsieur de Rubempré. You're in the presence of a magistrate who is anxious to undo the harm that the Law involuntarily does when it makes a preventive arrest that turns out to be groundless. I believe you are innocent, and you're going to be set free at once. I have here the proof of your innocence. This is a letter that your porter kept in your absence, and that she just brought to me. What with all the commotion caused by the appearance of the police and your own arrest in Fontainebleau, the woman forgot this letter that came from Mademoiselle Esther Gobseck. . . . Read it!"

Lucien took the letter, read it, and broke into tears. He sobbed, unable to articulate a single word. After fifteen minutes, during which time Lucien strove with difficulty to pull himself together, the clerk handed him the copy of the letter and asked him to please sign to indicate that it was *a copy conforming to the original, to be presented at once upon request for the duration of the inquiry,* and offering him the chance to compare the two; but Lucien naturally took Coquart's word as to the precision of the copy.

"Monsieur," said the magistrate in friendly, open-hearted tone, "it's still a little difficult to set you free until we fulfill certain formalities and I ask you a few questions. I'm asking these questions of you as a witness, and I must require you to answer them. When I'm dealing with a man such as yourself, I hardly need to say that swearing to speak the whole truth is not simply an appeal to your conscience but an actual necessity for your position here, which is not entirely clear quite yet. The truth can do you no harm, no matter what it is, but a lie could land you in the assize court and would force me to have you put back in the Conciergerie; but if you reply frankly to my questions, you'll be sleeping in your own home tonight, and your reputation will be rehabilitated by a line we'll have printed in the newspapers: 'Monsieur de Rubempré, arrested yesterday at Fontainebleau, was released immediately following an investigation.'"

This speech made a strong impression on Lucien, and, seeing that, the magistrate added, "I repeat, you were suspected of complicity in the murder by poisoning of Mademoiselle Esther, but we now have proof of her suicide, and that settles it, but the sum of seven hundred and fifty thousand francs was removed, and that money should have gone to you as her heir, We have, therefore, and unfortunately, a crime on our hands. This crime took place before her will was discovered. Now, the Law has reason to believe that a person who loves you, as much as you loved Mademoiselle Esther, committed this crime, to give the money to you. Don't interrupt," said Camusot, gesturing for Lucien to remain silent. "I am not asking you anything yet. I want you to understand that this situation has implications for your honor. Abandon the false, the miserable point of honor that binds accomplices together, and tell me the whole truth!"

We have already remarked upon the extreme disproportion in the weapons available to each in this duel between the prisoner and the examining magistrate. Certainly a denial that is consistent and well maintained is the best and a sufficient defense of the criminal; but it is also a little like a suit of armor that turns lethal when the opponent's dagger finds a joint in it. Once the denial ceases to account for certain evident facts, the prisoner finds himself entirely at the mercy of the magistrate. Suppose, for the moment, that a semicriminal like Lucien were to be preserved, saved from the shipwreck of his life by his virtue, and that he could amend his ways and become a useful citizen—such a person could still become entangled and tripped up in the various ambushes lying in wait for him during an interrogation. The magistrate writes up a dry, objective account of the questions and answers, but he includes none of the insidiously paternal discourse, none of the misleading warnings like the ones we've just seen. The judges and juries at the next stage of the process will see the results, but not the means that led to those results. And so some intelligent people have proposed that the jury itself should hear the interrogation, as they do in the English courts. France used a similar system for a while. Under the Code of Brumaire, Year IV, there was an examining jury, as opposed to a jury of judgment. When it comes to the final trial, if we were to reinstitute the examining jury, the trial would have to be the function of the royal courts, without the use of juries.

In Which Anyone Who Has Committed Any Crime Will Tremble at the Idea of Appearing before Any Kind of Court

"Now," said Camusot, after a pause, "what is your name? Monsieur Coquart, pay attention!" he added to the clerk.

"Lucien Chardon, de Rubempré."

"You were born . . ."

"In Angoulême."

Lucien added the day, the month, and the year.

"You inherited no property?"

"None."

"But you nonetheless spent, during your first stay in Paris, a great deal of money, relative to your lack of fortune?"

"Yes, monsieur. But in those days I had Mademoiselle Coralie, an exceptionally devoted friend who I had the misfortune to lose. My grief at her death is what led me to go back to my hometown."

"Fine, monsieur," said Camusot. "I commend your frankness—it's much appreciated."

As the reader may perhaps see, Lucien was starting down the path leading to a general confession.

"And you made even more considerable expenditures when you returned to Paris from Angoulême," Camusot continued. "You lived like a man with an income of sixty thousand francs."

"Yes, monsieur . . ."

"Who gave you that money?"

"My protector, the abbé Carlos Herrera."

"Where did you meet him?"

"I met him on the highway, just at the moment when I had decided to end my life. . . ."

"You never heard anyone in your family, such as your mother, speak of him?"

"Never."

"Your mother never told you she had met a Spaniard?"

"Never."

"Can you recall the month and year when you began your relationship with Mademoiselle Esther?"

"It was toward the end of 1823, at a small boulevard theater."

"At first she cost you money?"

"Yes, monsieur."

"More recently, out of your desire to marry Mademoiselle de Grandlieu, you bought up the remains of the Rubempré château and added lands to it, to the tune of a million. You told the Grandlieu family that your sister and brother-in-law had come into a considerable fortune, and that they gave you this money out of their own liberality. Did you tell that, monsieur, to the Grandlieu family?"

"Yes, monsieur."

"You don't know what caused the breakdown of your marriage plans?"

"Not at all, monsieur."

"Well, the Grandlieu family sent one of the most respectable lawyers in Paris down to visit your brother-in-law and gather some facts. In Angoulême the lawyer learned, directly from your sister and brother-in-law, that not only did they inherit relatively little, but most of the inheritance was in the form of land and buildings, important enough, of course, but the grand total of capital amounted to scarcely two hundred thousand francs. . . . Surely you cannot be surprised that a family such as the Grandlieus would turn their backs on a fortune whose origins are so murky—and this is where, monsieur, your lie led you."

Lucien was stunned by the revelation, and what little strength he had left abandoned him entirely now.

"The police and the justice system know all they need," said Camusot. "Remember that. Now," he continued, thinking of Jacques Collin's claim of fatherhood. "do you know who this man is, the one who claims to be Carlos Herrera?"

"Yes, monsieur, but I only learned it when it was too late. . . ."

"Too late? How so? Explain!"

"He's not a priest, and he's not a Spaniard; he's—"

"An escaped convict," the magistrate interrupted forcibly.

"Yes," replied Lucien. "When that fatal secret was revealed to me, I was already in his debt—I had thought I was involved with a respectable man of the church."

"Jacques Collin . . ." the magistrate began.

"Yes, Jacques Collin," Lucien repeated. "That's his name."

"Well. Jacques Collin," Monsieur Camusot went on, "has just now been recognized by someone, and if he continues to deny his identity it will be, I think, something he does in your interest. But I asked you if you knew who this man was in order to shed light on another imposture by Jacques Collin."

Lucien felt as if red-hot irons were penetrating his entrails as he waited for this terrifying question.

"Did you know," said the magistrate, "that he claims to be your father in order to justify the extraordinary affection he feels for you?"

"Him? My father? . . . Oh, monsieur! . . . He said that?"

"Did you have any suspicions regarding the origins of the money that he gave you? According to Mademoiselle Esther's letter, which you have there in your hand, that poor girl would appear to have done you similar services to those of Coralie earlier; and yet you lived, you tell me, quite splendidly for several years without receiving anything from her."

"But you would have to be the one to tell me, monsieur," cried Lucien, "where convicts get their money!... A Jacques Collin my father?... Oh, my poor mother ..."

And here he burst into tears.

"Clerk, read to the prisoner that part of the interrogation of the so-called Carlos Herrera in which he said he was the father of Lucien de Rubempré."

The poet listened to the reading in silence, but with an expression on his face that was painful to view.

"I'm lost!" he exclaimed.

"No one is lost, so long as they remain on the path of honor and truth," said the magistrate.

"But you'll be sending Jacques Collin up before the assize court?" asked Lucien.

"Certainly," said Camusot, who wanted to keep Lucien talking. "Finish your thought."

Two Moralities

But despite the efforts and the remonstrances of the magistrate, Lucien said nothing more. Reflection had come too late, as it always does with men who are slaves to sensation. And here we see the difference between the poet and the man of action: the one gives himself entirely to feeling in order to reproduce that feeling in powerful images, and he only reflects afterward; but the other feels and thinks at the same time. Lucien sat there solemn and pale, imagining himself at the foot of a precipice down which he had been hurled by the examining magistrate, the man who put on all that cheery friendliness to entrap him, the poet. He had just betrayed not only his benefactor but his accomplice, who had in fact defended their position with the courage of a lion and the skill to match. Where Jacques Collin had saved the day through his audacity, Lucien, the clever man, had lost everything through his failure to think, his failure to reflect. The ugly lie that made him so indignant really only screened off a deeper, ugly truth. Overwhelmed by the magistrate's subtlety and cowed by the cruelty of his rhetoric, by the rapidity of the blows that brought to light his weaknesses, and by the way in which these were used as hooks with which to dredge his conscience, Lucien sat there like an animal who just escaped the chopping block in the slaughterhouse. When he came into this office he had been free and innocent, but his own admissions had instantly turned him into a criminal. And as one last cruel joke upon him, the magistrate, calm and icy now, informed him that his revelations were the result of a misunderstanding. Camusot had been interested in Jacques Collin's claim to paternity, while Lucien had been so frightened at the thought of his connection with an escaped convict becoming public knowledge that he had imitated the famous inadvertent admission made by the murderers of Ibycus.[46]

It is one of the glories of Royer-Collard that he proclaimed the constant triumph of the natural feelings over those that are imposed upon us, that he supported the cause of the anteriority of oaths by claiming that the law of hospitality, for example, outweighed and might even annul the power of a judicial oath.[47] He proclaimed his theories openly and before all, in a French law court; he courageously praised the conspirators, arguing that it was properly human to obey the laws of friendship rather than the tyrannical laws dragged out from the arsenal of Society to be trained on this or that individual case. Natural Law makes demands upon us that have never been codified and that are more effective and more universally understood than those that Society forges. Lucien, to his own detriment, had failed to follow the law of solidarity that would oblige him to be silent and let Jacques Collin defend himself; and even worse: he had brought the charge against him! In his own interests, that man ought to have always been and ought always to remain Carlos Herrera.

Monsieur Camusot delighted in his triumph: he had two guilty parties in hand, he had used the fist of Justice to crush one of the fashionable dandies of the day, and he had unmasked the un-unmaskable Jacques Collin. He was going to be proclaimed one of the most capable of all examining magistrates. And so he let his prisoner be; but he continued to study him in his silent consternation, and he watched the beads of sweat breaking out on the man's overwrought face; they swelled in number, eventually joining and intermixing with two streams of tears.

The Hammer Blow

"Why this weeping, Monsieur de Rubempré? After all, you are, as I've told you, the heir of Mademoiselle Esther, who had no other heirs, direct or indirect, and her fortune comes to nearly eight million francs, if you can recoup the seven hundred and fifty thousand that were lost."

This was the final blow for the guilty Lucien. If he could have held on for ten minutes, as Jacques Collin had said in his note, Lucien would have realized all his greatest desires! He would have settled up with Jacques Collin, the two would have separated, and he would have married

Mademoiselle de Grandlieu. There is no better illustration of the power that examining magistrates are armed with when prisoners are kept isolated and separated, and nothing can better illustrate the value of the kind of communication Asia had managed to have with Jacques Collin.

"Ah, monsieur," Lucien replied, with all the bitterness and irony of a man who makes a kind of pedestal of his overwhelming misfortune, "how right they are to phrase it as '*undergoing interrogation*'! . . . Between the physical torture of the old days and the moral torture of our day, I wouldn't hesitate to choose the pains that the executioner used to inflict. What more do you want with me?" he concluded in a haughty voice.

"In this place, monsieur," said the magistrate, replying sneeringly to Lucien's sudden outburst of pridefulness, "I'm the only one who has the right to ask questions."

"I had the right not to reply to them," murmured poor Lucien, his intelligence now returning to him with full clarity.

"Clerk, read the interrogation out to the prisoner."

"So I'm a prisoner again!" Lucien said to himself.

While the clerk read, Lucien made a resolution, one that demanded he try to sweet-talk Monsieur Camusot. When Coquart's murmuring voice ceased, the poet gave a shudder, the kind a sleeping man makes when some sound he's been accustomed to suddenly stops.

"You need to sign the written report of your interrogation," said the magistrate.

"And then you'll set me free?" asked Lucien, adopting an ironic tone in turn.

"Not yet," Camusot replied. "But tomorrow, after your confrontation with Jacques Collin, you'll undoubtedly be free to go. First, Justice demands that we're satisfied you were not an accomplice to any crimes that that individual may have committed since his escape from prison, which was in 1820. But you won't have to stay in solitary. I'll write to the warden to put you in the best available *pistole* cell."

"Will I find writing materials there?"

"You'll be given anything you ask for—I'll inform the usher who conducts you back."

Lucien mechanically signed the report, putting his initials next to all the marginal spots that Coquart pointed to, all with the meekness of a victim resigned to his fate. One detail will say more about the state he was in than would the minutest description. The announcement that he would be facing Jacques Collin dried up all the little drops of sweat on his face; his eyes dried, and they now shone with a terrible gleam. In

316 | WHERE EVIL PATHWAYS LEAD

short, he had become, with the speed of a lightning bolt, the same thing
Jacques Collin was, a man of bronze.

People whose character is similar to Lucien's, that character so well
analyzed by Jacques Collin, experience these sudden transformations
from a state of utter demoralization to one that is practically ironclad;
the phenomenon is a striking example of the power of idea. The will
returns, like water gushing up from the spring, and it proceeds to infuse
itself throughout the entire machine, which has remained ready for the
play of its unknown powers; and then, the corpse becomes a man, and
the man springs forth, bursting with power, ready for supreme battles.

Lucien put Esther's letter next to his heart, along with the portrait she
had sent. He then gave Monsieur Camusot a disdainful bow and walked
off with a firm step into the corridors, along with the two gendarmes.

"What a scoundrel!" the magistrate exclaimed to his clerk in an effort
to avenge himself on the crushing contempt that the poet had just shown
him. "He thought he'd save himself by giving up his accomplice."

"Between the two of them," said Coquart timidly, "the convict is the
tougher one. . . ."

The Magistrate's Torture

"I'll set you free for today, Coquart," said the magistate. "That's enough.
Send away the people who are waiting out there, and tell them to come
back tomorrow. Oh! Do hurry over to the prosecutor-general's office to
see if he's still there. Oh, yes, he will be," he said after looking up at a
wretched wooden clock, painted green with gilt trim. "It's three forty-
five."

Though these interrogations, written down verbatim, are quickly
read, the questions and answers actually take an enormous amount of
time. This is one of the causes of criminal investigations moving at so
slow a pace, and of the length of time a person might be held in preventive detention. For people of modest means, it spells ruin; for the wealthy,
it's shame, because for them an immediate release might repair some of
the damage done by the arrest. This is why the two scenes that have just
been faithfully depicted took enough time for Asia to decipher her master's orders, to get the duchess out of her boudoir, and to instill some
energy into Madame de Sérisy.

At the moment, Camusot was thinking of how he could turn his skillful handling of the two prisoners into benefits for himself; he took up
the two reports, reread them, and decided he would show them to the

WHERE EVIL PATHWAYS LEAD | 317

prosecutor-general and seek his advice. While he stood there deliberating, his usher came in to tell him that the valet of Madame la Comtesse de Sérisy insisted upon speaking with him. At a sign from Camusot, a valet—who was dressed like a master—entered, looked at the usher, then at Camusot, and asked, "Is this Monsieur Camusot, to whom I have the honor . . ."

"Yes," replied both the usher and Camusot.

Camusot took a letter from the servant, which read as follows:

> For the sake of a number of interests that you will understand,
> dear Camusot, do not interrogate Monsieur de Rubempré; we'll
> be bringing you proofs of his innocence, so that he may be
> immediately set free.
>
> *D. de Maufrigneuse, L. de Sérisy*
>
> P.S. Burn this letter.

Camusot realized he had committed an enormous error in setting traps for Lucien, and he began by obeying the two great ladies. He lit a candle and destroyed the letter from the duchess. The valet bowed respectfully to him.

"Is Madame de Sérisy coming here?" Camuset asked.

"Her carriage is being brought around," said the valet.

Just then Coquart came to tell Monsieur Camusot that the prosecutor-general was waiting for him. Weighed down by the blunder he had committed against his ambition by putting Justice first, the magistrate—a man whose cunning and finesse were the results of seven years' practice in matching his wits against those of working-class girls—now recognized he had to find a way to defend himself from the resentment of the two great ladies. The candle with which he had burned the letter was still alight, so he used it to seal up the thirty notes the Duchesse de Maufrigneuse had sent Lucien, as well as the voluminous correspondence with Madame de Sérisy. Then he obeyed the summons of the prosecutor-general.

The Prosecutor-General

The Palais de Justice is a confused heap of buildings superimposed one upon the other, some quite grand, others shabby, and the effect of the whole spoiled by its lack of any unified design. The hall of the

Pas-Perdus is the largest of the known rooms, but its bareness makes it an appalling place, discouraging to the eye. The whole vast cathedral of legal chicanery annihilates what used to be a royal court. Now the Marchande gallery leads to two ghastly locales. In the gallery is a double staircase, a little bigger than the one for the correctional police, and below it a large folding door opens. The staircase leads to one assize court, and the lower door leads to another. In some years, there are so many crimes committed in the Seine Département that two courts are necessary. This is the way that leads to the prosecutor-general's office, the lawyers' room, their library, the offices of the prosecuting lawyers, and those of the prosecutor-general's deputies. All these spaces—for we can only use that most generic term—are connected by little spiral staircases and dark corridors that are a disgrace to architecture, to the city of Paris, and to France itself. In its interiors our highest levels of justice outdo the hideousness of the prisons. The writer determined to depict our times recoils before the necessity of describing the ignoble corridor, only about a meter in width, where the witnesses for the assize courts must sit and wait. And as for the stove intended to warm the room where the audience sits, it would dishonor a café on the Boulevard Montparnasse.

The office of the prosecutor-general is set within an octagon wing built out from the Marchande gallery on land that had until recently— recently, that is, relative to the age of the Palais—been part of the prison yard, on the side by the women's quarters. That whole side of the Palais is shadowed by the high, magnificent structure of the Sainte-Chapelle. And thus it is a somber, silent place.

Monsieur de Granville, that worthy successor to the great magistrates of the old *parlements*,[48] had not wanted to leave the Palais without finding a solution to the Lucien affair. He was waiting for news from Camusot, and the message he now received from the magistrate plunged him into the sort of involuntary reverie that long waiting arouses in even the strongest minds. He was sitting in the window bay of his office, and now he got up and paced back and forth, for that morning he had deliberately stationed himself in the path of Camusot, and he had found the man rather weak in understanding; now he felt a vague anxiety. He was worried, and this is why: The dignity of his station prohibited him from any meddling with the complete independence of the lower-level magistrate, but this case involved the honor and reputation of his best friend and one of his warmest protectors, the Comte de Sérisy, minister of State, member of the privy council, and vice president of the Council of State, and the man who would in the near future be the chancellor of France, once a certain old man who currently fulfilled those functions died. Monsieur de Sérisy had the misfortune of loving his wife *"no matter what,"* and he always made sure she was protected. Now, the prosecutor-general had no trouble picturing the horrible uproar that would be caused both in higher society and at the Royal Court if a man whose name had been so often and so long associated with that of the countess were to be declared guilty.

"Ah," he said to himself, crossing his arms, "in the old days the king had the power to step in with a case like this. . . . But our modern mania for equality will be our downfall."

The worthy magistrate knew where illicit attachments could lead, and the misery in which they could end. Esther and Lucien had rented, as we have seen, the apartment in which the Comte de Granville had lived secretly with Mademoiselle de Bellefeuille as man and wife, the place from which she fled one day, stolen away by a wretch. (See *A Double Marriage* in the series *Scenes from Private Life.*[49])

Just as the prosecutor-general was saying to himself, "This Camusot will end up doing something stupid," the examining magistrate knocked twice on his office door.

"Ah, my dear Camusot! Tell me, how is that little business we talked about this morning going?"

"Not well, *monsieur le comte.* Read these and judge for yourself!"

He handed the two interrogation reports to Monsieur de Granville, who put on his reading glasses and went back to the window bay. He read through them quickly.

"You've done your duty," said the prosecutor-general, sounding somewhat shaken. "It's all come out, and Justice will take its course . . . You've given proof of so much skill that we will always be in need of an examining magistrate like yourself."

Monsieur de Granville might have said, "You'll never be anything but an examining magistrate," but he could not have possibly been any more explicit than he was in his complimentary-sounding phrase.

"The Duchesse de Maufrigneuse, to whom I owe so much, begged me . . ."

"Ah, the Duchesse de Maufrigneuse," said Granville, interrupting the magistrate, "is a friend to Madame de Sérisy. I can plainly see that you have not given in to any outside influence. Well done, monsieur. You will be a great examining magistrate."

Is It Too Late?

At that moment, Comte Octave de Bauvan opened the door without knocking, and he said to the Comte de Granville: "My friend, I have a pretty woman here with me who didn't know where to turn, having got lost in our labyrinth. . . ."

And he brought in the Comtesse de Sérisy by the hand; she had been wandering through the Palais for a quarter of an hour.

"You here, madame!" cried the prosecutor-general, pushing a chair toward her. "And at such a moment! . . . This is Monsieur Camusot, madame," he added, nodding toward the magistrate. "Bauvan," he continued, addressing that illustrious ministerial orator, an ornament of the Restoration,[50] "wait for me in the president's office; he's still there, and I'll join you soon."

Comte Octave de Bauvan understood not only that he was *de tro,* but that the prosecutor-general wanted to have a reason to leave his office.

Madame de Sérisy had not made the mistake of arriving at the Palais in her magnificent carriage with its armorial mantling of blue, its coachman in his gold lace livery, and its two footmen in their short breeches and white silk stockings. When they were leaving, Asia made the two great ladies understand that they needed to take the cab in which she and the duchess had arrived; and she had also persuaded Lucien's mistress to wear the kind of outfit that, for men, is the plain gray cloak. The countess was wearing a brown jacket, an old black shawl, and a velvet hat, from which the flowers had been removed and replaced with a very thick black-lace veil.

"You received our letter. . . ." she said to Camusot, who stood there stupefied; she took this as a sign of admiration and respect.

"Too late, alas, *madame la comtesse,*" replied the magistrate, who only had any tact and intelligence when he was in his office interrogating prisoners.

"What do you mean, too late?"

She looked at Monsieur de Granville and saw the consternation on his face.

"It cannot be, it must not be too late!" she added, in the tone of a despot.

All That Women Do in Paris

Women—pretty women, women of position like Madame de Sérisy—are the spoiled children of French civilization. If the women of other nations had any idea of what a fashionable, rich, and titled woman was in Paris, they would all be making plans to move here and enjoy this magnificent, regal status. Women devoted solely to the bonds that their status imposes, to that collection of petty laws that has often been called the Female Code in the pages of the *Comédie humaine,* laugh at the laws men make. They say anything they please, flinch at no kind of blunder, at no species of folly; for they know perfectly well that they are responsible for nothing in life apart from their feminine honor and their children. They utter the most shocking things with a laugh. And in any kind of situation they will repeat the phrase used by the pretty Madame de Bauvan in the first years of her marriage, when she had come to fetch her husband at the Palais: "Hurry up and finish your judging, and come along!"

"Madame," said the prosecutor-general, "Monsieur Lucien de Rubempré is not guilty of either theft or poisoning, but Monsieur Camusot has got him to admit to an even greater crime than those!"

"What crime?" she asked.

"He has confessed," the prosecutor-general said quietly to her, "to having knowingly been the protégé of an escaped convict. The abbé Carlos Herrera, the Spaniard who lived with him for about seven years, turns out to be our famous Jacques Collin. . . ."

Madame de Sérisy felt each word he was saying like a blow from an iron club, but that famous name was the death blow.

"And the upshot of all this . . ." she asked in a voice that was little more than a breath.

"Is," Monsieur de Granville said, continuing the sentence the Comtesse had left hanging, and speaking himself in a very quiet voice, "that the convict will go before the assize court, and that even though Lucien doesn't seem to have been so close to him that he profited from the man's crimes, he will nonetheless have to appear as a witness, and one who has been gravely compromised. . . ."

"Oh, no, never that!" she cried out loud, with an extraordinary firmness. "For my part, I won't hesitate if I must choose between death and being seen as the companion of a man everyone has regarded as my best friend now being proclaimed the comrade of a convict. . . . No, the king is too fond of my husband."

"Madame," the prosecutor-general said aloud with a smile, "the king has not the slightest power over the most insignificant examining magistrate in the kingdom, nor over what takes place in the assize courts. And there you see the greatness of our new institutions. I myself have just congratulated Monsieur Camusot on his skill . . ."

"You mean his clumsiness," the countess interrupted vigorously, being considerably less disturbed at the thought of Lucien being involved with a convict than she was at his liaison with Esther.

"If you were to read the reports on the interrogations that Monsieur Camusot carried out with the two *prévenus,* you would see that everything depends upon him. . . ."

And with that final phrase, the only hint the prosecutor-general would permit himself, and after a glance of feminine, or should I say judicial, shrewdness, he turned to the door of his office. On the threshold he paused to add, "Please excuse me, madame! I need to talk to Bauvan. . . ."

This, spoken to the countess in the language of society, when translated meant "I can't be a witness to anything that passes between you and Camusot."

All That Women Can Do in Paris

"Now, what are these interrogation reports?" said Léontine sweetly to Camusot, who stood there sheepishly before the wife of one of the most important men of the State.

"Madame," replied Camusot, "a clerk writes down all the questions the magistrate asks and the answers that the *prévenu* gives; this report is then signed by the clerk, the magistrate, and the *prévenu*. These reports are then the basis of any trial, for they determine the exact nature of the accusation and the persons who are to be remanded to the assize court."

"Well," she asked, "what would happen if these reports were to be suppressed?"

"Oh, madame! That would be a crime that no magistrate would dare commit—a crime against society itself!"

"Having written them is a much greater crime, against me, but right now, this report is the only proof against Lucien. Let's see—read his interrogation report to me, and let's see if there isn't some way we can save all of us. My God, it's not only a matter of my suicide, which would be certain, but also of the welfare of Monsieur de Sérisy."

"Madame," said Camusot, "please don't think that I've forgotten the regard I owe you. If Monsieur Popinot, for example, had been in charge of this case, you would have been worse off than you are with me, because he would not have even consulted the prosecutor-general. No one would have known anything about it. And look, madame, they've seized all Lucien's papers, including your letters. . . ."

"Oh! My letters!"

"And here they are, sealed!" said the magistrate.

The countess, in her distraught state, rang the bell as if she were at her own home, and the office boy of the prosecutor-general hurried in.

"I need light," she said.

The boy lit a candle and set it on the mantel, while the countess examined her letters, counted them, crumpled them up, and then tossed them in the fireplace. The countess then took the top letter, twisted it, and lit it like a torch, and with it she set fire to the whole pile. Camusot stood and vacantly watched the pile of papers burn, holding the two interrogation reports in his hand. The countess appeared to be entirely focused on eliminating those traces of her love, but she was watching the magistrate out of the corner of her eye. She took her time, calculated her movements, and then, with the agility of a cat, she seized the two interrogation reports and threw them into the fire; but Camusot took them back, and at that the countess hurled herself upon the magistrate and again snatched the burning pages away. A struggle ensued, as Camusot cried out: "Madame! Madame! . . . You're attacking . . . Madame! . . ."

A man rushed into the office, and the countess could not repress an exclamation when she recognized the Comte de Sérisy, followed by de Granville and de Bauvan. Nonetheless, Léontine wanted to save Lucien at any cost, and she would not surrender those terrible official documents that she gripped as tightly as a vise even though the flames were already burning her delicate skin, making it look cauterized. Eventually Camusot, whose fingers had also been burned by the flames, seemed to feel a sense of shame in the situation, and he abandoned the papers; nothing was left of them but the scraps the two antagonists still clutched in their hands and that the fire had not had the time to devour. The whole scene took place in much less time than it takes to read about it.

A Funny Story

"What are you and Madame de Sérisy fighting about?" the minister of State asked Camusot.

Before the magistrate could reply, the countess took the scraps to the candle and then threw them on the remains of her letters that the fire had not entirely consumed.

"I will have to lodge a complaint," said Camusot, "against *madame la comtesse.*"

"And what is it that she's done?" asked the prosecutor-general, looking back and forth from the countess to the magistrate.

"I burned the interrogation reports," said the woman of fashion with a laugh, feeling so pleased with her actions that she didn't feel her burns. "If that's a crime, well, then, monsieur here can start his ridiculous scribbling all over again."

"That is correct," said Camusot, attempting to recover some shred of dignity.

"Well, it's all for the best," said the prosecutor-general. "But, my dear countess, you ought not to take such liberties with magistrates—they might fail to recognize who you are."

"Monsieur Camusot put up a brave resistance against a woman nobody can resist! The honor of the judicial robe is preserved!" said the Comte de Bauvan, laughing.

"Oh, Monsieur Camusot resisted?" said the prosecutor-general, also laughing. "That's very bold of him—I would never dare resist the countess!"

By now the entire, serious affair had become a pretty woman's joke, and even Camusot was laughing at it. But the prosecutor-general saw one man who wasn't laughing. Appropriately alarmed at the grave expression on the face of the Comte de Sérisy, Monsieur de Granville took him aside.

"My friend," he said quietly to him, "your suffering has made me decide—for the first and only time in my life, I'm going to compromise my duty."

The magistrate rang, and his office boy came in.

"Tell Monsieur de Chargeboeuf to come see me."

Monsieur de Chargeboeuf, a young lawyer still in his probationary period, was secretary to the prosecutor-general.

"My dear magistrate," the prosecutor-general said to Camusot, drawing him over to the window bay, "go back to your office and have a clerk help you reconstitute the interrogation report of the abbé Carlos Herrera—since he never signed it, you can redo it with no inconvenience. Then, tomorrow, you'll have this *Spanish diplomat* confronted by Messieurs de Rastignac and Bianchon, neither of whom will recognize Jacques Collin in him. Once he's assured that he's going to be freed, he will readily sign the report. As for Lucien de Rubempré, set him free this evening—he won't be the one who goes blabbing about a destroyed interrogation report, especially after the admonishment I'll give him. In the morning, the *Gazette des tribunaux* will be reporting that the young man was immediately released. Now, shall we consider whether Justice is injured by any of this? If the Spaniard is in fact the convict, we have thousands of ways of getting him arrested again and putting him on trial, for we're going to use diplomatic channels to find out what his Spanish connection is—Corentin, the counterespionage chief, will keep close watch on him for us, and in any case we won't let him out of our sight—so treat him well, no more solitary for him, have him transferred to a *pistole* cell for the night. Is it right that we kill the Comte and Comtesse de Sérisy and Lucien for the sake of the theft of seven hundred and fifty thousand francs—a theft that, after all, remains hypothetical and, if it were actually committed, was done for the sake of Lucien? . . . Wouldn't it be better for him to lose that money than to lose his reputation, especially when he would pull down with him a minister of State, his wife, and the Duchesse de Maufrigneuse? This young man is a bruised orange now—let's not let him go completely rotten. . . . All this will take you half an hour. Go on—we'll wait for you. It's now three-thirty, so you'll find judges still around. Let me know if you can get an official dismissal of the case—otherwise Lucien will have to wait till tomorrow morning."

Camusot bowed and left, but Madame de Sérisy, finally beginning to feel the pains of her burns, did not return his bow. Monsieur de Sérisy had abruptly left the office while the prosecutor-general was talking to the magistrate, and he now reappeared with a jar of virgin wax, which he began applying to his wife's hands, saying quietly to her, "Léontine, why did you come here without letting me know?"

"My poor friend!" she whispered to him. "Please pardon me, I must seem mad—but it concerns you as much as it does me."

"Love this young man, if that's what fate requires, but don't let the whole world see your passion," the poor husband replied.

"Come now, dear countess," said Monsieur de Granville, after speaking for a while with Comte Octave, "I hope you'll be able to take Monsieur de Rubempré home to dinner with you this evening."

That half-promise made such an impression on Madame de Sérisy that she burst into tears.

"I didn't think I had any more tears," she said with a smile. "Monsieur, couldn't you bring Monsieur de Rubempré here to wait?"

"I'll see if I can find some ushers to bring him to us, so he won't have to be accompanied by gendarmes," replied Monsieur de Granville.

"You're as good as God!" she exclaimed, and her powerful emotion made her voice sound like celestial music.

"It's always women like that," thought Comte Octave, "who are the most delicious, the most irresistible!"

And he was overwhelmed by melancholy as his thoughts turned to his wife. (See *Honorine,* in the series *Scenes from Private Life.*)

As he was leaving, Monsieur de Granville was stopped by young Chargeboeuf, to whom he gave instructions as to what he should tell Massol, one of the editors of the *Gazette des tribunaux.*

Dandy and Poet Are Reunited

While pretty women, ministers, and magistrates were all conspiring to save Lucien, here is what he was doing in the Conciergerie. As he passed through the wicket, he said that Monsieur Camusot had given him permission to write, and he asked for pens, ink, and paper, and upon a word whispered by Camusot's usher to the warden, the order was given to take them to him. During the few moments while the guard was off searching for the materials and getting them delivered to Lucien, the poor young man was thinking how a confrontation with Jacques Collin would be unendurable, and he fell into one of those fatal trains of thought that lead to the idea of suicide, an idea to which he had already succumbed once, though without finishing the deed, and the idea now took root and became an obsession. According to certain great medical *alienists,* suicide in certain personalities is the conclusion of a process of mental alienation; now, ever since his arrest, it had become an idée fixe for Lucien. Esther's letter, which he reread several times, only strengthened the intensity of his desire to die, bringing back for him the memory of Romeo rejoining Juliet. Here is what he wrote.

THIS IS MY LAST WILL AND TESTAMENT

At the Conciergerie, the 15th of May, 1830

I, the undersigned, give and bequeath to the children of my sister, Madame Ève Chardon, wife to David Séchard, former printer in Angoulême, and to Monsieur David Séchard, the entirety of the goods and lands that belong to me on the day of my death, with the deductions of certain payments and bequests that I beg my executor to make.

I entreat Monsieur de Sérisy to accept the task of being my executor.

There shall be paid, (1) to Monsieur l'Abbé Carlos Herrera the sum of three hundred thousand francs; (2) to Monsieur le Baron de Nucingen, the sum of fourteen hundred thousand francs, to be reduced to seven hundred and fifty thousand francs if the money taken from Mademoiselle Esther's is recovered.

I leave and bequeath, as heir of Mademoiselle Esther Gobseck, a sum of seven hundred sixty thousand francs to establish a home specifically for prostitutes who wish to quit their careers of vice and perdition.

I also bequeath the sum necessary to establish a personal income of thirty thousand francs at five per cent. The annual interest on this sum is to be used, twice per year, to free individuals imprisoned for debts, if their indebtedness is no more than two thousand francs. The administrators of the charity should choose from among the most honorable of those detained for debts.

I beg Monsieur de Sérisy to consecrate a sum of forty thousand francs to raising a monument in the East cemetery to Mademoiselle Esther, and I ask to be buried next to her. This tomb should be constructed like those of earlier times: it should be square, and our two statues in white marble should be lying on top, heads supported by cushions, hands joined and raised toward heaven. The tomb shall have no inscription.

I beg Monsieur de Sérisy to have the gold shaving set at my house sent to Monsieur Eugène de Rastignac, as a souvenir of me.

Finally, in the same way, I beg my executor to accept the gift I offer him of my personal library.

LUCIEN CHARDON DE RUBEMPRÉ

This will was put into an envelope that also contained a letter addressed to Monsieur le Comte de Granville, prosecutor-general of the Royal Court at Paris, as follows:

Monsieur le Comte,

I am sending you my last will and testament. When you unfold and read this sheet, I shall be no more. Out of a desire to regain my liberty, I responded in so craven a manner to Monsieur Camusot's underhanded questions that, despite my innocence, I may be implicated in a disgraceful court case. Even supposing that I were to be acquitted, without any censure, life after that would be impossible for me, given the tendencies of society.

I beg you, please send the enclosed letter to the Abbé Carlos Herrera without opening it, and please send the formal retraction, also enclosed, to Monsieur Camusot.

I don't think anyone would dare break the seal of an envelope addressed to you. In that confidence, I bid you adieu, offering

my respects for the last time, and entreating you to believe that
my writing to you is a token of my appreciation for all the kindnesses you have shown to your deceased servant,

LUCIEN DE R.

TO THE ABBÉ CARLOS HERRERA

My dear Abbé, I have never received anything but benefits from
you. My involuntary ingratitude is death to me and, when you
read these lines, I'll no longer be alive; you won't be here this
time to save me.

You gave me the absolute right to cast you aside like the butt
of a cigar if I ever found it would be advantageous to me to do
so; I've cast you off all right, but in the stupidest way. To get
myself out of a difficult spot, and seduced by the cunning techniques of an examining magistrate, I, your spiritual son, the man
you adopted, took the side of those who want to have you murdered, at any cost, by making people believe what I know to be
impossible, that you are the same as some French criminal. That
says it all.

Between a man of your great strength and me, the one you
tried to shape into a greater man than I ever could be, there is
no need for foolish sentimentality at the moment of our final
separation. You wanted to make me powerful and glorious, but
instead you've pushed me into the abyss of suicide—that is the
fact. For a long time now I've felt the great wings of this spiritual
vertigo beating behind me.

You told me once that Cain and Abel had differing posterities. In the great drama of humanity, Cain is the antagonist. You
are descended from Adam in that line, the line in which the
Devil continues to fan the fire of evil whose first spark arose in
Eve. Among the demons of that progeny arise, from time to time,
men of enormous power, men who contain within themselves all
human strengths, men who are like the feverish beasts of the desert, so strong that they require those vast open spaces in which
they live. Men like that are as dangerous in society as lions would
be in Normandy: they need their prey, and they devour vulgar,
ordinary men, and they snatch up the money of fools; and when
they play, their play is so dangerous that they end up killing the
humble dog they've adopted as their companion, their beloved
pet. When God wills it, these mysterious men might be a Moses,
an Attila, a Charlemagne, a Mohammed, or a Napoleon; but
when He allows these giant instruments to rust on the seafloor
of a generation, they merely become a Pugachev, a Robespierre, a

Louvel, or an Abbé Carlos Herrera.[51] Endowed with an immense power over tender souls, they draw the latter to them and grind them down. It is a grand thing, beautiful in its way. It is the poetry of evil. Men like you ought to live in caves, and never come out of them. You've made me live the life of a giant, and I'm damned well through with it now. And so I can pull my head back out of the Gordian knots of your intrigues, and slip it into the hangman's noose that I'm making of my cravat.

To make amends for my blunder, I'm sending the prosecutor-general a retraction of my interrogation. You'll know best how to make use of that.

I've drawn up a will in proper form, and you will be receiving, Monsieur l'Abbé, the sums belonging to your Order that you spent so imprudently on me out of the paternal tenderness you felt for me.

Farewell then, farewell, you splendid monument of evil and corruption, farewell, you who, if only you had taken a different path, could have been greater than Jiménez or Richelieu;[52] you kept all your promises; I have returned to what I was on the banks of the Charente, but I owe to you this long, enchanting dream; but unfortunately, it won't be the river of my youth where I'll drown my youthful sins, but the Seine, and the hole into which I'll sink will be a cell in the Conciergerie.

Don't have any regrets over me. My contempt for you is equal to my admiration.

LUCIEN

DECLARATION

I the undersigned retract the entirety of the interrogation that Monsieur Camusot made me undergo today.

The Abbé Carlos Herrera often called himself my spiritual father, and I was wrong to take that term in a different sense when the magistrate used it that way, no doubt by error.

I know that there is a politically motivated scheme to obscure certain secrets pertaining to the governments of the Tuileries and Spain, and to that end secret agents are trying to have the Abbé Carlos Herrera identified with a convict named Jacques Collin; but the Abbé Carlos Herrera has never told me anything beyond the fact that he was making efforts to find proof as to whether this Jacques Collin was still alive or not.

From the Conciergerie, May 15, 1830

LUCIEN DE RUBEMPRÉ

Difficulties in Committing Suicide in Prison

The suicide fever Lucien had contracted gave him a superb lucidity of mind, along with the activity of the hand that the fever of composition engenders in writers. This fever was so powerful that he wrote all four of these documents in less than half an hour. He made a single packet of them, sealed it with wax wafers, and using the signet ring on his finger, imprinted upon the wax, with a strength born of delirium, his coat of arms; he then very deliberately placed the packet in the middle of the floor. It would certainly have been difficult to behave with any more dignity in this wretched position into which all his infamy had plunged Lucien: it wiped all the disgrace from his memory and repaired the damage he had done to his accomplice—at least inasmuch as the nimble wit of the dandy could undo what the trusting soul of the poet had done.

If Lucien had been returned to one of the solitary confinement cells, he would have found it impossible to carry out his plan, because those cells, essentially boxes hewn out of stone, have nothing in them apart from a bed and a bucket for bodily needs. There is not a nail, not a chair, not so much as a stool. The camp bed is so solidly fixed in place that it cannot be moved without the kind of labor that would immediately attract the attention of the guard, for the iron Judas hole in the door always remains open. And, in fact, when a prisoner gives the staff any cause for uneasiness, they appoint a guard or a gendarme to keep him under perpetual surveillance. In the *pistole* cells, and particularly in the one to which Lucien was transferred, the examining magistrate having decided that a young man of high Parisian social standing deserved it, the movable bed, the table, and the chair could all actually make suicide more feasible, if not exactly easy. Lucien wore a long blue silk cravat; and as soon as he returned from his interrogation he was already thinking of the way Pichegru managed to end his life (whether voluntarily or not).[53] But to hang oneself one needs a point strong enough to hang from, as well as one high enough that the feet will not touch the floor. Now, the window of his cell, looking out over the prison yard, had no latch, and the iron bars on its exterior were separated from Lucien by the thickness of the wall, so there was no supporting point for him there.

But Lucien's faculty of invention soon suggested another method by which he might commit suicide: While the hood attached to the lower half of the window obstructed his view of the prison yard, it also kept guards outside from being able to see inside the cell; there were two wooden boards across the lower half of the window, but the upper part retained its small glass panes, separated each from each by the kind of framing typical of such windows. By climbing up on his table, Lucien could reach the glass portion of his window, and could knock out two of the panes, which allowed him to use the crossbar as his point of support. His plan was to pass his cravat around the crossbar, turn so as to draw it tightly around his neck, having first knotted it securely, and then kick the table away.

Therefore he pushed the table up close to the window without making a sound, removed his jacket and waistcoat, then climbed up on the table and, without hesitation, knocked holes in the pane immediately above the crossbar and the one immediately below it. When he was up on the table, he could see out into the prison yard, a magical spectacle that he was seeing for the first time. The Conciergerie warden, having received orders from Monsieur Camusot to treat Lucien as well as possible, had had him transferred to his new cell via interior corridors and through an underground passageway whose entrance is opposite the Tour d'Argent, thus keeping the elegant young man from the gaze of prisoners who were taking their exercise out in the yard. The reader may decide whether the sight of that exercise space was of the type to touch the soul of a poet.

A Hallucination

The Conciergerie's exercise yard extends to the quay between the Tour d'Argent and the Tour Bonbec; the space between those two is precisely the length of the yard. The gallery named Saint-Louis, which leads from the Galerie Marchande to the appeals court and the Tour Bonbec—where, people say, Saint Louis' study may still be seen—will give the curious an idea of the prison yard's length, for they have the same dimensions. Both the solitary cells and the *pistoles* are located below the Galerie Marchande. So Queen Marie Antoinette, whose dungeon was below the present solitary cells, was led to the revolutionary tribunal, which held its sessions in the current appeals courtroom, via a forbidding staircase hewn out of the thickness of the walls that support the Galerie Marchande, and which is today condemned. The Galerie Saint-Louis, which runs on the first floor along one side of the yard, offers to the viewer a succession of Gothic columns between which the architects of I don't know what period constructed two tiers of cells to house as many *prévenus* as possible, plugging up with plaster, grating, and sealing the capitals, the arches, and the vaults of this magnificent gallery. Below the so-called Saint Louis study in the Tour Bonbec winds a staircase that leads to these cells. This prostitution of one of France's finest structures is simply a hideous sight to behold.

At the height where Lucien was now, his gaze could take in at a slant that gallery and the details of the building that joins the Tour d'Argent and the Tour Bonbec; he could see the pointed roofs of both towers. He stood still, astonished at what he saw, his suicide postponed by the sheer wonder of the sight. Today the phenomena of hallucinations are so well recognized by medical science that these mirages of our senses, these strange powers of our minds, are no longer doubted. When a man is under the pressure of an emotion raised to the pitch of monomania by its intensity, he often finds himself in a state similar to those induced by opium, hashish, and nitrous oxide. Then specters arise, phantoms; then dreams take on bodily form, and things long dead come back to life in their original forms. What was originally only an idea in the mind now becomes a living, walking creature. Science is now hypothesizing that the brain, under the influence of passions that have risen to the heights of paroxysm, injects itself with blood, and this congestion is what produces the terrifying play of dreams coming to life during waking life—so reluctant people are to see thought as a vital, generative force (see *Louis Lambert* in the series *Études philosophiques*[54]). Now Lucien saw the Palais in all its primitive beauty. The colonnade was slender, young, fresh. The dwelling of Saint Louis appeared to him now as it once was, and he wondered at the Babylonian vastness of it, its Oriental fantasies. He accepted this sublime vision as a poetic farewell to the creations of the civilized world. While making his final preparations for death, he asked himself how such a marvel could exist and remain unknown in the heart of Paris. There were two Luciens: Lucien the poet was strolling through the Middle Ages, below the arcades and the turrets of Saint Louis, while the other Lucien was preparing his suicide.

A Drama in the Life of a Woman of Fashion

As Monsieur de Granville was concluding his instructions to his young secretary, the warden of the Conciergerie appeared, and the expression on his face gave the prosecutor-general a presentiment of some disaster.

"Did you see Monsieur Camusot?" he asked.

"No, monsieur," the warden replied. "His clerk Coquart told me to get the abbé Carlos Herrera out of solitary and to release Monsieur de Rubempré, but it's too late. . . ."

"My God! What happened?"

"Here, monsieur," said the warden, "is a packet of letters for you, and this will explain the whole catastrophe. The prisoner's guard heard the sound of windows being broken in the *pistole*, and Monsieur de Rubempré's neighbor in the next cell was shouting for help, for he could hear the young man's dying agony. The guard came back ashen from the sight of the prisoner hanging from the crossbar by his cravat. . . ."

Although the warden was saying all this very quietly, the shriek from Madame de Sérisy proved that, in such circumstances, our senses have an incalculable power. The countess had heard, or had guessed; but before Monsieur de Granville could turn around, and before either Monsieur de Sérisy or Monsieur de Bauvan could do anything to stop her rapid flight, she rushed out the door in a flash and ran to the Galerie Marchande, continuing to run all the way down it to the staircase that descends to the Rue de la Barillerie.

There was a lawyer there removing his robe and handing it in at one of the shops that have encumbered the gallery for so many years, where they sell shoes and where people can rent gowns and caps. The countess asked him the way to the Conciergerie.

"Straight down and turn to the left—the entry is on the Quai de l'Horloge, the first arcade."

"That woman looks insane," said the merchant. "Someone ought to follow her."

But nobody could have followed Léontine; she didn't run—she flew. Perhaps a doctor could explain how these society women, who never need to use their strength, find such inner resources in times of personal crisis. The countess rushed through the arcade and toward the wicket so quickly that the guard didn't even see her enter. She hurled herself up against the grating like a feather thrown there by a powerful wind, shaking the iron bars with such fury that she tore out the one she was gripping. Beating her breast with the two broken pieces until blood spurted forth, she fell to the floor shouting, "Open! Open!" in a voice that froze the blood of the onlookers.

The gatekeeper hurried over.

"Open it! I've been sent here by the prosecutor-general *to prevent a death!*"

While the countess was rushing along the Rue de la Barillerie and the Quai de l'Horloge, Monsieur de Granville and Monsieur de Sérisy were descending into the Conciergerie via the interior of the Palais, both of them inferring where the countess was heading; but despite their diligence, they only arrived just as she collapsed in a faint at the first grill, and as she was being picked up by gendarmes who had hurried down from the guardroom. At the sight of the Conciergerie's warden, the wicket was opened up, and the countess was carried into the office; she then stood up, then fell down onto her knees, her hands joined.

"To see him! . . . Just to see him! . . . Oh please, I won't cause any trouble! . . . But unless you want to see me die right here . . . let me see Lucien, whether he's dead or still alive. . . . Oh, there you are, my friend—choose between my death or . . ." Here she sank to the floor. "That's so good of you," she said. "I will always love you."

"Let's take her away," said Monsieur de Bauvan.

"No—let's go to the cell where Lucien is!" said Monsieur de Granville, reading the intention in Monsieur de Sérisy's eyes.

And he helped the countess up, holding her by one arm while Monsieur de Bauvan took hold of the other.

"Monsieur!" said Monsieur de Sérisy to the warden. "The silence of the grave concerning all this."

"Certainly," replied the warden. "You've made a wise choice. This lady . . ."

"My wife."

"Ah, pardon me, monsieur. Well, she will no doubt faint at the sight of the young man, and when she does she can be taken out to a carriage."

"That's what I was thinking too," said the count. "Have one of your men see my people, in the Cour de Harlay, and have them come to the wicket. My carriage is the only one there."

"We can still save him," the countess was saying as she walked along with a strength and a courage that surprised her guards. "There are ways of reviving people. . . ." And she swept the two magistrates along with her, crying out to the guard ahead: "Hurry, faster, a single second might mean the lives of three people!"

When the cell door was opened and the countess saw Lucien hanging, as if his garments had been hung on a coat hook, she leaped toward him, embracing and holding on to him tightly; but then she collapsed face down on the cell floor, uttering sharp, muffled cries, punctuated by what sounded like a dying gasp. Five minutes later, she was in the count's carriage being transported back to her home, lying flat on a cushion, her husband on his knees beside her. Comte de Bauvan had gone off in search of a doctor to perform first aid on the countess.

335 WHERE EVIL PATHWAYS LEAD

How It All Ended

The Conciergerie warden examined the grill outside the wicket, saying to his clerk: "We spared no expense! These iron bars were forged, they were tested, we paid a lot for them, and still there was some sort of flaw in this particular bar!"

The prosecutor-general went back to his office, where he had to give new instructions to his secretary.

Fortunately, Massol had not yet returned.

A few minutes after Monsieur de Granville had hurried off to the home of Monsieur de Sérisy, Massol found his ally Chargeboeuf in the prosecutor-general's office.

"My friend," the young secretary said to him, "if I may ask a kindness of you, please have what I'm about to dictate placed in your *Gazette* tomorrow, in the column where you put the judicial items. You should title it yourself."

"Let's have it!"

And he dictated as follows:

> It is understood that Mademoiselle Esther voluntarily committed suicide.
>
> The alibi given by Monsieur Lucien de Rubempré, along with his innocence, make his arrest all the more deplorable, especially since the young man died suddenly just as the examining magistrate was preparing the order for his release.

The young secretary said to Massol, "I hardly need to add, my friend, that you should exercise the greatest possible discretion with this little service we're asking of you."

"Since it's you who are doing me the honor of putting your confidence in me, I'll take the liberty," replied Massol, "of adding a comment. This note is going to give rise to some pretty damaging commentaries on the legal system."

"The system is strong enough to withstand them," the young secretary replied, with all the pride of a future magistrate under the protection of Monsieur de Granville.

"But allow me, my friend—a couple of sentences added can avoid all that."

He wrote as follows:

> The procedures of the legal system have no connection to a
> sad event like this. An autopsy was carried out at once, and it
> demonstrated that death was caused by the rupture of an aneu-
> rism in its last stages. If Monsieur de Rubempré had been
> upset by his arrest, death would have come even sooner. But
> we can confidently affirm that, far from being overwhelmed by
> his arrest, the poor young man laughed it off with those who
> brought him from Fontainebleau to Paris, confident that his
> innocence would be established as soon as he had the chance to
> speak to the examining magistrate.

"That fixes everything, don't you think?" asked the lawyer-journalist.

"You're absolutely right, my dear *maître*."

"The prosecutor-general will thank you tomorrow," Massol added with a wink.

So we see how the newspapers translate even life's greatest events into more or less true little tidbits in a column. And this is the way with much greater, much more important events than this one.

But meanwhile, for most of my readers, including the most astute among them, this particular study may seem not quite concluded with the deaths of Esther and Lucien; it may be that Jacques Collin, Asia, Europe, and Paccard, despite their infamous behavior, will be deemed interesting enough that one might want to know what became of them. This final act of our drama will in any case serve to complete our portrayal of contemporary life—which is the aim of the study—and will help to clarify the various interests that Lucien's life had brought together in so singular a manner, mingling ignoble convicts from the penal colonies together with people at the highest levels of society.

IV 𓆛

VAUTRIN'S LAST INCARNATION

The Two Robes

"What's wrong, Madeleine?" asked Madame Camusot, seeing her maid come in the room wearing the kind of expression that servants learn to affect at critical moments.

"Madame," Madeleine replied, "Monsieur is just back from the Palais, but he looks so upset, and he seems to be in such a state, that madame might want to go to his study and talk to him."

"Is something wrong?" asked Madame Camusot.

"No, madame; but we've never seen monsieur looking like this; it's as if he's coming down with something; he's all yellowish, and he seems to be falling to pieces."

Without waiting for her to finish her sentence, Madame Camusot rushed out of the room and ran to her husband. She found the examining magistrate sitting in an easy chair, his legs stretched out in front of him, his hands dangling, his face ashen, and a dazed look in his eyes, exactly as if he had just fainted.

"What's the matter, dear?" asked the young wife, frightened.

"Ah, poor Amélie, the most terrible thing has just happened—I'm still shaking from it. Imagine that the prosecutor-general . . . no, that Madame de Sérisy . . . that . . . Oh, I don't know where to begin."

"Start at the end!" said Madame Camusot.

"All right. Well, it was just when I was in the council chamber of the First Civil Court and Monsieur Popinot was signing the last signature necessary on the decision to drop charges and release Lucien de Rubempré. So, at last, it was all settled! The clerk went off with the record book, and I was just about to be finished with this whole affair—and in comes the president of the tribunal, and he looks at the paper, and he says:

"'You're about to release a dead man,' and he says it coldly, like he's mocking me. 'The young man has gone, as Monsieur de Bonald would say,[1] to his natural judge. He's just succumbed to an attack of apoplexy.'

"I breathed a sigh of relief, believing his death was accidental.

"'If I understand you correctly, *mon président*,'" Popinot said, "'it sounds like it was an attack of Pichegru apoplexy. . . .'"[2]

"'Messieurs,'" said the president gravely, "'you must understand that as far as the outside world is concerned, young Lucien de Rubempré died from a ruptured aneurism.'"

"At that, we all stared at each other.

"'There are important people involved in this deplorable affair,'" said the president. "'May God grant, for your sake, Monsieur Camusot, even though you were only doing your duty—may God grant that Madame de Sérisy recovers from her madness, which is the result of the blow she's received! I just met our prosecutor-general, who's in a state of such despair that it sickened me. Oh, you've really blundered, my dear Camusot!'" he added, whispering the last part in my ear.

"No, dear, listen, I could hardly find my way out of that room. My legs were trembling so that I didn't dare try to walk out on the street, so I went to rest in my office. Coquart was there arranging the day's paperwork on this horrible interrogation, and he told me about a beautiful lady who had come and made war on the Conciergerie, that she wanted to save the life of Lucien, with whom she was in love, and that she'd fainted dead away when she saw him hanging by his cravat from the window's crossbar in the *pistole*. The thought that the way I interrogated that unfortunate young man—who, just between us, was completely guilty—that it caused his suicide, that thought has haunted me ever since I left the Palais, and the thought still makes me feel like I'm about to faint . . .'"

"Oh, come now, you think you're a murderer because some prisoner hangs himself in his cell just when you're about to release him?" cried Madame Camusot. "An examining magistrate in a situation like that is just like a general who's had his horse shot out from under him—that's all!"

"Analogies like that, my dear, are fine for joking around, but this is no time for joking. *The dead seizes the living* in a case like this.[3] Lucien takes all our hopes into his coffin with him."

"Really?" asked Madame Camusot, in a tone of deep irony.

"Oh yes. My career is over. I'll never be anything more than a simple magistrate on the Seine tribunal. Monsieur de Granville, even before things took this fatal turn, was already strongly displeased with the way I handled the interrogation; I heard him saying to our president something that made it clear that as long as he, Monsieur de Granville, is prosecutor-general, I will never see a promotion!"

Promotion! There it was, the terrible word, and with it, the concept that turns a magistrate into a mere bureaucrat.

In earlier days, being a magistrate was all a magistrate needed to be. The three or four mortarboard hats of the chamber presidents were the ultimate that the ambitious could expect in any *parlement*. A de Brosses or a Molé, whether at Dijon or Paris, would have contented himself with being named councillor.[4] Such an office was worth a fortune, but it required a fortune to maintain it properly. In Paris, apart from the *parlement,* the men of the robe had only three superior options to which they could aspire: becoming controller-general, keeper of the seals, or chancellor. Also apart from *parlement* but on a lower level, becoming president of a lower court would be honor enough for a man to make him spend the rest of his life happily in that position. Compare the position of a councillor at the Royal Court of Paris in 1829, who has only his salary to live on, with that of a *parlement* councillor of 1729, and see how great is the difference! In our day, we have made money into the only universal guarantor of social position, and magistrates today do not need to be men of fortune, as was the case in the past; and therefore they become *députés,* or peers of France, piling up one magistrature upon another, becoming both judges and legislators, in an attempt to gain status by borrowing it from positions other than the very one in which they ought to seek to excel.

In short, magistrates seek distinction through promotion, the way one does in the military or the civil service.

And this fact, though it does not impair the independence of the magistrate, is so well known and has become so natural that its effects are everywhere to be seen, and as a result the magistracy loses much of its prestige in the eyes of the public. The salaries paid by the State turn the priest as well as the magistrate into State employees. Climbing from one grade to another nurtures ambition; ambition nurtures a readiness to defer to power; and added to that our modern mania for equality places the honorable man and the magistrate on the same social level. And thus the two pillars of all social order, Religion and Justice, are weakened in the nineteenth century, this era in which we pretend to be progressing in all things.

"But why won't you ever be promoted?" asked Amélie Camusot.

She looked at her husband mockingly, feeling the need to revive some energy in this man upon whom her own ambition depended, and upon whom she played as one does upon a musical instrument.

"Why this deep despair?" she continued, making a gesture that suggested how unimportant she found the death of this prisoner to be. "See, this suicide is going to be good news for Lucien's two enemies, Madame d'Espard and her cousin, the Comtesse Châtelet. Madame d'Espard is on excellent terms with the keeper of the seals, and through her you could get an audience with His Highness, and you could tell him the story of this whole affair. Now, if the minister of justice is on your side, what do you have to fear from your *président* and the prosecutor-general?"

"But Monsieur and Madame de Sérisy!" cried the poor magistrate. "Madame de Sérisy, I'm telling you, has lost her mind, and it's all because of me, they're saying!"

"Well, if she's crazy, she can't be much of a judge of things, can she?" exclaimed Madame Camusot with a laugh. "She can't hurt you! Come on, tell me everything about what happened today—give me all the details."

"My God," replied Camusot, "just when I'd finished taking that unfortunate young man's confession, in which he declared that the so-called Spanish priest was in fact Jacques Collin, the Duchesse de Maufrigneuse and Madame de Sérisy sent me, by a valet of hers, a little note begging me not to interrogate him. But it was all already done. . . ."

"But so what—so you lost your head!" said Amélie. "You're sure of your clerk, so you could have made Lucien come back, reassure him in a nice, skillful manner, and produce a corrected interrogation!"

"Oh, you're just like Madame de Sérisy, making a mockery of justice!" said Camusot, who could not endure any levity regarding his profession. "Madame de Sérisy took my interrogation reports and threw them in the fire!"

"Bravo! Now there's a woman!" cried Madame Camusot.

"Madame de Sérisy told me that she'd rather blow up the whole Palais de Justice than allow a young man who had enjoyed the good graces of the Duchesse de Maufrigneuse and her set be seen on the benches of a courtroom next to a convict!"

"But, Camusot," said Amélie, unable to suppress a smile of superiority, "your position is simply superb—"

"Oh, yes, very superb!"

"You've done your duty—"

"But unfortunately so, and despite the Jesuitical advice I had been given in the morning by Monsieur de Granville, who ran into me on the Quai Malaquais . . ."

"This morning?"

"This morning!"

"At what time?"

"Nine o'clock."

"Oh, Camusot!" cried Amélie, wringing her hands. "How many times must I remind you to always be on your guard. . . . My God, this isn't a man, it's a cartload of rocks I have to drag along! . . . Oh, Camusot, your prosecutor-general was waiting for you there, on purpose to give you some suggestions."

"Well, yes . . ."

"And you didn't understand! If you stay deaf like this, you'll never be anything but an examining magistrate, and one who never examines anything, at that! Have the wit to listen to people!" she said, hushing her husband who was trying to respond. "Do you think the whole business is over now?"

Camusot stared at his wife, his face taking on the expression a peasant has when confronted with a fast-talking salesman.

Amélie Makes Plans

"If the Duchesse de Maufrigneuse and the Comtesse de Sérisy are compromised, you'll need to ensure that they both become your patronesses," Amélie continued. "Do you see? Madame d'Espard will get you an audience with the keeper of the seals, you'll tell him the whole story, and he'll amuse the king with it, because every monarch loves to know what's going on beneath the surface of things, and understand the real motives behind events that the general public can only stare at, open mouthed. And from that point on, there's nothing to fear from the prosecutor-general, nor from Monsieur de Sérisy. . . ."

"What a treasure I have in a wife like you!" exclaimed the magistrate, feeling his courage returning. "After all, I did manage to beat Jacques Collin out of the weeds, and I'm going to have him up at the assize court, and I'm going to unmask all his crimes. A trial like that is a real feather in the cap of an examining magistrate, and a boost to his career—"

"Camusot," Amélie continued, observing with pleasure her husband's rebound from the moral and physical prostration to which the suicide of Lucien de Rubempré had led him, "the président of the tribunal told you that you had blundered, and now you're doing it again, but in the opposite direction! You've wandered off the path again, my friend!"

The examining magistrate stood still, staring at his wife stupidly.

"The king and the keeper of the seals will be delighted to know all the secrets of this affair, but they will not be delighted to see lawyers of the liberal persuasion dragging up to the bar of popular opinion, and the assize court, people of the stature of the Sérisys, the Maufrigneuses, and the Grandlieus, all the people involved directly or indirectly with this case!"

"Yes—they're all in it! I've got them!" Camusot exclaimed.

The magistrate got up and paced around his study, like Sganarelle on the stage when he's trying to get out of some difficult situation.[5]

"Listen, Amélie!" he said, stopping and standing directly in front of his wife. "I just remembered a detail, something that seemed insignificant but now, in the situation I'm in, it's hugely important. Picture it if you can, my dear one, this Jacques Collin, a colossus of intrigue, dissimulation, of deviousness, a man of such depths . . . He's like—what?— like the Cromwell of the prisons! I've never encountered a rogue like this one, and he very nearly bested me! . . . But in one of these criminal interrogations, if you take hold of a loose thread sometimes you follow it and find a whole ball of yarn, and that takes you into a labyrinth where consciences become shadowy, facts become dark and obscure. When Jacques Collin watched me paging through the documents seized from the home of Lucien de Rubempré, my little crook watched like a man who was waiting to see if some particular document were there or not, and I saw him make just the slightest expression of total satisfaction. It was the gaze of a thief estimating the value of some treasure, the expression of a prisoner saying to himself, 'I've still got my secret weapon!' And from that expression I learned a lot. You women, you're the only ones besides us and our prisoners who can pierce the secret of a glance, detect in it whole scenes of deception as complicated as a security lock. Whole volumes full of suspicion pass through the mind in a second! It's terrifying, really, the way life or death can depend on the blink of an eye. I thought, 'So our little con man has other letters in his possession!' But I was preoccupied with a thousand other details just then. I ignored it at the moment, because I thought I was going to get the two prisoners to confront each other, and we could return to this detail from the interrogation later. But now let's assume as a fact that Jacques Collin has in his possession, like these miserable wretches so often do, certain letters that are the very most compromising from the correspondence of this young man who was adored like—"

"And you trembled, Camusot! You! You're the one who's going to become president of the Royal Court, and a lot sooner than I ever thought!" cried Madame Camusot, her expression radiant. "Let's think it through! You need to conduct yourself so as to keep everybody happy, because now this whole affair has become so serious that if we aren't careful someone will *steal* it out from under us! . . . Now, they took from Popinot, didn't they, and entrusted them to you, the records and reports of the case of Madame d'Espard, when she tried to have Monsieur d'Espard declared incompetent?" she said, in response to his questioning gesture. "Well, if the prosecutor-general takes such a lively interest in the honor of Monsieur and Madame de Sérisy, couldn't he reopen this case in the Royal Court and get some councillor to start up the investigation again?"

"Oh, my love, where did you study criminal law?" cried Camusot. "You know everything; you're my *maître . . .*"

"Well, do you think that tomorrow morning Monsieur de Granville won't be terrified at the prospect of some liberal lawyer that this Jacques Collin could hire—because they'll swarm around him offering to pay *him* for the chance to defend him! . . . These women understand perfectly what kind of danger they're in, and better than you think they do—they'll inform the prosecutor-general, who can already picture these grand families being dragged into far too great a proximity to the courtroom, all because of the marriage between this convict and Lucien de Rubempré, the fiancé of Mademoiselle de Grandlieu, this Lucien, the lover of Mademoiselle Esther, previously lover of the Duchesse de Maufrigneuse, and the sweetheart of Madame de Sérisy. So you need to maneuver so as to be reconciled with the prosecutor-general and to gain the gratitude of Monsieur de Sérisy, as well as that of the Marquise d'Espard and the Comtesse Châtelet, and to get under the protective wing of Madame de Maufrigneuse as well as that of the Grandlieu family—all of which will result in your president showering compliments upon you. I'll see to Mesdames d'Espard, de Maufrigneuse, and de Grandlieu. Now tomorrow, you go to the home of your prosecutor-general. It's true, isn't it, that Monsieur de Granville doesn't live with his wife? Hasn't he had a mistress for the last twelve years, a woman named Mademoiselle de Bellefeuille, who has borne children for him out of their adultery? Well, our magistrate is no saint, but a man like any other—he can be seduced, he has his vulnerable spots—so all we need do is discover them and flatter him, ask his advice, make him see how dangerous the affair is. In short, be sure that others are compromised too, and you'll be—"

"No, no, I ought to fall down and kiss your feet," interrupted Camusot, taking hold of his wife by the waist and pressing her to his heart. "Amélie! You've saved me!"

"I'm the one who got you out of Alençon and into Mantes, and out of Mantes and into the tribunal of the Seine," Amélie replied. "So rest easy! . . . I want to be called Madame Présidente five years from now, but, my little one, please remember to think and think carefully before you make any resolution. The job of a magistrate is not like that of a fireman—your papers aren't on fire, you have the time to reflect—and that means that in a position like yours, a stupid move is never excusable. . . ."

After a long pause, the magistrate continued: "My most powerful advantage lies in the identity of the phony Spanish priest and Jacques Collin. Once that identity is firmly established, even if the court takes things out of my hands, that identity will always be a fact that no magistrate, judge, or lawyer can ignore. It will be like what children do when they tie a can to a cat's tail—no matter what happens, Jacques Collin's irons will always be clanking."

"Bravo!" said Amélie.

"And the prosecutor-general will much prefer coming to an understanding with me, the only one who can make this sword of Damocles hanging over the heart of the Faubourg Saint-Germain disappear, than with anybody else! But this magnificent result is going to require a lot of difficult work. The prosecutor-general and I, just now in his office, agreed to accept Jacques Collin's story, that he's really a canon of the Toledo chapter named Carlos Herrera. We agreed to recognize his diplomatic status, and to let the Spanish ambassador claim him. This was part of the plan in which I was to make out a report that would lead to the release of Lucien de Rubempré, and I had started making up new interrogation reports for my prisoners, turning them both white as snow. And tomorrow Messieurs de Rastignac, Bianchon, and I don't know who else were to come and look at the so-called canon of the royal chapter of Toledo and fail to recognize Jacques Collin in him, even though he had been arrested in their presence some ten years back, in a bourgeois *pension* where he went by the name of Vautrin."

A moment of silence followed, while Madame Camusot reflected.

"Are you sure your prisoner is Jacques Collin?"

"I am," said the magistrate, "and so is the prosecutor-peneral."

"Well, keep your kitty claws nicely hidden, but go to the Palais de Justice and see if you can raise a ruckus over it. If your man is still in solitary, go at once to the warden of the Conciergerie and have him put somewhere public where he'll be recognized. Instead of imitating children, imitate the way the ministers of police operate in absolutist countries— they invent conspiracies against the sovereign in order to give themselves the credit for discovering them and making themselves indispensable. Put three families in danger in order to have the glory of rescuing them."

"Oh—that reminds me! This is a piece of good luck. Coquart delivered the order to transfer Jacques Collin from solitary to the *pistoles;* he took it to Monsieur Gault, the Conciergerie warden. Now Bibi-Lupin, who's an enemy of Jacques Collin, had three criminals transferred from La Force to the Conciergerie, three men who knew him. So, if he goes down into the prison yard tomorrow, terrible scenes are expected...."

"Why?"

"Jacques Collin, my dear, acted as treasurer for the convicts, and he was in charge of considerable sums. They say he spent it all on ensuring luxury for Lucien, and they're going to be demanding an accounting. Bibi-Lupin tells me that they're bound to try to kill him, and the guards will have to intervene, and at that point the secret will be out. Jacques Collin's life will be at stake. If I get to the Palais early tomorrow, I'll be able to write up a report on the identification."

"Oh, if only they'd put an end to him and take him off your hands! Don't go to Monsieur de Granville's house after all—wait for him in his office, armed with this powerful new weapon! This is like a cannon trained on the three most important families of the Court and the peerage. Be bold, and propose to Monsieur de Granville that he take Jacques Collin to La Force, where the convicts know how to handle informers. I'll go to the Duchesse de Maufrigneuse, and she'll take me to the Grandlieus. I may also see Monsieur de Sérisy. Count on me to sound the alarm in every quarter. Send me a quick note to assure me that there's been a formal, judicial recognition that the Spanish priest is actually Jacques Collin. Arrange things so you can leave the Palais at two o'clock, and I'll have arranged an audience for you with the keeper of the seals—it might be at the home of the Marquise d'Espard."

Camusot stood still in a pose of sheer admiration for her, which made the clever Amélie smile.

"Come along, and let's have something to eat, and let's be cheerful," she said in conclusion. "Just think of it! We've only been in Paris two years, and by the end of the year you're likely to be named councillor.... And from there, my little one, to the presidency of a court is only the span of a little service rendered in some political matter."

This secret deliberation shows the extent to which the actions and even the most trivial words of Jacques Collin, the last of our characters in this study, involved the honor of those families into whose bosoms he had insinuated his deceased protégé.

Concerning Magnetism

Lucien's death and the Comtesse de Sérisy's invasion of the Conciergerie had thrown such a wrench into the works of the great machine that the warden had forgotten to have the so-called Spanish priest transferred out of solitary confinement.

Although the judicial annals offer us more than one example of it, the death of a prisoner in the course of an investigation is a rare enough occurrence that the guards, clerks, and warden were all shaken out of the tranquility in which they normally operate. But for them the truly startling event was not the way that handsome young man had so rapidly transformed himself into a corpse, but rather the breaking of an iron bar from the wicket's grillwork, at the delicate hands of a fashionable lady. Thus the warden, clerks, and guards all stood grouped together in front of the wicket, after the prosecutor-general and Comte Octave de Bauvan had departed in the carriage of the Comte de Sérisy along with his unconscious wife; they were joined there by Monsieur Lebrun, the prison doctor, who had been called to certify the death of Lucien along with the "death doctor" of the district in which the unfortunate young man had lived.

In Paris the term "death doctor" is used for the individual, in each district, charged with verifying the death and ascertaining its cause.

With that quick judgment that was his hallmark, Monsieur de Granville decided it was appropriate, for the honor of the compromised families, that Lucien's death certificate should be written up at the district that included the Quai Malaquais, where the deceased had lived, and to have him conveyed from his home to the church of Saint-Germain-des-Prés, where the funeral service would be held. Monsieur de Chargeboeuf, secretary to Monsieur de Granville, was given orders to that effect. Lucien's transferal was to be handled during the night. The young secretary had been charged with arranging everything with the town hall, the parish, and the funeral directors. Thus, in the eyes of the world Lucien had died a free man and in his own home; the procession would therefore leave from his home, and his friends would gather there for the ceremony.

Thus, at the moment when Camusot, his mind at peace, was sitting down to dinner with his ambitious better half, the warden of the Conciergerie and Monsieur Lebrun, the prison doctor, were standing outside the wicket, deploring the fragility of the iron bars and the strength of women in love.

"People don't realize," the doctor said to Monsieur Gault as he was leaving, "the sheer strength a person can exert when the passions are maximally excited! Physics and math don't have the concepts or the calculus to measure that strength. I can tell you about an experience I had yesterday that made me shudder, and that reveals the same kind of superhuman strength that little lady demonstrated here."

"Do tell me about it," said Monsieur Gault, "because I have a weakness for stories about magnetism—I don't believe in it, but it fascinates me."

"A doctor involved in magnetism—because there really are such people among us who do believe in it—" Doctor Lebrun continued, "proposed that I try out on myself an experiment that he described and that I doubted. Curious to see for myself one of those strange nervous paroxysms by which they prove the existence of magnetism, I agreed. Here are the facts. I'd certainly like to hear what our Academy of Medicine would say if they were to submit their members, one after the other, to this experiment that leaves no room for doubt. My old friend . . .

". . . This doctor," said Doctor Lebrun, opening up a parenthesis, "is an old man who was persecuted for his opinions by the faculty, since the time of Mesmer;[6] he's seventy, seventy-two years old, and his name is Bouvard.[7] He's a kind of patriarch of animal magnetism. I'm like a son to the old man, and I owe everything to him. So this elderly and respected Bouvard proposed demonstrating to me that the nervous power that the magnetizer sets in motion is not actually infinite, because man must submit to predetermined laws of nature, but that it springs from powers in nature whose absolute principles are mysterious to us still.

"'Thus,' he said to me, 'if you let your wrist be held by a somnambulist who, in the waking state, could not exert any unusual strength, you'll find that when he is in the state we clumsily name somnambulistic, his fingers are capable of exerting the kind of strength we find in a locksmith's lock-cutting machine!'

"Well, monsieur, when I allowed my wrist to be grasped by a woman who was, I won't say *asleep,* because Bouvard dislikes that term, but rather *isolated,* and when the old man commanded the woman to squeeze my wrist with all her strength, I had to beg him to stop her, because the blood was about to spurt out of my fingertips. Look here—look at the bracelet I've been sporting on this wrist for the last three months!"

"The devil!" said Monsieur Gault, examining the circular ecchymosis on his wrist, similar to the marking that a burn might have produced.

"My dear Gault," the doctor continued, "if they had clamped my wrist in an iron band, and a locksmith had turned a screw to tighten it on me, I would not have felt the pain of that metal collar as much as I felt the pain this woman's fingers imposed on me. Her grip was like inflexible steel, and I'm convinced she could have broken the bones in my wrist and torn my hand right off my wrist. At first I could barely feel the pressure, but it built up, adding ever new levels of strength on top of strength, until a tourniquet could not have been applied with any more precision than that woman's hand, which had turned into an instrument of torture. It seemed to me to prove the point that when ruled by passion—which is to say, the concentration of the will upon a single point—an incalculable quantity of animal strength can be deployed, in the same way that different types of electrical force can be, and the individual can bring into play his or her entire vital powers for either attack or repulsion, and focus them in this or that particular organ. . . . This little lady had, under the pressure of her own despair, directed all her vital forces into her fingers."

"But it takes a hell of a lot of vital force to rip through a bar of wrought iron," said the chief guard, shaking his head.

"Maybe there was a flaw in the bar!" suggested Monsieur Gault.

"If you ask me," said the doctor, "I don't dare assign any limits to the power of the nervous forces. You can observe it in those cases we hear about in which mothers, to save their children, can hypnotize lions, or walk through fire or along parapets where a cat would fear to tread, or endure the tortures of certain childbirths. And this explains why prisoners and convicts will struggle so mightily to regain their liberty. . . . We still don't understand how these vital forces work, but they share the power of nature itself, and we draw them up from unknown wellsprings!"

A guard hurried up to the warden, who was escorting Doctor Lebrun to the outer gate of the Conciergerie, and whispered to him: "Monsieur, the man in solitary number two claims to be ill and is asking for the doctor—he claims he's dying," the guard added.

"Really?" said the warden.

"He sounds like he's dying!" replied the guard.

"It's five o'clock," said the doctor, "and I haven't eaten. . . . But all right, I'm ready, let's go to him."

The Man in Solitary

"Solitary number two is, in fact, the Spanish priest suspected to be Jacques Collin," Monsieur Gault said to the doctor, "and he's implicated in the case of that poor young man. . . ."

"I already saw him this morning," said the doctor. "Monsieur Camusot wanted me to testify to the health of this con man, which, just between you and me, is excellent—the man could make a living portraying Hercules."

"He might want to kill himself too," said Monsieur Gault. "Let's take a walk to solitary, both of us, because I ought to be there, if only to have him transferred to a *pistole*. Monsieur Camusot ordered our extraordinary mystery man released from solitary. . . ."

Jacques Collin, the man nicknamed Deathcheater in the prisons, and the man who, from now on, shall be referred to only under that name, had been, ever since Camusot had sent him back to his cell in solitary, in the grip of an anxiety the likes of which he had never known in that life of his, though it was a life marked by so many crimes, by three prison escapes, and by two courtroom convictions. This man, who seems to sum up in himself all the life, the strength, the cunning, and the passions of the prisons, who may in fact be their very highest expression: is there not something beautiful, perhaps monstrously beautiful, in that devoted, canine-like attachment he formed for the young man he made into his friend? He was vile, and worthy of condemnation from every side, but that absolute devotion to his idol made him so genuinely interesting that our current tale, though already quite lengthy, would seem incomplete and abbreviated if the denouement of his life were not appended to that of Lucien de Rubempré. The little spaniel is dead, but the reader must be asking, what about the lion—is he still alive?

In real life, in society, every fact is so intimately entangled with other facts that we can hardly examine one without taking into account the others. The water in the river becomes a kind of moving, liquid platform; there is no wave, no matter how rebellious and no matter how high its jet might rise, that will not sink back into the great general mass of the water, and that mass is even stronger, because of the rapidity of its flow, than all the rebellions of the surges that end up moving along with it. Just as you can observe that onward flow despite the confused complications that shoot up from its surface, you might wish to contemplate the pressure exerted upon that whirlpool named Vautrin by the larger social powers, watch to see how long it takes before that rebellious wave sinks back into the abyss, and see what will be the ultimate fate of this truly diabolical man, who is, nevertheless, attached to the mass of humanity by love. That divine principle is so hard to kill off, even in the most gangrenous of hearts!

The ignoble convict embodied the poem so lovingly caressed by so many poets—by Moore, by Lord Byron, by Maturin, by Canalis[8]—in which a demon draws an angel down into Hell in order to refresh his soul with the dews of Heaven. This Jacques Collin, as will be evident if the reader has truly penetrated into that great heart of bronze, had renounced his very self for the past seven years. All his powerful faculties were absorbed by Lucien, and everything he did he did for Lucien; he rejoiced only in Lucien's progress, in his loves, in his ambition. Lucien was his soul made visible.

Deathcheater dined at the home of the Grandlieus, slipped into the boudoirs of great ladies, loved Esther—all by proxy. In short, he saw in Lucien a Jacques Collin who was beautiful, young, noble, and on his way to an ambassador's post.

Deathcheater had embodied the German superstition concerning the doppelgänger or double by the phenomenon of spiritual paternity, a phenomenon that women will recognize, especially those who have lived the lives of their beloved men, noble or wretched, happy or miserable, obscure or glorious—women who have felt, even at a great distance, a pain in their own leg if he had been injured there, who have felt it when he was fighting a duel, and who—to say it all in a single phrase—did not need to be told of his infidelity in order to know of it.

Conducted back into his cell, Jacques Collin said to himself: "They're interrogating the little one!"

And he shuddered, this man who killed as readily as a workingman drinks.

"Was he able to see his mistresses?" he asked himself. "Was my aunt able to find those damnable females? Those duchesses, those countesses—did they move in time, did they prevent his interrogation? . . . Did Lucien receive my instructions? And if it's his fate to be interrogated, how will he hold up? The poor little one—I'm the one who brought him to this! It's that crook Paccard and that snoop Europe who caused all this ruckus, by *swiping* that seven hundred and fifty thousand Nucingen had given to Esther. Those two idiots made us stumble just when we were on the last step, but they'll pay for their little trick! Just one more day and Lucien would have been rich! He would have married his Clotilde de Grandlieu. I wouldn't have Esther on my hands anymore. Lucien loved that whore too much, and he never really loved his scrawny lifeline, that Clotilde . . .[9] Oh, the little one would have been all mine! And to think that our fate depends on a single expression, a single blush from Lucien in front of that Camusot, who notices everything and has the typical cunning of an examining magistrate! Because when he was showing me those letters, we exchanged a look that both of us understood, and he realized that I could blackmail Lucien's mistresses! . . ."[10]

This monologue went on for three hours. The anguish was so powerful that it overwhelmed that constitution of iron and vitriol. Jacques Collin was so frantic that he felt as if his head was on fire, and he had a thirst so strong that he drained one of the two buckets that, along with a wooden plank bed, constitute the entire furnishings of a cell in solitary.

"If he loses his head, what will become of him? Because the dear boy doesn't have the inner strength of a Théodore . . ." he thought as he lay on the wooden bed in his cell.

Just a word or two about this Théodore who drifted into Jacques Collin's mind at this moment of supreme crisis. Théodore Calvi, a young Corsican, had been given a life sentence at the age of eighteen for eleven murders thanks to some influence that had cost a great deal, and he had been Jacques Collin's chainmate from 1819 to 1820. Jacques Collin's last escape had been one of his finest strokes of genius: he got out disguised as a gendarme escorting Théodore Calvi to the supervising guard. This superb escape had taken place in the penal colony of Rochefort, where convicts die routinely and where it was hoped these two dangerous characters would end their days. They escaped together, and chance events caused them to separate. Théodore was caught, and returned to the prison. After reaching Spain and transforming himself into Carlos Herrera, Jacques Collin returned to Rochefort to look for his Corsican, and this is when he met Lucien on the banks of the Charente. The hero of the banditti underworld, from whom Deathcheater had learned his Italian, was naturally sacrificed in favor of this new idol.

Life with Lucien, a boy who'd never been convicted of any crime and whose only self-reproaches were over mere peccadilloes, arose beautiful and magnificent in his imagination like sunrise on a summer's day, whereas with Théodore, Jacques Collin could foresee no possible end except the gallows, after an obligatory series of crimes.

The thought of some catastrophe caused by Lucien's weakness—for solitary confinement might very well lead him to lose his head—took on enormous proportions in the mind of Jacques Collin; and simply imagining that catastrophe, the wretch felt his eyes moistening with tears, a phenomenon that he had only experienced once since his childhood.

"I must have a raging fever," he thought, "so maybe if I can get a doctor to come I can offer him a big enough bribe to let me get in contact with Lucien."

Just then, the guard brought the prisoner his meal.

"It's no use, my boy—I can't possibly eat. Tell monsieur the warden to send me a doctor; I'm so sick I think my last hours have come."

And hearing the guttural wheezes that accompanied the convict's request, the guard nodded and left. Jacques Collin seized on this sudden hope with all his might; but when he saw the doctor come in accompanied by the warden, he assumed his plan was doomed, and he coolly awaited the outcome of the visit, holding out his wrist for the doctor to take his pulse.

"This man has a fever," the doctor said to Monsieur Gault, "but it's the kind of fever we often see with prisoners." Then, whispering to the false

Spaniard, "I've always thought a fever like this is proof of some criminality or other."

At that point the warden, to whom the prosecutor-general had given the letter from Lucien to Jacques Collin with instructions to deliver it, left the doctor and the prisoner with a guard and went back to get the letter.

"Monsieur," Jacques Collin said to the doctor, not knowing why the warden had left, and the guard being outside the door, "I would give thirty thousand francs to be able to send five lines to Lucien de Rubempré."

"I don't want to steal your money," said Doctor Lebrun. "No one can communicate with him any longer."

"No one?" asked Jacques Collin, stupefied. "Why?"

"He's hanged himself."

No tiger in the jungles of India, finding her babies stolen from her, ever uttered a cry as terrifying as that of Jacques Collin, who reared up on his feet like a tiger on her rear paws, shooting the doctor a look that burned like a bolt of lightning; then he collapsed on his plank bed, saying, "Oh! My son!"

"Poor man!" cried the doctor, moved at the sight of this terrible outburst of nature.

And that outburst was followed by complete and utter weakness, accompanied by the constant murmur of "Oh! My son!"

"Is this one going to drop dead on us too?" asked the guard.

"No, it isn't possible!" Jacques Collin continued, sitting up and staring at the two, who were witnessing the scene with an eye that now had neither flame nor even warmth. "You've made a mistake! It's not him! You didn't look properly. People can't hang themselves in solitary! Look around—how could I possibly hang myself here? All Paris is going to answer to me for that life! God owes it to me!"

The guard and the doctor were now, in their turn, stupefied, two men whom events had long ceased surprising. Monsieur Gault came back in, holding Lucien's letter. Seeing the warden's expression, Jacques Collin, crushed by the sheer violence of his explosion of grief, seemed to have calmed.

"Here's a letter the prosecutor-general gave me to deliver you, permitting you to have it unopened," said Monsieur Gault.

"It's from Lucien. . . ." said Jacques Collin.

"Yes, monsieur."

"The young man, monsieur, is . . ."

"Dead," the warden said. "Even though the doctor was on the premises, he unfortunately arrived too late.... The young man is dead ... in one of the *pistole* cells."

"May I see him for myself?" Jacques Collin asked timidly. "Would you let a father go weep over his son?"

"You may, if you like, have his cell, because my orders are to have you transferred to the *pistoles*. Your time in solitary is over, Monsieur."

The prisoner's eyes, denuded now of warmth and life, moved back and forth from the warden to the doctor inquisitively; Jacques Collin, fearing some kind of trap, hesitated to get up and leave.

"If you'd like to view the body," the doctor told him, "you'll need to hurry, because they'll be burying him tonight ..."

"If you have children, Monsieur," said Jacques Collin, "you'll understand why I seem to be acting like an imbecile; I can hardly see straight.... This blow is worse than death to me, but you can't understand what I'm saying.... You're not fathers, or if you are, not in the same way: you see, I'm his mother too! ... I—I think I'm losing my mind...."

Farewells

Using the corridors whose powerful doors open only for the warden, it is possible to get from the solitary cells to the *pistoles* very quickly. Those two rows of cells are separated by an underground passageway with thick walls, above which sits the gallery in the Palais de Justice that is known as the Galerie Marchande. And so Jacques Collin, a guard holding him by the arm, preceded by the warden and followed by the doctor, arrived in only a few minutes at the cell where Lucien had been laid on the bed.

At the sight, he fell upon the body, embracing it with such desperation that the three onlookers trembled at the force and passionate intensity of the embrace.

"Look," said the doctor to the warden; "this is an example of what I was telling you. This man is going to crush that body, and you don't know what a corpse is like—it's like stone ..."

"Leave me alone!" cried Jacques Collin in an exhausted voice. "I haven't got long to be with him, because they're going to come and take him to ..."

He couldn't quite say the words "bury him."

"Let me keep something from my dear child! ... Please have the kindness to clip, monsieur," he said to Doctor Lebrun, "a few locks from his hair; I can't do it."

"It really is his son!" said the doctor.

"You think so?" said the warden cautiously, which caused the doctor to slip into a kind of reverie for a moment.

The warden told the guard to leave the prisoner in the cell, and to cut a few locks of hair for the one who claimed to be the father, before they came to take away the body.

At five-thirty in the month of May, one can easily read a letter in the Conciergerie, despite the bars, the gratings, and the wire trellises across the windows. Jacques Collin therefore spelled out the terrible letter while holding on to Lucien's hand.

The man has not been found who can hold a piece of ice for ten minutes, gripping it tightly in the palm of his hand. The cold communicates itself with lethal rapidity to the very springs of life. But the effect of that terrible cold, which acts upon the body like a poison, is nothing compared to that produced upon the soul by the rigid, cold hand of a corpse held, gripped like this. Death, in such a case, speaks directly to Life, and tells black secrets that commit murder upon the feelings; for after all, when we make a feeling change, have we not killed it?

Let us reread Lucien's letter along with Jacques Collin, so that we can see how that dying communication was, to him, a poison.

TO THE ABBÉ CARLOS HERRERA[11]

My dear Abbé, I have never received anything but benefits from you. My involuntary ingratitude is death to me and, when you read these lines, I'll no longer be alive; you won't be here this time to save me.

You gave me the absolute right to cast you aside like the butt of a cigar if I ever found it would be advantageous to me to do so; I've cast you off all right, but in the stupidest way. To get myself out of a difficult spot, and seduced by the cunning techniques of an examining magistrate, I, your spiritual son, the man you adopted, took the side of those who want to have you murdered, at any cost, by making people believe what I know to be impossible, that you are the same as some French criminal. That says it all.

Between a man of your great strength and me, the one you tried to shape into a greater man than I ever could be, there is no need for foolish sentimentality at the moment of our final separation. You wanted to make me powerful and glorious, but instead you've pushed me into the abyss of suicide—that is the fact. For a long time now I've felt the great wings of this spiritual vertigo beating behind me.

You told me once that Cain and Abel had differing posterities. In the great drama of humanity, Cain is the antagonist. You are descended from Adam in that line, the line in which the Devil continues to fan the fire of evil whose first spark arose in Eve. Among the demons of that progeny arise, from time to time, men of enormous power, men who contain within themselves all human strengths, men who are like the feverish beasts of the desert, so strong that they require those vast open spaces in which they live. Men like that are as dangerous in society as lions would be in Normandy: they need their prey, and they devour vulgar, ordinary men, and they snatch up the money of fools; and when they play, their play is so dangerous that they end up killing the humble dog they've adopted as their companion, their beloved pet. When God wills it, these mysterious men might be a Moses, an Attila, a Charlemagne, a Mohammed, or a Napoleon; but when He allows these giant instruments to rust on the sea-floor of a generation, they merely become a Pugachev, a Robespierre, a Louvel, or an Abbé Carlos Herrera. Endowed with an immense power over tender souls, they draw the latter to them and grind them down. It is a grand thing, beautiful in its way. It is the poetry of evil. Men like you ought to live in caves, and never come out of them. You've made me live the life of a giant, and I'm damned well through with it now. And so I can pull my head back out of the Gordian knots of your intrigues, and slip it into the hangman's noose that I'm making of my cravat.

To make amends for my blunder, I'm sending the prosecutor-general a retraction of my interrogation. You'll know best how to make use of that.

I've drawn up a will in proper form, and you will be receiving, Monsieur l'Abbé, the sums belonging to your Order that you spent so imprudently on me out of the paternal tenderness you felt for me.

Farewell then, farewell, you splendid monument of evil and corruption, farewell, you who, if only you had taken a different path, could have been greater than Jiménez or Richelieu; you kept all your promises; I have returned to what I was on the banks of the Charente, but I owe to you this long, enchanting dream; but unfortunately, it won't be the river of my youth where I'll drown my youthful sins, but the Seine, and the hole into which I'll sink will be a cell in the Conciergerie.

Don't have any regrets over me. My contempt for you is equal to my admiration.

LUCIEN

Just before one in the morning, when they came to carry the body away, they found Jacques Collin kneeling next to the bed, the letter on the floor, dropped there no doubt in the same way the suicide drops the pistol that has killed him; but the poor wretch still gripped Lucien's hand tightly in his, and he was praying to God.

When the porters caught sight of the man in that position, they stopped still for a moment, for he resembled one of those stone sculptures kneeling for all eternity atop medieval tombs, images created by the stone-cutter's genius. The false priest, his eyes clear as a tiger's, his gaze preternaturally still, made such an impression on the men that they spoke gently as they asked him to arise.

"But why?" he asked timidly.

The bold, fearless Deathcheater had become as weak as a child.

The warden pointed this spectacle out to Monsieur de Chargeboeuf, who, seized by a deep respect for such extreme grief, and believing that Jacques Collin really was the father, explained to all what Monsieur de Granville's orders were with regard to the funeral and transport of Lucien, that he must definitely be taken to his home on the Quai Malaquais, where clergy were waiting to keep a vigil for him for the rest of the night.

The convict spoke out in a sorrowful tone: "I recognize in those orders the great soul of that magistrate. Tell him, monsieur, that he can rely on my gratitude. . . . Yes, I'm capable of doing him great service. Don't forget that phrase: for him, it's of the greatest importance. Ah, monsieur, great changes sweep through the heart of a man when he's wept for seven hours over a child like this one. . . . I'll never see him again!"

Brooding over Lucien like a mother who is being bereft of her son's body, Jacques Collin collapsed. Watching them pick up Lucien's body, he emitted such a groan that the porters tried to hurry.

The secretary of the prosecutor-general and the prison warden had already removed themselves from the spectacle.

Where had it gone, that nature of bronze with its ability to make decisions in the blink of an eye, with its union of thought and act springing forth like lightning, with its nerves hardened by three prison escapes, three sentences of hard labor, nerves as unbending and metallic as those of a savage? Iron will yield after a certain amount of hammering or after sustained pressure; its impenetrable molecules, purified by man and rendered homogeneous, will begin to break down; and without the fusion of smelting, the metal loses its ability to resist. Blacksmiths, locksmiths, and makers of edge-tools, indeed all those who work with this metal, use the same technical term: "the iron is retted," they say, importing a term usually reserved for hemp or flax, where steeping the material allows its parts to be separated. Well, the human person—or, if you prefer, the triple energy of body, heart, and mind—can be seen as analogous to iron under repeated shocks. Persons are then like hemp or like iron: they become retted. Science, the justice system, and the general public all seek out a thousand possible reasons for the terrible disasters that occur on the railroads, perhaps due to a cracked rail—the most horrific of which was at Bellvue[12]—but nobody thinks to ask the metal workers, who all say the same thing: "The iron was retted." And this danger cannot be predicted. Metal that has gone soft and metal that is still strong—they both look alike.

And it is in that kind of mental state that both confessors and examining magistrates often find great criminals. The terrible sensations caused by going before the assize court, or by the final preparations for the scaffold, almost always cause a breakdown in the nervous systems of even the strongest constitutions. Lips that were violently sealed now open, and confessions pour out; the strongest of hearts now begin to break; and—such a strange thing!—these confessions, removing at last the mask of innocence so stubbornly worn till now, take place when they serve no purpose at all, apart from giving some reassurance to the executioners, who are always somewhat uneasy at the prospect of putting an innocent person to death.

Napoleon knew this dissolution of the human person, this disintegration of all his inner powers, on the battlefield of Waterloo!

In the Prison Yard

At eight in the morning, when the guard of the *pistoles* entered Jacques Collin's cell, he found him pale and calm, like a man who had recovered his strength by the sheer violence of his willpower.

"It's time to go into the yard," said the jailer. "You've been locked up for three days now, so if you want to get some fresh air and walk around a little, now's the time!"

Jacques Collin, entirely absorbed in his thoughts and taking no interest in himself, feeling as if he were simply an empty set of clothes, an old rag, in no way suspected the trap that Bibi-Lupin had set for him, nor the importance of his entrance into the yard. The poor wretch walked out mechanically, threading his way along the corridor that runs alongside the cells hewn into what had been the cornices of the magnificent arcades in the Palais of the kings of France, beneath the gallery named for Saint Louis, through which today one passes to reach the various offices of the appeals court. This corridor joins up with the one by the *pistoles,* and—a circumstance worth noting—the cell where Louvel, one of the most famous of regicides, was held is the one at the point where the two corridors join up.[13] Beneath the attractive offices of the Tour Bonbec, at the end of the dark corridor, is a spiral staircase upon which the prisoners, whether those in the *pistoles* or those in the other cells, make their way to and from the yard.

All the prisoners, those scheduled to appear in the assize court as well as those whose cases have been heard, every prisoner in the Conciergerie except those in solitary confinement, come out to walk in this narrow, entirely paved space during certain hours of the day, and especially early in the morning on summer days. The yard is like the antechamber to both the scaffold and the prison, and on one side it ends there, while on the other it leads toward the outside world, though one must pass by gendarmes or be released by either the examining magistrate or the assize court. Thus its appearance is even more frightening than that of the scaffold. For the scaffold can be a pedestal by which one ascends to heaven; but the yard—all the infamies of the world gather together there, with no exit!

Whether it's at La Force or Poissy, at Melun or Sainte-Pélagie, a yard is a yard. The same aspects are reproduced everywhere, from the color of the walls to their height or to the size of the place. And therefore our STUDY OF MANNERS would be incomplete if we failed to give an exact description of this Parisian Pandemonium.[14]

Powerful arches support the audience chambers of the Appeals court, and beneath them, beneath the fourth arch, is a stone that, they say, was once used by Saint Louis for the distribution of alms, and which today is used as a counter on which food is sold to the prisoners. As soon as the yard opens to the prisoners, they can be seen grouping around this stone in search of prisoners' delicacies—brandy, rum, etc.

The first two arcades on this side of the yard, facing the magnificent Byzantine gallery, the last trace of the elegance that once marked the Palais of Saint Louis, are reserved as spaces where prisoners and their lawyers may confer, the entrance of which is closed off by a formidable wicket with enormous railings under the third archway. The railings separate off a double pathway, like the railings set up at theater entrances when the play is a great hit. This consulting room, situated at the end of the main entrance hall to the Conciergerie, in the past got its light through hooded windows, but now it's much better lit by framed windows on the wicket side, through which surveillance can be maintained on the lawyers and their clients. This innovation was necessitated by the all-too-powerful seductions that pretty women could exercise upon their defenders. Ah, where will the immorality stop? . . . Such precautions are like those premade sets of questions intended to serve as aids in the examination of one's conscience, but that end up suggesting all sorts of previously unheard-of monstrosities to imaginations that had been pure before. . . . In this conference room, the police sometimes allow friends and relatives to visit with the prisoners too.

The reader will now understand what the yard is to the two hundred prisoners of the Conciergerie: it is their garden, a garden with neither trees nor soil nor flowers—in short, a prison yard! The consultation area and the stone of Saint Louis, upon which authorized food and liquor are sold, constitute their only communication with the outside world.

The moments passed in the yard are the only ones in which the prisoner finds himself in the open air and in company; of course, in other prisons, prisoners have the opportunity to meet in workshops, but in the Conciergerie, no one is allowed to get involved in any occupation, except for prisoners in the *pistoles*. Here, the drama of the courtroom and the trial is the main topic on everyone's mind, since one is only held here for either interrogation or trial. The yard presents a hideous spectacle; you cannot really imagine it—you have to see it for yourself.

First, the meeting, in a space forty meters long and thirty wide, of some hundred prisoners, a mix of the *accusés* and the *prévenus*, hardly constitutes the better element of society. These wretches, who, for the most part, come from the lowest classes, are all poorly clothed; their physiognomies range from ignoble to horrible; a criminal who comes from a higher social sphere is, fortunately, fairly rare. Corruption, forgery, fraudulent bankruptcy—these are the only crimes that bring in people of the better sort, and in any case they tend to have the privilege of being placed in the *pistoles*, and they almost never leave their cells.

This exercise space, bordered by solid, formidable, blackened walls, by a colonnade transformed into cells, by fortification on the quay side, by the barred *pistole* cells on the north, and surveilled by careful watchers, occupied by a troop of ignoble criminals, none of whom can trust the others—all of this is sad enough simply to gaze upon; but the real terror sets in when you find yourself being stared at by all those hate-filled faces, faces expressing curiosity or despair, all of them dishonored and debased. No joy here! Everything is somber, the space itself as well as the men. Everything is mute, the walls as well as the consciences. Everything poses a danger for these unfortunates; apart from the sinister friendships that prisons engender, no one dares trust anyone else. The police hover

over them at all times, poisoning the atmosphere and corrupting everything, right down to the handshake between two guilty inmates who know each other well. A criminal encountering his best comrade cannot know whether the latter has repented, and has told some tales in order to save his life. This lack of security, this fear of the *stoolie,* destroys the already false freedom of the exercise yard. In prison jargon, the stoolie is an informer who appears to be in serious trouble, but whose proverbial cunning consists in having himself taken as a *pal.* This word "pal" signifies a lifelong, skilled thief who long ago broke all ties with society, who wants to remain a thief for the rest of his life, and who remains faithful *no matter what* to the *mob.*[15]

Crime and insanity have a lot in common. Watching the Conciergerie prisoners milling about the exercise yard and watching the madmen in the garden area of an asylum is a very similar thing. Both walk about while avoiding each other, both give each other strange, often hostile looks, depending on what's going through their minds at the moment, but these looks are never friendly, never serious, because they either know each other or fear each other. Awaiting their sentences gives the prisoners in the yard an anxious, haggard expression, much like that of madmen. It is only the most consummate criminals who seem assured, who seem to live in the kind of tranquility that an honest man does, with the sincerity of a clean conscience.

Men of the middle classes are unusual here, and a sense of shame keeps most of them in their cells, so most of those seen in the exercise yard are wearing the clothes of the working class. Work shirts, overalls, velvet jackets are the norm. These outfits, shabby or dirty, so well harmonizing with the vulgar, sinister physiognomies and the brutal manners—softened a little, true, by the sorrowful thoughts each prisoner is thinking—all contribute to the fear or disgust felt by the rare visitor who has been allowed the privilege of coming to observe the Conciergerie, owing to connections in high places.

Just as viewing an anatomical exhibit in which foul diseases are represented in wax inspires chaste and noble intentions in the young men brought to see it, so the sight of the yard and the Conciergerie, peopled with its guests destined to end up in the penal colony or on the scaffold or in some equally dreadful spot, instills a fear of human justice in those who do not fear the divine variety, though the voice of the latter speaks so vividly in our consciences, and they become honest, for quite a long time.

Philosophic, Linguistic, and Literary Essay on Slang, Whores, and Thieves

Since some of the men taking their exercise in the prison yard when Jacques Collin was about to arrive there would turn out to be actors in a critical scene in the life of Deathcheater, it seems worthwhile to paint the portrait of some of the principal figures in that terrible assembly.

Here, just like anywhere else that men are gathered together, at school for instance, what matters is strength, whether physical or moral. In school as in the prisons, criminality is the aristocracy. The one whose head is most endangered is the one who dominates all the others. The prison yard, as others have noted, is a school for criminal law, and its professors are far more effective than those who teach at the Panthéon. A common amusement is to act out the drama of an assize courtroom, with one prisoner playing the presiding judge, others the jury, a ministry representative, a lawyer, and to bring the trial to a decision. This ghastly farce is acted out inevitably when some famous crime is in the news. At this particular time, a major crime was the hideous murder of Monsieur and Madame Crottat, who were retired farmers, parents of a notary; the couple kept eight hundred thousand gold francs in their home, as the investigation showed.[16] One of the culprits in the double murder was the famous Dannepont, known as La Pouraille, an ex-convict who had kept one step ahead of the police for five years by using seven or eight different aliases. This rogue's disguises were so perfect that he had actually served a two-year term in prison under the name of Delsouq, who was one of his pupils, a famous thief, though his achievements never took him beyond the jurisdiction of ordinary magistrates' courts. La Pouraille was up to his third murder since his discharge from prison. The certainty that he would be facing a death sentence, not to mention the rumors of all the money he had acquired, made him both the terror and the idol of the prisoners; not one sou of his stolen money had ever been recovered. People still remember—despite the great events of July 1830—the fear the double murder caused throughout Paris, comparable in importance to the 1831 theft of medals from the Library[17]; there is an unfortunate tendency in our time to focus on numbers with every topic, and thus a murder involving a large stolen sum is considered more newsworthy.

La Pouraille, a small, thin man with a face like a weasel's, aged about forty-five, a celebrity in all three of the prisons he had successively inhabited since he was nineteen, knew Jacques Collin intimately, and we shall see how and why. Two other convicts had been transferred over from La

Force within the preceding twenty-four hours along with La Pouraille, and the other two immediately acknowledged, and made others acknowledge, right there in the yard, the sinister royalty of their *pal* destined for the scaffold. One of the two convicts, a parolee named Sélerier, sported a number aliases, including l'Auvergnat, Old Ralleau, the Roller, but in the society that in prison language is called the *mob,* he was known as Silk Thread, a nickname he had earned by demonstrating his skill in slipping out of the dangers entailed by his profession; he was one of the old associates of Deathcheater.

Now, Deathcheater had long suspected Silk Thread of playing a double role, of being at once in the counsels of the mob and in those of the police, and he believed he had played a role in Deathcheater's own arrest at the Vauquer pension (see *Père Goriot*) in 1819. Sélerier—who we will now call Silk Thread, just as Dannepont will be called La Pouraille—had been picked up for parole violation, and he was implicated in some serious thefts that, although involving no bloodshed at all, would nonetheless earn him a solid twenty more years. The other convict, named Riganson, had a girlfriend named La Biffe, and the two of them together formed one of the most formidable couples in the mob. Riganson, in an awkward relationship with the Law since his tenderest years, had been nicknamed Le Biffon: Biffon is the male version of Biffe, for nothing is sacred in the mob. Those savages have no respect for the law, or religion, or anything else, including what we might call "natural history," whose sacred nomenclature they parody, as in this example.

At this point a digression is necessary, for Jacques Collin's entrance into the yard, his appearance in the midst of his enemies, so well orchestrated by Bibi-Lupin and the examining magistrate, as well as the curious scenes that will follow—none of all this would be clear or comprehensible without some prior explanation concerning the world of thieves and prisons, their codes and customs, and above all their language, the grotesque poetry of which is indispensable for this part of our story. Let us begin, then, with a word or two on the language spoken by these Greeks, con men, thieves, and murderers, known as *argot,* which literature has of late used with a great deal of success—so much so that more than one example of this strange vocabulary has been heard on the pink lips of young ladies, has echoed from the gilded walls in boudoirs, has amused princes, more than one of whom has been heard to declare that he had been *ripped off!* Let us admit, though it may surprise some people, that there is no more energetic, colorful language than this of the underworld, this kind of language that has bubbled up from cellars, slums, the underbelly of society since the beginnings of empires and the founding of capital cities. It has bubbled up from the third cellar down, to use a theatrical term[18]—for, after all, we know that all the world's a stage, don't we? The third cellar is the ultimate basement level below the stage of the Opéra, where the various machinery is stored, and where the men are who operate it, seeing to the footlights, the apparitions, the blue devils that arise like flames from Hell, and so forth.

Every word of this language presents a brutal, ingenious, or terrible image. A man's underwear are his *uprights* (*montant*, a word we need explain no further). In argot, no one sleeps, they *roll up*: note the energy with which this phrase expresses the kind of sleep that a hunted, fatigued, wearied animal sleeps, the sleep of the thief who, once he feels secure, just lies down and rolls up into the abysses of a deep sleep, the heavy wings of Suspicion hovering just above him, just the way a wild animal sleeps, and snores, but never ceases listening!

Everything is savage in this language. The beginning and ending syllables of words are harsh, strangely shocking. A woman is a *largue*, for example.[19] And what poetry! A straw mat is a *Beauce featherbed*. Midnight is *when the lead hands meet*. It makes you shiver, doesn't it? Rifling a room is *wringing it dry*. How can the simple expression *going to bed* compete with *shedding your skin?* How vivid the imagery! To eat is to *play dominoes*; how else can hunted men eat?

Slang is always on the move, everywhere. It follows right behind civilization, right on its heels, enriching it with new expressions constantly. The potato, introduced into France by Louis XVI and Parmentier, is quickly turned by argot into *pigs' oranges*. Bank notes are invented, and the prison world soon calls them *garatted flimsies*, after Garat, the cashier whose name is printed on them. *Flimsies!* Doesn't it make you hear the very rustle of that thin paper? A thousand-franc note is a *male flimsy*, the five-hundred a *female flimsy*. Rest assured that the convicts will eventually rebaptize the hundred or two-hundred franc notes with some bizarre term.

In 1790 Guillotin discovered, in the interests of humanity, a mechanical expedient for resolving all the little problems that the death penalty caused. The convicts and ex–galley slaves took one look at this machine that served as a bridge between the old monarchical regime and the new republican one and renamed it *Climb-up Abbey!* Studying the angle at which the steel blade dropped, they invented the verb *scything!* When we recall that prison is called *the meadow*, people who study language really must admire the creation of these hideous "vocables," as Charles Nodier would call them.[20]

Let us also recognize the high antiquity of slang! About a tenth of its vocabulary stems from the Romanesque era, and another tenth is from the old Gaulish of Rabelais. *Effrondrer* (to beat or defeat), *otolondrer* (to annoy), *cambrioler* (anything done within an enclosed room), *aubert* (money), *gironde* (beautiful—the word comes from a river in the Languedoc region), *fouillousse* (pocket): these all come from the language of the fourteenth and fifteenth centuries. *Affe,* for "life," is of the greatest antiquity. Making trouble in one's *affe* gives us *affres,* from which stems our modern word *affreux* (hideous), best defined as anything that gives trouble to our lives, etc.

At least one hundred argot words come from the language of Panurge, who, in Rabelais' work, symbolizes the people, for his name is made up of two Greek words, meaning "the one who does everything." Science and technology change the face of our civilization by giving us the railroad; argot has already named it the *roulant vif* (noisy rattler).

The word for the head—while it is still on one's shoulders—is the *sorbonne,* which indicates the antique source of this language, used by the earliest novelists like Cervantes, as well as the Italian writers of *novelle,* and Aretino. In all ages the *whore,* the heroine of so many old tales, has been the protector, the companion, the consoler of gamblers, thieves, purse-snatchers, the con men, hustlers.

Prostitution and theft are two living protests, female and male, of the *state of nature* against the social state. And thus the great *philosophes,* as well as today's reformers and humanitarians, who carry the communists and the Fourierists in their train, always arrive, without knowing it, at the same two conclusions: prostitution and theft.[21] The thief does not write sophistical books questioning the validity of property, inheritance, social guarantees: no; he simply suppresses them. For him, stealing is taking possession of what's his. He doesn't write up a discussion of marriage nor does he denounce it, he does not ask, as the printed utopias do, for that mutual consent, that intimate union of souls too unique to generalize from: no; he simply couples, with the violence of the hammer of necessity. Modern reformers write up their ponderous theories, disjointed and nebulous, and sometimes embed them in philanthropic novels; but the thief acts! He's as clear as fact itself, as logical as a blow from a fist. And what a style!

One further observation! The world of whores, thieves, and murderers, of penal colonies and prisons, comprises a population of somewhere from sixty to eighty thousand individuals, male and female. Those who would depict the modern world and its ways cannot turn up their nose at representing this side of our society. The justice system, including the police forces, comprise an almost identical number—isn't that a strange thing? What a vast, far-reaching duel it is, between those who flee and those who pursue, and how eminently dramatic—as shown in the present study. Theft and the commerce in prostitution have much in common with the theater, with the police, with the priesthood, and with the military. In these six ways of life, the individual truly takes on his own unique, indelible character. He can no longer be anything but himself. The stigmata of divine ordination can never be removed, any more than those of the military life. And so it is with all those ways of life that are in such strong opposition, so contrary to civilized society. Their hallmarks are so violent, so bizarre, so singular, so *sui generis* that they render the prostitute, the thief, and the murderer so easy for their enemies, the spy and the policeman, to recognize that they become like game to the hunter: they have a certain color, a certain scent, specific *properties*, in short, that the pursuer cannot mistake. This accounts for the deep practice of disguise among the celebrities of the prison world.

The Grand Fanandels

And one further word about the nature of this world, which the abolition of the practice of branding and the softening of penalties and the dimwitted intelligence of juries renders so threatening. Honestly, in twenty years Paris is going to be completely surrounded by an army of forty thousand ex-convicts. The Département of the Seine with its fifteen hundred thousand inhabitants is the only place in France those wretches can hide. Paris is to them what virgin forest is to ferocious beasts.

The mob, which is the aristocracy, the Faubourg Saint-Germain of that world, was formed in 1816, following the peace that made life so difficult for so many, and the group was called the Grand Fanandels, the biggest or most important of the pals, consisting of the most famous gang leaders and a number of hardy individuals who then had no other way of making their living. This word "pals," or "fanandels," means "brothers," "friends," "comrades." All the thieves, convicts, prisoners—they're all fanandels. Now the Grand Fanandels, the very cream of the underworld, for some twenty years functioned as an appeals court, a school, and a legislature or chamber of peers for the larger group. The Grand Fanandels all had their own private fortune, and they also held a certain amount of capital in common, following a code of their own. They came to each other's aid in times of trouble, and they all knew each other. Moreover, they were immune to all the ruses and schemes of the police, having their own charter, their own passwords, their own means of identifying each other.

These dukes and peers of the prisons formed, between 1815 and 1819, the famous Society of Ten Thousand (see *Père Goriot*), the name deriving from their agreement that they would not bother with any job that would bring in less than ten thousand francs. At this point in our story, 1829–30, memoirs by a celebrated member of the police were beginning to appear in print, revealing the size of the society and naming its leaders.[22] Readers were shocked to learn of this highly skilled army of both men and women that was so formidable, so shrewd, so often successful, that thieves like Lévy, Pastourel, Collonge, Chimaux, their ages ranging from fifteen to sixty, had been in revolt against society since their childhoods.[23] . . . What an admission of impotence for the justice system, the existence of thieves of that age!

Jacques Collin acted as banker not only to the Ten Thousand but also to the Grand Fanandels, the heroes of the prison world. As competent authorities will confirm, there are always funds in prisons. It seems bizarre at first, but it makes sense: the money from thefts is almost never recovered. The convict, unable to take anything with him into the prison, is forced to entrust his money to men of proven capacity, just as in ordinary society we entrust our money to a banking house.

Long ago Bibi-Lupin—who had now been head of the Sûreté for ten years—had been a member of the Grand Fanandels. His treason resulted from wounded pride; he saw himself constantly being passed over in favor of the intelligence and strength of Deathcheater. This explains the famous Sûreté man's unrelenting desire for revenge on Jacques Collin. This also explains certain questionable dealings between Bibi-Lupin and his former comrades, which had begun to attract the attention of the magistrates.

So, in his desire for vengeance—which the examining magistrate had greatly facilitated by asking him to establish the identity of Jacques Collin—the head of the Sûreté police had very shrewdly chosen the men he would set against the false Spaniard—that is, La Pouraille, Silk Thread, and Biffon—for La Pouraille and Silk Thread belonged to the Ten Thousand, while Biffon was a Grand Fanandel.

Now, every one of these prison heroes has a kind of double in his devoted woman. La Biffe, for example, the formidable largue of Biffon who was so capable when it came to escaping the clutches of the police due to her ability to disguise herself as a proper lady, was presently at liberty. This woman, who knew so well how to turn herself into a marquise, a baroness, or a countess, had a coach and servants. She was a sort of Jacques Collin in skirts, the only woman comparable to Asia, Jacques Collin's right hand. Judicial records and the secret chronicles of the Palais will tell you this: no passion of an honest woman, not even that of a pious parishioner for her spiritual director, can match the attachment of a mistress who shares in the perils of a great criminal.

Passion is, with these people, almost always the basic motive behind their most audacious enterprises and even their murders. The excessive love impulse that, say the doctors, is constitutional with them draws them inevitably toward women and works to concentrate all the moral and physical strength of these energetic men. This is the cause of that idleness that marks most of their days; amatory excess requires repose and restorative meals. And this is the cause of that hatred for any kind of work, which forces the men to resort to rapid methods for acquiring some money. Nevertheless, the necessity of living, and of living well, violent as it already is, pales beside the prodigalities that the female inspires in these Medoros.[24] They lavish jewels and gowns upon them; the girl wants a shawl, so the lover steals one for her, and she takes this as a proof of his love. This situation is a sure path to theft, and one that, if we wish to examine the human heart closely, we will recognize as an almost natural sentiment in a man. Theft, in turn, is the path to murder, and murder takes the lover, step by step, up to the scaffold.

The wild, untamed physical love of these men might, if we listen to the medical authorities, be the cause of seven-tenths of the crimes that are committed. The proof of this is on display every time, strikingly, palpably, when an executed man is given an autopsy. And this is the cause of the adoration felt by the mistresses of these men, society's bogeymen. That female devotion can be seen hunkered down faithfully at the prison gates, always attempting to render the truth obscure and impenetrable to the law, endlessly occupied in undoing the efforts of the investigators, remaining incorruptible guardians of the darkest secrets. Herein lies both the strength and the weakness of the criminal. In the language of whores, *having integrity* means never failing in any of the laws of such an attachment, giving all one's money to one's man who is *on the inside,* keeping watch over his well-being, keeping absolute faith with him, doing anything and everything for him. The cruelest insult one whore can hurl in the face of another is to accuse her of infidelity to her man who's *locked up.* A whore like that is nothing more than a woman without a heart!

La Pouraille was passionately in love with a woman, as we will see. Silk Thread, a philosophical egoist for whom stealing was a way of life, strongly resembled Paccard, the henchman of Jacques Collin who had fled with Prudence Servien, the two of them richer by seven hundred and fifty thousand francs. He was attached to no one, didn't like women, and loved only Silk Thread. As for Biffon, as we saw earlier, he took

368 | VAUTRIN'S LAST INCARNATION

his name out of attachment to La Biffe. Now, these three exemplars of the mob had some points to dispute with Jacques Collin, accounts that would not be easy to settle.

Only the banker knew how many of his old associates still survived, and how much money each one had had. The special mortality rate among his clients had entered into the calculations of Deathcheater when he decided to *clean out the till* for Lucien.[25] By evading the attention both of his comrades and of the police for nine years, Jacques Collin could be pretty certain that he would be the heir, according to the charter of the Grand Fanandels, of two-thirds of the principal. And couldn't he also claim that he'd already made payments to certain associates who had been *mown down* since? There was no control, no system of supervision in place for this head of the Grand Fanandels. Their trust in him was, of necessity, absolute, for the wild-animal kind of life a convict lives in this wild world requires a great deal of delicacy. Out of the hundred thousand écus he had taken with him, Jacques Collin could at the moment perhaps come up with a hundred thousand francs. As we have seen, La Pouraille, one of his creditors, had only ninety days left to live. He no doubt had stashed away elsewhere a sum greater than the one his boss was keeping for him, so La Pouraille could probably turn out to be accommodating.

One of the infallible indices by which prison wardens, policemen and their assistants, and even examining magistrates recognize the old nags, that is, those who have already dined on the *special beans* (the food that the State gives the convict), is their relative ease in prison; the recidivists already know how things are done; they're at home here, and nothing surprises them.

Jacques Collin up to now had kept his guard up admirably, playing the innocent and the foreigner to perfection both at La Force and at the Conciergerie. But now, beaten down with grief, crushed by his double death—for on that fatal night, he died twice over—he became simply Jacques Collin. The guard was shocked to find that he didn't have to tell the Spanish priest the way down to the prison yard. The perfect actor had forgotten his role, and he made his way down the winding stairs of the Bonbec tower like someone who knew the Conciergerie well.

"Bibi-Lupin was right," the guard said to himself; "this one is an old nag, all right—it's Jacques Collin."

The Wild Boar Appears

The doorway of the tower forms a kind of frame, and in it appeared Deathcheater, just as the prisoners had completed making their purchases at the so-called Saint Louis stone counter and were now dispersed around the yard. Thus the new arrival was observed by everyone at once, with that rapidity and precision of perception that only prisoners seem to have, when they are all spread out around the yard, each one like a spider at the center of its web. And this comparison is mathematically exact, for the eye is bounded on all sides by high, black walls, so that the prisoner always sees, even without looking at it, the windows of the visiting room and staircase of the Bonbec tower, the only way out of the yard. In his profound isolation, everything is noteworthy to the prisoner, everything interests him; his boredom, similar to that of the caged tiger in the Jardin des Plantes, multiplies his powers of attention tenfold. It is not unimportant to point out that Jacques Collin, dressed as an ecclesiastic who is not too strict as to his appearance, was wearing black knee breeches with black stockings, shoes with silver buckles, a black waistcoat, and an odd dark maroon frock coat cut in a way that only priests wear, and the whole picture was completed by the characteristic hairstyle. Jacques Collin was wearing a supremely ecclesiastical wig, one that on him looked marvelously natural.

"Look! Look!" said La Pouraille to Biffon. "Bad luck here! A *wild boar*! How'd one of those get in here?"

"One of their tricks—some new type of *chef* [meaning spy]," Silk Thread replied. "It's a rope vendor in disguise, coming around to make a sale."

Argot provides various names for the police. When it's a policeman in pursuit of a thief, he's a *rope vendor*; when he's escorting the prisoner, he's a *carrier pigeon*; and when he leads the thief to the scaffold, he's a *guillotine guide*.

To complete our depiction of the prison yard, perhaps it's necessary to give brief descriptions of two other fanandels. First was Sélerier, called the Auvergnat, Old Ralleau, the Roller, and finally Silk Thread (he had thirty aliases and as many passports). We will call him only by this last designation, which is the only one he used among the mob. This deep thinker, who believed he smelled a policeman in the cleric's garb, was a little over five feet, with startlingly bulging muscles. Set in that enormous head of his were two small, burning eyes, heavy-lidded like those of birds of prey—gray eyes, dull and hard. At first he reminded you of a wolf, because of the size of his jaws and their sharp lines, their prominence; but that resemblance suggests cruelty, ferocity even, whereas the effect in him was counterbalanced by the shrewd, vivacious look he had on his smallpox-furrowed face. Those deep-cut scars made him look sharp-witted. You could read mockery in them. The life of a criminal with its hunger, its nights spent out of doors on quays and riverbanks, on bridges and streets, the orgies of strong liquor for celebrating some triumph—all this had laid, so to speak, its coat of varnish over that face. If Silk Thread had gone out without disguise, a policeman or gendarme would spot him at thirty paces; but he was the equal of Jacques Collin when it came to disguises and costumes. And now Silk Thread was in his ordinary guise, like some great actor who only takes trouble over his appearance when he's on stage, and was wearing a kind of hunter's jacket without buttons— the ripped button holes revealed the white of its lining—shabby old green slippers, nankeen breeches that were turning gray, and upon his head a cap without a peak, the cap threaded through with an old Madras bandana, heavily lined with rips and tears and much washing.

Next to Silk Thread sat Biffon, in perfect contrast. This famous thief, short, stocky, fat, and agile, with a livid complexion and black, deep-set eyes, was dressed like a kitchen assistant and planted on two very bowed legs; he frightened onlookers with a physiognomy that had all the features we associate with wild beasts.

Silk Thread and Biffon were paying court to La Pouraille, who had abandoned all his hopes. The recidivist murderer knew that he would be judged, sentenced, and executed within the next four months. So Silk Thread and Biffon, both pals of La Pouraille, started calling him *Father Superior*—that is, Father Superior of Climb-up Abbey. It's easy to see why Silk Thread and Biffon were making such a fuss over La Pouraille. The latter had buried two hundred and fifty thousand gold francs, his share in the loot from the murders of "Crottat husband and wife," as the official indictment phrased it. What a splendid inheritance to leave to these two fanandels, even though they were due to return to their prison in a few days. Biffon and Silk Thread were about to be sentenced for what are called "qualifying thefts"—that is, thefts with aggravating circumstances—to fifteen years, and not to be served concurrently with the ten years they'd gotten previously, a sentence they had taken the liberty of abbreviating. So, even though one of them had twenty-two and the other twenty-six years of hard labor staring them in the face, they both hoped to escape and seek out the pot of gold La Pouraille left behind. But the Man of the Ten Thousand kept his secret to himself, thinking there was no point in giving it up when he hadn't even been sentenced yet. A member of the highest level of the prison world's aristocracy, he had not even revealed his accomplices. His character was well known; Monsieur Popinot, the examining magistrate in this horrible affair, couldn't get anything out of him.

This terrible triumvirate had stationed themselves at the upper end of the prison yard, that is, right below the *pistoles*. Silk Thread was just finishing up a course of instruction for a young man who was in prison for the first time and who was looking for information about the various meadows.

"All right, sonny," Silk Thread was just saying to him in a professorial voice, "now let me tell you the difference between Brest, Toulon, and Rochefort."

"Good, old man," said the young one, with the curiosity of a novice.

This prisoner, son of a family under indictment for forgery, had come down into the yard from the *pistole* adjoining the one Lucien had been in.

"My boy," Silk Thread continued, "at Brest you're sure to find some beans in the third scoop with your spoon; at Toulon, it'll take you five, and at Rochefort, only the old pros get any at all."

With that, the deep philosopher rejoined La Pouraille and Biffon who, fascinated by the appearance of the wild boar, were beginning to descend and cross the yard, just as Jacques Collin, overwhelmed with grief, was walking up toward them. Deathcheater was absorbed in his sorrowful thoughts, the thoughts of an overthrown emperor, and had no idea he was the object of everyone else's attention; he moved along slowly, looking up at the fatal crossbar of the window where Lucien de Rubempré had hanged himself. None of the other prisoners knew anything about that event, for the young forger, Lucien's neighbor, had said nothing about it, for reasons that will soon become clear. The three fanandels lined up to form a barrier on the priest's path.

"This is no wild boar," said La Pouraille to Silk Thread. "It's an old nag. Look how he drags that right foot!"

Here we need to pause and explain, because not all of our readers will have taken the bizarre notion to actually visit a prison, that each convict is chained to another, always an old one together with a young one. The weight of this chain, riveted to a ring circling just above the ankle, is such that by the end of a year it causes the convict a permanent limp. Obliged to drag one leg along by exerting more strength than the other in order to cope with this *manacle* (the term used in the prison for this iron), the convict inevitably develops a habit from this effort. Later on, when he no longer has to wear the chain, the convict is like the amputee who continues to feel pain in his missing limb; the ex-convict always feels the presence of his manacle, and he can never rid himself of its effect on his manner of walking. The police like to say *he drags to the right*. This diagnosis, familiar to convicts as well as to the police, if it does not aid in identifying a comrade will at least serve to confirm it.

With Deathcheater, who had escaped eight years ago, this motion had been quite minimized; but now, due to his thoughts so occupying his attention, he was moving along at so slow and solemn a pace that, slight as his limp was, it couldn't help but stand out to a practiced eye like that of La Pouraille. It's easy to see how convicts, always in close proximity to each other in prisons, would have so thoroughly studied each other's physiognomies that they would be able to recognize certain little signs that would escape their systematic enemies—the informers, the gendarmes, the police inspectors. Thus the famous Coignard, lieutenant-colonel of the Seine Legion, owed his arrest to a little twitch of the muscles on his left cheek being recognized by a convict; for, despite Bibi-Lupin's certainty in the matter, the police dared not believe that the Comte Pontis de Sainte-Hélène was Coignard.[26]

His Majesty the Boss

"That's our *dab* (our boss)," exclaimed Silk Thread, when Jacques Collin glanced his way with the look of a man plunged into an abyss of despair.

"Dammit, you're right, it's Deathcheater," said Biffon, rubbing his hands together. "Wait—it's his size and his walk—but what's going on? He doesn't look himself."

"Oh, I get it," said Silk Thread. "He's got a plan! He wants to come see his *aunt,* the one who's going to be executed pretty soon."

To give some idea of the kind of person that the prisoners as well as the turnkeys call an "aunt," we need only recall the reply that one of the wardens of a central prison made to the late Lord Durham, who had been visiting all the prisons during his stay in Paris.[27] This lord, curious to learn all he could about the French justice system, went so far as to get the late Sanson, the executioner, to demonstrate his gear, asking for a calf to be killed in order to understand the workings of the machine made so famous by the French Revolution.[28]

The warden, after having shown him all around the prison, the yard, the workshops, the dungeons and so forth, pointed to a specific area while making a gesture of disgust.

"I won't take Your Lordship over there," he said. "That's where the aunts' quarters are."

"I say!" exclaimed Lord Durham. "What are they?"

"The third sex, my Lord."

"They're going to *put* Théodore *to ground* (guillotine him)!" exclaimed

La Pouraille. "A sweet boy! Such skills, too! And didn't he have guts! What a loss to society!"

"Yeah, Théodore Calvi *smoothed* (ate) his last mouthful," said Biffon. "Oh, his *largues* are going to give their eyeballs a good wash, because he was loved, the little beggar!"

"That you, old pal?" said La Pouraille to Jacques Collin.

And in concert with his two acolytes, the three of them linked arms, barring the path of the newcomer.

"Hey, boss, so now you're a wild boar?" added La Pouraille.

"I hear you went and got *sticky-fingered* with our *stash* (stole our money)," said Biffon in a threatening tone.

"You plan to *cough up our dough* (return our money), eh?" asked Silk Thread.

The three questions were fired at him as rapidly as pistol shots.

"Please don't play jokes on a poor priest who's been put here by mistake," Jacques Collin replied mechanically, but immediately recognizing his three comrades.

"His voice, all right, but don't look like his mug (face)," said La Pouraille, reaching out and gripping Jacques Collin by the shoulder.

That gesture, along with the sight of his three comrades, violently wrenched the boss out of his prostration and brought him back to reality; for during that preceding, fatal night, he had gone wandering through strange spiritual worlds and an infinity of emotions in search of some new pathway.

"Don't *get your boss in a stew* (don't arouse suspicions)!" said Jacques Collin in a low, threatening growl of a voice, reminiscent of a lion's. "The *screws* (police) are there; let them trip over their own feet. I'm acting this comedy for a *starving fanandel* (a comrade in desperate straits)."

This was enunciated with all the unction of a priest attempting to convert some poor wretches, and it was accompanied by a sweeping glance all around the yard, allowing Jacques Collin to take in the guards and watchers beneath the archways and, implicitly, to make his three comrades see and despise them too.

"See the kitchen boys all around? *Light your candles, time to wake up!* (Look around you and observe.) *Don't recon me, drop the veil, just another wild boar.* (Act as if you don't know me, be cautious, and treat me as you would a priest.) Otherwise *I'll sink you, and your largues and your goodies too.* (I'll destroy you, your women, and your fortune.)"

"*Don't know who we are?* (You aren't giving us enough credit)," said Silk Thread. "You're here to *buy out your aunt* (to rescue your friend)."

"Madeleine's *all dolled up and ready for her stage debut* (prepared to go to the scaffold)," said La Pouraille.

"Théodore!" exclaimed Jacques Collin, barely repressing a start and a cry.

This was the last turn of the screw torturing the fallen giant.

"They're going to drop him," La Pouraille went on. "*Got his passport* (was condemned to death) two months ago."

Jacques Collin felt a wave of weakness, his knees buckling beneath him, and his three friends reached out to steady him; he had the presence of mind to join his hands together in prayer and put on a show of piety. La Pouraille and Biffon respectfully supported the sacrilegious Death-cheater, while Silk Thread hurried over to the guard standing near the entrance to the visiting room.

"This venerable priest needs to sit down; give me a chair for him."

And so the trap set by Bibi-Lupin was a failure. Deathcheater, like Napoleon being recognized by his soldiers, got only submission and respect from the three convicts. Two words sufficed: your largues and your goodies, your women and your money, the summa of all man's real affections. The threat was, for the three convicts, the sign of supreme power; the boss still had their fortunes in his hands. Still all-powerful on the outside, their boss had not betrayed them, as some false friends had claimed. Their leader's colossal reputation for skill and ingenuity stimulated their curiosity; for in prison curiosity is the last stimulant available to the withered soul. Moreover, the sheer boldness of Jacques Collin's disguise, maintained even behind the locked doors of the Conciergerie, dazzled the three criminals.

"Locked up in solitary for four days . . . I didn't know Théodore was so close to the abbey," said Jacques Collin. "I came to save a poor youngster who hanged himself right up there, at four o'clock, and now here I am facing another misery. I don't have any more aces in my hand!"

"Poor boss!" said Silk Thread.

"Ah, the *baker* (the Devil) has abandoned me!" cried Jacques Collin, tearing himself out of his comrades' arms and taking on a more formidable stance. "Sooner or later there's a moment when the world is just too strong for us! The *Stork* (the Palais de Justice) swallows us whole in the end."

The Conciergerie's warden, having been informed that the Spanish priest had had a faint, came to the yard himself to spy on him. He sat down on a chair in the sun, observing the entire yard with that fearful clarity of mind that grows greater every day in a man with a position such as his, and that conceals itself behind a shield of apparent indifference.

"My God!" exclaimed Jacques Collin, "to be thrown among these people, the dregs of society, criminals, murderers!... But God will not abandon His servant. Dear warden, I plan to mark my passage through this place with acts of charity whose memory will remain after I've gone! I plan to convert these poor wretches, to teach them that they have an immortal soul, that eternal life awaits them, and that even if they've lost everything here on earth, Heaven awaits them, and Heaven is theirs, for the mere price of a sincere repentance."

Twenty or thirty prisoners had come up and grouped themselves behind the three terrible convicts, whose ferocious expressions had led them all to stay three paces away, and they all were now listening to this speech, enunciated with evangelical unction.

"That one, Monsieur Gault," said the fearsome La Pouraille, "we'll listen to him, I guess."

"I have been told," Jacques Collin continued, speaking to Monsieur Gault, "that there is a person in this prison who has been condemned to death."

"They're reading out the rejection of his appeal to him right now," said Monsieur Gault.

"I'm afraid I don't know what that means," said Jacques Collin naïvely, looking around as he did so.

"For God's sake, what a *sap*!" exclaimed the young man who had just been learning from Silk Thread about the food in the various prisons.

"Well, either today or tomorrow they're going to be *mowing him down*!" said another prisoner.

"Mowing him down?" asked Jacques Collin with such an air of innocence and ignorance that his three old comrades were stunned with admiration.

"In their language," the warden replied, "it means that the death sentence will be carried out. If the clerk is reading out the rejection of the appeal now, the executioner will soon be receiving his orders for the execution. The individual has consistently refused all offers of religious consolation. . . ."

"But, oh, monsieur warden, there's a soul to be saved!" cried Jacques Collin.

With that, the blasphemer joined his hands, putting on an expression of mingled love and despair, calculated to make the warden, who was watching him closely, think he had entered into a state of divine fervor.

"Oh, monsieur," Deathcheater continued, "let me prove to you who I am and what I can do by giving me permission to make the flower of penitence blossom in that hardened heart! God has blessed me with the ability of saying just a few words that can bring about grand changes. I break hearts in order to open them. . . . What is there to fear? Have your gendarmes accompany me, or other guards, or anyone you like."

"I'll see if the chaplain will let you take his place," said Monsieur Gault.

The warden left, struck by the indifferent yet curious air with which the other prisoners seemed to regard the priest, whose evangelical enthusiasm lent some charm to his half-French, half-Spanish speech.

Ruse against Ruse

"How did you come to be here, *monsieur l'abbé*?" asked Silk Thread's young interlocutor.

"Oh, it's all a mistake," replied Jacques Collin, looking the boy over. "They found me at the house of a courtesan who had been robbed after her death. Her death was known to be a suicide, and the thieves, who were probably the domestics, still haven't been arrested."

"And it's because of that theft that the young man hanged himself?"

"The poor boy no doubt couldn't tolerate the idea of his reputation being ruined by an unjust imprisonment," replied Deathcheater, casting his gaze up toward heaven.

"Yes," said the young man, "they had just decided to release him when he killed himself. What bad luck!"

"It's only the innocent ones who have their imaginations affected so strongly," said Jacques Collin. "And remember, the theft was actually of money belonging to him."

"How much money was it?" asked the deep, cunning Silk Thread.

"Seven hundred and fifty thousand francs," said Jacques Collin, quietly.

The three convicts looked at each other and then moved away, apart from the group that had gathered around the so-called ecclesiastic.

"So he's the one who *cleaned out* that whore's *cellar* (stole everything from her)!" Silk Thread whispered to Biffon. "And they're trying to *smoke us out* (make us concerned) about our *bag of marbles* (our money)."

"Nah—he'll always be the boss of the Grand Fanandels," replied La Pouraille. "No fears for our *heaps* (our money is safe)."

La Pouraille, looking for a man he could trust, had his own reasons for wanting to see Jacques Collin as an honest man. Prison is the place where people end up believing in what they hope is true.

"I'm betting he *skunks the Stork's boss* (outwits the prosecutor-general) and *gets his auntie off* (saves his friend)," said Silk Thread.

"If he does," said Biffon, "I ain't saying he's God almighty, but I'm saying he *shared a pipeful with the baker* (made a deal with the Devil)."

"Heard him just now, didn't you? 'The baker's abandoned me!'" said Silk Thread.

"Well," exclaimed La Pouraille, "if he decides to *get me off* (save my head), it's some life I'm going to be living with *my divvy of the heap* (my share of the fortune) and my *little yellow friends in the dark* (the stolen gold I recently hid away)."

"*Shoot with his bullets* (follow his instructions)!" said Silk Thread.

"You laughing?" La Pouraille said, looking at Biffon.

"What are you, a sap? You're *already stiff and headed up the abbey* (you're already condemned to death). There's no other door to take if you want to stay on your feet and go on eating, drinking, and thieving," Biffon replied. "Turn my back on him? Not likely."

"Now you said it," replied La Pouraille. "Nobody does tricks on the boss, or if they do, I'll be taking them along where I'm headed. . . ."

"He'll do it too!" said Silk Thread.

Even those people least likely to feel any sympathy for the inhabitants of this strange world will be able to imagine Jacques Collin's state of mind, finding himself between the corpse of the idol he had been worshipping all the preceding night and the upcoming death of his old companion in chains, the future corpse of Théodore, the young Corsican. Just getting in to see the boy would require extraordinary skill, but to save him—that would be a miracle! And that is just what he was pondering.

For the reader to understand what it was that Jacques Collin was about to attempt, we must begin by noting that the murderers, the thieves, all the populations of the prisons are far less fearsome than people think. In fact, with a few rare exceptions, they are quite cowardly, probably the result of their living in a state of constant fear that saps their spirits. Their minds are continually alert to the possibility of stealing, and since pulling off an important theft requires the complete concentration of all their powers, an agility of mind as well as body, and a focused attention that puts a strain on their morale, they become dull and stupid whenever those violent exertions of the will are no longer required, for the same reason that a singer or a dancer will collapse after a difficult solo or after one of those demanding duets that modern composers enjoy inflicting on the public. Criminals are in effect so stripped of the power of reason, or so oppressed by fear, that they become like children. Ridiculously credulous, the simplest ruse will entrap them. After a job has been completed, they're in such a state of absolute prostration

378 | VAUTRIN'S LAST INCARNATION

that they immediately abandon themselves to the debaucheries they find essential, and they get drunk on wine and liquors, hurling themselves into the arms of their women in a kind of rage in search of some sort of calm, some surrender of all their powers, seeking to blot out the memory of their crime along with their reason. At that point, they're at the mercy of the police. When they're arrested, they go blind, they lose their heads, and they need hope so badly that they'll believe in anything, no matter how absurd. An example will show just how stupid an arrested criminal is willing to be. Bibi-Lupin had recently gotten a nineteen-year-old murderer to confess by telling him that minors were never executed. When the boy was transferred to the Conciergerie for his punishment, after his appeal had been rejected, that terrible police agent came to see him.

"Are you sure you're under twenty?" he asked him.

"Yes, I'm only nineteen and a half," said the murderer, perfectly calm.

"Well then, rest easy: you won't see twenty."

"Why do you say that?"

"Because you'll be dead in three days," replied the head of the Sûreté.

The murderer, who had believed all along that, despite his death sentence, no one ever executed minors, collapsed like an omelet soufflé.

These men, so cruel because of the need to do away with witnesses—for they only murder in order to do away with evidence, one of the reasons people who are against capital punishment often cite—these giants of skill, know-how, these men who can use their hands and their eyes with the rapidity of savages, only become heroes of evil when they're on the stage of their own deeds. Once the crime is committed, only now do their difficulties begin, for now they're as confused and uncertain about what to do with their loot as they had been oppressed by their poverty before; now they're like women after childbirth, drained of all their strength. Energetic to a terrifying degree in their schemes, they become like children after a success. Again, they're like wild beasts: easy to kill after they've fed. In prison, these extraordinary men are truly men only in their dissimulation and in their discretion, though the latter does break down eventually when the men themselves are broken, beaten down by the sheer length of their detention.

We can understand, then, how it is that the three convicts, far from turning on their chief, wanted to serve him. They admired him: first, because they suspected him of having taken the seven hundred and fifty thousand francs; second, because of how calm he remained while locked up in the Conciergerie; and third, because they believed him capable of protecting them.

The Condemned Man's Cell

When Monsieur Gault left the false Spaniard, he went through the visiting room up to his office, and from there sought out Bibi-Lupin, who, during the twenty minutes that Jacques Collin had gone down to the yard from his cell, had been observing all, his eyes glued to a Judas hole that looked out on the yard.

"None of them recognized him," said Monsieur Gault. "Napolitas is keeping an eye on everything, and he hasn't heard anything. The poor priest, despite the horrible night he spent here, never said a word that would make anybody believe he was Jacques Collin."

"That just proves that he knows prisons very well," replied the chief of the Sûreté.

Napolitas, secretary to Bibi-Lupin, was unknown to anyone currently detained in the Conciergerie. He was playing the role of the young man from the family accused of forgery.

"Well, he's asking to be allowed to be confessor to the condemned man!" said the warden.

"All right—this is our last chance!" cried Bibi-Lupin. "I hadn't thought of this. The Corsican, Théodore Calvi, was Jacques Collin's chainmate, and when they were together in the meadow, Collin made him a nice set of footguards. . . ."

The convicts fabricate a kind of pad that they slip in between the iron ring and their flesh in an attempt to reduce the weight of the manacle on their ankles and insteps. These pads, made of oakum and linen, are called "footguards" by the prisoners.[29]

"Who's the guard on the condemned man?" Bibi-Lupin asked Monsieur Gault.

"It's old Metal-Ring."

"Good. I'll go *change my skin* and turn myself into a gendarme, so I'll be in the cell; I'll be able to hear them, and I take full responsibility."

"Aren't you worried that, if he is Jacques Collin, he'll recognize you and strangle you?" the Conciergerie warden asked Bibi-Lupin.

"As a gendarme, I'll have my saber," the chief replied, "and, anyway, if it is Jacques Collin he won't do anything to *let on,* and besides, if he's really a priest, I'm safe enough."

"No time to lose," said Monsieur Gault. "It's eight-thirty, and Father Sauteloup has just read him the rejection of his appeal. Monsieur Sanson is waiting in the hall for his orders."

"Yes, it's supposed to be today, and the Widow's Hussars"—another terrible term, referring to the assistants at the guillotine!—"are there," Bibi-Lupin replied. "I can understand why the prosecutor-general is hesitating. The boy continues to claim he's innocent, and if you ask me, the proofs against him aren't that convincing."

"He's a true Corsican," said Monsieur Gault. "He hasn't said a word, and nothing has broken him down."

These last words spoken by the warden to the head of the Sûreté summed up the somber history of men condemned to death. A man that the Justice system removes from the number of the living now belongs to the Bench. The Bench is sovereign: it answers to no one except its own conscience. The prison belongs to the Bench, where it is absolute master. Poetry recently took up this subject, so powerfully striking to the imagination, the *Condamné à mort*![30] Poetry has treated it sublimely, whereas prose has the real as its only resource, and yet the real is terrible enough to compete with lyricism. The life of a condemned man who has not admitted his crimes nor given up his accomplices is given up to terrible tortures. But these tortures are not the old ones of the boot that breaks the foot, nor of water pumped into the stomach, nor the distension of the limbs by ghastly machines—rather, this is the underhanded, one might even say negative, torture. The Bench leaves the condemned man entirely to himself, alone in the silence and the shadows, with a companion (a stool pigeon) he must distrust.

Our attractive modern philanthropy thinks that it is our age that discovered the horrible torture of isolation, but philanthropy is wrong.[31] Since the abolition of torture, the Bench, out of a natural desire to sooth the all-too-delicate consciences of juries, has learned about the terrible resource that solitude is, in terms of aiding Justice in its quest to elicit remorse. Solitude is a vacuum; and our moral nature has a natural abhorrence of a vacuum, just as physical nature does. Solitude is only habitable for the man of genius, who fills it up with his ideas, the daughters of the spiritual world, or for the contemplative, who finds it illuminated with the light of heaven and animated by the breath and the voice of God. But apart from those two kinds of people, both living so close to paradise, solitude is to torture what the mental is to the physical. The difference between solitude and torture is exactly the difference between a nervous malady and a surgical one: it multiplies the torment by infinity. The body approaches infinity via the nervous system, just as the mind does via thought. And so, in the annals of the Bench in Paris, the number of criminals who do not eventually confess can easily be counted.

This sinister situation, which takes on enormous proportions in certain cases, political ones for example, when the State or a dynasty is in question, will have its due treatment in the *Comédie humaine.*[32] But for now, our description of the box hewn out of stone in which, under the Restoration, the Paris Bench kept a prisoner who was condemned to death will suffice to suggest what the horror of the condemned man's last days must have been like.

Before the July Revolution, there existed, in the Conciergerie, and still exists today, a *condemned man's cell.* This cell backs up against the registry office, separated from it by a thick wall of hewn stone, and opposite to it is the wall, seven or eight feet thick, that supports one side of the great Pas-Perdus waiting room. You enter by the first door in the long, dark corridor, a corridor that attracts the eye from the middle of the vaulted hall. This sinister cell gets its light from a basement window, covered with formidable bars and barely visible from the entry point of the Conciergerie; it is placed in the narrow remaining space between the registry office's window, on the side of the wicket's grillwork, and the office of the Conciergerie clerk; the architect has tucked it in like a cupboard at the end of the entrance courtyard. Its situation explains why this little room, enclosed by four thick walls, was turned to its current funereal use when the Palais was reconstructed. Escape is simply impossible. The corridor leading to the solitary confinement cells and to the women's quarters ends at the big stove, where gendarmes and guards are constantly gathered. The basement window, the only outlet leading to the outside, is set nine feet above the flagstone floor and looks out upon the first courtyard, which is guarded by on-duty gendarmes staffing the entry gate to the Conciergerie. No human power could possibly breach those thick walls. In addition to all this, the condemned prisoner is put in a kind of straitjacket, which deprives him, as we know, of the use of his hands; moreover, he is chained to his camp bed; finally, he has, as his servant and guard, the informer. The floor of this cell is thick stones, and the light is so weak that one can barely see anything.

It is impossible not to feel a chill right down to the bones when entering this place even today, though the room has not served this purpose for some sixteen years now because of changes introduced in Paris concerning the procedures of the justice system. Imagine, reader, the criminal in the company only of his own remorse, in the silence and the darkness, two sources of horror, and ask yourself, Is this not enough to drive a man mad? What a constitution a man must have, what moral fiber to stand up to this treatment, and with the straitjacket too, adding the element of immobility!

Théodore Calvi, the twenty-seven-year-old Corsican, blanketed under the veils of absolute isolation for two months, had nonetheless resisted the effects of the solitary cell and the informer's endless yammering. The process by which the Corsican had come to be sentenced to capital punishment was an unusual one. Curious as it is, our analysis of it will be quite rapid.

It is impossible to take the reader on a lengthy digression at this point, near as we are to the denouement of a story that is already so long and that offers no interest beyond what happens to Jacques Collin, who is, so to speak, the vertebral column whose evil influence stitches together *Père Goriot* with *Lost Illusions,* and *Lost Illusions* with the present work. The reader's imagination in any case will be able to grasp this obscure matter quickly, which was causing, at the moment, a great deal of uneasiness among the jurors from the trial of Théodore Calvi. A week before, the criminal's appeal had been rejected by the court of appeals, and Monsieur de Granville's thoughts had been preoccupied with the subject, so much so that he had postponed the execution from day to day, hoping that he would be able to reassure the jurors that the condemned man, on the eve of his death, had finally admitted having done the crime.

A Remarkable Criminal Trial

A poor widow in Nanterre, whose house was located in an isolated district in that commune—which, as the reader knows, sits on an infertile plain stretching from Mont-Valérien and Saint-Germain,[33] between the hills of Sartrouville and d'Argenteuil—was murdered and robbed several days after receiving her share of an unexpected inheritance. Her part amounted to three thousand francs, a dozen silver place settings, a watch and chain, and some linen. Instead of depositing the three thousand francs in Paris, as was advised by the notary[34] representing the deceased wine merchant who left it to her, the old woman wanted to keep the whole sum with her. For one thing, she had never seen so much money, or had so much at one time, and then she distrusted everyone in every kind of business, as do most working-class and country people. After thinking it over and discussing it with a wine merchant in Nanterre, a relative of both her and the deceased man, the widow decided to use the money to set up an annuity for herself, to sell her Nanterre house, and to go live in Saint-Germain.

The house she lived in had a large garden attached to it, surrounded by a shabby fence; it was the kind of ignoble house that small farmers built for themselves outside Paris. The plaster and rubble stone that are so extremely abundant in Nanterre, a region covered with open quarries, had been constructed hastily and without the least architectural thought—as we see so often in the country around Paris. These places usually look like savage huts erected in the middle of a civilized country. The house consisted of a ground floor and an upper one, with an attic above.

The quarry worker, the woman's husband and the builder of the house, had installed solid iron bars in all the windows. The main door was solid, remarkably so. The deceased man knew he was alone out there in the country, and what country! His customers were major Paris builders, so most of what he sold was taken away by cart from his quarry, which stood only about five hundred paces away; the carts would return empty, and he chose many of the materials for his own house from demolition sites in Paris, bought them cheap, and brought them back in the carts. The windows, the ironwork, the doors, the shutters, the woodwork—all these came from authorized plundering, gifts his clients had offered him, and they were good gifts, well chosen. Presented with two window frames, he would choose the better one. The house, with a large yard and stables in front of it, was closed off from the road by a wall. A strong iron grating served as the gate. Guard dogs, moreover, lived in the stable, and one little dog lived inside the house. Behind the house stretched the garden, about a hectare in size.

When she was left a widow, and without children, the quarryman's wife lived on in the house with a single servant. She had sold off the quarry after his death, two years previous, which paid off the debts. All the widow needed was this house, where she raised chickens and cows, selling eggs and milk in Nanterre. No longer needing a stable boy or a driver or any of the other workers her deceased husband had kept busy around the place, she no longer cultivated the garden, instead simply picking the few herbs and vegetables that grew up naturally in the pebbly soil.

The price she would get for her house, together with the inheritance money, would amount to between seven and eight thousand francs, which would allow the woman to live comfortably in Saint-Germain, with an income of seven or eight hundred francs that she expected to get as an annuity from her eight thousand francs. She had already had a number of meetings with the notary of Saint-Germain, for she refused to surrender the money to the wine merchant to set up the annuity for her. This was the situation when, one day, nobody saw the widow Pigeau or her servant around. The courtyard gate, the main door to the house, the shutters, all were shut tight. After three days, the Law, informed of this strange state of things, descended upon the place. Monsieur Popinot, the examining magistrate, came out from Paris, accompanied by the prosecutor-general, and this is what they found.

There were no signs of any forced entry on the gate or the main door. The key was found in the door's lock, on the inside. None of the steel bars had been forced. All the locks, shutters, and fastenings were intact.

The walls provided no clues concerning the malefactor's entry. The chimneys gave no realistic access; no one could have gotten in that way. The roof ridges, sound and undamaged, suggested no violence. Proceeding into the bedrooms on the upper floor, the magistrates, the gendarmes, and Bibi-Lupin discovered the widow Pigeau strangled in her bed, and the servant strangled in hers, both with the neckerchiefs they wore at night. The three thousand francs had been taken, along with the silverware and jewels. The two bodies had begun to rot, as had those of the small house dog and a larger dog out in the courtyard. The fencing around the garden was examined, but showed no damage. In the garden itself, no footprints were found on the paths. The examining magistrate hypothesized that the murderer had walked only on the grass to avoid leaving footprints, if he in fact entered by that way, but how did he get in the house? The door on the garden side had a transom with three iron bars, all intact. On this side too, the key was found in the lock, just as with the front door.

Once these impossibilities had been attested to by Monsieur Popinot, by Bibi-Lupin, who stayed on an extra day to examine things, by the prosecutor-general himself, and by the police sergeant from Nanterre, the murder became a terrible problem that befuddled both the law and the political authorities.

This drama, written up and published in the *Gazette des tribunaux*, took place in the winter of 1828–29. God only knows how much interest this strange adventure aroused in Paris, but then Paris has new dramas to devour every morning, and Paris forgets all. The police, on the other hand, forget nothing. Three months after those first fruitless searches, a young prostitute attracted notice from Bibi-Lupin's agents by spending money very freely; they put her under surveillance because of her acquaintance with some thieves, and then she tried to get a friend to pawn the silverware and a gold watch. The friend refused. This came to the ears of Bibi-Lupin, who remembered the silverware and the gold watch and chain from the theft in Nanterre. Immediately, the various pawnbrokers and receivers of stolen goods in Paris were notified, and now Bibi-Lupin had Manon the Blonde under constant observation.

It soon became clear that Manon the Blonde was madly in love with a young man she rarely got to see, for he seemed to be deaf to the impassioned advances of blonde Manon. Mystery heaped upon mystery! The spies soon determined that the young man was an escaped convict, a celebrated hero of Corsican vendettas, the handsome Théodore Calvi, aka Madeleine.

One of the double-agent receivers of stolen goods, a man who worked with both thieves and the police, was dispatched to contact Théodore and offer to buy the silverware, along with the watch and gold chain. At ten-thirty that evening, the ironmonger from the Cour Saint-Guillaume was counting out the money for Théodore, who was disguised as a woman, and at that moment the police descended upon him and seized the goods.

The interrogation started up immediately. With such a feeble body of evidence, it would be impossible to get a death sentence, as the prosecutor-general wished. Calvi never contradicted himself. He never gave himself away, claiming now that a woman from the countryside had sold him the items in Argenteuil and that, after he had bought them, the news of the murder committed in Nanterre made it clear to him how dangerous possessing this silverware, this watch, and these jewels was; the inventory taken upon the death of the widow Pigeau's uncle, the wine merchant, listed the items, establishing that these were in fact the stolen items. Finally, he said, forced by poverty into selling the items, he had tried to get some noncompromised person to do it for him.

They could get nothing more out of the convict, whose silence and firm assurance led them to believe that the wine merchant in Nanterre had committed the crime, and that the woman from whom he had bought the items was the merchant's wife. So the widow Pigeau's unfortunate relative and his wife were arrested; but after a week's detention and a scrupulous investigation, it was established that neither the husband nor the wife had left their establishment at the time of the crime. Moreover, Calvi did not recognize the wine-dealer's wife as the person who had sold him the silverware and jewels.

Because Calvi's mistress, who was involved in the investigation, was known to have spent about a thousand francs between the time of the crime and the day that Calvi tried to sell the silverware and jewels, such evidence appeared sufficient for both the convict and the mistress to go to trial. This murder was the eighteenth committed by Théodore, and he was condemned to death, for he seemed to be the author of this crime, which had been so skillfully executed. Though he didn't recognize the Nanterre wine merchant, he was recognized by both the husband and the wife. The interrogation had established, through numerous witnesses, that Théodore had stayed in Nanterre for about a month; he had done some work for masons there, his face covered with plaster dust, and poorly dressed. Everyone in Nanterre guessed the boy was about eighteen, and he must have been *nursing this baby* (plotting the crime) for a month.

The Bench believed there had been accomplices. They measured the chimney flue to see whether Manon the Blonde could have gotten in that way; but even a child of six could not fit down the red-clay chimney that modern architecture favored, at the expense of the much larger chimneys of earlier times. If it hadn't been for this singular, frustrating mystery, Théodore would have been executed within a week. The prison's chaplain had, as we've seen, failed completely with him.

This case and the name of Calvi must have escaped the attention of Jacques Collin, preoccupied at the time with his duel with Contenson, Corentin, and Peyrade. Deathcheater, in any case, wanted to stay as far from his old pals as he could, not to mention anything involving the Palais de Justice. He trembled at the thought of any encounter that would have put him face to face with a fanandel or a boss who might have demanded a financial accounting that he would have been unable to provide.

Charlot

The Conciergerie warden went quickly to the office of the prosecutor-general, where he found the chief prosecutor conversing with Monsieur de Granville, the order for execution in his hand. Monsieur de Granville, who had just spent the whole night at the de Sérisy house, was heavily fatigued and depressed, for the doctors still dared not say whether Madame de Sérisy would recover her reason, and he was obliged by this sudden execution to return to doing the prosecutor's business. After having talked for a while with the warden, Monsieur de Granville took the execution order from his chief lawyer and handed it to Gault.

"Let the execution proceed," he said, "unless some unusual circumstance crops up, which you can determine—I trust your prudence. You can put off assembling the scaffold until ten-thirty, which gives you an hour. On a morning like this, hours feel like centuries, and a lot can happen in a century! Don't let him hope for any reprieve. Get him shaved and dressed, if need be, and if nothing extraordinary happens, send the order to Sanson at nine-thirty. Have him be at the ready!"

When the warden left the prosecutor-general's office, he ran into Monsieur Camusot below the arched passage that leads to the gallery; Camusot was on his way to the prosecutor's office. The warden had a short conversation with the examining magistrate, and after bringing him up to date on Jacques Collin, he went down to set up the meeting between Deathcheater and Madeleine, but he did not let the self-styled ecclesiastic have any communication with the condemned man until Bibi-Lupin, admirably disguised as a gendarme, had replaced the informer who was keeping watch over the Corsican.

It would be difficult to imagine the profound astonishment felt by the three convicts when they saw a guard come to get Jacques Collin to bring him to the condemned man's cell. They rushed over as one to crowd around the chair where Jacques Collin was seated.

"It's for today, then, right, Monsieur Julien?" Silk Thread asked the guard.

"Naturally. Charlot is there already," replied the guard with utter indifference.

This is what the inhabitants of the prisons call the Paris executioner, the sobriquet dating from 1789.[35] The name now produced an intense reaction. All the prisoners stopped and looked at each other.

"It's all settled!" the guard continued. "The order for the execution was delivered to Monsieur Gault, and the sentence was just read out."

"So," said La Pouraille, "the lovely Madeleine has received all the sacraments?" And he swallowed a deep gulp of air.

"Poor little Théodore . . ." cried Biffon. "He's such a sweet guy. He's too young to *sneeze in the sawdust.* . . ."

The guard walked over toward the wicket, thinking he was accompanied by Jacques Collin; but the Spaniard was moving slowly, and when he was about ten feet back from Julien, he seemed to weaken suddenly, and with a gesture asked for La Pouraille's arm.

"That one's a murderer!" exclaimed Napolitas to the priest, pointing to La Pouraille and offering his own arm.

"No, for me he's simply a poor unfortunate!" replied Deathcheater, with perfect presence of mind and all the unction of the Archbishop of Cambrai.

And he separated himself from Napolitas, having seen something suspicious about him from first sight.

"He's on the first step to Climb-up Abbey, but I'm the prior of the abbey! I'm going to show you all how to *get over on the Stork* (defeat the prosecutor). I plan to rip this little sorbonne right out of his claws."

"And all for the sake of what's in his pants!"[36] said Silk Thread with a smile.

"I wish to save this soul for heaven!" Jacques Collin replied solemnly, seeing himself surrounded by a number of prisoners.

And he turned to catch up with the guard at the wicket.

"He's here to save Madeleine," said Silk Thread. "We guessed right. Ah, what a boss!"

"But how? The guillotine hussars are there, and he won't be able to see him alone," said Biffon.

"He's got the baker on his side!" cried La Pouraille. "Ha!—him get sticky-fingered with our coins! . . . He loves his pals too much! He needs us too much. They wanted us to *rat him out*, but we aren't *a bunch of punks*! If he does manage to snatch off his Madeleine, I'll *blab* to him (tell him where my loot is)."

This last expression only fanned the flame of devotion that the three convicts felt for their god; for at this moment, their famous boss had become the embodiment of all their hopes.

Jacques Collin, despite the danger Madeleine was facing, did not let his mask slip. This man, who knew the Conciergerie as well as he did the three prison colonies, took wrong turns in so natural a manner that right up until they reached the office the guard was constantly saying to him, "This way—over here!" Once there, Jacques Collin saw at once, leaning by the stove, a tall, fat man whose long red visage did not lack a certain distinction, and he recognized Sanson.

"Ah, monsieur is the chaplain," he said, going up to him with a friendly air.

This was so horrific an error that it froze the spectators.

"No, monsieur; I perform other functions," said Sanson.

Sanson, father of the last public executioner of the same name, for he has been dismissed recently, was the son of the man who executed Louis XVI.[37]

After exercising this duty for four centuries, the heir to so many torturers was tempted to repudiate this hereditary burden. The Sansons, executioners in Rouen for two centuries before being promoted to the first rank of their field in the kingdom, had been executing the decrees of justice down through the generations since the thirteenth century. Few families can match this example of maintaining an office or a nobility and passing it down from father to son for six centuries. At the moment when the young man, who had become a captain in the cavalry, saw before him a fine future in the military, his father demanded that he come and help him with the execution of the king. Then he was made his father's second-in-command when, in 1793, two permanent scaffolds were erected—one at the Throne barrier, and the other at the Place de Grève. Aged now about sixty, this terrible functionary was remarkable for being extremely well dressed, with quiet, elegant manners, and for his contempt for Bibi-Lupin and his acolytes, the men who fed the machine. The only trait that betrayed him as a member of the old tribe of torturers from the Middle Ages was the formidable thickness and width of his hands. Reasonably well educated, serious about his duties as a citizen and elector, obsessed (people said) with gardening, this large, fat man with his low voice, his calm manner, his reticence, his high forehead with receding hairline, much more closely resembled a member of the English aristocracy than a public executioner. And so a Spanish priest might well have made the mistake unwittingly that Jacques Collin had made on purpose.

"That's no convict," said the head guard to the warden.

"I'm beginning to believe it," Monsieur Gault thought, nodding to his subordinate.

The Confession

Jacques Collin was taken into the cellarlike room where the young Théodore in his straitjacket was seated on the edge of an appalling camp bed. Deathcheater, momentarily illuminated by the light from the corridor, recognized Bibi-Lupin immediately in the gendarme who remained standing, leaning on his saber.

"Io sono Gaba-Morto! Parla nostro italiano," said Jacques Collin immediately. "Vengo ti salvar." (I am Deathcheater; let's speak our version of Italian; I've come to save you.)

Everything the two friends would say to each other would thus be unintelligible to the phony gendarme, and since Bibi-Lupin was supposedly there to guard the prisoner, he could not simply leave his post. The rage of the head of the Sûreté can only be imagined.

Théodore Calvi, a young man of a pale, olive-tinted complexion, with blond hair and deep-set, cloudy blue eyes but powerfully built, with a prodigious muscular force hidden behind that apparently lymphatic appearance so common in southerners, would have had the most charming face if it were not for those arched eyebrows and that low forehead, both suggesting something sinister, and if it were not for those red lips with their savage cruelty, and those muscles that denote the Corsican tendency to irritability, which explains their readiness to kill when they get into a fight.

Astonished to hear that voice, Théodore abruptly raised his head, thinking he might be having a hallucination; but having grown accustomed to the dark after two months of living in this cell hewn out of rock, he gazed upon the false ecclesiastic and emitted a deep sigh. He did not recognize Jacques Collin, whose face had been so scarred by sulfuric acid that it no longer seemed to be the face of his old boss.

"It's really me, your Jacques—I'm dressed up as a priest, and I've come to save you. Be smart, don't recognize me, and act as if you're making your confession."

This was said very rapidly.

"This young man is very dejected. He's afraid of dying, so he'll make a full confession," Jacques Collin said to the gendarme.

"Tell me something that proves you're really *him*—all you've got is his voice."

"Ah, you see, the poor wretch just told me that he's innocent," Jacques Collin said to the gendarme.

Bibi-Lupin dared not speak for fear of being recognized.

"Semprimi!" replied Jacques, turning back to Théodore, whispering the password in his ear.

"Sempriti!" said the young man, giving the password's reply. "So it really is my boss . . ."

"Did you do the crime?"

"Yes."

"Tell me all about it, while I figure out how I'm going to save you—and we need to do it now, because Charlot is already here."

And so the Corsican got down on his knees, seeming to want to confess. Bibi-Lupin was at a total loss, for the conversation went by more swiftly than the time it takes to read it. Théodore quickly ran through the already-known circumstances of the crime, though they were unknown to Jacques Collin.

"The jury found me guilty without evidence," he said in conclusion.

"My boy, you're arguing while they're coming to give you the final haircut!"

"But I could be charged with the attempt to sell the jewels. That's all. And there you see how they come to a judgment, and in Paris no less!"

"But how did you manage to do it?" asked Deathcheater.

"Well! Look—since you and I separated, I got acquainted with a little Corsican girl I met when I got to Pantin [Paris]."

"A man stupid enough to fall for a woman," exclaimed Jacques Collin, "always ends up dying for it! They're tigers roaming free, tigers that baby-talk and stare at themselves in mirrors. . . . Not so smart on your part."

"But . . ."

"Go on. What good did your damned largue do you?"

"That love of a woman, about as tall as a stick and skinny as an eel, slippery as a monkey, got in through the oven flue, and then she opened the door for me. The dogs ate some poisoned meatballs and dropped dead. I *iced* the two women. Once we got the loot, Ginetta locked up the door and climbed back up out of the oven."

"Good plan—good enough to deserve a life," said Jacques Collin, admiring the way the crime was done, the way a sculptor admires the modeling of a statuette.

"I was stupid to use all that talent for a measly thousand écus!"

"No, for a woman!" replied Jacques Collin. "And I told you how they make us stupid!"

And he gave Théodore a look dripping with scorn.

"But you weren't there!" replied the Corsican. "I was abandoned."

"Well, so, do you love this girl?" asked Jacques Collin, sensitive to the reproach.

"Ah, if I still want to live, it's for you more than for her."

"Rest easy! They don't call me Deathcheater for nothing. I'll see to it!"

"You mean it? Life?" cried the young Corsican, raising his straitjacketed arms up toward the damp vaulted ceiling of the cell.

"My little Madeleine, get ready to go back to the meadow for life," replied Jacques Collin. "You'll have to wait; they aren't going to give you a crown of roses, like an ox for the sacrifice! . . . If they've already got us *chained up* for Rochefort, it's because they just want to get rid of us! But I'll get you transferred to Toulon, and from there you'll escape and make your way back to Pantin, where I'll have a sweet little life all arranged for you. . . ."

A sigh like few ever exhaled beneath that inflexible vault, a sigh breathed out in the joy of deliverance, went forth and bumped up against the rock surface, which echoed it back like a note music never reached and into the ear of Bibi-Lupin, who stood there stupefied.

"You hear the effects of the absolution I've just promised him because of what he told me," Jacques Collin explained to the head of the Sûreté. "These Corsicans, *monsieur le gendarme,* are so filled with faith! But this one is as innocent as the Baby Jesus, and I'm going to try to save him. . . ."

"May God be with you, *monsieur l'abbé!*" said Théodore, in French.

Deathcheater, now more Carlos Herrera, more priest than ever, left the condemned man's cell, hurrying out into the corridor, pretending to be horrified as he approached Monsieur Gault.

"Monsieur warden, this young man is innocent; he's told me who the guilty party really is! . . . He's about to die for a false point of honor—that's a Corsican for you! Please go back to the prosecutor-general and ask him to give me five minutes. Monsieur de Granville will not refuse an immediate audience with a Spanish priest who's suffering so much from the mistakes of French justice!"

"I'm on my way!" replied Monsieur Gault, to the great surprise of all those who were spectators of the extraordinary scene.

"But," Jacques Collin continued, "please have me escorted back into the prison yard while I'm waiting, because I hope to complete the conversion of a criminal there whose heart I believe I've already softened. . . . And they do have hearts, these people!"

This speech stirred everyone who was there to hear it. The gendarmes, the prison registry clerk, Sanson, the guards, the executioner's assistants, who were waiting for the order to begin setting up the machine, as they say in prison—all these men, so rarely open to any feeling, were moved by curiosity, as can well be imagined.

In Which Mademoiselle Collin Enters the Scene

At that moment a ruckus could be heard outside, as a carriage with superb horses was pulling up outside the gates of the Conciergerie, on the quay, with what appeared to be the greatest importance. The carriage door was opened, and the steps were unfolded and lowered so adroitly that everyone assumed some grand personage had arrived. Then a lady emerged, waving a blue sheet of paper and, accompanied by a footman and a valet, proceeded at once to the wicket. Dressed entirely in black, in magnificent black, her hat covered by a veil, she was wiping away tears with a large embroidered handkerchief.

Jacques Collin at once recognized Asia, or, to give this woman her real name, Jacqueline Collin, his aunt. The hideous old woman, quite worthy of her nephew, all her thoughts concentrated on the prisoner she was defending with an intelligence, a perspicacity at least the equal of those on the side of the justice system, was carrying a permit, made out the preceding evening by the personal maid of the Duchesse de Maufrigneuse, on the recommendation of Monsieur de Sérisy, to meet with Lucien and the abbé Carlos Herrera as soon as they were released from solitary confinement, upon which the divisional chief in charge of prisons had added his own note. This sheet of paper by its color alone implied powerful influence; for permits, like the complimentary tickets theaters hand out, vary in their appearance.

At the sight of the paper, the guard opened the wicket, though he was just as impressed by the valet in his feathered green and gold livery, brilliant as the valet of a Russian general, implying that this was an aristocratic visitor, even a quasi-royal one.

"Ah, my dear abbé!" cried the false great lady, who burst into a torrent of tears upon catching sight of the ecclesiastic. "How could they have put you here, even for an instant—such a holy man!"

The warden took the permit and read: *Upon the recommendation of His Excellency the Comte de Sérisy.*

"Ah, Madame de San-Esteban, *madame la marquise,*" said Carlos Herrera, "what splendid devotion!"

"Madame, we should not have communication with prisoners in this manner," said the decent old Gault.

And he blocked the passage of that mass of black moiré silk and lace.

"But at such a distance!" said Jacques Collin. "And in front of all you? ..." he added, looking around at the group circling them.

The aunt, whose clothing must have stunned the clerk, the warden, the guards and the gendarmes, exuded a musky scent. She was wearing, besides lace that was worth a thousand écus, a black cashmere shawl that cost six thousand francs. The valet paraded around the Conciergerie courtyard with the insolence of a lackey who knows he is indispensable to a demanding princess. He didn't deign to speak with the footman, who took up his station at the iron gate, which always remained open during the day.

"What do you want me to do?" asked Madame de San-Esteban in the coded language used by aunt and nephew.

As we have already seen in "A Drama in the Prisons,"[38] this argot consisted in adding an *ar* or an *or,* an *al* or an *i* to words so as to disfigure the word by lengthening it, whether the word was proper French or slang. It was a kind of diplomatic code applied to spoken language.

"Put all the letters in a safe place, and take out the ones most compromising to the two women; then come back to the Pas-Perdus hall looking like a street thief, then wait there for my orders."

Asia, or Jacqueline, knelt as if to receive a blessing, and the false abbé blessed his aunt with suitably evangelical style.

"Addio, marchesa!" he said out loud. Then, returning to their coded language, he added, "Find Europe and Paccard with the seven hundred and fifty thousand they poached—we need them."

"Paccard is right over there," replied the pious marquise, indicating the valet with tears in her eyes.

Such perfect understanding drew not only a smile but even a little gesture of surprise from the man who could ever only be surprised by his aunt. The false marquise turned to the onlookers with the air of a woman who understood her status perfectly well.

"The poor man is in despair because he cannot attend the funeral of his child," she said to them in broken French. "Yes, I know all about this holy man's secret, and about this terrible miscarriage of justice! . . . I will attend the funeral Mass. Here, monsieur," she said to Monsieur Gault, handing him a purse filled with gold, "this is for the relief of the poor prisoners. . . ."

"Excellent touch!" her satisfied nephew whispered to her.

Jacques Collin followed his guard back to the prison yard.

Bibi-Lupin, in despair, had finally managed to get the attention of another, a real, gendarme by frequent "ahems!" The gendarme replaced him in the condemned man's cell, but the enemy of Deathcheater was too late to witness the great lady, who was whisked off in her brilliant coach and whose voice, though disguised, carried its hoarse whisky tones to his ears.

"Three hundred big ones for the detainees!" exclaimed the head guard, showing Bibi-Lupin the purse that Monsieur Gault had given to his clerk.

"Show me, Monsieur Jacomety," said Bibi-Lupin.

The chief of the Sûreté police took the purse, emptied the gold coins into his hand, and examined them carefully.

"It's gold, all right!" he said. "And the purse has her coat of arms on it! Oh, this scoundrel is good! Thinks of everything! He's got us all in the palm of his hand, every time! . . . He ought to be shot down like a dog!"

"What's the matter?" asked the clerk, taking the purse back.

"The matter? The matter is that woman's nothing but a *thief*!" cried Bibi-Lupin, stamping his foot on the flagstones next to the wicket in a fit of rage.

These words produced a strong sensation among the onlookers, grouped at a comfortable distance from Sanson, who remained standing all through the scene, his back leaning against the large stove at the center of the vast, vaulted room, awaiting an order to get the criminal shaved and to erect his scaffold on the Place de Grève.

A Seduction

Finding himself back in the prison yard, Jacques Collin directed his steps toward his pals, with the gait of a longtime prison denizen.

"What's eating you?" he asked La Pouraille.

"I'm finished," said the murderer, as Jacques Collin led off into a corner. "So now I need a *real* pal."

"Why?"

La Pouraille, after having told his chief all his crimes, using argot, finished by giving him the details of the murders and theft of the Crottat couple.

"I admire the job," said Jacques Collin. "You did it well, but I think you made one slip."

"Which was?"

"Once the business was over, you should have had a Russian passport, had yourself got up as a Russian prince, bought a nice carriage with a coat of arms on it, gone boldly to deposit the gold with a banker, gotten a letter of credit for Hamburg, taken a valet, a chambermaid, and your mistress all got up as a princess, and gone there quickly. Then, in Hamburg, taken a ship to Mexico. With two hundred eighty thousand francs in gold, a clever boy can do what he likes, and go where he likes, you sap!"

"Ah, you have ideas like that, because you're the boss! . . . You never lose your sorbonne, you! Not like me."

"Well, giving advice now in your situation—might as well be offering soup to a corpse," said Jacques Collin, casting his mesmerizing gaze at his fanandel.

"Right enough!" said La Pouraille, but with doubt in his voice. "But, you know, offer me some anyway, that soup of yours; if I can't eat it, I can use it to wash my feet. . . ."

"Here you are, nabbed by the Stork, with five aggravated thefts, three murders, the most recent of which were two wealthy bourgeois. Juries don't like it when you kill bourgeois. They'll bale you up and feed you to the machine. No hope!"

"Yeah, they told me all that," La Pouraille said pitifully.

"My aunt Jacqueline, with whom I just had a little chat right there in the office—you know her, she's the mama to the fanandels—she told me the Stork really wants to be done with you, because you scare it too much."

"But—" La Pouraille said, with a naïveté that proves just how much thieves are steeped in a sense that they have a natural right to steal—"I'm rich now, so what are they afraid of?"

"No time for philosophy," said Jacques Collin. "Let's get back to your situation."

"What do you want from me?" asked La Pouraille, interrupting his boss.

"You'll see! Even a dead dog is worth something."

"For somebody else, sure!" said La Pouraille.

"I'll take you into my game!" replied Jacques Collin.

"Well, that's something!" said the murderer. "And then?"

"I'm not asking where your money is, but what do you want done with it?"

La Pouraille stared at the impenetrable face of the boss, who continued impassively.

"Is there some largue you're in love with, or maybe some kid, or some fanandel you want to help out? I'm going to be out in an hour, and I can take care of anybody you want to help."

La Pouraille still hesitated, hanging fire with indecision. Jacques Collin tried one final argument.

"Your share in our funds comes to thirty thousand francs, so do you want to leave it to the fanandels or give it to somebody? Your share is guaranteed—I can hand it over this evening to anybody you tell me."

The murderer inadvertently gave a little start of pleasure.

"I've got him now!" thought Jacques Collin. He continued, speaking quietly into La Pouraille's ear: "Let's not waste time, so think about it! We've only got about ten minutes, old friend. . . . The prosecutor-general is going to call me in for a conference. I've got him, that man, and I can wring the Stork's neck! I'm sure I'm going to be able to save Madeleine."

"If you save Madeleine, my good old boss, how about me . . ."

"Don't waste your breath," said Jacques Collin, cutting him off. "Make your will."

"Well," La Pouraille replied, in a pitiful tone of voice, "I guess I'd like to give the money to Gonore."

"Really? So you were living with Moses' widow, that Jew who was running with the *rouletiers* in the south?"[39] asked Jacques Collin.

Like the great generals, Deathcheater had a commendably thorough knowledge of all the personnel in all the various troops.

"That's the one," said La Pouraille, highly flattered.

"Pretty girl!" said Jacques Collin, who knew very well how to manage the kind of trap he was setting. "That's one beauty of a largue! She knows everybody, and she does things right! And what a thief, too. Ah, so you got involved with Gonore! Stupid to get yourself arrested when you've got a largue like that. Idiot! You should have gone in for some honest little business, and live the good life! But what's her game now?"

"She got herself set up on the Rue Sainte-Barbe, running a house there. . . ."

"So, you want her to be your heir? Well, that's where they always lead us, these sluts, when we're dumb enough to fall for them."

"Yeah—but don't give her anything till they've popped me."

"Sacred duty," said Jacques Collin in a solemn tone. "Nothing for the fanandels?"

"Nothing—they're the ones squealed on me," La Pouraille said with hatred.

"Who sold you out? Want me to get your revenge?" asked Jacques Collin with feeling, trying to awaken in La Pouraille that last sentiment, the one that makes hearts like these thrill at the supreme moment. "Who knows, old friend—maybe I could get you some vengeance and at the same time make your peace with the Stork?"

The murderer stared at his boss, overwhelmed with happiness.

"But," the boss continued, as if in reply to that eloquent physiognomy, "right now I've got to concentrate on springing Théodore. But once this little piece of vaudeville is complete, well, when it comes to a friend— and you *are* my friend!—I'm capable of doing any number of things."

"If you can get that nasty ceremony for poor little Théodore postponed, look, I'll do anything you want."

"But it's already done—I'm definitely going to spring his sorbonne out of the Stork's claws. You know, La Pouraille, if you want to get out of a pit like this, you need to give others a hand too. . . . Nobody can do it by himself."

"You got that right!" cried the murderer.

His trust had by now been so firmly established, and his faith in his boss had become so fanatical, that La Pouraille hesitated no more.

Last Incarnation

La Pouraille went on to tell the secret of who his accomplices had been, a secret he had so carefully kept until now. This was all Jacques Collin wanted to know.

"So here's the scoop! On that little game, Ruffard, one of Bibi-Lupin's agents, was the third, along with me and Godet . . ."

"Woolripper?" cried Jacques Collin, using Ruffard's thieving alias.

"That's the one. Those crooks sold me out because I knew where their stash is and they don't know mine."

"Oh, my good friend, you're just giving my boots a shine!" said Jacques Collin.

"What do you mean?"

"Well, just look and see what you gain when you put your trust in me!" replied the boss. "Now your revenge is part of the game I'm putting together. . . . I'm not asking you where your stash is, tell me that at the last minute; but do tell me everything you can about Ruffard and Godet."

"You are, and you'll always be, our boss! I've got no secrets from you," replied La Pouraille. "My loot is in the *deep* (the cellar) of Gonore's house."

"You're not worried about your largue? Not at all?"

"Come on! No, she didn't even know I was messing around down there!" said La Pouraille. "I got her drunk—but anyway, she's a woman who wouldn't talk if her head was in the guillotine. But it's a lot of gold!"

"Yes, that's the kind of thing that'll tempt the purest!" replied Jacques Collin.

"So I was able to do the work without anybody eyeballing me! All the hens were upstairs on their roosts. The gold is buried three feet deep, over behind the wine bottles. And I put a layer of stones and mortar over it."

"Good!" said Jacques Collin. "And the others—where are their stashes?"

"Ruffard's heap is at Gonore's too, in the poor woman's bedroom. It's his way of having a hold on her, turning her into an accomplice, a receiver, so she'd end her days at Saint-Lazare."

"Oh, damn him! This is how the *bloodhounds* (the police) turn us into thieves!" said Jacques.

"Godet hid his heap at his sister's—she does laundry, the better stuff, an honest girl, might end up drawing five years in the Ors-fay.[40] The fanandel pulled up the floorboards, put them back down, and flew the coop."

"Know what I want from you?" said Jacques Collin, focusing his mesmerizing gaze on La Pouraille.

"What?"

"Take the fall for Madeleine's job. . . ."

La Pouraille jumped back abruptly, but he promptly reassumed his posture of obedience under the intense, fixed gaze of his boss.

"You're bucking and rearing already! I want you in my game! Look—four murders or three, what's the difference?"

"Maybe . . ."

"Oh, by the God of Thieves, you've got *water in your vermicelli* (no blood in your veins)! And here I was thinking I'd save you. . . ."

"But how?"

"Idiot! If we promised to give the gold back to the family, you'll only get life, you'll get gray on the big meadow. I wouldn't give a sou for your sorbonne otherwise, but right now you're worth seven hundred thousand francs, you idiot!"

"O, Boss, Boss!" cried La Pouraille, bursting with happiness.

"And," Jacques Collin went on, "we can even pin the murders on Ruffard. . . . And that'd be a smack in the head to Bibi-Lupin—I've got him!"

The idea left La Pouraille stupefied, and he stood like a statue, his eyes wide. He had been arrested three months before, just prior to his court appearance, and all his pals at La Force had given him their advice; he never gave up his accomplices, but he became so bitterly hopeless after his interrogation that a scheme like this one would never have occurred to his depressed mental powers. Thus, this little ray of hope rendered him practically imbecilic with happiness.

"Ruffard and Godet have already started their party, I suppose? Have they gone out tossing money around in public?" asked Jacques Collin.

"They don't dare," said La Pouraille. "Those clowns are waiting to hear my head's off. That's what I heard—my largue sent a message by Biffe, when she came to see Biffon."

"Well, we're going to have their stashes within twenty-four hours!" exclaimed Jacques Collin. "Those fools won't be able to do restitution, like you—you're going to be white as snow, and they'll be red as blood! I'm going to turn you into an innocent boy, led astray by them. I'll have your money to buy alibis for your other charges, and once you're back on the meadow, because that's where you'll be going, you'll figure out how to escape. . . . It's a lousy life, but at least it's life!"

La Pouraille's eyes betrayed his inner delirium.

"Old pal! With seven hundred thousand francs, you can buy as many heads as you need!" said Jacques Collin, getting his fanandel drunk on hopes.

"Oh, Boss! Boss!"

"I'll dazzle the minister of justice . . . Oh, Ruffard's going to dance— we're going to demolish that one. . . . Bibi-Lupin is toast."

"Well, that's it then!" exclaimed La Pouraille with savage joy. "You give the orders, I obey."

He caught Jacques Collin in his arms, letting him see the tears of joy in his eyes now that he thought it would be possible to save his head.

"That's not all," said Jacques Collin. "The Stork has digestion problems, especially when the *fever goes up* (when the revelation of a new fact leads to new charges). So now we need to *frame some largue* [get a woman charged in the case]."

"How? And what for?" asked the murderer.

"Just help me! You'll see!" Deathcheater replied.

Jacques Collin quickly told La Pouraille the secret concerning the

Nanterre crime, making him understand the necessity of getting a woman to play the role that Ginetta had played. Then he walked over to Biffon, followed by the now-joyous La Pouraille.

"I know how much you love your Biffe . . ." Jacques Collin said to Biffon.

The look Biffon gave him was a kind of horrible poem in itself.

"What will she do while you're out on the meadow?"

A tear swelled in the fierce eyes of Biffon.

"Well, what if I were to get her into *Ors-fay for largues* (the La Force for women, the prison known as Les Madelonnettes, or Saint-Lazare), for a year, about the time it'll take you to get settled, figure things out, and make your escape?"

"You can't do miracles. There's *zip on her* (she has no complicity in any crime)," replied the lover of La Biffe.

"Ah, Biffon, our boss can do as many miracles as God," said La Pouraille.

"What's your password with her?" Jacques Collin asked Biffon with the assurance of a master unaccustomed to being refused.

"*Sorgue in Pantin* (night in Paris). Use that, and she'll know you've come from me, and if you want her to obey you, show her a five-baller (a five-franc coin), and say this: *'Tondif!'*"[41]

"She'll get her sentence during La Pouraille's trial, and they'll let her out for informing after a year," said Jacques Collin sententiously, looking at La Pouraille.

La Pouraille understood his boss's plan, and with a look he made a promise to get Biffon to cooperate and have La Biffe pretend complicity in the crime.

"Good-bye then, kids. You're going to hear pretty soon that I managed to save my little one from the hands of Charlot," said Deathcheater. "Oh yes, Charlot was there at the office, with all his little handmaidens, ready to give Madeleine one last haircut! Oh, wait," he said. "They're coming to look for me, on the orders of the *Boss Stork* (the prosecutor-general)."

In fact, a guard had come through the wicket, signaling to this exceptional man, for whom the danger his young Corsican faced had been enough to restore all his savage strength and return him to the thick of his battle against society.

It will not be without interest to observe that at the moment Lucien's body was taken away from him, Jacques Collin made a decision, with supreme resolution, to attempt one final incarnation, this time not as a living creature but as a thing. He had taken the same final step that Napoleon took when he stepped onto the boat that took him to the

Bellerophon.[42] By a strange combination of circumstances, everything came together to aid this evil genius in his corrupt enterprise.

But even though the unexpected denouement of this criminal life will thereby lose a little of the sheen of the marvelous—for the marvelous, in our day, can only be achieved by the writer's abandoning all verisimilitude—still it is necessary, before we follow Jacques Collin into the office of the general prosecutor, to follow Madame Camusot to the homes she was visiting while all these events were transpiring at the Conciergerie. The historian who would depict the customs of our day has certain obligations that must never be shirked, one of which is never to spoil the truth by introducing supposedly dramatic circumstances, especially when the truth has taken the trouble to become just like a novel. The nature of human society, in Paris above all, comprises so many chance events, so many convolutions, so much conjecture, so much caprice, that it entirely surpasses anything the imagination of the writer could come up with. Truth is so bold that it rises to combinations forbidden to art because they are so improbable, or so indecent, that the writer has to find ways to tone them down, to prune them, to neuter them.

Madame Camusot's First Visit

Madame Camusot tried to dress and present herself in such a way that morning as to appear a model of good taste, a difficult thing to do for the wife of an examining magistrate who, up until the past six years, had always lived in the provinces. The great point was not to allow any room for critique from the gaze of the Marquise d'Espard nor that of the Duchesse de Maufrigneuse when coming to see them between eight and nine in the morning. Amélie-Cécile Camusot, though, we hasten to add, née Thirion, was half successful. But when it comes to clothes, doesn't that amount to a double blunder?

Many fail to realize how useful Parisian women are to the ambitious, in no matter what field; they are as necessary in the higher reaches of society as they are in the world of the thieves, where, as we have seen, they play an enormous role. For example, imagine a man who, on pain of being left behind in the arena, urgently needs to speak with that personage, so formidable during the Restoration, known as the keeper of the seals. Imagine our man is someone in a position that would seem most favorable to such a goal, a magistrate, someone who is even a familiar presence in the keeper's realm. The magistrate is obliged to go find either a division chief or a particular secretary or even the general secretary and to make his argument to them that his need for an audience is urgent. Can a keeper of the seals always be available on the spot? In the middle of the day, if he's not in the Chamber, he's in council with some state ministers, or he's signing documents, or he's already in audience with others. In the morning no one is sure where he has spent the night; in the evening he has both public and personal obligations. If every magistrate were to claim their private time with the keeper, for whatever reasons, the head of the justice system would be under perpetual siege. The justification for this particular, immediate audience must therefore be submitted to one of the intermediary powers, who thus become sometimes an obstacle, sometimes the opening of a door, and who are themselves the objects of competition. But a woman, ah! She can seek out another woman; she can enter into others' bedrooms immediately, arousing curiosity in both mistress and chambermaid, especially when the mistress is involved in some grand strategy serving someone's interest, or is weighted down by some personal necessity. Let us instance the female power known as the Marquise d'Espard, with whom ministers must come to terms; such a woman simply jots a little note on perfumed paper and has her valet deliver it to the minister's valet. The note is there to greet the minister as he awakens, and he reads it at once. While the minister has his business to attend to, the man is delighted to have to pay a visit to one of these queens of Paris, one of these powers of the Faubourg Saint-Germain, one of these favorites of Madame or the dauphine or the king. Casimir Périer, the only real prime minister following the July Revolution, dropped everything to go visit a former first gentleman of the bedchamber of King Charles X.[43]

This background will help explain the effect of the words spoken to the Marquise d'Espard by her chambermaid, the latter assuming the former was in fact awake: "Madame, Madame Camusot, on an extremely urgent matter, according to madame!"

The marquise exclaimed that Amélie was to be admitted immediately. The magistrate's wife had the marquise's full attention when she opened with this:

"*Madame la marquise,* we're all ruined through trying to avenge you. . . ."

"What are you saying, my pretty friend?" replied the marquise, looking at Madame Camusot in the shadowy light of the half-opened door. "Ah, you look divine this morning in that little hat. Where do you find shapes like that?"

"Oh, madame, you're so kind. . . . But you know that the manner in which Camusot interrogated Lucien de Rubempré reduced that young man to despair, and that he's hanged himself in his prison cell. . . ."

"What will become of Madame de Sérisy?" cried the marquise, playing ignorant in order to hear the whole tale all over again.

"Alas, they think she's lost her mind," replied Amélie. "But if you could see if His Highness would send for my husband by special messenger, the minister will learn of some strange mysteries, which will surely interest the king . . . Then Camusot's enemies would be reduced to silence."

"Who are Camusot's enemies?" asked the marquise.

"Well, the prosecutor-general, and now Monsieur de Sérisy . . ."

"Good, my little friend," said Madame d'Espard. It was to Messieurs de Granville and de Sérisy that she owed her defeat in her suit to have her husband declared mentally unfit. "I'll defend you. I never forget my friends, nor my enemies."

She rang and had the curtains opened, and daylight flooded into the room; she asked for her writing desk, and the chambermaid brought it. The marquise quickly jotted down a little note.

"So, mysterious things are afoot?" asked Madame d'Espard. "Tell me about them, dear. I take it Clotilde de Grandlieu is not mixed up in this affair?"

"*Madame la marquise* will hear all that from His Highness, because my husband hasn't told me anything except to warn me of this danger. It would be better for us if Madame de Sérisy were to die than to remain mad."

"Poor woman!" said the marquise. "But wasn't she already mad?"

Society women, by the hundred different ways they can pronounce any given phrase, can demonstrate to the listening world the infinite range of musical modes. The soul is present in its entirety in the voice, just as much as it is in the eyes; it imprints itself upon the light in the same way it does upon the air, the elements upon which the eyes and the larynx operate. The special accent the marquise gave to those two words, "poor woman," allowed the listener to infer the contentment of satisfied hatred and the happiness of victory. Oh, how much misery she wished to descend upon the protectress of Lucien! When vengeance transcends even the death of the hated object, it is never satisfied, and continues to cast a terrifying shadow. Madame Camusot, though she was herself of a bitter, hateful, and obsessive nature, was dumbstruck. Unable to think of anything to say, she remained silent.

"And Diane told me that Léontine actually went to the prison," Madame d'Espard continued. "That dear duchess is in despair over it all, because she was weak enough to care a great deal for Madame de Sérisy. But it makes a kind of sense, because they both were infatuated with that little imbecile Lucien, and at the same time, and there's nothing that will either unite or disunite two women more effectively than worshipping at the same altar. And so that dear friend spent two hours yesterday in Léontine's bedroom. I hear the countess said some truly horrible things. They say it was just disgusting! A decent woman would never let herself be overcome by such fits! . . . Foh! It was a purely physical passion. The duchess came to see me, pale as a corpse—she's so brave! There's something truly monstrous about this whole business. . . ."

"My husband will tell the whole story to the keeper of the seals in order to justify himself, because they wanted to save Lucien, and my husband, *madame la marquise,* did his duty. An examining magistrate must interrogate people who are in solitary confinement, and within the time span required by the law! . . . He had to put some questions to that little wretch, who didn't understand the interrogation was only a matter of a formality, and so he started right in confessing everything. . . ."

"He was a fool, and impertinent!" Madame d'Espard said dryly.

The magistrate's wife kept silent following that proclamation.

"If we lost our case against Monsieur d'Espard, it was not Camusot's fault, and I will always remember that!" the marquise continued after a pause. "It was Lucien, along with Messieurs de Sérisy, Bauvan, and de Granville, who brought us down. But in time God will be on my side! All of them are going to end badly. Rest easy—I'll send the Chevalier d'Espard to the keeper of the seals and have him hurry to call your husband in, if that seems as though it will be useful. . . ."

"Oh, madame!"

"Now listen!" said the marquise. "I promise you the Legion of Honor immediately, tomorrow! It'll be a very public demonstration of my satisfaction with your conduct in this affair. And yes, it'll be one more censure for Lucien, because it will declare that he was guilty! After all, people rarely hang themselves for the pleasure of it. . . . Enough now—farewell, my beautiful friend!"

Madame Camusot's Second Visit

Only ten minutes later, Madame Camusot entered the bedroom of the beautiful Diane de Maufrigneuse, who, though she had gone to bed at one o'clock in the morning, was still not asleep at nine.

Insensible and arrogant as duchesses may be, they are still women, and even if their hearts are made of stucco, they cannot watch one of their friends fall victim to madness without it making a deep impression on them.

And then the relationship between Diane and Lucien, though it had already been broken off for a year and a half, had left enough memories in the duchess's mind that the dreadful death of the boy had been a terrible blow to her too. All night long Diane had been picturing that handsome young man, so charming, so poetic, so good at lovemaking, hanging in the way Léontine had described him in her delirium, making wild gestures as her fever burned. She still retained letters from Lucien, eloquent, intoxicating letters, comparable to the ones Mirabeau wrote to Sophie[44] but more literary, more polished, for these letters had been dictated by the most violent of all our passions: vanity! Having the most ravishing of duchesses for a mistress, seeing her commit mad indiscretions for him—though quite discreet indiscretions, we must add—such happiness had gone to Lucien's head. The pride of the lover was inspiration to the poet. And so the duchess had kept these moving letters, the way some old men hang on to obscene engravings, for the sake of their hyperbolical elegies on all that was least "duchess" about her.

"And he's dead, dead in a foul prison!" she was saying to herself, clutching the letters tightly with a sensation of fear, when she heard her chambermaid gently rapping at the door.

"Madame Camusot, on some most serious business that directly concerns *madame la duchesse*," said the chambermaid.

Diane stood up rapidly in fright.

"Oh!" she exclaimed when she saw Amélie, who had put on an expression suitable for the occasion, "I understand everything! It's about my letters. . . . Ah, my letters! . . . Ah, my letters!" And with that she dropped down on a love seat. She suddenly remembered how she had responded to Lucien in the same tone, celebrating the poetry of the man as he sang the glories of the woman, and in what dithyrambs!

"Alas, yes, madame, I've come to save more than your life! It's a matter of your honor. . . . Pull yourself together, get dressed, and come with me to the Duchesse de Grandlieu—because, luckily for you, there are others compromised as well."

"But Léontine, yesterday, burned—they told me so, at the Palais—all the letters they took from poor Lucien's apartment, didn't she?"

"But, madame, Lucien was connected to Jacques Collin!" exclaimed the wife of the examining magistrate. "You're forgetting that disgusting companionship, which, no doubt, is the sole cause of the death of that charming, regrettable young man! Now, that Machiavelli of the prisons never loses *his* head! Monsieur Camusot is convinced that this monster has hidden away the most compromising letters from the mistresses of his . . ."

"His friend," said the Duchesse quickly. "You're right, my pretty little one—we need to go and talk this over with the Grandlieus. We're all involved in this affair, and we're all very fortunate to have Sérisy on our side."

Extreme danger exerts, as we have seen in the Conciergerie scenes, a power over the soul just as strong and as terrible as certain reagents have over the body. It is a moral voltaic battery. The day may not be far off in which we shall understand how feeling becomes condensed into a fluid, perhaps similar to electricity.

The phenomenon was the same with the convict as it was with the duchess. Beaten down, half dead, with no sleep, this duchess, who caused her maid such difficulty in dressing her, now found within herself the strength and ferocity of a lioness at bay, and the presence of mind of a general in the midst of battle. Diane picked out her own clothes and improvised dressing herself with all the agility of a seamstress who has to act as her own maid. The sight was so marvelous that the maid stood stock-still for an instant, so surprised was she to see her mistress in her nightwear, allowing the magistrate's wife a glimpse (and perhaps even taking some pleasure in allowing that glimpse), through the thin veil of linen, of a white body, as perfect as Canova's *Venus*. It was like a precious gem wrapped in thin tissue paper. Diane had suddenly realized where her front-fastening corset was, the one that saves a woman all the time of lacing up the back. By the time her maid brought her underskirt and gown, she had already fixed the lace of her chemise and nicely plumped the beauties of her bosom. While Amélie, at a sign from the chambermaid, helped fasten the gown behind and generally helped the duchess, the maid picked out the stockings of Scottish weave, velvet low boots, a shawl, and a hat. Amélie and the maid each took charge of one leg.

"You are the most beautiful woman I've ever seen," said Amélie skillfully, kissing Diane's smooth, polished knee with a passion.

"Madame has no equal," said the chambermaid.

"Enough, Josette—be quiet," replied the duchess.

"Did you bring a coach?" she asked Madame Camusot. "Come along, my little beauty, and we can talk on the way." The duchess proceeded to descend the grand staircase of the Cadignan home at a fast pace, slipping on her gloves as she went, a thing no one had ever witnessed before.

"To the Hôtel de Grandlieu, and hurry!" she ordered one of her domestics, making a signal for him to sit up behind.

The valet hesitated, seeing them getting up into a mere cab instead of a proper carriage.

"Ah, *madame la duchesse*, you never told me that the young man had letters from you! If we had known, Camusot would have handled it all differently. . . ."

"Léontine's situation had me so preoccupied that I forgot about myself altogether," she said. "The poor woman was half insane the day before yesterday, so you can imagine what kind of effect this would produce on her! Oh, my friend, if you only knew what our morning was like yesterday. . . . No, I swear, it's enough to make you swear off love. Yesterday the two of us, Léontine and I, were dragged off by a hideous old crone, a woman who sells used clothes, a damnably clever woman, into that sweaty, bloody underground pit they call the Palais de Justice, and I was saying to her, on our way there: 'Doesn't it make you want to get down on your knees and cry out, the way Madame de Nucingen did when she was on her way to Naples and got caught in one of those terrifying Mediterranean tempests: "My God! Save me this once, and I promise, never again!"' I'll never forget these two days. Aren't we stupid to write things down? . . . But you fall in love! And you receive letters that, just looking at them, set your heart on fire, and everything goes up in flames! And prudence right along with it! And so you write back. . . ."

"Why write back, when you can act!" said Madame Camusot.

"It's such a fine thing, losing yourself!" replied the duchess with some pridefulness. "It's the voluptuousness of the soul."

"Well, beautiful women," replied Madame Camusot modestly, "are excusable, because they have so many more occasions than the rest of us to fall!"

The duchess smiled.

"We're always too generous," Diane de Maufrigneuse continued. "I ought to be like that hideous Madame d'Espard."

"What does she do?" the magistrate's wife asked curiously.

"She's written a thousand love letters. . . ."

"As many as that!" exclaimed Madame Camusot, interrupting the duchess.

"Yes, but, my dear, you won't find a single compromising phrase in any one of them."

"Surely you'd be incapable of being so cold and calculating," replied Madame Camusot. "You're a woman, and you're one of those angels who can't resist the Devil."

"Well, I've vowed never to write again. In my whole life, the only one I did write to was that poor Lucien. I'll keep his letters to me until the day I die! Oh, my friend, it's fire, and you need that sometimes. . . ."

"But if they find them!" exclaimed Madame Camusot, with a bashful little gesture.

"Oh, I'd tell everyone that they were the beginning of a novel I was writing. Because I made copies of all of them, my dear, and I burned all the originals!"

"Oh, madame! What a reward you'd give me if you'd let me read them. . . ."

"Maybe," said the duchess. "And you'll see then, my dear, that he never wrote like that to Léontine!"

This last exclamation summed up the whole woman, and the woman of every era, and of every country.

An Important Person Destined to Oblivion

Like the frog in the La Fontaine fable,[45] Madame Camusot was ready to burst her skin with pride and pleasure in entering the home of the Grandlieus in the company of the beautiful Diane de Maufrigneuse. She would begin to forge, that morning, one of the links in the chain so necessary to ambition. She could already imagine herself being addressed as *"madame la présidente."* She felt that joy beyond words, that sense of having triumphed over immense obstacles, the biggest of which was her husband's incompetence, which was still a secret from the world but one that she knew well. Turning a mediocre man into a success! To a woman—as to a king—this is giving oneself the same kind of pleasure that seduces the great actors into performing a hundred times in a wretched play. It is the very intoxication of the ego! It is, in its way, a saturnalia of power. Power can only prove to itself that it really is power by crowning some absurdity with the wreath of success, thus insulting true genius, which is the one thing power itself can never acquire. Caligula promoting his horse, that imperial farce, has been played and replayed down through the centuries.[46]

In only a few minutes, Diane and Amélie had passed from the elegant disorder of the beautiful Diane's bedroom to the perfectly correct, severe, and grandiose luxury that was the home of the Duchesse de Grandlieu.

That very pious Portuguese got up each morning at eight to attend Mass at the little church of Sainte-Valère, which was an annex to Saint-Thomas-d'Aquin, then in the Esplanade des Invalides. This chapel, demolished now, was moved to the Rue de Bourgogne to make way for the construction of a Gothic church that would, people said, be dedicated to Sainte Clotilde.[47]

At the first words Diane de Maufrigneuse uttered quietly to the Duchesse de Grandlieu, that pious woman went off and promptly returned with Monsieur de Grandlieu. The duke cast upon Madame Camusot one of those rapid glances with which great lords instantly size up a whole life, and often the soul as well. The clothes and appearance of Amélie aided the duke greatly in deducing that this bourgeois had progressed from Alençon to Mantes, and from Mantes to Paris.

Ah! If the examining magistrate's wife had only understood this gift that dukes have, she would never have been able to endure gracefully that politely ironic gaze; she saw it only as polite. Sometimes ignorance is as good for us as perspicacity.

"This is Madame Camusot, the daughter of Thirion, one of the Cabinet clerks," the duchess said to her husband.

The duke bowed *very* politely to the judge's wife, and his face shed just a little of its gravity. The duke's valet arrived, his master having rung for him.

"Go to the Rue Honoré-Chevalier—take a carriage. Knock at a small door there, number ten. Tell the domestic who opens the door that I beg his master to come here. If monsieur is at home, bring him back with you. Use my name—that will be enough to deal with any difficulties. Try to get all this done and return in a quarter of an hour."

Another valet, this time the duchess's, appeared as soon as the duke's had departed.

"Go on my behalf to the home of the Duc de Chaulieu, and see that he gets this card." The duke gave him a card folded in a specific way. When those two close friends felt the need to see each other on some urgent and secret matter, one unsuitable to write about, they often used this method to communicate to each other.

Clearly, then, customs on each level of society resemble those on the others, differing only in their appearance. High society has its own slang, but this slang is called "form."

"Are you certain, madame, of the existence of these letters they claim were written to that young man by Clotilde de Grandlieu?" asked the Duc de Grandlieu. And again he cast a searching glance at Madame Camusot, like a mariner taking a sounding.

"I haven't seen them, but I fear that they do exist," she replied, trembling.

"My daughter could never write anything that we could not avow!" cried the duchess.

"Poor duchess!" thought Diane, looking across at the duke in a way that made him shudder.

"What do you think, my dear little Diane?" asked the duke privately to the Duchesse de Maufrigneuse, leading her over to a window recess.

"Clotilde is so mad about Lucien, my friend, that she arranged a rendezvous with him before her departure. If it weren't for little Lenon-court, she might have run off with him into the Fontainebleau forest! I know that Lucien wrote Clotilde the kind of letters that would seduce a saint! We're three daughters of Eve, all tangled up with the serpent of correspondence. . . ."

The duke and Diane came back from the window recess and walked over to the duchess and Madame Camusot, who were conversing in low tones. Amélie, hewing to the advice of the Duchesse de Maufrigneuse, was playing the religious devotee in order to gain the trust of the proud Portuguese.

"We are all at the mercy of a foul escaped convict!" said the duke with a certain shrug of the shoulders. "This is what one gets when one receives people of whom one is not absolutely sure! Before admitting someone into the home, one ought to know his financial situation, his relatives, his antecedents . . ."

And there, from the aristocratic point of view, we have the whole moral of this story.

"It's done now," said the Duchesse de Maufrigneuse. "Let's concentrate on trying to protect poor Madame de Sérisy, Clotilde, and me. . . ."

"We must wait for Henri. I've sent for him, but everything depends on the person Gentil has gone out to seek. May God grant that this person is presently in Paris! Madame," he said, turning to Madame Camusot, "I thank you for having thought of us. . . ."

That was Madame Camusot's dismissal. The daughter of the Cabinet clerk was clever enough to understand the duke, and she got up; but the Duchesse de Maufrigneuse, with that adorable grace that had won her so many friends and so much confidence, took Amélie by the hand and seemed to be presenting her formally to the duke and duchess.

"I simply want to say that because she got up this morning at dawn to try to save us all, I ask you to do more than remember my little Madame Camusot. For one thing, she has already done me services that one doesn't forget. Moreover, she is completely on our side, both her and her husband. I promised to help her Camusot advance, and I beg you to give him your protection and influence, for the sake of the friendship you have with me."

"No need for this recommendation," the duke said to Madame Camusot. "The Grandlieus never forget services people do them. The king's people will soon have the opportunity to distinguish themselves; they'll be asked to demonstrate their devotion, and your husband will find something opening up for him."[48]

Madame Camusot left the house swelling with pride, with happiness, almost bursting with it. She returned home triumphant, admiring herself, sneering at the hostility of the prosecutor-general. She said to herself, "What if we could force Monsieur de Granville out!"

The Obscure and Powerful Corentin

Indeed, it was high time that Madame Camusot depart. The Duc de Chaulieu, one of the king's favorites, passed that bourgeois woman on the steps.

"Henri," cried the Duc de Grandlieu when he heard the servant announce his friend's name, "hurry, I beg you, to the palace and try to see the king. Let me tell you what this is all about." And he drew the duke over to the window recess where he had recently been with the light and graceful Diane.

From time to time the Duc de Chaulieu stole a glance at the wild duchess, who, even while exchanging pieties with the devout duchess, was casting glances over at the Duc de Chaulieu.

When he was done talking privately with his friend, the Duc de Grandlieu said to her, "Dear child, you must be wiser! See here!" With that he took Diane's hands, saying, "Remember the proprieties and don't ever let yourself become compromised again. Never write letters! Letters, my dear, have caused as many private difficulties as public ones. . . . What would be pardonable in a young girl like Clotilde, in love for the first time, simply can't be excused for a—"

"For an old soldier who's seen battle!" said the duchess, making a pout to the duke. That combination of physiognomy and pleasantry brought smiles to the sorrowful faces of the two dukes, and even to that of the pious duchess. "But I haven't written a love letter in four years! . . . Are we going to be all right?" asked Diane, trying to conceal her anxiety behind playful childishness.

"Not yet!" said the Duc de Chaulieu. "You have no idea how difficult it is to commit an arbitrary act. What we're asking is, to a constitutional monarch, like what infidelity is to a married man. It's his adultery."

"His pet sin!" said the Duc de Grandlieu.

"Forbidden fruit!" said Diane with a smile. "Oh, I wish I could be the Government! I've got no fruit left—I've eaten it all."

"Oh, please, my dear!" said the pious duchess. "You go too far."

The two dukes, hearing a carriage pulling up by the front steps with the kind of clattering sounds that horses who have been galloping make, bowed to the two women and took their leave to go into the study of the Duc de Grandlieu, and there the inhabitant of the Rue Honoré-Chevalier was shown in as well. The latter was none other than the head of the king's special police force, the obscure and powerful Corentin.

"Do come in, come in, Monsieur de Saint-Denis," said the Duc de Grandlieu.

Corentin, surprised to see how well the duke remembered, bowed to both men and then preceded them into the study.

"We are still concerned with that same individual, monsieur," said the Duc de Grandlieu.

"But he's dead now," said Corentin.

"A friend of his remains," said the Duc de Chaulieu. "A very rough friend."

"The convict, Jacques Collin!" replied Corentin.

"Explain, Ferdinand," the Duc de Chaulieu said to the former ambassador.

"The wretch has given us something to fear," replied the Duc de Grandlieu, "because he's spirited away, for the purposes of blackmail, some letters that Mesdames de Sérisy and de Maufrigneuse wrote to that Lucien Chardon, who was his creature. It seems that this young man followed a system of extracting passionate letters in response to his own, and, they say, Mademoiselle de Grandlieu wrote some of them. In any case, that's what we're afraid of, and since she is abroad traveling, we can't know for sure. . . ."

"That little gentleman," Corentin replied, "was incapable of coming up with a scheme like this on his own! This is an elaborate precaution taken by the abbé Carlos Herrera!" Corentin rested his elbow on the arm of the chair he was sitting in and leaned his head against his hand to think. "Money? The man has more than we do," he said. "Esther Gobseck was the grubworm he baited his hook with, and he fished up nearly two million from that pond of gold pieces called Nucingen. . . . Gentlemen, if you get me full legal authority in this matter, I'll rid you of the man!"

"And . . . the letters?" the Duc de Grandlieu asked Corentin.

"Listen, messieurs," said Corentin, standing up and revealing his weasel-like face red with intensity. He put his hands into the pockets of his black flannel trousers. This great actor in the historical drama of our time had put on just a waistcoat and jacket, not even taking the time to change out of the trousers he had worn that morning, knowing very well how important promptness is for the great on certain occasions. Now he paced back and forth in the study, thinking aloud, as if he were at home.

"He's a convict! We could have him thrown secretly, no trial, into Bicêtre, cut him off from all communication, and let him rot there. . . . But he might have given instructions to his henchmen for just such a situation!"

"But he was put into solitary right off the bat," said the Duc de Grandlieu, "when they picked him up at the whore's house."

"Is any cell really solitary enough for that dog? He's as wily as—as me!"

The two dukes exchanged a glance that said, "What should we do?"

"We could return the clown to a penal colony at once—to Rochefort— and he'll be dead in six months! Oh, no illegal action required!" he added in response to a look from the Duc de Grandlieu. "It's just the way it is. A convict can't survive in the heat for more than six months when he's at hard labor in the mists of the Charente. But this option is only good if our man hasn't taken any precautions with the letters. If the clown was careful in thinking about his adversaries, which he probably was, we need to find out what those precautions were. If the person holding the letters is poor, he'll be corruptible. . . . So we have to get Jacques Collin talking! What a duel that would be—and I'd be the loser. The better thing would be to buy back the letters with other letters—I mean letters of amnesty—and then let me have that man in my shop. Jacques Collin is the only man capable of being my successor, now that poor Contenson and my dear Peyrade are dead. Jacques Collin took those two incomparable spies from me by killing them, as if he were clearing a place for himself. So you see, messieurs, you need to give me a free hand in this. Jacques Collin is in the Conciergerie. I'm going to go see Monsieur de Granville in his office. Send somebody you can trust there to join me, because I need either a letter to show Monsieur de Granville, who doesn't know me at all, a letter I would return to the president of the Council, or somebody sufficiently important as an interlocutor. . . . You have half an hour, because it will take about half an hour to get dressed, that is, to dress the way I should be dressed to meet the prosecutor-general."

"Monsieur," said the Duc de Chaulieu, "I'm aware of your deep shrewdness, so I only want a yes or a no. Will you succeed?"

"Yes, if I'm given full powers, and if I'm given your word never to have me questioned on the subject. My plan is ready."

This sinister response caused both of the great lords to shudder a little.

"Proceed, monsieur!" said the Duc de Chaulieu. "Charge any expenses to the account you're used to using."

Corentin bowed to the two lords and took his leave.

Henri de Lenoncourt, for whom Ferdinand de Grandlieu had arranged a carriage, went off immediately to the king, whom he was able to see at any time, due to the privileges of his office.

Thus the various interests that were knotted up together, ranging from the depths to the heights of society, were all brought together by necessity to meet in the office of the prosecutor-general, represented by three men: the law by Monsieur de Granville, the family by Corentin, and both facing their terrible adversary, Jacques Collin, who, in his savage energy, was the embodiment of social evil.

What a duel, then, between the law and arbitrary power, both united against the prison world and its cunning! The prison world, that symbol of the kind of audacity that abandons calculation and reflection, to which all means are good means, which does without the hypocrisy of arbitrary power, which symbolizes in its hideous way the interest of the starving belly, the bloody, swift-moving protest of hunger! It's both attack and defense, isn't it? Both theft and property? The terrible question of the social state vs. the natural state, facing off against each other in the narrowest arena possible? It was, in short, a terrible, living image of the antisocial compromises that the all-too-weak representatives of power have to make with the fiercest rebels.

The Pains of a Prosecutor-General

After Monsieur Camusot was announced to the prosecutor-general, he was gestured into the office. Monsieur de Granville was expecting the visit, and he wanted to come to an understanding as to how to terminate the Lucien affair. The plan he had made with Camusot the day before, before the poor poet's death, would no longer do.

"Have a seat, Monsieur Camusot," said Monsieur de Granville, throwing himself down in his own chair.

The prosecutor, alone now with the magistrate, made no attempt to conceal the despondency he felt. Camusot looked at Monsieur de Granville and saw how that firm face had turned pallid, almost gray, and how it had taken on a look of extreme fatigue, an utter prostration, denoting what might have been even greater suffering than what the condemned man felt when he heard his appeal was rejected. And yet when the prisoner hears that decision read according to the rules of the law, he knows it means prepare yourself; these are your last moments.

"I can come back another time, *monsieur le comte*," said Camusot, "though this business is rather urgent. . . ."

"No, stay," replied the prosecutor-general with dignity. "The true magistrate, monsieur, must accept his anguish and know how to conceal it. It's wrong of me to let my personal feelings show."

Camusot made a gesture.

"May God grant you never know, Monsieur Camusot, the most extreme demands of this life! A person could collapse under less! I just spent the night with one of my best friends, and I have only two such friends, Comte Octave de Bauvan and Comte de Sérisy. We were together, Monsieur de Sérisy, Comte Octave, and I, from six last night till six this morning, taking turns in the salon and at the bedside of Madame de Sérisy, fearing every time our turn came that we would find her either dead or permanently mad! Desplein, Bianchon, Sinard, and their two attendants never left the bedroom. The count adores his wife. Imagine the night I just spent, between a woman mad with love and my friend mad with despair. A statesman doesn't show his despair the way an imbecile does! Sérisy, as calm as if he were at a meeting of the Council of State, writhed in his armchair in an attempt to present an image of tranquility to us. But the sweat stood out on his brow to show the labor he was undertaking. I slept between five and seven-thirty, defeated by exhaustion, and I had to be here by eight-thirty to give orders for an execution. Believe me, Monsieur Camusot, when a prosecutor has been writhing all night long in the abysses of grief, feeling the hand of God weighing down on all things human and striking blow after blow upon noble hearts, he finds it awfully difficult to come in and sit over there and coldly give the order: 'Cut off a man's head at four! Annihilate a child of God full of life, strength, and health!' But this is my duty! . . . Overcome with grief, I had to give the order to erect the scaffold. . . .

"The condemned man doesn't know that the judge endures an agony equal to his. At such a moment he and I are linked together by a sheet of paper—and I act the part of society seeking its vengeance, he the part of a crime to be expiated. We're the same duty with different faces, two lives joined for an instant by the blade of the law. These miseries that the judge endures—who raises the lament for them? Who offers consolation for them? Our glory resides in our ability to keep them buried deep within our hearts! The priest offering his life to God, or the soldier offering his thousand deaths to his country, both seem better off to me than the magistrate with his doubts, his fears, his terrible responsibility.

"You know that we have to execute a young man," continued the prosecutor-general, "twenty-seven years old, as good-looking as the one who died yesterday, fair-skinned like him, too. His head became forfeit completely against our expectations, because the evidence against him only proved him guilty of receiving. Condemned to death, the boy has not admitted the crime! It's been seventy days now, and he's resisted every test, continuing to insist on his innocence. For these last two months I've felt like I've been carrying two heads on my shoulders! Oh! I'd give a year of my life to hear him confess! Jurors need to be assured. . . . And you can picture what a blow to justice it would be if someday we learn that another person did commit the crime, the crime for which this boy is about to die.

"In Paris everything takes on a terrible gravity—the smallest incidents in a judge's life become political.

"The jury, that institution that the legislators of the Revolution thought was such a powerful one, is in fact an instrument of social ruin, because it fails in its mission, it does not provide sufficient protection to society. The jury toys with its duties. There are two kinds of jurors. The first wants an end to the death penalty, and the result of that is the total destruction of true equality before the law. In one jurisdiction, a horrific crime like parricide will end in a not-guilty verdict, while in another, some ordinary crime will get the death penalty! What if here, in our jurisdiction, in Paris, we execute an innocent man?"

"Well, he *is* an escaped convict," Monsieur Camusot hazarded timidly.

"When the Opposition and the Press get hold of it, he'll be a Paschal Lamb!" cried Monsieur de Granville. "The Opposition would be able to whitewash him because he's a Corsican, and they'd claim he shared the fanatical ideas of Corsicans, and that the murder was the result of some *vendetta*! . . . On that island, you kill your enemy, and everybody considers you a perfectly righteous man.

"Oh, true magistrates are unhappy men! Listen! They need to live separate from all society, the way the high priests did in the old days. People only see them issuing forth from their cells at certain set times, solemn, elderly, venerable, making judgments just like the old high priests in the ancient world who exercised both judicial and sacerdotal powers! No one would ever see us except seated upon our legal benches. . . . But today we can be seen suffering or enjoying ourselves just like everybody else! People run into us in salons, in family groups, as citizens, having our own passions, and this makes us simply grotesque rather than terrible."

That supreme cry from the heart, punctuated by pauses and interjections, accompanied by gestures that added an eloquence difficult to represent on paper, made Camusot shiver.

What to Do?

"Speaking for myself, monsieur," said Camusot, "yesterday I began my apprenticeship in the miseries of our situation! . . . I nearly died myself over the death of that young man. He failed to see that I was trying to help him, and the poor wretch entrapped himself."

"Ah! He shouldn't have been interrogated," cried Monsieur de Granville. "It's so easy to be helpful by stepping back, by abstaining from certain things!"

"And the law?" replied Camusot. "The man had been in custody for two days."

"The damage is done," said the prosecutor-general. "I've done my best to try repairing what is irreparable. My carriage and my people will be part of the funeral cortege for that poor, weak poet. Sérisy's been doing the same, and in fact more, because he agreed to act as executor for the unfortunate young man's will. Promising to do so earned him a look from his wife that might suggest her reason returning. And Comte Octave will be attending the funeral in person."

"Well then, *monsieur le comte*," said Camusot, "let's finish our work. We still have a very dangerous prisoner on our hands. He is—you know it as well as I do—Jacques Collin. The wretch will be recognized for who he really is."

"Ah, then we're lost!" exclaimed Monsieur de Granville.

"Right now he's with your condemned man. The two of them had been in prison together, and in the prison he was to Collin what this Lucien had been in Paris—his special protégé! Bibi-Lupin is there too, disguised as a gendarme, listening in on the conversation."

"What does the Sûreté have to do with this?" asked the prosecutor-general. "They should not be involved without my orders!"

"The whole Conciergerie knows that we're holding Jacques Collin. . . . Well! I came to tell you that this great, audacious criminal evidently possesses some dangerous correspondence from Madame de Sérisy, the Duchesse de Maufrigneuse, and Mademoiselle Clotilde de Grandlieu."

"Are you certain of this?" asked Monsieur de Granville, unable to conceal his facial expression of dismal surprise.

"You can judge for yourself, Monsieur le Comte, whether I'm right to fear that it's correct. When I untied the bundle of letters that had been seized from the poor young man's home, Jacques Collin watched closely, and he let slip a little smile of satisfaction, the significance of which would be clear to any examining magistrate. An adversary as clever as

Jacques Collin would have been very careful not to let his weapons be taken from him. Just imagine those documents in the hands of some fool defender the wretch would choose from among the enemies of the Government and the aristocracy. My wife, to whom the Duchesse de Maufrigneuse has been very kind, has gone off to warn her, and as we speak they must be at the home of the Grandlieus to confer together."

"Putting the man on trial is impossible!" cried the prosecutor-general, getting up and striding across his office. "He must have put the documents away somewhere safe. . . ."

"I know where," said Camusot. And with that simple sentence, the examining magistrate erased all the prejudices the prosecutor-general had against him.

"Let's hear it!" said Monsieur de Granville, sitting back down.

"On my way from home to the Palais, I thought about this terrible affair the whole way. Jacques Collin has an aunt, a real one, not somebody in disguise, a woman the political police know about—they've sent a note about her to the prefecture. He's both the student of this woman and her idol—she's his father's sister, and her name is Jacqueline Collin. This amusing person runs a secondhand clothes shop, and with the help of various partners she's met in the course of running that business, she's become privy to a great many families' secrets. If Jacques Collin has entrusted those all-important papers to anyone, it's to this creature—we should move to arrest her. . . ."

The prosecutor-general shot a look at Camusot that seemed to say, "This man is not the fool I thought he was yesterday, but he's still young, and hasn't yet learned how to handle the reins of the law."

"But," Camusot continued, "if we're going to succeed, we have to take different measures than the ones we took yesterday, and I came here to ask for your advice, for your orders . . ."

The prosecutor-general took his paper-knife and tapped it gently against the edge of his desk in one of those gestures familiar with thinkers when they abandon themselves entirely to their thoughts.

"Three prominent aristocratic families in danger!" he exclaimed. "We dare not make even one false step! . . . You're right—we need to follow the Fouché principle: 'First, make the arrest!' We have to put Jacques Collin back in solitary immediately."

"But that amounts to declaring that he really is the convict, and that puts a stain on the memory of Lucien. . . ."

"What a horrible affair!" exclaimed Monsieur de Granville. "Danger everywhere!"

Just then the Conciergerie warden entered, having knocked first; but an office like that of the prosecutor-general is so well guarded that only well-known individuals are allowed close enough to knock.

"*Monsieur le comte,*" said Monsieur Gault, "the prisoner calling himself Carlos Herrera has asked to speak with you."

"Has he had any communication with anyone?" asked the prosecutor-general.

"With other prisoners, yes, because he's been out on the yard since about seven-thirty. He was allowed to see the condemned man, who apparently chatted with him."

A phrase of Camusot's came back to Monsieur de Granville now like a ray of light; he suddenly saw the value, when it came to getting the letters back, of a confession of intimacy between Jacques Collin and Théodore Calvi.

Enter Stage Right

Happy to have a reason to put off the execution, the prosecutor-general gestured for Monsieur Gault to come closer.

"I intend," he said, "to have the execution put off till tomorrow, but no one in the Conciergerie should know about this—complete silence! Let the executioner seem to be doing all his preparations. Have that Spanish priest brought here, under strong guard—the Spanish embassy has claimed him. Let the gendarmes bring Monsieur Carlos up by the private staircase so that he isn't able to see anyone. Tell two of your men to take him, one holding him by each arm, and not leaving his side until he's at my doorway. Are you absolutely sure, Monsieur Gault, that our dangerous foreigner has not been able to communicate with anyone but the prisoners?"

"Ah! Just when he was coming out of the condemned man's cell, there was a woman who wanted to see him."

At this, the two magistrates exchanged a look, and what a look!

"What woman?" asked Camusot.

"One of his penitents—some marquise," replied Monsieur Gault.

"Worse and worse!" exclaimed Monsieur de Granville, looking at Camusot.

"She was a real headache for the gendarmes and the guards," Monsieur Gault said, taken aback.

"There's no room for sloppiness in your position," said the prosecutor-general severely. "There aren't walls around the Conciergerie for nothing. How did this woman get in?"

"She had a permit, monsieur," the warden replied. "The lady was dressed stylishly, accompanied by a footman and a valet, and she arrived in a fine carriage to see her confessor before attending the funeral of the unfortunate young man you had taken away."

"Bring me her permit," said Monsieur de Granville.

"She was here on the recommendation of His Excellence the Comte de Sérisy."

"What was this woman like?" asked the prosecutor-general.

"She appeared to us to be a thoroughly respectable woman."

"Did you see her face?"

"She was wearing a black veil."

"What did they say to each other?"

"But she was a penitent, carrying a prayerbook—what do you think she'd say? . . . She asked for the abbé's blessing, she knelt down. . . ."

"How long did they talk together?" the magistrate asked.

"Not even five minutes. But none of us could understand what they were saying; they were probably speaking Spanish."

"Tell us everything, monsieur," said the prosecutor-general. "Let me repeat—the slightest detail will be of the greatest interest to us. Let this be an example to you!"

"She was weeping, monsieur."

"Really weeping?"

"We couldn't see, because she kept her face hidden behind her handkerchief. She left us three hundred gold francs for the prisoners."

"It's not her!" cried Camusot.

"Bibi-Lupin," Monsieur Gault continued, "exclaimed, 'She's a thief!'"

"He knows her, then," said Monsieur de Granville. "Get a warrant ready," he added, looking at Camusot, "and get everything in her place sealed immediately! But how could she have got a recommendation from Monsieur de Sérisy? . . . Bring me the permit from the prefecture—go on, Monsieur Gault! And have this abbé brought to me at once. Every minute we leave him there, the danger gets worse. In two hours' conversation, you can get pretty deeply into another man's mind."

"Especially a posecutor-general like yourself," said Camusot shrewdly.

"There'll be two of us there," the prosecutor-general replied politely. And then he returned to his reflections.

After a pause, he said: "There ought to be a position created for a supervisor in every visiting room in the prisons, an attractive position, well paid, something that would attract the most capable and best of the retired agents. Bibi-Lupin could finish out his years in such a position. Then we'd have sharp, observant eyes and ears in the places we most need them. Monsieur Gault couldn't give us anything decisive."

"He has so much to attend to," said Camusot. "But yes, between the solitary cells and us there's a real gap, and there shouldn't be. When we come through the Conciergerie to our offices, we pass through corridors and courtyards and up staircases. We can't expect perpetual attention from our men, but the prisoner is always focused solely on his own case.

"They told me that there already had been a woman present when Jacques Collin was on his way from his cell to his interrogation. She had made her way as far as the guardroom at the top of the little stairs by the Mousetrap. The guards told me about it, and I've reprimanded the gendarmes for it."

"Oh! The whole Palais de Justice ought to be rebuilt," said Monsieur de Granville, "but it would cost between twenty and thirty million! . . . Just try to get thirty million from the Chambre des Députés to improve the accommodations for Justice."

They could hear the approach of several persons, along with the clanking of arms. It had to be Jacques Collin.

The prosecutor-general put on a mask of utter gravity, and the individual man behind it disappeared. Camusot imitated his chief.

And, indeed, the office boy opened the door, and there stood Jacques Collin, completely calm, completely unsurprised.

"You said you wanted to talk to me," said the magistrate. "I'm listening."

"*Monsieur le comte,* I am Jacques Collin. I surrender to you!"

Camusot shuddered; the prosecutor-general remained calm.

Crime and Justice Have a Tête-à-Tête

"You must think I have some hidden motive for revealing myself," Jacques Collin went on, giving the two magistrates a mocking look. "I must be quite the embarrassment for you, because if I had remained the Spanish priest, you would have had your gendarmes take me to the Bayonne border, where Spanish bayonets would have done the job of getting me off your hands!"

The two magistrates remained impassive and silent.

"But, *monsieur le comte,*" the convict continued, "I have more serious reasons for doing this, though they are devilishly personal ones—ones I can only divulge to you. . . . Now, if you're afraid. . . ."

"Afraid? Afraid of whom? Of what?" The stance, the facial expression, the erect head, the gesture, the gaze—all came together to make the prosecutor-general into a living image of the Magistrature and into the finest example of civic courage. In that sudden reaction, he took on the grandeur of the magistrates from the old *parlements* from the era of the civil wars, when the presidents came face to face with death itself, themselves as unmoved as the marble of which their statues were later made.[49]

"Fear of being alone with an escaped convict, of course."

"Leave us, Monsieur Camusot," the prosecutor-general said quickly.

"I was about to suggest that you have my hands and feet bound," Jacques Collin said coldly, casting a formidable glare upon the two magistrates. He paused, and then said solemnly: "*Monsieur le comte,* you have always had my esteem, but now you have my admiration as well."

"So you think I should be afraid of you?" the magistrate asked with contempt in his voice.

"*Think* you should be afraid?" asked the convict. "What would be the point of *thinking* it? You should be—it's as simple as that." Jacques Collin sat down in a chair with all the ease of a man who knows his adversary's strengths and is ready to meet him as an equal.

Just then Monsieur Camusot, who had been about to close the door behind him, came back in, walked up to Monsieur de Granville, and handed him two folded documents.

"Look at this," the examining magistrate said to the prosecutor-general, indicating one of the papers.

"Call Monsieur Gault back!" cried the Comte de Granville as soon as he saw there the name of Madame de Maufrigneuse's chambermaid, whom he knew.

The warden came in.

The prosecutor-general whispered to him, "Describe the woman who came to see the prisoner."

"She was short, rather fat, stocky," said Monsieur Gault.

"The person for whom this permit was made out was tall and thin," said Monsieur de Granville. "How old was she?"

"About sixty."

"Does all this concern me, messieurs?" asked Jacques Collin. "Don't bother yourselves about it," he continued in a cheerful voice. "The individual happens to be my aunt, a real aunt, I mean, a woman, an older woman. I can spare you a lot of trouble—you'll never find my aunt without my help. If we let ourselves get bogged down like this, though, we'll never get anywhere."

"I see that *monsieur l'abbé* no longer speaks in his Spanish French," said Monsieur Gault. "He's dropped his dreadful accent."

"Ah, because we're all jumbled up enough right now, my dear Monsieur Gault!" said Jacques Collin with a bitter smile, addressing the warden by name.

Monsieur Gault hurried over to the prosecutor-general and whispered to him, "Stay on your guard, *monsieur le comte*! The man is in a fury."

Monsieur de Granville shot a quick glance at Jacques Collin, finding him calm enough; but he fully understood the truth of what the warden was saying. That calm pose masked the cold, terrible rage of a savage. He could see in the eyes of Jacques Collin a building volcanic eruption, and he could see that the man's fists were clenched. This was clearly the tiger readying himself to hurl himself onto his prey.

"Leave us alone," said the prosecutor-general in a solemn tone, addressing both the warden of the Conciergerie and the examining magistrate.

"That was a wise move, sending off the man who murdered Lucien!" said Jacques Collin, without caring whether Camusot could hear him or not. "I couldn't take it much longer—I was about to strangle him."

Monsieur de Granville shuddered at that. He had never before seen such bloodlust in a man's eyes, such pale intensity in his face, such sweat on his forehead, such taut contraction of all the muscles.

"What good would that murder do you?" the prosecutor-general asked the criminal calmly.

"You avenge yourself every day, or rather you tell yourself you're avenging Society, monsieur, and you ask me to explain why I'd want vengeance! . . . So you never felt the need for vengeance working in you like a blade, whetting itself in your veins? Can't you see that imbecile magistrate took him from us, murdered him? Because you loved him too, my Lucien, and he loved you! I know your heart, monsieur. That sweet boy told me everything, every evening when he returned home; I put him to bed, just the way a servant woman puts her little boy to bed, and I made him tell me everything. He confided in me, told me even his slightest sensations. . . . Oh, no good mother ever loved her only son more tenderly than I loved that angel. If you only knew! Good sprang up in his heart like wildflowers in a meadow. He was weak—that was his one fault—weak like the string of a lyre, the string that's so strong when it's taut. . . . The really beautiful natures are like that, their weakness somehow brings together their tenderness, their wonder, their faculty of coming to life in the sun of art, of love, of the beautiful that God has made for us all in so many forms! . . . Really, Lucien ought to have been born a woman. Oh, what did I say to that brute beast who just left the room. . . . Oh, monsieur, what I did, me, a prisoner before a magistrate, is what God Himself would have done to save his own son if, anxious to save him, He had gone along with him to face Pilate. . . ."

The Innocence of Théodore

Tears came down like torrents from the convict's clear, yellow eyes, which had so recently burned like those of a wolf starving for six months in the snows of the Ukraine. He continued: "That buzzard didn't want to listen, and he killed the boy!... Monsieur, I've bathed the little one's corpse with my tears, imploring *the One I don't know,* the One who's up there above us! Me—me, the one who doesn't believe in God! If I weren't a material-ist, I wouldn't be the man I am—that tells you everything.... You don't know, nobody can know this grief—only I know it. And the flames of that grief dried up my tears so that for the last night I couldn't weep any more. Oh, monsieur, may God—yes, I'm starting to believe!—may God keep you from ever becoming what I am now.... That damnable magistrate has ripped out my soul. Monsieur! Monsieur! They're out there burying him now, burying my life, my beauty, my virtue, my conscience, all my strength!... Imagine a dog that some scientist is draining of blood ... and there you have me! I'm that dog!... This is why I came here and said to you, 'I'm Jacques Collin, and I'm surrendering!'... I decided on it this morning, when they came and tore me away from that body that I was kissing like an insane man, like a mother, like the Virgin must have kissed Jesus in the tomb. I wanted to offer myself unconditionally to the service of Justice. I have to do it now, and I'm going to explain why."

"Are you speaking to Monsieur de Granville, or to the prosecutor-general?" asked the magistrate.

The two men, Crime and Justice, looked at each other. The convict had deeply moved the magistrate to a divine pity for the poor wretch; he had understood the man's life and the man's feelings. And the magistrate—for a magistrate is always a magistrate—who was unaware of Jacques Collin's conduct since his escape, thought that he was the one who could master this criminal, who, after all, was only guilty of a single forgery. And now he wanted to exercise his generosity toward that man of such a composite nature, a man like bronze, composed of both good and evil elements. Important too is the fact that Monsieur de Granville, having reached the age of fifty-three without ever having inspired love, naturally admired sensitive, feeling natures, just as do all men who have never been loved. Perhaps this despair, the lot of many men to whom women only accord their esteem and their friendship, was the secret bond that linked together Messieurs de Bauvan, de Granville, and de Sérisy; for an unhappiness in common will bring souls together into a harmony just as much as a shared happiness will.

"You have a future before you!" said the prosecutor-general, casting an inquiring gaze upon the dejected villain.

The man simply shrugged, with profound indifference.

"Lucien left a will, in which he gives you three hundred thousand francs."

"The poor little one! Oh, the poor little one!" cried Jacques Collin. "Always too good! I have all the wicked sentiments, but he had the good, the noble, the beautiful, the sublime! Beautiful souls like that never change! All he ever got from me was money, monsieur!"

This profound, complete surrender of his personality, which the magistrate was unable to reanimate, gave such proof of the man's terrible words that Monsieur de Granville passed over altogether onto the side of the criminal. Yet the prosecutor-general remained in control!

"If you don't care about anything anymore," asked Monsieur de Granville, "what did you come here to tell me?"

"Wasn't it enough that I came to surrender? You were getting warm, but you still hadn't got me! I would have remained just too much of a problem for you!"

"What an adversary!" thought the prosecutor-general.

"Monsieur, you're about to behead an innocent man, and I've discovered the guilty one," Jacques Collin went on gravely, wiping away his tears. "I came here not for them but for you. I came to keep you from remorse, because I love anyone who took any sort of interest in Lucien, just as I will always pursue with hatred all those who cut his life short. . . . What does some convict mean to me?" he continued, after a brief pause. "A convict to me is about what an ant is to you. I'm like those Italian brigands, those proud men! If a traveler is worth anything more than the price of a rifle shot, he'll be down on the ground, dead! I'm only thinking of you. I confessed the young man, who had nobody to confide in—he was my comrade on the chain gang. Théodore is good by nature. He tried to do a favor to a mistress by offering to sell some stolen goods for her, but he's no more guilty in that Nanterre affair than you are. He's a Corsican, so vengeance is second nature to him; they kill each other like flies down there.

"In Italy and Spain, there's no respect for a man's life, and the reason is simple. They think we all possess a soul, a something, an image of ourselves that will live on after us, that will live eternally. Go try to explain that kind of nonsense to a modern thinker! It's the atheist, philosophical countries where you have to pay dearly for taking the life of a man who's bothering you, and they're right, because for them there's only the material, only the present!

"If Calvi had turned and informed on the woman who gave him the stolen goods, you would have found—not the guilty party, because you already have him in your claws—but an accomplice that poor Théodore doesn't want to give up, because it's a woman. . . . What can I say? Every level in life has its points of honor, and the prisons and the thieves have theirs too! Right now, I know the murderer, the one who killed those two women and pulled the whole thing off, the whole strange, bizarre affair—I've been told the whole story in detail. Stop the execution of Calvi, and you'll learn it all; but first give me your word that you'll send him back to the penal colony, and commute his sentence. I'm in such a miserable state that there's no point in my taking the trouble of lying, and you know it. What I'm saying is the truth. . . ."

"In your case, Jacques Collin, even though it abases the dignity of the law, which should never allow itself compromises like this, I think I can relax the rigor of my duties and refer the matter to the right place."

"Do you grant me his life?"

"It could be done. . . ."

"Monsieur, I beg you! Give me your word—that's all I ask."

Monsieur de Granville made a gesture suggesting wounded pride.

The File of the Great Ladies

"I control the honor of three prominent families, and all you control is the fate of three convicts," Jacques Collin continued. "That makes me stronger than you."

"You could be returned to solitary—what could you do then?" asked the prosecutor-general.

"Oh, I see! We're still playing!" said Jacques Collin. "I was using *straight talk*! I was speaking to Monsieur de Granville, but if instead what I see before me is the prosecutor-general, I'll keep my cards closer to my chest. And there I was, all ready to hand over the letters Mademoiselle Clotilde de Grandlieu wrote to Lucien!" He said all this in a certain tone, with a coolness and an expression that revealed to Monsieur de Granville that, with this adversary, the slightest misstep could be fatal.

"Is that all you're asking me for?" the prosecutor-general asked.

"I'm going to speak to you for myself now," said Jacques Collin. "The honor of the Grandlieu family is what I'm offering to trade for the commutation of Théodore's sentence—that's giving a great deal to get very little in return. What's a convict with a life sentence? . . . If he escapes, you can easily be rid of him—it's a matter of signing a note of deferred payment to the guillotine! But since you'd pack him off, with distinctly

unpleasant intentions, to Rochefort, I want your promise to have him
sent to Toulon instead, along with your recommendation that he be
treated well. And now, for myself, here's what I want. I have documents
from Madame de Sérisy and the Duchesse de Maufrigneuse, and oh, what
letters they are! . . . Look, *monsieur le comte*, when a common whore
writes, she writes in high style with grand sentiments, while these great
ladies, who live in high style and have grand sentiments all day long,
when they turn to writing, they write the way the whores act. Maybe
the philosophers can explain this crisscross—I won't try. Woman is an
inferior being—she tends to obey her organs too often. For me, the only
beautiful woman is one who's like a man!

"And so these little duchesses, who are like men in their heads, oh,
they've written some real masterpieces. . . . Yes, it's beautiful stuff, from
beginning to end, just like that famous ode by Piron. . . ."[50]

"Really?"

"Want to see them?" asked Jacques Collin with a smile.

The magistrate felt ashamed.

"I can let you read them, but come on, let's quit the comedy. We're
talking straight, aren't we? . . . All right—you give me the letters back,
and you have to forbid anyone from following or even looking at the person who takes them."

"And this will take some time?" asked the prosecutor-general.

"Not at all—it's nine-thirty now," said Jacques Collin, glancing at the
clock. "Fine—in four minutes you'll have one letter from each of the
two ladies, and after you've read them, you can give orders to cancel the
guillotining! If all this weren't true, you wouldn't see me sitting here so
calmly. Anyway, the two ladies have been warned. . . ."

Monsieur de Granville jumped a little with surprise.

"While we're speaking here they must be busy already; probably
they've got the keeper of the seals involved, and who knows, they might
have gone as high up as the king . . . So, look—you'll give me your word
then, not to follow this person or have her followed for an hour?"

"Yes, I promise!"

"Good—and I'm sure you wouldn't want to play tricks on an escaped
convict. You're made of the same metal as Turenne, and you'll stick to
your word, even with thieves.[51] Well, in the Pas-Perdus hall there is, at
this very moment, a beggar in rags, an old woman, right in the middle of
the hall. She says she wants to speak to one of the public scriveners concerning a lawsuit over some shared wall—send your office boy to fetch
her, and have him say this to her: 'Dabor ti mandana.' She'll come . . . but
don't be cruel about it! Either you accept my proposition, or you don't

want to get mixed up with a convict. . . . Remember, I'm only a forger! . . . Well, meantime now, don't let poor Calvi go through the anguish of a man being shaved for execution. . . ."

"The execution has been countermanded. I don't want," Monsieur de Granville said to Jacques Collin, "justice to be any less worthy of respect than yourself!"

Jacques Collin looked at the prosecutor-general with a kind of astonishment, and he watched him pull the bell cord.

"May I ask you not to escape? Give me your word on it, and that will be enough for me. Go, find the woman."

The office boy appeared.

"Félix, send the gendarmes away," said Monsieur de Granville.

Jacques Collin was conquered.

In this duel with the magistrate, he had wanted to be the greater, the stronger, the more generous—but the magistrate had crushed him. Nevertheless, the convict felt he really was the superior one, because he was playing against the Law, convincing them that the guilty was innocent, and winning from them the head that was in contention; but that superiority had to remain silent, secret, hidden away, while the Stork overcame him in broad daylight, and majestically at that.

Jacques Collin's Debut in Comedy

As Jacques Collin was leaving Monsieur de Granville's office, the Comte des Lupeaulx, secretary-general of the council and a *député,* appeared, together with a sickly looking little old man. The latter was wrapped up in a puce-colored quilted overcoat, as if winter were still raging outside; he wore powder in his hair, and his face was pale and cold as he tottered along on gouty legs, his feet seeming outsized because of his Orléans calfskin shoes. He leaned on a cane with a gold knob, bareheaded, hat in hand, the decorations of seven orders in his boutonniere.

"What is it, my dear des Lupeaulx?" asked the prosecutor-general.

"The prince has sent me," des Lupeaulx whispered to Monsieur de Granville. "You have carte blanche to get back the letters from Madame de Sérisy and Madame de Maufrigneuse, together with those of Mademoiselle Clotilde de Grandlieu. You can work with this gentleman. . . ."

"Who is this?" the prosecutor-general whispered to des Lupeaulx.

"I have no secrets from you, my dear prosecutor-general. This is the famous Corentin. His Majesty wants you to tell him all the details of the affair, and what it will take to achieve success."

"Do me the favor," the prosecutor-general replied in a low voice to des Lupeaulx, "of telling the prince that it's all settled, and that I won't need this gentleman," he added, nodding toward Corentin. "I'll be going to get my orders from His Majesty, for the conclusion of the affair involves the keeper of the seals: there will need to be two reprieves."

"You're wise to have gone ahead on your own," said des Lupeaulx, reaching out and shaking the prosecutor-general's hand. "The king is on the verge of taking some significant steps, and he does not want to hear about any of the great families' reputations being tarnished and gossiped about at such a moment. . . . After all, it's no longer a shabby little criminal case—now it's an affair of State."

"Tell the Prince that when you got here it was all already settled!"

"Really?"

"I believe so."

"My friend, when the keeper of the seals is promoted to chancellor, you'll have his office."

"Oh, I'm not ambitious!" said the prosecutor-general.

At that, des Lupeaulx laughed and took his leave.

"Ask the prince if he can get me ten minutes with the king, around two-thirty," Monsieur de Granville added as he saw Comte des Lupeaulx out.

Des Lupeaulx cast a shrewd glance at Monsieur de Granville and commented, "You're not ambitious, you say? Come, you have two children, and you'd at least like to be made a peer of France. . . ."

"If monsieur the prosecutor-general already has the letters in his possession, he has no need of my intervention," said Corentin when he found himself alone with Monsieur de Granville, who looked at him with genuine, and quite understandable, curiosity.

"A man like you is never superfluous in a delicate business like this one," the prosecutor-general replied, seeing that Corentin had understood, or perhaps overheard, everything.

Corentin nodded, an almost patronizing gesture.

"Do you know, monsieur, the individual in question?"

"Yes, *monsieur le comte*—he's Jacques Collin, head of the Society of the Ten Thousand, banker for three of the penal colonies, a convict who has been hiding for five years inside the cassock of abbé Carlos Herrera. How could he possibly have been entrusted with a mission from the king of Spain for our late king? Trying to get at the truth in that affair has us all tangled up in knots. I'm awaiting a response from Madrid, where I've sent a man along with some letters. Here's a convict in possession of the secrets of two kings. . . ."

"He's an incredibly hardened case! We have only two options

with him—either recruit him for our own or get rid of him," said the prosecutor-general.

"We had exactly the same idea, which I regard as an honor for me," replied Corentin. "I am obliged to develop so many ideas on behalf of so many people that statistically speaking I'm bound to encounter a clever man now and then." This was said so dryly, so coolly, that the prosecutor-general made no reply but instead turned to arranging some papers.

When Jacques Collin appeared in the hall of the Pas-Perdus, it would be difficult to describe the astonishment felt by Mademoiselle Jacqueline Collin. She stood there, planted on her two feet, hands on her hips, dressed in the costume of a vegetable peddler. Accustomed as she was to the tours de force of which her nephew was capable, this one outdid them all.

"Well, if you're going to keep staring at me like I'm some kind of freak in a museum case," said Jacques Collin, taking his aunt by the arm and leading her out of the hall of the Pas-Perdus, "we're both going to look pretty odd, and maybe we'd get arrested, and that would be a waste of time." He proceeded down the staircase of the Galerie Marchand, which leads out to the Rue de la Barillerie. "Where's Paccard?"

"He's waiting for me at la Rousse's, pacing around on the Quai aux Fleurs."

"And Prudence?"

"She's at the same place—playing my goddaughter."

"Let's go."

"Make sure we aren't being followed."

The Tale of La Rousse

La Rousse[52] ran a hardware shop on the Quai aux Fleurs; she was the widow of a famous murderer, one of the Ten Thousand. In 1819 Jacques Collin had faithfully handed over to the girl more than twenty thousand francs from her lover, following his execution. Deathcheater was the only one who knew about the intimacy between the young woman, a milliner at the time, and her criminal friend.

"I'm your man's boss," said the man from Madame Vauquer's pension to the young milliner, meeting her in the Jardin des Plantes. "He must have mentioned me, little one. Anyone who betrays me won't live to see the end of the year! And anybody who's straight with me has nothing to be afraid of. I'm the kind of pal who'll die without saying a word to compromise anyone I care for. Stick with me like a soul sticking to the Devil, and you'll do all right for yourself. I promised your poor Auguste to get you set up properly, because he wanted you to have everything—he got himself sliced for you. Don't cry. Listen to me: nobody in the world except for me knows you were the mistress of a convict, a murderer who went under last Saturday, and I'll never say a word about it. You're twenty-two, you're pretty, and look, you're rich with twenty-six thousand francs. Forget Auguste, get married, and turn honest if you can. But in return for this nice quiet life, I'm asking you to be ready to do me some service, me and any people I send your way, and I'm asking you to do it without hesitation. I'll never ask you to do anything compromising, neither to you nor to your children nor your husband, if you have one, nor to your family. But in my profession I often have need of a place I can talk, a place I can hide. I need a discreet woman who can deliver a letter, do an errand. You'll be one of my mailboxes, one of my porter's lodges, one of my emissaries—nothing more, but nothing less. You're blonde, but Auguste and I always called you La Rousse, and I want you to hang on to that name. My aunt, a merchant over in the Temple area, will be the only person in the world you must obey. Tell her everything that's happened to you—she can get you married, and she'll be very useful to you."

And thus was concluded one of those diabolical pacts of the same kind as the one binding Prudence Servien and this man, who had concluded a great many of them; for he had this in common with the Demon, that he was an excellent recruiter.

Around 1821 Jacqueline Collin had got La Rousse married to the chief clerk of a wealthy wholesale hardware dealer. This head clerk, having purchased the commercial side of his patron's business, found himself well on the path to prosperity, father of two, and a deputy to the mayor of his district. La Rousse, now Madame Prélard, never had the slightest grounds for complaint concerning either Jacques Collin or his aunt, but every time some service was asked of her, she trembled from head to foot. And now, when she saw these two terrible characters walk into her shop, she turned pale.

"We need to talk business with you, madame," said Jacques Collin.

"My husband is here," she said.

"Ah. Well, we don't need much of your time at the moment—I never like to bother people unnecessarily."

"Go find a cab, my little friend," said Jacqueline Collin, "and tell my goddaughter to come down. I'm hoping to find her a position as chambermaid to a great lady, and the steward has asked me to bring her there."

Paccard, who looked like a plainclothes policeman, was inside talking with Monsieur Prélard about an important order for steel cable for a bridge project.

A clerk was sent out to find a cab, and a few minutes later Europe—or, to be done with that name under which she had served Esther, Prudence Servien along with Paccard, Jacques Collin, and his aunt were all (to the great relief of La Rousse) seated together in a cab. Deathcheater had told the driver to head for the Ivry barrier.

Prudence Servien and Paccard, trembling before their boss, looked like two guilty souls before the throne of God.

"Where are the seven hundred and *fifty* thousand francs?" the boss asked, fixing one of his fixed, intense gazes upon them, the kind that sets aboil the blood of damned souls caught in their sin; they could feel their hair standing on end like so many pins.

"The seven hundred and *thirty* thousand francs," Jacqueline Collin said to her nephew, "are safe. I deposited them this morning with La Romette, in a sealed envelope."

"If you hadn't handed the money over to Jacqueline," said Deathcheater, "you'd find yourselves right over there by now," he said, pointing to the Place de la Grève, which the cab was just passing.

Prudence Servien made the sign of the cross, as people do where she came from, as if she had just seen a thunderbolt strike.

"I forgive you," the boss continued, "on condition that you never make another false step like that again, and that from now on you'll act like these two fingers on my right hand," he said, holding up the index and middle fingers together, "because the thumb is this good largue here!" And with that he slapped his aunt's shoulder. "Now listen to me. Paccard, from now on you've got nothing to be afraid of—you can follow your nose and run off to Pantin as much as you please! You have my permission to marry Prudence."

How Paccard and Prudence Will Get Set Up

Paccard took Jacques Collin's hand and kissed it with the greatest respect.

"What do I have to do?" he asked.

"Nothing, and you'll have both income and women too, not counting your wife, because I know you, old friend; you're too Regency! . . . That's the problem when a man is just too good-looking!"

Paccard blushed at this satiric praise from his sultan.

"You, Prudence," Jacques went on, "you need a career, a position, a future, and you need to remain in my service. Listen carefully. On the Rue Sainte-Barbe, there's a very nice house belonging to that Madame Saint-Estève whose name my aunt sometimes uses . . . It's a good house, well stocked, brings in fifteen or twenty thousand francs a year. It's managed for Saint-Estève by . . ."

"La Gonore," said Jacqueline.

"Yes, the girlfriend of poor La Pouraille," said Paccard. "That's where I headed with Europe on the day that poor Madame Van Bogseck, our mistress, died. . . ."

"Who's mouthing off while I'm talking?" said Jacques Collin.

Complete silence descended upon the cab, and Prudence and Paccard didn't dare look at each other.

"The house is run by La Gonore," continued Jacques Collin. "If you did go there to hide with Prudence, Paccard, I can see that you're clever enough to *blind the funny boys* (trick the police), but not enough to fool the old girl," he said, caressing his aunt's chin. "Now I understand how she found you. . . . It all works out fine. You'll be going back there, back to La Gonore's—I'll go on. Jacqueline will negotiate the purchase of the establishment on the Rue Sainte-Barbe with Madame Nourisson, and you'll be able to make a fortune there if you're careful, little one!" he said, looking at Prudence. "Imagine—an abbess at your age! Just what a true daughter of France deserves," he added in a biting tone.

Prudence threw her arms around the neck of Deathcheater and kissed him, but the boss, with his extraordinary strength, pushed her away so powerfully that if it hadn't been for Paccard, her head would have gone through the window of the cab.

"Keep your paws to yourself! I don't like that kind of thing!" said the boss coldly. "It isn't respectful."

"He's right, dear," said Paccard. "Look, it's as if the boss had given you a hundred thousand francs. The business is worth that. It's on the boulevard, across from the Gymnase. We'll get people coming out of the theater. . . ."

"I'll do better than that—I'll buy the building too," said Deathcheater.

"And in six years, we'll be millionaires!" exclaimed Paccard.

Sick and tired of being interrupted, Deathcheater gave Paccard a kick in the shin hard enough to break the bone, but Paccard had nerves of rubber and bones of tinplate.

"Enough, boss! I'll shut up," he said.

"Do you think I'm playing games?" said Deathcheater, realizing that Paccard had evidently had a few too many drinks. "Listen. In the basement of that house are two hundred and fifty thousand gold francs. . . ."

The profoundest silence reigned anew in the cab.

"The gold is hidden under thick masonry . . . the trick is to get it out, and you've only got three nights to do it. Jacqueline will help you. A hundred thousand will be enough to buy the business, fifty thousand to buy the building, and you can keep the rest."

"Where?" asked Paccard.

"In the basement!" said Prudence.

"Silence!" said Jacqueline.

"All right, but to move all that we'll need cooperation from the *funny boys* (the police)," said Paccard.

"You'll have it," said Deathcheater dryly. "Is it your business?"

Jacqueline looked at her nephew, struck by the change in his face that was just visible behind the impassive mask that this so strong man used to conceal his emotions.

"Now, girl," Jacques Collin said to Prudence Severin, "my aunt will be returning to you the seven hundred and fifty thousand francs."

"Seven hundred and thirty," said Paccard.

"Fine—seven hundred thirty," Jacques Collin went on. "Tonight, find some pretext for going back to Madame Lucien's house. Get up on the roof, by the skylight, and get inside via the chimney, to the bedroom of your late mistress, and hide the packet of money she made inside the mattress . . ."

"Why not use the door?" asked Prudence Servien.

"Idiot—the seals are on the doors!" replied Jacques Collin. "They'll be doing the inventory in a few days, and then you'll be innocent of the theft . . ."

"Long live the boss!" cried Paccard. "Oh, how good he is!"

"Driver, stop!" commanded the powerful voice of Jacques Collin.

The coach had arrived at the taxi stand outside the Jardin des Plantes.

"Off with you now, my children," said Jacques Collin, "and don't do anything stupid! Be on the Pont des Arts at five o'clock and there you'll meet my aunt—she'll tell you if anything has changed. We have to think everything through carefully," he added to his aunt quietly. "Jacqueline will explain to you tomorrow," he continued, "how to extract that gold from the *depths*. It's a delicate operation."

Prudence and Paccard hopped out onto the street, happy as a couple of discharged thieves.

"Oh, that boss! What a man!" said Paccard.

"He'd be the king of men, if he only treated women better!"

"Ah, he's still the best!" cried Paccard. "Did you see the way he kicked my shins? Face it—we deserved to be sent off *ad patres*, because after all we're the ones who got him into this mess. . . ."

The clever, cunning Prudence replied, "As long as he doesn't get us involved in some crime that ends up sending us off to the meadows...."

"Him? Look, if that's what he wanted, he'd tell us—you don't know him! And look what a pretty future he's just given you! We're going to be bourgeois. How lucky! Oh, I tell you, when that man likes you, there's nobody more generous!"

The Prey Becomes the Predator

"Now, my sweetie!" said Jacques Collin to his aunt. "Take care of La Gonore—she needs to be handled right. In five days she'll be arrested, and they'll find in her bedroom one hundred and fifty thousand gold francs, the remainder of a share from the murder of the old Crottats, the father and mother of the notary."

"That'll land her in the Madelonnettes for five years," said Jacqueline.

"More or less," replied Jacques Collin. "And that makes a good reason for Nourisson to get rid of her house—she can't take care of it by herself, and good managers aren't easy to find. So you can arrange everything easily. Then we'll have an eye there.... But all three of these operations are subordinate to the negotiations I've started up for our letters. So rip open the seam on that dress and show me some sample merchandise. Where are the three packets?"

"My God! They're at La Rousse's!"

"Driver!" shouted Jacques Collin. "Back to the Palais de Justice, and as fast as you can! ... I promised that I'd hurry, and here I've been gone half an hour—and that's too much! You stay at La Rousse's, and give the sealed packets to the office boy who will come asking to see Madame de Saint-Estève. That 'de' will be the password, and he'll say to you, 'Madame, I've come on behalf of the prosecutor-general for you-know-what.' You should be standing out in front of La Rousse's door, keeping an eye on what goes on in the Flower Market, so as not to draw Prélard's attention. Once you've handed over the letters, you can start Paccard and Prudence working."

"I see what you're up to. You want to be the next Bibi-Lupin. That boy's death has turned your head!"

"And Théodore, who was scheduled to meet the reaper at four today!" cried Jacques Collin.

"Well, it's a thought, I suppose—we'll all end up good, respectable bourgeois, and retire to a nice property in the sunshine down in Touraine."

"What would I become otherwise? Lucien took my soul away with him, all my happiness. I might live another thirty long years, and I don't have the heart for it. Instead of being the boss of the prisons, I'll be the Figaro of Justice, and I'll avenge Lucien. The only way I can demolish Corentin is by getting myself inside the skin of the funny boys. That'll be living again—having a man to eat raw. And the part a man plays in this world—that's just appearances; the real is what's up here: the idea!" he added, tapping his forehead. "How much do we have in our treasury?"

"Nothing," said the aunt, frightened by the tone and the manners of her nephew. "I gave you everything for your little one. La Romette has only twenty thousand francs in the business. I took everything from Madame Nourisson, about sixty thousand francs. . . . Ah, we're sleeping in sheets that haven't been laundered for a year. The little one ate up all the loot from the fanandels, our own holdings, and everything Nourisson had."

"Which came to? . . ."

"Five hundred sixty thousand."

"We'll have a hundred and fifty in gold—Paccard and Prudence owe it to us. I'll tell you where you can get two hundred more—the rest will come from Esther's inheritance. Nourisson needs to be paid back. With Théodore, Paccard, Prudence, Nourisson, and you, I'll soon have the holy battalion I need. . . . Listen, we're almost there."

"Here, the three letters you wanted," said Jacqueline, having just finished snipping the seam of the lining of her dress.

"Good," Jacques Collin replied, taking the three precious handwritten documents, three sheets of fine paper, still scented with perfume. "Théodore did that Nanterre job."

"Ah, it was him! . . ."

"Quiet now—time is precious. He wanted to let a little Corsican bird named Ginetta wet her beak. Set Nourisson on the trail to find her; I'll get you the information you need from a letter that Gault will provide. Come to the Conciergerie gate two hours from now. We need to get that girl to a laundress, Godet's sister, and get her set up there. . . . Godet and Ruffard were involved with La Pouraille in the Crottat theft and murders. The four hundred thousand francs are intact, one-third in La Gonore's basement, which is La Pouraille's share, the second third in La Gonore's bedroom, and that's Ruffard's; the third is hidden with Godet's sister.

"We'll start by taking a hundred and fifty thousand francs out of La Pouraille's loot, then a hundred from Godet's, and a hundred from Ruffard's. Once Ruffard and Godet are *nabbed,* it'll look as if they're the ones who spent part of their loot. I'll get to Godet and get him to believe that we've set aside a hundred thousand for him, and I'll tell Ruffard and La

Pouraille that La Gonore has saved theirs!... Prudence and Paccard will go to work at La Gonore's. You and Ginetta, who seems to me like a pretty good little thing, you two work on Godet's sister. For my debut in the comedy, I'm going to let the Stork recover four hundred thousand francs from the Crottat theft, and I'll hand over the guilty parties. It'll look like I've cast light on the Nanterre case. We'll recover our dough, and there we are, in with the funny boys! We were the prey, now we're the predators— that's all there is to it. Give the driver three francs."

The cab had stopped in front of the Palais. Jacqueline, in a daze, paid the driver. Deathcheater walked up the stairs to see the prosecutor-general.

The English Gentlemen Get the First Shot

A total change of life is a violent thing, and so it was that, despite his resolution, Jacques Collin slowed down as he made his way up the stairs leading from the Rue de la Barillerie to the Galerie Marchande, where, beneath the peristyle of the Court of Assizes, the somber entrance to the court presents itself. Some political affair had occasioned a kind of gathering at the foot of the double stair that leads up to the Court of Assizes, and this led the convict to pause a moment, absorbed in his own thoughts, at the sight of the crowd. To the left of the double stairs stands, like an enormous pillar, one of the buttresses of the Palais, and in the side of its great mass is a a little door. This little door opens onto a spiral staircase that allows direct communication with the Conciergerie, a route used by the prosecutor-general, the warden, the presiding judges of the Court of Assizes, the lawyers, and the head of the police. There is a branch of this staircase, now condemned, up which Marie Antionette, Queen of France, was led to face the revolutionary tribunal which sat, as we know, in the great hall where the audience for the appeals court sits.

The sight of that horrible staircase makes the heart shrink when one thinks of Marie-Térèse's daughter having passed that way, she whose head-dress and hooped skirts once filled the stairways of Versailles! Perhaps it was expiation for her mother's crime, the hideous partitioning of Poland. Sovereigns who commit such acts rarely think of the payment Providence will eventually force upon them.

When Jacques Collin was just arriving under the vaulted ceilings above the stairway, on his way to the prosecutor-general, Bibi-Lupin came out from that little door hidden in the wall.

The head of the Sûreté was coming up from the Conciergerie, also on his way to Monsieur de Granville. The reader can imagine the astonishment Bibi-Lupin felt upon seeing Carlos Herrera in his frock coat, the same man he had studied so intently that morning; he hurried to catch up with him. Jacques Collin turned around. The two men stood still face to face and exchanged the same look, their eyes firing like two pistols in a duel, let off at the same second.

"This time I've got you, you crook!" exclaimed the chief of the Sûreté.

"Ah, do you, then?" exclaimed Jacques Collin with an ironic air. The thought flitted through his mind that Monsieur de Granville must have had him followed, and—strange as it may seem!—he felt hurt that the man was less great than he had taken him for.

Bibi-Lupin leaped bravely at Jacques Collin's throat, but the latter, keeping an eye on his adversary, struck him a blow that sent him flying back three feet; then, Deathcheater calmly strode over to Bibi-Lupin and stretched out his hand to help him up, for all the world like an English boxer who is entirely confident in his own strength and wishes nothing better than to go on with the fight. Bibi-Lupin was too strong a man to cry out; but he got up and rushed to the entry of the corridor to signal for a gendarme to come and stand there. Then, as swift as lightning, he turned back to his enemy, who was coolly watching what he did. Jacques Collin had worked out the alternatives: either the prosecutor-general had not kept his word or Bibi-Lupin had not been told about what was going on, and therefore he needed to clarify the situation.

"Do you want to arrest me?" Jacques Collin asked his enemy. "Say so and make it plain. Do you think I don't know that here in the house of the Stork, you're stronger than I am? I could kill you with a kick, but I'm not going to take on the whole troop of gendarmes. So be quiet about it. Where do you want to take me?"

"To Monsieur Camusot."

"Then let's go to Monsieur Camusot," replied Jacques Collin. "But why don't we go by the prosecutor-general's office? . . . After all, it's nearer," he added.

Bibi-Lupin knew he was not in good odor with the higher levels of judiciary power, for they suspected him of having made his fortune at the expense of criminals and their victims; therefore, he was not displeased at the idea of showing up in the prosecutor-general's office with such a prisoner.

"All right—that's fine with me! But since you're surrendering to me, let me get you set up—I'm not fond of your fists!" And with that he took a pair of thumb cuffs out of his pocket.

Jacques Collin held out his hands, and Bibi-Lupin put the cuffs on him.

"Now, since you're being a good boy," he continued, "tell me how you got out of the Conciergerie?"

"The same way anybody else would—by the smaller staircase."

"So you were able to pull a new trick on the guards?"

"No. Monsieur de Granville let me out on my word."

"You're conning me!"

"You'll see! . . . And you might be the one who ends up wearing these cuffs."

An Old Acquaintance

At that same moment, Corentin was speaking to the prosecutor-general: "Well, monsieur, your man has been gone an hour now, and aren't you a little afraid that he's making a fool of you? . . . He might be halfway to Spain by now, and we'll never find him there, because Spain is a fantastical place."

"Either I don't know men, or he'll be coming back—it's entirely in his own interests to do so. He needs me more than I need him. . . ."

Just then, Bibi-Lupin appeared.

"Monsieur le Comte," he began, "I've got good news for you. Jacques Collin escaped, but I've captured him."

"This is how you keep your word!" cried Jacques Collin. "Why don't you ask this two-faced agent of yours where he found me."

"Where?" asked the prosecutor-general.

"Just a few steps from your office, under the archway," replied Bibi-Lupin.

"Get your cuffs off that man," Monsieur de Granville told Bibi-Lupin with severity. "And understand this—until you're ordered to arrest him again, you're to leave this man alone. Go on now, leave us! . . . You're always acting as if you're both judge and police."

And the prosecutor-general turned his back on the head of the Sûreté as the latter turned pale, and all the more so as he caught the eye of Jacques Collin: in that glance he could read his own downfall.

"I have not left my office. I've been awaiting you here, and you need not fear that I won't keep my word, since you're keeping yours," Monsieur de Granville said to Jacques Collin.

"I did doubt you at first, monsieur, and perhaps in my place you would have too, but upon reflection I see that I was being unjust. I'm bringing more to you than you're giving me—it's not in your interest to trick me."

The magistrate exchanged a look with Corentin. This look did not escape the notice of Deathcheater, whose attention had been fixed on

Monsieur de Granville, and it made him focus now on that odd little old man sitting on a chair off in the corner. Immediately, thanks to that instinct, so sharp, so rapid, that announces the presence of an enemy, Jacques Collin began to examine this person; he detected immediately that the age in the man's eyes did not match the age implied by the costume, and he scented disguise. In a second, Jacques Collin had his revenge upon Corentin for the speed with which Corentin had unmasked him at Peyrade's.

"We're not alone! . . ." said Jacques Collin to Monsieur de Granville.

"No," replied the prosecutor-general simply.

"And monsieur here is," the convict continued, "a close acquaintance of mine. . . . Am I correct?"

He took a step forward and recognized Corentin, the true, avowed author of Lucien's fall. Jacques Collin's normally brick-red complexion turned, within an almost imperceptible instant, pale, almost white; all his blood went rushing to his heart, so ardent and frenetic was his urge to hurl himself upon this dangerous beast and crush it; but he repressed that brutal desire, holding it within himself with that strength that rendered him so terrible. He assumed an amiable air, even a tone of obsequious politeness, the air he was accustomed to using when he played the role of a high-ranking ecclesiastic, and he bowed to the little old man.

"Monsieur Corentin," he said, "is it just by chance that I have the pleasure of seeing you again, or could I be fortunate enough to be the object of your visit to the office today?"

The astonishment of the prosecutor-general was at its peak, and he could not help but stare at the two men in front of him. The movements of Jacques Collin, along with the forced way he was speaking, seemed to denote some sort of crisis within him, and he was curious to understand its cause. At this unexpected, almost miraculous recognition of his real identity, Corentin stood up like a snake whose tail has been trod upon.

"Yes, it is I, my dear Abbé Carlos Herrera."

"Have you come," asked Deathcheater, "to be a go-between for monsieur the prosecutor-general and myself? . . . Do I have the pleasure of being the subject of one of those negotiations that make your talents shine so brightly? But come, monsieur," the convict said, turning to the prosecutor-general, "I don't want to waste any time as precious as yours is, so please go ahead and read this little sample of my merchandise. . . ." And he handed Monsieur de Granville the three letters, drawing them out of his coat pocket. "While you're getting familiar with them, I'll chat, if you don't mind, with this gentleman."

One Perspective

"This is quite an honor for me," replied Corentin, though he could not suppress a shudder.

"You've managed to achieve a complete success in our business, monsieur," said Jacques Collin. "I've been defeated," he added lightly, in the manner of a gambler who's lost some money, "but you did leave some of your men on the field. . . . So it was a costly victory. . . ."

"Yes," replied Corentin, falling in with the tone of pleasantry. "If you've lost your queen, I've lost my two rooks. . . ."

"Oh, Contenson was only a pawn," replied Jacques Collin with a smile. "Easily replaced. You are—permit me to pay you this compliment now, face to face—you are, word of honor, a prodigious man."

"Oh, not at all—no, I bow to your superiority," replied Corentin, adopting the tone of a professional comedian, as if to say, "If you want to make jokes, let's make jokes." "After all, I had everything on my side, while you, you were, so to speak, operating all on your own."

"Oh!" said Jacques Collin.

"And you very nearly won, too," continued Corentin, noticing Collin's exclamation. "You're the most extraordinary man I've ever met, and I've met a lot of extraordinary men, because the kind of men I deal with are all remarkable for their audacity, the boldness of their schemes. I was, unfortunately, on grounds of some intimacy with the late Duc d'Otrante, and I worked for Louis XVIII when he reigned, and when he was exiled for the emperor, and before him for the Directory. . . . You have something of Louvel about you, the keenest political instrument I've ever seen, but in addition you're as supple as the prince of diplomats.[53] And what a group of auxiliaries! I'd give up a number of heads scheduled to be guillotined if I could have the cook who worked for that poor little Esther. . . . Where do you find beautiful creatures like the one who played the double for that Jew for a while with Monsieur de Nucingen? I never know where to find something like that when I need one."

"Monsieur, monsieur, this is all too much," said Jacques Collin. "Such praises coming from you are enough to turn a person's head. . . ."

"Oh, but all those praises are richly deserved! After all, you deceived Peyrade—he took you for an officer of the law. Him! . . . I tell you, if you hadn't had that little idiot to protect, you would have beaten all of us. . . ."

"Ah, monsieur, you're forgetting Contenson disguised as a mulatto . . . and Peyrade as an Englishman. Professional actors have all the resources of the theater to draw upon, but to act so perfectly in the harsh light of day, at every hour, no one can compare to you and yours. . . ."

"Well, then, let's think it over," said Corentin. "We're each fully persuaded of the other's worth, of our respective merits. We're each on our own, all alone—I'm missing my old friend, and you're missing your young protégé. I'm the stronger of the two for the moment, so why don't we do as they do in *L'Auberge des Adrets*?[54] We'll shake hands, and I'll say to you, 'Let's embrace and call an end to all this.' I offer you, here in the presence of the prosecutor-general, letters declaring your complete pardon, and in return you join us and become one of my men—the first among my men, and maybe even my successor."

"You're offering me a position?" asked Jacques Collin. "And an awfully nice one at that! So I'd be leaving the brunette for the blonde. . . ."

"You'll be in a sphere where your talents will be very well appreciated, where you'll be very well paid, and where you'll be the one who decides when and how to act. The political police, and the governmental too, have their dangers. I myself have been imprisoned by them two different times—and I'm none the worse for it. But a person has to go on! You become what you want to become. You operate the machinery behind big political dramas, and the great lords treat you with respect. . . . So come on, my dear Jacques Collin—are you in?"

"You've been given orders for this?" asked the convict.

"I'm fully empowered. . . ." replied Corentin, delighted with his idea.

"You must be playing with me. You're a powerful man, and you have to admit that a person has reason to distrust you. . . . You've sold off more than one man after enticing him to crawl into a sack, all of his own free will. I know all about the battles you've won—the Montauran affair, the Simeuse—oh, these are the Marengos of espionage!"[55]

"All right," said Corentin. "But you do esteem monsieur here, the prosecutor-general?"

"I do," said Jacques Collin, bowing his head respectfully. "I have only admiration for his fine character, his firmness, his nobility, and I'd give my life to make him happy. So let me begin by getting Madame de Sérisy out of the dangerous state she's been placed in."

The prosecutor-general gave a little sigh of relief.

"Well, then," Corentin went on, "ask him if I'm not fully empowered to pick you up out of the terrible situation you're in and attach you to myself."

"It's quite true," Monsieur de Granville said to the convict.

"Quite true! So I'll have absolution for my past, and the promise of succeeding you if I give you sufficient proofs of my abilities?"

"Between two men like ourselves, there should be no misunderstandings," said Corentin, revealing the kind of greatness of soul capable of attracting anyone.

"And the price of this transaction is, no doubt, the return of the three sets of letters?" asked Jacques Collin.

"I didn't think it was necessary even to say it. . . ."

Disappointment

"My dear Monsieur Corentin," said Deathcheater with an irony as grand as that of Talma in the role of Nicomède,[56] "I thank you—it's thanks to you that I've come to know my own worth, and just how important it is to get me disarmed. I'll never forget this. . . . I will be forever and always at your service, and instead of saying, as Robert Macaire does, 'Let us embrace,' I will simply embrace you myself."

He seized hold of Corentin around the waist with such speed that that latter could not defend himself from the powerful embrace. He was picked up like a doll, pressed tightly against Collin's heart, kissed on both cheeks, and then carried as lightly as a feather would have been until Death cheater, opening the office door, set him down outside it, bruised from the rough treatment.

"Farewell my friend," Jacques Collin said in a low voice so no one else could hear. "You and I are separated from each other by the length of three corpses. We've tried our swords and found they're of the same steel, the same strength. Let's have respect for each other, but I plan to be your equal, not your subordinate. . . . Armed as you are, you seem too dangerous a general for me to be your lieutenant. Let there be a ditch between us. And woe unto you if you cross onto my territory! . . . You call yourself the State, the way a lackey calls himself by his master's name. As for me, I'm going to be called Justice. We'll see each other often—we'll continue to treat each other with all the dignity, all the decorum appropriate to . . . a couple of foul gutter-dwellers," he whispered in Corentin's ear. "And now, I'll model all this by being the first to kiss you."

Corentin stood there, stupefied for the first time in his life, and he allowed his terrible adversary to take his hand and shake it.

"If that's the way it's going to be," he said, "I think it's in both our interests to remain friends."

"We'll each be the stronger for it, but we'll each be more dangerous for it too," said Jacques Collin in a low voice. "So tomorrow I hope you'll permit me to ask you to put down a deposit on our bargain. . . ."

"Very well," said Corentin with a friendly tone, "it appears you're going to take your affairs out of my hands and give them to the prosecutor-general. You're going to be the cause of his professional advancement, but I can't keep myself from saying, 'Yes, you're picking the right side....' Bibi-Lupin is too well known, his time is past. If you replace him, you'll be in the only position that really suits you. I'll be delighted to see you in it . . . word of honor."

"Good-bye, then. We'll meet again soon," said Jacques Collin.

Turning back into the office, Deathcheater found the prosecutor-general seated at his desk, his head in his hands.

"Are you really saying you know how to keep Madame de Sérisy from slipping into a permanent state of madness?" asked Monsieur de Granville.

"I can do it in five minutes," Jacques Collin replied.

"And you can get me all the letters from those women?"

"Did you read the three samples?"

"Oh, yes," said the prosecutor-general. "I feel ashamed for the ladies who wrote such things. . . ."

"Well, we're alone now. Close your door, and let's negotiate," said Jacques Collin.

"Permit me . . . Justice must have its due, and Monsieur Camusot has orders to have your aunt arrested."

"He'll never find her," said Jacques Collin.

"They're going to search for her in the Temple, at the home of a Mademoiselle Paccard who operates her shop."

"They'll find nothing but rags there, costumes, diamonds, uniforms. But Monsieur Camusot's zeal needs to be curbed."

Monsieur de Granville rang for an office boy, and told him to go fetch Monsieur Camusot; he wanted to talk with him.

"Come on," he said to Jacques Collin, "and let's get this all finished off! I'm dying to hear how you're going to cure the countess."

In Which Jacques Collin Abdicates as Boss

"*Monsieur le procureur général,*" Jacques Collin said, turning serious. "I was, as you know, sentenced to five years' hard labor for the crime of forgery. I love my liberty! . . . Now this love, like all loves, has been at cross-purposes with itself. Lovers quarrel sometimes, you know, because they're trying so hard to adore each other. By escaping, and being picked up one day, I was given an additional seven years. You only need to pardon me for the additional years I piled up in *the country*—excuse me, I mean in the penal colonies. Because in fact I've done my time, and until somebody catches me in some new crime, and I defy the Law and even Corentin himself to do that, I ought to have my rights as a French citizen restored. Banned from Paris, continually under police surveillance—is this a life? Where could I go? What could I do? You know my abilities. You've seen Corentin, that storehouse of subterfuge and betrayals, go white with fear at me, which does some justice to my talents. . . . That man has taken everything from me! It's him, only him—he's the one, using I don't know what means and in whose interest, who tore down the edifice of fortune Lucien was building. Corentin and Camusot, they're the ones who did it all. . . ."

"No recriminations," said Monsieur de Granville. "Let's stick with facts."

"All right—the facts—here they are. Last night, as I sat holding the cold hand of the dead boy, I made a promise to myself to give up the insane battle I'd been waging for twenty years against all society. You won't expect me to launch into Capuchin-style pieties, not after what I've already told you about my religious opinions. . . . Well! For these twenty years, I've seen the underside of the world, its cellars, and I've come to see that in the stream of events there's a power that you'll call Providence, and that I call chance, and that my companions call luck. Every evil act gets avenged eventually, no matter how swiftly it tries to hide itself. In this career of battling, even when you get a fine hand dealt you, when you're holding the best cards of all, all of a sudden the candle falls over, the cards burn up, or the gambler drops dead with apoplexy! . . . That's Lucien's whole story. That boy, that angel, never committed even the shadow of a crime—he let things take their course, he let things happen! He was going to marry Mademoiselle de Grandlieu, be made a marquis, have a fortune . . . yes, well, some whore poisons herself, hides the proceeds of an income she'd been given, and the whole edifice, so painstakingly built up, crumbles to the ground in an instant. And who's the first one to stab his sword at us? A man steeped in secret infamies, a monster who in the business world has committed such crimes [see *La Maison Nuchingen*] that every écu of his fortune is wet with the tears of some family—a Nucingen, a kind of legal Jacques Collin in the world of écus. But you know just as well as I do about all the bankruptcies, the hanging offenses of that man. My own chains will forever put their stamp on all my actions, even the most virtuous ones. Being batted back and forth between the one racket called prison and the other called the police—in a life like that, victory is an endless labor, and peace is obviously impossible. Jacques Collin is buried as of now, Monsieur de Granville, along with Lucien, upon whom they're sprinkling holy water right now as they prepare him for his trip to Père Lachaise. I need some place to go too, not to live, but some place to die. . . . The way things are now, you, I mean you as representing Justice, you don't want to bother about the civil or social state an ex-convict has to live in. Though the law is satisfied, society isn't; it continues to distrust him, and it does everything it can to prove to itself that its mistrust is justified. It ought to restore the man's rights to him, but instead it forbids him from living in certain zones. Society says to the wretch: Paris, the only place you could hide away, or any of its suburbs up to a certain point—you may not take up residence there! . . . Besides that, the ex-convict is subject to police surveillance. And you really think it's possible to live under conditions like that? If you want to live, you have to work, because nobody comes out of prison with a personal income. But you've set things up so that the convict must be clearly designated as such, recognized as such, walled in on all sides, and then you imagine that other citizens will trust him, while society, justice, the whole world do not. You condemn him either to hunger or to crime. He can't find work anywhere, and he's fatally pushed back toward his old way of life, the way that leads to the scaffold. This is why when I truly wanted to renounce my battle against the law, I was unable to find any place in the sun for myself. There's only one option open to me—to make myself the servant of that power that weighs down and crushes us—and when that thought occurred to me, the power I've spoken about became clear, rising up and manifesting itself clearly all around me.

"Three great families are in my hands. No, don't be afraid that I want to blackmail them.

"Blackmail is the most cowardly form of murder. In my view, it's actually a worse crime than murder. A murderer has to have a horrendous courage. And I'm formally putting my signature to this opinion, because those letters that comprise my personal security, that permit me to speak to you like this, that put me for the moment on the same level as you, me a criminal and you the representative of the law—those letters are yours now. . . .

"Your office boy can go pick them up for you—they'll be handed over to him. . . . And I'm not asking for any ransom, I'm not selling them! But oh, *monsieur le procureur général*, by hanging on to them I wasn't thinking of myself, but rather of the danger that might befall Lucien someday! If you don't yield to my request, I have more than enough courage, and more than enough disgust with life, to go blow my brains out and get myself off your hands forever. Or, with a passport, I could go to America and live there in solitude—I have all the inner qualities that a savage needs. . . . These are the kinds of thoughts that ran through my head last night. Your secretary must have passed on to you the message I gave him. . . . When I saw the precautions you took to keep Lucien's memory free of stain, I decided to devote my life to you, poor gift that it is! It doesn't mean anything to me anymore—I see that it's impossible without the light that shone upon it, the happiness that animated it, the thought that gave it meaning, the future prosperity of that young poet who was my sun, and I wanted to give you those three packets of letters. . . ."

Monsieur de Granville bowed his head.

What Followed the Abdication

"When I went down into the prison yard, I discovered the truth about who committed the Nanterre crime, and I also found my little chainmate facing the guillotine for his involuntary connection to the crime," Jacques Collin continued. "I saw that Bibi-Lupin was pulling a trick on the law, that in fact one of his own agents murdered the Crottats—providential, wouldn't you say? . . . That's when I thought that maybe I could do some good, make use of the gifts I've been given, these wretched people I've become acquainted with, and try to do something for society, to be useful instead of harmful, and I dared to count on your intelligence, on your good character."

The man's air of good will, of naïveté, of simplicity, making his confession freely and without bitterness, without that philosophy of vice that had previously made him so frightening to listen to—it all sounded like a true transformation. He was no longer the same man.

"And I do believe in you, so much that I want to put myself entirely at your disposal," he went on, with the humility of a penitent. "You see me at a crossroads, with three possible routes—suicide, America, and the Rue de Jérusalem.[57] Bibi-Lupin is rich—he's served his time, he's a man who works both sides of the street, and if you allow me to work against him, I'll have him collared red-handed in a week. And if you give me that rogue's position, you'll have done society a great service. I don't need anything for it. I'll be honest. I have all the credentials the job requires. I've got more education than Bibi-Lupin—they made me study, all the way to rhetoric. I'm not as stupid as him, and I have manners when I want to. My only ambition is to be an instrument of order and repression, and stop being the embodiment of corruption. I'll never again recruit anybody into serving in the great army of vice. And look, monsieur, in wartime when you take a general captive, you don't shoot him—you hand him back his sword, and give him a villa for his prison. Well, you see, I'm the general of the prisons, and here I am, surrendering to you. . . . It wasn't the Law that beat me—it was Death. . . . The sphere where I want to operate and live is the only one that will suit me, and I can sense that I'll grow even stronger there. So, decide . . ."

And with that, Jacques Collin assumed a modest, submissive posture.

"You've placed the letters at my disposal, then?" asked the prosecutor-general.

"You can send for them—they'll be handed over to the person you send. . . ."

"How?"

Jacques Collin could read the prosecutor-general's intent, and he therefore continued with his game.

"You promised to commute the death sentence of Calvi to twenty years' hard labor. Oh, I'm not reminding you of this in order to bargain with you," he added quickly, seeing the prosecutor-general making a gesture, "but that life ought to be preserved for other reasons. The boy is innocent. . . ."

"How can I get hold of those letters?" asked the prosecutor-general. "I have the right and the obligation to determine whether you're the man you say you are. I want you without any conditions. . . ."

"Send someone you trust to the Quai des Fleurs—he'll see there, on the steps of a hardware shop, below the sign of the Shield of Achilles . . ."

"The Shield establishment?"

"That's the one," said Jacques Collin with a bitter smile; "it's my own shield. Your man will find an old woman there, dressed, as I was about to say, in a fishmonger's outfit, wearing earrings and looking like a successful tradeswoman—he must ask her for Madame *de* Saint-Estève. Don't forget the *de*. And he should say to her: 'I've come from the prosecutor-general to find you-know-what. . . .' And then he'll immediately be given three sealed packets."

"And all the letters will be there?"

"Ha, I see you're a clever man! You didn't sneak your way into this job," said Jacques Collin with a smile. "I can see you think I'm capable of feeling you out by handing over nothing but blank pages. . . . But you don't know me!" he added. "I'm trusting you the way a son trusts his father. . . ."

"You'll be taken back to the Conciergerie," said the prosecutor-general, "and you'll wait there for our decision about your fate." Monsieur de

Granville then rang for the office boy; when he came in, he said to him, "Ask Monsieur Garnery to come in, if he's there."

Aside from the forty-eight police commissioners who keep watch over Paris like forty-eight separate little Providences,[58] and not counting the Sûreté police—in the slang of the thieves, those are called "quarter-eyes," because there are four of them in each arrondissement—there are two commissioners attached to both the police and the Palais de Justice to carry out delicate missions, replacing the examining magistrates in many cases. The office of these two commissioners—or rather magistrates, because the police commissioners are in fact magistrates—is called the Bureau of Delegations, because they are formally empowered to carry out investigations and make arrests. A position like this calls for a mature man, one with proven capacities, a strictly ethical man, and a man of absolute discretion; and it is one of the miracles that Providence showers upon Paris that such men are actually to be found. Our description of the Palais de Justice would be incomplete if it made no mention of these *preventative* magistracies, so to speak, which are among the most powerful instruments of the justice system; for if in the course of time Justice has lost some of her ancient pomp and splendor, we must at the same time grant that she has made material gains. In Paris especially, the mechanism has become perfected in the most admirable way.

Monsieur de Granville had sent off Monsieur de Chargeboeuf, his secretary, to attend Lucien's funeral, so he needed to replace him now for this mission, and he needed a man he could count on. Monsieur Garnery was one of the two Delegations commissioners.

The Burial

Jacques Collin said to the prosecutor-general: "Monsieur, I've given you sufficient proof of my honor. . . . You let me go free, and I returned. Now here it is eleven o'clock . . . the funeral mass for Lucien is coming to its end, and they'll be setting off for the cemetery . . . Instead of sending me back to the Conciergerie, let me accompany the boy's body to Père Lachaise; I'll return, and you can make me a prisoner again then."

"All right—go," said Monsieur de Granville with a note of kindness in his voice.

"One last thing, *monsieur le procureur général.* That whore's money—I mean Lucien's mistress's money—wasn't stolen. . . . During those few moments of liberty you granted me, I was able to question some people—and I'm as sure of them as you are of your two Delegations commissioners. The money from the financial transaction Mademoiselle Esther

Gobseck carried out will be found, when they lift the seals on her house, in her bedroom. The chambermaid told me that the deceased was, as they say, given to hiding things away, always distrustful, and she must have put the bank notes in her bed. Let the investigators search the bed carefully, take the bedstead apart, open up the mattress, and they'll find the money."

"You're sure of this?"

"I'm sure of the relative honesty of my little friends—they don't try to play games with me. I have the power of life and death over them—I'm the judge and I'm the one who hands down the sentences, and I make my arrests without any of your formalities. You'll be seeing evidence of my powers. I'll restore for you the money stolen from Monsieur and Madame Crottat; I'll *collar* one of Bibi-Lupin's agents, his right-hand man, and I'll reveal to you the whole truth about the Nanterre crime . . . And this is just a down payment! . . . Now, if you put me into the service of the Law and the police, at the end of the first year you'll be applauding the revelations I bring you—I'll be frankly and openly exactly what I should be, and I'll know how to handle any affair that you entrust to me."

"I can't promise you anything beyond my good will. What you're asking doesn't depend on me alone. Only the king, with the recommendation of the keeper of the seals, has the right to grant pardons, and the position you're asking for is at the disposal of the police prefect."

"Monsieur Garnery," said the office boy.

At a gesture from the prosecutor-general, the Delegations commissioner entered, casting a knowing glance at Jacques Collin and repressing any expression of his astonishment when he heard the following:

"Go now!" Monsieur de Granville said to Jacques Collin.

"Please permit me," replied Jacques Collin, "to stay on until Monsieur Garnery has delivered to you those items that comprise my entire strength, so that I can take along with me a sense that you're satisfied."

"No, go on!" said the magistrate. "I trust you."

Jacques Collin made a deep bow, expressing the complete submission of an inferior before his superior. Ten minutes later, Monsieur de Granville had in his possession the three packets of letters, all sealed and intact. But the importance of this matter along with the confession of Jacques Collin had made him forget the promise to cure Madame de Sérisy.

Once he was outside, Jacques Collin felt an incredible sensation of well-being. He felt free, reborn and ready for a new life; he walked along rapidly from the Palais to the church of Saint-Germain-des Prés, where the Mass had ended. Holy water was being sprinkled on the casket, and he was able to get there in time to make this Christian farewell to the mortal remains of that deeply loved boy, after which he got up into a cab and accompanied the corpse on its way to the cemetery.

With funerals in Paris, unless there are some extraordinary circumstances, or the deceased is some celebrity who has come to a natural end, the crowd at the church diminishes bit by bit as the coffin makes its way to Père Lachaise. People may have time to make an appearance at the church, but everyone has his own affairs to attend to and returns to them soon enough. Thus, out of the ten carriages that made the trip, not even four were full. When the convoy arrived at Père Lachaise, the followers were a mere dozen, Rastignac among them.

"Good that you remain faithful to *him*," Jacques Collin said to his old acquaintance.

Rastignac started with surprise to find Vautrin there.

"Don't worry," said the old boarder from Madame Vauquer's. "I'm your servant, your slave, for the simple reason that you've come here. My help is not something to turn up your nose at, and I am, or I will soon be, more powerful than ever. Now you, you've slipped your cable, and you've been pretty shrewd about it, but you might still have need of me someday, and I'll always be ready to serve you."

"But what are you going to do?"

"I'm going to be supplying the prisons rather than inhabiting them," replied Jacques Collin.

Rastignac made a gesture of disgust.

"Oh—if somebody robs you one day! . . ."

Rastignac strode off rapidly to put distance between himself and Jacques Collin.

"You never know the kind of circumstances you might find yourself in."

They had arrived at the open grave, next to that of Esther.

"Two creatures who loved each other, and who were happy!" said Jacques Collin. "They're reunited now. There's some happiness in rotting together. I want to be laid here too."

When they lowered Lucien's body into the grave, Jacques Collin fell down stiffly, fainting dead away. The man, otherwise so strong, could not endure the light sound the gravediggers make in shoveling some dirt down on the body before they come around to the mourners asking for tips. Two agents from the Sûreté came forward, recognizing Jacques Collin, and they picked him up and put him into a cab.

In Which Deathcheater Makes a Deal with the Stork

"What is it now?" asked Jacques Collin when he came to, looking around him in the cab. He saw himself between two police agents, one of whom was in fact Ruffard; he looked at the man closely, sounding the depths of the murderer's soul, all the way down to the secret of La Gonore.

"It's the prosecutor-general, he's asking for you," Ruffard replied; "we looked everywhere and finally found you out at the cemetery, where you'd just about gone head first into the grave of that young man."

Jacques Collin remained silent.

"Was it Bibi-Lupin who sent you looking for me?" he asked the other agent.

"No, Monsieur Garnery gave us our orders."

"He didn't say anything to you?"

The two agents exchanged a look, inquiring of each other as if in a pantomime.

"Come on! How did he give you the order?"

"He ordered us," said Ruffard, "to go find you as fast as we could, telling us you were at the Saint-Germain-des Prés church, but if the funeral procession had left, you'd be out at the cemetery."

"The prosecutor-general was asking for me?"

"Maybe."

"That's it," said Jacques Collin. "He needs me! . . ."

He turned silent again, which made the two agents nervous. At about two-thirty, Jacques Collin entered the office of Monsieur de Granville and saw a new individual there, Monsieur de Granville's predecessor, Comte Octave de Bauvan, one of the chief magistrates of the appeals court.

"You've forgotten the danger Madame de Sérisy is in, and you promised me you'd save her."

"*Monsieur le procureur général,*" he replied, signaling for the two agents to enter, "ask these two clowns what state I was in when they found me."

"He was unconscious, *monsieur le procureur général,* on the edge of the open grave of the young man they were burying."

"Save Madame de Sérisy," said Monsieur de Bauvan, "and you'll have everything you're asking for!"

"I'm not asking for anything," Jacques Collin said. "I've made an unconditional surrender, and monsieur the prosecutor-general should by now have received . . ."

"The whole set of letters!" said Monsieur de Granville. "But you promised you could bring Madame de Sérisy back to her reason—can you? Was that just boasting?"

"I hope I can," said Jacques Collin with modesty.

"All right then—come with me," said Comte Octave.

"No, monsieur," said Jacques Collin; "I don't want you to be seen in a coach with me. I'm still a convict. I want to turn and serve Justice now, and thus I don't want to start by dishonoring her. You go on to the home of *madame la comtesse,* and I'll follow shortly after. Tell her I'm Lucien's best friend, the abbé Carlos Herrera.... Just knowing that I'll be coming will inevitably have a powerful impact on her, and it will probably help bring about the end of her crisis. You'll pardon me, I hope, for assuming once again the false character of the Spanish canon, but it's in the service of a very great cause!"

"I'll see you there at four o'clock," said Monsieur de Granville, "because I have to go with the keeper of the seals to see the king."

Jacques Collin went to meet up with his aunt, who was waiting for him on the Quai des Fleurs.

"Well," she said, "so you've joined up with the Stork?"

"I have."

"Risky, don't you think?"

"No. I owed poor Théodore his life, and now he'll be reprieved."

"And yourself?"

"Me ... I'll become what I ought to be! I'll always be feared throughout our world! But now it's time to get to work. Go tell Paccard to get going at full speed, and tell Europe to carry out my orders."

"This won't be hard; I already know how to handle La Gonore!" said the terrible Jacqueline. "I haven't been sitting around picking posies!"

"Make sure that Corsican girl, Ginetta, turns up by tomorrow," said Jacques Collin, smiling at his aunt.

"Any clue where she is?"

"Start with Manon the Blonde," Jacques replied.

"We'll have it by this evening!" the aunt said. "You're busier than a rooster! Something good up?"

"I want my first steps to beat anything that Bibi-Lupin ever pulled off. I had a nice little chat with the monster who killed my Lucien, and all I'm living for is getting my revenge on him! He and I are going to be equal in strength, in our two positions, and we're going to have equally strong protectors! It'll take me a few years to get at that miserable wretch, but when I do strike the blow, he's going to feel it!"

"He must be grooming a dog to be ready to fight yours," said the aunt.

"He's taken in Peyrade's daughter—you remember, the kid we sold to Madame Nourisson."

"All right. So our first step will be to get one of our people in his house as a servant."

"That'll be tough. He's going to be on the watch!" said Jacqueline.

"Maybe so, but hatred makes you feel alive! Let's get to work on it!"

Jacques Collin got into a cab and went straight to the Quai Malaquais, to the little room he had been lodging in, one that was not connected to Lucien's apartment. The concierge was startled to see him, and wanted to tell him everything that had happened.

"I know all about it," said the abbé. "I was compromised, despite the sanctity of my character; but thanks to the intervention of the Spanish ambassador, I've been released."

With that he hurried up to his room, where he picked up his breviary, inside the cover of which was a letter that Lucien had written to Madame de Sérisy, when she had broken off with him after seeing him at the Italiens with Esther.

The Doctor

In his despair, Lucien had not bothered to send the letter, believing he had lost her forever; but Jacques Collin had read this masterpiece, and since everything connected with Lucien was sacred to him, he had slipped the letter into his breviary, cherishing the poetic expressions to which that vain love had given rise. When Monsieur de Granville had told him about Madame de Sérisy's state, the deep-thinking man had divined, correctly, that the great lady's despair and madness were born out of the quarrel she had had with Lucien, a quarrel she had allowed to fester. He knew women the way magistrates know criminals, saw into the deepest currents in their hearts, and he immediately thought that the countess must be thinking that her harshness had contributed to Lucien's death, and that she must be reproaching herself bitterly. Clearly, a man who was deeply in love with her would never end his own life. Knowing that she was truly and always loved, despite her harshness, ought to restore her reason.

If Jacques Collin was a great general to the convicts, it must also be admitted that he was no less a great doctor of souls. His appearance in the rooms of the de Sérisy house was a cause of both shame and hope. A number of people, including the count and the doctors, had been standing in the little room that led into the countess's bedroom; but to avoid any possible stain on his honor, the Comte de Bauvan sent them all away, and only he remained there, alone with his friend. It was already something of a blow for a vice president of the Council of State, a member of the king's private council, to have to see such a somber, sinister person entering his home.

Jacques Collin had changed his clothes. He was dressed now in trousers and a black frock coat, and his bearing, his gaze, his gestures were all perfectly appropriate. He bowed to the two statesmen, and asked if he could enter the countess's bedroom.

"She's waiting for you, and impatiently," said Monsieur de Bauvan.

"Impatiently? . . . That means she's going to be fine," said the terrifying yet magnetic Jacques Collin. And in fact, after half an hour's private talk, he opened the bedroom door and said: "Come in, *monsieur le comte*; you have nothing more to fear."

The countess was holding the letter tightly against her heart; she was calm, and appeared to be reconciled with herself. Seeing this, the count made an involuntary gesture of happiness.

"There they are, the people who decide our fates, and the fates of all the people!" thought Jacques Collin, shrugging his shoulders when the two friends were inside the bedroom. "Some female emits a sigh in the wrong way, and their minds are turned inside out like a glove! A glance makes them lose their heads! A skirt gets raised or lowered by an inch, and they go running all over Paris in utter despair! Some woman has a whim, and the whole State reacts! Oh, what strength a man acquires when he's like me, unaffected by that childish tyranny, that tendency to sacrifice loyalty for passion, those openly malicious actions, those barbaric schemes! Woman, with her executioner's mind, her special talents for torture, is and always will be the downfall of man. Prosecutor-general, minister of state, all of them blind, twisting and turning everything they can for the letters of a duchess or some girl, or for the sanity of a woman who's crazier when she's in her right mind than when she's out of it." He allowed himself a superb smile. "And," he thought, "they all believe me, they all act on the revelations I make to them, and they leave me alone and unhindered. I'm going to reign over this whole world, this world that has already been obeying me for twenty-five years. . . ."

Jacques Collin had made use of that supreme power that he once exercised over the poor Esther; for he possessed, as we have seen many times, the speech, the gaze, the gestures that readily tame the foolish and the mad, and he had depicted Lucien to her as having died with the countess's image in his heart.

No woman can resist the thought of being the only beloved.

"You have no more rivals!" he said, cold mockery in his tone, as he left her.

He remained another hour in that salon, alone and forgotten. Monsieur de Granville arrived and found him standing there, somber and lost in thought, like a man who has just experienced an 18th Brumaire in his life.[59]

The prosecutor-general walked up to the doorway of the countess's bedroom, but he stood there for a moment, then turned and approached Jacques Collin, saying:

"I assume you haven't changed your mind?"

"That's correct, monsieur."

"All right: you'll replace Bibi-Lupin, and the condemned man Calvi will get his reprieve."

"He won't be sent to Rochefort?"

"Not even to Toulon. You can employ him in your own service, but all these pardons depend on your conduct over the next six months, during which you'll be Bibi-Lupin's assistant."

Conclusion

A week later, Bibi-Lupin's assistant had recovered the Crottat family's four hundred thousand francs, and he had also arrested Ruffard and Godet.

The money from the sale of Esther Gobseck's certificates was found in the courtesan's bed, and Monsieur de Sérisy deposited in Jacques Collin's account the three hundred thousand francs left to him in the will of Lucien de Rubempré.

The funeral monument Lucien had ordered for himself and Esther is considered one of the finest in Père Lachaise; the plot it stands on belongs to Jacques Collin.

After having exercised his functions for some fifteen years, Jacques Collin retired, around the year 1845.[60]

TRANSLATOR'S NOTES

Translator's Introduction

1. Ellen Marriage (1865–1946), who translated about twenty-five novels from Balzac's *Comédie humaine* during the 1890s, felt she had to use a pseudonym for the more "daring" works, so her *A Harlot's Progress* appeared with the name of James Waring on the title page.

2. Rayner Heppenstall (1911–1981) published his translation in 1970.

3. The novel was *La Canne de Monsieur Balzac (Monsieur Balzac's Cane)*, by Delphine de Girardin, published in 1836.

4. Stefan Zweig, *Balzac,* translated by William and Dorothy Rose (New York: Viking, 1946). Zweig's unfinished text was completed by Richard Friedenthal. The two best biographies in English are Graham Robb, *Balzac: A Biography* (New York: W. W. Norton, 1994) and V. S. Pritchett, *Balzac* (New York: Knopf, 1973).

5. Théophile Gautier, *Honoré de Balzac* (Paris: Poulet-Malassis et de Boise, 1859), 11. Gautier's memoir was originally published in 1858, and it remains an excellent introduction to the man and his work.

6. The extremely complicated story of the book's long genesis is told in great detail in the introductions to the text Antoine Adam wrote for his Garnier edition (1958) and in the one by Pierre Citron in the Pléiade edition under the general editorship of Pierre-Georges Castex (1977). My abbreviated discussion is deeply indebted to the patient and precise work of Adam and Citron.

7. It may be only coincidence, but Socrates is also called a "torpedo-fish" in *Meno* 80b: "You seem, in appearance and in every other way, to be like the broad torpedo-fish, for it too makes anyone who comes close and touches it feel numb . . . for both my mind and my tongue are numb." Socrates jestingly replies that "if the torpedo-fish is itself numb and so makes others numb, then I resemble it, but not otherwise, for I myself do not have the answer when I perplex others" (80d; translated by G. M. A. Grube, in John M. Cooper, ed., *Plato: Complete Works* [Indianapolis: Hackett, 1997], 879).

8. "Lynx" (in French, *loup-cervier*) was the derogatory term for a financier,

implying a certain sharp-eyed quality as well as a decided ferocity. Nucingen is the lynx.

9. The dictionaries cited are available online at https://artfl-project.uchicago.edu/content/dictionnaires-dautrefois.

10. Parent-Duchâtelet lived from 1790 to 1836, his most important work being published shortly after his death: *De la Prostitution dans la ville de Paris, considérée sous le rapport de l'hygiène publique, de la morale et de l'administration.*

11. Jill Harsin, *Policing Prostitution in Nineteenth-Century Paris* (Princeton, N.J.: Princeton University Press, 1985), 102.

12. Antoine Adam, "Introduction," in Balzac, *Splendeurs et misères des courtisanes* (Paris: Garnier, 1958), xix.

13. Charles Bernheimer, *Figures of Ill Repute: Representing Prostitution in Nineteenth-Century France* (Cambridge, Mass.: Harvard University Press, 1989), 38.

14. Deborah Houk Schocket has suggested that Balzac presents Esther as "a kind of Robin Hood seeking vengeance and her seduction as a contribution both to social good and to Lucien's future, making her into an admirable figure of revolt against the evils of society" (*Modes of Seduction: Sexual Power in Balzac and Sand* [Madison, N.J.: Fairleigh Dickinson University Press, 2005], 98).

15. Jann Matlock, *Scenes of Seduction: Prostitution, Hysteria, and Reading Difference in Nineteenth-Century France* (New York: Columbia University Press, 1994). See especially chapter 3, 87–120.

16. Northrop Frye, *Anatomy of Criticism* (Princeton, N.J.: Princeton University Press, 1957), 47.

17. Christopher Prendergast, *Balzac: Fiction and Melodrama* (London: Edward Arnold, 1978), 87.

18. Shakespeare, *King Lear* 4.6.146–50, in Stephen Greenblatt et al., eds., *The Norton Shakespeare*, vol. 2 (New York: W. W. Norton, 2016). This is a play Balzac knew well; his novel *Père Goriot* is something of a modernized version of the tale of Lear and his daughters.

19. Georg Lukács, *Studies in European Realism: A Sociological Survey of the Writings of Balzac, Stendhal, Zola, Tolstoy, Gorki, and Others,* translated by Edith Bone (London: Hillway, 1950), 64.

20. Walter Benjamin, *The Arcades Project,* translated by Howard Eiland and Kevin McLaughlin (Cambridge, Mass.: Harvard University Press, 1999), 760.

21. Peter Brooks, "Foreword," in Eugène Sue, *The Mysteries of Paris,* translated by Carolyn Betensky and Jonathan Loesberg (New York: Penguin, 2015), xiii.

22. Both references are from Balzac's letters to Madame Hánska (the first from March [no day given] 1833 and the second from January 22, 1838), translated by Katherine Prescott Wormeley and available online via Project Gutenberg. All further quotations will be from https://www.gutenberg.org/files/54466/54466-h/54466-h.htm. Eveline, or Ewelina, Hańska (1805–1882) was a Polish noblewoman who began a correspondence with Balzac in 1832 that evolved into a close relationship; after the death of her husband, she and Balzac finally married in 1850, shortly before Balzac's death.

23. Prendergast, *Balzac: Fiction and Melodrama,* 36. Prendergast's tracing of the Balzac–Sue connection is careful and detailed, and my discussion of the subject is greatly indebted to him.

24. See Dominique Kalifa, *Vice, Crime, and Poverty: How the Western Imagination Invented the Underworld* (New York: Columbia University Press, 2013), especially chapter 3, "Dangerous Classes," 60–80.

25. Oscar Wilde, "The Decay of Lying" [1889], in Isobel Murray, ed., *Oscar Wilde* (The Oxford Authors) (New York: Oxford University Press, 1989), 222. There is an interesting exchange between Susan Sontag and Richard Ellman regarding this Wilde passage, available under the title "Vautrin's Cigar": https://www.nybooks.com/articles/1977/10/27/vautrins-cigar/.

26. Peter Brooks, *Body Work: Objects of Desire in Modern Narrative* (Cambridge, Mass.: Harvard University Press, 1993), 68.

27. Honoré de Balzac, *Lost Illusions* (Minneapolis: University of Minnesota Press, 2020), Part III, 153. On Vautrin's gender-switching, Janet Beizer offers a stimulating, psychoanalytic analysis in her *Family Plots: Balzac's Narrative Generations* (New Haven, Conn.: Yale University Press, 1986).

28. The story of Vidocq's memoirs is told in Roger Martin's introduction to his edition *Les Mémoires authentiques de Vidocq* (Paris: Archipoche, 2018). Also valuable is the narrative in Rosemary Peters, *Stealing Things: Theft and the Author in Nineteenth-Century France* (Lanham, Md.: Lexington, 2013).

29. Bernheimer, *Figures of Ill Repute,* 73.

30. Baudelaire, "Crowds," in *Paris spleen and La Fanfarlo,* translated by Raymond N. MacKenzie (Indianapolis: Hackett, 2008), 22.

31. D. A. Miller, "Balzac's Illusions Lost and Found," *Yale French Studies* 67 (1984): 181.

32. Harry Levin, *The Gates of Horn: A Study of Five French Realists* (New York: Oxford University Press, 1963), 199.

33. Many of Balzac's stories turn on imprisonment for debt, and he frequently editorializes against the practice. Elisabeth Bruyère provides good context for this in "Balzac and the Criticism of the French Civil Code in the First Half of the Nineteenth Century," in V. Amorosi and V. M. Minale, eds., *History of the Law and Other Humanities* (Madrid: Universidad Carlos III de Madrid, 2019), 329–36. See also Erika Vause, *In the Red and in the Black: Debt, Dishonor, and the Law in France between Revolutions* (Charlottesville: University of Virginia Press, 2018), especially chapter 5, "The Economy of Discredit," 152–86.

34. Maurice Samuels, *Inventing the Israelite: Jewish Fiction in Nineteenth-Century France* (Stanford, Calif.: Stanford University Press, 2009), 21. Helpful background on the topic is in Dorian Bell's study *Globalizing Race: Antisemitism and Empire in French and European Culture* (Evanston, Ill.: Northwestern University Press, 2018), especially chapter 2, 81–131.

35. An important example is the character Jean-Esther van Gobseck. Balzac's early (1830) story about him was at one point titled *L'Usurier* (*The Usurer*) but later was retitled *Gobseck.* The miserly moneylender turns out to be related to Esther, and he leaves his millions to her. In the tale *Gobseck,* the old man is humanized and made sympathetic in the affection he develops for the young lawyer Derville.

60

36. In a remarkable psychoanalytical analysis, Esther Rashkin suggests that Balzac's complicated representations of Jews imply "a need to unconsciously enact or work through an anxiety about the future of the Christian in France." See her *Unspeakable Secrets and the Psychoanalysis of Culture* (Albany, N.Y.: SUNY Press, 2008), especially 113–35. One might add that Balzac's relationship to Christianity was at least as complex.

37. Theodor Adorno, "Reading Balzac," in *Notes to Literature,* ed. Rolf Tiedemann, translated by Shierry Weber Nicholson (New York: Columbia University Press, 2019), 134.

38. On the Balzac–Genet continuum, see Éric Marty, *Radical French Thought and the Return of the "Jewish Question"* (Bloomington: Indiana University Press, 2015), especially chapter 1, "Jean Genet's Anxiety in the Face of the Good," 1–52.

39. Patrick Pollard gives a useful overview of the major instances of homosexuality in Balzac's works in his study *André Gide: Homosexual Moralist* (New Haven, Conn.: Yale University Press, 1991), 211–16. A number of critics have insisted there is no homosexual intent with the character of Collin, but the point seems to me too obvious to need arguing.

40. Print runs and sales figures indicating the relative popularity of Balzac's works are given in David Bellos, *Balzac Criticism in France, 1850–1900: The Making of a Reputation* (New York: Oxford University Press, 1976).

41. This is the count given by Fernand Lotte in his *Dictionnaire biographique des personnages fictifs de La Comédie humaine* (Paris: José Corti, 1952).

42. Robert Tranchida has compiled a good brief history of the Furne project (in French) online at http://www.v1.paris.fr/commun/v2asp/musees/balzac/furne/historique.htm.

43. Criminal slang remained a fascination well into twentieth-century French culture: consider the deliberately impenetrable titles of some of the great French crime thrillers, like *Touchez pas au grisbi* (1954), *Rififi chez les hommes* (1955), or *Razzia sur la chnouf* (1955).

44. An older but still helpful discussion of the uses of slang in the novel is Stephen Ullmann, *Style in the French Novel* (New York: Cambridge University Press, 1957), especially 81–93.

45. Edmond and Jules de Goncourt, *Journal,* September [no day given], 1857. The French original of the passage can be found online at Project Gutenberg: http://www.gutenberg.org/cache/epub/14799/pg14799-images.html.

I. How Women Love

1. The Bal de l'Opéra, held during the Carnival season preceding Lent, was an institution dating back to 1715; it only finally began to die out in the 1920s. To some extent it was an imitation of the masked balls of Venice, but the Paris balls took on their own character. In 1824, the final ball of the season would probably have been on February 28.

2. Frascati's was a famous casino, located on the Rue Richelieu; at one point in his life, Balzac had rooms above Frascati's.

3. Coralie was the actress who loved Lucien devotedly in *Lost Illusions,* right up to her death. Being known as the lover of a mere actress (in a day when the line between actress and prostitute was often blurred) harmed Lucien's

reputation in higher society, but ironically Coralie is one of the most faithful, appealing, and sympathetic characters in all of Balzac's works.

4. *Sargine, or Love's Student (Sargine, ou L'Élève de l'amour)* was a comic opera from 1788 by Nicolas Dalayrac and Jaques-Marie Boutet de Monvel.

5. Châtelet puns on the word *argent,* which means "silver" in Lucien's coat of arms, but which also means "money."

6. In this fencing match of one-upmanship, Lucien deliberately drops the particle "du" that ordinarily prefaces Châtelet's name, further downgrading his social standing.

7. In *Père Goriot* (1834–35), Rastignac and the mysterious man had both roomed at the establishment run by Madame Vauquer.

8. A man does awaken to find a panther next to him in Balzac's 1830 tale "Une passion dans le desert" ("A Passion in the Desert").

9. The story of the gifts sent to Lucien in Angoulême so he could have his triumph is told in *Lost Illusions,* Part III. At his request, his old circle in Paris sent him a set of fine clothes and accessories to enhance his social impact in the provincial town.

10. In La Fontaine's 1679 edition of *Fables,* the ape Bertrand talks Raton the cat into getting chestnuts from the fire for him; Bertrand gets his nuts, but the cat burns his paws and gets nothing for his trouble ("Le Singe et le chat," *Fables* IX, 17).

11. The outspoken Alceste and the more polite and restrained Philinte are characters in Molière's *Le Misanthrope* (1666).

12. Lucien implies he is supported by the conservative Royalist party. The story of his cynically switching political parties is told in *Lost Illusions,* Part II.

13. *Quibuscumque viis*: in one way or another.

14. The Latin *fuge, late, tace* (flee, hide, be silent) was inscribed in the monastery of the Grande Chartreuse, which Balzac had visited. The phrase, and Balzac's use of it both here and in *Le Médecin de campagne (The Country Doctor,* 1833), is discussed by Andrew Bennett in his *Suicide Century: Literature and Suicide from James Joyce to David Foster Wallace* (New York: Cambridge University Press, 2017), 82–84.

15. Bixiou's sentence is clear enough in its 1824 setting, but for Balzac's readers in the 1840s it might recall the satiric newspaper *Le Charivari,* which had a long life, beginning in 1832 and only ceasing publication in 1937. Another slight anachronism in this passage is Bixiou's exclamation "Charles X!" In 1824, when the scene is set, Louis XVIII was still on the throne. Bixiou could be implying that Lucien is already looking ahead to the next administration.

16. Lointier's, on the Rue de Richelieu near the Bourse, was one of the finest restaurants of the era.

17. The French word *torpille* means torpedo, but not the armament; rather, the electric fish, the fish that stuns and numbs. Given the usual use of "torpedo" in English, it seemed best to retain the French word. Balzac explains the origins of the nickname a little later.

18. Aspasia of Miletus was a celebrated courtesan, an immigrant to Greece who became the lover of the Athenian leader Pericles about 445 BCE.

19. Blondet's lengthy catalog of famous courtesans is pompous and overdone, with the kind of exaggerated, semi-sarcastic rhetoric he enjoys, but it

does work also to help put La Torpille and her story against a grander historical background.

20. Blondet writes for the *Journal des débats,* the most prestigious and most widely read of the weekly papers at the time.

21. Thérésa Cabarrus, Madame Tallien, one of the most famous personalities during the 1790s and later in Paris, presided over a famous salon and was known to dress (and live) flamboyantly. There is a superb portrait of her, done in 1806 by Duvivier, in the Brooklyn Museum.

22. In *Lost Illusions* we learn that Finot is the son of a hatmaker.

23. Rabelais discusses the powers of salt in Book II, chapter 3, of *Gargantua et Pantagruel* (1534).

24. We read about Esther's mother, Sarah Gobseck, in Balzac's 1835 novella *Gobseck* and in the 1837 novel *César Birotteau* (*Histoire de la grandeur et de la décadence de César Birotteau*); in both of those she is known as "the beautiful Hollander" (*la belle Hollandaise*). Maxime de Trailles, an especially dangerous rogue, appears in those two works, too, as well as many others.

25. Marie-Antoine Carême (1784–1833) was a celebrated French chef who developed what became known as "grande cuisine." Taglioni could refer to the dancer Marie Taglioni (1804–1884) or to her equally famous father, the choreographer Filippo Taglioni (1777–1871). The Englishman Thomas Lawrence (1769–1830) was in high demand as a portrait painter. André-Charles Boulle (1642–1732) was a designer whose armoires and cabinets remained in high demand during Balzac's time.

26. "The English" (*les Anglais*) is old slang for creditors, bill collectors.

27. Giovanni Bellini (circa 1430–1516), a Venetian, was a prolific painter; he did a number of Madonnas, but none quite like what Balzac describes here.

28. Antoine Adam points out that prostitutes in the early nineteenth century often adopted nicknames, *noms de guerre,* such as this one, making it harder for the police to identify them. The practice was outlawed in 1828, though of course that did not put an end to it.

29. The Rue de Langlade and the area Balzac describes were all swept away in the great reconstruction of Paris in the 1860s.

30. The eerie episode of the frozen words is in Book 4 of Rabelais. Panurge and Pantagruel hear strange, disembodied words in the air, and they speculate that they might be words from the ancient world that had frozen, perhaps even the words of Plato.

31. The Wooden Galleries, adjacent to the Palais-Royal, operated from 1786 to 1829. The place, a kind of indoor arcade, was home to the publishing trade and, by night, to crowds of prostitutes. Balzac describes the Wooden Galleries at length in *Lost Illusions,* Part II.

32. A sink (Balzac uses the term *plomb*) was an open drain for dirty water and other matter, installed in the foyer on each floor; the contents would flow through pipes and out, sometimes into the sewers, sometimes into the street. Balzac calls these sinks "horrible," no doubt because of the smell.

33. The Théâtre de la Porte Saint-Martin was originally opened in 1781. Though it burned down once and was rebuilt, it has remained in continuous operation at its original site, 18 Boulevard Saint-Martin.

34. Francisco Zurbarán (1598–1664) was a Spanish painter of religious subjects; his use of darkness and shade in his work suggests the influence of Caravaggio.

35. The list of famous ancients in love includes the less familiar Cethegus, a Roman senator of the first century BCE who was said to be so in love with the beautiful courtesan Praecia that he would do nothing without consulting her. See Nicholas K. Rauh, "Prostitutes, Pimps, and Political Conspiracies," in Allison Glazebrook and Madeleine M. Henry, eds., *Greek Prostitutes in the Ancient Mediterranean, 800 BCE–200 CE* (Madison: University of Wisconsin Press, 2011), 198–99.

36. Adam notes that Balzac, evidently pleased with this description of Esther, cited it in his 1839 preface to *Une fille d'Ève (A Daughter of Eve)*: writing such a description, Balzac said, "can cost us an entire night's work, the reading of several volumes, and the posing of great scientific questions" (Adam, 52).

37. Balzac had written admiringly about the Jesuits in Paraguay in his *Histoire impartiale des Jésuits* (1824).

38. In Judges 11, Jephthah promises the Lord that he will sacrifice the first person he encounters after the battle. It turns out to be his daughter, and after allowing her two months grace, he does sacrifice her; in ensuing years, all the daughters of Israel ritually recall and lament her death.

39. *The Prairie* (1827), a novel by James Fenimore Cooper, was known in France by the title *Les Puritains d'Amérique*. The heroine's name is Ruth, but after a series of events that result in her being raised by American Indians, she takes the name Narra-Matah.

40. Antoine Adam suggests the doctor is Étienne-Jean Georget (1795–1828) (Adam, 56). Georget wrote on monomania and melancholy and is considered the father of forensic psychiatry. He was a disciple of the psychologist Jean-Étienne Dominique Esquirol (1772–1840), with whom Balzac was acquainted.

41. Françoise d'Aubigné, Marquise de Maintenon (1635–1719), the second wife of Louis XIV, may have been born in a prison, hence the reference to her "native mud." The story about the fish is widely reported, though they are sometimes said to have been goldfish; it apparently originated with Sébastien Nicolas de Chamfort (1741–94).

42. François Habeneck (1781–1849) was conductor at the Paris Conservatoire and then the Opéra.

43. Antoine Adam points out that the phrase "Church and Monarchy man" (*religieux et monarchique*) was common in the Restoration for the class known as the *bien-pensants*, those who thought "correctly" and thus remained on good terms with, and benefited from, the restored regime.

44. The Rocher-de-Cancale, established in 1734, was in Balzac's time one of the most expensive restaurants in Paris; it is still in operation today, at 78 Rue Montorgueil.

45. "Putting the body to the question" means torture. The phrase often refers specifically to water torture.

46. The *Rey netto* is the "pure" king, that is, the rightful monarch with all his powers restored. Ferdinand VII of Spain (1784–1833) had been taken prisoner and forced to accept a liberal constitution in 1820, but by the time of the events in

the novel (1824), he was already on the path back to absolutism; his next ten years would be increasingly repressive. In 1823 the French under the Duc d'Angoulême had invaded and restored him to power.

47. The *camarilla* was Ferdinand's circle of advisers and supporters; the Cortes is the Spanish parliament.

48. In the 1838 version of the novel, Balzac had made Herrera a liberal, but in 1843 he changed his background and political orientation completely.

49. This digression on seventeenth-century French history reflects Balzac's research into the period in 1837, when he was writing articles for a volume edited by William Duckett, *Dictionnaire de la conversation*. The general public was reading about that same era in the wildly popular historical novel by Alfred de Vigny, Cinq-Mars (1826).

50. Raphael's mistress, Marghareta Luti, was known as La Fornarina (The Baker); his famous painting of her (c. 1518) is given that title.

51. The *bocchettino* is the hookah's mouthpiece.

52. *Manlius Capitolinus* was a hit play by Antoine de la Fosse. The famous actor François-Joseph Talma (1763–1826) played the title role to great acclaim.

53. Caroline Bellefeuille's story is told in Balzac's *Une double famille* (*A Double Family*), which was written, published, revised, and republished a number of times between 1830 and 1842. It was translated by Clara Bell under the title *A Second Home.*

54. Littré's 1873 *Dictionnaire* explains that a "tiger" is the groom of a fashionable man (*groom d'un élégant*).

55. Marie-Antoine Carême (1784–1833) was a celebrated French chef, architect of the so-called grand cuisine.

56. Monrose was the stage name of Claude Barizain (1783–1843), a French actor who was noted for playing servants' roles in comedies like *Le Bàrbier de Séville.*

57. *Madelonnette* was a slang term for a reformed prostitute (from Madeleine/ Magdalene), as well as the prison where prostitutes were taken.

58. Locusta was a famous maker of poisons in first-century Rome, a favorite of the emperor Nero.

59. Her real last name is Gobseck.

60. The two main characters in the novel *Paul et Virginie* (1787) by Bernardin de Saint-Pierre are innocent lovers in an Edenic setting, an island paradise.

61. "The man who feels the bumps" is the phrenologist, who can tell one's character and one's leading passion by feeling bumps on the head. Balzac makes frequent reference to phrenology.

62. The reference is to the conservative group known as La Congrégation de la Sainte-Vierge (The Congregation of the Holy Virgin), a group of lay Catholics who had considerable influence during the Restoration.

63. The story of Godefroid de Beaudenord, and his carefully chosen apartment in the "right" neighborhood, is told in the 1838 novella *La Maison Nucingen* (translated as *The Nucingen Firm*).

64. The higher the floor, the less prestige: Herrera is effacing himself, sacrificing his own comfort and status, so as to keep Lucien always in the forefront.

65. Balzac (and other French writers of the era, too, notably Stendhal) frequently contrasts what he sees as easy, natural familiarity in social intercourse among the French with the stiff and cold distance of the English.

66. Madame de Sérisy figures in a number of other works by Balzac, notably *Ferragus* (1833) and *Ursule Mirouët* (1841).

67. The Grand Chaplaincy (La Grande-Aumônerie) is the clergy, or group of clergy, responsible for the religious practices in the king's household and beyond. Its influence grew dramatically during the Restoration, and it was finally disbanded after the July Revolution of 1830.

68. Antoine Adam points out that there appears to be no such word as *Reinganum*. He speculates that Balzac may have imperfectly remembered a term used in parts of Switzerland, *ringulum*, to signify a kind of toy top (88).

69. The term "lynx" (*loup-cervier*) was used in the era to denote unscrupulous financiers, or any person who was rapacious concerning money.

70. Nucingen's Alsatian accent is thick, and that combined with his shaky grasp on grammar sometimes makes him nearly incomprehensible. This translation will try to err on the side of comprehensibility, or close to it.

71. The Rue Vivienne was known as a haven for prostitution.

72. A heyduck (*heiduque* in Balzac's French) is, here, a generalized term for a manservant; the word originally denoted a kind of bandit or brigand.

73. "Rational-style love" is an attempt to translate *amour-goût,* the kind of love that one seeks out consciously, the kind embodied today in internet dating. The term comes from the opening chapter of Stendhal's *De l'amour* (1822); Stendhal saw *amour-goût* coming to dominate modern life in novels and memoirs that began to be published around 1760. Stendhal's book was not widely read in its day; Balzac was one of the first, and one of the few in the era, to recognize Stendhal's genius.

74. Friedrich von Gentz (1764–1832), German diplomat and writer who played an important role after the fall of Napoleon, experienced a powerful infatuation late in life with the beautiful young Austrian dancer Fanny Elssler (1810–84); he is said to have died in her arms.

75. The Holy Ampulla (Sainte Ampoule) is a glass vial dating back to the twelfth century; it held the oil used to anoint the kings of France.

76. Balzac reminds us that Delphine is the daughter of one of his most famous characters, the retired merchant Jean-Joachim Goriot from the novel *Père Goriot.*

77. The Gardes du Commerce, established by Napoleon in 1808, combined the functions of bailiffs and detectives, focusing on business-related rather than purely criminal matters; the courts often gave them the authority to arrest a debtor on the street. They were also *gardes* in the sense that they could be installed within a debtor's house to ensure that he or she did not try to sell off any of the household goods.

78. Balzac puns on the word *étranger,* which means both "stranger" and "foreigner": Herrera was *plus étrange qu'étranger.*

79. Pierre Coignard (1774–1834) was a convict who escaped and turned up in Spain in 1805 under the title of the Comte de Sainte-Hélène. He managed his false identity well, asserting a vigorous royalism, and he rose to the post of

lieutenant-colonel in 1816, during the Restoration; the following year he was finally recognized. He fled and was recaptured in 1818; he returned to prison, where he ultimately died.

80. The "fateful letters" that were branded on convicts' backs were T. F., for *travaux forcés*: forced labor.

81. Scholars have been unable to trace this tale about the dervish and the youth, which sounds so much like the tale of Carlos and Lucien that it may be Balzac's invention.

82. The three main penal colonies (*bagnes*) within France were at Rochefort, Toulon, and Brest, though there were others, some of them infamous, in the colonies.

83. The reference is to Voltaire's 1736 play *Le Fanatisme, ou Mahomet le prophète*. In the play, the character Seid falls victim to religious fanaticism.

84. *Incedo per ignes*: I walk through the flames. From Horace, *Odes*, II.2.

85. *Caveo non timeo*: I take care, but I do not fear. The italicized phrase is heraldic jargon, which describes the coat of arms of the Duc de Grandlieu.

86. The story of Derville and the viscountess is told in *Gobseck*; we will meet Derville later in this story. The "exile" of the viscountess would have been what came to be called the Emigration, the flight of the aristocrats from France following the Revolution; some, like the Grandlieus, drifted back during Napoleon's reign, but most returned after 1814, when the monarchy was restored.

87. "Monsieur" is the old way of discreetly referring to the king's brother, that is, the next in line for the throne; in this case that was Louis' brother Charles, who would become Charles X.

88. Armand-Benoît Roussel (1773–1852), known simply as Armand, was one of the era's most celebrated actors.

89. A Maître Jacques is a right-hand man. During the time the novel took place, this would have been Jules, Prince de Polignac (1780–1847), who was raised to a position of very great power by Charles X in 1829. His extremist views led to the declaration of the infamous Four Ordinances of 1830, which were a primary cause of the July Revolution.

90. The death of Baron de Macumer figures in Balzac's *Mémoires de deux jeunes mariées* (translated by Jordan Stump as *The Memoirs of Two Young Wives* [New York: NYTB Books, 2018]), 1841.

91. The *fichu menteur* was a thick neckerchief; it was designed to be tucked so as to cover the bust, but Clotilde's chest is evidently too flat for it be usable.

92. Sainte-Pélagie was a prison in Paris in the 5th arrondissement. It was torn down in 1899.

93. The story of Madame d'Espard's attempt to have her husband certified as mentally ill is told in Balzac's *L'Interdiction* (translated as *The Commission in Lunacy*).

94. The *Gazette des tribunaux*, established in 1825, published news items relating to court cases and would certainly have seized on the d'Espard story as a sensational one.

95. For more detail on the somewhat elaborate administrative structure of the French police in the post-Napoleonic era, see Clive Emsley, "Policing the Streets of Nineteenth-Century Paris," *French History* 1, no. 2 (October 1987):

257–82; and John Merriman, *Police Stories: Building the French State, 1815–1851* (New York: Oxford University Press, 2006). Balzac's description here (rather, Louchard's) is a little misleading but close enough for narrative purposes.

96. The character Turcaret gave his name to a satirical play by Alain-René Lesage (1708). Turcaret is a vulgar and ruthless financier.

97. Lansmatt, whose name was actually Lansmartre, was a valet and master of the hunt to Louis XV, not a doorkeeper or concierge.

98. Frédérick Lemaître (1880–1876) was a famous French actor. He portrayed Balzac's Vautrin in the play of that name (1840).

99. The term *petites maisons* (little houses) refers, in this context, to "pleasure houses," small places, located on back streets, that one could rent for keeping an affair secret.

100. Joseph Fouché (1759–1820) was minister of police under Napoleon, and before Napoleon's ascendancy to emperor, under the Directory and the Consulate. A friend of Robespierre, he was highly efficient, even ruthless at times.

101. Louis XVIII did away with the Ministry of Police in 1814, but when Napoleon returned for the Hundred Days, he reinstated it. After Napoleon's final fall, it was disbanded and reorganized in 1818.

102. The story of Nucingen's shrewd but hardly ethical rise is told in *La Maison Nucingen.*

103. A horseshoe found in the street turned into the chief clue in solving an attempted assassination of Napoleon in 1800. The *machine infernale* was a cart loaded with gunpowder and rigged to explode as Napoleon passed by. The story of the plot is told concisely by Tom Holmberg and Max Sewell in "The Infernal Machine," http://www.napoleon-series.org/research/miscellaneous/c_infernal .html.

104. The secret police agent Corentin is fictional; he appears in many of Balzac's works, including the early novel *Les Chouans* (1829).

105. Fouché was associated with the order of Oratorians during his school years and for some time after, but he never took orders and became a priest. The belief that the fierce minister of police had once been a priest was, however, widespread.

106. The Café David, despite Balzac's specificity as to its location, is apparently fictional.

107. All are characters who figure in other Balzac works, especially *Histoire de la grandeur et de la décadence de César Birotteau* (1837). Camusot plays a minor but significant role in *Illusions perdues* (1837–43). Guillaume figures in *La Maison du chat qui pelote* (1842).

108. The *Petites-Affiches* was a newspaper devoted to local legal and news items in the Département of the Seine.

109. Vitellius (15–69 CE) was renowned for his gluttony and other excesses; he reigned as emperor of Rome for a mere eight months before being murdered by soldiers loyal to Vespasian.

110. Jean Lenoir and Joseph Albert alternately held the post of lieutenant-general of police between 1774 and 1785.

111. Balzac's history gives a good general picture but is not correct in every detail; see the works cited Emsley and Merriman cited in note 95.

112. La Force was located in what is now the 4th arrondissement of Paris. It was originally the home of the Duc de la Force and was made into a prison in 1780; it was torn down in 1845. It will feature later in the story.

113. Walcheren is an island in the mouth of the Scheldt River, not far from Antwerp. Some forty thousand English troops landed there on July 30, 1809, but the invasion went no further, a severe sickness spreading through the camp and the expedition returning home in December. The Duc d'Otrante was Joseph Fouché.

114. Jean-Jacques-Régis de Cambacérès, duke of Parma (1753–1824), an early supporter of Napoleon, rose so high during the Empire that he effectively governed France while Napoleon's attention was focused on military conquest.

115. The painter Joseph-Marie Vien (1716–1809) was a powerful influence on the young Jacques-Louis David (1748–1825).

116. Balzac cites his own novel *Une ténébreuse affaire*, 1843. Herbert J. Hunt translated it as *A Murky Business* (London: Penguin, 1972).

117. Balzac's early novel *Les Chouans* was published in 1829. Antirevolutionary insurgents in the 1790s in the regions of Brittany and Normandy were nicknamed Chouans, a regional term for "owls," probably because of their nocturnal activities. In the novel a woman is sent as "bait" to catch a Chouan leader, but she ends up falling in love with him.

118. Anne Jean Marie René Savary (1774–1833) was a successful general; Napoleon gave him the title of Duc de Rovigo. He was put in charge of the police following the dismissal of Fouché in 1810.

119. Eugène-François Vidocq (1775–1857) is regarded as the founder of the modern French police force. He was legendary, having been a criminal before turning his considerable intelligence to working for rather than against the law. He captured Balzac's imagination and that of many others ever since. He continues to be the subject of historical studies and fiction, and he even figures in at least one modern video game, *Assassin's Creed Unity* (Ubisoft, 2014).

120. The Cercle des Étrangers, founded in 1794, was a kind of gourmand club; its cuisine was famous in its day.

121. The *Courrier français* was a liberal paper, and hence one critical of the government, so the implication perhaps is that "imbeciles" would read such a paper. But in the first printed version of the novel, Balzac had named the *Journal des débats*, which was more supportive of the government.

122. "Mère Godichon" is an old traditional song; the phrase "to sing 'Mère Godichon'" means to be festive, to party.

123. This alludes to what is known as the affair of the diamond necklace (which took place in 1784–85); the story is told, and considerably embroidered upon, by Dumas in his novel *La Collier de la reine* (*The Queen's Necklace*, 1849). Nothing in the story quite matches the anecdote Balzac seems to have in mind, however.

124. The prince referred to is the Duc d'Orléans, a rival of Louis' brother Charles to the throne. Peyrade and Corentin were indeed foresighted, for Charles X would ultimately inherit just such a revolution in 1830.

125. Wilhelm Schmucke, German musician and music teacher, is fictional. He appears in other Balzac works, notably *Ursule Mirouët* (1841) and *Le Cousin Pons* (1847).

126. *Les Frères de la Consolation* was a working title for a novel that was eventually published under the title *L'Envers de l'histoire contemporaine,* translated by Jordan Stump as *The Wrong Side of Paris* (New York: Random House, 2003).

127. Balzac uses slang ("faces") and professional jargon ("the house"), providing his own translation in brackets.

128. Elsewhere Balzac calls Nucingen an Alsatian. Perhaps this is a slip, or perhaps the phrase should be read "in his hideous accent so similar to that of a Polish Jew. . . ."

129. The Pont Louis XVI was renamed Pont de la Concorde in 1830, the name it bears today.

130. "The boys from the fields" is translated from *les amis du pré,* a slang phrase for the convicts who had been in the penal camps and/or galleys together. "Alms" is the translation of the slang term *thunes,* and "five-ballers," *cinq balles,* five-franc pieces. Citron, in the Pléiade edition, points out that this little burst of criminal slang was added only in the final revision.

131. The powerful alcoholic concoction known as *liqueur des braves* came into fashion around 1819.

132. The story of Corentin, Gondreville, and "those Simeuse people" is told in *Une ténébreuse affaire (A Murky Business).*

133. The Bal Mabille was a popular outdoor dancing establishment in Paris. It opened in 1831 and was so successful that it didn't close until 1875.

134. Braschon the interior decorator *(tapissier)* is fictional; he appears in other Balzac works, notably *Histoire de la grandeur et de la décadence de César Birotteau* (1837).

135. The gold coin, the *louis d'or,* was worth twenty francs. Under the Empire, the same coin was called a "napoleon."

136. Amber pills were taken as a kind of aphrodisiac. The servant is worried that taking them without sexual release might be dangerous.

137. There were four licensed gambling establishments in the Palais-Royal, known by their street addresses. There is a painting from 1815, titled *Le 113,* by Georg Emmanuel Opitz showing prostitutes gathering outside the establishment. See https://commons.wikimedia.org/wiki/File:Palais-royal_1815.jpg.

138. In the early versions, Balzac used the vulgarism *gougé avec,* translated here as "got on top of." In the Furne edition he toned this down to read "until he had had" her.

139. The "Boulogne near Paris" is today a suburb, Boulogne-Billancourt, not to be confused with the town on the northern coast, Boulogne-sur-Mer.

140. Georges d'Estourny figures in other Balzac novels, *Modeste Mignon* (1841) and *Un homme d'affaires* (1845).

141. Jean-Baptiste Sylvère Gay, First Viscount of Martignac (1778–1832), was a moderate Royalist, minister of the interior from 1828 until 1829.

142. Cérizet plays a hypocritical, near villainous role in Part III of Balzac's *Lost Illusions,* where he betrays the trust of his employer, David Séchard (Lucien's brother-in-law).

143. Ninon de l'Enclos (1620–1705), the famous courtesan and woman of letters in the era of Louis XIV, was said to have been entrusted with sixty thousand francs by Jean Hérault de Gourville, who deposited an equal amount with the

supposedly pious Notre-Dame official who held the title of *grand pénitencier*. When, some time later, de Gourville returned to France, Ninon returned his money immediately, but the *grand pénitencier* cited religious reasons for keeping it. Voltaire wrote a satirical play on this Molière-worthy subject, *Le Dépositaire* (1769).

144. In Part III of *Lost Illusions,* Cérizet had sided with the scheming lawyer Petit-Claud and the equally scheming businessmen the Cointet brothers, in bringing about what they expected to be the ruin of the naïve and honest David Séchard.

145. Asia, we learn later, uses this name from time to time. Antoine Adam points out that the famous (real life) detective Vidocq sometimes used the name himself.

II. What Love Costs an Old Man

1. Balzac invokes the Roman satirist Juvenal (circa 50–120 CE) to suggest a force that chastens the proud and the powerful.

2. A minor slip on Balzac's part: he told us in Part I that Asia had "that copper-colored face typical of Malays," and here he suggests that she really was Malaysian. We will learn much later that this is not the case.

3. The Théâtre du Gymnase, on the Boulevard Bonne-Nouvelle, opened in 1820.

4. The phrase translated here as "an obscene gesture" was originally *une geste digne de la Halle* (a gesture worthy of Les Halles). Les Halles, the main food market in Paris, was a place of sharp negotiation and, inevitably, of harsh, obscene language.

5. "Mademoiselle Dupont" is probably Caroline Dupont (born 1794), who was active on the Paris stage between 1810 and 1840.

6. Saint-Lazare was a prison for women in the 10th arrondissement; it was demolished in 1935.

7. Stanislaus Baudry's Omnibus line, horse-drawn vehicles that could carry from twelve to eighteen passengers, was launched in Paris in April 1828, following a successful trial in Nantes. The new buses were a popular success, but at first they lost a great deal of money; the losses led Baudry to commit suicide in 1830.

8. Louis Mandrin (1725–55) was a notorious smuggler.

9. Jean-François Regnard's comedy *Le Joueur (The Gambler)* was first produced in 1696.

10. Grindot is fictional; he appears briefly as a noted architect in a number of other works, including *César Birotteau* and *Eugénie Grandet.*

11. "Take my bear" *(Prenez mon ours)* comes from Eugène Scribe's farce *L'Ours et le pascha* (1834). The phrase became a common sarcastic idiom, meaning, roughly, you've put too high a price on the goods you're offering.

12. Anne-Marie Bigot de Cornuel (1605–1694), known for her wit, hosted a literary salon in Paris. She is thought to have been the originator of the saying "No man is a hero to his valet."

13. Sébastien Zamet (1549–1614), Italian born, was a financier who rose to

prominence in France under Henri IV. His son, also named Sébastien, was bishop of Langres and director of Port Royal.

14. Sextus Julius Frontinus (circa 40–103) was an exceptionally competent civil engineer, best known for his work on the aqueduct systems; he rose politically to become consul under the emperors Nerva and Trajan.

15. Martin Garat (1748–1830) was director-general of the Banque de France between 1800 and 1830.

16. Marie Anne Adelaide Lenormand (1772–1843) operated as a psychic and fortune-teller whose clients included the Empress Joséphine and the Czar Alexander I. The Cabaret Ramponneau was frequented by elegant, higher-society patrons during the late eighteenth and early nineteenth centuries, but by Balzac's time it was beginning to attract members of the working and domestic classes.

17. In Book II of *Gargantua and Pantagruel* the character Panurge indulges in tricky sleight of hand with money, giving away (or seeming to) much more than he actually has.

18. Asia is no doubt referring to the case of Dr. Edmé-Samuel Castaing (1796–1823), who befriended two wealthy brothers who were both lawyers and was arrested later for poisoning both of them separately, using morphine. Castaing did have a mistress, with whom he had had two children, and they were in financial difficulties. Accounts of his 1823 trial were published that same year, and though he continued to maintain his innocence, he was guillotined in December.

19. The mythical Babylonian queen Semiramis was the subject of a heroic tragedy by Voltaire (1748); Asia is striking a theatrical pose of feigned nobility.

20. In the spring of 1800, Napoleon, then first consul, led his army through the Great Saint Bernard Pass and into Italy.

21. Robert d'Arbrissel (circa 1045–1116) was an itinerant preacher whose primary theme was chastity; he founded the Abbey of Fontrevault in Anjou.

22. Vincenzo Bellini's opera *I Puritani (The Puritans)* premiered in Paris in January 1835 to great acclaim. The soprano Maria Amigo appeared in the role of Henrietta Maria, the wife of Charles I.

23. Octave Uzanne describes the "madwoman" or *à la folle* style of bonnet as "trimmed with a multi-colored scarf, and blonde, and lace, which half hid the wearer's face" (*Fashion in Paris*, trans. Lady Mary Lloyd [London: Heinemann, 1901], 16).

24. Chevet's shop was also located in the Palais-Royal suite of shops. The "Review of Two Worlds" reference involves a rather labored joke: at Chevet's or the restaurant Rocher-de-Cancale one can eat foods from two worlds, both the Old World and the New. But the phrase "Revue des Deux Mondes" is the title of the famous magazine, founded in 1829. Balzac had quarreled with its editor, and the joke here is that the publication *Revue des deux mondes* is not true or delicious.

25. The Duke of Torlonia (1769–1865) was almost proverbial for his enormous wealth; the Torlonia family were bankers to the Vatican.

26. The painters Hippolyte Schinner and Léon de Lora are fictional, both appearing in other Balzac works. Alexandre du Sommerard (1779–1842) was a French archaeologist and art collector whose collection formed the basis of today's Musée de Cluny.

27. Alexandre Dumas's play *Richard d'Arlington* (1831) was based on Walter Scott's novel *Kenilworth*. Since it premiered in 1831, this is another minor anachronism on Balzac's part.

28. The story of Philippe Bridau, now Comte de Brambourg, is told in Balzac's 1842 novel *La Rabouilleuse* (translated by Donald Adamson as *The Black Sheep*).

29. The term "nabob" was used to refer to any wealthy Englishman, many Englishmen having made a fortune in India.

30. "Nabot" is a pejorative term for a dwarf. Antoine Adam explains that the person known as the Bailli de Ferrette was indeed short and also very thin. He was a habitué of the Opéra, known to be a "protector" to some performers. Pierre Citron adds that Balzac referred to him in two other stories as well.

31. The Rue de Jérusalem, swept away in the general reconstruction of Paris later in the century, was the site of the Prefecture of Police.

32. In Balzac's *Ursule Mirouët* (1842), the Vicomte de Portenduère is briefly imprisoned for debt in Sainte-Pélagie but is ultimately united with his beloved Ursule, a humble orphan.

33. Balzac uses the English word *parties,* in italics. The marriage of Théodore Gaillard and Suzanne du Val-Noble is referred to in *Béatrix* (1839).

34. The painter Musson was known as a professional *mystificateur,* translated here as "hoaxer." There was a brief vogue in Balzac's time for hiring a *mystificateur* to come in disguise to a dinner or gathering; one of the guests would be preselected as the target or butt of the joke, and the *mystificateur* would proceed to befuddle or embarrass the unwitting guest, providing comedy for the rest of the party.

35. Charles had never been popular, and charges against his legitimacy were mounting; the Algerian expedition, intended to increase the regime's standing with the people, took place in July 1830, but that same month saw revolution at home, and Charles abdicated on August 2.

36. Peyrade has chosen the names of two men famous in the history of the French police. Antoine de Sartine (1729–1801) was lieutenant-general of the Paris police, and his protégé was the lawyer Jean-Charles-Pierre Lenoir (1732–1807).

37. The man in the cab holds the rank of *officier de paix,* or peace officer, a police rank established in 1791. The *officier de paix* was authorized to make an arrest and take the offender to a magistrate. In 1829 the rank of *sergent* was established, and these *sergents* were under the authority of the *officiers de paix.*

38. The headquarters of the General Police was on the Rue de Grenelle and of the prefecture on the Rue de Jérusalem.

39. The firms of Huret and of Fichet were both manufacturers of strongboxes and safes. Alexandre Fichet was originally a locksmith, and the firm he founded in 1829 is still manufacturing locks; today it's known as Fichet-Bauche.

40. A well-known scandal of the summer of 1828 involved the sixty-year-old Marquis de Lauriston (1768–1828), who died in the arms of his mistress, a young dancer. The newspaper account, in an attempt to save his reputation, stated that he had died "in the arms of Religion." The mistress from then on was referred to as Mademoiselle la Réligion.

41. We have already met the doctors Bianchon and Desplein; Haudry is a third who also features in a number of Balzac's works.

42. The Duc de Chaulieu figures in several of Balzac's works, notably *Mémoires de deux jeunes mariées* (translated by Jordan Stump as *The Memoirs of Two Young Wives,* where he gives a memorable, impassioned defense of the high conservatism of the aristocrat.

43. The Cadran-Bleu (Blue Dial) was a restaurant favored by middle-class businesspeople. It was located on the Boulevard du Temple.

44. In English in the original. Balzac's command of English was imperfect, and he assumes French pluralization, so that the phrase appears in the French text as "very fines." The cacophony among the characters' languages seems to be contagious.

45. Jean Anthelme Brillat-Savarin (1755–1826) was a French lawyer who had become famous as a gourmet and for his writing about food.

46. The story of David Séchard, his papermaking invention, and the Cointet brothers is told in Part III of *Lost Illusions.*

47. The *tribunal de première instance* is a lower court, used primarily for misdemeanors and the like. It was also called the *justice de paix* court during the nineteenth century. Derville works for the tribunal of the Seine prefecture.

48. La Verberie is the name of the house Eve Séchard bought, adjoining old Séchard's property and vineyards.

49. "Look under the *buchons*" refers to an old tradition of placing a kind of branch (*buchon*) over the door of an inn or tavern to signify that wine was sold there.

50. To sleep *à la belle étoile* is to sleep under the stars, in the open air.

51. Handmade tapestries and carpets are still produced today in the little town of Aubusson, about 250 miles south of Paris. The town's craft apparently dates back at least to the fourteenth century.

52. Public executions were carried out on the Place de Grève (which today is called the Place de l'Hôtel de Ville). The "final shave" *(rasé)* refers to the blade of the guillotine.

53. Charenton was an asylum located in Saint-Maurice, a suburb today but then a village just southeast of Paris.

54. Pierre Citron points out on page 1401 that the phrase "no one's ever been able to figure that out" *(on n'a jamais pu le savoir)* had become a standing joke, a deliberate piece of non sequitur silliness, in Balzac's era.

55. A song by Pierre-Jean de Béranger, "Les Moutons" ("The Sheep"), includes a similar refrain. Balzac also quotes it in *Cousin Pons* (1847): *"Pauvres moutons... on vous tondra, toujours on vous tondra"* ("Poor sheep ... they shear you, they're always shearing you").

56. The banker Nicolas Beaujon (1718–1786) was famed for his philanthropy, having endowed a home for orphans.

57. The poet is Alphonse de Lamartine (1790–1869). One of the most famous and most widely reproduced portraits of him, by Henri Decaisne in 1830, depicts him with two whippet dogs.

58. The Hôtel-Dieu, established in the seventh century, is the oldest hospital in Paris; it is still in operation today.

59. Esther exclaims *"Des planches!"* (planks) in one version of the text and *"Des voliges!"* (roof supports) in another. "Stepping-stone" seems to get the point across, but "plank" might include a swipe at Clotilde's skinny frame.

60. On Habeneck and the Conservatory, see Part I, note 42.

61. Louis François Armand de Vignerot du Plessis, Duc de Richelieu (1696–1788) was married three times. His third marriage, at age eighty-four, was to a woman thirty-eight years younger. Antoine de Rivarol (1753–1801) was a Royalist writer, translator, and epigrammatist.

62. Balzac italicizes "the curious" as a piece of criminal slang for judges, interrogators, and so on.

63. Balzac consistently misspells the name of Bourron, a village about four miles south of Fontainebleau, as "Bouron."

64. A britska was a long carriage, designed so that passengers could stretch out full length.

65. The berline was a smaller carriage with two interior seats as well as a hooded perch on the back, where a footman or valet could ride; it was named for the city of Berlin, where it was first designed.

III. Where Evil Pathways Lead

1. The compartmentalized police van *(voiture cellulaire)* had individual cells inside, so prisoners could not see or touch each other.

2. In the Abbé Prévost's 1731 novel *Manon Lescaut,* Manon is in and out of trouble with the law constantly; at one point she is arrested and carried through Paris in a similar kind of cart or tumbril.

3. *A Murky Business* (London: Penguin, 1978) is Herbert J. Hunt's translation of the 1841 novel *Une ténébreuse affaire.* In the short-lived revolutionary calendar, Brumaire, Year IV, would be the period from October 22 to November 22, 1792.

4. Bibi-Lupin is fictional, but his name suggests that Balzac was modeling him, in part, on a real-life ex-convict who had turned informer and then policeman, Coco-Latour. Bibi-Lupin is the head of the undercover police force, known as the Sûreté. This term is usually translated as "security," but the Sûreté, founded by the famous Vidocq in 1812, is closer to what we might call a detective bureau.

5. Balzac refers to *"intonations illinoises"* (Illinoisan intonations)—Illinois, to him, being an exotic wilderness, home of Native tribes, something like the setting for novels by James Fenimore Cooper.

6. This was the signal for what is known as the Saint Bartholomew's Day Massacre, on the night of August 24–25, 1572, when at the instigation of Catherine de Medici thousands of Protestants were murdered, both in Paris and elsewhere in the country.

7. Saint Louis is King Louis IX (1214–1270). Louis commissioned the building of the Sainte-Chapelle in 1238, and it housed (and still houses) his collection of relics, the most important of which is the crown of thorns.

8. King Charles V (1338–1380) abandoned the Palais in 1358. He moved first to the Louvre and began construction of the royal residence complex called the Hôtel Saint-Pol in 1361.

9. The word *bastille* meant a small fortress.

10. *Lanterne* is the term for a small observation deck just above the great cupola of the Paris Panthéon, affording a spectacular view of the city.

11. *Études philosophiques (Philosophical Studies)* is a set of books in the *Comédie humaine* in which Balzac placed his attempt at the historical novel, eventually titled *Sur Catherine de Médicis*.

12. The prisons known as La Roquette, in the 11th arrondissement of Paris, were opened in 1837. The larger one was for adults and was known as La Grande Roquette; it was closed in 1900. La Petite Roquette, for young people, continued in operation and was not demolished until 1974.

13. The Mousetrap (*la Souricière*) is a two-level sequence of cells where prisoners were held while awaiting interrogation; Balzac describes it more fully in the following chapter.

14. This roll call of famous victims of capital punishment spans several centuries.

15. Antoine Quentin Fouquier-Tinville (1746–1795) was the much-feared prosecutor during the Reign of Terror.

16. Pierre-Denis, Comte de Peyronnet (1778–1854) was minister of justice from 1821 to 1828. He was one of the extreme right-wing ministers whose policies were so repressive that they provoked the July 1830 Revolution.

17. Gabriel-Julien Ouvrard (1770–1846) was a noted and highly influential financier who, in 1809, was imprisoned for debt in Sainte-Pélagie; then, in 1823, he came to bankruptcy and ruin and was imprisoned for a time in the Conciergerie.

18. Lehon was a notary whose trial for embezzlement fascinated the public in 1841. The Prince de Bergues reference is more obscure, but he was probably the man who lived from 1791 until 1864 and was imprisoned for financial fraud. Both men are, interestingly, contemporaries who were in the prison at the time of writing, rather than during the time frame of the novel.

19. Antoine Marie Chamans, Comte de Lavalette, was imprisoned following Napoleon's Hundred Days and escaped with his wife's help, apparently by putting on her clothes and fooling the guards, while the wife remained in the cell. His wife was kept in prison for another two months and then released.

20. *Pistoles* were sparsely furnished cells that were available to prisoners who could not afford better ones, but the *pistoles* were far superior to the worst cells, the *oubliettes,* where those with no money were put.

21. Lucien lived in just this kind of place when he first came to Paris; see Part II of *Lost Illusions.*

22. The queen is Marie Antoinette; Madame Élisabeth is the Princess Élisabeth (1764–1794), younger sister of Louis XVI. Both were held in the Conciergerie before their executions. The Catholic Church regards Élisabeth as a martyr.

23. Susse was a Parisian firm that manufactured many very diverse items, one of which was the tiny pencil; the firm is still in business, known today as Susse Fondeur.

24. This Camusot, examining magistrate, is the son of the Camusot, silk merchant and lover of Coralie, from *Lost Illusions.* Camusot the son appears in a number of other works, notably *Cousin Pons* (1847) and *Le Cabinet des antiques* (1838), which has been variously translated as *Jealousies of a Country Town: The Collection of Antiquities* and *The Cabinet of Antiquities.*

25. *L'Interdiction* (1836), translated by Clara Bell as *A Commission in Lunacy,* tells the story of Madame d'Espard's attempt to have her husband declared mentally incompetent.

26. See Part I, note 79.

27. Jean-Louis Lefebvre de Cheverus (1768–1836) was elevated to the rank of Cardinal-Archbishop of Bordeaux in 1826; prior to that he had worked extensively, and with much distinction, in the United States. He had a reputation for integrity that made him widely admired in both countries.

28. Two historical allusions: the first involves an episode from 1524, in which a clerk named Gentil indirectly caused the downfall and execution, in 1527, of the superintendent of finances, Jacques de Beaune, Baron de Semblançay. The second reference is to events in 1811, when a clerk named Michel sold military documents to the Russian diplomat Czernicheff; Michel was discovered when he began living flamboyantly with the money and was ultimately guillotined.

29. On the designer André-Charles Boulle, see Part I, note 25. Such a clock would be an expensive item.

30. Citron points out that the count is making a slightly bawdy joke here: "the reverse side of the medal" (*la médaille à revers*) means a woman's derriere.

31. The slang term Balzac uses is *chevaux de retour,* literally "return horses."

32. Anthime Collet (1785–1840) was a criminal considered a master of disguise, and at one time he did indeed disguise himself as a priest. He published his memoirs in 1839.

33. A *grève,* in this sense of the word, is the shoreline of a river.

34. *Pas-Perdus* means "lost steps." The term is used more widely to refer not just to the hall in the Palais de Justice but to any waiting room in a courthouse or other place where lawyers gather.

35. Balzac evidently planned such a work, but it was never written.

36. Massol figures in a number of Balzac's works, including *Les Comédiens sans le savoir* (1846), translated by Katherine Prescott Wormeley as *Unconscious Comedians.*

37. The simile, worthy of Raymond Chandler, also appears in *Père Goriot,* as Antoine Adam points out (412).

38. Dorine is the quick-witted servant girl in Molière's *Tartuffe.*

39. On the case of Dr. Edmé-Samuel Castaing (executed in 1823), see Part II, note 18.

40. The "Savages" here are another reminiscence from Balzac's reading of American writer James Fenimore Cooper.

41. Quatre-Voleurs (four thieves) was a brand name, though Balzac does not capitalize it. The (probably apocryphal) story behind the name tells of four thieves who concocted this particular vinegar during an outbreak of plague in Marseilles in 1720. They would soak their handkerchiefs in it and then cover their mouths with the handkerchiefs as they went out to plunder plague victims, the vinegar supposedly making them immune to the disease.

42. Balzac's playful but untranslatable title for this chapter is "Fin contre fin, quelle en sera la fin."

43. A *palatine* was a fur piece women wore over their bare shoulders like a mini cape. Madame Poiret is referring to the man's chest hair.

44. Lizinska de Mirbel (1796–1849) was a celebrated painter specializing in miniature portraits.

45. The term "raca" is biblical, meaning a curse or imprecation: in Matthew 5:22, there is a warning against anyone "who shall say to his brother, raca . . ." Many translations of the Bible (whether into French or English) leave the word in its original Syrian. It's possible that Esther might have encountered the word in a sermon or Bible study at the convent school.

46. Ibycus was a lyric poet of the sixth century BCE. The story goes that while he was being murdered in the desert by a gang of bandits, he looked to the sky, saw cranes flying overhead, and declared, "The cranes will avenge me." Some time later, in a city, one of the bandits saw cranes and exclaimed, "Look, the avengers of Ibycus!" That exclamation proved their guilt in his murder.

47. Pierre Paul Royer-Collard (1763–1845) was a statesman and philosopher whose views were a mix of monarchist and liberal. Balzac here makes him sound Rousseauist.

48. Before the French Revolution, the *parlements* were effectively a higher court system, similar to appellate courts. They were abolished in 1790.

49. The novel Balzac refers to was titled *Une double famille* (*A Double Family*), published in 1842.

50. Balzac tells the story of Octave de Bauvan in the novel *Honorine* (1844).

51. Yemelan Pugachev (1742–1775) was a disaffected Cossack officer who led a rebellion against Catherine the Great. Louis-Pierre Louvel (1783–1820) was a radical antimonarchist who assassinated the Duc de Berry in 1820. In other versions of the text, the list substitutes Joseph Fouché (1759–1820), the famous founder of the police force during the 1790s, for that of Robespierre. Interestingly, the first version of the preceding list (Moses, Attila, and so on) puts Robespierre in the place that later became Mohammed's.

52. Cardinal Francisco Jiménez de Cisneros (1436–1517) rose to become a chief adviser and policy maker for the regime of Ferdinand II of Spain. Cardinal Richelieu (1585–1642) played a similar role for Louis XIII of France. Does Lucien still believe that Carlos Herrera/Jacques Collin really is a churchman?

53. Jean-Charles Pichegru (1761–1804) was a French general who, having been arrested following a coup attempt against Napoleon, was found strangled in his jail cell. The death was reported as suicide, but there have always been doubts.

54. Balzac's philosophical novel *Louis Lambert* dates from 1832. The character of Lambert, something of a self-portrait, has much in common with Balzac, especially in the depiction of his early life, but his impassioned intellect slowly begins to overwhelm him, and he ultimately goes mad. He is mentioned in *Lost Illusions* as a friend of the idealistic group to which Lucien once belonged, the Cénacle.

IV. Vautrin's Last Incarnation

1. Louis de Bonald (1754–1840) was one of the chief conservative, antirevolutionary thinkers and writers of the day. In 1825 Charles X had instigated a new law against sacrilege and blasphemy, offenders to be subject to capital punishment. Bonald vigorously supported the law and the punishment before the National Assembly, using similar phrasing: capital punishment simply brings the offender more swiftly before his natural judge. The law was revoked in 1830.

2. Pichegru: see Part III, note 53.

3. Camusot uses legal phraseology: the French phrase *le mort saisit le vif* means that the heir succeeds to the goods of the deceased from the moment of death. But in this case, it takes on a grim irony: Camusot will "inherit" the misfortune of the deceased Lucien.

4. Charles de Brosses (1754–1840) was a highly respected member of the Burgundy *parlement.* Louis-Mathieu Molé (1754–1840) had been a member of the Council of State under Napoleon and served as prime minister from 1836 until 1839.

5. There are two characters named Sganarelle in Molière's works. His comedy *Sganarelle, ou Le Cocu imaginaire (Sganarelle, or The Imaginary Cuckold)* was first produced in 1660, and *Dom Juan,* in which Sganarelle is the valet, premiered in 1665. Balzac probably has the latter in mind.

6. Franz Mesmer lived from 1734 until 1815. His theory of animal magnetism was presented as science but borders on the occult, and it fascinated people all across Europe and America, from Balzac to Poe. Balzac saw great scientific and even social value in Mesmer's ideas. See K. Melissa Marcus, *The Representation of Mesmerism in Balzac's "La Comédie humaine"* (New York: Peter Lang, 1995).

7. Doctor Bouvard also appears in Balzac's *Ursule Mirouët* (1841). Flaubert may have remembered him when he wrote his satire on useless knowledge, *Bouvard et Pécuchet* (1881).

8. Balzac mixes the fictional Canalis with three real writers. In an earlier version, instead of Canalis he listed "the author of *Eloa*"—that is, *Eloa, ou La Soeur des anges (Eloa, or The Sister of Angels)*, by Alfred de Vigny (1824). Poems concerning demons and fallen angels by the others include Thomas Moore's *The Loves of the Angels* (1823; Balzac no doubt read it in its very popular French translation), Byron's *Cain* and *Heaven and Earth* (1820–21), and Charles Maturin's *Melmoth the Wanderer* (1820). Only Vigny's poem actually corresponds to the summary Balzac gives.

9. Jacques Collin puns here: he refers to Clotilde as Lucien's *planche de salut,* his "plank of salvation," as in the plank one would cling to after a shipwreck, but that phrase hints again at Clotilde being flat like a board.

10. Balzac uses a slang phrase for "blackmail," and, as he often does, calls attention to the slang by italicizing it. The phrase is *faire chanter,* or "make sing," so the sentence literally translates as "I could make those mistresses of Lucien's sing!"

11. Repeating the entire letter seems odd, but Balzac printed *Vautrin's Last Incarnation,* which we know as Part IV of the novel, separately, and some of his readers would not necessarily have seen the material in Part III.

12. On May 8, 1842, France experienced its first major railway disaster on the line between Meudon and Bellevue, when the train broke an axle, derailed, and caught on fire. Estimates of the dead range from fifty to two hundred. The train was returning from Versailles, so the incident is often called the Versailles rail disaster.

13. On Louvel, see Part III, note 51.

14. Balzac uses the term "Pandemonium" in its original sense (the place of all demons or all evils), not in its more recent sense of a chaotic place.

15. Balzac italicizes prison slang: here, *stoolie* translates *mouton* (literally, a sheep), and *mob* translates *la haute pègre* (the professional criminal underworld).

16. The fictional Crottats figure in Balzac's novel *César Birotteau* (1837).

17. The daring theft of rare and extremely valuable coins and medals from the Royal Library (Bibliothèque Royale) took place in November 1831; the culprit was named Fossard, and though he was caught and sentenced to prison (where he died of cholera), he never revealed where he had hidden the medals. They were recovered in 1832, in the possession of the Vicomtesse de Nays-Candau, who had been Fossard's lover.

18. The "third cellar down" translates *le troisième dessous*, a term whose origin is the Paris Opéra, which indeed had three levels of cellars below stage. To fall into *le troisième dessous* is to be in a very difficult situation.

19. The derivation of "largue" is uncertain. The word was a nautical one; to *prendre la largue* was to take to the open seas. How it came to be applied to women in underworld slang, though, is not clear.

20. Charles Nodier (1780–1844), who wrote a number of remarkable novels and tales, was head librarian at the Bibliothèque de l'Arsenal from 1824 until his death. He wrote on linguistics and was considered an expert in that field.

21. Charles Fourier (1772–1830) was the famous founder of utopian socialism, and Fourierism became shorthand for any radical political or social scheme. Balzac's novel predates Marx (*The Communist Manifesto* dates from 1848), so the "communism" he refers to is more like what we would consider a general tendency toward radical social reform rather than Marxian communism.

22. Balzac refers to the memoirs of Eugène-François Vidocq; see the Translator's Introduction.

23. All the criminals mentioned were real people; Balzac got their names, probably, from Vidocq.

24. Medoro is the deeply romantic, devoted lover of Angelica in Ariosto's chivalric epic *Orlando Furioso* (1516, 1532).

25. The phrase translated as "clean out the till" is a much more picturesque French idiom: *manger la grenouille,* or "eat the frog."

26. On the escaped convict Pierre Coignard, see Part I, note 9.

27. John Lambton, First Earl of Durham (1792–1840), British statesman, was appointed lord of the privy seal in 1830. He made his tour of the French prisons in 1834.

28. Henri Sanson (1767–1840) was the public executioner at the time. His father, Charles-Henri Sanson (1739–1806), had held the same post, and he executed King Louis XVI. Henri had the distinction of having guillotined Marie Antoinette. Barbara Soloff Levy's book treats the entire family: *Legacy of Death: The Remarkable Saga of the Sanson Family* (New York: Prentice-Hall, 1973).

29. The term translated here as "footguard" is more colorful in the original; the French word is *patarasse,* a nautical term that refers to material used in caulking a ship.

30. Balzac slightly misremembers the title of Victor Hugo's 1829 novel *La Dernier Jour d'un condamné,* translated by Christopher Moncrieff as *The Last Day of a Condemned Man.*

31. Antoine Adam (553) notes that Balzac is referring to the prolonged

isolation of the prisoner in solitary over five or even ten years, the so-called Philadelphia system, or the *régime pennsylvanien,* imported from American practice. Extended solitary confinement was on the rise in the 1840s, and Balzac is protesting, as we would today, what he sees as an inhumane system.

32. Unfortunately, Balzac never wrote the book projected here. We do know that the title would have been *Le Régicide.*

33. This is Saint-Germain-en-Laye, then a small town west of Paris (now a suburb), not to be confused with the district in central Paris known as the Faubourg Saint-Germain.

34. A notary in France holds a position of importance and has much more legal responsibility than in the United States. Notaries function almost like lawyers, especially in smaller towns, offering legal advice and overseeing contracts.

35. Citron (1476) points out that the nickname is recorded as early as 1615.

36. The slang term Silk Thread uses is *montante,* usually glossed as "breeches" but with a sexual connotation: the word can also mean an upright bar or rod, which seems to justify the present translation.

37. This is Henri-Clément Sanson (1799–1889), who held the post of executioner after his father's death. He was dismissed from the post in 1847 for pawning the guillotine to cope with his debts.

38. "A Drama in the Prisons" ("Un Drame dans les prisons") was an earlier title for Part III, "Where Evil Pathways Lead."

39. *Rouletiers* (Balzac uses the term *rouleurs*) were thieves, sometimes working in groups, who preyed on coaches, especially mail coaches.

40. Balzac's slang term is *lorcefé,* which twists around the name of the prison, La Force.

41. The meaning of *tondif* is not clear. Citron (1487) argues that the word is a typographical error for *fonbif,* but that word is no clearer.

42. In 1815, following the battle of Waterloo, Napoleon boarded the British ship *Bellerophon* to sign the documents for his surrender.

43. Casimir Périer (1777–1832), despite his initial skepticism concerning the July Revolution, Louis-Philippe, and his constitutional monarchy, was respected by the new king; he was called to the office of chief minister in 1831, holding it until his death, from cholera, in 1832.

44. Honoré Gabriel Riqueti, Comte de Mirabeau (1749–1791), is best remembered today as one of the leaders during the early days of the French Revolution, but earlier in life he had famously fallen in love with Marie-Thérèse, known as Sophie, the young wife of the elderly Marquis de Monnier. They eloped, then were caught, and she was sent to a convent, while he was imprisoned for a time. He wrote a series of often deeply passionate letters to her, which were first published in 1783.

45. La Fontaine's fable (I.III) was titled "La Grenouille qui veut se faire aussi grosse que le boeuf" (the frog who wanted to be as big as the ox). The frog swells herself up desperately, to the point of bursting her skin open.

46. Suetonius *(The Lives of the Twelve Caesars)* claims that Caligula intended to name his beloved horse Incitatus a consul of the empire.

47. The Basilica of Sainte-Clotilde was begun in 1846 and completed in 1857.

48. The Duc de Grandlieu refers to the plans that Charles X was about to

undertake in July 1830. Together with his chief minister, Polignac, he devised a set of "ordinances" designed to restore order and shore up his monarchy. These included suspending the freedom of the press, reducing the size of the electorate, and dismissing the Chamber of Deputies. The ordinances infuriated the public, and within days he was deposed in what is known as the July Revolution.

49. Balzac is probably thinking of the heroism of the Parlement of Paris during the period known as the Fronde (1643–52). The *parlement* stood up for the nobility against the unlimited powers of the king, though royal absolutism won out.

50. The poet and dramatist Alexis Piron (1689–1773) had, in his youth, written a semi-obscene "Ode à Priape" ("Ode to Priapus"). The memory of that ode caused King Louis XV to prevent his election to the Académie Française in 1753.

51. Henri de La Tour d'Auvergne, Vicomte de Turenne (1611–1675), was renowned as a general, for his valor and his vigorous support of the monarchy of Louis XIV.

52. A *rousse* is a redhead.

53. The Duc d'Otrante is the title Napoleon granted Joseph Fouché, founder of the modern French police. Louis-Pierre Louvel assassinated the Duc de Berry in 1820. The "prince of diplomats" probably refers to the highly flexible politician Talleyrand (Charles-Maurice de Talleyrand-Périgord, 1754–1838).

54. *L'Auberge des Adrets* was a comedy-melodrama by Benjamin Antier (1787–1870) and two cowriters, Saint-Amand (pen name of Jean-Armand Lacoste, 1797–1885) and Polyanthe (pen name of Alexandre Chaponnier, 1793–1852). It was first staged in 1823, but Balzac would have seen the revival in 1832. The play introduced to the French stage the character Robert Macaire, a comic villain who appeared in many imitations and spinoffs.

55. Nicolas de Montauran's story is told in Balzac's *Les Chouans* (1829). The Simeuse affair is detailed in his *Une ténébreuse affaire* (1841; translated as *A Murky Business*). The Battle of Marengo in 1800 was one of Napoleon's great military triumphs.

56. François-Joseph Talmawq (1763-1826) was the most celebrated actor of his day. *Nicomède* (1651), one of Corneille's great tragedies, concerns the coolly ironic king of the title who must foil various plots against him.

57. The police prefecture was located on the Rue de Jérusalem.

58. In Balzac's day, Paris was divided into twelve arrondissements, with four police stations in each.

59. Napoleon's bloodless coup d'état took place on November 9, 1799, or 18 Brumaire, Year VII, in the new revolutionary calendar. It marks the end of the Revolution and the beginning of what would be Napoleon's empire.

60. In the version serialized in *La Presse,* a clause was added to the last sentence: "and readers of the *Comédie humaine* will see the results of his underground duel with the famous Corentin." Balzac evidently planned to continue the story, but this was never written.

HONORÉ DE BALZAC (1799–1850) worked as a clerk, printer, and publisher before devoting himself to writing fiction. He wrote more than one hundred volumes of stories, novellas, and novels, most of which were included in his comprehensive study of all aspects of contemporary French life, *La Comédie humaine.*

RAYMOND N. MACKENZIE is professor of English at the University of St. Thomas in St. Paul, Minnesota. He has translated works by Montesquieu, Flaubert, Baudelaire, and Mauriac. Among his translations for the University of Minnesota Press are Barbey d'Aurevilly's *Diaboliques,* Stendhal's *Italian Chronicles,* Lamartine's *Graziella,* and Balzac's *Lost Illusions.*